AF517108

The yellowbacks... classics of popular fiction

The yellowjackets or yellowbacks were a great series of bestselling adventure and crime thrillers that had their origins in the mid to late 19th century following on from the 'penny dreadfuls'. They virtually began the mass market revolution of the early 20th century with a clear standard format and imprint/series livery (what would today be called branding). Hodder & Stoughton published the yellowjackets in two main series with series run dates of: 1923-1939 and later 1949-1957.

As the tagline ('where thrillers really began') on the back cover implies, the imprint and series focused on thrillers that were the bestsellers of their time. This current reissue or retro revival if you will, brings back many of these masterpieces, now classics in their own way and extends it further by including key titles from that period that were either great crime or thriller or even general commercial fiction (including sub-genres of noir, horror, gothic, romance, westerns, etc.) influences of their time. There are some perennial favourites and many rarities either lost or not easily available being revived in the current series. Writers and characters ranged from adventure heroes like Bulldog Drummond, Allan Quatermain, Richard Hannay or the Saint through thriller grandmasters Edgar Wallace and E. Phillips Oppenheim, crime and mystery maestros like Patricia Wentworth, GK Chesterton, Agatha Christie and the Detection club, to western and swashbucklers like Zane Grey, Max Brand, Captain Blood and even romance or general fiction classics like Hermina Black, Denise Robins, Marie Corelli or Stella Morton. These were books that had storytelling at their heart and always entertained.

The yellowbacks had both hardback (with varying design elements) and paperback (which built the series look) versions with the latter still carrying the imprint 'yellowjacket'. The current reissues pay tribute to both and use an amalgam of elements from both editions while retaining the complete yellow (or 'mustard-plaster') livery with the author's name in blue beveled type with a 'simulated emboss' effect and a white outer 'outline', and the book title in black. These reissues retain the distinctive size of the original mass market paperback and follow the three main category variations—the thrillers (crime, westerns, mystery, adventure) had blue lettering for the author's name, while romance and softer general fiction had red; and other categories like humour had green.

For more detail and a full list of titles visit https://www.hachetteindia.com/home/yellowbacks

THE CAPTAIN BLOOD OMNIBUS

THE CAPTAIN BLOOD OMNIBUS

Rafael Sabatini (1875–1950) was an Italian/British writer of novels of romance and adventure. At a young age, Rafael was exposed to many languages. By the time he was seventeen, he was the master of five languages. He quickly added a sixth language - English - to his linguistic collection. After a brief stint in the business world, Sabatini went to work as a writer. He wrote short stories in the 1890s, and his first novel came out in 1902. Sabatini was a prolific writer; he produced a new book approximately every year. He consciously chose to write in his adopted language, because, he said, "all the best stories are written in English." In all, he produced thirty one novels, eight short story collections, six nonfiction books, numerous uncollected short stories, and a play. He is best known for his world-wide bestsellers: *The Sea Hawk* (1915), *Scaramouche* (1921), *Captain Blood* (1922) and *Bellarion the Fortunate* (1926). Other famous works by Sabatini are *The Lion's Skin* (1911), *The Strolling Saint* (1913) and *The Snare* (1917).

THE CAPTAIN BLOOD OMNIBUS

Rafael Sabatini

Captain Blood: His Odyssey
The Chronicles of Captain Blood
The Fortunes of Captain Blood

hachette

The Captain Blood Omnibus
First published by Houghton Mifflin Company in 1922

1

The texts in these editions in most cases have been reprinted as is, with minimal editorial changes and by and large no bowdlerizing for political correctness; though in some editions, a few words and phrases considered archaic, or those considered offensive now, along with archaic punctuation may have been modified in places to make the text more accessible to today's readers. The narratives, language, beliefs, social mores and/or cultural depictions, in these volumes are a reflection of their times and must be viewed as such. They may also contain certain cultural, racial and gender prejudices and stereotypes that may be outdated or clearly wrong then and wrong today; but their removal would be tantamount to claiming these prejudices never existed. The Publisher does not endorse or support those depictions or stereotypes; and these books have been made available for a discerning audience that will read it for entertainment value and a chronicle/record of popular fiction of past times.

Cover design by Priya Singh adapted from the original classic yellowjacket by Hodder & Stoughton.

Cover illustration: Hodder original.

Series note: Some of the books in the series (unless otherwise credited) may have cover or inside illustrations from the original yellowbacks or early editions, and while full restoration has been attempted, some images may be grainy or faded due to the condition of the original material. The end notes or bonus material or blurb details may have been sourced from the public domain or free use publications such as Wikipedia and attribution is hereby made also allowing similar free use reproduction from here. Sources requiring further specific attribution may write in and further detailing and/or corrections shall be made in subsequent printings/editions.

Reprint specifications may be subject to change including but not limited to finishes, paper, colour sections.

ISBN: 978-93-5731-876-1

Hachette Book Publishing India Pvt. Ltd.
4th & 5th Floors, Corporate Centre,
Plot No. 94, Sector 44, Gurugram - 122 003, India

Typeset in Electra LT STD 10/12.5 pt by Manipal Technologies Limited, Manipal

Printed and bound in India by Manipal Technologies Limited, Manipal

CONTENTS

CAPTAIN BLOOD: HIS ODYSSEY

CONTENTS

I

THE MESSENGER

Peter Blood, bachelor of medicine and several other things besides, smoked a pipe and tended the geraniums boxed on the sill of his window above Water Lane in the town of Bridgewater.

Sternly disapproving eyes considered him from a window opposite, but went disregarded. Mr. Blood's attention was divided between his task and the stream of humanity in the narrow street below; a stream which poured for the second time that day towards Castle Field, where earlier in the afternoon Ferguson, the Duke's chaplain, had preached a sermon containing more treason than divinity.

These straggling, excited groups were mainly composed of men with green boughs in their hats and the most ludicrous of weapons in their hands. Some, it is true, shouldered fowling pieces, and here and there a sword was brandished; but more of them were armed with clubs, and most of them trailed the mammoth pikes fashioned out of scythes, as formidable to the eye as they were clumsy to the hand. There were weavers, brewers, carpenters, smiths, masons, bricklayers, cobblers, and representatives of every other of the trades of peace among these improvised men of war. Bridgewater, like Taunton, had yielded so generously of its manhood to the service of the bastard Duke that for any to abstain whose age and strength admitted of his bearing arms was to brand himself a coward or a papist.

Yet Peter Blood, who was not only able to bear arms, but trained and skilled in their use, who was certainly no coward, and a papist only when it suited him, tended his geraniums and smoked his pipe on that warm July evening as indifferently as if nothing were afoot. One other thing he did. He flung after those war-fevered enthusiasts a line of Horace—a poet for whose work he had early conceived an inordinate affection:

"Quo, quo, scelesti, ruitis?"

And now perhaps you guess why the hot, intrepid blood inherited from the roving sires of his Somersetshire mother remained cool amidst all this frenzied fanatical heat of rebellion; why the turbulent spirit which had forced him once from the sedate academical bonds his father would have imposed upon him, should now remain quiet in the very midst of turbulence. You realize how he regarded these men who were rallying to the banners of liberty—the banners woven by the virgins of Taunton, the girls from the seminaries of Miss Blake and Mrs. Musgrove, who—as the ballad runs—had ripped open their silk petticoats to make colours for King Monmouth's army. That Latin line, contemptuously flung after them as they clattered down the cobbled street, reveals his mind. To him they were fools rushing in wicked frenzy upon their ruin.

You see, he knew too much about this fellow Monmouth and the pretty brown slut who had borne him, to be deceived by the legend of legitimacy, on the strength of which this standard of rebellion had been raised. He had read the absurd proclamation posted at the Cross at Bridgewater—as it had been posted also at Taunton and elsewhere—setting forth that "upon the decease of our Sovereign Lord Charles the Second, the right of succession to the Crown of England, Scotland, France, and Ireland, with the dominions and territories thereunto belonging, did legally descend and devolve upon the most illustrious and high-born Prince James, Duke of Monmouth, son and heir apparent to the said King Charles the Second."

It had moved him to laughter, as had the further announcement that "James Duke of York did first cause the said late King to be poysoned, and immediately thereupon did usurp and invade the Crown."

He knew not which was the greater lie. For Mr. Blood had spent a third of his life in the Netherlands, where this same James Scott—who now proclaimed himself James the Second, by the grace of God, King, et cetera—first saw the light some six-and-thirty years ago, and he was acquainted with the story current there of the fellow's real paternity. Far from being legitimate—by virtue of a pretended secret marriage between Charles Stuart and Lucy Walter—it was possible that this Monmouth who now proclaimed himself King of England was not even the illegitimate child of the late sovereign. What but ruin and disaster could be the end of this grotesque pretension? How could it be hoped that England would ever swallow such a Perkin? And it was on his behalf, to uphold his fantastic claim, that these West Country clods, led by a few armigerous Whigs, had been seduced into rebellion!

"Quo, quo, scelesti, ruitis?"

He laughed and sighed in one; but the laugh dominated the sigh, for Mr. Blood was unsympathetic, as are most self-sufficient men; and he was very self-sufficient; adversity had taught him so to be. A more tender-hearted man, possessing his vision and his knowledge, might have found cause for tears in the contemplation of these ardent, simple, Nonconformist sheep going forth to the shambles—escorted to the rallying ground on Castle Field by wives and daughters, sweethearts and mothers, sustained by the delusion that they were to take the field in defence of Right, of Liberty, and of Religion. For he knew, as all Bridgewater knew and had known now for some hours, that it was Monmouth's intention to deliver battle that same night. The Duke was to lead a surprise attack upon the Royalist army under Feversham that was now encamped on Sedgemoor. Mr. Blood assumed that Lord Feversham would be equally well-informed, and if in this assumption he was wrong, at least he was justified of it. He was not to suppose the Royalist commander so indifferently skilled in the trade he followed.

Mr. Blood knocked the ashes from his pipe, and drew back to close his window. As he did so, his glance travelling straight across the street met at last the glance of those hostile eyes that watched him. There were two pairs, and they belonged to the Misses Pitt, two amiable, sentimental maiden ladies who yielded to none in Bridgewater in their worship of the handsome Monmouth.

Mr. Blood smiled and inclined his head, for he was on friendly terms with these ladies, one of whom, indeed, had been for a little while his patient. But there was no response to his greeting. Instead, the eyes gave him back a stare of cold disdain. The smile on his thin lips grew a little broader, a little less pleasant. He understood the reason of that hostility, which had been daily growing in this past week since Monmouth had come to turn the brains of women of all ages. The Misses Pitt, he apprehended, contemned him that he, a young and vigorous man, of a military training which might now be valuable to the Cause, should stand aloof; that he should placidly smoke his pipe and tend his geraniums on this evening of all evenings, when men of spirit were rallying to the Protestant Champion, offering their blood to place him on the throne where he belonged.

If Mr. Blood had condescended to debate the matter with these ladies, he might have urged that having had his fill of wandering and adventuring, he was now embarked upon the career for which he had been originally intended and for which his studies had equipped him; that he was a man of medicine and not of war; a healer, not a slayer. But they would have answered him, he knew, that in such a cause it behoved every man who deemed himself a man to take up arms. They would have pointed out that their own nephew Jeremiah, who was by trade a sailor, the master of a ship—which by an ill-chance for that young man had come to anchor at this season in Bridgewater Bay—had quitted the helm to snatch up a musket in defence of Right. But Mr. Blood was not of those who argue. As I have said, he was a self-sufficient man.

He closed the window, drew the curtains, and turned to the pleasant, candle-lighted room, and the table on which Mrs. Barlow, his housekeeper, was in the very act of spreading supper. To her, however, he spoke aloud his thought.

"It's out of favour I am with the vinegary virgins over the way."

He had a pleasant, vibrant voice, whose metallic ring was softened and muted by the Irish accent which in all his wanderings he had never lost. It was a voice that could woo seductively and caressingly, or command in such a way as to compel obedience. Indeed, the man's whole nature was in that voice of his. For the rest of him, he was tall and spare, swarthy of tint as a gipsy, with eyes that were startlingly blue in that dark face and under those level black brows. In their glance those eyes, flanking a high-bridged, intrepid nose, were of singular penetration and of a steady haughtiness that went well with his firm lips. Though dressed in black as became his calling, yet it was with an elegance derived from the love of clothes that is peculiar to the adventurer he had been, rather than to the staid medicus he now was. His coat was of fine camlet, and it was laced with silver; there were ruffles of Mechlin at his wrists and a Mechlin cravat encased his throat. His great black periwig was as sedulously curled as any at Whitehall.

Seeing him thus, and perceiving his real nature, which was plain upon him, you might have been tempted to speculate how long such a man would be content to lie by in this little backwater of the world into which chance had swept him some six months ago; how long he would continue to pursue the trade for which he had qualified himself before he had begun to live. Difficult of belief though it may be when you know his history, previous and subsequent, yet it is possible that but for the trick that Fate was about to play him, he might have continued this peaceful existence, settling down completely to the life of a doctor in this Somersetshire haven. It is possible, but not probable.

He was the son of an Irish medicus, by a Somersetshire lady in whose veins ran the rover blood of the Frobishers, which may account for a certain wildness that had early manifested itself in his disposition. This wildness had profoundly alarmed his father, who for an Irishman was of a singularly peace-loving nature. He had early resolved that the boy should follow his own honourable profession, and Peter Blood, being quick to learn and oddly greedy of knowledge, had satisfied his parent by receiving at the age of twenty the degree of baccalaureus medicinae at Trinity College, Dublin. His father survived that satisfaction by three months only. His mother had then been dead some years already. Thus Peter Blood came into an inheritance of some few hundred pounds, with which he had set out to see the world and give for a season a free rein to that restless spirit by which he was imbued. A set of curious chances led him to take service with the Dutch, then at war with France; and a predilection for the sea made him elect that this service should be upon that element. He had the advantage of a commission under the famous de Ruyter, and fought in the Mediterranean engagement in which that great Dutch admiral lost his life.

After the Peace of Nimeguen his movements are obscure. But we know that he spent two years in a Spanish prison, though we do not know how he contrived to get there. It may be due to this that upon his release he took his sword to France, and saw service with the French in their warring upon the Spanish Netherlands. Having reached, at last, the age of thirty-two, his appetite for adventure surfeited, his health having grown indifferent as the result of a neglected wound, he was suddenly overwhelmed by homesickness. He took ship from Nantes with intent to cross to Ireland. But the vessel being driven by stress of weather into Bridgewater Bay, and Blood's health having grown worse during the voyage, he decided to go ashore there, additionally urged to it by the fact that it was his mother's native soil.

Thus in January of that year 1685 he had come to Bridgewater, possessor of a fortune that was approximately the same as that with which he had originally set out from Dublin eleven years ago.

Because he liked the place, in which his health was rapidly restored to him, and because he conceived that he had passed through adventures enough for a man's lifetime, he determined to settle there, and take up at last the profession of medicine from which he had, with so little profit, broken away.

That is all his story, or so much of it as matters up to that night, six months later, when the battle of Sedgemoor was fought.

Deeming the impending action no affair of his, as indeed it was not, and indifferent to the activity with which Bridgewater was that night agog, Mr. Blood closed his ears to the sounds of it, and went early to bed. He was peacefully asleep long before eleven o'clock, at which hour, as you know, Monmouth rode but with his rebel host along the Bristol Road, circuitously to avoid the marshland that lay directly between himself and the Royal Army. You also know that his numerical advantage—possibly counter-balanced by the greater steadiness of the regular troops on the other side—and the advantages he derived from falling by surprise upon an army that was more or less asleep, were all lost to him by blundering and bad leadership before ever he was at grips with Feversham.

The armies came into collision in the neighbourhood of two o'clock in the morning. Mr. Blood slept undisturbed through the distant boom of cannon. Not until four o'clock, when the sun was rising to dispel the last wisps of mist over that stricken field of battle, did he awaken from his tranquil slumbers.

He sat up in bed, rubbed the sleep from his eyes, and collected himself. Blows were thundering upon the door of his house, and a voice was calling incoherently. This was the noise that had aroused him. Conceiving that he had to do with some urgent obstetrical case, he reached for bedgown and slippers, to go below. On the landing he almost collided with Mrs. Barlow, new-risen and unsightly, in a state of panic. He quieted her cluckings with a word of reassurance, and went himself to open.

There in slanting golden light of the new-risen sun stood a breathless, wild-eyed man and a steaming horse. Smothered in dust and grime, his clothes in disarray, the left sleeve of his doublet hanging in rags, this young man opened his lips to speak, yet for a long moment remained speechless.

In that moment Mr. Blood recognized him for the young shipmaster, Jeremiah Pitt, the nephew of the maiden ladies opposite, one who had been drawn by the general enthusiasm into the vortex of that rebellion. The street was rousing, awakened by the sailor's noisy advent; doors were opening, and lattices were being unlatched for the protrusion of anxious, inquisitive heads.

"Take your time, now," said Mr. Blood. "I never knew speed made by overhaste."

But the wild-eyed lad paid no heed to the admonition. He plunged, headlong, into speech, gasping, breathless.

"It is Lord Gildoy," he panted. "He is sore wounded... at Oglethorpe's Farm by the river. I bore him thither... and... and he sent me for you. Come away! Come away!"

He would have clutched the doctor, and haled him forth by force in bedgown and slippers as he was. But the doctor eluded that too eager hand.

"To be sure, I'll come," said he. He was distressed. Gildoy had been a very friendly, generous patron to him since his settling in these parts. And Mr. Blood was eager enough to do what he now could to discharge the debt, grieved that the occasion should have arisen, and in such a manner—for he knew quite well that the rash young nobleman had been an active agent of the Duke's. "To be sure, I'll come. But first give me leave to get some clothes and other things that I may need."

"There's no time to lose."

"Be easy now. I'll lose none. I tell ye again, ye'll go quickest by going leisurely. Come in... take a chair..." He threw open the door of a parlour.

Young Pitt waved aside the invitation.

"I'll wait here. Make haste, in God's name." Mr. Blood went off to dress and to fetch a case of instruments.

Questions concerning the precise nature of Lord Gildoy's hurt could wait until they were on their way. Whilst he pulled on his boots, he gave Mrs. Barlow instructions for the day, which included the matter of a dinner he was not destined to eat.

When at last he went forth again, Mrs. Barlow clucking after him like a disgruntled fowl, he found young Pitt smothered in a crowd of scared, half-dressed townsfolk—mostly women—who had come hastening for news of how the battle had sped. The news he gave them was to be read in the lamentations with which they disturbed the morning air.

At sight of the doctor, dressed and booted, the case of instruments tucked under his arm, the messenger disengaged himself from those who pressed about, shook off his weariness and the two tearful aunts that clung most closely, and seizing the bridle of his horse, he climbed to the saddle.

"Come along, sir," he cried. "Mount behind me."

Mr. Blood, without wasting words, did as he was bidden. Pitt touched the horse with his spur. The little crowd gave way, and thus, upon the crupper of that doubly-laden horse, clinging to the belt of his companion, Peter Blood set out upon his Odyssey. For this Pitt, in whom he beheld no more than the messenger of a wounded rebel gentleman, was indeed the very messenger of Fate.

II

KIRKE'S DRAGOONS

Oglethorpe's farm stood a mile or so to the south of Bridgewater on the right bank of the river. It was a straggling Tudor building showing grey above the ivy that clothed its lower parts. Approaching it now, through the fragrant orchards amid which it seemed to drowse in Arcadian peace beside the waters of the Parrett, sparkling in the morning sunlight, Mr. Blood might have had a difficulty in believing it part of a world tormented by strife and bloodshed.

On the bridge, as they had been riding out of Bridgewater, they had met a vanguard of fugitives from the field of battle, weary, broken men, many of them wounded, all of them terror-stricken, staggering in speedless haste with the last remnants of their strength into the shelter which it was their vain illusion the town would afford them. Eyes glazed with lassitude and fear looked up piteously out of haggard faces at Mr. Blood and his companion as they rode forth; hoarse voices cried a warning that merciless pursuit was not far behind. Undeterred, however, young Pitt rode amain along the dusty road by which these poor fugitives from that swift rout on Sedgemoor came flocking in ever-increasing numbers. Presently he swung aside, and quitting the road took to a pathway that crossed the dewy meadowlands. Even here they met odd groups of these human derelicts, who were scattering in all directions, looking fearfully behind them as they came through the long grass, expecting at every moment to see the red coats of the dragoons.

But as Pitt's direction was a southward one, bringing them ever nearer to Feversham's headquarters, they were presently clear of that human flotsam and jetsam of the battle, and riding through the peaceful orchards heavy with the ripening fruit that was soon to make its annual yield of cider.

At last they alighted on the kidney stones of the courtyard, and Baynes, the master, of the homestead, grave of countenance and flustered of manner, gave them welcome.

In the spacious, stone-flagged hall, the doctor found Lord Gildoy—a very tall and dark young gentleman, prominent of chin and nose—stretched on a cane day-bed under one of the tall mullioned windows, in the care of Mrs. Baynes and her comely daughter. His cheeks were leaden-hued, his eyes closed, and from his blue lips came with each laboured breath a faint, moaning noise.

Mr. Blood stood for a moment silently considering his patient. He deplored that a youth with such bright hopes in life as Lord Gildoy's should have risked all, perhaps existence itself, to forward the ambition of a worthless adventurer. Because he had liked and honoured this brave lad he paid his case the tribute of a sigh. Then he knelt to his task, ripped away doublet and underwear to lay bare his lordship's mangled side, and called for water and linen and what else he needed for his work.

He was still intent upon it a half-hour later when the dragoons invaded the homestead. The clatter of hooves and hoarse shouts that heralded their approach disturbed him not at all. For one thing, he was not easily disturbed; for another, his task absorbed him. But his lordship, who had now recovered consciousness, showed considerable alarm, and the battle-stained Jeremy Pitt sped to cover in a clothes-press. Baynes was uneasy, and his wife and daughter trembled. Mr. Blood reassured them.

"Why, what's to fear?" he said. "It's a Christian country, this, and Christian men do not make war upon the wounded, nor upon those who harbour them." He still had, you see, illusions about Christians. He held a glass of cordial, prepared under his directions, to his lordship's lips. "Give your mind peace, my lord. The worst is done."

And then they came rattling and clanking into the stone-flagged hall—a round dozen jack-booted, lobster-coated troopers of the Tangiers Regiment, led by a sturdy, black-browed fellow with a deal of gold lace about the breast of his coat.

Baynes stood his ground, his attitude half-defiant, whilst his wife and daughter shrank away in renewed fear. Mr. Blood, at the head of the day-bed, looked over his shoulder to take stock of the invaders.

The officer barked an order, which brought his men to an attentive halt, then swaggered forward, his gloved hand bearing down the pummel of his sword, his spurs jingling musically as he moved. He announced his authority to the yeoman.

"I am Captain Hobart, of Colonel Kirke's dragoons. What rebels do you harbour?"

The yeoman took alarm at that ferocious truculence. It expressed itself in his trembling voice.

"I... I am no harbourer of rebels, sir. This wounded gentleman..."

"I can see for myself." The Captain stamped forward to the day-bed, and scowled down upon the grey-faced sufferer.

"No need to ask how he came in this state and by his wounds. A damned rebel, and that's enough for me." He flung a command at his dragoons. "Out with him, my lads."

Mr. Blood got between the day-bed and the troopers.

"In the name of humanity, sir!" said he, on a note of anger. "This is England, not Tangiers. The gentleman is in sore case. He may not be moved without peril to his life."

Captain Hobart was amused.

"Oh, I am to be tender of the lives of these rebels! Odds blood! Do you think it's to benefit his health we're taking him? There's gallows being planted along the road from Weston to Bridgewater, and he'll serve for one of them as well as another. Colonel Kirke'll learn these nonconforming oafs something they'll not forget in generations."

"You're hanging men without trial? Faith, then, it's mistaken I am. We're in Tangiers, after all, it seems, where your regiment belongs."

The Captain considered him with a kindling eye. He looked him over from the soles of his riding-boots to the crown of his periwig. He noted the spare, active frame, the arrogant poise of the head, the air of authority that invested Mr. Blood, and soldier recognized soldier. The Captain's eyes narrowed. Recognition went further.

"Who the hell may you be?" he exploded.

"My name is Blood, sir—Peter Blood, at your service."

"Aye—aye! Codso! That's the name. You were in French service once, were you not?"

If Mr. Blood was surprised, he did not betray it.

"I was."

"Then I remember you—five years ago, or more, you were in Tangiers."

"That is so. I knew your colonel."

"Faith, you may be renewing the acquaintance." The Captain laughed unpleasantly. "What brings you here, sir?"

"This wounded gentleman. I was fetched to attend him. I am a medicus."

"A doctor—you?" Scorn of that lie—as he conceived it—rang in the heavy, hectoring voice.

"Medicinae baccalaureus," said Mr. Blood.

"Don't fling your French at me, man," snapped Hobart. "Speak English!"

Mr. Blood's smile annoyed him.

"I am a physician practising my calling in the town of Bridgewater."

The Captain sneered. "Which you reached by way of Lyme Regis in the following of your bastard Duke."

It was Mr. Blood's turn to sneer. "If your wit were as big as your voice, my dear, it's the great man you'd be by this."

For a moment the dragoon was speechless. The colour deepened in his face.

"You may find me great enough to hang you."

"Faith, yes. Ye've the look and the manners of a hangman. But if you practise your trade on my patient here, you may be putting a rope round your own neck. He's not the kind you may string up and no questions asked. He has the right to trial, and the right to trial by his peers."

"By his peers?"

The Captain was taken aback by these three words, which Mr. Blood had stressed.

"Sure, now, any but a fool or a savage would have asked his name before ordering him to the gallows. The gentleman is my Lord Gildoy."

And then his lordship spoke for himself, in a weak voice.

"I make no concealment of my association with the Duke of Monmouth. I'll take the consequences. But, if you please, I'll take them after trial—by my peers, as the doctor has said."

The feeble voice ceased, and was followed by a moment's silence. As is common in many blustering men, there was a deal of timidity deep down in Hobart. The announcement of his lordship's rank had touched those depths. A servile upstart, he stood in awe of titles. And he stood in awe of his colonel. Percy Kirke was not lenient with blunderers.

By a gesture he checked his men. He must consider. Mr. Blood, observing his pause, added further matter for his consideration.

"Ye'll be remembering, Captain, that Lord Gildoy will have friends and relatives on the Tory side, who'll have something to say to Colonel Kirke if his lordship should be handled like a common felon. You'll go warily, Captain, or, as I've said, it's a halter for your neck ye'll be weaving this morning."

Captain Hobart swept the warning aside with a bluster of contempt, but he acted upon it none the less. "Take up the day-bed," said he, "and convey him on that to Bridgewater. Lodge him in the gaol until I take order about him."

"He may not survive the journey," Blood remonstrated. "He's in no case to be moved."

"So much the worse for him. My affair is to round up rebels." He confirmed his order by a gesture. Two of his men took up the day-bed, and swung to depart with it.

Gildoy made a feeble effort to put forth a hand towards Mr. Blood. "Sir," he said, "you leave me in your debt. If I live I shall study how to discharge it."

Mr. Blood bowed for answer; then to the men: "Bear him steadily," he commanded. "His life depends on it."

As his lordship was carried out, the Captain became brisk. He turned upon the yeoman.

"What other cursed rebels do you harbour?"

"None other, sir. His lordship..."

"We've dealt with his lordship for the present. We'll deal with you in a moment when we've searched your house. And, by God, if you've lied to me..." He broke off, snarling, to give an order. Four of his dragoons went out. In a moment they were heard moving noisily in the adjacent room. Meanwhile, the Captain was questing about the hall, sounding the wainscoting with the butt of a pistol.

Mr. Blood saw no profit to himself in lingering.

"By your leave, it's a very good day I'll be wishing you," said he.

"By my leave, you'll remain awhile," the Captain ordered him.

Mr. Blood shrugged, and sat down. "You're tiresome," he said. "I wonder your colonel hasn't discovered it yet."

But the Captain did not heed him. He was stooping to pick up a soiled and dusty hat in which there was pinned a little bunch of oak leaves. It had been lying near the clothes-press in which the unfortunate Pitt had taken refuge. The Captain smiled malevolently. His eyes raked the room, resting first sardonically on the yeoman, then on the two women in the background, and finally on Mr. Blood, who sat with one leg thrown over the other in an attitude of indifference that was far from reflecting his mind.

Then the Captain stepped to the press, and pulled open one of the wings of its massive oaken door. He took the huddled inmate by the collar of his doublet, and lugged him out into the open.

"And who the devil's this?" quoth he. "Another nobleman?"

Mr. Blood had a vision of those gallows of which Captain Hobart had spoken, and of this unfortunate young shipmaster going to adorn one of them, strung up without trial, in the place of the other victim of whom the Captain had been cheated. On the spot he invented not only a title but a whole family for the young rebel.

"Faith, ye've said it, Captain. This is Viscount Pitt, first cousin to Sir Thomas Vernon, who's married to that slut Moll Kirke, sister to your own colonel, and sometime lady in waiting upon King James's queen."

Both the Captain and his prisoner gasped. But whereas thereafter young Pitt discreetly held his peace, the Captain rapped out a nasty oath. He considered his prisoner again.

"He's lying, is he not?" he demanded, seizing the lad by the shoulder, and glaring into his face. "He's rallying rue, by God!"

"If ye believe that," said Blood, "hang him, and see what happens to you."

The dragoon glared at the doctor and then at his prisoner. "Pah!" He thrust the lad into the hands of his men. "Fetch him along to Bridgewater. And make fast that fellow also," he pointed to Baynes. "We'll show him what it means to harbour and comfort rebels."

There was a moment of confusion. Baynes struggled in the grip of the troopers, protesting vehemently. The terrified women screamed until silenced by a greater terror. The Captain strode across to them. He took the girl by the shoulders. She was a pretty, golden-headed creature, with soft blue eyes that looked up entreatingly, piteously into the face of the dragoon. He leered upon her, his eyes aglow, took her chin in his hand, and set her shuddering by his brutal kiss.

"It's an earnest," he said, smiling grimly. "Let that quiet you, little rebel, till I've done with these rogues."

And he swung away again, leaving her faint and trembling in the arms of her anguished mother. His men stood, grinning, awaiting orders, the two prisoners now fast pinioned.

"Take them away. Let Cornet Drake have charge of them." His smouldering eye again sought the cowering girl. "I'll stay awhile—to search out this place. There may be other rebels hidden here." As an afterthought, he added: "And take this fellow with you." He pointed to Mr. Blood. "Bestir!"

Mr. Blood started out of his musings. He had been considering that in his case of instruments there was a lancet with which he might perform on Captain Hobart a beneficial operation. Beneficial, that is, to humanity. In any case, the dragoon was obviously plethoric and would be the better for a blood-letting. The difficulty lay in making the opportunity. He was beginning to wonder if he could lure the Captain aside with some tale of hidden treasure, when this untimely interruption set a term to that interesting speculation.

He sought to temporize.

"Faith it will suit me very well," said he. "For Bridgewater is my destination, and but that ye detained me I'd have been on my way thither now."

"Your destination there will be the gaol."

"Ah, bah! Ye're surely joking!"

"There's a gallows for you if you prefer it. It's merely a question of now or later."

Rude hands seized Mr. Blood, and that precious lancet was in the case on the table out of reach. He twisted out of the grip of the dragoons, for he was strong and agile, but they closed with him again immediately, and bore him down. Pinning him to the ground, they tied his wrists behind his back, then roughly pulled him to his feet again.

"Take him away," said Hobart shortly, and turned to issue his orders to the other waiting troopers. "Go search the house, from attic to cellar; then report to me here."

The soldiers trailed out by the door leading to the interior. Mr. Blood was thrust by his guards into the courtyard, where Pitt and Baynes already waited. From the threshold of the hall, he looked back at Captain Hobart, and his sapphire eyes were blazing. On his lips trembled a threat of what he would do to Hobart if he should happen to survive this business. Betimes he remembered that to utter it were probably to extinguish his chance of living to execute it. For today the King's men were masters in the West, and the West was regarded as enemy country, to be subjected to the worst horror of war by the victorious side. Here a captain of horse was for the moment lord of life and death.

Under the apple-trees in the orchard Mr. Blood and his companions in misfortune were made fast each to a trooper's stirrup leather. Then at the sharp order of the cornet, the little troop started for Bridgewater. As they set out there was the fullest confirmation of Mr. Blood's hideous assumption that to the dragoons this was a conquered enemy country. There were sounds of rending timbers, of furniture smashed and overthrown, the shouts and laughter of brutal men, to announce that this hunt for rebels was no more than a pretext for pillage and destruction. Finally above all other sounds came the piercing screams of a woman in acutest agony.

Baynes checked in his stride, and swung round writhing, his face ashen. As a consequence he was jerked from his feet by the rope that attached him to the stirrup leather, and he was dragged helplessly a yard or two before the trooper reined in, cursing him foully, and striking him with the flat of his sword.

It came to Mr. Blood, as he trudged forward under the laden apple-trees on that fragrant, delicious July morning, that man—as he had long suspected—was the vilest work of God, and that only a fool would set himself up as a healer of a species that was best exterminated.

III

THE LORD CHIEF JUSTICE

It was not until two months later—on the 19th of September, if you must have the actual date—that Peter Blood was brought to trial, upon a charge of high treason. We know that he was not guilty of this; but we need not doubt that he was quite capable of it by the time he was indicted. Those two months of inhuman, unspeakable imprisonment had moved his mind to a cold and deadly hatred of King James and his representatives. It says something for his fortitude that in all the circumstances he should still have had a mind at all. Yet, terrible as was the position of this entirely innocent man, he had cause for thankfulness on two counts. The first of these was that he should have been brought to trial at all; the second, that his trial took place on the date named, and not a day earlier. In the very delay which exacerbated him lay—although he did not realize it—his only chance of avoiding the gallows.

Easily, but for the favour of Fortune, he might have been one of those haled, on the morrow of the battle, more or less haphazard from the overflowing gaol at Bridgewater to be summarily hanged in the market-place by the bloodthirsty Colonel Kirke. There was about the Colonel of the Tangiers Regiment a deadly despatch which might have disposed in like fashion of all those prisoners, numerous as they were, but for the vigorous intervention of Bishop Mews, which put an end to the drumhead courts-martial.

Even so, in that first week after Sedgemoor, Kirke and Feversham contrived between them to put to death over a hundred men after a trial so summary as to be no trial at all. They required human freights for the gibbets with which they were planting the countryside, and they little cared how they procured them or what innocent lives they took. What, after all, was the life of a clod? The executioners were kept busy with rope and chopper and cauldrons of pitch. I spare you the details of that nauseating picture. It is, after all, with the fate of Peter Blood that we are concerned rather than with that of the Monmouth rebels.

He survived to be included in one of those melancholy droves of prisoners who, chained in pairs, were marched from Bridgewater to Taunton. Those who were too sorely wounded to march were conveyed in carts, into which they were brutally crowded, their wounds undressed and festering. Many were fortunate enough to die upon the way. When Blood insisted upon his right to exercise his art so as to relieve some of this suffering, he was accounted importunate and threatened with a flogging. If he had one regret now it was that he had not been out with Monmouth. That, of course, was illogical; but you can hardly expect logic from a man in his position.

His chain companion on that dreadful march was the same Jeremy Pitt who had been the agent of his present misfortunes. The young shipmaster had remained his close companion after their common arrest. Hence, fortuitously, had they been chained together in the crowded prison, where they were almost suffocated by the heat and the stench during those days of July, August, and September.

Scraps of news filtered into the gaol from the outside world. Some may have been deliberately allowed to penetrate. Of these was the tale of Monmouth's execution. It created profoundest dismay amongst those men who were suffering for the Duke and for the religious cause he had professed to champion. Many refused utterly to believe it. A wild story began to circulate that a man resembling Monmouth had offered himself up in the Duke's stead, and that Monmouth survived to come again in glory to deliver Zion and make war upon Babylon.

Mr. Blood heard that tale with the same indifference with which he had received the news of Monmouth's death. But one shameful thing he heard in connection with this which left him not quite so unmoved, and served to nourish the contempt he was forming for King James. His Majesty had consented to see Monmouth. To have done so unless he intended to pardon him was a thing execrable and damnable beyond belief; for the only other object in granting that interview could be the evilly mean satisfaction of spurning the abject penitence of his unfortunate nephew.

Later they heard that Lord Grey, who after the Duke—indeed, perhaps, before him—was the main leader of the rebellion, had purchased his own pardon for forty thousand pounds. Peter Blood found this of a piece with the rest. His contempt for King James blazed out at last.

"Why, here's a filthy mean creature to sit on a throne. If I had known as much of him before as I know today, I don't doubt I should have given cause to be where I am now." And then on a sudden thought: "And where will Lord Gildoy be, do you suppose?" he asked.

Young Pitt, whom he addressed, turned towards him a face from which the ruddy tan of the sea had faded almost completely during those months of captivity. His grey eyes were round and questioning. Blood answered him.

"Sure, now, we've never seen his lordship since that day at Oglethorpe's. And where are the other gentry that were taken?—the real leaders of this plaguey rebellion. Grey's case explains their absence, I think. They are wealthy men that can ransom themselves. Here awaiting the gallows are none but the unfortunates who followed; those who had the honour to lead them go free. It's a curious and instructive reversal of the usual way of these things. Faith, it's an uncertain world entirely!"

He laughed, and settled down into that spirit of scorn, wrapped in which he stepped later into the great hall of Taunton Castle to take his trial. With him went Pitt and the yeoman Baynes. The three of them were to be tried together, and their case was to open the proceedings of that ghastly day.

The hall, even to the galleries—thronged with spectators, most of whom were ladies—was hung in scarlet; a pleasant conceit, this, of the Lord Chief Justice's, who naturally enough preferred the colour that should reflect his own bloody mind.

At the upper end, on a raised dais, sat the Lords Commissioners, the five judges in their scarlet robes and heavy dark periwigs, Baron Jeffreys of Wem enthroned in the middle place.

The prisoners filed in under guard. The crier called for silence under pain of imprisonment, and as the hum of voices gradually became hushed, Mr. Blood considered with interest the twelve good men and true that composed the jury. Neither good nor true did they look. They were scared, uneasy, and hangdog as any set of thieves caught with their hands in the pockets of their neighbours. They were twelve shaken men, each of whom stood between the sword of the Lord Chief Justice's recent bloodthirsty charge and the wall of his own conscience.

From them Mr. Blood's calm, deliberate glance passed on to consider the Lords Commissioners, and particularly the presiding Judge, that Lord Jeffreys, whose terrible fame had come ahead of him from Dorchester.

He beheld a tall, slight man on the young side of forty, with an oval face that was delicately beautiful. There were dark stains of suffering or sleeplessness under the low-lidded eyes, heightening their brilliance and their gentle melancholy. The face was very pale, save for the vivid colour of the full lips and the hectic flush on the rather high but inconspicuous cheek-bones. It was something in those lips that marred the perfection of that countenance; a fault, elusive but undeniable, lurked there to belie the fine sensitiveness of those nostrils, the tenderness of those dark, liquid eyes and the noble calm of that pale brow.

The physician in Mr. Blood regarded the man with peculiar interest knowing as he did the agonizing malady from which his lordship suffered, and the amazingly irregular, debauched life that he led in spite of it—perhaps because of it.

"Peter Blood, hold up your hand!"

Abruptly he was recalled to his position by the harsh voice of the clerk of arraigns. His obedience was mechanical, and the clerk droned out the wordy indictment which pronounced Peter Blood a false traitor against the Most Illustrious and Most Excellent Prince, James the Second, by the grace of God, of England, Scotland, France, and Ireland King, his supreme and natural lord. It informed him that, having no fear of God in his heart, but being moved and seduced by the instigation of the Devil, he had failed in the love and true and due natural obedience towards his said lord the King, and had moved to disturb the peace and tranquillity of the kingdom and to stir up war and rebellion to depose his said lord the King from the title, honour, and the regal name of the imperial crown—and much more of the same kind, at the end of all of which he was invited to say whether he was guilty or not guilty. He answered more than was asked.

"It's entirely innocent I am."

A small, sharp-faced man at a table before and to the right of him bounced up. It was Mr. Pollexfen, the Judge-Advocate.

"Are you guilty or not guilty?" snapped this peppery gentleman. "You must take the words."

"Words, is it?" said Peter Blood. "Oh—not guilty." And he went on, addressing himself to the bench. "On this same subject of words, may it please your lordships, I am guilty of nothing to justify any of those words I have heard used to describe me, unless it be of a want of patience at having been closely confined for two months and longer in a foetid gaol with great peril to my health and even life."

Being started, he would have added a deal more; but at this point the Lord Chief Justice interposed in a gentle, rather plaintive voice.

"Look you, sir: because we must observe the common and usual methods of trial, I must interrupt you now. You are no doubt ignorant of the forms of law?"

"Not only ignorant, my lord, but hitherto most happy in that ignorance. I could gladly have forgone this acquaintance with them."

A pale smile momentarily lightened the wistful countenance.

"I believe you. You shall be fully heard when you come to your defence. But anything you say now is altogether irregular and improper."

Enheartened by that apparent sympathy and consideration, Mr. Blood answered thereafter, as was required of him, that he would be tried by God and his country. Whereupon, having prayed to God to send him a good deliverance, the clerk called upon Andrew Baynes to hold up his hand and plead.

From Baynes, who pleaded not guilty, the clerk passed on to Pitt, who boldly owned his guilt. The Lord Chief Justice stirred at that.

"Come; that's better," quoth he, and his four scarlet brethren nodded. "If all were as obstinate as his two fellow-rebels, there would never be an end."

After that ominous interpolation, delivered with an inhuman iciness that sent a shiver through the court, Mr. Pollexfen got to his feet. With great prolixity he stated the general case against the three men, and the particular case against Peter Blood, whose indictment was to be taken first.

The only witness called for the King was Captain Hobart. He testified briskly to the manner in which he had found and taken the three prisoners, together with Lord Gildoy. Upon the orders of his colonel he would have hanged Pitt out of hand, but was restrained by the lies of the prisoner Blood, who led him to believe that Pitt was a peer of the realm and a person of consideration.

As the Captain's evidence concluded, Lord Jeffreys looked across at Peter Blood.

"Will the prisoner Blood ask the witness any questions?"

"None, my lord. He has correctly related what occurred."

"I am glad to have your admission of that without any of the prevarications that are usual in your kind. And I will say this, that here prevarication would avail you little. For we always have the truth in the end. Be sure of that."

Baynes and Pitt similarly admitted the accuracy of the Captain's evidence, whereupon the scarlet figure of the Lord Chief Justice heaved a sigh of relief.

"This being so, let us get on, in God's name; for we have much to do." There was now no trace of gentleness in his voice. It was brisk and rasping, and the lips through which it passed were curved in scorn. "I take it, Mr. Pollexfen, that the wicked treason of these three rogues being established—indeed, admitted by them—there is no more to be said."

Peter Blood's voice rang out crisply, on a note that almost seemed to contain laughter.

"May it please your lordship, but there's a deal more to be said."

His lordship looked at him, first in blank amazement at his audacity, then gradually with an expression of dull anger. The scarlet lips fell into unpleasant, cruel lines that transfigured the whole countenance.

"How now, rogue? Would you waste our time with idle subterfuge?"

"I would have your lordship and the gentlemen of the jury hear me on my defence, as your lordship promised that I should be heard."

"Why, so you shall, villain; so you shall." His lordship's voice was harsh as a file. He writhed as he spoke, and for an instant his features were distorted. A delicate dead-white hand, on which the veins showed blue, brought forth a handkerchief with which he dabbed his lips and then his brow. Observing him with his physician's eye, Peter Blood judged him a prey to the pain of the disease that was destroying him. "So you shall. But after the admission made, what defence remains?"

"You shall judge, my lord."

"That is the purpose for which I sit here."

"And so shall you, gentlemen." Blood looked from judge to jury. The latter shifted uncomfortably under the confident flash of his blue eyes. Lord Jeffreys's bullying charge had whipped the spirit out of them. Had they, themselves, been prisoners accused of treason, he could not have arraigned them more ferociously.

Peter Blood stood boldly forward, erect, self-possessed, and saturnine. He was freshly shaven, and his periwig, if out of curl, was at least carefully combed and dressed.

"Captain Hobart has testified to what he knows—that he found me at Oglethorpe's Farm on the Monday morning after the battle at Weston. But he has not told you what I did there."

Again the Judge broke in. "Why, what should you have been doing there in the company of rebels, two of whom—Lord Gildoy and your fellow there—have already admitted their guilt?"

"That is what I beg leave to tell your lordship."

"I pray you do, and in God's name be brief, man. For if I am to be troubled with the say of all you traitor dogs, I may sit here until the Spring Assizes."

"I was there, my lord, in my quality as a physician, to dress Lord Gildoy's wounds."

"What's this? Do you tell us that you are a physician?"

"A graduate of Trinity College, Dublin."

"Good God!" cried Lord Jeffreys, his voice suddenly swelling, his eyes upon the jury. "What an impudent rogue is this! You heard the witness say that he had known him in Tangiers some years ago, and that he was then an officer in the French service. You heard the prisoner admit that the witness had spoken the truth?"

"Why, so he had. Yet what I am telling you is also true, so it is. For some years I was a soldier; but before that I was a physician, and I have been one again since January last, established in Bridgewater, as I can bring a hundred witnesses to prove."

"There's not the need to waste our time with that. I will convict you out of your own rascally mouth. I will ask you only this: How came you, who represent yourself as a physician peacefully following your calling in the town of Bridgewater, to be with the army of the Duke of Monmouth?"

"I was never with that army. No witness has sworn to that, and I dare swear that no witness will. I never was attracted to the late rebellion. I regarded the adventure as a wicked madness. I take leave to ask your lordship" (his brogue became more marked than ever) "what should I, who was born and bred a papist, be doing in the army of the Protestant Champion?"

"A papist thou?" The judge gloomed on him a moment. "Art more like a snivelling, canting Jack Presbyter. I tell you, man, I can smell a Presbyterian forty miles."

"Then I'll take leave to marvel that with so keen a nose your lordship can't smell a papist at four paces."

There was a ripple of laughter in the galleries, instantly quelled by the fierce glare of the Judge and the voice of the crier.

Lord Jeffreys leaned farther forward upon his desk. He raised that delicate white hand, still clutching its handkerchief, and sprouting from a froth of lace.

"We'll leave your religion out of account for the moment, friend," said he. "But mark what I say to you." With a minatory forefinger he beat the time of his words. "Know, friend, that there is no religion a man can pretend to can give a countenance to lying. Thou hast a precious immortal soul, and there is nothing in the world equal to it in value. Consider that the great God of Heaven and Earth, before Whose tribunal thou and we and all persons are to stand at the last day, will take vengeance on thee for every falsehood, and justly strike thee into eternal flames, make thee drop into the bottomless pit of fire and brimstone, if thou offer to deviate the least from the truth and nothing but the truth. For I tell thee God is not mocked. On that I charge you to answer truthfully. How came you to be taken with these rebels?"

Peter Blood gaped at him a moment in consternation. The man was incredible, unreal, fantastic, a nightmare judge. Then he collected himself to answer.

"I was summoned that morning to succour Lord Gildoy, and I conceived it to be the duty imposed upon me by my calling to answer that summons."

"Did you so?" The Judge, terrible now of aspect—his face white, his twisted lips red as the blood for which they thirsted—glared upon him in evil mockery. Then he controlled himself as if by an effort. He sighed. He resumed his earlier gentle plaintiveness. "Lord! How you waste our time. But I'll have patience with you. Who summoned you?"

"Master Pitt there, as he will testify."

"Oh! Master Pitt will testify—he that is himself a traitor self-confessed. Is that your witness?"

"There is also Master Baynes here, who can answer to it."

"Good Master Baynes will have to answer for himself; and I doubt not he'll be greatly exercised to save his own neck from a halter. Come, come, sir; are these your only witnesses?"

"I could bring others from Bridgewater, who saw me set out that morning upon the crupper of Master Pitt's horse."

His lordship smiled. "It will not be necessary. For, mark me, I do not intend to waste more time on you. Answer me only this: When Master Pitt, as you pretend, came to summon you, did you know that he had been, as you have heard him confess, of Monmouth's following?"

"I did, My lord."

"You did! Ha!" His lordship looked at the cringing jury and uttered a short, stabbing laugh. "Yet in spite of that you went with him?"

"To succour a wounded man, as was my sacred duty."

"Thy sacred duty, sayest thou?" Fury blazed out of him again. "Good God! What a generation of vipers do we live in! Thy sacred duty, rogue, is to thy King and to God. But let it pass. Did he tell you whom it was that you were desired to succour?"

"Lord Gildoy—yes."

"And you knew that Lord Gildoy had been wounded in the battle, and on what side he fought?"

"I knew."

"And yet, being, as you would have us believe, a true and loyal subject of our Lord the King, you went to succour him?"

Peter Blood lost patience for a moment. "My business, my lord, was with his wounds, not with his politics."

A murmur from the galleries and even from the jury approved him. It served only to drive his terrible judge into a deeper fury.

"Jesus God! Was there ever such an impudent villain in the world as thou?" He swung, white-faced, to the jury. "I hope, gentlemen of the jury, you take notice of the horrible carriage of this traitor rogue, and withal you cannot but observe the spirit of this sort of people, what a villainous and devilish one it is. Out of his own mouth he has said enough to hang him a dozen times. Yet is there more. Answer me this, sir: When you cozened Captain Hobart with your lies concerning the station of this other traitor Pitt, what was your business then?"

"To save him from being hanged without trial, as was threatened."

"What concern was it of yours whether or how the wretch was hanged?"

"Justice is the concern of every loyal subject, for an injustice committed by one who holds the King's commission is in some sense a dishonour to the King's majesty."

It was a shrewd, sharp thrust aimed at the jury, and it reveals, I think, the alertness of the man's mind, his self-possession ever steadiest in moments of dire peril. With any other jury it must have made the impression that he hoped to make. It may even have made its impression upon these poor pusillanimous sheep. But the dread judge was there to efface it.

He gasped aloud, then flung himself violently forward.

"Lord of Heaven!" he stormed. "Was there ever such a canting, impudent rascal? But I have done with you. I see thee, villain, I see thee already with a halter round thy neck."

Having spoken so, gloatingly, evilly, he sank back again, and composed himself. It was as if a curtain fell. All emotion passed again from his pale face. Back to invest it again came that gentle melancholy. Speaking after a moment's pause, his voice was soft, almost tender, yet every word of it carried sharply through that hushed court.

"If I know my own heart it is not in my nature to desire the hurt of anybody, much less to delight in his eternal perdition. It is out of compassion for you that I have used all these words—because I would have you have some regard for your immortal soul, and not ensure its damnation by obdurately persisting in falsehood and prevarication. But I see that all the pains in the world, and all compassion and charity are lost upon you, and therefore I will say no more to you." He turned again to the jury that countenance of wistful beauty. "Gentlemen, I must tell you for law, of which we are the judges, and not you, that if any person be in actual rebellion against the King, and another person—who really and actually was not in rebellion—does knowingly receive, harbour, comfort, or succour him, such a person is as much a traitor as he who indeed bore arms. We are bound by our oaths and consciences to declare to you what is law; and you are bound by your oaths and your consciences to deliver and to declare to us by your verdict the truth of the facts."

Upon that he proceeded to his summing-up, showing how Baynes and Blood were both guilty of treason, the first for having harboured a traitor, the second for having succoured that traitor by dressing his wounds. He interlarded his address by sycophantic allusions to his natural lord and lawful sovereign, the King, whom God had set over them, and with vituperations of Nonconformity and of Monmouth, of whom—in his own words—he dared boldly affirm that the meanest subject within the kingdom that was of legitimate birth had a better title to the crown. "Jesus God! That ever we should have such a generation of vipers among us," he burst out in rhetorical frenzy. And then he sank back as if exhausted by the violence he had used. A moment he was still, dabbing his lips again; then he moved uneasily; once more his features were twisted by pain, and in a few snarling, almost incoherent words he dismissed the jury to consider the verdict.

Peter Blood had listened to the intemperate, the blasphemous, and almost obscene invective of that tirade with a detachment that afterwards, in retrospect, surprised him. He was so amazed by the man, by the reactions taking place in him between mind and body, and by his methods of bullying and coercing the jury into bloodshed, that he almost forgot that his own life was at stake.

The absence of that dazed jury was a brief one. The verdict found the three prisoners guilty. Peter Blood looked round the scarlet-hung court. For an instant that foam of white faces seemed to heave before him. Then he was himself again, and a voice was asking him what he had to say for himself, why sentence of death should not be passed upon him, being convicted of high treason.

He laughed, and his laugh jarred uncannily upon the deathly stillness of the court. It was all so grotesque, such a mockery of justice administered by that wistful-eyed jack-pudding in scarlet, who was himself a mockery—the venal instrument of a brutally spiteful and vindictive king. His laughter shocked the austerity of that same jack-pudding.

"Do you laugh, sirrah, with the rope about your neck, upon the very threshold of that eternity you are so suddenly to enter into?"

And then Blood took his revenge.

"Faith, it's in better case I am for mirth than your lordship. For I have this to say before you deliver judgment. Your lordship sees me—an innocent man whose only offence is that I practised charity—with a halter round my neck. Your lordship, being the justiciar, speaks with knowledge of what is to come to me. I, being a physician, may speak with knowledge of what is to come to your lordship. And I tell you that I would not now change places with you—that I would not exchange this halter that you fling about my neck for the stone that you carry in your body. The death to which you may doom me is a light pleasantry by contrast with the death to which your lordship has been doomed by that Great Judge with whose name your lordship makes so free."

The Lord Chief Justice sat stiffly upright, his face ashen, his lips twitching, and whilst you might have counted ten there was no sound in that paralyzed court after Peter Blood had finished speaking. All those who knew Lord Jeffreys regarded this as the lull before the storm, and braced themselves for the explosion. But none came.

Slowly, faintly, the colour crept back into that ashen face. The scarlet figure lost its rigidity, and bent forward. His lordship began to speak. In a muted voice and briefly—much more briefly than his wont on such occasions and in a manner entirely mechanical, the manner of a man whose thoughts are elsewhere while his lips are speaking—he delivered sentence of death in the prescribed form, and without the least allusion to what Peter Blood had said. Having delivered it, he sank back exhausted, his eyes half-closed, his brow agleam with sweat.

The prisoners filed out.

Mr. Pollexfen—a Whig at heart despite the position of Judge-Advocate which he occupied—was overheard by one of the jurors to mutter in the ear of a brother counsel:

"On my soul, that swarthy rascal has given his lordship a scare. It's a pity he must hang. For a man who can frighten Jeffreys should go far."

IV

HUMAN MERCHANDISE

Mr. Pollexfen was at one and the same time right and wrong—a condition much more common than is generally supposed.

He was right in his indifferently expressed thought that a man whose mien and words could daunt such a lord of terror as Jeffreys, should by the dominance of his nature be able to fashion himself a considerable destiny. He was wrong—though justifiably so—in his assumption that Peter Blood must hang.

I have said that the tribulations with which he was visited as a result of his errand of mercy to Oglethorpe's Farm contained—although as yet he did not perceive it, perhaps—two sources of thankfulness: one that he was tried at all; the other that his trial took place on the 19th of September. Until the 18th, the sentences passed by the court of the Lords Commissioners had been carried out literally and expeditiously. But on the morning of the 19th there arrived at Taunton a courier from Lord Sunderland, the Secretary of State, with a letter for Lord Jeffreys wherein he was informed that His Majesty had been graciously pleased to command that eleven hundred rebels should be furnished for transportation to some of His Majesty's southern plantations, Jamaica, Barbados, or any of the Leeward Islands.

You are not to suppose that this command was dictated by any sense of mercy. Lord Churchill was no more than just when he spoke of the King's heart as being as insensible as marble. It had been realized that in these wholesale hangings there was taking place a reckless waste of valuable material. Slaves were urgently required in the plantations, and a healthy, vigorous man could be reckoned worth at least from ten to fifteen pounds. Then, there were at court many gentlemen who had some claim or other upon His Majesty's bounty. Here was a cheap and ready way to discharge these claims. From amongst the convicted rebels a certain number might be set aside to be bestowed upon those gentlemen, so that they might dispose of them to their own profit.

My Lord Sunderland's letter gives precise details of the royal munificence in human flesh. A thousand prisoners were to be distributed among some eight courtiers and others, whilst a postscriptum to his lordship's letter asked for a further hundred to be held at the disposal of the Queen. These prisoners were to be transported at once to His Majesty's southern plantations, and to be kept there for the space of ten years before being restored to liberty, the parties to whom they were assigned entering into security to see that transportation was immediately effected.

We know from Lord Jeffreys's secretary how the Chief Justice inveighed that night in drunken frenzy against this misplaced clemency to which His Majesty had been persuaded. We know how he attempted by letter to induce the King to reconsider his decision. But James adhered to it. It was—apart from the indirect profit he derived from it—a clemency full worthy of him. He knew that to spare lives in this fashion was to convert them into living deaths. Many must succumb in torment to the horrors of West Indian slavery, and so be the envy of their surviving companions.

Thus it happened that Peter Blood, and with him Jeremy Pitt and Andrew Baynes, instead of being hanged, drawn, and quartered as their sentences directed, were conveyed to Bristol and there shipped with some fifty others aboard the Jamaica Merchant. From close confinement under hatches, ill-nourishment and foul water, a sickness broke out amongst them, of which eleven died. Amongst these was the unfortunate yeoman from Oglethorpe's Farm, brutally torn from his quiet homestead amid the fragrant cider orchards for no other sin but that he had practised mercy.

The mortality might have been higher than it was but for Peter Blood. At first the master of the Jamaica Merchant had answered with oaths and threats the doctor's expostulations against permitting men to perish in this fashion, and his insistence that he should be made free of the medicine chest and given leave to minister to the sick. But presently Captain Gardner came to see that he might be brought to task for these too heavy losses of human merchandise and because of this he was belatedly glad to avail himself of the skill of Peter Blood. The doctor went to work zealously and zestfully, and wrought so ably that, by his ministrations and by improving the condition of his fellow-captives, he checked the spread of the disease.

Towards the middle of December the Jamaica Merchant dropped anchor in Carlisle Bay, and put ashore the forty-two surviving rebels-convict.

If these unfortunates had imagined—as many of them appear to have done—that they were coming into some wild, savage country, the prospect, of which they had a glimpse before they were hustled over the ship's side into the waiting boats, was enough to correct the impression. They beheld a town of sufficiently imposing proportions composed of houses built upon European notions of architecture, but without any of the huddle usual in European cities. The spire of a church rose dominantly above the red roofs, a fort guarded the entrance of the wide harbour, with guns thrusting their muzzles between the crenels, and the wide facade of Government House revealed itself dominantly placed on a gentle hill above the town. This hill was vividly green as is an English hill in April, and the day was such a day as April gives to England, the season of heavy rains being newly ended.

On a wide cobbled space on the sea front they found a guard of red-coated militia drawn up to receive them, and a crowd—attracted by their arrival—which in dress and manner differed little from a crowd in a seaport at home save that it contained fewer women and a great number of negroes.

To inspect them, drawn up there on the mole, came Governor Steed, a short, stout, red-faced gentleman, in blue taffetas burdened by a prodigious amount of gold lace, who limped a little and leaned heavily upon a stout ebony cane. After him, in the uniform of a colonel of the Barbados Militia, rolled a tall, corpulent man who towered head and shoulders above the Governor, with malevolence plainly written on his enormous yellowish countenance. At his side, and contrasting oddly with his grossness, moving with an easy stripling grace, came a slight young lady in a modish riding-gown. The broad brim of a grey hat with scarlet sweep of ostrich plume shaded an oval face upon which the climate of the Tropic of Cancer had made no impression, so delicately fair was its complexion. Ringlets of red-brown hair hung to her shoulders. Frankness looked out from her hazel eyes which were set wide; commiseration repressed now the mischievousness that normally inhabited her fresh young mouth.

Peter Blood caught himself staring in a sort of amazement at that piquant face, which seemed here so out of place, and finding his stare returned, he shifted uncomfortably. He grew conscious of the sorry figure that he cut. Unwashed, with rank and matted hair and a disfiguring black beard upon his face, and the erstwhile splendid suit of black camlet in which he had been taken prisoner now reduced to rags that would have disgraced a scarecrow, he was in no case for inspection by such dainty eyes as these. Nevertheless, they continued to inspect him with round-eyed, almost childlike wonder and pity. Their owner put forth a hand to touch the scarlet sleeve of her companion, whereupon with an ill-tempered grunt the man swung his great bulk round so that he directly confronted her.

Looking up into his face, she was speaking to him earnestly, but the Colonel plainly gave her no more than the half of his attention. His little beady eyes, closely flanking a fleshly, pendulous nose, had passed from her and were fixed upon fair-haired, sturdy young Pitt, who was standing beside Blood.

The Governor had also come to a halt, and for a moment now that little group of three stood in conversation. What the lady said, Peter could not hear at all, for she lowered her voice; the Colonel's reached him in a confused rumble, but the Governor was neither considerate nor indistinct; he had a high-pitched voice which carried far, and believing himself witty, he desired to be heard by all.

"But, my dear Colonel Bishop, it is for you to take first choice from this dainty nosegay, and at your own price. After that we'll send the rest to auction."

Colonel Bishop nodded his acknowledgment. He raised his voice in answering. "Your excellency is very good. But, faith, they're a weedy lot, not likely to be of much value in the plantation." His beady eyes scanned them again, and his contempt of them deepened the malevolence of his face. It was as if he were annoyed with them for being in no better condition. Then he beckoned forward Captain Gardner, the master of the Jamaica Merchant, and for some minutes stood in talk with him over a list which the latter produced at his request.

Presently he waved aside the list and advanced alone towards the rebels-convict, his eyes considering them, his lips pursed. Before the young Somersetshire shipmaster he came to a halt, and stood an instant pondering him. Then he fingered the muscles of the young man's arm, and bade him open his mouth that he might see his teeth. He pursed his coarse lips again and nodded.

He spoke to Gardner over his shoulder.

"Fifteen pounds for this one."

The Captain made a face of dismay. "Fifteen pounds! It isn't half what I meant to ask for him."

"It is double what I had meant to give," grunted the Colonel.

"But he would be cheap at thirty pounds, your honour."

"I can get a black man for that. These white swine don't live. They're not fit for the labour."

Gardner broke into protestations of Pitt's health, youth, and vigour. It was not a man he was discussing; it was a beast of burden. Pitt, a sensitive lad, stood mute and unmoving. Only the ebb and flow of colour in his cheeks showed the inward struggle by which he maintained his self-control.

Peter Blood was nauseated by the loathsome haggle.

In the background, moving slowly away down the line of prisoners, went the lady in conversation with the Governor, who smirked and preened himself as he limped beside her. She was unconscious of the loathly business the Colonel was transacting. Was she, wondered Blood, indifferent to it?

Colonel Bishop swung on his heel to pass on.

"I'll go as far as twenty pounds. Not a penny more, and it's twice as much as you are like to get from Crabston."

Captain Gardner, recognizing the finality of the tone, sighed and yielded. Already Bishop was moving down the line. For Mr. Blood, as for a weedy youth on his left, the Colonel had no more than a glance of contempt. But the next man, a middle-aged Colossus named Wolverstone, who had lost an eye at Sedgemoor, drew his regard, and the haggling was recommenced.

Peter Blood stood there in the brilliant sunshine and inhaled the fragrant air, which was unlike any air that he had ever breathed. It was laden with a strange perfume, blend of logwood flower, pimento, and aromatic cedars. He lost himself in unprofitable speculations born of that singular fragrance. He was in no mood for conversation, nor was Pitt, who stood dumbly at his side, and who was afflicted mainly at the moment by the thought that he was at last about to be separated from this man with whom he had stood shoulder to shoulder throughout all these troublous months, and whom he had come to love and depend upon for guidance and sustenance. A sense of loneliness and misery pervaded him by contrast with which all that he had endured seemed as nothing. To Pitt, this separation was the poignant climax of all his sufferings.

Other buyers came and stared at them, and passed on. Blood did not heed them. And then at the end of the line there was a movement. Gardner was speaking in a loud voice, making an announcement to the general public of buyers that had waited until Colonel Bishop had taken his choice of that human merchandise. As he finished, Blood, looking in his direction, noticed that the girl was speaking to Bishop, and pointing up the line with a silver-hilted riding-whip she carried. Bishop shaded his eyes with his hand to look in the direction in which she was pointing. Then slowly, with his ponderous, rolling gait, he approached again accompanied by Gardner, and followed by the lady and the Governor.

On they came until the Colonel was abreast of Blood. He would have passed on, but that the lady tapped his arm with her whip.

"But this is the man I meant," she said.

"This one?" Contempt rang in the voice. Peter Blood found himself staring into a pair of beady brown eyes sunk into a yellow, fleshly face like currants into a dumpling. He felt the colour creeping into his face under the insult of that contemptuous inspection. "Bah! A bag of bones. What should I do with him?"

He was turning away when Gardner interposed.

"He maybe lean, but he's tough; tough and healthy. When half of them was sick and the other half sickening, this rogue kept his legs and doctored his fellows. But for him there'd ha' been more deaths than there was. Say fifteen pounds for him, Colonel. That's cheap enough. He's tough, I tell your honour—tough and strong, though he be lean. And he's just the man to bear the heat when it comes. The climate'll never kill him."

There came a chuckle from Governor Steed. "You hear, Colonel. Trust your niece. Her sex knows a man when it sees one." And he laughed, well pleased with his wit.

But he laughed alone. A cloud of annoyance swept across the face of the Colonel's niece, whilst the Colonel himself was too absorbed in the consideration of this bargain to heed the Governor's humour. He twisted his lip a little, stroking his chin with his hand the while. Jeremy Pitt had almost ceased to breathe.

"I'll give you ten pounds for him," said the Colonel at last.

Peter Blood prayed that the offer might be rejected. For no reason that he could have given you, he was taken with repugnance at the thought of becoming the property of this gross animal, and in some sort the property of that hazel-eyed young girl. But it would need more than repugnance to save him from his destiny. A slave is a slave, and has no power to shape his fate. Peter Blood was sold to Colonel Bishop—a disdainful buyer—for the ignominious sum of ten pounds.

V

ARABELLA BISHOP

One sunny morning in January, about a month after the arrival of the Jamaica Merchant at Bridgetown, Miss Arabella Bishop rode out from her uncle's fine house on the heights to the northwest of the city. She was attended by two black men who trotted after her at a respectful distance, and her destination was Government House, whither she went to visit the Governor's lady, who had lately been ailing. Reaching the summit of a gentle, grassy slope, she met a tall, lean man dressed in a sober, gentlemanly fashion, who was walking in the opposite direction. He was a stranger to her, and strangers were rare enough in the island. And yet in some vague way he did not seem quite a stranger.

Miss Arabella drew rein, affecting to pause that she might admire the prospect, which was fair enough to warrant it. Yet out of the corner of those hazel eyes she scanned this fellow very attentively as he came nearer. She corrected her first impression of his dress. It was sober enough, but hardly gentlemanly. Coat and breeches were of plain homespun; and if the former sat so well upon him it was more by virtue of his natural grace than by that of tailoring. His stockings were of cotton, harsh and plain, and the broad castor, which he respectfully doffed as he came up with her, was an old one unadorned by band or feather. What had seemed to be a periwig at a little distance was now revealed for the man's own lustrous coiling black hair.

Out of a brown, shaven, saturnine face two eyes that were startlingly blue considered her gravely. The man would have passed on but that she detained him.

"I think I know you, sir," said she.

Her voice was crisp and boyish, and there was something of boyishness in her manner—if one can apply the term to so dainty a lady. It arose perhaps from an ease, a directness, which disdained the artifices of her sex, and set her on good terms with all the world. To this it may be due that Miss Arabella had reached the age of five and twenty not merely unmarried but unwooed. She used with all men a sisterly frankness which in itself contains a quality of aloofness, rendering it difficult for any man to become her lover.

Her black men had halted at some distance in the rear, and they squatted now upon the short grass until it should be her pleasure to proceed upon her way.

The stranger came to a standstill upon being addressed.

"A lady should know her own property," said he.

"My property?"

"Your uncle's, leastways. Let me present myself. I am called Peter Blood, and I am worth precisely ten pounds. I know it because that is the sum your uncle paid for me. It is not every man has the same opportunities of ascertaining his real value."

She recognized him then. She had not seen him since that day upon the mole a month ago, and that she should not instantly have known him again despite the interest he had then aroused in her is not surprising, considering the change he had wrought in his appearance, which now was hardly that of a slave.

"My God!" said she. "And you can laugh!"

"It's an achievement," he admitted. "But then, I have not fared as ill as I might."

"I have heard of that," said she.

What she had heard was that this rebel-convict had been discovered to be a physician. The thing had come to the ears of Governor Steed, who suffered damnably from the gout, and Governor Steed had borrowed the fellow from his purchaser. Whether by skill or good fortune, Peter Blood had afforded the Governor that relief which his excellency had failed to obtain from the ministrations of either of the two physicians practising in Bridgetown. Then the Governor's lady had desired him to attend her for the megrims. Mr. Blood had found her suffering from nothing worse than peevishness—the result of a natural petulance aggravated by the dulness of life in Barbados to a lady of her social aspirations. But he had prescribed for her none the less, and she had conceived herself the better for his prescription. After that the fame of him had gone through Bridgetown, and Colonel Bishop had found that there was more profit to be made out of this new slave by leaving him to pursue his profession than by setting him to work on the plantations, for which purpose he had been originally acquired.

"It is yourself, madam, I have to thank for my comparatively easy and clean condition," said Mr. Blood, "and I am glad to take this opportunity of doing so."

The gratitude was in his words rather than in his tone. Was he mocking, she wondered, and looked at him with the searching frankness that another might have found disconcerting. He took the glance for a question, and answered it.

"If some other planter had bought me," he explained, "it is odds that the facts of my shining abilities might never have been brought to light, and I should be hewing and hoeing at this moment like the poor wretches who were landed with me."

"And why do you thank me for that? It was my uncle who bought you."

"But he would not have done so had you not urged him. I perceived your interest. At the time I resented it."

"You resented it?" There was a challenge in her boyish voice.

"I have had no lack of experiences of this mortal life; but to be bought and sold was a new one, and I was hardly in the mood to love my purchaser."

"If I urged you upon my uncle, sir, it was that I commiserated you." There was a slight severity in her tone, as if to reprove the mixture of mockery and flippancy in which he seemed to be speaking.

She proceeded to explain herself. "My uncle may appear to you a hard man. No doubt he is. They are all hard men, these planters. It is the life, I suppose. But there are others here who are worse. There is Mr. Crabston, for instance, up at Speightstown. He was there on the mole, waiting to buy my uncle's leavings, and if you had fallen into his hands... A dreadful man. That is why."

He was a little bewildered.

"This interest in a stranger..." he began. Then changed the direction of his probe. "But there were others as deserving of commiseration."

"You did not seem quite like the others."

"I am not," said he.

"Oh!" She stared at him, bridling a little. "You have a good opinion of yourself."

"On the contrary. The others are all worthy rebels. I am not. That is the difference. I was one who had not the wit to see that England requires purifying. I was content to pursue a doctor's trade in Bridgewater whilst my betters were shedding their blood to drive out an unclean tyrant and his rascally crew."

"Sir!" she checked him. "I think you are talking treason."

"I hope I am not obscure," said he.

"There are those here who would have you flogged if they heard you."

"The Governor would never allow it. He has the gout, and his lady has the megrims."

"Do you depend upon that?" She was frankly scornful.

"You have certainly never had the gout; probably not even the megrims," said he.

She made a little impatient movement with her hand, and looked away from him a moment, out to sea. Quite suddenly she looked at him again; and now her brows were knit.

"But if you are not a rebel, how come you here?"

He saw the thing she apprehended, and he laughed. "Faith, now, it's a long story," said he.

"And one perhaps that you would prefer not to tell?"

Briefly on that he told it her.

"My God! What an infamy!" she cried, when he had done.

"Oh, it's a sweet country England under King James! There's no need to commiserate me further. All things considered I prefer Barbados. Here at least one can believe in God."

He looked first to right, then to left as he spoke, from the distant shadowy bulk of Mount Hillbay to the limitless ocean ruffled by the winds of heaven. Then, as if the fair prospect rendered him conscious of his own littleness and the insignificance of his woes, he fell thoughtful.

"Is that so difficult elsewhere?" she asked him, and she was very grave.

"Men make it so."

"I see." She laughed a little, on a note of sadness, it seemed to him. "I have never deemed Barbados the earthly mirror of heaven," she confessed. "But no doubt you know your world better than I." She touched her horse with her little silver-hilted whip. "I congratulate you on this easing of your misfortunes."

He bowed, and she moved on. Her black men sprang up, and went trotting after her.

Awhile Peter Blood remained standing there, where she left him, conning the sunlit waters of Carlisle Bay below, and the shipping in that spacious haven about which the gulls were fluttering noisily.

It was a fair enough prospect, he reflected, but it was a prison, and in announcing that he preferred it to England, he had indulged that almost laudable form of boasting which lies in belittling our misadventures.

He turned, and resuming his way, went off in long, swinging strides towards the little huddle of huts built of mud and wattles—a miniature village enclosed in a stockade which the plantation slaves inhabited, and where he, himself, was lodged with them.

Through his mind sang the line of Lovelace:

> *"Stone walls do not a prison make,*
> *Nor iron bars a cage."*

But he gave it a fresh meaning, the very converse of that which its author had intended. A prison, he reflected, was a prison, though it had neither walls nor bars, however spacious it might be. And as he realized it that morning so he was to realize it increasingly as time sped on. Daily he came to think more of his clipped wings, of his exclusion from the world, and less of the fortuitous liberty he enjoyed. Nor did the contrasting of his comparatively easy lot with that of his unfortunate fellow-convicts bring him the satisfaction a differently constituted mind might have derived from it. Rather did the contemplation of their misery increase the bitterness that was gathering in his soul.

Of the forty-two who had been landed with him from the Jamaica Merchant, Colonel Bishop had purchased no less than twenty-five. The remainder had gone to lesser planters, some of them to Speightstown, and others still farther north. What may have been the lot of the latter he could not tell, but amongst Bishop's slaves Peter Blood came and went freely, sleeping in their quarters, and their lot he knew to be a brutalizing misery. They toiled in the sugar plantations from sunrise to sunset, and if their labours flagged, there were the whips of the overseer and his men to quicken them. They went in rags, some almost naked; they dwelt in squalor, and they were ill-nourished on salted meat and maize dumplings—food which to many of them was for a season at least so nauseating that two of them sickened and died before Bishop remembered that their lives had a certain value in labour to him and yielded to Blood's intercessions for a better care of such as fell ill. To curb insubordination, one of them who had rebelled against Kent, the brutal overseer, was lashed to death by black men under his comrades' eyes, and another who had been so misguided as to run away into the woods was tracked, brought back, flogged, and then branded on the forehead with the letters "F. T.," that all might know him for a fugitive traitor as long as he lived. Fortunately for him the poor fellow died as a consequence of the flogging.

After that a dull, spiritless resignation settled down upon the remainder. The most mutinous were quelled, and accepted their unspeakable lot with the tragic fortitude of despair.

Peter Blood alone, escaping these excessive sufferings, remained outwardly unchanged, whilst inwardly the only change in him was a daily deeper hatred of his kind, a daily deeper longing to escape from this place where man defiled so foully the lovely work of his Creator. It was a longing too vague to amount to a hope. Hope here was inadmissible. And yet he did not yield to despair. He set a mask of laughter on his saturnine countenance and went his way, treating the sick to the profit of Colonel Bishop, and encroaching further and further upon the preserves of the two other men of medicine in Bridgetown.

Immune from the degrading punishments and privations of his fellow-convicts, he was enabled to keep his self-respect, and was treated without harshness even by the soulless planter to whom he had been sold. He owed it all to gout and megrims.

He had won the esteem of Governor Steed, and—what is even more important—of Governor Steed's lady, whom he shamelessly and cynically flattered and humoured.

Occasionally he saw Miss Bishop, and they seldom met but that she paused to hold him in conversation for some moments, evincing her interest in him. Himself, he was never disposed to linger. He was not, he told himself, to be deceived by her delicate exterior, her sapling grace, her easy, boyish ways and pleasant, boyish voice. In all his life—and it had been very varied—he had never met a man whom he accounted more beastly than her uncle, and he could not dissociate her from the man. She was his niece, of his own blood, and some of the vices of it, some of the remorseless cruelty of the wealthy planter must, he argued, inhabit that pleasant body of hers. He argued this very often to himself, as if answering and convincing some instinct that pleaded otherwise, and arguing it he avoided her when it was possible, and was frigidly civil when it was not.

Justifiable as his reasoning was, plausible as it may seem, yet he would have done better to have trusted the instinct that was in conflict with it. Though the same blood ran in her veins as in those of Colonel Bishop, yet hers was free of the vices that tainted her uncle's, for these vices were not natural to that blood; they were, in his case, acquired. Her father, Tom Bishop—that same Colonel Bishop's brother—had been a kindly, chivalrous, gentle soul, who, broken-hearted by the early death of a young wife, had abandoned the Old World and sought an anodyne for his grief in the New. He had come out to the Antilles, bringing with him his little daughter, then five years of age, and had given himself up to the life of a planter. He had prospered from the first, as men sometimes will who care nothing for prosperity. Prospering, he had bethought him of his younger brother, a soldier at home reputed somewhat wild. He had advised him to come out to Barbados; and the advice, which at another season William Bishop might have scorned, reached him at a moment when his wildness was beginning to bear such fruit that a change of climate was desirable. William came, and was admitted by his generous brother to a partnership in the prosperous plantation. Some six years later, when Arabella was fifteen, her father died, leaving her in her uncle's guardianship. It was perhaps his one mistake. But the goodness of his own nature coloured his views of other men; moreover, himself, he had conducted the education of his daughter, giving her an independence of character upon which perhaps he counted unduly. As things were, there was little love between uncle and niece. But she was dutiful to him, and he was circumspect in his behaviour before her. All his life, and for all his wildness, he had gone in a certain awe of his brother, whose worth he had the wit to recognize; and now it was almost as if some of that awe was transferred to his brother's child, who was also, in a sense, his partner, although she took no active part in the business of the plantations.

Peter Blood judged her—as we are all too prone to judge—upon insufficient knowledge.

He was very soon to have cause to correct that judgment. One day towards the end of May, when the heat was beginning to grow oppressive, there crawled into Carlisle Bay a wounded, battered English ship, the Pride of Devon, her freeboard scarred and broken, her coach a gaping wreck, her mizzen so shot away that only a jagged stump remained to tell the place where it had stood. She had been in action off Martinique with two Spanish treasure ships, and although her captain swore that the Spaniards had beset him without provocation, it is difficult to avoid a suspicion that the encounter had been brought about quite otherwise. One of the Spaniards had fled from the combat, and if the Pride of Devon had not given chase it was probably because she was by then in no case to do so. The other had been sunk, but not before the English ship had transferred to her own hold a good deal of the treasure aboard the Spaniard. It was, in fact, one of those piratical affrays which were a perpetual source of trouble between the courts of St. James's and the Escurial, complaints emanating now from one and now from the other side.

Steed, however, after the fashion of most Colonial governors, was willing enough to dull his wits to the extent of accepting the English seaman's story, disregarding any evidence that might belie it. He shared the hatred so richly deserved by arrogant, overbearing Spain that was common to men of every other nation from the Bahamas to the Main. Therefore he gave the Pride of Devon the shelter she sought in his harbour and every facility to careen and carry out repairs.

But before it came to this, they fetched from her hold over a score of English seamen as battered and broken as the ship herself, and together with these some half-dozen Spaniards in like case, the only survivors of a boarding party from the Spanish galleon that had invaded the English ship and found itself unable to retreat. These wounded men were conveyed to a long shed on the wharf, and the medical skill of Bridgetown was summoned to their aid. Peter Blood was ordered to bear a hand in this work, and partly because he spoke Castilian—and he spoke it as fluently as his own native tongue—partly because of his inferior condition as a slave, he was given the Spaniards for his patients.

Now Blood had no cause to love Spaniards. His two years in a Spanish prison and his subsequent campaigning in the Spanish Netherlands had shown him a side of the Spanish character which he had found anything but admirable. Nevertheless he performed his doctor's duties zealously and painstakingly, if emotionlessly, and even with a certain superficial friendliness towards each of his patients. These were so surprised at having their wounds healed instead of being summarily hanged that they manifested a docility very unusual in their kind. They were shunned, however, by all those charitably disposed inhabitants of Bridgetown who flocked to the improvised hospital with gifts of fruit and flowers and delicacies for the injured English seamen. Indeed, had the wishes of some of these inhabitants been regarded, the Spaniards would have been left to die like vermin, and of this Peter Blood had an example almost at the very outset.

With the assistance of one of the black men sent to the shed for the purpose, he was in the act of setting a broken leg, when a deep, gruff voice, that he had come to know and dislike as he had never disliked the voice of living man, abruptly challenged him.

"What are you doing there?"

Blood did not look up from his task. There was not the need. He knew the voice, as I have said.

"I am setting a broken leg," he answered, without pausing in his labours.

"I can see that, fool." A bulky body interposed between Peter Blood and the window. The half-naked man on the straw rolled his black eyes to stare up fearfully out of a clay-coloured face at this intruder. A knowledge of English was unnecessary to inform him that here came an enemy. The harsh, minatory note of that voice sufficiently expressed the fact. "I can see that, fool; just as I can see what the rascal is. Who gave you leave to set Spanish legs?"

"I am a doctor, Colonel Bishop. The man is wounded. It is not for me to discriminate. I keep to my trade."

"Do you, by God! If you'd done that, you wouldn't now be here."

"On the contrary, it is because I did it that I am here."

"Aye, I know that's your lying tale." The Colonel sneered; and then, observing Blood to continue his work unmoved, he grew really angry. "Will you cease that, and attend to me when I am speaking?"

Peter Blood paused, but only for an instant. "The man is in pain," he said shortly, and resumed his work.

"In pain, is he? I hope he is, the damned piratical dog. But will you heed me, you insubordinate knave?"

The Colonel delivered himself in a roar, infuriated by what he conceived to be defiance, and defiance expressing itself in the most unruffled disregard of himself. His long bamboo cane was raised to strike. Peter Blood's blue eyes caught the flash of it, and he spoke quickly to arrest the blow.

"Not insubordinate, sir, whatever I may be. I am acting upon the express orders of Governor Steed."

The Colonel checked, his great face empurpling. His mouth fell open.

"Governor Steed!" he echoed. Then he lowered his cane, swung round, and without another word to Blood rolled away towards the other end of the shed where the Governor was standing at the moment.

Peter Blood chuckled. But his triumph was dictated less by humanitarian considerations than by the reflection that he had baulked his brutal owner.

The Spaniard, realizing that in this altercation, whatever its nature, the doctor had stood his friend, ventured in a muted voice to ask him what had happened. But the doctor shook his head in silence, and pursued his work. His ears were straining to catch the words now passing between Steed and Bishop. The Colonel was blustering and storming, the great bulk of him towering above the wizened little overdressed figure of the Governor. But the little fop was not to be browbeaten. His excellency was conscious that he had behind him the force of public opinion to support him. Some there might be, but they were not many, who held such ruthless views as Colonel Bishop. His excellency asserted his authority. It was by his orders that Blood had devoted himself to the wounded

Spaniards, and his orders were to be carried out. There was no more to be said.

Colonel Bishop was of another opinion. In his view there was a great deal to be said. He said it, with great circumstance, loudly, vehemently, obscenely—for he could be fluently obscene when moved to anger.

"You talk like a Spaniard, Colonel," said the Governor, and thus dealt the Colonel's pride a wound that was to smart resentfully for many a week. At the moment it struck him silent, and sent him stamping out of the shed in a rage for which he could find no words.

It was two days later when the ladies of Bridgetown, the wives and daughters of her planters and merchants, paid their first visit of charity to the wharf, bringing their gifts to the wounded seamen.

Again Peter Blood was there, ministering to the sufferers in his care, moving among those unfortunate Spaniards whom no one heeded. All the charity, all the gifts were for the members of the crew of the Pride of Devon. And this Peter Blood accounted natural enough. But rising suddenly from the redressing of a wound, a task in which he had been absorbed for some moments, he saw to his surprise that one lady, detached from the general throng, was placing some plantains and a bundle of succulent sugar cane on the cloak that served one of his patients for a coverlet. She was elegantly dressed in lavender silk and was followed by a half-naked black man carrying a basket.

Peter Blood, stripped of his coat, the sleeves of his coarse shirt rolled to the elbow, and holding a bloody rag in his hand, stood at gaze a moment. The lady, turning now to confront him, her lips parting in a smile of recognition, was Arabella Bishop.

"The man's a Spaniard," said he, in the tone of one who corrects a misapprehension, and also tinged never so faintly by something of the derision that was in his soul.

The smile with which she had been greeting him withered on her lips. She frowned and stared at him a moment, with increasing haughtiness.

"So I perceive. But he's a human being none the less," said she.

That answer, and its implied rebuke, took him by surprise.

"Your uncle, the Colonel, is of a different opinion," said he, when he had recovered. "He regards them as vermin to be left to languish and die of their festering wounds."

She caught the irony now more plainly in his voice. She continued to stare at him.

"Why do you tell me this?"

"To warn you that you may be incurring the Colonel's displeasure. If he had had his way, I should never have been allowed to dress their wounds."

"And you thought, of course, that I must be of my uncle's mind?" There was a crispness about her voice, an ominous challenging sparkle in her hazel eyes.

"I'd not willingly be rude to a lady even in my thoughts," said he. "But that you should bestow gifts on them, considering that if your uncle came to hear of it..." He paused, leaving the sentence unfinished. "Ah, well—there it is!" he concluded.

But the lady was not satisfied at all.

"First you impute to me inhumanity, and then cowardice. Faith! For a man who would not willingly be rude to a lady even in his thoughts, it's none so bad." Her boyish laugh trilled out, but the note of it jarred his ears this time.

He saw her now, it seemed to him, for the first time, and saw how he had misjudged her.

"Sure, now, how was I to guess that... that Colonel Bishop could have an angel for his niece?" said he recklessly, for he was reckless as men often are in sudden penitence.

"You wouldn't, of course. I shouldn't think you often guess aright." Having withered him with that and her glance, she turned to her black man and the basket that he carried. From this she lifted now the fruits and delicacies with which it was laden, and piled them in such heaps upon the beds of the six Spaniards that by the time she had so served the last of them her basket was empty, and there was nothing left for her own fellow-countrymen. These, indeed, stood in no need of her bounty—as she no doubt observed—since they were being plentifully supplied by others.

Having thus emptied her basket, she called her negro, and without another word or so much as another glance at Peter Blood, swept out of the place with her head high and chin thrust forward.

Peter watched her departure. Then he fetched a sigh.

It startled him to discover that the thought that he had incurred her anger gave him concern. It could not have been so yesterday. It became so only since he had been vouchsafed this revelation of her true nature. "Bad cess to it now, it serves me right. It seems I know nothing at all of human nature. But how the devil was I to guess that a family that can breed a devil like Colonel Bishop should also breed a saint like this?"

VI

PLANS OF ESCAPE

After that Arabella Bishop went daily to the shed on the wharf with gifts of fruit, and later of money and of wearing apparel for the Spanish prisoners. But she contrived so to time her visits that Peter Blood never again met her there. Also his own visits were growing shorter in a measure as his patients healed. That they all throve and returned to health under his care, whilst fully one third of the wounded in the care of Whacker and Bronson—the two other surgeons—died of their wounds, served to increase the reputation in which this rebel-convict stood in Bridgetown. It may have been no more than the fortune of war. But the townsfolk did not choose so to regard it. It led to a further dwindling of the practices of his free colleagues and a further increase of his own labours and his owner's profit. Whacker and Bronson laid their heads together to devise a scheme by which this intolerable state of things should be brought to an end. But that is to anticipate.

One day, whether by accident or design, Peter Blood came striding down the wharf a full half-hour earlier than usual, and so met Miss Bishop just issuing from the shed. He doffed his hat and stood aside to give her passage. She took it, chin in the air, and eyes which disdained to look anywhere where the sight of him was possible.

"Miss Arabella," said he, on a coaxing, pleading note.

She grew conscious of his presence, and looked him over with an air that was faintly, mockingly searching.

"La!" said she. "It's the delicate-minded gentleman!"

Peter groaned. "Am I so hopelessly beyond forgiveness? I ask it very humbly."

"What condescension!"

"It is cruel to mock me," said he, and adopted mock-humility. "After all, I am but a slave. And you might be ill one of these days."

"What, then?"

"It would be humiliating to send for me if you treat me like an enemy."

"You are not the only doctor in Bridgetown."

"But I am the least dangerous."

She grew suddenly suspicious of him, aware that he was permitting himself to rally her, and in a measure she had already yielded to it. She stiffened, and looked him over again.

"You make too free, I think," she rebuked him.

"A doctor's privilege."

"I am not your patient. Please to remember it in future." And on that, unquestionably angry, she departed.

"Now is she a vixen or am I a fool, or is it both?" he asked the blue vault of heaven, and then went into the shed.

It was to be a morning of excitements. As he was leaving an hour or so later, Whacker, the younger of the other two physicians, joined him—an unprecedented condescension this, for hitherto neither of them had addressed him beyond an occasional and surly "good-day!"

"If you are for Colonel Bishop's, I'll walk with you a little way, Doctor Blood," said he. He was a short, broad man of five-and-forty with pendulous cheeks and hard blue eyes.

Peter Blood was startled. But he dissembled it.

"I am for Government House," said he.

"Ah! To be sure! The Governor's lady." And he laughed; or perhaps he sneered. Peter Blood was not quite certain. "She encroaches a deal upon your time, I hear. Youth and good looks, Doctor Blood! Youth and good looks! They are inestimable advantages in our profession as in others—particularly where the ladies are concerned."

Peter stared at him. "If you mean what you seem to mean, you had better say it to Governor Steed. It may amuse him."

"You surely misapprehend me."

"I hope so."

"You're so very hot, now!" The doctor linked his arm through Peter's. "I protest I desire to be your friend—to serve you. Now, listen." Instinctively his voice grew lower. "This slavery in which you find yourself must be singularly irksome to a man of parts such as yourself."

"What intuitions!" cried sardonic Mr. Blood. But the doctor took him literally.

"I am no fool, my dear doctor. I know a man when I see one, and often I can tell his thoughts."

"If you can tell me mine, you'll persuade me of it," said Mr. Blood.

Dr. Whacker drew still closer to him as they stepped along the wharf. He lowered his voice to a still more confidential tone. His hard blue eyes peered up into the swart, sardonic face of his companion, who was a head taller than himself.

"How often have I not seen you staring out over the sea, your soul in your eyes! Don't I know what you are thinking? If you could escape from this hell of slavery, you could exercise the profession of which you are an ornament as a free man with pleasure and profit to yourself. The world is large. There are many nations besides England where a man of your parts would be warmly welcomed. There are many colonies besides these English ones." Lower still came the voice until it was no more than a whisper. Yet there was no one within earshot. "It is none so far now to the Dutch settlement of Curacao. At this time of the year the voyage may safely be undertaken in a light craft. And Curacao need be no more than a stepping-stone to the great world, which would lie open to you once you were delivered from this bondage."

Dr. Whacker ceased. He was pale and a little out of breath. But his hard eyes continued to study his impassive companion.

"Well?" he said alter a pause. "What do you say to that?"

Yet Blood did not immediately answer. His mind was heaving in tumult, and he was striving to calm it that he might take a proper survey of this thing flung into it to create so monstrous a disturbance. He began where another might have ended.

"I have no money. And for that a handsome sum would be necessary."

"Did I not say that I desired to be your friend?"

"Why?" asked Peter Blood at point-blank range.

But he never heeded the answer. Whilst Dr. Whacker was professing that his heart bled for a brother doctor languishing in slavery, denied the opportunity which his gifts entitled him to make for himself, Peter Blood pounced like a hawk upon the obvious truth. Whacker and his colleague desired to be rid of one who threatened to ruin them. Sluggishness of decision was never a fault of Blood's. He leapt where another crawled. And so this thought of evasion never entertained until planted there now by Dr. Whacker sprouted into instant growth.

"I see, I see," he said, whilst his companion was still talking, explaining, and to save Dr. Whacker's face he played the hypocrite. "It is very noble in you—very brotherly, as between men of medicine. It is what I myself should wish to do in like case."

The hard eyes flashed, the husky voice grew tremulous as the other asked almost too eagerly:

"You agree, then? You agree?"

"Agree?" Blood laughed. "If I should be caught and brought back, they'd clip my wings and brand me for life."

"Surely the thing is worth a little risk?" More tremulous than ever was the tempter's voice.

"Surely," Blood agreed. "But it asks more than courage. It asks money. A sloop might be bought for twenty pounds, perhaps."

"It shall be forthcoming. It shall be a loan, which you shall repay us—repay me, when you can."

That betraying "us" so hastily retrieved completed Blood's understanding. The other doctor was also in the business.

They were approaching the peopled part of the mole. Quickly, but eloquently, Blood expressed his thanks, where he knew that no thanks were due.

"We will talk of this again, sir—tomorrow," he concluded. "You have opened for me the gates of hope."

In that at least he tittered no more than the bare truth, and expressed it very baldly. It was, indeed, as if a door had been suddenly flung open to the sunlight for escape from a dark prison in which a man had thought to spend his life.

He was in haste now to be alone, to straighten out his agitated mind and plan coherently what was to be done. Also he must consult another. Already he had hit upon that other. For such a voyage a navigator would be necessary, and a navigator was ready to his hand in Jeremy Pitt. The first thing was to take counsel with the young shipmaster, who must be associated with him in this business if it were to be undertaken. All that day his mind was in turmoil with this new hope, and he was sick with impatience for night and a chance to discuss the matter with his chosen partner. As a result Blood was betimes that evening in the spacious stockade that enclosed the huts of the slaves together with the big white house of the overseer, and he found an opportunity of a few words with Pitt, unobserved by the others.

"Tonight when all are asleep, come to my cabin. I have something to say to you."

The young man stared at him, roused by Blood's pregnant tone out of the mental lethargy into which he had of late been lapsing as a result of the dehumanizing life he lived. Then he nodded understanding and assent, and they moved apart.

The six months of plantation life in Barbados had made an almost tragic mark upon the young seaman. His erstwhile bright alertness was all departed. His face was growing vacuous, his eyes were dull and lack-lustre, and he moved in a cringing, furtive manner, like an over-beaten dog. He had survived the ill-nourishment, the excessive work on the sugar plantation under a pitiless sun, the lashes of the overseer's whip when his labours flagged, and the deadly, unrelieved animal life to which he was condemned. But the price he was paying for survival was the usual price. He was in danger of becoming no better than an animal, of sinking to the level of the black men who sometimes toiled beside him. The man, however, was still there, not yet dormant, but merely torpid from a surfeit of despair; and the man in him promptly shook off that torpidity and awoke at the first words Blood spoke to him that night—awoke and wept.

"Escape?" he panted. "O God!" He took his head in his hands, and fell to sobbing like a child.

"Sh! Steady now! Steady!" Blood admonished him in a whisper, alarmed by the lad's blubbering. He crossed to Pitt's side, and set a restraining hand upon his shoulder. "For God's sake, command yourself. If we're overheard we shall both be flogged for this."

Among the privileges enjoyed by Blood was that of a hut to himself, and they were alone in this. But, after all, it was built of wattles thinly plastered with mud, and its door was composed of bamboos, through which sound passed very easily. Though the stockade was locked for the night, and all within it asleep by now—it was after midnight—yet a prowling overseer was not impossible, and a sound of voices must lead to discovery. Pitt realized this, and controlled his outburst of emotion.

Sitting close thereafter they talked in whispers for an hour or more, and all the while those dulled wits of Pitt's were sharpening themselves anew upon this precious whetstone of hope. They would need to recruit others into their enterprise, a half-dozen at least, a half-score if possible, but no more than that. They must pick the best out of that score of survivors of the Monmouth men that Colonel Bishop had acquired. Men who understood the sea were desirable. But of these there were only two in that unfortunate gang, and their knowledge was none too full. They were Hagthorpe, a gentleman who had served in the Royal Navy, and Nicholas Dyke, who had been a petty officer in the late king's time, and there was another who had been a gunner, a man named Ogle.

It was agreed before they parted that Pitt should begin with these three and then proceed to recruit some six or eight others. He was to move with the utmost caution, sounding his men very carefully before making anything in the nature of a disclosure, and even then avoid rendering that disclosure so full that its betrayal might frustrate the plans which as yet had to be worked out in detail. Labouring with them in the plantations, Pitt would not want for opportunities of broaching the matter to his fellow-slaves.

"Caution above everything," was Blood's last recommendation to him at parting. "Who goes slowly, goes safely, as the Italians have it. And remember that if you betray yourself, you ruin all, for you are the only navigator amongst us, and without you there is no escaping."

Pitt reassured him, and slunk off back to his own hut and the straw that served him for a bed.

Coming next morning to the wharf, Blood found Dr. Whacker in a generous mood. Having slept on the matter, he was prepared to advance the convict any sum up to thirty pounds that would enable him to acquire a boat capable of taking him away from the settlement. Blood expressed his thanks becomingly, betraying no sign that he saw clearly into the true reason of the other's munificence.

"It's not money I'll require," said he, "but the boat itself. For who will be selling me a boat and incurring the penalties in Governor Steed's proclamation? Ye'll have read it, no doubt?"

Dr. Whacker's heavy face grew overcast. Thoughtfully he rubbed his chin. "I've read it—yes. And I dare not procure the boat for you. It would be discovered. It must be. And the penalty is a fine of two hundred pounds besides imprisonment. It would ruin me. You'll see that?"

The high hopes in Blood's soul, began to shrink. And the shadow of his despair overcast his face.

"But then..." he faltered. "There is nothing to be done."

"Nay, nay: things are not so desperate." Dr. Whacker smiled a little with tight lips. "I've thought of it. You will see that the man who buys the boat must be one of those who goes with you—so that he is not here to answer questions afterwards."

"But who is to go with me save men in my own case? What I cannot do, they cannot."

"There are others detained on the island besides slaves. There are several who are here for debt, and would be glad enough to spread their wings. There's a fellow Nuttall, now, who follows the trade of a shipwright, whom I happen to know would welcome such a chance as you might afford him."

"But how should a debtor come with money to buy a boat? The question will be asked."

"To be sure it will. But if you contrive shrewdly, you'll all be gone before that happens."

Blood nodded understanding, and the doctor, setting a hand upon his sleeve, unfolded the scheme he had conceived.

"You shall have the money from me at once. Having received it, you'll forget that it was I who supplied it to you. You have friends in England—relatives, perhaps—who sent it out to you through the agency of one of your Bridgetown patients, whose name as a man of honour you will on no account divulge lest you bring trouble upon him. That is your tale if there are questions."

He paused, looking hard at Blood. Blood nodded understanding and assent. Relieved, the doctor continued:

"But there should be no questions if you go carefully to work. You concert matters with Nuttall. You enlist him as one of your companions and a shipwright should be a very useful member of your crew. You engage him to discover a likely sloop whose owner is disposed to sell. Then let your preparations all be made before the purchase is effected, so that your escape may follow instantly upon it before the inevitable questions come to be asked. You take me?"

So well did Blood take him that within an hour he contrived to see Nuttall, and found the fellow as disposed to the business as Dr. Whacker had predicted. When he left the shipwright, it was agreed that Nuttall should seek the boat required, for which Blood would at once produce the money.

The quest took longer than was expected by Blood, who waited impatiently with the doctor's gold concealed about his person. But at the end of some three weeks, Nuttall—whom he was now meeting daily—informed him that he had found a serviceable wherry, and that its owner was disposed to sell it for twenty-two pounds. That evening, on the beach, remote from all eyes, Peter Blood handed that sum to his new associate, and Nuttall went off with instructions to complete the purchase late on the following day. He was to bring the boat to the wharf, where under cover of night Blood and his fellow-convicts would join him and make off.

Everything was ready. In the shed, from which all the wounded men had now been removed and which had since remained untenanted, Nuttall had concealed the necessary stores: a hundredweight of bread, a quantity of cheese, a cask of water and some few bottles of Canary, a compass, quadrant, chart, half-hour glass, log and line, a tarpaulin, some carpenter's tools, and a lantern and candles. And in the stockade, all was likewise in readiness. Hagthorpe, Dyke, and Ogle had agreed to join the venture, and eight others had been carefully recruited. In Pitt's hut, which he shared with five other rebels-convict, all of whom were to join in this bid for liberty, a ladder had been constructed in secret during those nights of waiting. With this they were to surmount the stockade and gain the open. The risk of detection, so that they made little noise, was negligible. Beyond locking them all into that stockade at night, there was no great precaution taken. Where, after all, could any so foolish as to attempt escape hope to conceal himself in that island? The chief risk lay in discovery by those of their companions who were to be left behind. It was because of these that they must go cautiously and in silence.

The day that was to have been their last in Barbados was a day of hope and anxiety to the twelve associates in that enterprise, no less than to Nuttall in the town below.

Towards sunset, having seen Nuttall depart to purchase and fetch the sloop to the prearranged moorings at the wharf, Peter Blood came sauntering towards the stockade, just as the slaves were being driven in from the fields. He stood aside at the entrance to let them pass, and beyond the message of hope flashed by his eyes, he held no communication with them.

He entered the stockade in their wake, and as they broke their ranks to seek their various respective huts, he beheld Colonel Bishop in talk with Kent, the overseer. The pair were standing by the stocks, planted in the middle of that green space for the punishment of offending slaves.

As he advanced, Bishop turned to regard him, scowling. "Where have you been this while?" he bawled, and although a minatory note was normal to the Colonel's voice, yet Blood felt his heart tightening apprehensively.

"I've been at my work in the town," he answered. "Mrs. Patch has a fever and Mr. Dekker has sprained his ankle."

"I sent for you to Dekker's, and you were not there. You are given to idling, my fine fellow. We shall have to quicken you one of these days unless you cease from abusing the liberty you enjoy. D'ye forget that ye're a rebel convict?"

"I am not given the chance," said Blood, who never could learn to curb his tongue.

"By God! Will you be pert with me?"

Remembering all that was at stake, growing suddenly conscious that from the huts surrounding the enclosure anxious ears were listening, he instantly practised an unusual submission.

"Not pert, sir. I... I am sorry I should have been sought..."

"Aye, and you'll be sorrier yet. There's the Governor with an attack of gout, screaming like a wounded horse, and you nowhere to be found. Be off, man—away with you at speed to Government House! You're awaited, I tell you. Best lend him a horse, Kent, or the lout'll be all night getting there."

They bustled him away, choking almost from a reluctance that he dared not show. The thing was unfortunate; but after all not beyond remedy. The escape was set for midnight, and he should easily be back by then. He mounted the horse that Kent procured him, intending to make all haste.

"How shall I reenter the stockade, sir?" he enquired at parting.

"You'll not reenter it," said Bishop. "When they've done with you at Government House, they may find a kennel for you there until morning."

Peter Blood's heart sank like a stone through water.

"But..." he began.

"Be off, I say. Will you stand there talking until dark? His excellency is waiting for you." And with his cane Colonel

Bishop slashed the horse's quarters so brutally that the beast bounded forward all but unseating her rider.

Peter Blood went off in a state of mind bordering on despair. And there was occasion for it. A postponement of the escape at least until tomorrow night was necessary now, and postponement must mean the discovery of Nuttall's transaction and the asking of questions it would be difficult to answer.

It was in his mind to slink back in the night, once his work at Government House were done, and from the outside of the stockade make known to Pitt and the others his presence, and so have them join him that their project might still be carried out. But in this he reckoned without the Governor, whom he found really in the thrall of a severe attack of gout, and almost as severe an attack of temper nourished by Blood's delay.

The doctor was kept in constant attendance upon him until long after midnight, when at last he was able to ease the sufferer a little by a bleeding. Thereupon he would have withdrawn. But Steed would not hear of it. Blood must sleep in his own chamber to be at hand in case of need. It was as if Fate made sport of him. For that night at least the escape must be definitely abandoned.

Not until the early hours of the morning did Peter Blood succeed in making a temporary escape from Government House on the ground that he required certain medicaments which he must, himself, procure from the apothecary.

On that pretext, he made an excursion into the awakening town, and went straight to Nuttall, whom he found in a state of livid panic. The unfortunate debtor, who had sat up waiting through the night, conceived that all was discovered and that his own ruin would be involved. Peter Blood quieted his fears.

"It will be for tonight instead," he said, with more assurance than he felt, "if I have to bleed the Governor to death. Be ready as last night."

"But if there are questions meanwhile?" bleated Nuttall. He was a thin, pale, small-featured, man with weak eyes that now blinked desperately.

"Answer as best you can. Use your wits, man. I can stay no longer." And Peter went off to the apothecary for his pretexted drugs.

Within an hour of his going came an officer of the Secretary's to Nuttall's miserable hovel. The seller of the boat had—as by law required since the coming of the rebels-convict—duly reported the sale at the Secretary's office, so that he might obtain the reimbursement of the ten-pound surety into which every keeper of a small boat was compelled to enter. The Secretary's office postponed this reimbursement until it should have obtained confirmation of the transaction.

"We are informed that you have bought a wherry from Mr. Robert Farrell," said the officer.

"That is so," said Nuttall, who conceived that for him this was the end of the world.

"You are in no haste, it seems, to declare the same at the Secretary's office." The emissary had a proper bureaucratic haughtiness.

Nuttall's weak eyes blinked at a redoubled rate.

"To... to declare it?"

"Ye know it's the law."

"I... I didn't, may it please you."

"But it's in the proclamation published last January."

"I... I can't read, sir. I... I didn't know."

"Faugh!" The messenger withered him with his disdain.

"Well, now you're informed. See to it that you are at the Secretary's office before noon with the ten pounds surety into which you are obliged to enter."

The pompous officer departed, leaving Nuttall in a cold perspiration despite the heat of the morning. He was thankful that the fellow had not asked the question he most dreaded, which was how he, a debtor, should come by the money to buy a wherry. But this he knew was only a respite. The question would presently be asked of a certainty, and then hell would open for him. He cursed the hour in which he had been such a fool as to listen to Peter Blood's chatter of escape. He thought it very likely that the whole plot would be discovered, and that he would probably be hanged, or at least branded and sold into slavery like those other damned rebels-convict, with whom he had been so mad as to associate himself. If only he had the ten pounds for this infernal surety, which until this moment had never entered into their calculations, it was possible that the thing might be done quickly and questions postponed until later. As the Secretary's messenger had overlooked the fact that he was a debtor, so might the others at the Secretary's office, at least for a day or two; and in that time he would, he hoped, be beyond the reach of their questions. But in the meantime what was to be done about this money? And it was to be found before noon!

Nuttall snatched up his hat, and went out in quest of Peter Blood. But where look for him? Wandering aimlessly up the irregular, unpaved street, he ventured to enquire of one or two if they had seen Dr. Blood that morning. He affected to be feeling none so well, and indeed his appearance bore out the deception. None could give him information; and since Blood had never told him of Whacker's share in this business, he walked in his unhappy ignorance past the door of the one man in Barbados who would eagerly have saved him in this extremity.

Finally he determined to go up to Colonel Bishop's plantation. Probably Blood would be there. If he were not, Nuttall would find Pitt, and leave a message with him. He was acquainted with Pitt and knew of Pitt's share in this business. His pretext for seeking Blood must still be that he needed medical assistance.

And at the same time that he set out, insensitive in his anxiety to the broiling heat, to climb the heights to the north of the town, Blood was setting out from Government House at last, having so far eased the Governor's condition as to be permitted to depart. Being mounted, he would, but for an unexpected delay, have reached the stockade ahead of Nuttall, in which case several unhappy events might have been averted. The unexpected delay was occasioned by Miss Arabella Bishop.

They met at the gate of the luxuriant garden of Government House, and Miss Bishop, herself mounted, stared to see Peter Blood on horseback. It happened that he was in good spirits. The fact that the Governor's condition had so far improved as to restore him his freedom of movement had sufficed to remove the depression under which he had been labouring for the past twelve hours and more. In its rebound the mercury of his mood had shot higher far than present circumstances warranted. He was disposed to be optimistic. What had failed last night would certainly not fail again tonight. What was a day, after all? The Secretary's office might be troublesome, but not really troublesome for another twenty-four hours at least; and by then they would be well away.

This joyous confidence of his was his first misfortune. The next was that his good spirits were also shared by Miss Bishop, and that she bore no rancour. The two things conjoined to make the delay that in its consequences was so deplorable.

"Good-morning, sir," she hailed him pleasantly. "It's close upon a month since last I saw you."

"Twenty-one days to the hour," said he. "I've counted them."

"I vow I was beginning to believe you dead."

"I have to thank you for the wreath."

"The wreath?"

"To deck my grave," he explained.

"Must you ever be rallying?" she wondered, and looked at him gravely, remembering that it was his rallying on the last occasion had driven her away in dudgeon.

"A man must sometimes laugh at himself or go mad," said he. "Few realize it. That is why there are so many madmen in the world."

"You may laugh at yourself all you will, sir. But sometimes I think you laugh at me, which is not civil."

"Then, faith, you're wrong. I laugh only at the comic, and you are not comic at all."

"What am I, then?" she asked him, laughing.

A moment he pondered her, so fair and fresh to behold, so entirely maidenly and yet so entirely frank and unabashed.

"You are," he said, "the niece of the man who owns me his slave." But he spoke lightly. So lightly that she was encouraged to insistence.

"Nay, sir, that is an evasion. You shall answer me truthfully this morning."

"Truthfully? To answer you at all is a labour. But to answer truthfully! Oh, well, now, I should say of you that he'll be lucky who counts you his friend." It was in his mind to add more. But he left it there.

"That's mighty civil," said she. "You've a nice taste in compliments, Mr. Blood. Another in your place..."

"Faith, now, don't I know what another would have said? Don't I know my fellow-man at all?"

"Sometimes I think you do, and sometimes I think you don't. Anyway, you don't know your fellow-woman. There was that affair of the Spaniards."

"Will ye never forget it?"

"Never."

"Bad cess to your memory. Is there no good in me at all that you could be dwelling on instead?"

"Oh, several things."

"For instance, now?" He was almost eager.

"You speak excellent Spanish."

"Is that all?" He sank back into dismay.

"Where did you learn it? Have you been in Spain?"

"That I have. I was two years in a Spanish prison."

"In prison?" Her tone suggested apprehensions in which he had no desire to leave her.

"As a prisoner of war," he explained. "I was taken fighting with the French—in French service, that is."

"But you're a doctor!" she cried.

"That's merely a diversion, I think. By trade I am a soldier—at least, it's a trade I followed for ten years. It brought me no great gear, but it served me better than medicine, which, as you may observe, has brought me into slavery. I'm thinking it's more pleasing in the sight of Heaven to kill men than to heal them. Sure it must be."

"But how came you to be a soldier, and to serve the French?"

"I am Irish, you see, and I studied medicine. Therefore—since it's a perverse nation we are—... Oh, but it's a long story, and the Colonel will be expecting my return." She was not in that way to be defrauded of her entertainment. If he would wait a moment they would ride back together. She had but come to enquire of the Governor's health at her uncle's request.

So he waited, and so they rode back together to Colonel Bishop's house. They rode very slowly, at a walking pace, and some whom they passed marvelled to see the doctor-slave on such apparently intimate terms with his owner's niece. One or two may have promised themselves that they would drop a hint to the Colonel. But the two rode oblivious of all others in the world that morning. He was telling her the story of his early turbulent days, and at the end of it he dwelt more fully than hitherto upon the manner of his arrest and trial.

The tale was barely done when they drew up at the Colonel's door, and dismounted, Peter Blood surrendering his nag to one of the black man grooms, who informed them that the Colonel was from home at the moment.

Even then they lingered a moment, she detaining him.

"I am sorry, Mr. Blood, that I did not know before," she said, and there was a suspicion of moisture in those clear hazel eyes. With a compelling friendliness she held out her hand to him.

"Why, what difference could it have made?" he asked.

"Some, I think. You have been very hardly used by Fate."

"Och, now..." He paused. His keen sapphire eyes considered her steadily a moment from under his level black brows. "It might have been worse," he said, with a significance which brought a tinge of colour to her cheeks and a flutter to her eyelids.

He stooped to kiss her hand before releasing it, and she did not deny him. Then he turned and strode off towards the stockade a half-mile away, and a vision of her face went with him, tinted with a rising blush and a sudden unusual shyness. He forgot in that little moment that he was a rebel-convict with ten years of slavery before him; he forgot that he had planned an escape, which was to be carried into effect that night; forgot even the peril of discovery which as a result of the Governor's gout now overhung him.

VII

PIRATES

Mr. James Nuttall made all speed, regardless of the heat, in his journey from Bridgetown to Colonel Bishop's plantation, and if ever man was built for speed in a hot climate that man was Mr. James Nuttall, with his short, thin body, and his long, fleshless legs. So withered was he that it was hard to believe there were any juices left in him, yet juices there must have been, for he was sweating violently by the time he reached the stockade.

At the entrance he almost ran into the overseer Kent, a squat, bow-legged animal with the arms of a Hercules and the jowl of a bulldog.

"I am seeking Doctor Blood," he announced breathlessly.

"You are in a rare haste," growled Kent. "What the devil is it? Twins?"

"Eh? Oh! Nay, nay. I'm not married, sir. It's a cousin of mine, sir."

"What is?"

"He is taken bad, sir," Nuttall lied promptly upon the cue that Kent himself had afforded him. "Is the doctor here?"

"That's his hut yonder." Kent pointed carelessly. "If he's not there, he'll be somewhere else." And he took himself off. He was a surly, ungracious beast at all times, readier with the lash of his whip than with his tongue.

Nuttall watched him go with satisfaction, and even noted the direction that he took. Then he plunged into the enclosure, to verify in mortification that Dr. Blood was not at home. A man of sense might have sat down and waited, judging that to be the quickest and surest way in the end. But Nuttall had no sense. He flung out of the stockade again, hesitated a moment as to which direction he should take, and finally decided to go any way but the way that Kent had gone. He sped across the parched savannah towards the sugar plantation which stood solid as a rampart and gleaming golden in the dazzling June sunshine. Avenues intersected the great blocks of ripening amber cane. In the distance down one of these he espied some slaves at work. Nuttall entered the avenue and advanced upon them. They eyed him dully, as he passed them. Pitt was not of their number, and he dared not ask for him. He continued his search for best part of an hour, up one of those lanes and then down another. Once an overseer challenged him, demanding to know his business. He was looking, he said, for Dr. Blood. His cousin was taken ill. The overseer bade him go to the devil, and get out of the plantation. Blood was not there. If he was anywhere he would be in his hut in the stockade.

Nuttall passed on, upon the understanding that he would go. But he went in the wrong direction; he went on towards the side of the plantation farthest from the stockade, towards the dense woods that fringed it there. The overseer was too contemptuous and perhaps too languid in the stifling heat of approaching noontide to correct his course.

Nuttall blundered to the end of the avenue, and round the corner of it, and there ran into Pitt, alone, toiling with a wooden spade upon an irrigation channel. A pair of cotton drawers, loose and ragged, clothed him from waist to knee; above and below he was naked, save for a broad hat of plaited straw that sheltered his unkempt golden head from the rays of the tropical sun. At sight of him Nuttall returned thanks aloud to his Maker. Pitt stared at him, and the shipwright poured out his dismal news in a dismal tone. The sum of it was that he must have ten pounds from Blood that very morning or they were all undone. And all he got for his pains and his sweat was the condemnation of Jeremy Pitt.

"Damn you for a fool!" said the slave. "If it's Blood you're seeking, why are you wasting your time here?"

"I can't find him," bleated Nuttall. He was indignant at his reception. He forgot the jangled state of the other's nerves after a night of anxious wakefulness ending in a dawn of despair. "I thought that you..."

"You thought that I could drop my spade and go and seek him for you? Is that what you thought? My God! that our lives should depend upon such a dummerhead. While you waste your time here, the hours are passing! And if an overseer should catch you talking to me? How'll you explain it?"

For a moment Nuttall was bereft of speech by such ingratitude. Then he exploded.

"I would to Heaven I had never had no hand in this affair. I would so! I wish that..."

What else he wished was never known, for at that moment round the block of cane came a big man in biscuit-coloured taffetas followed by two black men in cotton drawers who were armed with cutlasses. He was not ten yards away, but his approach over the soft, yielding marl had been unheard.

Mr. Nuttall looked wildly this way and that a moment, then bolted like a rabbit for the woods, thus doing the most foolish and betraying thing that in the circumstances it was possible for him to do. Pitt groaned and stood still, leaning upon his spade.

"Hi, there! Stop!" bawled Colonel Bishop after the fugitive, and added horrible threats tricked out with some rhetorical indecencies.

But the fugitive held amain, and never so much as turned his head. It was his only remaining hope that Colonel Bishop might not have seen his face; for the power and influence of Colonel Bishop was quite sufficient to hang any man whom he thought would be better dead.

Not until the runagate had vanished into the scrub did the planter sufficiently recover from his indignant amazement to remember the two black men who followed at his heels like a brace of hounds. It was a bodyguard without which he never moved in his plantations since a slave had made an attack upon him and all but strangled him a couple of years ago.

"After him, you black swine!" he roared at them. But as they started he checked them. "Wait! Get to heel, damn you!"

It occurred to him that to catch and deal with the fellow there was not the need to go after him, and perhaps spend the day hunting him in that cursed wood. There was Pitt here ready to his hand, and Pitt should tell him the identity of his bashful friend, and also the subject of that close and secret talk he had disturbed. Pitt might, of course, be reluctant. So much the worse for Pitt. The ingenious Colonel Bishop knew a dozen ways—some of them quite diverting—of conquering stubbornness in these convict dogs.

He turned now upon the slave a countenance that was inflamed by heat internal and external, and a pair of heady eyes that were alight with cruel intelligence. He stepped forward swinging his light bamboo cane.

"Who was that runagate?" he asked with terrible suavity. Leaning over on his spade, Jeremy Pitt hung his head a little, and shifted uncomfortably on his bare feet. Vainly he groped for an answer in a mind that could do nothing but curse the idiocy of Mr. James Nuttall.

The planter's bamboo cane fell on the lad's naked shoulders with stinging force.

"Answer me, you dog! What's his name?"

Jeremy looked at the burly planter out of sullen, almost defiant eyes.

"I don't know," he said, and in his voice there was a faint note at least of the defiance aroused in him by a blow which he dared not, for his life's sake, return. His body had remained unyielding under it, but the spirit within writhed now in torment.

"You don't know? Well, here's to quicken your wits." Again the cane descended. "Have you thought of his name yet?"

"I have not."

"Stubborn, eh?" For a moment the Colonel leered. Then his passion mastered him. "'Swounds! You impudent dog! D'you trifle with me? D'you think I'm to be mocked?"

Pitt shrugged, shifted sideways on his feet again, and settled into dogged silence. Few things are more provocative; and Colonel Bishop's temper was never one that required much provocation. Brute fury now awoke in him. Fiercely now he lashed those defenceless shoulders, accompanying each blow by blasphemy and foul abuse, until, stung beyond endurance, the lingering embers of his manhood fanned into momentary flame, Pitt sprang upon his tormentor.

But as he sprang, so also sprang the watchful blacks. Muscular bronze arms coiled crushingly about the frail white body, and in a moment the unfortunate slave stood powerless, his wrists pinioned behind him in a leathern thong.

Breathing hard, his face mottled, Bishop pondered him a moment. Then: "Fetch him along," he said.

Down the long avenue between those golden walls of cane standing some eight feet high, the wretched Pitt was thrust by his black captors in the Colonel's wake, stared at with fearful eyes by his fellow-slaves at work there. Despair went with him. What torments might immediately await him he cared little, horrible though he knew they would be. The real source of his mental anguish lay in the conviction that the elaborately planned escape from this unutterable hell was frustrated now in the very moment of execution.

They came out upon the green plateau and headed for the stockade and the overseer's white house. Pitt's eyes looked out over Carlisle Bay, of which this plateau commanded a clear view from the fort on one side to the long sheds of the wharf on the other. Along this wharf a few shallow boats were moored, and Pitt caught himself wondering which of these was the wherry in which with a little luck they might have been now at sea. Out over that sea his glance ranged miserably.

In the roads, standing in for the shore before a gentle breeze that scarcely ruffled the sapphire surface of the Caribbean, came a stately red-hulled frigate, flying the English ensign.

Colonel Bishop halted to consider her, shading his eyes with his fleshly hand. Light as was the breeze, the vessel spread no canvas to it beyond that of her foresail. Furled was her every other sail, leaving a clear view of the majestic lines of her hull, from towering stern castle to gilded beakhead that was aflash in the dazzling sunshine.

So leisurely an advance argued a master indifferently acquainted with these waters, who preferred to creep forward cautiously, sounding his way. At her present rate of progress it would be an hour, perhaps, before she came to anchorage within the harbour. And whilst the Colonel viewed her, admiring, perhaps, the gracious beauty of her, Pitt was hurried forward into the stockade, and clapped into the stocks that stood there ready for slaves who required correction.

Colonel Bishop followed him presently, with leisurely, rolling gait.

"A mutinous cur that shows his fangs to his master must learn good manners at the cost of a striped hide," was all he said before setting about his executioner's job.

That with his own hands he should do that which most men of his station would, out of self-respect, have relegated to one of the negroes, gives you the measure of the man's beastliness. It was almost as if with relish, as if gratifying some feral instinct of cruelty, that he now lashed his victim about head and shoulders. Soon his cane was reduced, to splinters by his violence. You know, perhaps, the sting of a flexible bamboo cane when it is whole. But do you realize its murderous quality when it has been split into several long lithe blades, each with an edge that is of the keenness of a knife?

When, at last, from very weariness, Colonel Bishop flung away the stump and thongs to which his cane had been reduced, the wretched slave's back was bleeding pulp from neck to waist.

As long as full sensibility remained, Jeremy Pitt had made no sound. But in a measure as from pain his senses were mercifully dulled, he sank forward in the stocks, and hung there now in a huddled heap, faintly moaning.

Colonel Bishop set his foot upon the crossbar, and leaned over his victim, a cruel smile on his full, coarse face.

"Let that teach you a proper submission," said he. "And now touching that shy friend of yours, you shall stay here without meat or drink—without meat or drink, d' ye hear me?—until you please to tell me his name and business." He took his foot from the bar. "When you've had enough of this, send me word, and we'll have the branding-irons to you."

On that he swung on his heel, and strode out of the stockade, his black men following.

Pitt had heard him, as we hear things in our dreams. At the moment so spent was he by his cruel punishment, and so deep was the despair into which he had fallen, that he no longer cared whether he lived or died.

Soon, however, from the partial stupor which pain had mercifully induced, a new variety of pain aroused him. The stocks stood in the open under the full glare of the tropical sun, and its blistering rays streamed down upon that mangled, bleeding back until he felt as if flames of fire were searing it. And, soon, to this was added a torment still more unspeakable. Flies, the cruel flies of the Antilles, drawn by the scent of blood, descended in a cloud upon him.

Small wonder that the ingenious Colonel Bishop, who so well understood the art of loosening stubborn tongues, had not deemed it necessary to have recourse to other means of torture. Not all his fiendish cruelty could devise a torment more cruel, more unendurable than the torments Nature would here procure a man in Pitt's condition.

The slave writhed in his stocks until he was in danger of breaking his limbs, and writhing, screamed in agony.

Thus was he found by Peter Blood, who seemed to his troubled vision to materialize suddenly before him. Mr. Blood carried a large palmetto leaf. Having whisked away with this the flies that were devouring Jeremy's back, he slung it by a strip of fibre from the lad's neck, so that it protected him from further attacks as well as from the rays of the sun. Next, sitting down beside him, he drew the sufferer's head down on his own shoulder, and bathed his face from a pannikin of cold water. Pitt shuddered and moaned on a long, indrawn breath.

"Drink!" he gasped. "Drink, for the love of Christ!" The pannikin was held to his quivering lips. He drank greedily, noisily, nor ceased until he had drained the vessel. Cooled and revived by the draught, he attempted to sit up.

"My back!" he screamed.

There was an unusual glint in Mr. Blood's eyes; his lips were compressed. But when he parted them to speak, his voice came cool and steady.

"Be easy, now. One thing at a time. Your back's taking no harm at all for the present, since I've covered it up. I'm wanting to know what's happened to you. D' ye think we can do without a navigator that ye go and provoke that beast Bishop until he all but kills you?"

Pitt sat up and groaned again. But this time his anguish was mental rather than physical.

"I don't think a navigator will be needed this time, Peter."

"What's that?" cried Mr. Blood.

Pitt explained the situation as briefly as he could, in a halting, gasping speech. "I'm to rot here until I tell him the identity of my visitor and his business."

Mr. Blood got up, growling in his throat. "Bad cess to the filthy slaver!" said he. "But it must be contrived, nevertheless. To the devil with Nuttall! Whether he gives surety for the boat or not, whether he explains it or not, the boat remains, and we're going, and you're coming with us."

"You're dreaming, Peter," said the prisoner. "We're not going this time. The magistrates will confiscate the boat since the surety's not paid, even if when they press him Nuttall does not confess the whole plan and get us all branded on the forehead."

Mr. Blood turned away, and with agony in his eyes looked out to sea over the blue water by which he had so fondly hoped soon to be travelling back to freedom.

The great red ship had drawn considerably nearer shore by now. Slowly, majestically, she was entering the bay. Already one or two wherries were putting off from the wharf to board her. From where he stood, Mr. Blood could see the glinting of the brass cannons mounted on the prow above the curving beak-head, and he could make out the figure of a seaman in the forechains on her larboard side, leaning out to heave the lead.

An angry voice aroused him from his unhappy thoughts.

"What the devil are you doing here?"

The returning Colonel Bishop came striding into the stockade, his black men following ever.

Mr. Blood turned to face him, and over that swarthy countenance—which, indeed, by now was tanned to the golden brown of a half-caste Indian—a mask descended.

"Doing?" said he blandly. "Why, the duties of my office."

The Colonel, striding furiously forward, observed two things. The empty pannikin on the seat beside the prisoner, and the palmetto leaf protecting his back. "Have you dared to do this?" The veins on the planter's forehead stood out like cords.

"Of course I have." Mr. Blood's tone was one of faint surprise.

"I said he was to have neither meat nor drink until I ordered it."

"Sure, now, I never heard ye."

"You never heard me? How should you have heard me when you weren't here?"

"Then how did ye expect me to know what orders ye'd given?" Mr. Blood's tone was positively aggrieved. "All that I knew was that one of your slaves was being murthered by the sun and the flies. And I says to myself, this is one of the Colonel's slaves, and I'm the Colonel's doctor, and sure it's my duty to be looking after the Colonel's property. So I just gave the fellow a spoonful of water and covered his back from the sun. And wasn't I right now?"

"Right?" The Colonel was almost speechless.

"Be easy, now, be easy!" Mr. Blood implored him. "It's an apoplexy ye'll be contacting if ye give way to heat like this."

The planter thrust him aside with an imprecation, and stepping forward tore the palmetto leaf from the prisoner's back.

"In the name of humanity, now..." Mr. Blood was beginning.

The Colonel swung upon him furiously. "Out of this!" he commanded. "And don't come near him again until I send for you, unless you want to be served in the same way."

He was terrific in his menace, in his bulk, and in the power of him. But Mr. Blood never flinched. It came to the Colonel, as he found himself steadily regarded by those light-blue eyes that looked so arrestingly odd in that tawny face—like pale sapphires set in copper—that this rogue had for some time now been growing presumptuous. It was a matter that he must presently correct. Meanwhile Mr. Blood was speaking again, his tone quietly insistent.

"In the name of humanity," he repeated, "ye'll allow me to do what I can to ease his sufferings, or I swear to you that I'll forsake at once the duties of a doctor, and that it's devil another patient will I attend in this unhealthy island at all."

For an instant the Colonel was too amazed to speak. Then—

"By God!" he roared. "D'ye dare take that tone with me, you dog? D'ye dare to make terms with me?"

"I do that." The unflinching blue eyes looked squarely into the Colonel's, and there was a devil peeping out of them, the devil of recklessness that is born of despair.

Colonel Bishop considered him for a long moment in silence. "I've been too soft with you," he said at last. "But that's to be mended." And he tightened his lips. "I'll have the rods to you, until there's not an inch of skin left on your dirty back."

"Will ye so? And what would Governor Steed do, then?"

"Ye're not the only doctor on the island."

Mr. Blood actually laughed. "And will ye tell that to his excellency, him with the gout in his foot so bad that he can't stand? Ye know very well it's devil another doctor will he tolerate, being an intelligent man that knows what's good for him."

But the Colonel's brute passion thoroughly aroused was not so easily to be baulked. "If you're alive when my blacks have done with you, perhaps you'll come to your senses."

He swung to his black men to issue an order. But it was never issued. At that moment a terrific rolling thunderclap drowned his voice and shook the very air. Colonel Bishop jumped, his black men jumped with him, and so even did the apparently imperturbable Mr. Blood. Then the four of them stared together seawards.

Down in the bay all that could be seen of the great ship, standing now within a cable's-length of the fort, were her topmasts thrusting above a cloud of smoke in which she was enveloped. From the cliffs a flight of startled seabirds had risen to circle in the blue, giving tongue to their alarm, the plaintive curlew noisiest of all.

As those men stared from the eminence on which they stood, not yet understanding what had taken place, they saw the British Jack dip from the main truck and vanish into the rising cloud below. A moment more, and up through that cloud to replace the flag of England soared the gold and crimson banner of Castile. And then they understood.

"Pirates!" roared the Colonel, and again, "Pirates!"

Fear and incredulity were blent in his voice. He had paled under his tan until his face was the colour of clay, and there was a wild fury in his beady eyes. His black men looked at him, grinning idiotically, all teeth and eyeballs.

VIII

SPANIARDS

The stately ship that had been allowed to sail so leisurely into Carlisle Bay under her false colours was a Spanish privateer, coming to pay off some of the heavy debt piled up by the predaceous Brethren of the Coast, and the recent defeat by the Pride of Devon of two treasure galleons bound for Cadiz. It happened that the galleon which escaped in a more or less crippled condition was commanded by Don Diego de Espinosa y Valdez, who was own brother to the Spanish Admiral Don Miguel de Espinosa, and who was also a very hasty, proud, and hot-tempered gentleman.

Galled by his defeat, and choosing to forget that his own conduct had invited it, he had sworn to teach the English a sharp lesson which they should remember. He would take a leaf out of the book of Morgan and those other robbers of the sea, and make a punitive raid upon an English settlement. Unfortunately for himself and for many others, his brother the Admiral was not at hand to restrain him when for this purpose he fitted out the Cinco Llagas at San Juan de Porto Rico. He chose for his objective the island of Barbados, whose natural strength was apt to render her defenders careless. He chose it also because thither had the Pride of Devon been tracked by his scouts, and he desired a measure of poetic justice to invest his vengeance. And he chose a moment when there were no ships of war at anchor in Carlisle Bay.

He had succeeded so well in his intentions that he had aroused no suspicion until he saluted the fort at short range with a broadside of twenty guns.

And now the four gaping watchers in the stockade on the headland beheld the great ship creep forward under the rising cloud of smoke, her mainsail unfurled to increase her steering way, and go about close-hauled to bring her larboard guns to bear upon the unready fort.

With the crashing roar of that second broadside, Colonel Bishop awoke from stupefaction to a recollection of where his duty lay. In the town below drums were beating frantically, and a trumpet was bleating, as if the peril needed further advertising. As commander of the Barbados Militia, the place of Colonel Bishop was at the head of his scanty troops, in that fort which the Spanish guns were pounding into rubble.

Remembering it, he went off at the double, despite his bulk and the heat, his black men trotting after him.

Mr. Blood turned to Jeremy Pitt. He laughed grimly. "Now that," said he, "is what I call a timely interruption. Though what'll come of it," he added as an afterthought, "the devil himself knows."

As a third broadside was thundering forth, he picked up the palmetto leaf and carefully replaced it on the back of his fellow-slave.

And then into the stockade, panting and sweating, came Kent followed by best part of a score of plantation workers, some of whom were black and all of whom were in a state of panic. He led them into the low white house, to bring them forth again, within a moment, as it seemed, armed now with muskets and hangers and some of them equipped with bandoleers.

By this time the rebels-convict were coming in, in twos and threes, having abandoned their work upon finding themselves unguarded and upon scenting the general dismay.

Kent paused a moment, as his hastily armed guard dashed forth, to fling an order to those slaves.

"To the woods!" he bade them. "Take to the woods, and lie close there, until this is over, and we've gutted these Spanish swine."

On that he went off in haste after his men, who were to be added to those massing in the town, so as to oppose and overwhelm the Spanish landing parties.

The slaves would have obeyed him on the instant but for Mr. Blood.

"What need for haste, and in this heat?" quoth he. He was surprisingly cool, they thought. "Maybe there'll be no need to take to the woods at all, and, anyway, it will be time enough to do so when the Spaniards are masters of the town."

And so, joined now by the other stragglers, and numbering in all a round score—rebels-convict all—they stayed to watch from their vantage-ground the fortunes of the furious battle that was being waged below.

The landing was contested by the militia and by every islander capable of bearing arms with the fierce resoluteness of men who knew that no quarter was to be expected in defeat. The ruthlessness of Spanish soldiery was a byword, and not at his worst had Morgan or L'Ollonais ever perpetrated such horrors as those of which these Castilian gentlemen were capable.

But this Spanish commander knew his business, which was more than could truthfully be said for the Barbados Militia. Having gained the advantage of a surprise blow, which had put the fort out of action, he soon showed them that he was master of the situation. His guns turned now upon the open space behind the mole, where the incompetent Bishop had marshalled his men, tore the militia into bloody rags, and covered the landing parties which were making the shore in their own boats and in several of those which had rashly gone out to the great ship before her identity was revealed.

All through the scorching afternoon the battle went on, the rattle and crack of musketry penetrating ever deeper into the town to show that the defenders were being driven steadily back. By sunset two hundred and fifty Spaniards were masters of Bridgetown, the islanders were disarmed, and at Government House, Governor Steed—his gout forgotten in his panic—supported by Colonel Bishop and some lesser officers, was being informed by Don Diego, with an urbanity that was itself a mockery, of the sum that would be required in ransom.

For a hundred thousand pieces of eight and fifty head of cattle, Don Diego would forbear from reducing the place to ashes. And what time that suave and courtly commander was settling these details with the apoplectic British Governor, the Spaniards were smashing and looting, feasting, drinking, and ravaging after the hideous manner of their kind.

Mr. Blood, greatly daring, ventured down at dusk into the town. What he saw there is recorded by Jeremy Pitt to whom he subsequently related it—in that voluminous log from which the greater part of my narrative is derived. I have no intention of repeating any of it here. It is all too loathsome and nauseating, incredible, indeed, that men however abandoned could ever descend such an abyss of bestial cruelty and lust.

What he saw was fetching him in haste and white-faced out of that hell again, when in a narrow street a girl hurtled into him, wild-eyed, her unbound hair streaming behind her as she ran. After her, laughing and cursing in a breath, came a heavy-booted Spaniard. Almost he was upon her, when suddenly Mr. Blood got in his way. The doctor had taken a sword from a dead man's side some little time before and armed himself with it against an emergency.

As the Spaniard checked in anger and surprise, he caught in the dusk the livid gleam of that sword which Mr. Blood had quickly unsheathed.

"Ah, perro ingles!" he shouted, and flung forward to his death.

"It's hoping I am ye're in a fit state to meet your Maker," said Mr. Blood, and ran him through the body. He did the thing skilfully: with the combined skill of swordsman and surgeon. The man sank in a hideous heap without so much as a groan.

Mr. Blood swung to the girl, who leaned panting and sobbing against a wall. He caught her by the wrist.

"Come!" he said.

But she hung back, resisting him by her weight. "Who are you?" she demanded wildly.

"Will ye wait to see my credentials?" he snapped. Steps were clattering towards them from beyond the corner round which she had fled from that Spanish ruffian. "Come," he urged again. And this time, reassured perhaps by his clear English speech, she went without further questions.

They sped down an alley and then up another, by great good fortune meeting no one, for already they were on the outskirts of the town. They won out of it, and white-faced, physically sick, Mr. Blood dragged her almost at a run up the hill towards Colonel Bishop's house. He told her briefly who and what he was, and thereafter there was no conversation between them until they reached the big white house. It was all in darkness, which at least was reassuring. If the Spaniards had reached it, there would be lights. He knocked, but had to knock again and yet again before he was answered. Then it was by a voice from a window above.

"Who is there?" The voice was Miss Bishop's, a little tremulous, but unmistakably her own.

Mr. Blood almost fainted in relief. He had been imagining the unimaginable. He had pictured her down in that hell out of which he had just come. He had conceived that she might have followed her uncle into Bridgetown, or committed some other imprudence, and he turned cold from head to foot at the mere thought of what might have happened to her.

"It is I—Peter Blood," he gasped.

"What do you want?"

It is doubtful whether she would have come down to open. For at such a time as this it was no more than likely that the wretched plantation slaves might be in revolt and prove as great a danger as the Spaniards. But at the sound of her voice, the girl Mr. Blood had rescued peered up through the gloom.

"Arabella!" she called. "It is I, Mary Traill."

"Mary!" The voice ceased above on that exclamation, the head was withdrawn. After a brief pause the door gaped wide. Beyond it in the wide hall stood Miss Arabella, a slim, virginal figure in white, mysteriously revealed in the gleam of a single candle which she carried.

Mr. Blood strode in followed by his distraught companion, who, falling upon Arabella's slender bosom, surrendered herself to a passion of tears. But he wasted no time.

"Whom have you here with you? What servants?" he demanded sharply.

The only male was James, an old black man groom.

"The very man," said Blood. "Bid him get out horses. Then away with you to Speightstown, or even farther north, where you will be safe. Here you are in danger—in dreadful danger."

"But I thought the fighting was over..." she was beginning, pale and startled.

"So it is. But the deviltry's only beginning. Miss Traill will tell you as you go. In God's name, madam, take my word for it, and do as I bid you."

"He... he saved me," sobbed Miss Traill.

"Saved you?" Miss Bishop was aghast. "Saved you from what, Mary?"

"Let that wait," snapped Mr. Blood almost angrily. "You've all the night for chattering when you're out of this, and away beyond their reach. Will you please call James, and do as I say—and at once!"

"You are very peremptory..."

"Oh, my God! I am peremptory! Speak, Miss Trail!, tell her whether I've cause to be peremptory."

"Yes, yes," the girl cried, shuddering. "Do as he says—Oh, for pity's sake, Arabella."

Miss Bishop went off, leaving Mr. Blood and Miss Traill alone again.

"I... I shall never forget what you did, sir," said she, through her diminishing tears. She was a slight wisp of a girl, a child, no more.

"I've done better things in my time. That's why I'm here," said Mr. Blood, whose mood seemed to be snappy.

She didn't pretend to understand him, and she didn't make the attempt.

"Did you... did you kill him?" she asked, fearfully.

He stared at her in the flickering candlelight. "I hope so. It is very probable, and it doesn't matter at all," he said. "What matters is that this fellow James should fetch the horses." And he was stamping off to accelerate these preparations for departure, when her voice arrested him.

"Don't leave me! Don't leave me here alone!" she cried in terror.

He paused. He turned and came slowly back. Standing above her he smiled upon her.

"There, there! You've no cause for alarm. It's all over now. You'll be away soon—away to Speightstown, where you'll be quite safe."

The horses came at last—four of them, for in addition to James who was to act as her guide, Miss Bishop had her woman, who was not to be left behind.

Mr. Blood lifted the slight weight of Mary Traill to her horse, then turned to say goodbye to Miss Bishop, who was already mounted. He said it, and seemed to have something to add. But whatever it was, it remained unspoken. The horses started, and receded into the sapphire starlit night, leaving him standing there before Colonel Bishop's door. The last he heard of them was Mary Traill's childlike voice calling back on a quavering note—

"I shall never forget what you did, Mr. Blood. I shall never forget."

But as it was not the voice he desired to hear, the assurance brought him little satisfaction. He stood there in the dark watching the fireflies amid the rhododendrons, till the hoofbeats had faded. Then he sighed and roused himself. He had much to do. His journey into the town had not been one of idle curiosity to see how the Spaniards conducted themselves in victory. It had been inspired by a very different purpose, and he had gained in the course of it all the information he desired. He had an extremely busy night before him, and must be moving.

He went off briskly in the direction of the stockade, where his fellow-slaves awaited him in deep anxiety and some hope.

IX

THE REBELS-CONVICT

There were, when the purple gloom of the tropical night descended upon the Caribbean, not more than ten men on guard aboard the Cinco Llagas, so confident—and with good reason—were the Spaniards of the complete subjection of the islanders. And when I say that there were ten men on guard, I state rather the purpose for which they were left aboard than the duty which they fulfilled. As a matter of fact, whilst the main body of the Spaniards feasted and rioted ashore, the Spanish gunner and his crew—who had so nobly done their duty and ensured the easy victory of the day—were feasting on the gun-deck upon the wine and the fresh meats fetched out to them from shore. Above, two sentinels only kept vigil, at stem and stern. Nor were they as vigilant as they should have been, or else they must have observed the two wherries that under cover of the darkness came gliding from the wharf, with well-greased rowlocks, to bring up in silence under the great ship's quarter.

From the gallery aft still hung the ladder by which Don Diego had descended to the boat that had taken him ashore. The sentry on guard in the stern, coming presently round this gallery, was suddenly confronted by the black shadow of a man standing before him at the head of the ladder.

"Who's there?" he asked, but without alarm, supposing it one of his fellows.

"It is I," softly answered Peter Blood in the fluent Castillan of which he was master.

"Is it you, Pedro?" The Spaniard came a step nearer.

"Peter is my name; but I doubt I'll not be the Peter you're expecting."

"How?" quoth the sentry, checking.

"This way," said Mr. Blood.

The wooden taffrail was a low one, and the Spaniard was taken completely by surprise. Save for the splash he made as he struck the water, narrowly missing one of the crowded boats that waited under the counter, not a sound announced his misadventure. Armed as he was with corselet, cuissarts, and headpiece, he sank to trouble them no more.

"Whist!" hissed Mr. Blood to his waiting rebels-convict. "Come on, now, and without noise."

Within five minutes they had swarmed aboard, the entire twenty of them overflowing from that narrow gallery and crouching on the quarter-deck itself. Lights showed ahead. Under the great lantern in the prow they saw the black figure of the other sentry, pacing on the forecastle. From below sounds reached them of the orgy on the gun-deck: a rich male voice was singing an obscene ballad to which the others chanted in chorus:

"Y estos son los usos de Castilla y de Leon!"

"From what I've seen today I can well believe it," said Mr. Blood, and whispered: "Forward—after me."

Crouching low, they glided, noiseless as shadows, to the quarter-deck rail, and thence slipped without sound down into the waist. Two thirds of them were armed with muskets, some of which they had found in the overseer's house, and others supplied from the secret hoard that Mr. Blood had so laboriously assembled against the day of escape. The remainder were equipped with knives and cutlasses.

In the vessel's waist they hung awhile, until Mr. Blood had satisfied himself that no other sentinel showed above decks but that inconvenient fellow in the prow. Their first attention must be for him. Mr. Blood, himself, crept forward with two companions, leaving the others in the charge of that Nathaniel Hagthorpe whose sometime commission in the King's Navy gave him the best title to this office.

Mr. Blood's absence was brief. When he rejoined his comrades there was no watch above the Spaniards' decks.

Meanwhile the revellers below continued to make merry at their ease in the conviction of complete security. The garrison of Barbados was overpowered and disarmed, and their companions were ashore in complete possession of the town, glutting themselves hideously upon the fruits of victory. What, then, was there to fear? Even when their quarters were invaded and they found themselves surrounded by a score of wild, hairy, half-naked men, who—save that they appeared once to have been white—looked like a horde of savages, the Spaniards could not believe their eyes.

Who could have dreamed that a handful of forgotten plantation-slaves would have dared to take so much upon themselves?

The half-drunken Spaniards, their laughter suddenly quenched, the song perishing on their lips, stared, stricken and bewildered at the levelled muskets by which they were checkmated.

And then, from out of this uncouth pack of savages that beset them, stepped a slim, tall fellow with light-blue eyes in a tawny face, eyes in which glinted the light of a wicked humour. He addressed them in the purest Castilian.

"You will save yourselves pain and trouble by regarding yourselves my prisoners, and suffering yourselves to be quietly bestowed out of harm's way."

"Name of God!" swore the gunner, which did no justice at all to an amazement beyond expression.

"If you please," said Mr. Blood, and thereupon those gentlemen of Spain were induced without further trouble beyond a musket prod or two to drop through a scuttle to the deck below.

After that the rebels-convict refreshed themselves with the good things in the consumption of which they had interrupted the Spaniards. To taste palatable Christian food after months of salt fish and maize dumplings was in itself a feast to these unfortunates. But there were no excesses. Mr. Blood saw to that, although it required all the firmness of which he was capable.

Dispositions were to be made without delay against that which must follow before they could abandon themselves fully to the enjoyment of their victory. This, after all, was no more than a preliminary skirmish, although it was one that afforded them the key to the situation. It remained to dispose so that the utmost profit might be drawn from it. Those dispositions occupied some very considerable portion of the night. But, at least, they were complete before the sun peeped over the shoulder of Mount Hilibay to shed his light upon a day of some surprises.

It was soon after sunrise that the rebel-convict who paced the quarter-deck in Spanish corselet and headpiece, a Spanish musket on his shoulder, announced the approach of a boat. It was Don Diego de Espinosa y Valdez coming aboard with four great treasure-chests, containing each twenty-five thousand pieces of eight, the ransom delivered to him at dawn by Governor Steed. He was accompanied by his son, Don Esteban, and by six men who took the oars.

Aboard the frigate all was quiet and orderly as it should be. She rode at anchor, her larboard to the shore, and the main ladder on her starboard side. Round to this came the boat with Don Diego and his treasure. Mr. Blood had disposed effectively. It was not for nothing that he had served under de Ruyter. The swings were waiting, and the windlass manned. Below, a gun-crew held itself in readiness under the command of Ogle, who—as I have said—had been a gunner in the Royal Navy before he went in for politics and followed the fortunes of the Duke of Monmouth. He was a sturdy, resolute fellow who inspired confidence by the very confidence he displayed in himself.

Don Diego mounted the ladder and stepped upon the deck, alone, and entirely unsuspicious. What should the poor man suspect?

Before he could even look round, and survey this guard drawn up to receive him, a tap over the head with a capstan bar efficiently handled by Hagthorpe put him to sleep without the least fuss.

He was carried away to his cabin, whilst the treasure-chests, handled by the men he had left in the boat, were being hauled to the deck. That being satisfactorily accomplished, Don Esteban and the fellows who had manned the boat came up the ladder, one by one, to be handled with the same quiet efficiency. Peter Blood had a genius for these things, and almost, I suspect, an eye for the dramatic. Dramatic, certainly, was the spectacle now offered to the survivors of the raid.

With Colonel Bishop at their head, and gout-ridden Governor Steed sitting on the ruins of a wall beside him, they glumly watched the departure of the eight boats containing the weary Spanish ruffians who had glutted themselves with rapine, murder, and violences unspeakable.

They looked on, between relief at this departure of their remorseless enemies, and despair at the wild ravages which, temporarily at least, had wrecked the prosperity and happiness of that little colony.

The boats pulled away from the shore, with their loads of laughing, jeering Spaniards, who were still flinging taunts across the water at their surviving victims. They had come midway between the wharf and the ship, when suddenly the air was shaken by the boom of a gun.

A round shot struck the water within a fathom of the foremost boat, sending a shower of spray over its occupants. They paused at their oars, astounded into silence for a moment. Then speech burst from them like an explosion. Angrily voluble they anathematized this dangerous carelessness on the part of their gunner, who should know better than to fire a salute from a cannon loaded with shot. They were still cursing him when a second shot, better aimed than the first, came to crumple one of the boats into splinters, flinging its crew, dead and living, into the water.

But if it silenced these, it gave tongue, still more angry, vehement, and bewildered to the crews of the other seven boats. From each the suspended oars stood out poised over the water, whilst on their feet in the excitement the Spaniards screamed oaths at the ship, begging Heaven and Hell to inform them what madman had been let loose among her guns.

Plump into their middle came a third shot, smashing a second boat with fearful execution. Followed again a moment of awful silence, then among those Spanish pirates all was gibbering and jabbering and splashing of oars, as they attempted to pull in every direction at once. Some were for going ashore, others for heading straight to the vessel and there discovering what might be amiss. That something was very gravely amiss there could be no further doubt, particularly as whilst they discussed and fumed and cursed two more shots came over the water to account for yet a third of their boats.

The resolute Ogle was making excellent practice, and fully justifying his claims to know something of gunnery. In their consternation the Spaniards had simplified his task by huddling their boats together.

After the fourth shot, opinion was no longer divided amongst them. As with one accord they went about, or attempted to do so, for before they had accomplished it two more of their boats had been sunk.

The three boats that remained, without concerning themselves with their more unfortunate fellows, who were struggling in the water, headed back for the wharf at speed.

If the Spaniards understood nothing of all this, the forlorn islanders ashore understood still less, until to help their wits they saw the flag of Spain come down from the mainmast of the Cinco Llagas, and the flag of England soar to its empty place. Even then some bewilderment persisted, and it was with fearful eyes that they observed the return of their enemies, who might vent upon them the ferocity aroused by these extraordinary events.

Ogle, however, continued to give proof that his knowledge of gunnery was not of yesterday. After the fleeing Spaniards went his shots. The last of their boats flew into splinters as it touched the wharf, and its remains were buried under a shower of loosened masonry.

That was the end of this pirate crew, which not ten minutes ago had been laughingly counting up the pieces of eight that would fall to the portion of each for his share in that act of villainy. Close upon threescore survivors contrived to reach the shore. Whether they had cause for congratulation, I am unable to say in the absence of any records in which their fate may be traced. That lack of records is in itself eloquent. We know that they were made fast as they landed, and considering the offence they had given I am not disposed to doubt that they had every reason to regret the survival.

The mystery of the succour that had come at the eleventh hour to wreak vengeance upon the Spaniards, and to preserve for the island the extortionate ransom of a hundred thousand pieces of eight, remained yet to be probed. That the Cinco

Llagas was now in friendly hands could no longer be doubted after the proofs it had given. But who, the people of Bridgetown asked one another, were the men in possession of her, and whence had they come? The only possible assumption ran the truth very closely. A resolute party of islanders must have got aboard during the night, and seized the ship. It remained to ascertain the precise identity of these mysterious saviours, and do them fitting honour.

Upon this errand—Governor Steed's condition not permitting him to go in person—went Colonel Bishop as the Governor's deputy, attended by two officers.

As he stepped from the ladder into the vessel's waist, the Colonel beheld there, beside the main hatch, the four treasure-chests, the contents of one of which had been contributed almost entirely by himself. It was a gladsome spectacle, and his eyes sparkled in beholding it.

Ranged on either side, athwart the deck, stood a score of men in two well-ordered files, with breasts and backs of steel, polished Spanish morions on their heads, overshadowing their faces, and muskets ordered at their sides.

Colonel Bishop could not be expected to recognize at a glance in these upright, furbished, soldierly figures the ragged, unkempt scarecrows that but yesterday had been toiling in his plantations. Still less could he be expected to recognize at once the courtly gentleman who advanced to greet him—a lean, graceful gentleman, dressed in the Spanish fashion, all in black with silver lace, a gold-hilted sword dangling beside him from a gold embroidered baldrick, a broad castor with a sweeping plume set above carefully curled ringlets of deepest black.

"Be welcome aboard the Cinco Llagas, Colonel, darling," a voice vaguely familiar addressed the planter. "We've made the best of the Spaniards' wardrobe in honour of this visit, though it was scarcely yourself we had dared hope to expect. You find yourself among friends—old friends of yours, all."

The Colonel stared in stupefaction. Mr. Blood tricked out in all this splendour—indulging therein his natural taste—his face carefully shaven, his hair as carefully dressed, seemed transformed into a younger man. The fact is he looked no more than the thirty-three years he counted to his age.

"Peter Blood!" It was an ejaculation of amazement. Satisfaction followed swiftly. "Was it you, then...?"

"Myself it was—myself and these, my good friends and yours." Mr. Blood tossed back the fine lace from his wrist, to wave a hand towards the file of men standing to attention there.

The Colonel looked more closely. "Gad's my life!" he crowed on a note of foolish jubilation. "And it was with these fellows that you took the Spaniard and turned the tables on those dogs! Oddswounds! It was heroic!"

"Heroic, is it? Bedad, it's epic! Ye begin to perceive the breadth and depth of my genius."

Colonel Bishop sat himself down on the hatch-coaming, took off his broad hat, and mopped his brow.

"Y'amaze me!" he gasped. "On my soul, y'amaze me! To have recovered the treasure and to have seized this fine ship and all she'll hold! It will be something to set against the other losses we have suffered. As Gad's my life, you deserve well for this."

"I am entirely of your opinion."

"Damme! You all deserve well, and damme, you shall find me grateful."

"That's as it should be," said Mr. Blood. "The question is how well we deserve, and how grateful shall we find you?"

Colonel Bishop considered him. There was a shadow of surprise in his face.

"Why—his excellency shall write home an account of your exploit, and maybe some portion of your sentences shall be remitted."

"The generosity of King James is well known," sneered Nathaniel Hagthorpe, who was standing by, and amongst the ranged rebels-convict some one ventured to laugh.

Colonel Bishop started up. He was pervaded by the first pang of uneasiness. It occurred to him that all here might not be as friendly as appeared.

"And there's another matter," Mr. Blood resumed. "There's a matter of a flogging that's due to me. Ye're a man of your word in such matters, Colonel—if not perhaps in others—and ye said, I think, that ye'd not leave a square inch of skin on my back."

The planter waved the matter aside. Almost it seemed to offend him.

"Tush! Tush! After this splendid deed of yours, do you suppose I can be thinking of such things?"

"I'm glad ye feel like that about it. But I'm thinking it's mighty lucky for me the Spaniards didn't come to day instead of yesterday, or it's in the same plight as Jeremy Pitt I'd be this minute. And in that case where was the genius that would have turned the tables on these rascally Spaniards?"

"Why speak of it now?"

Mr. Blood resumed: "ye'll please to understand that I must, Colonel, darling. Ye've worked a deal of wickedness and cruelty in your time, and I want this to be a lesson to you, a lesson that ye'll remember—for the sake of others who may come after us. There's Jeremy up there in the round-house with a back that's every colour of the rainbow; and the poor lad'll not be himself again for a month. And if it hadn't been for the Spaniards maybe it's dead he'd be by now, and maybe myself with him."

Hagthorpe lounged forward. He was a fairly tall, vigorous man with a clear-cut, attractive face which in itself announced his breeding.

"Why will you be wasting words on the hog?" wondered that sometime officer in the Royal Navy. "Fling him overboard and have done with him."

The Colonel's eyes bulged in his head. "What the devil do you mean?" he blustered.

"It's the lucky man ye are entirely, Colonel, though ye don't guess the source of your good fortune."

And now another intervened—the brawny, one-eyed Wolverstone, less mercifully disposed than his more gentlemanly fellow-convict.

"String him up from the yardarm," he cried, his deep voice harsh and angry, and more than one of the slaves standing to their arms made echo.

Colonel Bishop trembled. Mr. Blood turned. He was quite calm.

"If you please, Wolverstone," said he, "I conduct affairs in my own way. That is the pact. You'll please to remember it." His eyes looked along the ranks, making it plain that he addressed them all. "I desire that Colonel Bishop should have his life. One reason is that I require him as a hostage. If ye insist on hanging him, ye'll have to hang me with him, or in the alternative I'll go ashore."

He paused. There was no answer. But they stood hang-dog and half-mutinous before him, save Hagthorpe, who shrugged and smiled wearily.

Mr. Blood resumed: "Ye'll please to understand that aboard a ship there is one captain. So." He swung again to the startled Colonel. "Though I promise you your life, I must—as you've heard—keep you aboard as a hostage for the good behaviour of Governor Steed and what's left of the fort until we put to sea."

"Until you..." Horror prevented Colonel Bishop from echoing the remainder of that incredible speech.

"Just so," said Peter Blood, and he turned to the officers who had accompanied the Colonel. "The boat is waiting, gentlemen. You'll have heard what I said. Convey it with my compliments to his excellency."

"But, sir..." one of them began.

"There is no more to be said, gentlemen. My name is Blood—Captain Blood, if you please, of this ship the Cinco Llagas, taken as a prize of war from Don Diego de Espinosa y Valdez, who is my prisoner aboard. You are to understand that I have turned the tables on more than the Spaniards. There's the ladder. You'll find it more convenient than being heaved over the side, which is what'll happen if you linger."

They went, though not without some hustling, regardless of the bellowings of Colonel Bishop, whose monstrous rage was fanned by terror at finding himself at the mercy of these men of whose cause to hate him he was very fully conscious.

A half-dozen of them, apart from Jeremy Pitt, who was utterly incapacitated for the present, possessed a superficial knowledge of seamanship. Hagthorpe, although he had been a fighting officer, untrained in navigation, knew how to handle a ship, and under his directions they set about getting under way.

The anchor catted, and the mainsail unfurled, they stood out for the open before a gentle breeze, without interference from the fort.

As they were running close to the headland east of the bay, Peter Blood returned to the Colonel, who, under guard and panic-stricken, had dejectedly resumed his seat on the coamings of the main batch.

"Can ye swim, Colonel?"

Colonel Bishop looked up. His great face was yellow and seemed in that moment of a preternatural flabbiness; his beady eyes were beadier than ever.

"As your doctor, now, I prescribe a swim to cool the excessive heat of your humours." Blood delivered the explanation pleasantly, and, receiving still no answer from the Colonel, continued: "It's a mercy for you I'm not by nature as bloodthirsty as some of my friends here. And it's the devil's own labour I've had to prevail upon them not to be vindictive. I doubt if ye're worth the pains I've taken for you."

He was lying. He had no doubt at all. Had he followed his own wishes and instincts, he would certainly have strung the Colonel up, and accounted it a meritorious deed. It was the thought of Arabella Bishop that had urged him to mercy, and had led him to oppose the natural vindictiveness of his fellow-slaves until he had been in danger of precipitating a mutiny. It was entirely to the fact that the Colonel was her uncle, although he did not even begin to suspect such a cause, that he owed such mercy as was now being shown him.

"You shall have a chance to swim for it," Peter Blood continued. "It's not above a quarter of a mile to the headland yonder, and with ordinary luck ye should manage it. Faith, you're fat enough to float. Come on! Now, don't be hesitating or it's a long voyage ye'll be going with us, and the devil knows what may happen to you. You're not loved any more than you deserve."

Colonel Bishop mastered himself, and rose. A merciless despot, who had never known the need for restraint in all these years, he was doomed by ironic fate to practise restraint in the very moment when his feelings had reached their most violent intensity.

Peter Blood gave an order. A plank was run out over the gunwale, and lashed down.

"If you please, Colonel," said he, with a graceful flourish of invitation.

The Colonel looked at him, and there was hell in his glance. Then, taking his resolve, and putting the best face upon it, since no other could help him here, he kicked off his shoes, peeled off his fine coat of biscuit-coloured taffetas, and climbed upon the plank.

A moment he paused, steadied by a hand that clutched the ratlines, looking down in terror at the green water rushing past some five-and-twenty feet below.

"Just take a little walk, Colonel, darling," said a smooth, mocking voice behind him.

Still clinging, Colonel Bishop looked round in hesitation, and saw the bulwarks lined with swarthy faces—the faces of men that as lately as yesterday would have turned pale under his frown, faces that were now all wickedly agrin.

For a moment rage stamped out his fear. He cursed them aloud venomously and incoherently, then loosed his hold and stepped out upon the plank. Three steps he took before he lost his balance and went tumbling into the green depths below.

When he came to the surface again, gasping for air, the Cinco Llagas was already some furlongs to leeward. But the roaring cheer of mocking valediction from the rebels-convict reached him across the water, to drive the iron of impotent rage deeper into his soul.

X

DON DIEGO

Don Diego de Espinosa y Valdez awoke, and with languid eyes in aching head, he looked round the cabin, which was flooded with sunlight from the square windows astern. Then he uttered a moan, and closed his eyes again, impelled to this by the monstrous ache in his head. Lying thus, he attempted to think, to locate himself in time and space. But between the pain in his head and the confusion in his mind, he found coherent thought impossible.

An indefinite sense of alarm drove him to open his eyes again, and once more to consider his surroundings.

There could be no doubt that he lay in the great cabin of his own ship, the Cinco Llagas, so that his vague disquiet must be, surely, ill-founded. And yet, stirrings of memory coming now to the assistance of reflection, compelled him uneasily to insist that here something was not as it should be. The low position of the sun, flooding the cabin with golden light from those square ports astern, suggested to him at first that it was early morning, on the assumption that the vessel was headed westward. Then the alternative occurred to him. They might be sailing eastward, in which case the time of day would be late afternoon. That they were sailing he could feel from the gentle forward heave of the vessel under him. But how did they come to be sailing, and he, the master, not to know whether their course lay east or west, not to be able to recollect whither they were bound?

His mind went back over the adventure of yesterday, if of yesterday it was. He was clear on the matter of the easily successful raid upon the Island of Barbados; every detail stood vividly in his memory up to the moment at which, returning aboard, he had stepped on to his own deck again. There memory abruptly and inexplicably ceased.

He was beginning to torture his mind with conjecture, when the door opened, and to Don Diego's increasing mystification he beheld his best suit of clothes step into the cabin. It was a singularly elegant and characteristically Spanish suit of black taffetas with silver lace that had been made for him a year ago in Cadiz, and he knew each detail of it so well that it was impossible he could now be mistaken.

The suit paused to close the door, then advanced towards the couch on which Don Diego was extended, and inside the suit came a tall, slender gentleman of about Don Diego's own height and shape. Seeing the wide, startled eyes of the Spaniard upon him, the gentleman lengthened his stride.

"Awake, eh?" said he in Spanish.

The recumbent man looked up bewildered into a pair of light-blue eyes that regarded him out of a tawny, sardonic face set in a cluster of black ringlets. But he was too bewildered to make any answer.

The stranger's fingers touched the top of Don Diego's head, whereupon Don Diego winced and cried out in pain.

"Tender, eh?" said the stranger. He took Don Diego's wrist between thumb and second finger. And then, at last, the intrigued Spaniard spoke.

"Are you a doctor?"

"Among other things." The swarthy gentleman continued his study of the patient's pulse. "Firm and regular," he announced at last, and dropped the wrist. "You've taken no great harm."

Don Diego struggled up into a sitting position on the red velvet couch.

"Who the devil are you?" he asked. "And what the devil are you doing in my clothes and aboard my ship?"

The level black eyebrows went up, a faint smile curled the lips of the long mouth.

"You are still delirious, I fear. This is not your ship. This is my ship, and these are my clothes."

"Your ship?" quoth the other, aghast, and still more aghast he added: "Your clothes? But... then..." Wildly his eyes looked about him. They scanned the cabin once again, scrutinizing each familiar object. "Am I mad?" he asked at last. "Surely this ship is the Cinco Llagas?"

"The Cinco Llagas it is."

"Then..." The Spaniard broke off. His glance grew still more troubled. "Valga me Dios!" he cried out, like a man in anguish. "Will you tell me also that you are Don Diego de Espinosa?"

"Oh, no, my name is Blood—Captain Peter Blood. This ship, like this handsome suit of clothes, is mine by right of conquest. Just as you, Don Diego, are my prisoner."

Startling as was the explanation, yet it proved soothing to Don Diego, being so much less startling than the things he was beginning to imagine.

"But... Are you not Spanish, then?"

"You flatter my Castilian accent. I have the honour to be Irish. You were thinking that a miracle had happened. So it has—a miracle wrought by my genius, which is considerable."

Succinctly now Captain Blood dispelled the mystery by a relation of the facts. It was a narrative that painted red and white by turns the Spaniard's countenance. He put a hand to the back of his head, and there discovered, in confirmation of the story, a lump as large as a pigeon's egg. Lastly, he stared wild-eyed at the sardonic Captain Blood.

"And my son? What of my son?" he cried out. "He was in the boat that brought me aboard."

"Your son is safe; he and the boat's crew together with your gunner and his men are snugly in irons under hatches."

Don Diego sank back on the couch, his glittering dark eyes fixed upon the tawny face above him. He composed himself. After all, he possessed the stoicism proper to his desperate trade. The dice had fallen against him in this venture. The tables had been turned upon him in the very moment of success. He accepted the situation with the fortitude of a fatalist.

With the utmost calm he enquired:

"And now, Senor Capitan?"

"And now," said Captain Blood—to give him the title he had assumed—"being a humane man, I am sorry to find that ye're not dead from the tap we gave you. For it means that you'll be put to the trouble of dying all over again."

"Ah!" Don Diego drew a deep breath. "But is that necessary?" he asked, without apparent perturbation.

Captain Blood's blue eyes approved his bearing. "Ask yourself," said he. "Tell me, as an experienced and bloody pirate, what in my place would you do, yourself?"

"Ah, but there is a difference." Don Diego sat up to argue the matter. "It lies in the fact that you boast yourself a humane man."

Captain Blood perched himself on the edge of the long oak table. "But I am not a fool," said he, "and I'll not allow a natural Irish sentimentality to stand in the way of my doing what is necessary and proper. You and your ten surviving scoundrels are a menace on this ship. More than that, she is none so well found in water and provisions. True, we are fortunately a small number, but you and your party inconveniently increase it. So that on every hand, you see, prudence suggests to us that we should deny ourselves the pleasure of your company, and, steeling our soft hearts to the inevitable, invite you to be so obliging as to step over the side."

"I see," said the Spaniard pensively. He swung his legs from the couch, and sat now upon the edge of it, his elbows on his knees. He had taken the measure of his man, and met him with a mock-urbanity and a suave detachment that matched his own. "I confess," he admitted, "that there is much force in what you say."

"You take a load from my mind," said Captain Blood. "I would not appear unnecessarily harsh, especially since I and my friends owe you so very much. For, whatever it may have been to others, to us your raid upon Barbados was most opportune. I am glad, therefore, that you agree the I have no choice."

"But, my friend, I did not agree so much."

"If there is any alternative that you can suggest, I shall be most happy to consider it."

Don Diego stroked his pointed black beard.

"Can you give me until morning for reflection? My head aches so damnably that I am incapable of thought. And this, you will admit, is a matter that asks serious thought."

Captain Blood stood up. From a shelf he took a half-hour glass, reversed it so that the bulb containing the red sand was uppermost, and stood it on the table.

"I am sorry to press you in such a matter, Don Diego, but one glass is all that I can give you. If by the time those sands have run out you can propose no acceptable alternative, I shall most reluctantly be driven to ask you to go over the side with your friends."

Captain Blood bowed, went out, and locked the door. Elbows on his knees and face in his hands, Don Diego sat watching the rusty sands as they filtered from the upper to the lower bulb. And what time he watched, the lines in his lean brown face grew deeper. Punctually as the last grains ran out, the door reopened.

The Spaniard sighed, and sat upright to face the returning Captain Blood with the answer for which he came.

"I have thought of an alternative, sir captain; but it depends upon your charity. It is that you put us ashore on one of the islands of this pestilent archipelago, and leave us to shift for ourselves."

Captain Blood pursed his lips. "It has its difficulties," said he slowly.

"I feared it would be so." Don Diego sighed again, and stood up. "Let us say no more."

The light-blue eyes played over him like points of steel.

"You are not afraid to die, Don Diego?"

The Spaniard threw back his head, a frown between his eyes. "The question is offensive, sir."

"Then let me put it in another way—perhaps more happily: You do not desire to live?"

"Ah, that I can answer. I do desire to live; and even more do I desire that my son may live. But the desire shall not make a coward of me for your amusement, master mocker." It was the first sign he had shown of the least heat or resentment.

Captain Blood did not directly answer. As before he perched himself on the corner of the table.

"Would you be willing, sir, to earn life and liberty—for yourself, your son, and the other Spaniards who are on board?"

"To earn it?" said Don Diego, and the watchful blue eyes did not miss the quiver that ran through him. "To earn it, do you say? Why, if the service you would propose is one that cannot hurt my honour..."

"Could I be guilty of that?" protested the Captain. "I realize that even a pirate has his honour." And forthwith he propounded his offer. "If you will look from those windows, Don Diego, you will see what appears to be a cloud on the horizon. That is the island of Barbados well astern. All day we have been sailing east before the wind with but one intent—to set as great a distance between Barbados and ourselves as possible. But now, almost out of sight of land, we are in a difficulty. The only man among us schooled in the art of navigation is fevered, delirious, in fact, as a result of certain ill-treatment he received ashore before we carried him away with us. I can handle a ship in action, and there are one or two men aboard who can assist me; but of the higher mysteries of seamanship and of the art of finding a way over the trackless wastes of ocean, we know nothing. To hug the land, and go blundering about what you so aptly call this pestilent archipelago, is for us to court disaster, as you can perhaps conceive. And so it comes to this: We desire to make for the Dutch settlement of Curacao as straightly as possible. Will you pledge me your honour, if I release you upon parole, that you will navigate us thither? If so, we will release you and your surviving men upon arrival there."

Don Diego bowed his head upon his breast, and strode away in thought to the stern windows. There he stood looking out upon the sunlit sea and the dead water in the great ship's wake—his ship, which these English dogs had wrested from him; his ship, which he was asked to bring safely into a port where she would be completely lost to him and refitted perhaps to make war upon his kin. That was in one scale; in the other were the lives of sixteen men. Fourteen of them mattered little to him, but the remaining two were his own and his son's.

He turned at length, and his back being to the light, the Captain could not see how pale his face had grown.

"I accept," he said.

XI

FILIAL PIETY

By virtue of the pledge he had given, Don Diego de Espinosa enjoyed the freedom of the ship that had been his, and the navigation which he had undertaken was left entirely in his hands. And because those who manned her were new to the seas of the Spanish Main, and because even the things that had happened in Bridgetown were not enough to teach them to regard every Spaniard as a treacherous, cruel dog to be slain at sight, they used him with the civility which his own suave urbanity invited. He took his meals in the great cabin with Blood and the three officers elected to support him: Hagthorpe, Wolverstone, and Dyke.

They found Don Diego an agreeable, even an amusing companion, and their friendly feeling towards him was fostered by his fortitude and brave equanimity in this adversity.

That Don Diego was not playing fair it was impossible to suspect. Moreover, there was no conceivable reason why he should not. And he had been of the utmost frankness with them. He had denounced their mistake in sailing before the wind upon leaving Barbados. They should have left the island to leeward, heading into the Caribbean and away from the archipelago. As it was, they would now be forced to pass through this archipelago again so as to make Curacao, and this passage was not to be accomplished without some measure of risk to themselves. At any point between the islands they might come upon an equal or superior craft; whether she were Spanish or English would be equally bad for them, and being undermanned they were in no case to fight. To lessen this risk as far as possible, Don Diego directed at first a southerly and then a westerly course; and so, taking a line midway between the islands of Tobago and Grenada, they won safely through the danger-zone and came into the comparative security of the Caribbean Sea.

"If this wind holds," he told them that night at supper, after he had announced to them their position, "we should reach Curacao inside three days."

For three days the wind held, indeed it freshened a little on the second, and yet when the third night descended upon them they had still made no landfall. The Cinco Llagas was ploughing through a sea contained on every side by the blue bowl of heaven. Captain Blood uneasily mentioned it to Don Diego.

"It will be for tomorrow morning," he was answered with calm conviction.

"By all the saints, it is always 'tomorrow morning' with you Spaniards; and tomorrow never comes, my friend."

"But this tomorrow is coming, rest assured. However early you may be astir, you shall see land ahead, Don Pedro."

Captain Blood passed on, content, and went to visit Jerry Pitt, his patient, to whose condition Don Diego owed his chance of life. For twenty-four hours now the fever had left the sufferer, and under Peter Blood's dressings, his lacerated back was beginning to heal satisfactorily. So far, indeed, was he recovered that he complained of his confinement, of the heat in his cabin. To indulge him Captain Blood consented that he should take the air on deck, and so, as the last of the daylight was fading from the sky, Jeremy Pitt came forth upon the Captain's arm.

Seated on the hatch-coamings, the Somersetshire lad gratefully filled his lungs with the cool night air, and professed himself revived thereby. Then with the seaman's instinct his eyes wandered to the darkling vault of heaven, spangled already with a myriad golden points of light. Awhile he scanned it idly, vacantly; then, his attention became sharply fixed. He looked round and up at Captain Blood, who stood beside him.

"D'ye know anything of astronomy, Peter?" quoth he.

"Astronomy, is it? Faith, now, I couldn't tell the Belt of Orion from the Girdle of Venus."

"Ah! And I suppose all the others of this lubberly crew share your ignorance."

"It would be more amiable of you to suppose that they exceed it."

Jeremy pointed ahead to a spot of light in the heavens over the starboard bow. "That is the North Star," said he.

"Is it now? Glory be, I wonder ye can pick it out from the rest."

"And the North Star ahead almost over your starboard bow means that we're steering a course, north, northwest, or maybe north by west, for I doubt if we are standing more than ten degrees westward."

"And why shouldn't we?" wondered Captain Blood.

"You told me—didn't you?—that we came west of the archipelago between Tobago and Grenada, steering for Curacao. If that were our present course, we should have the North Star abeam, out yonder."

On the instant Mr. Blood shed his laziness. He stiffened with apprehension, and was about to speak when a shaft of light clove the gloom above their heads, coming from the door of the poop cabin which had just been opened. It closed again, and presently there was a step on the companion. Don Diego was approaching. Captain Blood's fingers pressed Jerry's shoulder with significance. Then he called the Don, and spoke to him in English as had become his custom when others were present.

"Will ye settle a slight dispute for us, Don Diego?" said he lightly. "We are arguing, Mr. Pitt and I, as to which is the North Star."

"So?" The Spaniard's tone was easy; there was almost a suggestion that laughter lurked behind it, and the reason for this was yielded by his next sentence. "But you tell me Mr. Pitt he is your navigant?"

"For lack of a better," laughed the Captain, good-humouredly contemptuous. "Now I am ready to wager him a hundred pieces of eight that that is the North Star." And he flung out an arm towards a point of light in the heavens straight abeam. He afterwards told Pitt that had Don Diego confirmed him, he would have run him through upon that instant. Far from that, however, the Spaniard freely expressed his scorn.

"You have the assurance that is of ignorance, Don Pedro; and you lose. The North Star is this one." And he indicated it.

"You are sure?"

"But my dear Don Pedro!" The Spaniard's tone was one of amused protest. "But is it possible that I mistake? Besides, is there not the compass? Come to the binnacle and see there what course we make."

His utter frankness, and the easy manner of one who has nothing to conceal resolved at once the doubt that had leapt so suddenly in the mind of Captain Blood. Pitt was satisfied less easily.

"In that case, Don Diego, will you tell me, since Curacao is our destination, why our course is what it is?"

Again there was no faintest hesitation on Don Diego's part. "You have reason to ask," said he, and sighed. "I had hope" it would not be observed. I have been careless—oh, of a carelessness very culpable. I neglect observation. Always it is my way. I make too sure. I count too much on dead reckoning. And so today I find when at last I take out the quadrant that we do come by a half-degree too much south, so that Curacao is now almost due north. That is what cause the delay. But we will be there tomorrow."

The explanation, so completely satisfactory, and so readily and candidly forthcoming, left no room for further doubt that Don Diego should have been false to his parole. And when presently Don Diego had withdrawn again, Captain Blood confessed to Pitt that it was absurd to have suspected him. Whatever his antecedents, he had proved his quality when he announced himself ready to die sooner than enter into any undertaking that could hurt his honour or his country.

New to the seas of the Spanish Main and to the ways of the adventurers who sailed it, Captain Blood still entertained illusions. But the next dawn was to shatter them rudely and for ever.

Coming on deck before the sun was up, he saw land ahead, as the Spaniard had promised them last night. Some ten miles ahead it lay, a long coast-line filling the horizon east and west, with a massive headland jutting forward straight before them. Staring at it, he frowned. He had not conceived that Curacao was of such considerable dimensions. Indeed, this looked less like an island than the main itself.

Beating out a weather, against the gentle landward breeze he beheld a great ship on their starboard bow, that he conceived to be some three or four miles off, and—as well as he could judge her at that distance—of a tonnage equal if not superior to their own. Even as he watched her she altered her course, and going about came heading towards them, close-hauled.

A dozen of his fellows were astir on the forecastle, looking eagerly ahead, and the sound of their voices and laughter reached him across the length of the stately Cinco Llagas.

"There," said a soft voice behind him in liquid Spanish, "is the Promised Land, Don Pedro."

It was something in that voice, a muffled note of exultation, that awoke suspicion in him, and made whole the half-doubt he had been entertaining. He turned sharply to face Don Diego, so sharply that the sly smile was not effaced from the Spaniard's countenance before Captain Blood's eyes had flashed upon it.

"You find an odd satisfaction in the sight of it—all things considered," said Mr. Blood.

"Of course." The Spaniard rubbed his hands, and Mr. Blood observed that they were unsteady. "The satisfaction of a mariner."

"Or of a traitor—which?" Blood asked him quietly. And as the Spaniard fell back before him with suddenly altered countenance that confirmed his every suspicion, he flung an arm out in the direction of the distant shore. "What land is that?" he demanded. "Will you have the effrontery to tell me that is the coast of Curacao?"

He advanced upon Don Diego suddenly, and Don Diego, step by step, fell back. "Shall I tell you what land it is? Shall I?" His fierce assumption of knowledge seemed to dazzle and daze the Spaniard. For still Don Diego made no answer. And then Captain Blood drew a bow at a venture—or not quite at a venture. Such a coast-line as that, if not of the main itself, and the main he knew it could not be, must belong to either Cuba or Hispaniola. Now knowing Cuba to lie farther north and west of the two, it followed, he reasoned swiftly, that if Don Diego meant betrayal he would steer for the nearer of these Spanish territories. "That land, you treacherous, forsworn Spanish dog, is the island of Hispaniola."

Having said it, he closely watched the swarthy face now overspread with pallor, to see the truth or falsehood of his guess reflected there. But now the retreating Spaniard had come to the middle of the quarter-deck, where the mizzen sail made a screen to shut them off from the eyes of the Englishmen below. His lips writhed in a snarling smile.

"Ah, perro ingles! You know too much," he said under his breath, and sprang for the Captain's throat.

Tight-locked in each other's arms, they swayed a moment, then together went down upon the deck, the Spaniard's feet jerked from under him by the right leg of Captain Blood. The Spaniard had depended upon his strength, which was considerable. But it proved no match for the steady muscles of the Irishman, tempered of late by the vicissitudes of slavery. He had depended upon choking the life out of Blood, and so gaining the half-hour that might be necessary to bring up that fine ship that was beating towards them—a Spanish ship, perforce, since none other would be so boldly cruising in these Spanish waters off Hispaniola. But all that Don Diego had accomplished was to betray himself completely, and to no purpose. This he realized when he found himself upon his back, pinned down by Blood, who was kneeling on his chest, whilst the men summoned by their Captain's shout came clattering up the companion.

"Will I say a prayer for your dirty soul now, whilst I am in this position?" Captain Blood was furiously mocking him.

But the Spaniard, though defeated, now beyond hope for himself, forced his lips to smile, and gave back mockery for mockery.

"Who will pray for your soul, I wonder, when that galleon comes to lie board and board with you?"

"That galleon!" echoed Captain Blood with sudden and awful realization that already it was too late to avoid the consequences of Don Diego's betrayal of them.

"That galleon," Don Diego repeated, and added with a deepening sneer: "Do you know what ship it is? I will tell you. It is the Encarnacion, the flagship of Don Miguel de Espinosa, the Lord Admiral of Castile, and Don Miguel is my brother. It is a very fortunate encounter. The Almighty, you see, watches over the destinies of Catholic Spain."

There was no trace of humour or urbanity now in Captain Blood. His light eyes blazed: his face was set.

He rose, relinquishing the Spaniard to his men. "Make him fast," he bade them. "Truss him, wrist and heel, but don't hurt him—not so much as a hair of his precious head."

The injunction was very necessary. Frenzied by the thought that they were likely to exchange the slavery from which they had so lately escaped for a slavery still worse, they would have torn the Spaniard limb from limb upon the spot. And if they now obeyed their Captain and refrained, it was only because the sudden steely note in his voice promised for Don Diego Valdez something far more exquisite than death.

"You scum! You dirty pirate! You man of no honour!" Captain Blood apostrophized his prisoner.

But Don Diego looked up at him and laughed.

"You underrated me." He spoke English, so that all might hear. "I tell you that I was not fear death, and I show you that I was not fear it. You no understand. You just an English dog."

"Irish, if you please," Captain Blood corrected him. "And your parole, you tyke of Spain?"

"You think I give my parole to leave you sons of filth with this beautiful Spanish ship, to go make war upon other Spaniards! Ha!" Don Diego laughed in his throat. "You fool! You can kill me. Pish! It is very well. I die with my work well done. In less than an hour you will be the prisoners of Spain, and the Cinco Llagas will go belong to Spain again."

Captain Blood regarded him steadily out of a face which, if impassive, had paled under its deep tan. About the prisoner, clamant, infuriated, ferocious, the rebels-convict surged, almost literally "athirst for his blood."

"Wait," Captain Blood imperiously commanded, and turning on his heel, he went aside to the rail. As he stood there deep in thought, he was joined by Hagthorpe, Wolverstone, and Ogle the gunner. In silence they stared with him across the water at that other ship. She had veered a point away from the wind, and was running now on a line that must in the end converge with that of the Cinco Llagas.

"In less than half-an-hour," said Blood presently, "we shall have her athwart our hawse, sweeping our decks with her guns."

"We can fight," said the one-eyed giant with an oath.

"Fight!" sneered Blood. "Undermanned as we are, mustering a bare twenty men, in what case are we to fight? No, there would be only one way. To persuade her that all is well aboard, that we are Spaniards, so that she may leave us to continue on our course."

"And how is that possible?" Hagthorpe asked.

"It isn't possible," said Blood. "If it..." And then he broke off, and stood musing, his eyes upon the green water. Ogle, with a bent for sarcasm, interposed a suggestion bitterly.

"We might send Don Diego de Espinosa in a boat manned by his Spaniards to assure his brother the Admiral that we are all loyal subjects of his Catholic Majesty."

The Captain swung round, and for an instant looked as if he would have struck the gunner. Then his expression changed: the light of inspiration Was in his glance.

"Bedad! ye've said it. He doesn't fear death, this damned pirate; but his son may take a different view. Filial piety's mighty strong in Spain." He swung on his heel abruptly, and strode back to the knot of men about his prisoner. "Here!" he shouted to them. "Bring him below." And he led the way down to the waist, and thence by the booby hatch to the gloom of the 'tween-decks, where the air was rank with the smell of tar and spun yarn. Going aft he threw open the door of the spacious wardroom, and went in followed by a dozen of the hands with the pinioned Spaniard. Every man aboard would have followed him but for his sharp command to some of them to remain on deck with Hagthorpe.

In the ward-room the three stern chasers were in position, loaded, their muzzles thrusting through the open ports, precisely as the Spanish gunners had left them.

"Here, Ogle, is work for you," said Blood, and as the burly gunner came thrusting forward through the little throng of gaping men, Blood pointed to the middle chaser; "Have that gun hauled back," he ordered.

When this was done, Blood beckoned those who held Don Diego.

"Lash him across the mouth of it," he bade them, and whilst, assisted by another two, they made haste to obey, he turned to the others. "To the roundhouse, some of you, and fetch the Spanish prisoners. And you, Dyke, go up and bid them set the flag of Spain aloft."

Don Diego, with his body stretched in an arc across the cannon's mouth, legs and arms lashed to the carriage on either side of it, eyeballs rolling in his head, glared maniacally at Captain Blood. A man may not fear to die, and yet be appalled by the form in which death comes to him.

From frothing lips he hurled blasphemies and insults at his tormentor.

"Foul barbarian! Inhuman savage! Accursed heretic! Will it not content you to kill me in some Christian fashion?" Captain Blood vouchsafed him a malignant smile, before he turned to meet the fifteen manacled Spanish prisoners, who were thrust into his presence.

Approaching, they had heard Don Diego's outcries; at close quarters now they beheld with horror-stricken eyes his plight. From amongst them a comely, olive-skinned stripling, distinguished in bearing and apparel from his companions, started forward with an anguished cry of "Father!"

Writhing in the arms that made haste to seize and hold him, he called upon heaven and hell to avert this horror, and lastly, addressed to Captain Blood an appeal for mercy that was at once fierce and piteous. Considering him, Captain Blood thought with satisfaction that he displayed the proper degree of filial piety.

He afterwards confessed that for a moment he was in danger of weakening, that for a moment his mind rebelled against the pitiless thing it had planned. But to correct the sentiment he evoked a memory of what these Spaniards had performed in Bridgetown. Again he saw the white face of that child Mary Traill as she fled in horror before the jeering ruffian whom he had slain, and other things even more unspeakable seen on that dreadful evening rose now before the eyes of his memory to stiffen his faltering purpose. The Spaniards had shown themselves without mercy or sentiment or decency of any kind; stuffed with religion, they were without a spark of that Christianity, the Symbol of which was mounted on the mainmast of the approaching ship. A moment ago this cruel, vicious Don Diego had insulted the Almighty by his assumption that He kept a specially benevolent watch over the destinies of Catholic Spain. Don Diego should be taught his error.

Recovering the cynicism in which he had approached his task, the cynicism essential to its proper performance, he commanded Ogle to kindle a match and remove the leaden apron from the touch-hole of the gun that bore Don Diego. Then, as the younger Espinosa broke into fresh intercessions mingled with imprecations, he wheeled upon him sharply.

"Peace!" he snapped. "Peace, and listen! It is no part of my intention to blow your father to hell as he deserves, or indeed to take his life at all."

Having surprised the lad into silence by that promise—a promise surprising enough in all the circumstances—he proceeded to explain his aims in that faultless and elegant

Castilian of which he was fortunately master—as fortunately for Don Diego as for himself.

"It is your father's treachery that has brought us into this plight and deliberately into risk of capture and death aboard that ship of Spain. Just as your father recognized his brother's flagship, so will his brother have recognized the Cinco Llagas. So far, then, all is well. But presently the Encarnacion will be sufficiently close to perceive that here all is not as it should be. Sooner or later, she must guess or discover what is wrong, and then she will open fire or lay us board and board. Now, we are in no case to fight, as your father knew when he ran us into this trap. But fight we will, if we are driven to it. We make no tame surrender to the ferocity of Spain."

He laid his hand on the breech of the gun that bore Don Diego.

"Understand this clearly: to the first shot from the Encarnacion this gun will fire the answer. I make myself clear, I hope?"

White-faced and trembling, young Espinosa stared into the pitiless blue eyes that so steadily regarded him.

"If it is clear?" he faltered, breaking the utter silence in which all were standing. "But, name of God, how should it be clear? How should I understand? Can you avert the fight? If you know a way, and if I, or these, can help you to it—if that is what you mean—in Heaven's name let me hear it."

"A fight would be averted if Don Diego de Espinosa were to go aboard his brother's ship, and by his presence and assurances inform the Admiral that all is well with the Cinco Llagas, that she is indeed still a ship of Spain as her flag now announces. But of course Don Diego cannot go in person, because he is... otherwise engaged. He has a slight touch of fever—shall we say?—that detains him in his cabin. But you, his son, may convey all this and some other matters together with his homage to your uncle. You shall go in a boat manned by six of these Spanish prisoners, and I—a distinguished Spaniard delivered from captivity in Barbados by your recent raid—will accompany you to keep you in countenance. If I return alive, and without accident of any kind to hinder our free sailing hence, Don Diego shall have his life, as shall every one of you. But if there is the least misadventure, be it from treachery or ill-fortune—I care not which—the battle, as I have had the honour to explain, will be opened on our side by this gun, and your father will be the first victim of the conflict."

He paused a moment. There was a hum of approval from his comrades, an anxious stirring among the Spanish prisoners. Young Espinosa stood before him, the colour ebbing and flowing in his cheeks. He waited for some direction from his father. But none came. Don Diego's courage, it seemed, had sadly waned under that rude test. He hung limply in his fearful bonds, and was silent. Evidently he dared not encourage his son to defiance, and presumably was ashamed to urge him to yield. Thus, he left decision entirely with the youth.

"Come," said Blood. "I have been clear enough, I think. What do you say?"

Don Esteban moistened his parched lips, and with the back of his hand mopped the anguish-sweat from his brow. His eyes gazed wildly a moment upon the shoulders of his father, as if beseeching guidance. But his father remained silent. Something like a sob escaped the boy.

"I... I accept," he answered at last, and swung to the Spaniards. "And you—you will accept too," he insisted passionately. "For Don Diego's sake and for your own—for all our sakes. If you do not, this man will butcher us all without mercy."

Since he yielded, and their leader himself counselled no resistance, why should they encompass their own destruction by a gesture of futile heroism? They answered without much hesitation that they would do as was required of them.

Blood turned, and advanced to Don Diego.

"I am sorry to inconvenience you in this fashion, but..." For a second he checked and frowned as his eyes intently observed the prisoner. Then, after that scarcely perceptible pause, he continued, "but I do not think that you have anything beyond this inconvenience to apprehend, and you may depend upon me to shorten it as far as possible." Don Diego made him no answer.

Peter Blood waited a moment, observing him; then he bowed and stepped back.

XII

DON PEDRO SANGRE

The Cinco Llagas and the Encarnacion, after a proper exchange of signals, lay hove to within a quarter of a mile of each other, and across the intervening space of gently heaving, sunlit waters sped a boat from the former, manned by six Spanish seamen and bearing in her stern sheets Don Esteban de Espinosa and Captain Peter Blood.

She also bore two treasure-chests containing fifty thousand pieces of eight. Gold has at all times been considered the best of testimonies of good faith, and Blood was determined that in all respects appearances should be entirely on his side. His followers had accounted this a supererogation of pretence. But Blood's will in the matter had prevailed. He carried further a bulky package addressed to a grande of Spain, heavily sealed with the arms of Espinosa—another piece of evidence hastily manufactured in the cabin of the Cinco Llagas—and he was spending these last moments in completing his instructions to his young companion.

Don Esteban expressed his last lingering uneasiness:

"But if you should betray yourself?" he cried.

"It will be unfortunate for everybody. I advised your father to say a prayer for our success. I depend upon you to help me more materially."

"I will do my best. God knows I will do my best," the boy protested.

Blood nodded thoughtfully, and no more was said until they bumped alongside the towering mass of the Encarnadon. Up the ladder went Don Esteban closely followed by Captain Blood. In the waist stood the Admiral himself to receive them, a handsome, self-sufficient man, very tall and stiff, a little older and greyer than Don Diego, whom he closely resembled. He was supported by four officers and a friar in the black and white habit of St. Dominic.

Don Miguel opened his arms to his nephew, whose lingering panic he mistook for pleasurable excitement, and having enfolded him to his bosom turned to greet Don Esteban's companion.

Peter Blood bowed gracefully, entirely at his ease, so far as might be judged from appearances.

"I am," he announced, making a literal translation of his name, "Don Pedro Sangre, an unfortunate gentleman of Leon, lately delivered from captivity by Don Esteban's most gallant father." And in a few words he sketched the imagined conditions of his capture by, and deliverance from, those accursed heretics who held the island of Barbados. "Benedicamus Domino," said the friar to his tale.

"Ex hoc nunc et usque in seculum," replied Blood, the occasional papist, with lowered eyes.

The Admiral and his attending officers gave him a sympathetic hearing and a cordial welcome. Then came the dreaded question.

"But where is my brother? Why has he not come, himself, to greet me?"

It was young Espinosa who answered this:

"My father is afflicted at denying himself that honour and pleasure. But unfortunately, sir uncle, he is a little indisposed—oh, nothing grave; merely sufficient to make him keep his cabin. It is a little fever, the result of a slight wound taken in the recent raid upon Barbados, which resulted in this gentleman's happy deliverance."

"Nay, nephew, nay," Don Miguel protested with ironic repudiation. "I can have no knowledge of these things. I have the honour to represent upon the seas His Catholic Majesty, who is at peace with the King of England. Already you have told me more than it is good for me to know. I will endeavour to forget it, and I will ask you, sirs," he added, glancing at his officers, "to forget it also." But he winked into the twinkling eyes of Captain Blood; then added matter that at once extinguished that twinkle. "But since Diego cannot come to me, why, I will go across to him."

For a moment Don Esteban's face was a mask of pallid fear. Then Blood was speaking in a lowered, confidential voice that admirably blended suavity, impressiveness, and sly mockery.

"If you please, Don Miguel, but that is the very thing you must not do—the very thing Don Diego does not wish you to do. You must not see him until his wounds are healed. That is his own wish. That is the real reason why he is not here. For the truth is that his wounds are not so grave as to have prevented his coming. It was his consideration of himself and the false position in which you would be placed if you had direct word from him of what has happened. As your excellency has said, there is peace between His Catholic Majesty and the King of England, and your brother Don Diego..." He paused a moment. "I am sure that I need say no more. What you hear from us is no more than a mere rumour. Your excellency understands."

His excellency frowned thoughtfully. "I understand... in part," said he.

Captain Blood had a moment's uneasiness. Did the Spaniard doubt his bona fides? Yet in dress and speech he knew himself to be impeccably Spanish, and was not Don Esteban there to confirm him? He swept on to afford further confirmation before the Admiral could say another word.

"And we have in the boat below two chests containing fifty thousand pieces of eight, which we are to deliver to your excellency."

His excellency jumped; there was a sudden stir among his officers.

"They are the ransom extracted by Don Diego from the Governor of..."

"Not another word, in the name of Heaven!" cried the Admiral in alarm. "My brother wishes me to assume charge of this money, to carry it to Spain for him? Well, that is a family matter between my brother and myself. So, it can be done. But I must not know..." He broke off. "Hum! A glass of Malaga in my cabin, if you please," he invited them, "whilst the chests are being hauled aboard."

He gave his orders touching the embarkation of these chests, then led the way to his regally appointed cabin, his four officers and the friar following by particular invitation.

Seated at table there, with the tawny wine before them, and the servant who had poured it withdrawn, Don Miguel laughed and stroked his pointed, grizzled beard.

"Virgen santisima! That brother of mine has a mind that thinks of everything. Left to myself, I might have committed a fine indiscretion by venturing aboard his ship at such a moment. I might have seen things which as Admiral of Spain it would be difficult for me to ignore."

Both Esteban and Blood made haste to agree with him, and then Blood raised his glass, and drank to the glory of Spain and the damnation of the besotted James who occupied the throne of England. The latter part of his toast was at least sincere.

The Admiral laughed.

"Sir, sir, you need my brother here to curb your imprudences. You should remember that His Catholic Majesty and the King of England are very good friends. That is not a toast to propose in this cabin. But since it has been proposed, and by one who has such particular personal cause to hate these English hounds, why, we will honour it—but unofficially."

They laughed, and drank the damnation of King James—quite unofficially, but the more fervently on that account. Then Don Esteban, uneasy on the score of his father, and remembering that the agony of Don Diego was being protracted with every moment that they left him in his dreadful position, rose and announced that they must be returning.

"My father," he explained, "is in haste to reach San Domingo. He desired me to stay no longer than necessary to embrace you. If you will give us leave, then, sir uncle."

In the circumstances "sir uncle" did not insist.

As they returned to the ship's side, Blood's eyes anxiously scanned the line of seamen leaning over the bulwarks in idle talk with the Spaniards in the cock-boat that waited at the ladder's foot. But their manner showed him that there was no ground for his anxiety. The boat's crew had been wisely reticent.

The Admiral took leave of them—of Esteban affectionately, of Blood ceremoniously.

"I regret to lose you so soon, Don Pedro. I wish that you could have made a longer visit to the Encarnacion."

"I am indeed unfortunate," said Captain Blood politely.

"But I hope that we may meet again."

"That is to flatter me beyond all that I deserve."

They reached the boat; and she cast off from the great ship. As they were pulling away, the Admiral waving to them from the taffrail, they heard the shrill whistle of the bo'sun piping the hands to their stations, and before they had reached the Cinco Llagas, they beheld the Encarnacion go about under sail. She dipped her flag to them, and from her poop a gun fired a salute.

Aboard the Cinco Llagas some one—it proved afterwards to be Hagthorpe—had the wit to reply in the same fashion. The comedy was ended. Yet there was something else to follow as an epilogue, a thing that added a grim ironic flavour to the whole.

As they stepped into the waist of the Cinco Llagas, Hagthorpe advanced to receive them. Blood observed the set, almost scared expression on his face.

"I see that you've found it," he said quietly.

Hagthorpe's eyes looked a question. But his mind dismissed whatever thought it held.

"Don Diego..." he was beginning, and then stopped, and looked curiously at Blood.

Noting the pause and the look, Esteban bounded forward, his face livid.

"Have you broken faith, you curs? Has he come to harm?" he cried—and the six Spaniards behind him grew clamorous with furious questionings.

"We do not break faith," said Hagthorpe firmly, so firmly that he quieted them. "And in this case there was not the need. Don Diego died in his bonds before ever you reached the Encarnacion."

Peter Blood said nothing.

"Died?" screamed Esteban. "You killed him, you mean. Of what did he die?"

Hagthorpe looked at the boy. "If I am a judge," he said, "Don Diego died of fear."

Don Esteban struck Hagthorpe across the face at that, and Hagthorpe would have struck back, but that Blood got between, whilst his followers seized the lad.

"Let be," said Blood. "You provoked the boy by your insult to his father."

"I was not concerned to insult," said Hagthorpe, nursing his cheek. "It is what has happened. Come and look."

"I have seen," said Blood. "He died before I left the Cinco Llagas. He was hanging dead in his bonds when I spoke to him before leaving."

"What are you saying?" cried Esteban.

Blood looked at him gravely. Yet for all his gravity he seemed almost to smile, though without mirth.

"If you had known that, eh?" he asked at last. For a moment Don Esteban stared at him wide-eyed, incredulous. "I don't believe you," he said at last.

"Yet you may. I am a doctor, and I know death when I see it."

Again there came a pause, whilst conviction sank into the lad's mind.

"If I had known that," he said at last in a thick voice, "you would be hanging from the yardarm of the Encarnacion at this moment."

"I know," said Blood. "I am considering it—the profit that a man may find in the ignorance of others."

"But you'll hang there yet," the boy raved.

Captain Blood shrugged, and turned on his heel. But he did not on that account disregard the words, nor did Hagthorpe, nor yet the others who overheard them, as they showed at a council held that night in the cabin.

This council was met to determine what should be done with the Spanish prisoners. Considering that Curacao now lay beyond their reach, as they were running short of water and provisions, and also that Pitt was hardly yet in case to undertake the navigation of the vessel, it had been decided that, going east of Hispaniola, and then sailing along its northern coast, they should make for Tortuga, that haven of the buccaneers, in which lawless port they had at least no danger of recapture to apprehend. It was now a question whether they should convey the Spaniards thither with them, or turn them off in a boat to make the best of their way to the coast of Hispaniola, which was but ten miles off. This was the course urged by Blood himself.

"There's nothing else to be done," he insisted. "In Tortuga they would be flayed alive."

"Which is less than the swine deserve," growled Wolverstone.

"And you'll remember, Peter," put in Hagthorpe, "that boy's threat to you this morning. If he escapes, and carries word of all this to his uncle, the Admiral, the execution of that threat will become more than possible."

It says much for Peter Blood that the argument should have left him unmoved. It is a little thing, perhaps, but in a narrative in which there is so much that tells against him, I cannot—since my story is in the nature of a brief for the defence—afford to slur a circumstance that is so strongly in his favour, a circumstance revealing that the cynicism attributed to him proceeded from his reason and from a brooding over wrongs rather than from any natural instincts. "I care nothing for his threats."

"You should," said Wolverstone. "The wise thing'd be to hang him, along o' all the rest."

"It is not human to be wise," said Blood. "It is much more human to err, though perhaps exceptional to err on the side of mercy. We'll be exceptional. Oh, faugh! I've no stomach for cold-blooded killing. At daybreak pack the Spaniards into a boat with a keg of water and a sack of dumplings, and let them go to the devil."

That was his last word on the subject, and it prevailed by virtue of the authority they had vested in him, and of which he had taken so firm a grip. At daybreak Don Esteban and his followers were put off in a boat.

Two days later, the Cinco Llagas sailed into the rock-bound bay of Cayona, which Nature seemed to have designed for the stronghold of those who had appropriated it.

XIII

TORTUGA

It is time fully to disclose the fact that the survival of the story of Captain Blood's exploits is due entirely to the industry of Jeremy Pitt, the Somersetshire shipmaster. In addition to his ability as a navigator, this amiable young man appears to have wielded an indefatigable pen, and to have been inspired to indulge its fluency by the affection he very obviously bore to Peter Blood.

He kept the log of the forty-gun frigate Arabella, on which he served as master, or, as we should say today, navigating officer, as no log that I have seen was ever kept. It runs into some twenty-odd volumes of assorted sizes, some of which are missing altogether and others of which are so sadly depleted of leaves as to be of little use. But if at times in the laborious perusal of them—they are preserved in the library of Mr. James Speke of Comerton—I have inveighed against these lacunae, at others I have been equally troubled by the excessive prolixity of what remains and the difficulty of disintegrating from the confused whole the really essential parts.

I have a suspicion that Esquemeling—though how or where I can make no surmise—must have obtained access to these records, and that he plucked from them the brilliant feathers of several exploits to stick them into the tail of his own hero,

Captain Morgan. But that is by the way. I mention it chiefly as a warning, for when presently I come to relate the affair of Maracaybo, those of you who have read Esquemeling may be in danger of supposing that Henry Morgan really performed those things which here are veraciously attributed to Peter Blood. I think, however, that when you come to weigh the motives actuating both Blood and the Spanish Admiral, in that affair, and when you consider how integrally the event is a part of Blood's history—whilst merely a detached incident in Morgan's—you will reach my own conclusion as to which is the real plagiarist.

The first of these logs of Pitt's is taken up almost entirely with a retrospective narrative of the events up to the time of Blood's first coming to Tortuga. This and the Tannatt Collection of State Trials are the chief—though not the only—sources of my history so far.

Pitt lays great stress upon the fact that it was the circumstances upon which I have dwelt, and these alone, that drove Peter Blood to seek an anchorage at Tortuga. He insists at considerable length, and with a vehemence which in itself makes it plain that an opposite opinion was held in some quarters, that it was no part of the design of Blood or of any of his companions in misfortune to join hands with the buccaneers who, under a semi-official French protection, made of Tortuga a lair whence they could sally out to drive their merciless piratical trade chiefly at the expense of Spain.

It was, Pitt tells us, Blood's original intention to make his way to France or Holland. But in the long weeks of waiting for a ship to convey him to one or the other of these countries, his resources dwindled and finally vanished. Also, his chronicler thinks that he detected signs of some secret trouble in his friend, and he attributes to this the abuses of the potent West Indian spirit of which Blood became guilty in those days of inaction, thereby sinking to the level of the wild adventurers with whom ashore he associated.

I do not think that Pitt is guilty in this merely of special pleading, that he is putting forward excuses for his hero. I think that in those days there was a good deal to oppress Peter Blood. There was the thought of Arabella Bishop—and that this thought loomed large in his mind we are not permitted to doubt. He was maddened by the tormenting lure of the unattainable. He desired Arabella, yet knew her beyond his reach irrevocably and for all time. Also, whilst he may have desired to go to France or Holland, he had no clear purpose to accomplish when he reached one or the other of these countries. He was, when all is said, an escaped slave, an outlaw in his own land and a homeless outcast in any other. There remained the sea, which is free to all, and particularly alluring to those who feel themselves at war with humanity. And so, considering the adventurous spirit that once already had sent him a-roving for the sheer love of it, considering that this spirit was heightened now by a recklessness begotten of his outlawry, that his training and skill in militant seamanship clamorously supported the temptations that were put before him, can you wonder, or dare you blame him, that in the end he succumbed? And remember that these temptations proceeded not only from adventurous buccaneering acquaintances in the taverns of that evil haven of Tortuga, but even from M. d'Ogeron, the governor of the island, who levied as his harbour dues a percentage of one tenth of all spoils brought into the bay, and who profited further by commissions upon money which he was desired to convert into bills of exchange upon France.

A trade that might have worn a repellent aspect when urged by greasy, half-drunken adventurers, boucan-hunters, lumbermen, beach-combers, English, French, and Dutch, became a dignified, almost official form of privateering when advocated by the courtly, middle-aged gentleman who in representing the French West India Company seemed to represent France herself.

Moreover, to a man—not excluding Jeremy Pitt himself, in whose blood the call of the sea was insistent and imperative—those who had escaped with Peter Blood from the Barbados plantations, and who, consequently, like himself, knew not whither to turn, were all resolved upon joining the great Brotherhood of the Coast, as those rovers called themselves. And they united theirs to the other voices that were persuading Blood, demanding that he should continue now in the leadership which he had enjoyed since they had left Barbados, and swearing to follow him loyally whithersoever he should lead them.

And so, to condense all that Jeremy has recorded in the matter, Blood ended by yielding to external and internal pressure, abandoned himself to the stream of Destiny. "Fata viam invenerunt," is his own expression of it.

If he resisted so long, it was, I think, the thought of Arabella Bishop that restrained him. That they should be destined never to meet again did not weigh at first, or, indeed, ever. He conceived the scorn with which she would come to hear of his having turned pirate, and the scorn, though as yet no more than imagined, hurt him as if it were already a reality. And even when he conquered this, still the thought of her was ever present. He compromised with the conscience that her memory kept so disconcertingly active. He vowed that the thought of her should continue ever before him to help him keep his hands as clean as a man might in this desperate trade upon which he was embarking. And so, although he might entertain no delusive hope of ever winning her for his own, of ever even seeing her again, yet the memory of her was to abide in his soul as a bitter-sweet, purifying influence. The love that is never to be realized will often remain a man's guiding ideal. The resolve being taken, he went actively to work. Ogeron, most accommodating of governors, advanced him money for the proper equipment of his ship the Cinco Llagas, which he renamed the Arabella. This after some little hesitation, fearful of thus setting his heart upon his sleeve. But his Barbados friends accounted it merely an expression of the ever-ready irony in which their leader dealt.

To the score of followers he already possessed, he added threescore more, picking his men with caution and discrimination—and he was an exceptional judge of men—from amongst the adventurers of Tortuga. With them all he entered into the articles usual among the Brethren of the Coast under which each man was to be paid by a share in the prizes captured. In other respects, however, the articles were different. Aboard the Arabella there was to be none of the ruffianly indiscipline that normally prevailed in buccaneering vessels. Those who shipped with him undertook obedience and submission in all things to himself and to the officers appointed by election. Any to whom this clause in the articles was distasteful might follow some other leader.

Towards the end of December, when the hurricane season had blown itself out, he put to sea in his well-found, well-manned ship, and before he returned in the following May from a protracted and adventurous cruise, the fame of Captain Peter Blood had run like ripples before the breeze across the face of the Caribbean Sea. There was a fight in the Windward Passage at the outset with a Spanish galleon, which had resulted in the gutting and finally the sinking of the Spaniard. There was a daring raid effected by means of several appropriated piraguas upon a Spanish pearl fleet in the Rio de la Hacha, from which they had taken a particularly rich haul of pearls. There was an overland expedition to the goldfields of Santa Maria, on the Main, the full tale of which is hardly credible, and there were lesser adventures through all of which the crew of the Arabella came with credit and profit if not entirely unscathed.

And so it happened that before the Arabella came homing to Tortuga in the following May to refit and repair—for she was not without scars, as you conceive—the fame of her and of Peter Blood her captain had swept from the Bahamas to the Windward Isles, from New Providence to Trinidad.

An echo of it had reached Europe, and at the Court of St. James's angry representations were made by the Ambassador of Spain, to whom it was answered that it must not be supposed that this Captain Blood held any commission from the King of England; that he was, in fact, a proscribed rebel, an escaped slave, and that any measures against him by His Catholic Majesty would receive the cordial approbation of King James II.

Don Miguel de Espinosa, the Admiral of Spain in the West Indies, and his nephew Don Esteban who sailed with him, did not lack the will to bring the adventurer to the yardarm. With them this business of capturing Blood, which was now an international affair, was also a family matter.

Spain, through the mouth of Don Miguel, did not spare her threats. The report of them reached Tortuga, and with it the assurance that Don Miguel had behind him not only the authority of his own nation, but that of the English King as well.

It was a brutum fulmen that inspired no terrors in Captain Blood. Nor was he likely, on account of it, to allow himself to run to rust in the security of Tortuga. For what he had suffered at the hands of Man he had chosen to make Spain the scapegoat. Thus he accounted that he served a twofold purpose: he took compensation and at the same time served, not indeed the Stuart King, whom he despised, but England and, for that matter, all the rest of civilized mankind which cruel, treacherous, greedy, bigoted Castile sought to exclude from intercourse with the New World.

One day as he sat with Hagthorpe and Wolverstone over a pipe and a bottle of rum in the stifling reek of tar and stale tobacco of a waterside tavern, he was accosted by a splendid ruffian in a gold-laced coat of dark-blue satin with a crimson sash, a foot wide, about the waist.

"C'est vous qu'on appelle Le Sang?" the fellow hailed him.

Captain Blood looked up to consider the questioner before replying. The man was tall and built on lines of agile strength, with a swarthy, aquiline face that was brutally handsome. A diamond of great price flamed on the indifferently clean hand resting on the pummel of his long rapier, and there were gold rings in his ears, half-concealed by long ringlets of oily chestnut hair.

Captain Blood took the pipe-stem from between his lips.

"My name," he said, "is Peter Blood. The Spaniards know me for Don Pedro Sangre and a Frenchman may call me Le Sang if he pleases."

"Good," said the gaudy adventurer in English, and without further invitation he drew up a stool and sat down at that greasy table. "My name," he informed the three men, two of whom at least were eyeing him askance, "it is Levasseur. You may have heard of me."

They had, indeed. He commanded a privateer of twenty guns that had dropped anchor in the bay a week ago, manned by a crew mainly composed of French boucanhunters from Northern Hispaniola, men who had good cause to hate the Spaniard with an intensity exceeding that of the English. Levasseur had brought them back to Tortuga from an indifferently successful cruise. It would need more, however, than lack of success to abate the fellow's monstrous vanity. A roaring, quarrelsome, hard-drinking, hard-gaming scoundrel, his reputation as a buccaneer stood high among the wild Brethren of the Coast. He enjoyed also a reputation of another sort. There was about his gaudy, swaggering raffishness something that the women found singularly alluring. That he should boast openly of his bonnes fortunes did not seem strange to Captain Blood; what he might have found strange was that there appeared to be some measure of justification for these boasts.

It was current gossip that even Mademoiselle d'Ogeron, the Governor's daughter, had been caught in the snare of his wild attractiveness, and that Levasseur had gone the length of audacity of asking her hand in marriage of her father. M. d'Ogeron had made him the only possible answer. He had shown him the door. Levasseur had departed in a rage, swearing that he would make mademoiselle his wife in the teeth of all the fathers in Christendom, and that M. d'Ogeron should bitterly rue the affront he had put upon him.

This was the man who now thrust himself upon Captain Blood with a proposal of association, offering him not only his sword, but his ship and the men who sailed in her.

A dozen years ago, as a lad of barely twenty, Levasseur had sailed with that monster of cruelty L'Ollonais, and his own subsequent exploits bore witness and did credit to the school in which he had been reared. I doubt if in his day there was a greater scoundrel among the Brethren of the Coast than this Levasseur. And yet, repulsive though he found him, Captain Blood could not deny that the fellow's proposals displayed boldness, imagination, and resource, and he was forced to admit that jointly they could undertake operations of a greater magnitude than was possible singly to either of them. The climax of Levasseur's project was to be a raid upon the wealthy mainland city of Maracaybo; but for this, he admitted, six hundred men at the very least would be required, and six hundred men were not to be conveyed in the two bottoms they now commanded. Preliminary cruises must take place, having for one of their objects the capture of further ships.

Because he disliked the man, Captain Blood would not commit himself at once. But because he liked the proposal he consented to consider it. Being afterwards pressed by both Hagthorpe and Wolverstone, who did not share his own personal dislike of the Frenchman, the end of the matter was that within a week articles were drawn up between Levasseur and Blood, and signed by them and—as was usual—by the chosen representatives of their followers.

These articles contained, inter alia, the common provisions that, should the two vessels separate, a strict account must afterwards be rendered of all prizes severally taken, whilst the vessel taking a prize should retain three fifths of its value, surrendering two fifths to its associate. These shares were subsequently to be subdivided among the crew of each vessel, in accordance with the articles already obtaining between each captain and his own men. For the rest, the articles contained all the clauses that were usual, among which was the clause that any man found guilty of abstracting or concealing any part of a prize, be it of the value of no more than a peso, should be summarily hanged from the yardarm.

All being now settled they made ready for sea, and on the very eve of sailing, Levasseur narrowly escaped being shot in a romantic attempt to scale the wall of the Governor's garden, with the object of taking passionate leave of the infatuated Mademoiselle d'Ogeron. He desisted after having been twice fired upon from a fragrant ambush of pimento trees where the Governor's guards were posted, and he departed vowing to take different and very definite measures on his return.

That night he slept on board his ship, which with characteristic flamboyance he had named La Foudre, and there on the following day he received a visit from Captain Blood, whom he greeted half-mockingly as his admiral. The Irishman came to settle certain final details of which all that need concern us is an understanding that, in the event of the two vessels becoming separated by accident or design, they should rejoin each other as soon as might be at Tortuga.

Thereafter Levasseur entertained his admiral to dinner, and jointly they drank success to the expedition, so copiously on the part of Levasseur that when the time came to separate he was as nearly drunk as it seemed possible for him to be and yet retain his understanding.

Finally, towards evening, Captain Blood went over the side and was rowed back to his great ship with her red bulwarks and gilded ports, touched into a lovely thing of flame by the setting sun.

He was a little heavy-hearted. I have said that he was a judge of men, and his judgment of Levasseur filled him with misgivings which were growing heavier in a measure as the hour of departure approached.

He expressed it to Wolverstone, who met him as he stepped aboard the Arabella:

"You over persuaded me into those articles, you blackguard; and it'll surprise me if any good comes of this association."

The giant rolled his single bloodthirsty eye, and sneered, thrusting out his heavy jaw. "We'll wring the dog's neck if there's any treachery."

"So we will—if we are there to wring it by then." And on that, dismissing the matter: "We sail in the morning, on the first of the ebb," he announced, and went off to his cabin.

XIV

LEVASSEUR'S HEROICS

It would be somewhere about ten o'clock on the following morning, a full hour before the time appointed for sailing, when a canoe brought up alongside La Foudre, and a half-caste Indian stepped out of her and went up the ladder. He was clad in drawers of hairy, untanned hide, and a red blanket served him for a cloak. He was the bearer of a folded scrap of paper for Captain Levasseur.

The Captain unfolded the letter, sadly soiled and crumpled by contact with the half-caste's person. Its contents may be roughly translated thus:

"My well-beloved—I am in the Dutch brig Jongvrow, which is about to sail. Resolved to separate us for ever, my cruel father is sending me to Europe in my brother's charge. I implore you, come to my rescue. Deliver me, my well-beloved hero!—Your desolated Madeleine, who loves you."

The well-beloved hero was moved to the soul of him by that passionate appeal. His scowling glance swept the bay for the Dutch brig, which he knew had been due to sail for Amsterdam with a cargo of hides and tobacco.

She was nowhere to be seen among the shipping in that narrow, rock-bound harbour. He roared out the question in his mind.

In answer the half-caste pointed out beyond the frothing surf that marked the position of the reef constituting one of the stronghold's main defences. Away beyond it, a mile or so distant, a sail was standing out to sea. "There she go," he said.

"There!" The Frenchman gazed and stared, his face growing white. The man's wicked temper awoke, and turned to vent itself upon the messenger. "And where have you been that you come here only now with this? Answer me!"

The half-caste shrank terrified before his fury. His explanation, if he had one, was paralyzed by fear. Levasseur took him by the throat, shook him twice, snarling the while, then hurled him into the scuppers. The man's head struck the gunwale as he fell, and he lay there, quite still, a trickle of blood issuing from his mouth.

Levasseur dashed one hand against the other, as if dusting them.

"Heave that muck overboard," he ordered some of those who stood idling in the waist. "Then up anchor, and let us after the Dutchman."

"Steady, Captain. What's that?" There was a restraining hand upon his shoulder, and the broad face of his lieutenant Cahusac, a burly, callous Breton scoundrel, was stolidly confronting him.

Levasseur made clear his purpose with a deal of unnecessary obscenity.

Cahusac shook his head. "A Dutch brig!" said he. "Impossible! We should never be allowed."

"And who the devil will deny us?" Levasseur was between amazement and fury.

"For one thing, there's your own crew will be none too willing. For another there's Captain Blood."

"I care nothing for Captain Blood..."

"But it is necessary that you should. He has the power, the weight of metal and of men, and if I know him at all he'll sink us before he'll suffer interference with the Dutch. He has his own views of privateering, this Captain Blood, as I warned you."

"Ah!" said Levasseur, showing his teeth. But his eyes, riveted upon that distant sail, were gloomily thoughtful. Not for long. The imagination and resource which Captain Blood had detected in the fellow soon suggested a course.

Cursing in his soul, and even before the anchor was weighed, the association into which he had entered, he was already studying ways of evasion. What Cahusac implied was true: Blood would never suffer violence to be done in his presence to a Dutchman; but it might be done in his absence; and, being done, Blood must perforce condone it, since it would then be too late to protest.

Within the hour the Arabella and La Foudre were beating out to sea together. Without understanding the change of plan involved, Captain Blood, nevertheless, accepted it, and weighed anchor before the appointed time upon perceiving his associate to do so.

All day the Dutch brig was in sight, though by evening she had dwindled to the merest speck on the northern horizon. The course prescribed for Blood and Levasseur lay eastward along the northern shores of Hispaniola. To that course the Arabella continued to hold steadily throughout the night. When day broke again, she was alone. La Foudre under cover of the darkness had struck away to The northeast with every rag of canvas on her yards.

Cahusac had attempted yet again to protest against this.

"The devil take you!" Levasseur had answered him. "A ship's a ship, be she Dutch or Spanish, and ships are our present need. That will suffice for the men."

His lieutenant said no more. But from his glimpse of the letter, knowing that a girl and not a ship was his captain's real objective, he gloomily shook his head as he rolled away on his bowed legs to give the necessary orders.

Dawn found La Foudre close on the Dutchman's heels, not a mile astern, and the sight of her very evidently flustered the Jongvrow. No doubt mademoiselle's brother recognizing Levasseur's ship would be responsible for the Dutch uneasiness. They saw the Jongvrow crowding canvas in a futile endeavour to outsail them, whereupon they stood off to starboard and raced on until they were in a position whence they could send a warning shot across her bow. The Jongvrow veered, showed them her rudder, and opened fire with her stern chasers. The small shot went whistling through La Foudre's shrouds with some slight damage to her canvas. Followed a brief running fight in the course of which the Dutchman let fly a broadside.

Five minutes after that they were board and board, the Jongvrow held tight in the clutches of La Foudre's grapnels, and the buccaneers pouring noisily into her waist.

The Dutchman's master, purple in the face, stood forward to beard the pirate, followed closely by an elegant, pale-faced young gentleman in whom Levasseur recognized his brother-in-law elect.

"Captain Levasseur, this is an outrage for which you shall be made to answer. What do you seek aboard my ship?"

"At first I sought only that which belongs to me, something of which I am being robbed. But since you chose war and opened fire on me with some damage to my ship and loss of life to five of my men, why, war it is, and your ship a prize of war."

From the quarter rail Mademoiselle d'Ogeron looked down with glowing eyes in breathless wonder upon her well-beloved hero. Gloriously heroic he seemed as he stood towering there, masterful, audacious, beautiful. He saw her, and with a glad shout sprang towards her. The Dutch master got in his way with hands upheld to arrest his progress. Levasseur did not stay to argue with him: he was too impatient to reach his mistress. He swung the poleaxe that he carried, and the Dutchman went down in blood with a cloven skull. The eager lover stepped across the body and came on, his countenance joyously alight.

But mademoiselle was shrinking now, in horror. She was a girl upon the threshold of glorious womanhood, of a fine height and nobly moulded, with heavy coils of glossy black hair above and about a face that was of the colour of old ivory. Her countenance was cast in lines of arrogance, stressed by the low lids of her full dark eyes.

In a bound her well-beloved was beside her, flinging away his bloody poleaxe, he opened wide his arms to enfold her. But she still shrank even within his embrace, which would not be denied; a look of dread had come to temper the normal arrogance of her almost perfect face.

"Mine, mine at last, and in spite of all!" he cried exultantly, theatrically, truly heroic.

But she, endeavouring to thrust him back, her hands against his breast, could only falter: "Why, why did you kill him?"

He laughed, as a hero should; and answered her heroically, with the tolerance of a god for the mortal to whom he condescends: "He stood between us. Let his death be a symbol, a warning. Let all who would stand between us mark it and beware."

It was so splendidly terrific, the gesture of it was so broad and fine and his magnetism so compelling, that she cast her silly tremors and yielded herself freely, intoxicated, to his fond embrace. Thereafter he swung her to his shoulder, and stepping with ease beneath that burden, bore her in a sort of triumph, lustily cheered by his men, to the deck of his own ship. Her inconsiderate brother might have ruined that romantic scene but for the watchful Cahusac, who quietly tripped him up, and then trussed him like a fowl.

Thereafter, what time the Captain languished in his lady's smile within the cabin, Cahusac was dealing with the spoils of war. The Dutch crew was ordered into the longboat, and bidden go to the devil. Fortunately, as they numbered fewer than thirty, the longboat, though perilously overcrowded, could yet contain them. Next, Cahusac having inspected the cargo, put a quartermaster and a score of men aboard the Jongvrow, and left her to follow La Foudre, which he now headed south for the Leeward Islands.

Cahusac was disposed to be ill-humoured. The risk they had run in taking the Dutch brig and doing violence to members of the family of the Governor of Tortuga, was out of all proportion to the value of their prize. He said so, sullenly, to Levasseur.

"You'll keep that opinion to yourself," the Captain answered him. "Don't think I am the man to thrust my neck into a noose, without knowing how I am going to take it out again. I shall send an offer of terms to the Governor of Tortuga that he will be forced to accept. Set a course for the Virgen Magra. We'll go ashore, and settle things from there. And tell them to fetch that milksop Ogeron to the cabin."

Levasseur went back to the adoring lady.

Thither, too, the lady's brother was presently conducted. The Captain rose to receive him, bending his stalwart height to avoid striking the cabin roof with his head. Mademoiselle rose too.

"Why this?" she asked Levasseur, pointing to her brother's pinioned wrists—the remains of Cahusac's precautions.

"I deplore it," said he. "I desire it to end. Let M. d'Ogeron give me his parole..."

"I give you nothing," flashed the white-faced youth, who did not lack for spirit.

"You see." Levasseur shrugged his deep regret, and mademoiselle turned protesting to her brother.

"Henri, this is foolish! You are not behaving as my friend. You..."

"Little fool," her brother answered her—and the "little" was out of place; she was the taller of the twain. "Little fool, do you think I should be acting as your friend to make terms with this blackguard pirate?"

"Steady, my young cockerel!" Levasseur laughed. But his laugh was not nice.

"Don't you perceive your wicked folly in the harm it has brought already? Lives have been lost—men have died—that this monster might overtake you. And don't you yet realize where you stand—in the power of this beast, of this cur born in a kennel and bred in thieving and murder?"

He might have said more but that Levasseur struck him across the mouth. Levasseur, you see, cared as little as another to hear the truth about himself.

Mademoiselle suppressed a scream, as the youth staggered back under the blow. He came to rest against a bulkhead, and leaned there with bleeding lips. But his spirit was unquenched, and there was a ghastly smile on his white face as his eyes sought his sister's.

"You see," he said simply. "He strikes a man whose hands are bound."

The simple words, and, more than the words, their tone of ineffable disdain, aroused the passion that never slumbered deeply in Levasseur.

"And what should you do, puppy, if your hands were unbound?" He took his prisoner by the breast of his doublet and shook him. "Answer me! What should you do? Tchah! You empty windbag! You..." And then came a torrent of words unknown to mademoiselle, yet of whose foulness her intuitions made her conscious.

With blanched cheeks she stood by the cabin table, and cried out to Levasseur to stop. To obey her, he opened the door, and flung her brother through it.

"Put that rubbish under hatches until I call for it again," he roared, and shut the door.

Composing himself, he turned to the girl again with a deprecatory smile. But no smile answered him from her set face. She had seen her beloved hero's nature in curl-papers, as it were, and she found the spectacle disgusting and terrifying. It recalled the brutal slaughter of the Dutch captain, and suddenly she realized that what her brother had just said of this man was no more than true. Fear growing to panic was written on her face, as she stood there leaning for support against the table.

"Why, sweetheart, what is this?" Levasseur moved towards her. She recoiled before him. There was a smile on his face, a glitter in his eyes that fetched her heart into her throat.

He caught her, as she reached the uttermost limits of the cabin, seized her in his long arms and pulled her to him.

"No, no!" she panted.

"Yes, yes," he mocked her, and his mockery was the most terrible thing of all. He crushed her to him brutally, deliberately hurtful because she resisted, and kissed her whilst she writhed in his embrace. Then, his passion mounting, he grew angry and stripped off the last rag of hero's mask that still may have hung upon his face. "Little fool, did you not hear your brother say that you are in my power? Remember it, and remember that of your own free will you came. I am not the man with whom a woman can play fast and loose. So get sense, my girl, and accept what you have invited." He kissed her again, almost contemptuously, and flung her off. "No more scowls," he said. "You'll be sorry else."

Some one knocked. Cursing the interruption, Levasseur strode off to open. Cahusac stood before him. The Breton's face was grave. He came to report that they had sprung a leak between wind and water, the consequence of damage sustained from one of the Dutchman's shots. In alarm Levasseur went off with him. The leakage was not serious so long as the weather kept fine; but should a storm overtake them it might speedily become so. A man was slung overboard to make a partial stoppage with a sail-cloth, and the pumps were got to work.

Ahead of them a low cloud showed on the horizon, which Cahusac pronounced one of the northernmost of the Virgin Islands.

"We must run for shelter there, and careen her," said Levasseur. "I do not trust this oppressive heat. A storm may catch us before we make land."

"A storm or something else," said Cahusac grimly. "Have you noticed that?" He pointed away to starboard.

Levasseur looked, and caught his breath. Two ships that at the distance seemed of considerable burden were heading towards them some five miles away.

"If they follow us what is to happen?" demanded Cahusac.

"We'll fight whether we're in case to do so or not," swore Levasseur.

"Counsels of despair." Cahusac was contemptuous. To mark it he spat upon the deck. "This comes of going to sea with a lovesick madman. Now, keep your temper, Captain, for the hands will be at the end of theirs if we have trouble as a result of this Dutchman business."

For the remainder of that day Levasseur's thoughts were of anything but love. He remained on deck, his eyes now upon the land, now upon those two slowly gaining ships. To run for the open could avail him nothing, and in his leaky condition would provide an additional danger. He must stand at bay and fight. And then, towards evening, when within three miles of shore and when he was about to give the order to strip for battle, he almost fainted from relief to hear a voice from the crow's-nest above announce that the larger of the two ships was the Arabella. Her companion was presumably a prize.

But the pessimism of Cahusac abated nothing.

"That is but the lesser evil," he growled. "What will Blood say about this Dutchman?"

"Let him say what he pleases." Levasseur laughed in the immensity of his relief.

"And what about the children of the Governor of Tortuga?"

"He must not know."

"He'll come to know in the end."

"Aye, but by then, morbleu, the matter will be settled. I shall have made my peace with the Governor. I tell you I know the way to compel Ogeron to come to terms."

Presently the four vessels lay to off the northern coast of La Virgen Magra, a narrow little island arid and treeless, some twelve miles by three, uninhabited save by birds and turtles and unproductive of anything but salt, of which there were considerable ponds to the south.

Levasseur put off in a boat accompanied by Cahusac and two other officers, and went to visit Captain Blood aboard the Arabella.

"Our brief separation has been mighty profitable," was Captain Blood's greeting. "It's a busy morning we've both had." He was in high good-humour as he led the way to the great cabin for a rendering of accounts.

The tall ship that accompanied the Arabella was a Spanish vessel of twenty-six guns, the Santiago from Puerto Rico with a hundred and twenty thousand weight of cacao, forty thousand pieces of eight, and the value of ten thousand more in jewels. A rich capture of which two fifths under the articles went to Levasseur and his crew. Of the money and jewels a division was made on the spot. The cacao it was agreed should be taken to Tortuga to be sold.

Then it was the turn of Levasseur, and black grew the brow of Captain Blood as the Frenchman's tale was unfolded. At the end he roundly expressed his disapproval. The Dutch were a friendly people whom it was a folly to alienate, particularly for so paltry a matter as these hides and tobacco, which at most would fetch a bare twenty thousand pieces.

But Levasseur answered him, as he had answered Cahusac, that a ship was a ship, and it was ships they needed against their projected enterprise. Perhaps because things had gone well with him that day, Blood ended by shrugging the matter aside. Thereupon Levasseur proposed that the Arabella and her prize should return to Tortuga there to unload the cacao and enlist the further adventurers that could now be shipped. Levasseur meanwhile would effect certain necessary repairs, and then proceeding south, await his admiral at Saltatudos, an island conveniently situated—in the latitude of 11 deg. 11' N.—for their enterprise against Maracaybo.

To Levasseur's relief, Captain Blood not only agreed, but pronounced himself ready to set sail at once.

No sooner had the Arabella departed than Levasseur brought his ships into the lagoon, and set his crew to work upon the erection of temporary quarters ashore for himself, his men, and his enforced guests during the careening and repairing of La Foudre.

At sunset that evening the wind freshened; it grew to a gale, and from that to such a hurricane that Levasseur was thankful to find himself ashore and his ships in safe shelter. He wondered a little how it might be faring with Captain Blood out there at the mercy of that terrific storm; but he did not permit concern to trouble him unduly.

XV

THE RANSOM

In the glory of the following morning, sparkling and clear after the storm, with an invigorating, briny tang in the air from the salt-ponds on the south of the island, a curious scene was played on the beach of the Virgen Magra, at the foot of a ridge of bleached dunes, beside the spread of sail from which Levasseur had improvised a tent.

Enthroned upon an empty cask sat the French filibuster to transact important business: the business of making himself safe with the Governor of Tortuga.

A guard of honour of a half-dozen officers hung about him; five of them were rude boucan-hunters, in stained jerkins and leather breeches; the sixth was Cahusac. Before him, guarded by two half-naked negroes, stood young d'Ogeron, in frilled shirt and satin small-clothes and fine shoes of Cordovan leather. He was stripped of doublet, and his hands were tied behind him. The young gentleman's comely face was haggard. Near at hand, and also under guard, but unpinioned, mademoiselle his sister sat hunched upon a hillock of sand. She was very pale, and it was in vain that she sought to veil in a mask of arrogance the fears by which she was assailed.

Levasseur addressed himself to M. d'Ogeron. He spoke at long length. In the end—

"I trust, monsieur," said he, with mock suavity, "that I have made myself quite clear. So that there may be no misunderstandings, I will recapitulate. Your ransom is fixed at twenty thousand pieces of eight, and you shall have liberty on parole to go to Tortuga to collect it. In fact, I shall provide the means to convey you thither, and you shall have a month in which to come and go. Meanwhile, your sister remains with me as a hostage. Your father should not consider such a sum excessive as the price of his son's liberty and to provide a dowry for his daughter. Indeed, if anything, I am too modest, pardi! M. d'Ogeron is reputed a wealthy man."

M. d'Ogeron the younger raised his head and looked the Captain boldly in the face.

"I refuse—utterly and absolutely, do you understand? So do your worst, and be damned for a filthy pirate without decency and without honour."

"But what words!" laughed Levasseur. "What heat and what foolishness! You have not considered the alternative. When you do, you will not persist in your refusal. You will not do that in any case. We have spurs for the reluctant. And I warn you against giving me your parole under stress, and afterwards playing me false. I shall know how to find and punish you. Meanwhile, remember your sister's honour is in pawn to me. Should you forget to return with the dowry, you will not consider it unreasonable that I forget to marry her."

Levasseur's smiling eyes, intent upon the young man's face, saw the horror that crept into his glance. M. d'Ogeron cast a wild glance at mademoiselle, and observed the grey despair that had almost stamped the beauty from her face. Disgust and fury swept across his countenance.

Then he braced himself and answered resolutely:

"No, you dog! A thousand times, no!"

"You are foolish to persist." Levasseur spoke without anger, with a coldly mocking regret. His fingers had been busy tying knots in a length of whipcord. He held it up. "You know this? It is a rosary of pain that has wrought the conversion of many a stubborn heretic. It is capable of screwing the eyes out of a man's head by way of helping him to see reason. As you please."

He flung the length of knotted cord to one of the negroes, who in an instant made it fast about the prisoner's brows. Then between cord and cranium the black inserted a short length of metal, round and slender as a pipe-stem. That done he rolled his eyes towards Levasseur, awaiting the Captain's signal.

Levasseur considered his victim, and beheld him tense and braced, his haggard face of a leaden hue, beads of perspiration glinting on his pallid brow just beneath the whipcord.

Mademoiselle cried out, and would have risen: but her guards restrained her, and she sank down again, moaning.

"I beg that you will spare yourself and your sister," said the Captain, "by being reasonable. What, after all, is the sum I have named? To your wealthy father a bagatelle. I repeat, I have been too modest. But since I have said twenty thousand pieces of eight, twenty thousand pieces it shall be."

"And for what, if you please, have you said twenty thousand pieces of eight?"

In execrable French, but in a voice that was crisp and pleasant, seeming to echo some of the mockery that had invested Levasseur's, that question floated over their heads.

Startled, Levasseur and his officers looked up and round. On the crest of the dunes behind them, in sharp silhouette against the deep cobalt of the sky, they beheld a tall, lean figure scrupulously dressed in black with silver lace, a crimson ostrich plume curled about the broad brim of his hat affording the only touch of colour. Under that hat was the tawny face of Captain Blood.

Levasseur gathered himself up with an oath of amazement. He had conceived Captain Blood by now well below the horizon, on his way to Tortuga, assuming him to have been so fortunate as to have weathered last night's storm.

Launching himself upon the yielding sand, into which he sank to the level of the calves of his fine boots of Spanish leather, Captain Blood came sliding erect to the beach. He was followed by Wolverstone, and a dozen others. As he came to a standstill, he doffed his hat, with a flourish, to the lady. Then he turned to Levasseur.

"Good-morning, my Captain," said he, and proceeded to explain his presence. "It was last night's hurricane compelled our return. We had no choice but to ride before it with stripped poles, and it drove us back the way we had gone. Moreover—as the devil would have it!—the Santiago sprang her mainmast; and so I was glad to put into a cove on the west of the island a couple of miles away, and we've walked across to stretch our legs, and to give you good-day. But who are these?" And he designated the man and the woman.

Cahusac shrugged his shoulders, and tossed his long arms to heaven.

"Voila!" said he, pregnantly, to the firmament.

Levasseur gnawed his lip, and changed colour. But he controlled himself to answer civilly:

"As you see, two prisoners."

"Ah! Washed ashore in last night's gale, eh?"

"Not so." Levasseur contained himself with difficulty before that irony. "They were in the Dutch brig."

"I don't remember that you mentioned them before."

"I did not. They are prisoners of my own—a personal matter. They are French."

"French!" Captain Blood's light eyes stabbed at Levasseur, then at the prisoners.

M. d'Ogeron stood tense and braced as before, but the grey horror had left his face. Hope had leapt within him at this interruption, obviously as little expected by his tormentor as by himself. His sister, moved by a similar intuition, was leaning forward with parted lips and gaping eyes.

Captain Blood fingered his lip, and frowned thoughtfully upon Levasseur.

"Yesterday you surprised me by making war upon the friendly Dutch. But now it seems that not even your own countrymen are safe from you."

"Have I not said that these... that this is a matter personal to me?"

"Ah! And their names?"

Captain Blood's crisp, authoritative, faintly disdainful manner stirred Levasseur's quick anger. The blood crept slowly back into his blenched face, and his glance grew in insolence, almost in menace. Meanwhile the prisoner answered for him.

"I am Henri d'Ogeron, and this is my sister."

"D'Ogeron?" Captain Blood stared. "Are you related by chance to my good friend the Governor of Tortuga?"

"He is my father."

Levasseur swung aside with an imprecation. In Captain Blood, amazement for the moment quenched every other emotion.

"The saints preserve us now! Are you quite mad, Levasseur? First you molest the Dutch, who are our friends; next you take prisoners two persons that are French, your own countrymen; and now, faith, they're no less than the children of the Governor of Tortuga, which is the one safe place of shelter that we enjoy in these islands..."

Levasseur broke in angrily:

"Must I tell you again that it is a matter personal to me? I make myself alone responsible to the Governor of Tortuga."

"And the twenty thousand pieces of eight? Is that also a matter personal to you?"

"It is."

"Now I don't agree with you at all." Captain Blood sat down on the cask that Levasseur had lately occupied, and looked up blandly. "I may inform you, to save time, that I heard the entire proposal that you made to this lady and this gentleman, and I'll also remind you that we sail under articles that admit no ambiguities. You have fixed their ransom at twenty thousand pieces of eight. That sum then belongs to your crews and mine in the proportions by the articles established. You'll hardly wish to dispute it. But what is far more grave is that you have concealed from me this part of the prizes taken on your last cruise, and for such an offence as that the articles provide certain penalties that are something severe in character."

"Ho, ho!" laughed Levasseur unpleasantly. Then added: "If you dislike my conduct we can dissolve the association."

"That is my intention. But we'll dissolve it when and in the manner that I choose, and that will be as soon as you have satisfied the articles under which we sailed upon this cruise.

"What do you mean?"

"I'll be as short as I can," said Captain Blood. "I'll waive for the moment the unseemliness of making war upon the Dutch, of taking French prisoners, and of provoking the anger of the Governor of Tortuga. I'll accept the situation as I find it. Yourself you've fixed the ransom of this couple at twenty thousand pieces, and, as I gather, the lady is to be your perquisite. But why should she be your perquisite more than another's, seeing that she belongs by the articles to all of us, as a prize of war?"

Black as thunder grew the brow of Levasseur.

"However," added Captain Blood, "I'll not dispute her to you if you are prepared to buy her."

"Buy her?"

"At the price you have set upon her."

Levasseur contained his rage, that he might reason with the Irishman. "That is the ransom of the man. It is to be paid for him by the Governor of Tortuga."

"No, no. Ye've parcelled the twain together—very oddly, I confess. Ye've set their value at twenty thousand pieces, and for that sum you may have them, since you desire it; but you'll pay for them the twenty thousand pieces that are ultimately to come to you as the ransom of one and the dowry of the other; and that sum shall be divided among our crews. So that you do that, it is conceivable that our followers may take a lenient view of your breach of the articles we jointly signed."

Levasseur laughed savagely. "Ah ca! Credieu! The good jest!"

"I quite agree with you," said Captain Blood.

To Levasseur the jest lay in that Captain Blood, with no more than a dozen followers, should come there attempting to hector him who had a hundred men within easy call. But it seemed that he had left out of his reckoning something which his opponent had counted in. For as, laughing still, Levasseur swung to his officers, he saw that which choked the laughter in his throat. Captain Blood had shrewdly played upon the cupidity that was the paramount inspiration of those adventurers. And Levasseur now read clearly on their faces how completely they adopted Captain Blood's suggestion that all must participate in the ransom which their leader had thought to appropriate to himself.

It gave the gaudy ruffian pause, and whilst in his heart he cursed those followers of his, who could be faithful only to their greed, he perceived—and only just in time—that he had best tread warily.

"You misunderstand," he said, swallowing his rage. "The ransom is for division, when it comes. The girl, meanwhile, is mine on that understanding."

"Good!" grunted Cahusac. "On that understanding all arranges itself."

"You think so?" said Captain Blood. "But if M. d'Ogeron should refuse to pay the ransom? What then?" He laughed, and got lazily to his feet. "No, no. If Captain Levasseur is meanwhile to keep the girl, as he proposes, then let him pay this ransom, and be his the risk if it should afterwards not be forthcoming."

"That's it!" cried one of Levasseur's officers. And Cahusac added: "It's reasonable, that! Captain Blood is right. It is in the articles."

"What is in the articles, you fools?" Levasseur was in danger of losing his head. "Sacre Dieu! Where do you suppose that I have twenty thousand pieces? My whole share of the prizes of this cruise does not come to half that sum. I'll be your debtor until I've earned it. Will that content you?"

All things considered, there is not a doubt that it would have done so had not Captain Blood intended otherwise.

"And if you should die before you have earned it? Ours is a calling fraught with risks, my Captain."

"Damn you!" Levasseur flung upon him livid with fury. "Will nothing satisfy you?"

"Oh, but yes. Twenty thousand pieces of eight for immediate division."

"I haven't got it."

"Then let some one buy the prisoners who has."

"And who do you suppose has it if I have not?"

"I have," said Captain Blood.

"You have!" Levasseur's mouth fell open. "You... you want the girl?"

"Why not? And I exceed you in gallantry in that I will make sacrifices to obtain her, and in honesty in that I am ready to pay for what I want."

Levasseur stared at him foolishly agape. Behind him pressed his officers, gaping also.

Captain Blood sat down again on the cask, and drew from an inner pocket of his doublet a little leather bag. "I am glad to be able to resolve a difficulty that at one moment seemed insoluble." And under the bulging eyes of Levasseur and his officers, he untied the mouth of the bag and rolled into his left palm four or five pearls each of the size of a sparrow's egg. There were twenty such in the bag, the very pick of those taken in that raid upon the pearl fleet. "You boast a knowledge of pearls, Cahusac. At what do you value this?"

The Breton took between coarse finger and thumb the proffered lustrous, delicately iridescent sphere, his shrewd eyes appraising it.

"A thousand pieces," he answered shortly.

"It will fetch rather more in Tortuga or Jamaica," said Captain Blood, "and twice as much in Europe. But I'll accept your valuation. They are almost of a size, as you can see. Here are twelve, representing twelve thousand pieces of eight, which is La Foudre's share of three fifths of the prize, as provided by the articles. For the eight thousand pieces that go to the Arabella, I make myself responsible to my own men. And now, Wolverstone, if you please, will you take my property aboard the Arabella?" He stood up again, indicating the prisoners.

"Ah, no!" Levasseur threw wide the floodgates of his fury. "Ah, that, no, by example! You shall not take her..." He would have sprung upon Captain Blood, who stood aloof, alert, tight-lipped, and watchful.

But it was one of Levasseur's own officers who hindered him.

"Nom de Dieu, my Captain! What will you do? It is settled; honourably settled with satisfaction to all."

"To all?" blazed Levasseur. "Ah ca! To all of you, you animals! But what of me?"

Cahusac, with the pearls clutched in his capacious hand, stepped up to him on the other side. "Don't be a fool, Captain. Do you want to provoke trouble between the crews? His men outnumber us by nearly two to one. What's a girl more or less? In Heaven's name, let her go. He's paid handsomely for her, and dealt fairly with us."

"Dealt fairly?" roared the infuriated Captain. "You..." In all his foul vocabulary he could find no epithet to describe his lieutenant. He caught him a blow that almost sent him sprawling. The pearls were scattered in the sand.

Cahusac dived after them, his fellows with him. Vengeance must wait. For some moments they groped there on hands and knees, oblivious of all else. And yet in those moments vital things were happening.

Levasseur, his hand on his sword, his face a white mask of rage, was confronting Captain Blood to hinder his departure.

"You do not take her while I live!" he cried.

"Then I'll take her when you're dead," said Captain Blood, and his own blade flashed in the sunlight. "The articles provide that any man of whatever rank concealing any part of a prize, be it of the value of no more than a peso, shall be hanged at the yardarm. It's what I intended for you in the end. But since ye prefer it this way, ye muckrake, faith, I'll be humouring you."

He waved away the men who would have interfered, and the blades rang together.

M. d'Ogeron looked on, a man bemused, unable to surmise what the issue either way could mean for him. Meanwhile, two of Blood's men who had taken the place of the Frenchman's black man guards, had removed the crown of whipcord from his brow. As for mademoiselle, she had risen, and was leaning forward, a hand pressed tightly to her heaving breast, her face deathly pale, a wild terror in her eyes.

It was soon over. The brute strength, upon which Levasseur so confidently counted, could avail nothing against the Irishman's practised skill. When, with both lungs transfixed, he lay prone on the white sand, coughing out his rascally life, Captain Blood looked calmly at Cahusac across the body.

"I think that cancels the articles between us," he said. With soulless, cynical eyes Cahusac considered the twitching body of his recent leader. Had Levasseur been a man of different temper, the affair might have ended in a very different manner. But, then, it is certain that Captain Blood would have adopted in dealing with him different tactics. As it was, Levasseur commanded neither love nor loyalty. The men who followed him were the very dregs of that vile trade, and cupidity was their only inspiration. Upon that cupidity Captain Blood had deftly played, until he had brought them to find Levasseur guilty of the one offence they deemed unpardonable, the crime of appropriating to himself something which might be converted into gold and shared amongst them all.

Thus now the threatening mob of buccaneers that came hastening to the theatre of that swift tragi-comedy were appeased by a dozen words of Cahusac's.

Whilst still they hesitated, Blood added something to quicken their decision.

"If you will come to our anchorage, you shall receive at once your share of the booty of the Santiago, that you may dispose of it as you please."

They crossed the island, the two prisoners accompanying them, and later that day, the division made, they would have parted company but that Cahusac, at the instances of the men who had elected him Levasseur's successor, offered Captain Blood anew the services of that French contingent.

"If you will sail with me again," the Captain answered him, "you may do so on the condition that you make your peace with the Dutch, and restore the brig and her cargo."

The condition was accepted, and Captain Blood went off to find his guests, the children of the Governor of Tortuga.

Mademoiselle d'Ogeron and her brother—the latter now relieved of his bonds—sat in the great cabin of the Arabella, whither they had been conducted.

Wine and food had been placed upon the table by Benjamin, Captain Blood's black man steward and cook, who had intimated to them that it was for their entertainment. But it had remained untouched. Brother and sister sat there in agonized bewilderment, conceiving that their escape was but from frying-pan to fire. At length, overwrought by the suspense, mademoiselle flung herself upon her knees before her brother to implore his pardon for all the evil brought upon them by her wicked folly.

M. d'Ogeron was not in a forgiving mood.

"I am glad that at least you realize what you have done. And now this other filibuster has bought you, and you belong to him. You realize that, too, I hope."

He might have said more, but he checked upon perceiving that the door was opening. Captain Blood, coming from settling matters with the followers of Levasseur, stood on the threshold. M. d'Ogeron had not troubled to restrain his high-pitched voice, and the Captain had overheard the Frenchman's last two sentences. Therefore he perfectly understood why mademoiselle should bound up at sight of him, and shrink back in fear.

"Mademoiselle," said he in his vile but fluent French, "I beg you to dismiss your fears. Aboard this ship you shall be treated with all honour. So soon as we are in case to put to sea again, we steer a course for Tortuga to take you home to your father. And pray do not consider that I have bought you, as your brother has just said. All that I have done has been to provide the ransom necessary to bribe a gang of scoundrels to depart from obedience to the arch-scoundrel who commanded them, and so deliver you from all peril. Count it, if you please, a friendly loan to be repaid entirely at your convenience."

Mademoiselle stared at him in unbelief. M. d'Ogeron rose to his feet.

"Monsieur, is it possible that you are serious?"

"I am. It may not happen often nowadays. I may be a pirate. But my ways are not the ways of Levasseur, who should have stayed in Europe, and practised purse-cutting. I have a sort of honour—shall we say, some rags of honour?—remaining me from better days." Then on a brisker note he added: "We dine in an hour, and I trust that you will honour my table with your company. Meanwhile, Benjamin will see, monsieur, that you are more suitably provided in the matter of wardrobe."

He bowed to them, and turned to depart again, but mademoiselle detained him.

"Monsieur!" she cried sharply.

He checked and turned, whilst slowly she approached him, regarding him between dread and wonder.

"Oh, you are noble!"

"I shouldn't put it as high as that myself," said he.

"You are, you are! And it is but right that you should know all."

"Madelon!" her brother cried out, to restrain her.

But she would not be restrained. Her surcharged heart must overflow in confidence.

"Monsieur, for what befell I am greatly at fault. This man—this Levasseur..."

He stared, incredulous in his turn. "My God! Is it possible? That animal!"

Abruptly she fell on her knees, caught his hand and kissed it before he could wrench it from her.

"What do you do?" he cried.

"An amende. In my mind I dishonoured you by deeming you his like, by conceiving your fight with Levasseur a combat between jackals. On my knees, monsieur, I implore you to forgive me."

Captain Blood looked down upon her, and a smile broke on his lips, irradiating the blue eyes that looked so oddly light in that tawny face.

"Why, child," said he, "I might find it hard to forgive you the stupidity of having thought otherwise."

As he handed her to her feet again, he assured himself that he had behaved rather well in the affair. Then he sighed. That dubious fame of his that had spread so quickly across the Caribbean would by now have reached the ears of Arabella Bishop. That she would despise him, he could not doubt, deeming him no better than all the other scoundrels who drove this villainous buccaneering trade. Therefore he hoped that some echo of this deed might reach her also, and be set by her against some of that contempt. For the whole truth, which he withheld from Mademoiselle d'Ogeron, was that in venturing his life to save her, he had been driven by the thought that the deed must be pleasing in the eyes of Miss Bishop could she but witness it.

XVI

THE TRAP

That affair of Mademoiselle d'Ogeron bore as its natural fruit an improvement in the already cordial relations between Captain Blood and the Governor of Tortuga. At the fine stone house, with its green-jalousied windows, which M. d'Ogeron had built himself in a spacious and luxuriant garden to the east of Cayona, the Captain became a very welcome guest. M. d'Ogeron was in the Captain's debt for more than the twenty thousand pieces of eight which he had provided for mademoiselle's ransom; and shrewd, hard bargain-driver though he might be, the Frenchman could be generous and understood the sentiment of gratitude. This he now proved in every possible way, and under his powerful protection the credit of Captain Blood among the buccaneers very rapidly reached its zenith.

So when it came to fitting out his fleet for that enterprise against Maracaybo, which had originally been Levasseur's project, he did not want for either ships or men to follow him. He recruited five hundred adventurers in all, and he might have had as many thousands if he could have offered them accommodation. Similarly without difficulty he might have increased his fleet to twice its strength of ships but that he preferred to keep it what it was. The three vessels to which he confined it were the Arabella, the La Foudre, which Cahusac now commanded with a contingent of some sixscore Frenchmen, and the Santiago, which had been refitted and rechristened the Elizabeth, after that Queen of England whose seamen had humbled Spain as Captain Blood now hoped to humble it again. Hagthorpe, in virtue of his service in the navy, was appointed by Blood to command her, and the appointment was confirmed by the men.

It was some months after the rescue of Mademoiselle d'Ogeron—in August of that year 1687—that this little fleet, after some minor adventures which I pass over in silence, sailed into the great lake of Maracaybo and effected its raid upon that opulent city of the Main.

The affair did not proceed exactly as was hoped, and Blood's force came to find itself in a precarious position. This is best explained in the words employed by Cahusac—which Pitt has carefully recorded—in the course of an altercation that broke out on the steps of the Church of Nuestra Senora del Carmen, which Captain Blood had impiously appropriated for the purpose of a corps-de-garde. I have said already that he was a papist only when it suited him.

The dispute was being conducted by Hagthorpe, Wolverstone, and Pitt on the one side, and Cahusac, out of whose uneasiness it all arose, on the other. Behind them in the sun-scorched, dusty square, sparsely fringed by palms, whose fronds drooped listlessly in the quivering heat, surged a couple of hundred wild fellows belonging to both parties, their own excitement momentarily quelled so that they might listen to what passed among their leaders.

Cahusac appeared to be having it all his own way, and he raised his harsh, querulous voice so that all might hear his truculent denunciation. He spoke, Pitt tells us, a dreadful kind of English, which the shipmaster, however, makes little attempt to reproduce. His dress was as discordant as his speech. It was of a kind to advertise his trade, and ludicrously in contrast with the sober garb of Hagthorpe and the almost foppish daintiness of Jeremy Pitt. His soiled and blood-stained shirt of blue cotton was open in front, to cool his hairy breast, and the girdle about the waist of his leather breeches carried an arsenal of pistols and a knife, whilst a cutlass hung from a leather baldrick loosely slung about his body; above his countenance, broad and flat as a Mongolian's, a red scarf was swathed, turban-wise, about his head.

"Is it that I have not warned you from the beginning that all was too easy?" he demanded between plaintiveness and fury. "I am no fool, my friends. I have eyes, me. And I see. I see an abandoned fort at the entrance of the lake, and nobody there to fire a gun at us when we came in. Then I suspect the trap. Who would not that had eyes and brain? Bah! we come on. What do we find? A city, abandoned like the fort; a city out of which the people have taken all things of value. Again I warn Captain Blood. It is a trap, I say. We are to come on; always to come on, without opposition, until we find that it is too late to go to sea again, that we cannot go back at all. But no one will listen to me. You all know so much more. Name of God! Captain Blood, he will go on, and we go on. We go to Gibraltar. True that at last, after long time, we catch the Deputy-Governor; true, we make him pay big ransom for Gibraltar; true between that ransom and the loot we return here with some two thousand pieces of eight. But what is it, in reality, will you tell me? Or shall I tell you? It is a piece of cheese—a piece of cheese in a mousetrap, and we are the little mice. Goddam! And the cats—oh, the cats they wait for us! The cats are those four Spanish ships of war that have come meantime. And they wait for us outside the bottle-neck of this lagoon. Mort de Dieu! That is what comes of the damned obstinacy of your fine Captain Blood."

Wolverstone laughed. Cahusac exploded in fury.

"Ah, sangdieu! Tu ris, animal? You laugh! Tell me this: How do we get out again unless we accept the terms of Monsieur the Admiral of Spain?"

From the buccaneers at the foot of the steps came an angry rumble of approval. The single eye of the gigantic Wolverstone rolled terribly, and he clenched his great fists as if to strike the Frenchman, who was exposing them to mutiny. But Cahusac was not daunted. The mood of the men enheartened him.

"You think, perhaps, this your Captain Blood is the good God. That he can make miracles, eh? He is ridiculous, you know, this Captain Blood; with his grand air and his..."

He checked. Out of the church at that moment, grand air and all, sauntered Peter Blood. With him came a tough, long-legged French sea-wolf named Yberville, who, though still young, had already won fame as a privateer commander before the loss of his own ship had driven him to take service under Blood. The Captain advanced towards that disputing group, leaning lightly upon his long ebony cane, his face shaded by a broad-plumed hat. There was in his appearance nothing of the buccaneer. He had much more the air of a lounger in the Mall or the Alameda—the latter rather, since his elegant suit of violet taffetas with gold-embroidered button-holes was in the Spanish fashion. But the long, stout, serviceable rapier, thrust up behind by the left hand resting lightly on the pummel, corrected the impression. That and those steely eyes of his announced the adventurer.

"You find me ridiculous, eh, Cahusac?" said he, as he came to a halt before the Breton, whose anger seemed already to have gone out of him. "What, then, must I find you?" He spoke quietly, almost wearily. "You will be telling them that we have delayed, and that it is the delay that has brought about our danger. But whose is the fault of that delay? We have been a month in doing what should have been done, and what but for your blundering would have been done, inside of a week."

"Ah ca! Nom de Dieu! Was it my fault that..."

"Was it any one else's fault that you ran your ship La Foudre aground on the shoal in the middle of the lake? You would not be piloted. You knew your way. You took no soundings even. The result was that we lost three precious days in getting canoes to bring off your men and your gear. Those three days gave the folk at Gibraltar not only time to hear of our coming, but time in which to get away. After that, and because of it, we had to follow the Governor to his infernal island fortress, and a fortnight and best part of a hundred lives were lost in reducing it. That's how we come to have delayed until this Spanish fleet is fetched round from La Guayra by a guarda-costa; and if ye hadn't lost La Foudre, and so reduced our fleet from three ships to two, we should even now be able to fight our way through with a reasonable hope of succeeding. Yet you think it is for you to come hectoring here, upbraiding us for a situation that is just the result of your own ineptitude."

He spoke with a restraint which I trust you will agree was admirable when I tell you that the Spanish fleet guarding the bottle-neck exit of the great Lake of Maracaybo, and awaiting there the coming forth of Captain Blood with a calm confidence based upon its overwhelming strength, was commanded by his implacable enemy, Don Miguel de Espinosa y Valdez, the Admiral of Spain. In addition to his duty to his country, the Admiral had, as you know, a further personal incentive arising out of that business aboard the Encarnacion a year ago, and the death of his brother Don Diego; and with him sailed his nephew Esteban, whose vindictive zeal exceeded the Admiral's own.

Yet, knowing all this, Captain Blood could preserve his calm in reproving the cowardly frenzy of one for whom the situation had not half the peril with which it was fraught for himself. He turned from Cahusac to address the mob of buccaneers, who had surged nearer to hear him, for he had not troubled to raise his voice. "I hope that will correct some of the misapprehension that appears to have been disturbing you," said he.

"There's no good can come of talking of what's past and done," cried Cahusac, more sullen now than truculent. Whereupon Wolverstone laughed, a laugh that was like the neighing of a horse. "The question is: what are we to do now?"

"Sure, now, there's no question at all," said Captain Blood.

"Indeed, but there is," Cahusac insisted. "Don Miguel, the Spanish Admiral, have offer us safe passage to sea if we will depart at once, do no damage to the town, release our prisoners, and surrender all that we took at Gibraltar."

Captain Blood smiled quietly, knowing precisely how much Don Miguel's word was worth. It was Yberville who replied, in manifest scorn of his compatriot:

"Which argues that, even at this disadvantage as he has us, the Spanish Admiral is still afraid of us."

"That can be only because he not know our real weakness," was the fierce retort. "And, anyway, we must accept these terms. We have no choice. That is my opinion."

"Well, it's not mine, now," said Captain Blood. "So, I've refused them."

"Refuse'!" Cahusac's broad face grew purple. A muttering from the men behind enheartened him. "You have refused? You have refused already—and without consulting me?"

"Your disagreement could have altered nothing. You'd have been outvoted, for Hagthorpe here was entirely of my own mind. Still," he went on, "if you and your own French followers wish to avail yourselves of the Spaniard's terms, we shall not hinder you. Send one of your prisoners to announce it to the Admiral. Don Miguel will welcome your decision, you may be sure."

Cahusac glowered at him in silence for a moment. Then, having controlled himself, he asked in a concentrated voice:

"Precisely what answer have you make to the Admiral?"

A smile irradiated the face and eyes of Captain Blood. "I have answered him that unless within four-and-twenty hours we have his parole to stand out to sea, ceasing to dispute our passage or hinder our departure, and a ransom of fifty thousand pieces of eight for Maracaybo, we shall reduce this beautiful city to ashes, and thereafter go out and destroy his fleet."

The impudence of it left Cahusac speechless. But among the English buccaneers in the square there were many who savoured the audacious humour of the trapped dictating terms to the trappers. Laughter broke from them. It spread into a roar of acclamation; for bluff is a weapon dear to every adventurer. Presently, when they understood it, even Cahusac's French followers were carried off their feet by that wave of jocular enthusiasm, until in his truculent obstinacy Cahusac remained the only dissentient. He withdrew in mortification. Nor was he to be mollified until the following day brought him his revenge. This came in the shape of a messenger from Don Miguel with a letter in which the Spanish Admiral solemnly vowed to God that, since the pirates had refused his magnanimous offer to permit them to surrender with the honours of war, he would now await them at the mouth of the lake there to destroy them on their coming forth. He added that should they delay their departure, he would so soon as he was reinforced by a fifth ship, the Santo Nino, on its way to join him from La Guayra, himself come inside to seek them at Maracaybo.

This time Captain Blood was put out of temper.

"Trouble me no more," he snapped at Cahusac, who came growling to him again. "Send word to Don Miguel that you have seceded from me. He'll give you safe conduct, devil a doubt. Then take one of the sloops, order your men aboard and put to sea, and the devil go with you."

Cahusac would certainly have adopted that course if only his men had been unanimous in the matter. They, however, were torn between greed and apprehension. If they went they must abandon their share of the plunder, which was considerable, as well as the slaves and other prisoners they had taken. If they did this, and Captain Blood should afterwards contrive to get away unscathed—and from their knowledge of his resourcefulness, the thing, however unlikely, need not be impossible—he must profit by that which they now relinquished. This was a contingency too bitter for contemplation. And so, in the end, despite all that Cahusac could say, the surrender was not to Don Miguel, but to Peter Blood. They had come into the venture with him, they asserted, and they would go out of it with him or not at all. That was the message he received from them that same evening by the sullen mouth of Cahusac himself.

He welcomed it, and invited the Breton to sit down and join the council which was even then deliberating upon the means to be employed. This council occupied the spacious patio of the Governor's house—which Captain Blood had appropriated to his own uses—a cloistered stone quadrangle in the middle of which a fountain played coolly under a trellis of vine. Orange-trees grew on two sides of it, and the still, evening air was heavy with the scent of them. It was one of those pleasant exterior-interiors which Moorish architects had introduced to Spain and the Spaniards had carried with them to the New World.

Here that council of war, composed of six men in all, deliberated until late that night upon the plan of action which Captain Blood put forward.

The great freshwater lake of Maracaybo, nourished by a score of rivers from the snow-capped ranges that surround it on two sides, is some hundred and twenty miles in length and almost the same distance across at its widest. It is—as has been indicated—in the shape of a great bottle having its neck towards the sea at Maracaybo.

Beyond this neck it widens again, and then the two long, narrow strips of land known as the islands of Vigilias and Palomas block the channel, standing lengthwise across it. The only passage out to sea for vessels of any draught lies in the narrow strait between these islands. Palomas, which is some ten miles in length, is unapproachable for half a mile on either side by any but the shallowest craft save at its eastern end, where, completely commanding the narrow passage out to sea, stands the massive fort which the buccaneers had found deserted upon their coming. In the broader water between this passage and the bar, the four Spanish ships were at anchor in mid-channel. The Admiral's Encarnacion, which we already know, was a mighty galleon of forty-eight great guns and eight small. Next in importance was the Salvador with thirty-six guns; the other two, the Infanta and the San Felipe, though smaller vessels, were still formidable enough with their twenty guns and a hundred and fifty men apiece.

Such was the fleet of which the gauntlet was to be run by Captain Blood with his own Arabella of forty guns, the Elizabeth of twenty-six, and two sloops captured at Gibraltar, which they had indifferently armed with four culverins each. In men they had a bare four hundred survivors of the five hundred-odd that had left Tortuga, to oppose to fully a thousand Spaniards manning the galleons.

The plan of action submitted by Captain Blood to that council was a desperate one, as Cahusac uncompromisingly pronounced it.

"Why, so it is," said the Captain. "But I've done things more desperate." Complacently he pulled at a pipe that was loaded with that fragrant Sacerdotes tobacco for which Gibraltar was famous, and of which they had brought away some hogsheads. "And what is more, they've succeeded. Audaces fortuna juvat. Bedad, they knew their world, the old Romans."

He breathed into his companions and even into Cahusac some of his own spirit of confidence, and in confidence all went busily to work. For three days from sunrise to sunset, the buccaneers laboured and sweated to complete the preparations for the action that was to procure them their deliverance. Time pressed. They must strike before Don Miguel de Espinosa received the reenforcement of that fifth galleon, the Santo Nino, which was coming to join him from La Guayra.

Their principal operations were on the larger of the two sloops captured at Gibraltar; to which vessel was assigned the leading part in Captain Blood's scheme. They began by tearing down all bulkheads, until they had reduced her to the merest shell, and in her sides they broke open so many ports that her gunwale was converted into the semblance of a grating. Next they increased by a half-dozen the scuttles in her deck, whilst into her hull they packed all the tar and pitch and brimstone that they could find in the town, to which they added six barrels of gunpowder, placed on end like guns at the open ports on her larboard side. On the evening of the fourth day, everything being now in readiness, all were got aboard, and the empty, pleasant city of Maracaybo was at last abandoned. But they did not weigh anchor until some two hours after midnight. Then, at last, on the first of the ebb, they drifted silently down towards the bar with all canvas furled save only their spiltsails, which, so as to give them steering way, were spread to the faint breeze that stirred through the purple darkness of the tropical night.

The order of their going was as follows: Ahead went the improvised fire-ship in charge of Wolverstone, with a crew of six volunteers, each of whom was to have a hundred pieces of eight over and above his share of plunder as a special reward. Next came the Arabella. She was followed at a distance by the Elizabeth, commanded by Hagthorpe, with whom was the now shipless Cahusac and the bulk of his French followers. The rear was brought up by the second sloop and some eight canoes, aboard of which had been shipped the prisoners, the slaves, and most of the captured merchandise. The prisoners were all pinioned, and guarded by four buccaneers with musketoons who manned these boats in addition to the two fellows who were to sail them. Their place was to be in the rear and they were to take no part whatever in the coming fight.

As the first glimmerings of opalescent dawn dissolved the darkness, the straining eyes of the buccaneers were able to make out the tall rigging of the Spanish vessels, riding at anchor less than a quarter of a mile ahead. Entirely without suspicion as the Spaniards were, and rendered confident by their own overwhelming strength, it is unlikely that they used a vigilance keener than their careless habit. Certain it is that they did not sight Blood's fleet in that dim light until some time after Blood's fleet had sighted them. By the time that they had actively roused themselves, Wolverstone's sloop was almost upon them, speeding under canvas which had been crowded to her yards the moment the galleons had loomed into view.

Straight for the Admiral's great ship, the Encarnacion, did Wolverstone head the sloop; then, lashing down the helm, he kindled from a match that hung ready lighted beside him a great torch of thickly plaited straw that had been steeped in bitumen. First it glowed, then as he swung it round his head, it burst into flame, just as the slight vessel went crashing and bumping and scraping against the side of the flagship, whilst rigging became tangled with rigging, to the straining of yards and snapping of spars overhead. His six men stood at their posts on the larboard side, stark naked, each armed with a grapnel, four of them on the gunwale, two of them aloft. At the moment of impact these grapnels were slung to bind the Spaniard to them, those aloft being intended to complete and preserve the entanglement of the rigging.

Aboard the rudely awakened galleon all was confused hurrying, scurrying, trumpeting, and shouting. At first there had been a desperately hurried attempt to get up the anchor; but this was abandoned as being already too late; and conceiving themselves on the point of being boarded, the Spaniards stood to arms to ward off the onslaught. Its slowness in coming intrigued them, being so different from the usual tactics of the buccaneers. Further intrigued were they by the sight of the gigantic Wolverstone speeding naked along his deck with a great flaming torch held high. Not until he had completed his work did they begin to suspect the truth—that he was lighting slow-matches—and then one of their officers rendered reckless by panic ordered a boarding-party on to the sloop.

The order came too late. Wolverstone had seen his six fellows drop overboard after the grapnels were fixed, and then had sped, himself, to the starboard gunwale. Thence he flung his flaming torch down the nearest gaping scuttle into the hold, and thereupon dived overboard in his turn, to be picked up presently by the longboat from the Arabella. But before that happened the sloop was a thing of fire, from which explosions were hurling blazing combustibles aboard the Encarnacion, and long tongues of flame were licking out to consume the galleon, beating back those daring Spaniards who, too late, strove desperately to cut her adrift.

And whilst the most formidable vessel of the Spanish fleet was thus being put out of action at the outset, Blood had sailed in to open fire upon the Salvador. First athwart her hawse he had loosed a broadside that had swept her decks with terrific effect, then going on and about, he had put a second broadside into her hull at short range. Leaving her thus half-crippled, temporarily, at least, and keeping to his course, he had bewildered the crew of the Infanta by a couple of shots from the chasers on his beak-head, then crashed alongside to grapple and board her, whilst Hagthorpe was doing the like by the San Felipe.

And in all this time not a single shot had the Spaniards contrived to fire, so completely had they been taken by surprise, and so swift and paralyzing had been Blood's stroke.

Boarded now and faced by the cold steel of the buccaneers, neither the San Felipe nor the Infanta offered much resistance.

The sight of their admiral in flames, and the Salvador drifting crippled from the action, had so utterly disheartened them that they accounted themselves vanquished, and laid down their arms.

If by a resolute stand the Salvador had encouraged the other two undamaged vessels to resistance, the Spaniards might well have retrieved the fortunes of the day. But it happened that the Salvador was handicapped in true Spanish fashion by being the treasure-ship of the fleet, with plate on board to the value of some fifty thousand pieces. Intent above all upon saving this from falling into the hands of the pirates, Don Miguel, who, with a remnant of his crew, had meanwhile transferred himself aboard her, headed her down towards Palomas and the fort that guarded the passage. This fort the Admiral, in those days of waiting, had taken the precaution secretly to garrison and rearm. For the purpose he had stripped the fort of Cojero, farther out on the gulf, of its entire armament, which included some cannon-royal of more than ordinary range and power.

With no suspicion of this, Captain Blood gave chase, accompanied by the Infanta, which was manned now by a prize-crew under the command of Yberville. The stern chasers of the Salvador desultorily returned the punishing fire of the pursuers; but such was the damage she, herself, sustained, that presently, coming under the guns of the fort, she began to sink, and finally settled down in the shallows with part of her hull above water. Thence, some in boats and some by swimming, the Admiral got his crew ashore on Palomas as best he could.

And then, just as Captain Blood accounted the victory won, and that his way out of that trap to the open sea beyond lay clear, the fort suddenly revealed its formidable and utterly unsuspected strength. With a roar the cannons-royal proclaimed themselves, and the Arabella staggered under a blow that smashed her bulwarks at the waist and scattered death and confusion among the seamen gathered there.

Had not Pitt, her master, himself seized the whipstaff and put the helm hard over to swing her sharply off to starboard, she must have suffered still worse from the second volley that followed fast upon the first.

Meanwhile it had fared even worse with the frailer Infanta. Although hit by one shot only, this had crushed her larboard timbers on the waterline, starting a leak that must presently have filled her, but for the prompt action of the experienced Yberville in ordering her larboard guns to be flung overboard. Thus lightened, and listing now to starboard, he fetched her about, and went staggering after the retreating Arabella, followed by the fire of the fort, which did them, however, little further damage.

Out of range, at last, they lay to, joined by the Elizabeth and the San Felipe, to consider their position.

XVII

THE DUPES

It was a crestfallen Captain Blood who presided over that hastily summoned council held on the poop-deck of the Arabella in the brilliant morning sunshine. It was, he declared afterwards, one of the bitterest moments in his career. He was compelled to digest the fact that having conducted the engagement with a skill of which he might justly be proud, having destroyed a force so superior in ships and guns and men that Don Miguel de Espinosa had justifiably deemed it overwhelming, his victory was rendered barren by three lucky shots from an unsuspected battery by which they had been surprised. And barren must their victory remain until they could reduce the fort that still remained to defend the passage.

At first Captain Blood was for putting his ships in order and making the attempt there and then. But the others dissuaded him from betraying an impetuosity usually foreign to him, and born entirely of chagrin and mortification, emotions which will render unreasonable the most reasonable of men. With returning calm, he surveyed the situation. The Arabella was no longer in case to put to sea; the Infanta was merely kept afloat by artifice, and the San Felipe was almost as sorely damaged by the fire she had sustained from the buccaneers before surrendering.

Clearly, then, he was compelled to admit in the end that nothing remained but to return to Maracaybo, there to refit the ships before attempting to force the passage.

And so, back to Maracaybo came those defeated victors of that short, terrible fight. And if anything had been wanting further to exasperate their leader, he had it in the pessimism of which Cahusac did not economize expressions. Transported at first to heights of dizzy satisfaction by the swift and easy victory of their inferior force that morning, the Frenchman was now plunged back and more deeply than ever into the abyss of hopelessness. And his mood infected at least the main body of his own followers.

"It is the end," he told Captain Blood. "This time we are checkmated."

"I'll take the liberty of reminding you that you said the same before," Captain Blood answered him as patiently as he could. "Yet you've seen what you've seen, and you'll not deny that in ships and guns we are returning stronger than we went. Look at our present fleet, man."

"I am looking at it," said Cahusac.

"Pish! Ye're a white-livered cur when all is said."

"You call me a coward?"

"I'll take that liberty."

The Breton glared at him, breathing hard. But he had no mind to ask satisfaction for the insult. He knew too well the kind of satisfaction that Captain Blood was likely to afford him. He remembered the fate of Levasseur. So he confined himself to words.

"It is too much! You go too far!" he complained bitterly.

"Look you, Cahusac: it's sick and tired I am of your perpetual whining and complaining when things are not as smooth as a convent dining-table. If ye wanted things smooth and easy, ye shouldn't have taken to the sea, and ye should never ha' sailed with me, for with me things are never smooth and easy. And that, I think, is all I have to say to you this morning."

Cahusac flung away cursing, and went to take the feeling of his men.

Captain Blood went off to give his surgeon's skill to the wounded, among whom he remained engaged until late afternoon. Then, at last, he went ashore, his mind made up, and returned to the house of the Governor, to indite a truculent but very scholarly letter in purest Castilian to Don Miguel.

"I have shown your excellency this morning of what I am capable," he wrote. "Although outnumbered by more than two to one in men, in ships, and in guns, I have sunk or captured the vessels of the great fleet with which you were to come to Maracaybo to destroy us. So that you are no longer in case to carry out your boast, even when your reinforcements on the Santo Nino, reach you from La Guayra. From what has occurred, you may judge of what must occur. I should not trouble your excellency with this letter but that I am a humane man, abhorring bloodshed. Therefore before proceeding to deal with your fort, which you may deem invincible, as I have dealt already with your fleet, which you deemed invincible, I make you, purely out of humanitarian considerations, this last offer of terms. I will spare this city of Maracaybo and forthwith evacuate it, leaving behind me the forty prisoners I have taken, in consideration of your paying me the sum of fifty thousand pieces of eight and one hundred head of cattle as a ransom, thereafter granting me unmolested passage of the bar. My prisoners, most of whom are persons of consideration, I will retain as hostages until after my departure, sending them back in the canoes which we shall take with us for that purpose. If your excellency should be so ill-advised as to refuse these terms, and thereby impose upon me the necessity of reducing your fort at the cost of some lives, I warn you that you may expect no quarter from us, and that I shall begin by leaving a heap of ashes where this pleasant city of Maracaybo now stands."

The letter written, he bade them bring him from among the prisoners the Deputy-Governor of Maracaybo, who had been taken at Gibraltar. Disclosing its contents to him, he despatched him with it to Don Miguel.

His choice of a messenger was shrewd. The Deputy-Governor was of all men the most anxious for the deliverance of his city, the one man who on his own account would plead most fervently for its preservation at all costs from the fate with which Captain Blood was threatening it. And as he reckoned so it befell. The Deputy-Governor added his own passionate pleading to the proposals of the letter.

But Don Miguel was of stouter heart. True, his fleet had been partly destroyed and partly captured. But then, he argued, he had been taken utterly by surprise. That should not happen again. There should be no surprising the fort. Let Captain Blood do his worst at Maracaybo, there should be a bitter reckoning for him when eventually he decided—as, sooner or later, decide he must—to come forth. The Deputy-Governor was flung into panic. He lost his temper, and said some hard things to the Admiral. But they were not as hard as the thing the Admiral said to him in answer.

"Had you been as loyal to your King in hindering the entrance of these cursed pirates as I shall be in hindering their going forth again, we should not now find ourselves in our present straits. So weary me no more with your coward counsels. I make no terms with Captain Blood. I know my duty to my King, and I intend to perform it. I also know my duty to myself. I have a private score with this rascal, and I intend to settle it. Take you that message back."

So back to Maracaybo, back to his own handsome house in which Captain Blood had established his quarters, came the Deputy-Governor with the Admiral's answer. And because he had been shamed into a show of spirit by the Admiral's own stout courage in adversity, he delivered it as truculently as the Admiral could have desired. "And is it like that?" said Captain Blood with a quiet smile, though the heart of him sank at this failure of his bluster. "Well, well, it's a pity now that the Admiral's so headstrong. It was that way he lost his fleet, which was his own to lose. This pleasant city of Maracaybo isn't. So no doubt he'll lose it with fewer misgivings. I am sorry. Waste, like bloodshed, is a thing abhorrent to me. But there ye are! I'll have the faggots to the place in the morning, and maybe when he sees the blaze tomorrow night he'll begin to believe that Peter Blood is a man of his word. Ye may go, Don Francisco."

The Deputy-Governor went out with dragging feet, followed by guards, his momentary truculence utterly spent.

But no sooner had he departed than up leapt Cahusac, who had been of the council assembled to receive the Admiral's answer. His face was white and his hands shook as he held them out in protest.

"Death of my life, what have you to say now?" he cried, his voice husky. And without waiting to hear what it might be, he raved on: "I knew you not frighten the Admiral so easy. He hold us entrap', and he knows it; yet you dream that he will yield himself to your impudent message. Your fool letter it have seal' the doom of us all."

"Have ye done?" quoth Blood quietly, as the Frenchman paused for breath.

"No, I have not."

"Then spare me the rest. It'll be of the same quality, devil a doubt, and it doesn't help us to solve the riddle that's before us."

"But what are you going to do? Is it that you will tell me?" It was not a question, it was a demand.

"How the devil do I know? I was hoping you'd have some ideas yourself. But since Ye're so desperately concerned to save your skin, you and those that think like you are welcome to leave us. I've no doubt at all the Spanish Admiral will welcome the abatement of our numbers even at this late date. Ye shall have the sloop as a parting gift from us, and ye can join Don Miguel in the fort for all I care, or for all the good ye're likely to be to us in this present pass."

"It is to my men to decide," Cahusac retorted, swallowing his fury, and on that stalked out to talk to them, leaving the others to deliberate in peace.

Next morning early he sought Captain Blood again. He found him alone in the patio, pacing to and fro, his head sunk on his breast. Cahusac mistook consideration for dejection. Each of us carries in himself a standard by which to measure his neighbour.

"We have take' you at your word, Captain," he announced, between sullenness and defiance. Captain Blood paused, shoulders hunched, hands behind his back, and mildly regarded the buccaneer in silence. Cahusac explained himself. "Last night I send one of my men to the Spanish Admiral with a letter. I make him offer to capitulate if he will accord us passage with the honours of war. This morning I receive his answer. He accord us this on the understanding that we carry nothing away with us. My men they are embarking them on the sloop. We sail at once."

"Bon voyage," said Captain Blood, and with a nod he turned on his heel again to resume his interrupted mediation.

"Is that all that you have to say to me?" cried Cahusac.

"There are other things," said Blood over his shoulder. "But I know ye wouldn't like them."

"Ha! Then it's adieu, my Captain." Venomously he added: "It is my belief that we shall not meet again."

"Your belief is my hope," said Captain Blood.

Cahusac flung away, obscenely vituperative. Before noon he was under way with his followers, some sixty dejected men who had allowed themselves to be persuaded by him into that empty-handed departure—in spite even of all that Yberville could do to prevent it. The Admiral kept faith with him, and allowed him free passage out to sea, which, from his knowledge of Spaniards, was more than Captain Blood had expected.

Meanwhile, no sooner had the deserters weighed anchor than Captain Blood received word that the Deputy-Governor begged to be allowed to see him again. Admitted, Don Francisco at once displayed the fact that a night's reflection had quickened his apprehensions for the city of Maracaybo and his condemnation of the Admiral's intransigence.

Captain Blood received him pleasantly.

"Good-morning to you, Don Francisco. I have postponed the bonfire until nightfall. It will make a better show in the dark."

Don Francisco, a slight, nervous, elderly man of high lineage and low vitality, came straight to business.

"I am here to tell you, Don Pedro, that if you will hold your hand for three days, I will undertake to raise the ransom you demand, which Don Miguel de Espinosa refuses."

Captain Blood confronted him, a frown contracting the dark brows above his light eyes:

"And where will you be raising it?" quoth he, faintly betraying his surprise.

Don Francisco shook his head. "That must remain my affair," he answered. "I know where it is to be found, and my compatriots must contribute. Give me leave for three days on parole, and I will see you fully satisfied. Meanwhile my son remains in your hands as a hostage for my return." And upon that he fell to pleading. But in this he was crisply interrupted.

"By the Saints! Ye're a bold man, Don Francisco, to come to me with such a tale—to tell me that ye know where the ransom's to be raised, and yet to refuse to say. D'ye think now that with a match between your fingers ye'd grow more communicative?"

If Don Francisco grew a shade paler, yet again he shook his head.

"That was the way of Morgan and L'Ollonais and other pirates. But it is not the way of Captain Blood. If I had doubted that I should not have disclosed so much."

The Captain laughed. "You old rogue," said he. "Ye play upon my vanity, do you?"

"Upon your honour, Captain."

"The honour of a pirate? Ye're surely crazed!"

"The honour of Captain Blood," Don Francisco insisted. "You have the repute of making war like a gentleman."

Captain Blood laughed again, on a bitter, sneering note that made Don Francisco fear the worst. He was not to guess that it was himself the Captain mocked.

"That's merely because it's more remunerative in the end. And that is why you are accorded the three days you ask for. So about it, Don Francisco. You shall have what mules you need. I'll see to it."

Away went Don Francisco on his errand, leaving Captain Blood to reflect, between bitterness and satisfaction, that a reputation for as much chivalry as is consistent with piracy is not without its uses.

Punctually on the third day the Deputy-Governor was back in Maracaybo with his mules laden with plate and money to the value demanded and a herd of a hundred head of cattle driven in by black man slaves.

These bullocks were handed over to those of the company who ordinarily were boucan-hunters, and therefore skilled in the curing of meats, and for best part of a week thereafter they were busy at the waterside with the quartering and salting of carcases.

While this was doing on the one hand and the ships were being refitted for sea on the other, Captain Blood was pondering the riddle on the solution of which his own fate depended. Indian spies whom he employed brought him word that the Spaniards, working at low tide, had salved the thirty guns of the Salvador, and thus had added yet another battery to their already overwhelming strength. In the end, and hoping for inspiration on the spot, Captain Blood made a reconnaissance in person. At the risk of his life, accompanied by two friendly Indians, he crossed to the island in a canoe under cover of dark. They concealed themselves and the canoe in the short thick scrub with which that side of the island was densely covered, and lay there until daybreak. Then Blood went forward alone, and with infinite precaution, to make his survey. He went to verify a suspicion that he had formed, and approached the fort as nearly as he dared and a deal nearer than was safe.

On all fours he crawled to the summit of an eminence a mile or so away, whence he found himself commanding a view of the interior dispositions of the stronghold. By the aid of a telescope with which he had equipped himself he was able to verify that, as he had suspected and hoped, the fort's artillery was all mounted on the seaward side.

Satisfied, he returned to Maracaybo, and laid before the six who composed his council—Pitt, Hagthorpe, Yberville, Wolverstone, Dyke, and Ogle—a proposal to storm the fort from the landward side. Crossing to the island under cover of night, they would take the Spaniards by surprise and attempt to overpower them before they could shift their guns to meet the onslaught.

With the exception of Wolverstone, who was by temperament the kind of man who favours desperate chances, those officers received the proposal coldly. Hagthorpe incontinently opposed it.

"It's a harebrained scheme, Peter," he said gravely, shaking his handsome head. "Consider now that we cannot depend upon approaching unperceived to a distance whence we might storm the fort before the cannon could be moved. But even if we could, we can take no cannon ourselves; we must depend entirely upon our small arms, and how shall we, a bare three hundred" (for this was the number to which Cahusac's defection had reduced them), "cross the open to attack more than twice that number under cover?"

The others—Dyke, Ogle, Yberville, and even Pitt, whom loyalty to Blood may have made reluctant—loudly approved him. When they had done, "I have considered all," said Captain Blood. "I have weighed the risks and studied how to lessen them. In these desperate straits..."

He broke off abruptly. A moment he frowned, deep in thought; then his face was suddenly alight with inspiration. Slowly he drooped his head, and sat there considering, weighing, chin on breast. Then he nodded, muttering, "Yes," and again, "Yes." He looked up, to face them. "Listen," he cried. "You may be right. The risks may be too heavy. Whether or not, I have thought of a better way. That which should have been the real attack shall be no more than a feint. Here, then, is the plan I now propose."

He talked swiftly and clearly, and as he talked one by one his officers' faces became alight with eagerness. When he had done, they cried as with one voice that he had saved them.

"That is yet to be proved in action," said he.

Since for the last twenty-four hours all had been in readiness for departure, there was nothing now to delay them, and it was decided to move next morning.

Such was Captain Blood's assurance of success that he immediately freed the prisoners held as hostages, and even the black man slaves, who were regarded by the others as legitimate plunder. His only precaution against those released prisoners was to order them into the church and there lock them up, to await deliverance at the hands of those who should presently be coming into the city.

Then, all being aboard the three ships, with the treasure safely stowed in their holds and the slaves under hatches, the buccaneers weighed anchor and stood out for the bar, each vessel towing three piraguas astern.

The Admiral, beholding their stately advance in the full light of noon, their sails gleaming white in the glare of the sunlight, rubbed his long, lean hands in satisfaction, and laughed through his teeth.

"At last!" he cried. "God delivers him into my hands!" He turned to the group of staring officers behind him. "Sooner or later it had to be," he said. "Say now, gentlemen, whether I am justified of my patience. Here end today the troubles caused to the subjects of the Catholic King by this infamous Don Pedro Sangre, as he once called himself to me."

He turned to issue orders, and the fort became lively as a hive. The guns were manned, the gunners already kindling fuses, when the buccaneer fleet, whilst still heading for Palomas, was observed to bear away to the west. The Spaniards watched them, intrigued.

Within a mile and a half to westward of the fort, and within a half-mile of the shore—that is to say, on the very edge of the shoal water that makes Palomas unapproachable on either side by any but vessels of the shallowest draught—the four ships cast anchor well within the Spaniards' view, but just out of range of their heaviest cannon.

Sneeringly the Admiral laughed.

"Aha! They hesitate, these English dogs! Por Dios, and well they may."

"They will be waiting for night," suggested his nephew, who stood at his elbow quivering with excitement.

Don Miguel looked at him, smiling. "And what shall the night avail them in this narrow passage, under the very muzzles of my guns? Be sure, Esteban, that tonight your father will be paid for."

He raised his telescope to continue his observation of the buccaneers. He saw that the piraguas towed by each vessel were being warped alongside, and he wondered a little what this manoeuver might portend. Awhile those piraguas were hidden from view behind the hulls. Then one by one they reappeared, rowing round and away from the ships, and each boat, he observed, was crowded with armed men. Thus laden, they were headed for the shore, at a point where it was densely wooded to the water's edge. The eyes of the wondering Admiral followed them until the foliage screened them from his view.

Then he lowered his telescope and looked at his officers.

"What the devil does it mean?" he asked.

None answered him, all being as puzzled as he was himself.

After a little while, Esteban, who kept his eyes on the water, plucked at his uncle's sleeve. "There they go!" he cried, and pointed.

And there, indeed, went the piraguas on their way back to the ships. But now it was observed that they were empty, save for the men who rowed them. Their armed cargo had been left ashore.

Back to the ships they pulled, to return again presently with a fresh load of armed men, which similarly they conveyed to Palomas. And at last one of the Spanish officers ventured an explanation:

"They are going to attack us by land—to attempt to storm the fort."

"Of course." The Admiral smiled. "I had guessed it. Whom the gods would destroy they first make mad."

"Shall we make a sally?" urged Esteban, in his excitement.

"A sally? Through that scrub? That would be to play into their hands. No, no, we will wait here to receive this attack. Whenever it comes, it is themselves will be destroyed, and utterly. Have no doubt of that."

But by evening the Admiral's equanimity was not quite so perfect. By then the piraguas had made a half-dozen journeys with their loads of men, and they had landed also—as Don Miguel had clearly observed through his telescope—at least a dozen guns.

His countenance no longer smiled; it was a little wrathful and a little troubled now as he turned again to his officers.

"Who was the fool who told me that they number but three hundred men in all? They have put at least twice that number ashore already."

Amazed as he was, his amazement would have been deeper had he been told the truth: that there was not a single buccaneer or a single gun ashore on Palomas. The deception had been complete. Don Miguel could not guess that the men he had beheld in those piraguas were always the same; that on the journeys to the shore they sat and stood upright in full view; and that on the journeys back to the ships, they lay invisible at the bottom of the boats, which were thus made to appear empty.

The growing fears of the Spanish soldiery at the prospect of a night attack from the landward side by the entire buccaneer force—and a force twice as strong as they had suspected the pestilent Blood to command—began to be communicated to the Admiral.

In the last hours of fading daylight, the Spaniards did precisely what Captain Blood so confidently counted that they would do—precisely what they must do to meet the attack, preparations for which had been so thoroughly simulated. They set themselves to labour like the damned at those ponderous guns emplaced to command the narrow passage out to sea.

Groaning and sweating, urged on by the curses and even the whips of their officers, they toiled in a frenzy of panic-stricken haste to shift the greater number and the more powerful of their guns across to the landward side, there to emplace them anew, so that they might be ready to receive the attack which at any moment now might burst upon them from the woods not half a mile away.

Thus, when night fell, although in mortal anxiety of the onslaught of those wild devils whose reckless courage was a byword on the seas of the Main, at least the Spaniards were tolerably prepared for it. Waiting, they stood to their guns.

And whilst they waited thus, under cover of the darkness and as the tide began to ebb, Captain Blood's fleet weighed anchor quietly; and, as once before, with no more canvas spread than that which their sprits could carry, so as to give them steering way—and even these having been painted black—the four vessels, without a light showing, groped their way by soundings to the channel which led to that narrow passage out to sea.

The Elizabeth and the Infanta, leading side by side, were almost abreast of the fort before their shadowy bulks and the soft gurgle of water at their prows were detected by the Spaniards, whose attention until that moment had been all on the other side. And now there arose on the night air such a sound of human baffled fury as may have resounded about Babel at the confusion of tongues. To heighten that confusion, and to scatter disorder among the Spanish soldiery, the Elizabeth emptied her larboard guns into the fort as she was swept past on the swift ebb.

At once realizing—though not yet how—he had been duped, and that his prey was in the very act of escaping after all, the Admiral frantically ordered the guns that had been so laboriously moved to be dragged back to their former emplacements, and commanded his gunners meanwhile to the slender batteries that of all his powerful, but now unavailable, armament still remained trained upon the channel. With these, after the loss of some precious moments, the fort at last made fire.

It was answered by a terrific broadside from the Arabella, which had now drawn abreast, and was crowding canvas to her yards. The enraged and gibbering Spaniards had a brief vision of her as the line of flame spurted from her red flank, and the thunder of her broadside drowned the noise of the creaking halyards. After that they saw her no more. Assimilated by the friendly darkness which the lesser Spanish guns were speculatively stabbing, the escaping ships fired never another shot that might assist their baffled and bewildered enemies to locate them.

Some slight damage was sustained by Blood's fleet. But by the time the Spaniards had resolved their confusion into some order of dangerous offence, that fleet, well served by a southerly breeze, was through the narrows and standing out to sea.

Thus was Don Miguel de Espinosa left to chew the bitter cud of a lost opportunity, and to consider in what terms he would acquaint the Supreme Council of the Catholic King that Peter Blood had got away from Maracaybo, taking with him two twenty-gun frigates that were lately the property of Spain, to say nothing of two hundred and fifty thousand pieces of eight and other plunder. And all this in spite of Don Miguel's four galleons and his heavily armed fort that at one time had held the pirates so securely trapped.

Heavy, indeed, grew the account of Peter Blood, which Don Miguel swore passionately to Heaven should at all costs to himself be paid in full.

Nor were the losses already detailed the full total of those suffered on this occasion by the King of Spain. For on the following evening, off the coast of Oruba, at the mouth of the Gulf of Venezuela, Captain Blood's fleet came upon the belated Santo Nino, speeding under full sail to reenforce Don Miguel at Maracaybo.

At first the Spaniard had conceived that she was meeting the victorious fleet of Don Miguel, returning from the destruction of the pirates. When at comparatively close quarters the pennon of St. George soared to the Arabella's masthead to disillusion her, the Santo Nino chose the better part of valour, and struck her flag.

Captain Blood ordered her crew to take to the boats, and land themselves at Oruba or wherever else they pleased. So considerate was he that to assist them he presented them with several of the piraguas which he still had in tow.

"You will find," said he to her captain, "that Don Miguel is in an extremely bad temper. Commend me to him, and say that I venture to remind him that he must blame himself for all the ills that have befallen him. The evil has recoiled upon him which he loosed when he sent his brother unofficially to make a raid upon the island of Barbados. Bid him think twice before he lets his devils loose upon an English settlement again."

With that he dismissed the Captain, who went over the side of the Santo Nino, and Captain Blood proceeded to investigate the value of this further prize. When her hatches were removed, a human cargo was disclosed in her hold.

"Slaves," said Wolverstone, and persisted in that belief cursing Spanish devilry until Cahusac crawled up out of the dark bowels of the ship, and stood blinking in the sunlight.

There was more than sunlight to make the Breton pirate blink. And those that crawled out after him—the remnants of his crew—cursed him horribly for the pusillanimity which had brought them into the ignominy of owing their deliverance to those whom they had deserted as lost beyond hope.

Their sloop had encountered and had been sunk three days ago by the Santo Nino, and Cahusac had narrowly escaped hanging merely that for some time he might be a mock among the Brethren of the Coast.

For many a month thereafter he was to hear in Tortuga the jeering taunt:

"Where do you spend the gold that you brought back from Maracaybo?"

XVIII

THE MILAGROSA

The affair at Maracaybo is to be considered as Captain Blood's buccaneering masterpiece. Although there is scarcely one of the many actions that he fought—recorded in such particular detail by Jeremy Pitt—which does not afford some instance of his genius for naval tactics, yet in none is this more shiningly displayed than in those two engagements by which he won out of the trap which Don Miguel de Espinosa had sprung upon him.

The fame which he had enjoyed before this, great as it already was, is dwarfed into insignificance by the fame that followed. It was a fame such as no buccaneer—not even Morgan—has ever boasted, before or since.

In Tortuga, during the months he spent there refitting the three ships he had captured from the fleet that had gone out to destroy him, he found himself almost an object of worship in the eyes of the wild Brethren of the Coast, all of whom now clamoured for the honour of serving under him. It placed him in the rare position of being able to pick and choose the crews for his augmented fleet, and he chose fastidiously. When next he sailed away it was with a fleet of five fine ships in which went something over a thousand men. Thus you behold him not merely famous, but really formidable. The three captured Spanish vessels he had renamed with a certain scholarly humour the Clotho, Lachesis, and Atropos, a grimly jocular manner of conveying to the world that he made them the arbiters of the fate of any Spaniards he should henceforth encounter upon the seas.

In Europe the news of this fleet, following upon the news of the Spanish Admiral's defeat at Maracaybo, produced something of a sensation. Spain and England were variously and unpleasantly exercised, and if you care to turn up the diplomatic correspondence exchanged on the subject, you will find that it is considerable and not always amiable.

And meanwhile in the Caribbean, the Spanish Admiral Don Miguel de Espinosa might be said—to use a term not yet invented in his day—to have run amok. The disgrace into which he had fallen as a result of the disasters suffered at the hands of Captain Blood had driven the Admiral all but mad. It is impossible, if we impose our minds impartially, to withhold a certain sympathy from Don Miguel. Hate was now this unfortunate man's daily bread, and the hope of vengeance an obsession to his mind. As a madman he went raging up and down the Caribbean seeking his enemy, and in the meantime, as an hors d'oeuvre to his vindictive appetite, he fell upon any ship of England or of France that loomed above his horizon.

I need say no more to convey the fact that this illustrious sea-captain and great gentleman of Castile had lost his head, and was become a pirate in his turn. The Supreme Council of Castile might anon condemn him for his practices. But how should that matter to one who already was condemned beyond redemption? On the contrary, if he should live to lay the audacious and ineffable Blood by the heels, it was possible that Spain might view his present irregularities and earlier losses with a more lenient eye.

And so, reckless of the fact that Captain Blood was now in vastly superior strength, the Spaniard sought him up and down the trackless seas. But for a whole year he sought him vainly. The circumstances in which eventually they met are very curious.

An intelligent observation of the facts of human existence will reveal to shallow-minded folk who sneer at the use of coincidence in the arts of fiction and drama that life itself is little more than a series of coincidences. Open the history of the past at whatsoever page you will, and there you shall find coincidence at work bringing about events that the merest chance might have averted. Indeed, coincidence may be defined as the very tool used by Fate to shape the destinies of men and nations.

Observe it now at work in the affairs of Captain Blood and of some others.

On the 15th September of the year 1688—a memorable year in the annals of England—three ships were afloat upon the Caribbean, which in their coming conjunctions were to work out the fortunes of several persons.

The first of these was Captain Blood's flagship the Arabella, which had been separated from the buccaneer fleet in a hurricane off the Lesser Antilles. In somewhere about 17 deg. N. Lat., and 74 deg. Long., she was beating up for the Windward Passage, before the intermittent southeasterly breezes of that stifling season, homing for Tortuga, the natural rendezvous of the dispersed vessels.

The second ship was the great Spanish galleon, the Milagrosa, which, accompanied by the smaller frigate Hidalga, lurked off the Caymites, to the north of the long peninsula that thrusts out from the southwest corner of Hispaniola. Aboard the Milagrosa sailed the vindictive Don Miguel.

The third and last of these ships with which we are at present concerned was an English man-of-war, which on the date I have given was at anchor in the French port of St. Nicholas on the northwest coast of Hispaniola. She was on her way from

Plymouth to Jamaica, and carried on board a very distinguished passenger in the person of Lord Julian Wade, who came charged by his kinsman, my Lord Sunderland, with a mission of some consequence and delicacy, directly arising out of that vexatious correspondence between England and Spain.

The French Government, like the English, excessively annoyed by the depredations of the buccaneers, and the constant straining of relations with Spain that ensued, had sought in vain to put them down by enjoining the utmost severity against them upon her various overseas governors. But these, either—like the Governor of Tortuga—throve out of a scarcely tacit partnership with the filibusters, or—like the Governor of French Hispaniola—felt that they were to be encouraged as a check upon the power and greed of Spain, which might otherwise be exerted to the disadvantage of the colonies of other nations. They looked, indeed, with apprehension upon recourse to any vigorous measures which must result in driving many of the buccaneers to seek new hunting-grounds in the South Sea.

To satisfy King James's anxiety to conciliate Spain, and in response to the Spanish Ambassador's constant and grievous expostulations, my Lord Sunderland, the Secretary of State, had appointed a strong man to the deputy-governorship of Jamaica. This strong man was that Colonel Bishop who for some years now had been the most influential planter in Barbados.

Colonel Bishop had accepted the post, and departed from the plantations in which his great wealth was being amassed with an eagerness that had its roots in a desire to pay off a score of his own with Peter Blood.

From his first coming to Jamaica, Colonel Bishop had made himself felt by the buccaneers. But do what he might, the one buccaneer whom he made his particular quarry—that Peter Blood who once had been his slave—eluded him ever, and continued undeterred and in great force to harass the Spaniards upon sea and land, and to keep the relations between England and Spain in a state of perpetual ferment, particularly dangerous in those days when the peace of Europe was precariously maintained.

Exasperated not only by his own accumulated chagrin, but also by the reproaches for his failure which reached him from London, Colonel Bishop actually went so far as to consider hunting his quarry in Tortuga itself and making an attempt to clear the island of the buccaneers it sheltered. Fortunately for himself, he abandoned the notion of so insane an enterprise, deterred not only by the enormous natural strength of the place, but also by the reflection that a raid upon what was, nominally at least, a French settlement, must be attended by grave offence to France. Yet short of some such measure, it appeared to Colonel Bishop that he was baffled. He confessed as much in a letter to the Secretary of State.

This letter and the state of things which it disclosed made my Lord Sunderland despair of solving this vexatious problem by ordinary means. He turned to the consideration of extraordinary ones, and bethought him of the plan adopted with Morgan, who had been enlisted into the King's service under Charles II. It occurred to him that a similar course might be similarly effective with Captain Blood. His lordship did not omit the consideration that Blood's present outlawry might well have been undertaken not from inclination, but under stress of sheer necessity; that he had been forced into it by the circumstances of his transportation, and that he would welcome the opportunity of emerging from it.

Acting upon this conclusion, Sunderland sent out his kinsman, Lord Julian Wade, with some commissions made out in blank, and full directions as to the course which the Secretary considered it desirable to pursue and yet full discretion in the matter of pursuing them. The crafty Sunderland, master of all labyrinths of intrigue, advised his kinsman that in the event of his finding Blood intractable, or judging for other reasons that it was not desirable to enlist him in the King's service, he should turn his attention to the officers serving under him, and by seducing them away from him leave him so weakened that he must fall an easy victim to Colonel Bishop's fleet.

The Royal Mary—the vessel bearing that ingenious, tolerably accomplished, mildly dissolute, entirely elegant envoy of my Lord Sunderland's—made a good passage to St. Nicholas, her last port of call before Jamaica. It was understood that as a preliminary Lord Julian should report himself to the Deputy-Governor at Port Royal, whence at need he might have himself conveyed to Tortuga. Now it happened that the Deputy-Governor's niece had come to St. Nicholas some months earlier on a visit to some relatives, and so that she might escape the insufferable heat of Jamaica in that season. The time for her return being now at hand, a passage was sought for her aboard the Royal Mary, and in view of her uncle's rank and position promptly accorded.

Lord Julian hailed her advent with satisfaction. It gave a voyage that had been full of interest for him just the spice that it required to achieve perfection as an experience. His lordship was one of your gallants to whom existence that is not graced by womankind is more or less of a stagnation. Miss Arabella Bishop—this straight up and down slip of a girl with her rather boyish voice and her almost boyish ease of movement—was not perhaps a lady who in England would have commanded much notice in my lord's discerning eyes. His very sophisticated, carefully educated tastes in such matters inclined him towards the plump, the languishing, and the quite helplessly feminine. Miss Bishop's charms were undeniable. But they were such that it would take a delicate-minded man to appreciate them; and my Lord Julian, whilst of a mind that was very far from gross, did not possess the necessary degree of delicacy. I must not by this be understood to imply anything against him.

It remained, however, that Miss Bishop was a young woman and a lady; and in the latitude into which Lord Julian had strayed this was a phenomenon sufficiently rare to command attention. On his side, with his title and position, his personal grace and the charm of a practised courtier, he bore about him the atmosphere of the great world in which normally he had his being—a world that was little more than a name to her, who had spent most of her life in the Antilles. It is not therefore wonderful that they should have been attracted to each other before the Royal Mary was warped out of St. Nicholas. Each could tell the other much upon which the other desired information. He could regale her imagination with stories of St. James's—in many of which he assigned himself a heroic, or at least a distinguished part—and she could enrich his mind with information concerning this new world to which he had come.

Before they were out of sight of St. Nicholas they were good friends, and his lordship was beginning to correct his first impressions of her and to discover the charm of that frank, straightforward attitude of comradeship which made her treat every man as a brother. Considering how his mind was obsessed with the business of his mission, it is not wonderful that he should have come to talk to her of Captain Blood. Indeed, there was a circumstance that directly led to it.

"I wonder now," he said, as they were sauntering on the poop, "if you ever saw this fellow Blood, who was at one time on your uncle's plantations as a slave."

Miss Bishop halted. She leaned upon the taffrail, looking out towards the receding land, and it was a moment before she answered in a steady, level voice:

"I saw him often. I knew him very well."

"Ye don't say!" His lordship was slightly moved out of an imperturbability that he had studiously cultivated. He was a young man of perhaps eight-and-twenty, well above the middle height in stature and appearing taller by virtue of his exceeding leanness. He had a thin, pale, rather pleasing hatchet-face, framed in the curls of a golden periwig, a sensitive mouth and pale blue eyes that lent his countenance a dreamy expression, a rather melancholy pensiveness. But they were alert, observant eyes notwithstanding, although they failed on this occasion to observe the slight change of colour which his question had brought to Miss Bishop's cheeks or the suspiciously excessive composure of her answer.

"Ye don't say!" he repeated, and came to lean beside her. "And what manner of man did you find him?"

"In those days I esteemed him for an unfortunate gentleman."

"You were acquainted with his story?"

"He told it me. That is why I esteemed him—for the calm fortitude with which he bore adversity. Since then, considering what he has done, I have almost come to doubt if what he told me of himself was true."

"If you mean of the wrongs he suffered at the hands of the Royal Commission that tried the Monmouth rebels, there's little doubt that it would be true enough. He was never out with Monmouth; that is certain. He was convicted on a point of law of which he may well have been ignorant when he committed what was construed into treason. But, faith, he's had his revenge, after a fashion."

"That," she said in a small voice, "is the unforgivable thing. It has destroyed him—deservedly."

"Destroyed him?" His lordship laughed a little. "Be none so sure of that. He has grown rich, I hear. He has translated, so it is said, his Spanish spoils into French gold, which is being treasured up for him in France. His future father-in-law, M. d'Ogeron, has seen to that."

"His future father-in-law?" said she, and stared at him round-eyed, with parted lips. Then added: "M. d'Ogeron? The Governor of Tortuga?"

"The same. You see the fellow's well protected. It's a piece of news I gathered in St. Nicholas. I am not sure that I welcome it, for I am not sure that it makes any easier a task upon which my kinsman, Lord Sunderland, has sent me hither. But there it is. You didn't know?"

She shook her head without replying. She had averted her face, and her eyes were staring down at the gently heaving water. After a moment she spoke, her voice steady and perfectly controlled.

"But surely, if this were true, there would have been an end to his piracy by now. If he... if he loved a woman and was betrothed, and was also rich as you say, surely he would have abandoned this desperate life, and..."

"Why, so I thought," his lordship interrupted, "until I had the explanation. D'Ogeron is avaricious for himself and for his child. And as for the girl, I'm told she's a wild piece, fit mate for such a man as Blood. Almost I marvel that he doesn't marry her and take her a-roving with him. It would be no new experience for her. And I marvel, too, at Blood's patience. He killed a man to win her."

"He killed a man for her, do you say?" There was horror now in her voice.

"Yes—a French buccaneer named Levasseur. He was the girl's lover and Blood's associate on a venture. Blood coveted the girl, and killed Levasseur to win her. Pah! It's an unsavoury tale, I own. But men live by different codes out in these parts..."

She had turned to face him. She was pale to the lips, and her hazel eyes were blazing, as she cut into his apologies for Blood.

"They must, indeed, if his other associates allowed him to live after that."

"Oh, the thing was done in fair fight, I am told."

"Who told you?"

"A man who sailed with them, a Frenchman named Cahusac, whom I found in a waterside tavern in St. Nicholas.

He was Levasseur's lieutenant, and he was present on the island where the thing happened, and when Levasseur was killed."

"And the girl? Did he say the girl was present, too?"

"Yes. She was a witness of the encounter. Blood carried her off when he had disposed of his brother-buccaneer."

"And the dead man's followers allowed it?" He caught the note of incredulity in her voice, but missed the note of relief with which it was blent. "Oh, I don't believe the tale. I won't believe it!"

"I honour you for that, Miss Bishop. It strained my own belief that men should be so callous, until this Cahusac afforded me the explanation."

"What?" She checked her unbelief, an unbelief that had uplifted her from an inexplicable dismay. Clutching the rail, she swung round to face his lordship with that question. Later he was to remember and perceive in her present behaviour a certain oddness which went disregarded now.

"Blood purchased their consent, and his right to carry the girl off. He paid them in pearls that were worth more than twenty thousand pieces of eight." His lordship laughed again with a touch of contempt. "A handsome price! Faith, they're scoundrels all—just thieving, venal curs. And faith, it's a pretty tale this for a lady's ear."

She looked away from him again, and found that her sight was blurred. After a moment in a voice less steady than before she asked him:

"Why should this Frenchman have told you such a tale? Did he hate this Captain Blood?"

"I did not gather that," said his lordship slowly. "He related it... oh, just as a commonplace, an instance of buccaneering ways.

"A commonplace!" said she. "My God! A commonplace!"

"I dare say that we are all savages under the cloak that civilization fashions for us," said his lordship. "But this Blood, now, was a man of considerable parts, from what else this Cahusac told me. He was a bachelor of medicine."

"That is true, to my own knowledge."

"And he has seen much foreign service on sea and land. Cahusac said—though this I hardly credit—that he had fought under de Ruyter."

"That also is true," said she. She sighed heavily. "Your Cahusac seems to have been accurate enough. Alas!"

"You are sorry, then?"

She looked at him. She was very pale, he noticed.

"As we are sorry to hear of the death of one we have esteemed. Once I held him in regard for an unfortunate but worthy gentleman. Now..."

She checked, and smiled a little crooked smile. "Such a man is best forgotten."

And upon that she passed at once to speak of other things. The friendship, which it was her great gift to command in all she met, grew steadily between those two in the little time remaining, until the event befell that marred what was promising to be the pleasantest stage of his lordship's voyage.

The marplot was the mad-dog Spanish Admiral, whom they encountered on the second day out, when halfway across the Gulf of Gonaves. The Captain of the Royal Mary was not disposed to be intimidated even when Don Miguel opened fire on him. Observing the Spaniard's plentiful seaboard towering high above the water and offering him so splendid a mark, the Englishman was moved to scorn. If this Don who flew the banner of Castile wanted a fight, the Royal Mary was just the ship to oblige him. It may be that he was justified of his gallant confidence, and that he would that day have put an end to the wild career of Don Miguel de Espinosa, but that a lucky shot from the Milagrosa got among some powder stored in his forecastle, and blew up half his ship almost before the fight had started. How the powder came there will never now be known, and the gallant Captain himself did not survive to enquire into it.

Before the men of the Royal Mary had recovered from their consternation, their captain killed and a third of their number destroyed with him, the ship yawing and rocking helplessly in a crippled state, the Spaniards boarded her.

In the Captain's cabin under the poop, to which Miss Bishop had been conducted for safety, Lord Julian was seeking to comfort and encourage her, with assurances that all would yet be well, at the very moment when Don Miguel was stepping aboard. Lord Julian himself was none so steady, and his face was undoubtedly pale. Not that he was by any means a coward. But this cooped-up fighting on an unknown element in a thing of wood that might at any moment founder under his feet into the depths of ocean was disturbing to one who could be brave enough ashore. Fortunately Miss Bishop did not appear to be in desperate need of the poor comfort he was in case to offer. Certainly she, too, was pale, and her hazel eyes may have looked a little larger than usual. But she had herself well in hand. Half sitting, half leaning on the Captain's table, she preserved her courage sufficiently to seek to calm the octoroon waiting-woman who was grovelling at her feet in a state of terror.

And then the cabin-door flew open, and Don Miguel himself, tall, sunburned, and aquiline of face, strode in. Lord Julian span round, to face him, and clapped a hand to his sword.

The Spaniard was brisk and to the point.

"Don't be a fool," he said in his own tongue, "or you'll come by a fool's end. Your ship is sinking."

There were three or four men in morions behind Don Miguel, and Lord Julian realized the position. He released his hilt, and a couple of feet or so of steel slid softly back into the scabbard. But Don Miguel smiled, with a flash of white teeth behind his grizzled beard, and held out his hand.

"If you please," he said.

Lord Julian hesitated. His eyes strayed to Miss Bishop's. "I think you had better," said that composed young lady, whereupon with a shrug his lordship made the required surrender.

"Come you—all of you—aboard my ship," Don Miguel invited them, and strode out.

They went, of course. For one thing the Spaniard had force to compel them; for another a ship which he announced to be sinking offered them little inducement to remain. They stayed no longer than was necessary to enable Miss Bishop to collect some spare articles of dress and my lord to snatch up his valise.

As for the survivors in that ghastly shambles that had been the Royal Mary, they were abandoned by the Spaniards to their own resources. Let them take to the boats, and if those did not suffice them, let them swim or drown. If Lord Julian and Miss Bishop were retained, it was because Don Miguel perceived their obvious value. He received them in his cabin with great urbanity. Urbanely he desired to have the honour of being acquainted with their names.

Lord Julian, sick with horror of the spectacle he had just witnessed, commanded himself with difficulty to supply them. Then haughtily he demanded to know in his turn the name of their aggressor. He was in an exceedingly ill temper. He realized that if he had done nothing positively discreditable in the unusual and difficult position into which Fate had thrust him, at least he had done nothing creditable. This might have mattered less but that the spectator of his indifferent performance was a lady. He was determined if possible to do better now.

"I am Don Miguel de Espinosa," he was answered. "Admiral of the Navies of the Catholic King."

Lord Julian gasped. If Spain made such a hubbub about the depredations of a runagate adventurer like Captain Blood, what could not England answer now?

"Will you tell me, then, why you behave like a damned pirate?" he asked. And added: "I hope you realize what will be the consequences, and the strict account to which you shall be brought for this day's work, for the blood you have murderously shed, and for your violence to this lady and to myself."

"I offer you no violence," said the Admiral, smiling, as only the man who holds the trumps can smile. "On the contrary, I have saved your lives..."

"Saved our lives!" Lord Julian was momentarily speechless before such callous impudence. "And what of the lives you have destroyed in wanton butchery? By God, man, they shall cost you dear."

Don Miguel's smile persisted. "It is possible. All things are possible. Meantime it is your own lives that will cost you dear. Colonel Bishop is a rich man; and you, milord, are no doubt also rich. I will consider and fix your ransom."

"So that you're just the damned murderous pirate I was supposing you," stormed his lordship. "And you have the impudence to call yourself the Admiral of the Navies of the Catholic King? We shall see what your Catholic King will have to say to it."

The Admiral ceased to smile. He revealed something of the rage that had eaten into his brain. "You do not understand," he said. "It is that I treat you English heretic dogs just as you English heretic dogs have treated Spaniards upon the seas—you robbers and thieves out of hell! I have the honesty to do it in my own name—but you, you perfidious beasts, you send your Captain Bloods, your Hagthorpes, and your Morgans against us and disclaim responsibility for what they do. Like Pilate, you wash your hands." He laughed savagely. "Let Spain play the part of Pilate. Let her disclaim responsibility for me, when your ambassador at the Escurial shall go whining to the Supreme Council of this act of piracy by Don Miguel de Espinosa."

"Captain Blood and the rest are not admirals of England!" cried Lord Julian.

"Are they not? How do I know? How does Spain know? Are you not liars all, you English heretics?"

"Sir!" Lord Julian's voice was harsh as a rasp, his eyes flashed. Instinctively he swung a hand to the place where his sword habitually hung. Then he shrugged and sneered: "Of course," said he, "it sorts with all I have heard of Spanish honour and all that I have seen of yours that you should insult a man who is unarmed and your prisoner."

The Admiral's face flamed scarlet. He half raised his hand to strike. And then, restrained, perhaps, by the very words that had cloaked the retorting insult, he turned on his heel abruptly and went out without answering.

XIX

THE MEETING

As the door slammed after the departing Admiral, Lord Julian turned to Arabella, and actually smiled. He felt that he was doing better, and gathered from it an almost childish satisfaction—childish in all the circumstances. "Decidedly I think I had the last word there," he said, with a toss of his golden ringlets.

Miss Bishop, seated at the cabin-table, looked at him steadily, without returning his smile. "Does it matter, then, so much, having the last word? I am thinking of those poor fellows on the Royal Mary. Many of them have had their last word, indeed. And for what? A fine ship sunk, a score of lives lost, thrice that number now in jeopardy, and all for what?"

"You are overwrought, ma'am. I..."

"Overwrought!" She uttered a single sharp note of laughter. "I assure you I am calm. I am asking you a question, Lord Julian. Why has this Spaniard done all this? To what purpose?"

"You heard him." Lord Julian shrugged angrily. "Blood-lust," he explained shortly.

"Blood-lust?" she asked. She was amazed. "Does such a thing exist, then? It is insane, monstrous."

"Fiendish," his lordship agreed. "Devil's work."

"I don't understand. At Bridgetown three years ago there was a Spanish raid, and things were done that should have been impossible to men, horrible, revolting things which strain belief, which seem, when I think of them now, like the illusions of some evil dream. Are men just beasts?"

"Men?" said Lord Julian, staring. "Say Spaniards, and I'll agree." He was an Englishman speaking of hereditary foes. And yet there was a measure of truth in what he said. "This is the Spanish way in the New World. Faith, almost it justifies such men as Blood of what they do."

She shivered, as if cold, and setting her elbows on the table, she took her chin in her hands, and sat staring before her.

Observing her, his lordship noticed how drawn and white her face had grown. There was reason enough for that, and for worse. Not any other woman of his acquaintance would have preserved her self-control in such an ordeal; and of fear, at least, at no time had Miss Bishop shown any sign. It is impossible that he did not find her admirable.

A Spanish steward entered bearing a silver chocolate service and a box of Peruvian candies, which he placed on the table before the lady.

"With the Admiral's homage," he said, then bowed, and withdrew.

Miss Bishop took no heed of him or his offering, but continued to stare before her, lost in thought. Lord Julian took a turn in the long low cabin, which was lighted by a skylight above and great square windows astern. It was luxuriously appointed: there were rich Eastern rugs on the floor, well-filled bookcases stood against the bulkheads, and there was a carved walnut sideboard laden with silverware. On a long, low chest standing under the middle stern port lay a guitar that was gay with ribbons. Lord Julian picked it up, twanged the strings once as if moved by nervous irritation, and put it down.

He turned again to face Miss Bishop.

"I came out here," he said, "to put down piracy. But—blister me!—I begin to think that the French are right in desiring piracy to continue as a curb upon these Spanish scoundrels."

He was to be strongly confirmed in that opinion before many hours were past. Meanwhile their treatment at the hands of Don Miguel was considerate and courteous. It confirmed the opinion, contemptuously expressed to his lordship by Miss Bishop, that since they were to be held to ransom they need not fear any violence or hurt. A cabin was placed at the disposal of the lady and her terrified woman, and another at Lord Julian's. They were given the freedom of the ship, and bidden to dine at the Admiral's table; nor were his further intentions regarding them mentioned, nor yet his immediate destination.

The Milagrosa, with her consort the Hidalga rolling after her, steered a south by westerly course, then veered to the southeast round Cape Tiburon, and thereafter, standing well out to sea, with the land no more than a cloudy outline to larboard, she headed directly east, and so ran straight into the arms of Captain Blood, who was making for the Windward Passage, as we know. That happened early on the following morning. After having systematically hunted his enemy in vain for a year, Don Miguel chanced upon him in this unexpected and entirely fortuitous fashion. But that is the ironic way of Fortune. It was also the way of Fortune that Don Miguel should thus come upon the Arabella at a time when, separated from the rest of the fleet, she was alone and at a disadvantage. It looked to Don Miguel as if the luck which so long had been on Blood's side had at last veered in his own favour.

Miss Bishop, newly risen, had come out to take the air on the quarter-deck with his lordship in attendance—as you would expect of so gallant a gentleman—when she beheld the big red ship that had once been the Cinco Llagas out of Cadiz. The vessel was bearing down upon them, her mountains of snowy canvas bellying forward, the long pennon with the cross of St. George fluttering from her main truck in the morning breeze, the gilded portholes in her red hull and the gilded beak-head aflash in the morning sun.

Miss Bishop was not to recognize this for that same Cinco Llagas which she had seen once before—on a tragic day in Barbados three years ago. To her it was just a great ship that was heading resolutely, majestically, towards them, and an Englishman to judge by the pennon she was flying. The sight thrilled her curiously; it awoke in her an uplifting sense of pride that took no account of the danger to herself in the encounter that must now be inevitable.

Beside her on the poop, whither they had climbed to obtain a better view, and equally arrested and at gaze, stood Lord Julian. But he shared none of her exultation. He had been in his first sea-fight yesterday, and he felt that the experience would suffice him for a very considerable time. This, I insist, is no reflection upon his courage.

"Look," said Miss Bishop, pointing; and to his infinite amazement he observed that her eyes were sparkling. Did she realize, he wondered, what was afoot? Her next sentence resolved his doubt. "She is English, and she comes resolutely on. She means to fight."

"God help her, then," said his lordship gloomily. "Her captain must be mad. What can he hope to do against two such heavy hulks as these? If they could so easily blow the Royal Mary out of the water, what will they do to this vessel? Look at that devil Don Miguel. He's utterly disgusting in his glee."

From the quarter-deck, where he moved amid the frenzy of preparation, the Admiral had turned to flash a backward glance at his prisoners. His eyes were alight, his face transfigured. He flung out an arm to point to the advancing ship, and bawled something in Spanish that was lost to them in the noise of the labouring crew.

They advanced to the poop-rail, and watched the bustle. Telescope in hand on the quarter-deck, Don Miguel was issuing his orders. Already the gunners were kindling their matches; sailors were aloft, taking in sail; others were spreading a stout rope net above the waist, as a protection against falling spars. And meanwhile Don Miguel had been signalling to his consort, in response to which the Hidalga had drawn steadily forward until she was now abeam of the Milagrosa, half cable's length to starboard, and from the height of the tall poop my lord and Miss Bishop could see her own bustle of preparation. And they could discern signs of it now aboard the advancing English ship as well. She was furling tops and mainsail, stripping in fact to mizzen and sprit for the coming action. Thus, almost silently without challenge or exchange of signals, had action been mutually determined.

Of necessity now, under diminished sail, the advance of the Arabella was slower; but it was none the less steady. She was already within saker shot, and they could make out the figures stirring on her forecastle and the brass guns gleaming on her prow. The gunners of the Milagrosa raised their linstocks and blew upon their smouldering matches, looking up impatiently at the Admiral.

But the Admiral solemnly shook his head.

"Patience," he exhorted them. "Save your fire until we have him. He is coming straight to his doom—straight to the yardarm and the rope that have been so long waiting for him."

"Stab me!" said his lordship. "This Englishman may be gallant enough to accept battle against such odds. But there are times when discretion is a better quality than gallantry in a commander."

"Gallantry will often win through, even against overwhelming strength," said Miss Bishop. He looked at her, and noted in her bearing only excitement. Of fear he could still discern no trace. His lordship was past amazement. She was not by any means the kind of woman to which life had accustomed him.

"Presently," he said, "you will suffer me to place you under cover."

"I can see best from here," she answered him. And added quietly: "I am praying for this Englishman. He must be very brave."

Under his breath Lord Julian damned the fellow's bravery.

The Arabella was advancing now along a course which, if continued, must carry her straight between the two Spanish ships. My lord pointed it out. "He's crazy surely!" he cried. "He's driving straight into a death-trap. He'll be crushed to splinters between the two. No wonder that black-faced Don is holding his fire. In his place, I should do the same."

But even at that moment the Admiral raised his hand; in the waist, below him, a trumpet blared, and immediately the gunner on the prow touched off his guns. As the thunder of them rolled out, his lordship saw ahead beyond the English ship and to larboard of her two heavy splashes. Almost at once two successive spurts of flame leapt from the brass cannon on the Arabella's beak-head, and scarcely had the watchers on the poop seen the shower of spray, where one of the shots struck the water near them, then with a rending crash and a shiver that shook the Milagrosa from stem to stern, the other came to lodge in her forecastle. To avenge that blow, the Hidalga blazed at the Englishman with both her forward guns. But even at that short range—between two and three hundred yards—neither shot took effect.

At a hundred yards the Arabella's forward guns, which had meanwhile been reloaded, fired again at the Milagrosa, and this time smashed her bowsprit into splinters; so that for a moment she yawed wildly to port. Don Miguel swore profanely, and then, as the helm was put over to swing her back to her course, his own prow replied. But the aim was too high, and whilst one of the shots tore through the Arabella's shrouds and scarred her mainmast, the other again went wide. And when the smoke of that discharge had lifted, the English ship was found almost between the Spaniards, her bows in line with theirs and coming steadily on into what his lordship deemed a death-trap.

Lord Julian held his breath, and Miss Bishop gasped, clutching the rail before her. She had a glimpse of the wickedly grinning face of Don Miguel, and the grinning faces of the men at the guns in the waist.

At last the Arabella was right between the Spanish ships prow to poop and poop to prow. Don Miguel spoke to the trumpeter, who had mounted the quarter-deck and stood now at the Admiral's elbow. The man raised the silver bugle that was to give the signal for the broadsides of both ships. But even as he placed it to his lips, the Admiral seized his arm, to arrest him. Only then had he perceived what was so obvious—or should have been to an experienced sea-fighter: he had delayed too long and Captain Blood had outmanoeuvred him. In attempting to fire now upon the Englishman, the Milagrosa and her consort would also be firing into each other. Too late he ordered his helmsman to put the tiller hard over and swing the ship to larboard, as a preliminary to manoeuvring for a less impossible position of attack. At that very moment the Arabella seemed to explode as she swept by. Eighteen guns from each of her flanks emptied themselves at that point-blank range into the hulls of the two Spanish vessels.

Half stunned by that reverberating thunder, and thrown off her balance by the sudden lurch of the ship under her feet, Miss Bishop hurtled violently against Lord Julian, who kept his feet only by clutching the rail on which he had been leaning. Billowing clouds of smoke to starboard blotted out everything, and its acrid odour, taking them presently in the throat, set them gasping and coughing.

From the grim confusion and turmoil in the waist below arose a clamour of fierce Spanish blasphemies and the screams of maimed men. The Milagrosa staggered slowly ahead, a gaping rent in her bulwarks; her foremast was shattered, fragments of the yards hanging in the netting spread below. Her beak-head was in splinters, and a shot had smashed through into the great cabin, reducing it to wreckage.

Don Miguel was bawling orders wildly, and peering ever and anon through the curtain of smoke that was drifting slowly astern, in his anxiety to ascertain how it might have fared with the Hidalga.

Suddenly, and ghostly at first through that lifting haze, loomed the outline of a ship; gradually the lines of her red hull became more and more sharply defined as she swept nearer with poles all bare save for the spread of canvas on her sprit.

Instead of holding to her course as Don Miguel had expected she would, the Arabella had gone about under cover of the smoke, and sailing now in the same direction as the Milagrosa, was converging sharply upon her across the wind, so sharply that almost before the frenzied Don Miguel had realized the situation, his vessel staggered under the rending impact with which the other came hurtling alongside. There was a rattle and clank of metal as a dozen grapnels fell, and tore and caught in the timbers of the Milagrosa, and the Spaniard was firmly gripped in the tentacles of the English ship.

Beyond her and now well astern the veil of smoke was rent at last and the Hidalga was revealed in desperate case. She was bilging fast, with an ominous list to larboard, and it could be no more than a question of moments before she settled down. The attention of her hands was being entirely given to a desperate endeavour to launch the boats in time.

Of this Don Miguel's anguished eyes had no more than a fleeting but comprehensive glimpse before his own decks were invaded by a wild, yelling swarm of boarders from the grappling ship. Never was confidence so quickly changed into despair, never was hunter more swiftly converted into helpless prey. For helpless the Spaniards were. The swiftly executed boarding manoeuvre had caught them almost unawares in the moment of confusion following the punishing broadside they had sustained at such short range. For a moment there was a valiant effort by some of Don Miguel's officers to rally the men for a stand against these invaders. But the Spaniards, never at their best in close-quarter fighting, were here demoralized by knowledge of the enemies with whom they had to deal. Their hastily formed ranks were smashed before they could be steadied; driven across the waist to the break of the poop on the one side, and up to the forecastle bulkheads on the other, the fighting resolved itself into a series of skirmishes between groups. And whilst this was doing above, another horde of buccaneers swarmed through the hatch to the main deck below to overpower the gun-crews at their stations there.

On the quarter deck, towards which an overwhelming wave of buccaneers was sweeping, led by a one-eyed giant, who was naked to the waist, stood Don Miguel, numbed by despair and rage. Above and behind him on the poop, Lord Julian and Miss Bishop looked on, his lordship aghast at the fury of this cooped-up fighting, the lady's brave calm conquered at last by horror so that she reeled there sick and faint.

Soon, however, the rage of that brief fight was spent. They saw the banner of Castile come fluttering down from the masthead. A buccaneer had slashed the halyard with his cutlass. The boarders were in possession, and on the upper deck groups of disarmed Spaniards stood huddled now like herded sheep.

Suddenly Miss Bishop recovered from her nausea, to lean forward staring wild-eyed, whilst if possible her cheeks turned yet a deadlier hue than they had been already.

Picking his way daintily through that shambles in the waist came a tall man with a deeply tanned face that was shaded by a Spanish headpiece. He was armed in back-and-breast of black steel beautifully damascened with golden arabesques. Over this, like a stole, he wore a sling of scarlet silk, from each end of which hung a silver-mounted pistol. Up the broad companion to the quarter-deck he came, toying with easy assurance, until he stood before the Spanish Admiral. Then he bowed stiff and formally. A crisp, metallic voice, speaking perfect Spanish, reached those two spectators on the poop, and increased the admiring wonder in which Lord Julian had observed the man's approach.

"We meet again at last, Don Miguel," it said. "I hope you are satisfied. Although the meeting may not be exactly as you pictured it, at least it has been very ardently sought and desired by you."

Speechless, livid of face, his mouth distorted and his breathing laboured, Don Miguel de Espinosa received the irony of that man to whom he attributed his ruin and more beside. Then he uttered an inarticulate cry of rage, and his hand swept to his sword. But even as his fingers closed upon the hilt, the other's closed upon his wrist to arrest the action.

"Calm, Don Miguel!" he was quietly but firmly enjoined. "Do not recklessly invite the ugly extremes such as you would, yourself, have practised had the situation been reversed."

A moment they stood looking into each other's eyes.

"What do you intend by me?" the Spaniard enquired at last, his voice hoarse.

Captain Blood shrugged. The firm lips smiled a little. "All that I intend has been already accomplished. And lest it increase your rancour, I beg you to observe that you have brought it entirely upon yourself. You would have it so." He turned and pointed to the boats, which his men were heaving from the boom amidships. "Your boats are being launched. You are at liberty to embark in them with your men before we scuttle this ship. Yonder are the shores of Hispaniola. You should make them safely. And if you'll take my advice, sir, you'll not hunt me again. I think I am unlucky to you. Get you home to Spain, Don Miguel, and to concerns that you understand better than this trade of the sea."

For a long moment the defeated Admiral continued to stare his hatred in silence, then, still without speaking, he went down the companion, staggering like a drunken man, his useless rapier clattering behind him. His conqueror, who had not even troubled to disarm him, watched him go, then turned and faced those two immediately above him on the poop. Lord Julian might have observed, had he been less taken up with other things, that the fellow seemed suddenly to stiffen, and that he turned pale under his deep tan. A moment he stood at gaze; then suddenly and swiftly he came up the steps. Lord Julian stood forward to meet him.

"Ye don't mean, sir, that you'll let that Spanish scoundrel go free?" he cried.

The gentleman in the black corselet appeared to become aware of his lordship for the first time.

"And who the devil may you be?" he asked, with a marked Irish accent. "And what business may it be of yours, at all?"

His lordship conceived that the fellow's truculence and utter lack of proper deference must be corrected. "I am Lord Julian Wade," he announced, with that object.

Apparently the announcement made no impression.

"Are you, indeed! Then perhaps ye'll explain what the plague you're doing aboard this ship?"

Lord Julian controlled himself to afford the desired explanation. He did so shortly and impatiently.

"He took you prisoner, did he—along with Miss Bishop there?"

"You are acquainted with Miss Bishop?" cried his lordship, passing from surprise to surprise.

But this mannerless fellow had stepped past him, and was making a leg to the lady, who on her side remained unresponsive and forbidding to the point of scorn. Observing this, he turned to answer Lord Julian's question.

"I had that honour once," said he. "But it seems that Miss Bishop has a shorter memory."

His lips were twisted into a wry smile, and there was pain in the blue eyes that gleamed so vividly under his black brows, pain blending with the mockery of his voice. But of all this it was the mockery alone that was perceived by Miss Bishop; she resented it.

"I do not number thieves and pirates among my acquaintance, Captain Blood," said she; whereupon his lordship exploded in excitement.

"Captain Blood!" he cried. "Are you Captain Blood?"

"What else were ye supposing?"

Blood asked the question wearily, his mind on other things. "I do not number thieves and pirates among my acquaintance." The cruel phrase filled his brain, reechoing and reverberating there.

But Lord Julian would not be denied. He caught him by the sleeve with one hand, whilst with the other he pointed after the retreating, dejected figure of Don Miguel.

"Do I understand that ye're not going to hang that Spanish scoundrel?"

"What for should I be hanging him?"

"Because he's just a damned pirate, as I can prove, as I have proved already."

"Ah!" said Blood, and Lord Julian marvelled at the sudden haggardness of a countenance that had been so devil-may-care but a few moments since. "I am a damned pirate, myself; and so I am merciful with my kind. Don Miguel goes free."

Lord Julian gasped. "After what I've told you that he has done? After his sinking of the Royal Mary? After his treatment of me—of us?" Lord Julian protested indignantly.

"I am not in the service of England, or of any nation, sir. And I am not concerned with any wrongs her flag may suffer."

His lordship recoiled before the furious glance that blazed at him out of Blood's haggard face. But the passion faded as swiftly as it had arisen. It was in a level voice that the Captain added:

"If you'll escort Miss Bishop aboard my ship, I shall be obliged to you. I beg that you'll make haste. We are about to scuttle this hulk."

He turned slowly to depart. But again Lord Julian interposed. Containing his indignant amazement, his lordship delivered himself coldly. "Captain Blood, you disappoint me. I had hopes of great things for you."

"Go to the devil," said Captain Blood, turning on his heel, and so departed.

XX

THIEF AND PIRATE

Captain Blood paced the poop of his ship alone in the tepid dusk, and the growing golden radiance of the great poop lantern in which a seaman had just lighted the three lamps. About him all was peace. The signs of the day's battle had been effaced, the decks had been swabbed, and order was restored above and below. A group of men squatting about the main hatch were drowsily chanting, their hardened natures softened, perhaps, by the calm and beauty of the night. They were the men of the larboard watch, waiting for eight bells which was imminent.

Captain Blood did not hear them; he did not hear anything save the echo of those cruel words which had dubbed him thief and pirate.

Thief and pirate!

It is an odd fact of human nature that a man may for years possess the knowledge that a certain thing must be of a certain fashion, and yet be shocked to discover through his own senses that the fact is in perfect harmony with his beliefs. When first, three years ago, at Tortuga he had been urged upon the adventurer's course which he had followed ever since, he had known in what opinion Arabella Bishop must hold him if he succumbed. Only the conviction that already she was for ever lost to him, by introducing a certain desperate recklessness into his soul had supplied the final impulse to drive him upon his rover's course.

That he should ever meet her again had not entered his calculations, had found no place in his dreams. They were, he conceived, irrevocably and for ever parted. Yet, in spite of this, in spite even of the persuasion that to her this reflection that was his torment could bring no regrets, he had kept the thought of her ever before him in all those wild years of filibustering. He had used it as a curb not only upon himself, but also upon those who followed him. Never had buccaneers been so rigidly held in hand, never had they been so firmly restrained, never so debarred from the excesses of rapine and lust that were usual in their kind as those who sailed with Captain Blood. It was, you will remember, stipulated in their articles that in these as in other matters they must submit to the commands of their leader. And because of the singular good fortune which had attended his leadership, he had been able to impose that stern condition of a discipline unknown before among buccaneers. How would not these men laugh at him now if he were to tell them that this he had done out of respect for a slip of a girl of whom he had fallen romantically enamoured? How would not that laughter swell if he added that this girl had that day informed him that she did not number thieves and pirates among her acquaintance.

Thief and pirate!

How the words clung, how they stung and burnt his brain!

It did not occur to him, being no psychologist, nor learned in the tortuous workings of the feminine mind, that the fact that she should bestow upon him those epithets in the very moment and circumstance of their meeting was in itself curious. He did not perceive the problem thus presented; therefore he could not probe it. Else he might have concluded that if in a moment in which by delivering her from captivity he deserved her gratitude, yet she expressed herself in bitterness, it must be because that bitterness was anterior to the gratitude and deep-seated. She had been moved to it by hearing of the course he had taken. Why? It was what he did not ask himself, or some ray of light might have come to brighten his dark, his utterly evil despondency. Surely she would never have been so moved had she not cared—had she not felt that in what he did there was a personal wrong to herself. Surely, he might have reasoned, nothing short of this could have moved her to such a degree of bitterness and scorn as that which she had displayed.

That is how you will reason. Not so, however, reasoned Captain Blood. Indeed, that night he reasoned not at all. His soul was given up to conflict between the almost sacred love he had borne her in all these years and the evil passion which she had now awakened in him. Extremes touch, and in touching may for a space become confused, indistinguishable. And the extremes of love and hate were tonight so confused in the soul of Captain Blood that in their fusion they made up a monstrous passion.

Thief and pirate!

That was what she deemed him, without qualification, oblivious of the deep wrongs he had suffered, the desperate case in which he found himself after his escape from Barbados, and all the rest that had gone to make him what he was. That he should have conducted his filibustering with hands as clean as were possible to a man engaged in such undertakings had also not occurred to her as a charitable thought with which to mitigate her judgment of a man she had once esteemed. She had no charity for him, no mercy. She had summed him up, convicted him and sentenced him in that one phrase. He was thief and pirate in her eyes; nothing more, nothing less. What, then, was she? What are those who have no charity? he asked the stars.

Well, as she had shaped him hitherto, so let her shape him now. Thief and pirate she had branded him. She should be justified. Thief and pirate should he prove henceforth; no more nor less; as bowelless, as remorseless, as all those others who had deserved those names. He would cast out the maudlin ideals by which he had sought to steer a course; put an end to this idiotic struggle to make the best of two worlds. She had shown him clearly to which world he belonged. Let him now justify her. She was aboard his ship, in his power, and he desired her.

He laughed softly, jeeringly, as he leaned on the taffrail, looking down at the phosphorescent gleam in the ship's wake, and his own laughter startled him by its evil note. He checked suddenly, and shivered. A sob broke from him to end that ribald burst of mirth. He took his face in his hands and found a chill moisture on his brow.

Meanwhile, Lord Julian, who knew the feminine part of humanity rather better than Captain Blood, was engaged in solving the curious problem that had so completely escaped the buccaneer. He was spurred to it, I suspect, by certain vague stirrings of jealousy. Miss Bishop's conduct in the perils through which they had come had brought him at last to perceive that a woman may lack the simpering graces of cultured femininity and yet because of that lack be the more admirable. He wondered what precisely might have been her earlier relations with Captain Blood, and was conscious of a certain uneasiness which urged him now to probe the matter.

His lordship's pale, dreamy eyes had, as I have said, a habit of observing things, and his wits were tolerably acute.

He was blaming himself now for not having observed certain things before, or, at least, for not having studied them more closely, and he was busily connecting them with more recent observations made that very day.

He had observed, for instance, that Blood's ship was named the Arabella, and he knew that Arabella was Miss Bishop's name. And he had observed all the odd particulars of the meeting of Captain Blood and Miss Bishop, and the curious change that meeting had wrought in each.

The lady had been monstrously uncivil to the Captain. It was a very foolish attitude for a lady in her circumstances to adopt towards a man in Blood's; and his lordship could not imagine Miss Bishop as normally foolish. Yet, in spite of her rudeness, in spite of the fact that she was the niece of a man whom Blood must regard as his enemy, Miss Bishop and his lordship had been shown the utmost consideration aboard the Captain's ship. A cabin had been placed at the disposal of each, to which their scanty remaining belongings and Miss Bishop's woman had been duly transferred. They were given the freedom of the great cabin, and they had sat down to table with Pitt, the master, and Wolverstone, who was Blood's lieutenant, both of whom had shown them the utmost courtesy. Also there was the fact that Blood, himself, had kept almost studiously from intruding upon them.

His lordship's mind went swiftly but carefully down these avenues of thought, observing and connecting. Having exhausted them, he decided to seek additional information from Miss Bishop. For this he must wait until Pitt and Wolverstone should have withdrawn. He was hardly made to wait so long, for as Pitt rose from table to follow Wolverstone, who had already departed, Miss Bishop detained him with a question:

"Mr. Pitt," she asked, "were you not one of those who escaped from Barbados with Captain Blood?"

"I was. I, too, was one of your uncle's slaves."

"And you have been with Captain Blood ever since?"

"His shipmaster always, ma'am."

She nodded. She was very calm and self-contained; but his lordship observed that she was unusually pale, though considering what she had that day undergone this afforded no matter for wonder.

"Did you ever sail with a Frenchman named Cahusac?"

"Cahusac?" Pitt laughed. The name evoked a ridiculous memory. "Aye. He was with us at Maracaybo."

"And another Frenchman named Levasseur?"

His lordship marvelled at her memory of these names.

"Aye. Cahusac was Levasseur's lieutenant, until he died."

"Until who died?"

"Levasseur. He was killed on one of the Virgin Islands two years ago."

There was a pause. Then, in an even quieter voice than before, Miss Bishop asked:

"Who killed him?"

Pitt answered readily. There was no reason why he should not, though he began to find the catechism intriguing.

"Captain Blood killed him."

"Why?"

Pitt hesitated. It was not a tale for a maid's ears.

"They quarrelled," he said shortly.

"Was it about a... a lady?" Miss Bishop relentlessly pursued him.

"You might put it that way."

"What was the lady's name?"

Pitt's eyebrows went up; still he answered.

"Miss d'Ogeron. She was the daughter of the Governor of Tortuga. She had gone off with this fellow Levasseur, and... and Peter delivered her out of his dirty clutches. He was a black-hearted scoundrel, and deserved what Peter gave him."

"I see. And... and yet Captain Blood has not married her?"

"Not yet," laughed Pitt, who knew the utter groundlessness of the common gossip in Tortuga which pronounced Mdlle. d'Ogeron the Captain's future wife.

Miss Bishop nodded in silence, and Jeremy Pitt turned to depart, relieved that the catechism was ended. He paused in the doorway to impart a piece of information.

"Maybe it'll comfort you to know that the Captain has altered our course for your benefit. It's his intention to put you both ashore on the coast of Jamaica, as near Port Royal as we dare venture. We've gone about, and if this wind holds ye'll soon be home again, mistress."

"Vastly obliging of him," drawled his lordship, seeing that Miss Bishop made no shift to answer. Sombre-eyed she sat, staring into vacancy.

"Indeed, ye may say so," Pitt agreed. "He's taking risks that few would take in his place. But that's always been his way."

He went out, leaving his lordship pensive, those dreamy blue eyes of his intently studying Miss Bishop's face for all their dreaminess; his mind increasingly uneasy. At length Miss Bishop looked at him, and spoke.

"Your Cahusac told you no more than the truth, it seems."

"I perceived that you were testing it," said his lordship. "I am wondering precisely why."

Receiving no answer, he continued to observe her silently, his long, tapering fingers toying with a ringlet of the golden periwig in which his long face was set.

Miss Bishop sat bemused, her brows knit, her brooding glance seeming to study the fine Spanish point that edged the tablecloth. At last his lordship broke the silence.

"He amazes me, this man," said he, in his slow, languid voice that never seemed to change its level. "That he should alter his course for us is in itself matter for wonder; but that he should take a risk on our behalf—that he should venture into Jamaica waters... It amazes me, as I have said."

Miss Bishop raised her eyes, and looked at him. She appeared to be very thoughtful. Then her lip flickered curiously, almost scornfully, it seemed to him. Her slender fingers drummed the table.

"What is still more amazing is that he does not hold us to ransom," said she at last.

"It's what you deserve."

"Oh, and why, if you please?"

"For speaking to him as you did."

"I usually call things by their names."

"Do you? Stab me! I shouldn't boast of it. It argues either extreme youth or extreme foolishness." His lordship, you see, belonged to my Lord Sunderland's school of philosophy. He added after a moment: "So does the display of ingratitude."

A faint colour stirred in her cheeks. "Your lordship is evidently aggrieved with me. I am disconsolate. I hope your lordship's grievance is sounder than your views of life. It is news to me that ingratitude is a fault only to be found in the young and the foolish."

"I didn't say so, ma'am." There was a tartness in his tone evoked by the tartness she had used. "If you would do me the honour to listen, you would not misapprehend me. For if unlike you I do not always say precisely what I think, at least I say precisely what I wish to convey. To be ungrateful may be human; but to display it is childish."

"I... I don't think I understand." Her brows were knit. "How have I been ungrateful and to whom?"

"To whom? To Captain Blood. Didn't he come to our rescue?"

"Did he?" Her manner was frigid. "I wasn't aware that he knew of our presence aboard the Milagrosa."

His lordship permitted himself the slightest gesture of impatience.

"You are probably aware that he delivered us," said he. "And living as you have done in these savage places of the world, you can hardly fail to be aware of what is known even in England: that this fellow Blood strictly confines himself to making war upon the Spaniards. So that to call him thief and pirate as you did was to overstate the case against him at a time when it would have been more prudent to have understated it."

"Prudence?" Her voice was scornful. "What have I to do with prudence?"

"Nothing—as I perceive. But, at least, study generosity. I tell you frankly, ma'am, that in Blood's place I should never have been so nice. Sink me! When you consider what he has suffered at the hands of his fellow-countrymen, you may marvel with me that he should trouble to discriminate between Spanish and English. To be sold into slavery! Ugh!" His lordship shuddered. "And to a damned colonial planter!" He checked abruptly. "I beg your pardon, Miss Bishop. For the moment..."

"You were carried away by your heat in defence of this... sea-robber." Miss Bishop's scorn was almost fierce.

His lordship stared at her again. Then he half-closed his large, pale eyes, and tilted his head a little. "I wonder why you hate him so," he said softly.

He saw the sudden scarlet flame upon her cheeks, the heavy frown that descended upon her brow. He had made her very angry, he judged. But there was no explosion. She recovered.

"Hate him? Lord! What a thought! I don't regard the fellow at all."

"Then ye should, ma'am." His lordship spoke his thought frankly. "He's worth regarding. He'd be an acquisition to the King's navy—a man that can do the things he did this morning. His service under de Ruyter wasn't wasted on him. That was a great seaman, and—blister me!—the pupil's worthy the master if I am a judge of anything. I doubt if the Royal Navy can show his equal. To thrust himself deliberately between those two, at point-blank range, and so turn the tables on them! It asks courage, resource, and invention. And we land-lubbers were not the only ones he tricked by his manoeuvre. That Spanish Admiral never guessed the intent until it was too late and Blood held him in check. A great man, Miss Bishop. A man worth regarding."

Miss Bishop was moved to sarcasm.

"You should use your influence with my Lord Sunderland to have the King offer him a commission."

His lordship laughed softly. "Faith, it's done already. I have his commission in my pocket." And he increased her amazement by a brief exposition of the circumstances. In that amazement he left her, and went in quest of Blood. But he was still intrigued. If she were a little less uncompromising in her attitude towards Blood, his lordship would have been happier.

He found the Captain pacing the quarter-deck, a man mentally exhausted from wrestling with the Devil, although of this particular occupation his lordship could have no possible suspicion. With the amiable familiarity he used, Lord Julian slipped an arm through one of the Captain's, and fell into step beside him.

"What's this?" snapped Blood, whose mood was fierce and raw. His lordship was not disturbed.

"I desire, sir, that we be friends," said he suavely.

"That's mighty condescending of you!"

Lord Julian ignored the obvious sarcasm.

"It's an odd coincidence that we should have been brought together in this fashion, considering that I came out to the Indies especially to seek you."

"Ye're not by any means the first to do that," the other scoffed. "But they've mainly been Spaniards, and they hadn't your luck."

"You misapprehend me completely," said Lord Julian. And on that he proceeded to explain himself and his mission.

When he had done, Captain Blood, who until that moment had stood still under the spell of his astonishment, disengaged his arm from his lordship's, and stood squarely before him.

"Ye're my guest aboard this ship," said he, "and I still have some notion of decent behaviour left me from other days, thief and pirate though I may be. So I'll not be telling you what I think of you for daring to bring me this offer, or of my Lord Sunderland—since he's your kinsman for having the impudence to send it. But it does not surprise me at all that one who is a minister of James Stuart's should conceive that every man is to be seduced by bribes into betraying those who trust him." He flung out an arm in the direction of the waist, whence came the half-melancholy chant of the lounging buccaneers.

"Again you misapprehend me," cried Lord Julian, between concern and indignation. "That is not intended. Your followers will be included in your commission."

"And d' ye think they'll go with me to hunt their brethren—the Brethren of the Coast? On my soul, Lord Julian, it is yourself does the misapprehending. Are there not even notions of honour left in England? Oh, and there's more to it than that, even. D'ye think I could take a commission of King James's? I tell you I wouldn't be soiling my hands with it—thief and pirate's hands though they be. Thief and pirate is what you heard Miss Bishop call me today—a thing of scorn, an outcast. And who made me that? Who made me thief and pirate?"

"If you were a rebel...?" his lordship was beginning.

"Ye must know that I was no such thing—no rebel at all. It wasn't even pretended. If it were, I could forgive them. But not even that cloak could they cast upon their foulness. Oh, no; there was no mistake. I was convicted for what I did, neither more nor less. That bloody vampire Jeffreys—bad cess to him!—sentenced me to death, and his worthy master James Stuart afterwards sent me into slavery, because I had performed an act of mercy; because compassionately and without thought for creed or politics I had sought to relieve the sufferings of a fellow-creature; because I had dressed the wounds of a man who was convicted of treason. That was all my offence. You'll find it in the records. And for that I was sold into slavery: because by the law of England, as administered by James Stuart in violation of the laws of God, who harbours or comforts a rebel is himself adjudged guilty of rebellion. D'ye dream man, what it is to be a slave?"

He checked suddenly at the very height of his passion. A moment he paused, then cast it from him as if it had been a cloak. His voice sank again. He uttered a little laugh of weariness and contempt.

"But there! I grow hot for nothing at all. I explain myself, I think, and God knows, it is not my custom. I am grateful to you, Lord Julian, for your kindly intentions. I am so. But ye'll understand, perhaps. Ye look as if ye might."

Lord Julian stood still. He was deeply stricken by the other's words, the passionate, eloquent outburst that in a few sharp, clear-cut strokes had so convincingly presented the man's bitter case against humanity, his complete apologia and justification for all that could be laid to his charge. His lordship looked at that keen, intrepid face gleaming lividly in the light of the great poop lantern, and his own eyes were troubled. He was abashed.

He fetched a heavy sigh. "A pity," he said slowly. "Oh, blister me—a cursed pity!" He held out his hand, moved to it on a sudden generous impulse. "But no offence between us, Captain Blood!"

"Oh, no offence. But... I'm a thief and a pirate." He laughed without mirth, and, disregarding the proffered hand, swung on his heel.

Lord Julian stood a moment, watching the tall figure as it moved away towards the taffrail. Then letting his arms fall helplessly to his sides in dejection, he departed.

Just within the doorway of the alley leading to the cabin, he ran into Miss Bishop. Yet she had not been coming out, for her back was towards him, and she was moving in the same direction. He followed her, his mind too full of Captain Blood to be concerned just then with her movements.

In the cabin he flung into a chair, and exploded, with a violence altogether foreign to his nature.

"Damme if ever I met a man I liked better, or even a man I liked as well. Yet there's nothing to be done with him."

"So I heard," she admitted in a small voice. She was very white, and she kept her eyes upon her folded hands.

He looked up in surprise, and then sat conning her with brooding glance. "I wonder, now," he said presently, "if the mischief is of your working. Your words have rankled with him. He threw them at me again and again. He wouldn't take the King's commission; he wouldn't take my hand even. What's to be done with a fellow like that? He'll end on a yardarm for all his luck. And the quixotic fool is running into danger at the present moment on our behalf."

"How?" she asked him with a sudden startled interest.

"How? Have you forgotten that he's sailing to Jamaica, and that Jamaica is the headquarters of the English fleet? True, your uncle commands it..."

She leaned across the table to interrupt him, and he observed that her breathing had grown labored, that her eyes were dilating in alarm.

"But there is no hope for him in that!" she cried. "Oh, don't imagine it! He has no bitterer enemy in the world! My uncle is a hard, unforgiving man. I believe that it was nothing but the hope of taking and hanging Captain Blood that made my uncle leave his Barbados plantations to accept the deputy-governorship of Jamaica. Captain Blood doesn't know that, of course...." She paused with a little gesture of helplessness.

"I can't think that it would make the least difference if he did," said his lordship gravely. "A man who can forgive such an enemy as Don Miguel and take up this uncompromising attitude with me isn't to be judged by ordinary rules. He's chivalrous to the point of idiocy."

"And yet he has been what he has been and done what he has done in these last three years," said she, but she said it sorrowfully now, without any of her earlier scorn.

Lord Julian was sententious, as I gather that he often was. "Life can be infernally complex," he sighed.

XXI

THE SERVICE OF KING JAMES

Miss Arabella Bishop was aroused very early on the following morning by the brazen voice of a bugle and the insistent clanging of a bell in the ship's belfry. As she lay awake, idly watching the rippled green water that appeared to be streaming past the heavily glazed porthole, she became gradually aware of the sounds of swift, laboured bustle—the clatter of many feet, the shouts of hoarse voices, and the persistent trundlings of heavy bodies in the ward-room immediately below the deck of the cabin. Conceiving these sounds to portend a more than normal activity, she sat up, pervaded by a vague alarm, and roused her still slumbering woman.

In his cabin on the starboard side Lord Julian, disturbed by the same sounds, was already astir and hurriedly dressing. When presently he emerged under the break of the poop, he found himself staring up into a mountain of canvas. Every foot of sail that she could carry had been crowded to the Arabella's yards, to catch the morning breeze. Ahead and on either side stretched the limitless expanse of ocean, sparkling golden in the sun, as yet no more than a half-disc of flame upon the horizon straight ahead.

About him in the waist, where all last night had been so peaceful, there was a frenziedly active bustle of some threescore men. By the rail, immediately above and behind Lord Julian, stood Captain Blood in altercation with a one-eyed giant, whose head was swathed in a red cotton kerchief, whose blue shirt hung open at the waist. As his lordship, moving forward, revealed himself, their voices ceased, and Blood turned to greet him.

"Good-morning to you," he said, and added "I've blundered badly, so I have. I should have known better than to come so close to Jamaica by night. But I was in haste to land you. Come up here. I have something to show you."

Wondering, Lord Julian mounted the companion as he was bidden. Standing beside Captain Blood, he looked astern, following the indication of the Captain's hand, and cried out in his amazement. There, not more than three miles away, was land—an uneven wall of vivid green that filled the western horizon. And a couple of miles this side of it, bearing after them, came speeding three great white ships.

"They fly no colours, but they're part of the Jamaica fleet." Blood spoke without excitement, almost with a certain listlessness. "When dawn broke we found ourselves running to meet them. We went about, and it's been a race ever since. But the Arabella 's been at sea these four months, and her bottom's too foul for the speed we're needing."

Wolverstone hooked his thumbs into his broad leather belt, and from his great height looked down sardonically upon Lord Julian, tall man though his lordship was. "So that you're like to be in yet another sea-fight afore ye've done wi' ships, my lord."

"That's a point we were just arguing," said Blood. "For I hold that we're in no case to fight against such odds."

"The odds be damned!" Wolverstone thrust out his heavy jowl. "We're used to odds. The odds was heavier at Maracaybo; yet we won out, and took three ships. They was heavier yesterday when we engaged Don Miguel."

"Aye—but those were Spaniards."

"And what better are these?—Are ye afeard of a lubberly Barbados planter? Whatever ails you, Peter? I've never known ye scared afore."

A gun boomed out behind them.

"That'll be the signal to lie to," said Blood, in the same listless voice; and he fetched a sigh.

Wolverstone squared himself defiantly before his captain

"I'll see Colonel Bishop in hell or ever I lies to for him." And he spat, presumably for purposes of emphasis.

His lordship intervened.

"Oh, but—by your leave—surely there is nothing to be apprehended from Colonel Bishop. Considering the service you have rendered to his niece and to me..."

Wolverstone's horse-laugh interrupted him. "Hark to the gentleman!" he mocked. "Ye don't know Colonel Bishop, that's clear. Not for his niece, not for his daughter, not for his own mother, would he forgo the blood what he thinks due to him. A drinker of blood, he is. A nasty beast. We knows, the Cap'n and me. We been his slaves."

"But there is myself," said Lord Julian, with great dignity.

Wolverstone laughed again, whereat his lordship flushed. He was moved to raise his voice above its usual languid level.

"I assure you that my word counts for something in England."

"Oh, aye—in England. But this ain't England, damme."

Came the roar of a second gun, and a round shot splashed the water less than half a cable's-length astern. Blood leaned over the rail to speak to the fair young man immediately below him by the helmsman at the whipstaff.

"Bid them take in sail, Jeremy," he said quietly. "We lie to."

But Wolverstone interposed again.

"Hold there a moment, Jeremy!" he roared. "Wait!" He swung back to face the Captain, who had placed a hand on is shoulder and was smiling, a trifle wistfully.

"Steady, Old Wolf! Steady!" Captain Blood admonished him.

"Steady, yourself, Peter. Ye've gone mad! Will ye doom us all to hell out of tenderness for that cold slip of a girl?"

"Stop!" cried Blood in sudden fury.

But Wolverstone would not stop. "It's the truth, you fool. It's that cursed petticoat's making a coward of you. It's for her that ye're afeard—and she, Colonel Bishop's niece! My God, man, ye'll have a mutiny aboard, and I'll lead it myself sooner than surrender to be hanged in Port Royal."

Their glances met, sullen defiance braving dull anger, surprise, and pain.

"There is no question," said Blood, "of surrender for any man aboard save only myself. If Bishop can report to England that I am taken and hanged, he will magnify himself and at the same time gratify his personal rancour against me. That should satisfy him. I'll send him a message offering to surrender aboard his ship, taking Miss Bishop and Lord Julian with me, but only on condition that the Arabella is allowed to proceed unharmed. It's a bargain that he'll accept, if I know him at all."

"It's a bargain he'll never be offered," retorted Wolverstone, and his earlier vehemence was as nothing to his vehemence now. "Ye're surely daft even to think of it, Peter!"

"Not so daft as you when you talk of fighting that." He flung out an arm as he spoke to indicate the pursuing ships, which were slowly but surely creeping nearer. "Before we've run another half-mile we shall be within range."

Wolverstone swore elaborately, then suddenly checked. Out of the tail of his single eye he had espied a trim figure in grey silk that was ascending the companion. So engrossed had they been that they had not seen Miss Bishop come from the door of the passage leading to the cabin. And there was something else that those three men on the poop, and Pitt immediately below them, had failed to observe. Some moments ago Ogle, followed by the main body of his gun-deck crew, had emerged from the booby hatch, to fall into muttered, angrily vehement talk with those who, abandoning the gun-tackles upon which they were labouring, had come to crowd about him.

Even now Blood had no eyes for that. He turned to look at Miss Bishop, marvelling a little, after the manner in which yesterday she had avoided him, that she should now venture upon the quarter-deck. Her presence at this moment, and considering the nature of his altercation with Wolverstone, was embarrassing.

Very sweet and dainty she stood before him in her gown of shimmering grey, a faint excitement tinting her fair cheeks and sparkling in her clear, hazel eyes, that looked so frank and honest. She wore no hat, and the ringlets of her gold-brown hair fluttered distractingly in the morning breeze.

Captain Blood bared his head and bowed silently in a greeting which she returned composedly and formally.

"What is happening, Lord Julian?" she enquired.

As if to answer her a third gun spoke from the ships towards which she was looking intent and wonderingly. A frown rumpled her brow. She looked from one to the other of the men who stood there so glum and obviously ill at ease.

"They are ships of the Jamaica fleet," his lordship answered her.

It should in any case have been a sufficient explanation. But before more could be added, their attention was drawn at last to Ogle, who came bounding up the broad ladder, and to the men lounging aft in his wake, in all of which, instinctively, they apprehended a vague menace.

At the head of the companion, Ogle found his progress barred by Blood, who confronted him, a sudden sternness in his face and in every line of him.

"What's this?" the Captain demanded sharply. "Your station is on the gun-deck. Why have you left it?"

Thus challenged, the obvious truculence faded out of Ogle's bearing, quenched by the old habit of obedience and the natural dominance that was the secret of the Captain's rule over his wild followers. But it gave no pause to the gunner's intention. If anything it increased his excitement.

"Captain," he said, and as he spoke he pointed to the pursuing ships, "Colonel Bishop holds us. We're in no case either to run or fight."

Blood's height seemed to increase, as did his sternness.

"Ogle," said he, in a voice cold and sharp as steel, "your station is on the gun-deck. You'll return to it at once, and take your crew with you, or else..."

But Ogle, violent of mien and gesture, interrupted him.

"Threats will not serve, Captain."

"Will they not?"

It was the first time in his buccaneering career that an order of his had been disregarded, or that a man had failed in the obedience to which he pledged all those who joined him. That this insubordination should proceed from one of those whom he most trusted, one of his old Barbados associates, was in itself a bitterness, and made him reluctant to that which instinct told him must be done. His hand closed over the butt of one of the pistols slung before him.

"Nor will that serve you," Ogle warned him, still more fiercely. "The men are of my thinking, and they'll have their way."

"And what way may that be?"

"The way to make us safe. We'll neither sink nor hang whiles we can help it."

From the three or four score men massed below in the waist came a rumble of approval. Captain Blood's glance raked the ranks of those resolute, fierce-eyed fellows, then it came to rest again on Ogle. There was here quite plainly a vague threat, a mutinous spirit he could not understand. "You come to give advice, then, do you?" quoth he, relenting nothing of his sternness.

"That's it, Captain; advice. That girl, there." He flung out a bare arm to point to her. "Bishop's girl; the Governor of Jamaica's niece... We want her as a hostage for our safety."

"Aye!" roared in chorus the buccaneers below, and one or two of them elaborated that affirmation.

In a flash Captain Blood saw what was in their minds. And for all that he lost nothing of his outward stern composure, fear invaded his heart.

"And how," he asked, "do you imagine that Miss Bishop will prove such a hostage?"

"It's a providence having her aboard; a providence. Heave to, Captain, and signal them to send a boat, and assure themselves that Miss is here. Then let them know that if they attempt to hinder our sailing hence, we'll hang the doxy first and fight for it after. That'll cool Colonel Bishop's heat, maybe."

"And maybe it won't." Slow and mocking came Wolverstone's voice to answer the other's confident excitement, and as he spoke he advanced to Blood's side, an unexpected ally. "Some o' them dawcocks may believe that tale." He jerked a contemptuous thumb towards the men in the waist, whose ranks were steadily being increased by the advent of others from the forecastle. "Although even some o' they should know better, for there's still a few was on Barbados with us, and are acquainted like me and you with Colonel Bishop. If ye're counting on pulling Bishop's heartstrings, ye're a bigger fool, Ogle, than I've always thought you was with anything but guns. There's no heaving to for such a matter as that unless you wants to make quite sure of our being sunk. Though we had a cargo of Bishop's nieces it wouldn't make him hold his hand. Why, as I was just telling his lordship here, who thought like you that having Miss Bishop aboard would make us safe, not for his mother would that filthy slaver forgo what's due to him. And if ye' weren't a fool, Ogle, you wouldn't need me to tell you this. We've got to fight, my lads..."

"How can we fight, man?" Ogle stormed at him, furiously battling the conviction which Wolverstone's argument was imposing upon his listeners. "You may be right, and you may be wrong. We've got to chance it. It's our only chance..."

The rest of his words were drowned in the shouts of the hands insisting that the girl be given up to be held as a hostage. And then louder than before roared a gun away to leeward, and away on their starboard beam they saw the spray flung up by the shot, which had gone wide.

"They are within range," cried Ogle. And leaning from the rail, "Put down the helm," he commanded.

Pitt, at his post beside the helmsman, turned intrepidly to face the excited gunner.

"Since when have you commanded on the main deck, Ogle? I take my orders from the Captain."

"You'll take this order from me, or, by God, you'll..."

"Wait!" Blood bade him, interrupting, and he set a restraining hand upon the gunner's arm. "There is, I think, a better way."

He looked over his shoulder, aft, at the advancing ships, the foremost of which was now a bare quarter of a mile away. His glance swept in passing over Miss Bishop and Lord Julian standing side by side some paces behind him. He observed her pale and tense, with parted lips and startled eyes that were fixed upon him, an anxious witness of this deciding of her fate. He was thinking swiftly, reckoning the chances if by pistolling Ogle he were to provoke a mutiny. That some of the men would rally to him, he was sure. But he was no less sure that the main body would oppose him, and prevail in spite of all that he could do, taking the chance that holding Miss Bishop to ransom seemed to afford them. And if they did that, one way or the other, Miss Bishop would be lost. For even if Bishop yielded to their demand, they would retain her as a hostage.

Meanwhile Ogle was growing impatient. His arm still gripped by Blood, he thrust his face into the Captain's.

"What better way?" he demanded. "There is none better. I'll not be bubbled by what Wolverstone has said. He may be right, and he may be wrong. We'll test it. It's our only chance, I've said, and we must take it."

The better way that was in Captain Blood's mind was the way that already he had proposed to Wolverstone. Whether the men in the panic Ogle had aroused among them would take a different view from Wolverstone's he did not know. But he saw quite clearly now that if they consented, they would not on that account depart from their intention in the matter of Miss Bishop; they would make of Blood's own surrender merely an additional card in this game against the Governor of Jamaica.

"It's through her that we're in this trap," Ogle stormed on. "Through her and through you. It was to bring her to Jamaica that you risked all our lives, and we're not going to lose our lives as long as there's a chance to make ourselves safe through her."

He was turning again to the helmsman below, when Blood's grip tightened on his arm. Ogle wrenched it free, with an oath. But Blood's mind was now made up. He had found the only way, and repellent though it might be to him, he must take it.

"That is a desperate chance," he cried. "Mine is the safe and easy way. Wait!" He leaned over the rail. "Put the helm down," he bade Pitt. "Heave her to, and signal to them to send a boat."

A silence of astonishment fell upon the ship—of astonishment and suspicion at this sudden yielding. But Pitt, although he shared it, was prompt to obey. His voice rang out, giving the necessary orders, and after an instant's pause, a score of hands sprang to execute them. Came the creak of blocks and the rattle of slatting sails as they swung aweather, and Captain Blood turned and beckoned Lord Julian forward. His lordship, after a moment's hesitation, advanced in surprise and mistrust—a mistrust shared by Miss Bishop, who, like his lordship and all else aboard, though in a different way, had been taken aback by Blood's sudden submission to the demand to lie to.

Standing now at the rail, with Lord Julian beside him, Captain Blood explained himself.

Briefly and clearly he announced to all the object of Lord Julian's voyage to the Caribbean, and he informed them of the offer which yesterday Lord Julian had made to him.

"That offer I rejected, as his lordship will tell you, deeming myself affronted by it. Those of you who have suffered under the rule of King James will understand me. But now in the desperate case in which we find ourselves—outsailed, and likely to be outfought, as Ogle has said—I am ready to take the way of Morgan: to accept the King's commission and shelter us all behind it."

It was a thunderbolt that for a moment left them all dazed. Then Babel was reenacted. The main body of them welcomed the announcement as only men who have been preparing to die can welcome a new lease of life. But many could not resolve one way or the other until they were satisfied upon several questions, and chiefly upon one which was voiced by Ogle.

"Will Bishop respect the commission when you hold it?"

It was Lord Julian who answered:

"It will go very hard with him if he attempts to flout the King's authority. And though he should dare attempt it, be sure that his own officers will not dare to do other than oppose him."

"Aye," said Ogle, "that is true."

But there were some who were still in open and frank revolt against the course. Of these was Wolverstone, who at once proclaimed his hostility.

"I'll rot in hell or ever I serves the King," he bawled in a great rage.

But Blood quieted him and those who thought as he did.

"No man need follow me into the King's service who is reluctant. That is not in the bargain. What is in the bargain is that I accept this service with such of you as may choose to follow me. Don't think I accept it willingly. For myself, I am entirely of Wolverstone's opinion. I accept it as the only way to save us all from the certain destruction into which my own act may have brought us. And even those of you who do not choose to follow me shall share the immunity of all, and shall afterwards be free to depart. Those are the terms upon which I sell myself to the King. Let Lord Julian, the representative of the Secretary of State, say whether he agrees to them."

Prompt, eager, and clear came his lordship's agreement. And that was practically the end of the matter. Lord Julian, the butt now of good-humouredly ribald jests and half-derisive acclamations, plunged away to his cabin for the commission, secretly rejoicing at a turn of events which enabled him so creditably to discharge the business on which he had been sent.

Meanwhile the bo'sun signalled to the Jamaica ships to send a boat, and the men in the waist broke their ranks and went noisily flocking to line the bulwarks and view the great stately vessels that were racing down towards them.

As Ogle left the quarter-deck, Blood turned, and came face to face with Miss Bishop. She had been observing him with shining eyes, but at sight of his dejected countenance, and the deep frown that scarred his brow, her own expression changed. She approached him with a hesitation entirely unusual to her. She set a hand lightly upon his arm.

"You have chosen wisely, sir," she commended him, "however much against your inclinations."

He looked with gloomy eyes upon her for whom he had made this sacrifice.

"I owed it to you—or thought I did," he said.

She did not understand. "Your resolve delivered me from a horrible danger," she admitted. And she shivered at the memory of it. "But I do not understand why you should have hesitated when first it was proposed to you. It is an honourable service."

"King James's?" he sneered.

"England's," she corrected him in reproof. "The country is all, sir; the sovereign naught. King James will pass; others will come and pass; England remains, to be honourably served by her sons, whatever rancour they may hold against the man who rules her in their time."

He showed some surprise. Then he smiled a little. "Shrewd advocacy," he approved it. "You should have spoken to the crew."

And then, the note of irony deepening in his voice: "Do you suppose now that this honourable service might redeem one who was a pirate and a thief?"

Her glance fell away. Her voice faltered a little in replying. "If he... needs redeeming. Perhaps... perhaps he has been judged too harshly."

The blue eyes flashed, and the firm lips relaxed their grim set.

"Why... if ye think that," he said, considering her, an odd hunger in his glance, "life might have its uses, after all, and even the service of King James might become tolerable."

Looking beyond her, across the water, he observed a boat putting off from one of the great ships, which, hove to now, were rocking gently some three hundred yards away. Abruptly his manner changed. He was like one recovering, taking himself in hand again. "If you will go below, and get your gear and your woman, you shall presently be sent aboard one of the ships of the fleet." He pointed to the boat as he spoke.

She left him, and thereafter with Wolverstone, leaning upon the rail, he watched the approach of that boat, manned by a dozen sailors, and commanded by a scarlet figure seated stiffly in the stern sheets. He levelled his telescope upon that figure.

"It'll not be Bishop himself," said Wolverstone, between question and assertion.

"No." Blood closed his telescope. "I don't know who it is."

"Ha!" Wolverstone vented an ejaculation of sneering mirth. "For all his eagerness, Bishop'd be none so willing to come, hisself. He's been aboard this hulk afore, and we made him swim for it that time. He'll have his memories. So he sends a deputy."

This deputy proved to be an officer named Calverley, a vigorous, self-sufficient fellow, comparatively fresh from England, whose manner made it clear that he came fully instructed by Colonel Bishop upon the matter of how to handle the pirates.

His air, as he stepped into the waist of the Arabella, was haughty, truculent, and disdainful.

Blood, the King's commission now in his pocket, and Lord Julian standing beside him, waited to receive him, and Captain Calverley was a little taken aback at finding himself confronted by two men so very different outwardly from anything that he had expected. But he lost none of his haughty poise, and scarcely deigned a glance at the swarm of fierce, half-naked fellows lounging in a semicircle to form a background.

"Good-day to you, sir," Blood hailed him pleasantly. "I have the honour to give you welcome aboard the Arabella. My name is Blood—Captain Blood, at your service. You may have heard of me."

Captain Calverley stared hard. The airy manner of this redoubtable buccaneer was hardly what he had looked for in a desperate fellow, compelled to ignominious surrender. A thin, sour smile broke on the officer's haughty lips.

"You'll ruffle it to the gallows, no doubt," he said contemptuously. "I suppose that is after the fashion of your kind. Meanwhile it's your surrender I require, my man, not your impudence."

Captain Blood appeared surprised, pained. He turned in appeal to Lord Julian.

"D'ye hear that now? And did ye ever hear the like? But what did I tell ye? Ye see, the young gentleman's under a misapprehension entirely. Perhaps it'll save broken bones if your lordship explains just who and what I am."

Lord Julian advanced a step and bowed perfunctorily and rather disdainfully to that very disdainful but now dumbfounded officer. Pitt, who watched the scene from the quarter-deck rail, tells us that his lordship was as grave as a parson at a hanging. But I suspect this gravity for a mask under which Lord Julian was secretly amused.

"I have the honour to inform you, sir," he said stiffly, "that Captain Blood holds a commission in the King's service under the seal of my Lord Sunderland, His Majesty's Secretary of State."

Captain Calverley's face empurpled; his eyes bulged. The buccaneers in the background chuckled and crowed and swore among themselves in their relish of this comedy. For a long moment Calverley stared in silence at his lordship, observing the costly elegance of his dress, his air of calm assurance, and his cold, fastidious speech, all of which savoured distinctly of the great world to which he belonged.

"And who the devil may you be?" he exploded at last.

Colder still and more distant than ever grew his lordship's voice.

"You're not very civil, sir, as I have already noticed. My name is Wade—Lord Julian Wade. I am His Majesty's envoy to these barbarous parts, and my Lord Sunderland's near kinsman. Colonel Bishop has been notified of my coming."

The sudden change in Calverley's manner at Lord Julian's mention of his name showed that the notification had been received, and that he had knowledge of it.

"I... I believe that he has," said Calverley, between doubt and suspicion. "That is: that he has been notified of the coming of Lord Julian Wade. But... but... aboard this ship...?" The officer made a gesture of helplessness, and, surrendering to his bewilderment, fell abruptly silent.

"I was coming out on the Royal Mary..."

"That is what we were advised."

"But the Royal Mary fell a victim to a Spanish privateer, and I might never have arrived at all but for the gallantry of Captain Blood, who rescued me."

Light broke upon the darkness of Calverley's mind. "I see. I understand."

"I will take leave to doubt it." His lordship's tone abated nothing of its asperity. "But that can wait. If Captain Blood will show you his commission, perhaps that will set all doubts at rest, and we may proceed. I shall be glad to reach Port Royal."

Captain Blood thrust a parchment under Calverley's bulging eyes. The officer scanned it, particularly the seals and signature. He stepped back, a baffled, impotent man. He bowed helplessly.

"I must return to Colonel Bishop for my orders," he informed them.

At that moment a lane was opened in the ranks of the men, and through this came Miss Bishop followed by her octoroon woman. Over his shoulder Captain Blood observed her approach.

"Perhaps, since Colonel Bishop is with you, you will convey his niece to him. Miss Bishop was aboard the Royal Mary also, and I rescued her together with his lordship. She will be able to acquaint her uncle with the details of that and of the present state of affairs."

Swept thus from surprise to surprise, Captain Calverley could do no more than bow again.

"As for me," said Lord Julian, with intent to make Miss Bishop's departure free from all interference on the part of the buccaneers, "I shall remain aboard the Arabella until we reach Port Royal. My compliments to Colonel Bishop. Say that I look forward to making his acquaintance there."

XXII

HOSTILITIES

In the great harbour of Port Royal, spacious enough to have given moorings to all the ships of all the navies of the world, the Arabella rode at anchor. Almost she had the air of a prisoner, for a quarter of a mile ahead, to starboard, rose the lofty, massive single round tower of the fort, whilst a couple of cables'-length astern, and to larboard, rode the six men-of-war that composed the Jamaica squadron.

Abeam with the Arabella, across the harbour, were the flat-fronted white buildings of that imposing city that came down to the very water's edge. Behind these the red roofs rose like terraces, marking the gentle slope upon which the city was built, dominated here by a turret, there by a spire, and behind these again a range of green hills with for ultimate background a sky that was like a dome of polished steel.

On a cane day-bed that had been set for him on the quarter-deck, sheltered from the dazzling, blistering sunshine by an improvised awning of brown sailcloth, lounged Peter Blood, a calf-bound, well-thumbed copy of Horace's Odes neglected in his hands.

From immediately below him came the swish of mops and the gurgle of water in the scuppers, for it was still early morning, and under the directions of Hayton, the bo'sun, the swabbers were at work in the waist and forecastle. Despite the heat and the stagnant air, one of the toilers found breath to croak a ribald buccaneering ditty:

"For we laid her board and board,
And we put her to the sword,
And we sank her in the deep blue sea.
So It's heigh-ho, and heave-a-ho!
Who'll sail for the Main with me?"

Blood fetched a sigh, and the ghost of a smile played over his lean, sun-tanned face. Then the black brows came together above the vivid blue eyes, and thought swiftly closed the door upon his immediate surroundings.

Things had not sped at all well with him in the past fortnight since his acceptance of the King's commission. There had been trouble with Bishop from the moment of landing. As Blood and Lord Julian had stepped ashore together, they had been met by a man who took no pains to dissemble his chagrin at the turn of events and his determination to change it. He awaited them on the mole, supported by a group of officers.

"You are Lord Julian Wade, I understand," was his truculent greeting. For Blood at the moment he had nothing beyond a malignant glance.

Lord Julian bowed. "I take it I have the honour to address Colonel Bishop, Deputy-Governor of Jamaica." It was almost as if his lordship were giving the Colonel a lesson in deportment. The Colonel accepted it, and belatedly bowed, removing his broad hat. Then he plunged on.

"You have granted, I am told, the King's commission to this man." His very tone betrayed the bitterness of his rancour. "Your motives were no doubt worthy... your gratitude to him for delivering you from the Spaniards. But the thing itself is unthinkable, my lord. The commission must be cancelled."

"I don't think I understand," said Lord Julian distantly.

"To be sure you don't, or you'd never ha' done it. The fellow's bubbled you. Why, he's first a rebel, then an escaped slave, and lastly a bloody pirate. I've been hunting him this year past."

"I assure you, sir, that I was fully informed of all. I do not grant the King's commission lightly."

"Don't you, by God! And what else do you call this? But as His Majesty's Deputy-Governor of Jamaica, I'll take leave to correct your mistake in my own way."

"Ah! And what way may that be?"

"There's a gallows waiting for this rascal in Port Royal."

Blood would have intervened at that, but Lord Julian forestalled him.

"I see, sir, that you do not yet quite apprehend the circumstances. If it is a mistake to grant Captain Blood a commission, the mistake is not mine. I am acting upon the instructions of my Lord Sunderland; and with a full knowledge of all the facts, his lordship expressly designated Captain Blood for this commission if Captain Blood could be persuaded to accept it."

Colonel Bishop's mouth fell open in surprise and dismay.

"Lord Sunderland designated him?" he asked, amazed.

"Expressly."

His lordship waited a moment for a reply. None coming from the speechless Deputy-Governor, he asked a question: "Would you still venture to describe the matter as a mistake, sir? And dare you take the risk of correcting it?"

"I... I had not dreamed..."

"I understand, sir. Let me present Captain Blood."

Perforce Bishop must put on the best face he could command. But that it was no more than a mask for his fury and his venom was plain to all.

From that unpromising beginning matters had not improved; rather had they grown worse.

Blood's thoughts were upon this and other things as he lounged there on the day-bed. He had been a fortnight in Port

Royal, his ship virtually a unit now in the Jamaica squadron. And when the news of it reached Tortuga and the buccaneers who awaited his return, the name of Captain Blood, which had stood so high among the Brethren of the Coast, would become a byword, a thing of execration, and before all was done his life might pay forfeit for what would be accounted a treacherous defection. And for what had he placed himself in this position? For the sake of a girl who avoided him so persistently and intentionally that he must assume that she still regarded him with aversion. He had scarcely been vouchsafed a glimpse of her in all this fortnight, although with that in view for his main object he had daily haunted her uncle's residence, and daily braved the unmasked hostility and baffled rancour in which Colonel Bishop held him. Nor was that the worst of it. He was allowed plainly to perceive that it was the graceful, elegant young trifler from St. James's, Lord Julian Wade, to whom her every moment was devoted. And what chance had he, a desperate adventurer with a record of outlawry, against such a rival as that, a man of parts, moreover, as he was bound to admit?

You conceive the bitterness of his soul. He beheld himself to be as the dog in the fable that had dropped the substance to snatch at a delusive shadow.

He sought comfort in a line on the open page before him:

"levius fit patientia quicquid corrigere est nefas."

Sought it, but hardly found it.

A boat that had approached unnoticed from the shore came scraping and bumping against the great red hull of the Arabella, and a raucous voice sent up a hailing shout. From the ship's belfry two silvery notes rang clear and sharp, and a moment or two later the bo'sun's whistle shrilled a long wail.

The sounds disturbed Captain Blood from his disgruntled musings. He rose, tall, active, and arrestingly elegant in a scarlet, gold-laced coat that advertised his new position, and slipping the slender volume into his pocket, advanced to the carved rail of the quarter-deck, just as Jeremy Pitt was setting foot upon the companion.

"A note for you from the Deputy-Governor," said the master shortly, as he proffered a folded sheet.

Blood broke the seal, and read. Pitt, loosely clad in shirt and breeches, leaned against the rail the while and watched him, unmistakable concern imprinted on his fair, frank countenance.

Blood uttered a short laugh, and curled his lip. "It is a very peremptory summons," he said, and passed the note to his friend.

The young master's grey eyes skimmed it. Thoughtfully he stroked his golden beard.

"You'll not go?" he said, between question and assertion.

"Why not? Haven't I been a daily visitor at the fort...?"

"But it'll be about the Old Wolf that he wants to see you. It gives him a grievance at last. You know, Peter, that it is Lord Julian alone has stood between Bishop and his hate of you. If now he can show that..."

"What if he can?" Blood interrupted carelessly. "Shall I be in greater danger ashore than aboard, now that we've but fifty men left, and they lukewarm rogues who would as soon serve the King as me? Jeremy, dear lad, the Arabella's a prisoner here, bedad, 'twixt the fort there and the fleet yonder. Don't be forgetting that."

Jeremy clenched his hands. "Why did ye let Wolverstone and the others go?" he cried, with a touch of bitterness. "You should have seen the danger."

"How could I in honesty have detained them? It was in the bargain. Besides, how could their staying have helped me?" And as Pitt did not answer him: "Ye see?" he said, and shrugged. "I'll be getting my hat and cane and sword, and go ashore in the cock-boat. See it manned for me."

"Ye're going to deliver yourself into Bishop's hands," Pitt warned him.

"Well, well, maybe he'll not find me quite so easy to grasp as he imagines. There's a thorn or two left on me." And with a laugh Blood departed to his cabin.

Jeremy Pitt answered the laugh with an oath. A moment he stood irresolute where Blood had left him. Then slowly, reluctance dragging at his feet, he went down the companion to give the order for the cock-boat.

"If anything should happen to you, Peter," he said, as Blood was going over the side, "Colonel Bishop had better look to himself. These fifty lads may be lukewarm at present, as you say, but—sink me!—they'll be anything but lukewarm if there's a breach of faith."

"And what should be happening to me, Jeremy? Sure, now, I'll be back for dinner, so I will."

Blood climbed down into the waiting boat. But laugh though he might, he knew as well as Pitt that in going ashore that morning he carried his life in his hands. Because of this, it may have been that when he stepped on to the narrow mole, in the shadow of the shallow outer wall of the fort through whose crenels were thrust the black noses of its heavy guns, he gave order that the boat should stay for him at that spot. He realized that he might have to retreat in a hurry.

Walking leisurely, he skirted the embattled wall, and passed through the great gates into the courtyard. Half-a-dozen soldiers lounged there, and in the shadow cast by the wall, Major Mallard, the Commandant, was slowly pacing. He stopped short at sight of Captain Blood, and saluted him, as was his due, but the smile that lifted the officer's stiff mostachios was grimly sardonic. Peter Blood's attention, however, was elsewhere.

On his right stretched a spacious garden, beyond which rose the white house that was the residence of the Deputy-Governor. In that garden's main avenue, that was fringed with palm and sandalwood, he had caught sight of Miss Bishop alone. He crossed the courtyard with suddenly lengthened stride.

"Good-morning to ye, ma'am," was his greeting as he overtook her; and hat in hand now, he added on a note of protest: "Sure, it's nothing less than uncharitable to make me run in this heat."

"Why do you run, then?" she asked him coolly, standing slim and straight before him, all in white and very maidenly save in her unnatural composure. "I am pressed," she informed him. "So you will forgive me if I do not stay."

"You were none so pressed until I came," he protested, and if his thin lips smiled, his blue eyes were oddly hard.

"Since you perceive it, sir, I wonder that you trouble to be so insistent."

That crossed the swords between them, and it was against Blood's instincts to avoid an engagement.

"Faith, you explain yourself after a fashion," said he. "But since it was more or less in your service that I donned the King's coat, you should suffer it to cover the thief and pirate."

She shrugged and turned aside, in some resentment and some regret. Fearing to betray the latter, she took refuge in the former. "I do my best," said she.

"So that ye can be charitable in some ways!" He laughed softly. "Glory be, now, I should be thankful for so much. Maybe I'm presumptuous. But I can't forget that when I was no better than a slave in your uncle's household in Barbados, ye used me with a certain kindness."

"Why not? In those days you had some claim upon my kindness. You were just an unfortunate gentleman then."

"And what else would you be calling me now?"

"Hardly unfortunate. We have heard of your good fortune on the seas—how your luck has passed into a byword. And we have heard other things: of your good fortune in other directions."

She spoke hastily, the thought of Mademoiselle d'Ogeron in her mind. And instantly would have recalled the words had she been able. But Peter Blood swept them lightly aside, reading into them none of her meaning, as she feared he would.

"Aye—a deal of lies, devil a doubt, as I could prove to you."

"I cannot think why you should trouble to put yourself on your defence," she discouraged him.

"So that ye may think less badly of me than you do."

"What I think of you can be a very little matter to you, sir."

This was a disarming stroke. He abandoned combat for expostulation.

"Can ye say that now? Can ye say that, beholding me in this livery of a service I despise? Didn't ye tell me that I might redeem the past? It's little enough I am concerned to redeem the past save only in your eyes. In my own I've done nothing at all that I am ashamed of, considering the provocation I received."

Her glance faltered, and fell away before his own that was so intent.

"I... I can't think why you should speak to me like this," she said, with less than her earlier assurance.

"Ah, now, can't ye, indeed?" he cried. "Sure, then, I'll be telling ye."

"Oh, please." There was real alarm in her voice. "I realize fully what you did, and I realize that partly, at least, you may have been urged by consideration for myself. Believe me, I am very grateful. I shall always be grateful."

"But if it's also your intention always to think of me as a thief and a pirate, faith, ye may keep your gratitude for all the good it's like to do me."

A livelier colour crept into her cheeks. There was a perceptible heave of the slight breast that faintly swelled the flimsy bodice of white silk. But if she resented his tone and his words, she stifled her resentment. She realized that perhaps she had, herself, provoked his anger. She honestly desired to make amends.

"You are mistaken," she began. "It isn't that."

But they were fated to misunderstand each other.

Jealousy, that troubler of reason, had been over-busy with his wits as it had with hers.

"What is it, then?" quoth he, and added the question: "Lord Julian?"

She started, and stared at him blankly indignant now.

"Och, be frank with me," he urged her, unpardonably. "'Twill be a kindness, so it will."

For a moment she stood before him with quickened breathing, the colour ebbing and flowing in her cheeks. Then she looked past him, and tilted her chin forward.

"You... you are quite insufferable," she said. "I beg that you will let me pass."

He stepped aside, and with the broad feathered hat which he still held in his hand, he waved her on towards the house.

"I'll not be detaining you any longer, ma'am. After all, the cursed thing I did for nothing can be undone. Ye'll remember afterwards that it was your hardness drove me."

She moved to depart, then checked, and faced him again. It was she now who was on her defence, her voice quivering with indignation.

"You take that tone! You dare to take that tone!" she cried, astounding him by her sudden vehemence. "You have the effrontery to upbraid me because I will not take your hands when I know how they are stained; when I know you for a murderer and worse?"

He stared at her open-mouthed.

"A murderer—I?" he said at last.

"Must I name your victims? Did you not murder Levasseur?"

"Levasseur?" He smiled a little. "So they've told you about that!"

"Do you deny it?"

"I killed him, it is true. I can remember killing another man in circumstances that were very similar. That was in Bridgetown on the night of the Spanish raid. Mary Traill would tell you of it. She was present."

He clapped his hat on his head with a certain abrupt fierceness, and strode angrily away, before she could answer or even grasp the full significance of what he had said.

XXIII

HOSTAGES

Peter Blood stood in the pillared portico of Government House, and with unseeing eyes that were laden with pain and anger, stared out across the great harbour of Port Royal to the green hills rising from the farther shore and the ridge of the Blue Mountains beyond, showing hazily through the quivering heat.

He was aroused by the return of the black man who had gone to announce him, and following now this slave, he made his way through the house to the wide piazza behind it, in whose shade Colonel Bishop and my Lord Julian Wade took what little air there was.

"So ye've come," the Deputy-Governor hailed him, and followed the greeting by a series of grunts of vague but apparently ill-humoured import.

He did not trouble to rise, not even when Lord Julian, obeying the instincts of finer breeding, set him the example. From under scowling brows the wealthy Barbados planter considered his sometime slave, who, hat in hand, leaning lightly upon his long beribboned cane, revealed nothing in his countenance of the anger which was being steadily nourished by this cavalier reception.

At last, with scowling brow and in self-sufficient tones, Colonel Bishop delivered himself.

"I have sent for you, Captain Blood, because of certain news that has just reached me. I am informed that yesterday evening a frigate left the harbour having on board your associate Wolverstone and a hundred men of the hundred and fifty that were serving under you. His lordship and I shall be glad to have your explanation of how you came to permit that departure."

"Permit?" quoth Blood. "I ordered it."

The answer left Bishop speechless for a moment. Then:

"You ordered it?" he said in accents of unbelief, whilst Lord Julian raised his eyebrows. "'Swounds! Perhaps you'll explain yourself? Whither has Wolverstone gone?"

"To Tortuga. He's gone with a message to the officers commanding the other four ships of the fleet that is awaiting me there, telling them what's happened and why they are no longer to expect me."

Bishop's great face seemed to swell and its high colour to deepen. He swung to Lord Julian.

"You hear that, my lord? Deliberately he has let Wolverstone loose upon the seas again—Wolverstone, the worst of all that gang of pirates after himself. I hope your lordship begins at last to perceive the folly of granting the King's commission to such a man as this against all my counsels. Why, this thing is... it's just mutiny... treason! By God! It's matter for a court-martial."

"Will you cease your blather of mutiny and treason and courts-martial?" Blood put on his hat, and sat down unbidden. "I have sent Wolverstone to inform Hagthorpe and Christian and Yberville and the rest of my lads that they've one clear month in which to follow my example, quit piracy, and get back to their boucans or their logwood, or else sail out of the Caribbean Sea. That's what I've done."

"But the men?" his lordship interposed in his level, cultured voice. "This hundred men that Wolverstone has taken with him?"

"They are those of my crew who have no taste for King James's service, and have preferred to seek work of other kinds. It was in our compact, my lord, that there should be no constraining of my men."

"I don't remember it," said his lordship, with sincerity.

Blood looked at him in surprise. Then he shrugged. "Faith, I'm not to blame for your lordship's poor memory. I say that it was so; and I don't lie. I've never found it necessary. In any case ye couldn't have supposed that I should consent to anything different."

And then the Deputy-Governor exploded.

"You have given those damned rascals in Tortuga this warning so that they may escape! That is what you have done. That is how you abuse the commission that has saved your own neck!"

Peter Blood considered him steadily, his face impassive. "I will remind you," he said at last, very quietly, "that the object in view was—leaving out of account your own appetites which, as every one knows, are just those of a hangman—to rid the Caribbean of buccaneers. Now, I've taken the most effective way of accomplishing that object. The knowledge that I've entered the King's service should in itself go far towards disbanding the fleet of which I was until lately the admiral."

"I see!" sneered the Deputy-Governor malevolently. "And if it does not?"

"It will be time enough then to consider what else is to be done."

Lord Julian forestalled a fresh outburst on the part of Bishop.

"It is possible," he said, "that my Lord Sunderland will be satisfied, provided that the solution is such as you promise."

It was a courteous, conciliatory speech. Urged by friendliness towards Blood and understanding of the difficult position in which the buccaneer found himself, his lordship was disposed to take his stand upon the letter of his instructions. Therefore he now held out a friendly hand to help him over the latest and most difficult obstacle which Blood himself had enabled Bishop to place in the way of his redemption. Unfortunately the last person from whom Peter Blood desired assistance at that moment was this young nobleman, whom he regarded with the jaundiced eyes of jealousy.

"Anyway," he answered, with a suggestion of defiance and more than a suggestion of a sneer, "it's the most ye should expect from me, and certainly it's the most ye'll get."

His lordship frowned, and dabbed his lips with a handkerchief.

"I don't think that I quite like the way you put it. Indeed, upon reflection, Captain Blood, I am sure that I do not."

"I am sorry for that, so I am," said Blood impudently. "But there it is. I'm not on that account concerned to modify it."

His lordship's pale eyes opened a little wider. Languidly he raised his eyebrows.

"Ah!" he said. "You're a prodigiously uncivil fellow. You disappoint me, sir. I had formed the notion that you might be a gentleman."

"And that's not your lordship's only mistake," Bishop cut in. "You made a worse when you gave him the King's commission, and so sheltered the rascal from the gallows I had prepared for him in Port Royal."

"Aye—but the worst mistake of all in this matter of commissions," said Blood to his lordship, "was the one that trade this greasy slaver Deputy-Governor of Jamaica instead of its hangman, which is the office for which he's by nature fitted."

"Captain Blood!" said his lordship sharply in reproof. "Upon my soul and honour, sir, you go much too far. You are..."

But here Bishop interrupted him. He had heaved himself to his feet, at last, and was venting his fury in unprintable abuse. Captain Blood, who had also risen, stood apparently impassive, for the storm to spend itself. When at last this happened, he addressed himself quietly to Lord Julian, as if Colonel Bishop had not spoken.

"Your lordship was about to say?" he asked, with challenging smoothness.

But his lordship had by now recovered his habitual composure, and was again disposed to be conciliatory. He laughed and shrugged.

"Faith! here's a deal of unnecessary heat," said he. "And God knows this plaguey climate provides enough of that. Perhaps, Colonel Bishop, you are a little uncompromising; and you, sir, are certainly a deal too peppery. I have said, speaking on behalf of my Lord Sunderland, that I am content to await the result of your experiment."

But Bishop's fury had by now reached a stage in which it was not to be restrained.

"Are you, indeed?" he roared. "Well, then, I am not. This is a matter in which your lordship must allow me to be the better judge. And, anyhow, I'll take the risk of acting on my own responsibility."

Lord Julian abandoned the struggle. He smiled wearily, shrugged, and waved a hand in implied resignation. The Deputy-Governor stormed on.

"Since my lord here has given you a commission, I can't regularly deal with you out of hand for piracy as you deserve. But you shall answer before a court-martial for your action in the matter of Wolverstone, and take the consequences."

"I see," said Blood. "Now we come to it. And it's yourself as Deputy-Governor will preside over that same court-martial. So that ye can wipe off old scores by hanging me, it's little ye care how ye do it!" He laughed, and added: "Praemonitus, praemunitus."

"What shall that mean?" quoth Lord Julian sharply.

"I had imagined that your lordship would have had some education."

He was at pains, you see, to be provocative.

"It's not the literal meaning I am asking, sir," said Lord Julian, with frosty dignity. "I want to know what you desire me to understand?"

"I'll leave your lordship guessing," said Blood. "And I'll be wishing ye both a very good day." He swept off his feathered hat, and made them a leg very elegantly.

"Before you go," said Bishop, "and to save you from any idle rashness, I'll tell you that the Harbour-Master and the Commandant have their orders. You don't leave Port Royal, my fine gallows bird. Damme, I mean to provide you with permanent moorings here, in Execution Dock."

Peter Blood stiffened, and his vivid blue eyes stabbed the bloated face of his enemy. He passed his long cane into his left hand, and with his right thrust negligently into the breast of his doublet, he swung to Lord Julian, who was thoughtfully frowning.

"Your lordship, I think, promised me immunity from this."

"What I may have promised," said his lordship, "your own conduct makes it difficult to perform." He rose. "You did me a service, Captain Blood, and I had hoped that we might be friends. But since you prefer to have it otherwise..." He shrugged, and waved a hand towards the Deputy-Governor.

Blood completed the sentence in his own way:

"Ye mean that ye haven't the strength of character to resist the urgings of a bully." He was apparently at his ease, and actually smiling. "Well, well—as I said before—praemonitus, praemunitus. I'm afraid that ye're no scholar, Bishop, or ye'd know that I means forewarned, forearmed."

"Forewarned? Ha!" Bishop almost snarled. "The warning comes a little late. You do not leave this house." He took a step in the direction of the doorway, and raised his voice. "Ho there..." he was beginning to call.

Then with a sudden audible catch in his breath, he stopped short. Captain Blood's right hand had reemerged from the breast of his doublet, bringing with it a long pistol with silver mountings richly chased, which he levelled within a foot of the Deputy-Governor's head.

"And forearmed," said he. "Don't stir from where you are, my lord, or there may be an accident."

And my lord, who had been moving to Bishop's assistance, stood instantly arrested. Chap-fallen, with much of his high colour suddenly departed, the Deputy-Governor was swaying on unsteady legs. Peter Blood considered him with a grimness that increased his panic.

"I marvel that I don't pistol you without more ado, ye fat blackguard. If I don't, it's for the same reason that once before I gave ye your life when it was forfeit. Ye're not aware of the reason, to be sure; but it may comfort ye to know that it exists. At the same time I'll warn ye not to put too heavy a strain on my generosity, which resides at the moment in my trigger-finger. Ye mean to hang me, and since that's the worst that can happen to me anyway, you'll realize that I'll not boggle at increasing the account by spilling your nasty blood." He cast his cane from him, thus disengaging his left hand. "Be good enough to give me your arm, Colonel Bishop. Come, come, man, your arm."

Under the compulsion of that sharp tone, those resolute eyes, and that gleaming pistol, Bishop obeyed without demur. His recent foul volubility was stemmed. He could not trust himself to speak. Captain Blood tucked his left arm through the Deputy-Governor's proffered right. Then he thrust his own right hand with its pistol back into the breast of his doublet.

"Though invisible, it's aiming at ye none the less, and I give you my word of honour that I'll shoot ye dead upon the very least provocation, whether that provocation is yours or another's. Ye'll bear that in mind, Lord Julian. And now, ye greasy hangman, step out as brisk and lively as ye can, and behave as naturally as ye may, or it's the black stream of Cocytus ye'll be contemplating." Arm in arm they passed through the house, and down the garden, where Arabella lingered, awaiting Peter Blood's return.

Consideration of his parting words had brought her first turmoil of mind, then a clear perception of what might be indeed the truth of the death of Levasseur. She perceived that the particular inference drawn from it might similarly have been drawn from Blood's deliverance of Mary Traill. When a man so risks his life for a woman, the rest is easily assumed. For the men who will take such risks without hope of personal gain are few. Blood was of those few, as he had proved in the case of Mary Traill.

It needed no further assurances of his to convince her that she had done him a monstrous injustice. She remembered words he had used—words overheard aboard his ship (which he had named the Arabella) on the night of her deliverance from the Spanish admiral; words he had uttered when she had approved his acceptance of the King's commission; the words he had spoken to her that very morning, which had but served to move her indignation. All these assumed a fresh meaning in her mind, delivered now from its unwarranted preconceptions.

Therefore she lingered there in the garden, awaiting his return that she might make amends; that she might set a term to all misunderstanding. In impatience she awaited him. Yet her patience, it seemed, was to be tested further. For when at last he came, it was in company—unusually close and intimate company—with her uncle. In vexation she realized that explanations must be postponed. Could she have guessed the extent of that postponement, vexation would have been changed into despair.

He passed, with his companion, from that fragrant garden into the courtyard of the fort. Here the Commandant, who had been instructed to hold himself in readiness with the necessary men against the need to effect the arrest of Captain Blood, was amazed by the curious spectacle of the Deputy-Governor of Jamaica strolling forth arm in arm and apparently on the friendliest terms with the intended prisoner. For as they went, Blood was chatting and laughing briskly.

They passed out of the gates unchallenged, and so came to the mole where the cock-boat from the Arabella was waiting. They took their places side by side in the stern sheets, and were pulled away together, always very close and friendly, to the great red ship where Jeremy Pitt so anxiously awaited news.

You conceive the master's amazement to see the Deputy-Governor come toiling up the entrance ladder, with Blood following very close behind him.

"Sure, I walked into a trap, as ye feared, Jeremy," Blood hailed him. "But I walked out again, and fetched the trapper with me. He loves his life, does this fat rascal."

Colonel Bishop stood in the waist, his great face blenched to the colour of clay, his mouth loose, almost afraid to look at the sturdy ruffians who lounged about the shot-rack on the main hatch.

Blood shouted an order to the bo'sun, who was leaning against the forecastle bulkhead.

"Throw me a rope with a running noose over the yardarm there, against the need of it. Now, don't be alarming yourself, Colonel, darling. It's no more than a provision against your being unreasonable, which I am sure ye'll not be. We'll talk the matter over whiles we are dining, for I trust ye'll not refuse to honour my table by your company."

He led away the will-less, cowed bully to the great cabin. Benjamin, the black man steward, in white drawers and cotton shirt, made haste by his command to serve dinner.

Colonel Bishop collapsed on the locker under the stern ports, and spoke now for the first time.

"May I ask wha... what are your intentions?" he quavered.

"Why, nothing sinister, Colonel. Although ye deserve nothing less than that same rope and yardarm, I assure you that it's to be employed only as a last resource. Ye've said his lordship made a mistake when he handed me the commission which the Secretary of State did me the honour to design for me. I'm disposed to agree with you; so I'll take to the sea again. Cras ingens iterabimus aequor. It's the fine Latin scholar ye'll be when I've done with ye. I'll be getting back to Tortuga and my buccaneers, who at least are honest, decent fellows. So I've fetched ye aboard as a hostage."

"My God!" groaned the Deputy-Governor. "Ye... ye never mean that ye'll carry me to Tortuga!"

Blood laughed outright. "Oh, I'd never serve ye such a bad turn as that. No, no. All I want is that ye ensure my safe departure from Port Royal. And, if ye're reasonable, I'll not even trouble you to swim for it this time. Ye've given certain orders to your Harbour-Master, and others to the Commandant of your plaguey fort. Ye'll be so good as to send for them both aboard here, and inform them in my presence that the Arabella is leaving this afternoon on the King's service and is to pass out unmolested. And so as to make quite sure of their obedience, they shall go a little voyage with us, themselves. Here's what you require. Now write—unless you prefer the yardarm."

Colonel Bishop heaved himself up in a pet. "You constrain me with violence..." he was beginning.

Blood smoothly interrupted him.

"Sure, now, I am not constraining you at all. I'm giving you a perfectly free choice between the pen and the rope. It's a matter for yourself entirely."

Bishop glared at him; then shrugging heavily, he took up the pen and sat down at the table. In an unsteady hand he wrote that summons to his officers. Blood despatched it ashore; and then bade his unwilling guest to table.

"I trust, Colonel, your appetite is as stout as usual."

The wretched Bishop took the seat to which he was commanded. As for eating, however, that was not easy to a man in his position; nor did Blood press him. The Captain, himself, fell to with a good appetite. But before he was midway through the meal came Hayton to inform him that Lord Julian Wade had just come aboard, and was asking to see him instantly.

"I was expecting him," said Blood. "Fetch him in."

Lord Julian came. He was very stern and dignified. His eyes took in the situation at a glance, as Captain Blood rose to greet him.

"It's mighty friendly of you to have joined us, my lord."

"Captain Blood," said his lordship with asperity, "I find your humour a little forced. I don't know what may be your intentions; but I wonder do you realize the risks you are running."

"And I wonder does your lordship realize the risk to yourself in following us aboard as I had counted that you would."

"What shall that mean, sir?"

Blood signalled to Benjamin, who was standing behind Bishop.

"Set a chair for his lordship. Hayton, send his lordship's boat ashore. Tell them he'll not be returning yet awhile."

"What's that?" cried his lordship. "Blister me! D'ye mean to detain me? Are ye mad?"

"Better wait, Hayton, in case his lordship should turn violent," said Blood. "You, Benjamin, you heard the message. Deliver it."

"Will you tell me what you intend, sir?" demanded his lordship, quivering with anger.

"Just to make myself and my lads here safe from Colonel Bishop's gallows. I've said that I trusted to your gallantry not to leave him in the lurch, but to follow him hither, and there's a note from his hand gone ashore to summon the Harbour-

Master and the Commandant of the fort. Once they are aboard, I shall have all the hostages I need for our safety."

"You scoundrel!" said his lordship through his teeth.

"Sure, now, that's entirely a matter of the point of view," said Blood. "Ordinarily it isn't the kind of name I could suffer any man to apply to me. Still, considering that ye willingly did me a service once, and that ye're likely unwillingly to do me another now, I'll overlook your discourtesy, so I will."

His lordship laughed. "You fool," he said. "Do you dream that I came aboard your pirate ship without taking my measures? I informed the Commandant of exactly how you had compelled Colonel Bishop to accompany you. Judge now whether he or the Harbour-Master will obey the summons, or whether you will be allowed to depart as you imagine."

Blood's face became grave. "I'm sorry for that," said he.

I thought you would be, answered his lordship.

"Oh, but not on my own account. It's the Deputy-Governor there I'm sorry for. D'ye know what Ye've done? Sure, now, ye've very likely hanged him."

"My God!" cried Bishop in a sudden increase of panic.

"If they so much as put a shot across my bows, up goes their Deputy-Governor to the yardarm. Your only hope, Colonel, lies in the fact that I shall send them word of that intention. And so that you may mend as far as you can the harm you have done, it's yourself shall bear them the message, my lord."

"I'll see you damned before I do," fumed his lordship.

"Why, that's unreasonable and unreasoning. But if ye insist, why, another messenger will do as well, and another hostage aboard—as I had originally intended—will make my hand the stronger."

Lord Julian stared at him, realizing exactly what he had refused.

"You'll think better of it now that ye understand?" quoth Blood.

"Aye, in God's name, go, my lord," spluttered Bishop, "and make yourself obeyed. This damned pirate has me by the throat."

His lordship surveyed him with an eye that was not by any means admiring. "Why, if that is your wish..." he began. Then he shrugged, and turned again to Blood.

"I suppose I can trust you that no harm will come to Colonel Bishop if you are allowed to sail?"

"You have my word for it," said Blood. "And also that I shall put him safely ashore again without delay."

Lord Julian bowed stiffly to the cowering Deputy-Governor. "You understand, sir, that I do as you desire," he said coldly.

"Aye, man, aye!" Bishop assented hastily.

"Very well." Lord Julian bowed again and took his departure. Blood escorted him to the entrance ladder at the foot of which still swung the Arabella's own cock-boat.

"It's goodbye, my lord," said Blood. "And there's another thing." He proffered a parchment that he had drawn from his pocket. "It's the commission. Bishop was right when he said it was a mistake."

Lord Julian considered him, and considering him his expression softened.

"I am sorry," he said sincerely.

"In other circumstances..." began Blood. "Oh, but there! Ye'll understand. The boat's waiting."

Yet with his foot on the first rung of the ladder, Lord Julian hesitated.

"I still do not perceive—blister me if I do!—why you should not have found some one else to carry your message to the Commandant, and kept me aboard as an added hostage for his obedience to your wishes."

Blood's vivid eyes looked into the other's that were clear and honest, and he smiled, a little wistfully. A moment he seemed to hesitate. Then he explained himself quite fully.

"Why shouldn't I tell you? It's the same reason that's been urging me to pick a quarrel with you so that I might have the satisfaction of slipping a couple of feet of steel into your vitals. When I accepted your commission, I was moved to think it might redeem me in the eyes of Miss Bishop—for whose sake, as you may have guessed, I took it. But I have discovered that such a thing is beyond accomplishment. I should have known it for a sick man's dream. I have discovered also that if she's choosing you, as I believe she is, she's choosing wisely between us, and that's why I'll not have your life risked by keeping you aboard whilst the message goes by another who might bungle it. And now perhaps ye'll understand."

Lord Julian stared at him bewildered. His long, aristocratic face was very pale.

"My God!" he said. "And you tell me this?"

"I tell you because... Oh, plague on it!—so that ye may tell her; so that she may be made to realize that there's something of the unfortunate gentleman left under the thief and pirate she accounts me, and that her own good is my supreme desire. Knowing that, she may... faith, she may remember me more kindly—if it's only in her prayers. That's all, my lord."

Lord Julian continued to look at the buccaneer in silence. In silence, at last, he held out his hand; and in silence Blood took it.

"I wonder whether you are right," said his lordship, "and whether you are not the better man."

"Where she is concerned see that you make sure that I am right. Goodbye to you."

Lord Julian wrung his hand in silence, went down the ladder, and was pulled ashore. From the distance he waved to Blood, who stood leaning on the bulwarks watching the receding cock-boat.

The Arabella sailed within the hour, moving lazily before a sluggish breeze. The fort remained silent and there was no movement from the fleet to hinder her departure. Lord Julian had carried the message effectively, and had added to it his own personal commands.

XXIV

WAR

Five miles out at sea from Port Royal, whence the details of the coast of Jamaica were losing their sharpness, the Arabella hove to, and the sloop she had been towing was warped alongside.

Captain Blood escorted his compulsory guest to the head of the ladder. Colonel Bishop, who for two hours and more had been in a state of mortal anxiety, breathed freely at last; and as the tide of his fears receded, so that of his deep-rooted hate of this audacious buccaneer resumed its normal flow. But he practised circumspection. If in his heart he vowed that once back in Port Royal there was no effort he would spare, no nerve he would not strain, to bring Peter Blood to final moorings in Execution Dock, at least he kept that vow strictly to himself.

Peter Blood had no illusions. He was not, and never would be, the complete pirate. There was not another buccaneer in all the Caribbean who would have denied himself the pleasure of stringing Colonel Bishop from the yardarm, and by thus finally stifling the vindictive planter's hatred have increased his own security. But Blood was not of these. Moreover, in the case of Colonel Bishop there was a particular reason for restraint. Because he was Arabella Bishop's uncle, his life must remain sacred to Captain Blood.

And so the Captain smiled into the sallow, bloated face and the little eyes that fixed him with a malevolence not to be dissembled.

"A safe voyage home to you, Colonel, darling," said he in valediction, and from his easy, smiling manner you would never have dreamt of the pain he carried in his breast. "It's the second time ye've served me for a hostage. Ye'll be well advised to avoid a third. I'm not lucky to you, Colonel, as you should be perceiving."

Jeremy Pitt, the master, lounging at Blood's elbow, looked darkly upon the departure of the Deputy-Governor. Behind them a little mob of grim, stalwart, sun-tanned buccaneers were restrained from cracking Bishop like a flea only by their submission to the dominant will of their leader. They had learnt from Pitt while yet in Port Royal of their Captain's danger, and whilst as ready as he to throw over the King's service which had been thrust upon them, yet they resented the manner in which this had been rendered necessary, and they marvelled now at Blood's restraint where Bishop was concerned. The Deputy-Governor looked round and met the lowering hostile glances of those fierce eyes. Instinct warned him that his life at that moment was held precariously, that an injudicious word might precipitate an explosion of hatred from which no human power could save him. Therefore he said nothing. He inclined his head in silence to the Captain, and went blundering and stumbling in his haste down that ladder to the sloop and its waiting black man crew.

They pushed off the craft from the red hull of the Arabella, bent to their sweeps, then, hoisting sail, headed back for Port Royal, intent upon reaching it before darkness should come down upon them. And Bishop, the great bulk of him huddled in the stem sheets, sat silent, his black brows knitted, his coarse lips pursed, malevolence and vindictiveness so whelming now his recent panic that he forgot his near escape of the yardarm and the running noose.

On the mole at Port Royal, under the low, embattled wall of the fort, Major Mallard and Lord Julian waited to receive him, and it was with infinite relief that they assisted him from the sloop.

Major Mallard was disposed to be apologetic.

"Glad to see you safe, sir," said he. "I'd have sunk Blood's ship in spite of your excellency's being aboard but for your own orders by Lord Julian, and his lordship's assurance that he had Blood's word for it that no harm should come to you so that no harm came to him. I'll confess I thought it rash of his lordship to accept the word of a damned pirate..."

"I have found it as good as another's," said his lordship, cropping the Major's too eager eloquence. He spoke with an unusual degree of that frosty dignity he could assume upon occasion. The fact is that his lordship was in an exceedingly bad humour. Having written jubilantly home to the Secretary of State that his mission had succeeded, he was now faced with the necessity of writing again to confess that this success had been ephemeral. And because Major Mallard's crisp mostachios were lifted by a sneer at the notion of a buccaneer's word being acceptable, he added still more sharply: "My justification is here in the person of Colonel Bishop safely returned. As against that, sir, your opinion does not weigh for very much. You should realize it."

"Oh, as your lordship says." Major Mallard's manner was tinged with irony. "To be sure, here is the Colonel safe and sound. And out yonder is Captain Blood, also safe and sound, to begin his piratical ravages all over again."

"I do not propose to discuss the reasons with you, Major Mallard."

"And, anyway, it's not for long," growled the Colonel, finding speech at last. "No, by..." He emphasized the assurance by an unprintable oath. "If I spend the last shilling of my fortune and the last ship of the Jamaica fleet, I'll have that rascal in a hempen necktie before I rest. And I'll not be long about it." He had empurpled in his angry vehemence, and the veins of his forehead stood out like whipcord. Then he checked.

"You did well to follow Lord Julian's instructions," he commended the Major. With that he turned from him, and took his lordship by the arm. "Come, my lord. We must take order about this, you and I."

They went off together, skirting the redoubt, and so through courtyard and garden to the house where Arabella waited anxiously. The sight of her uncle brought her infinite relief, not only on his own account, but on account also of Captain Blood.

"You took a great risk, sir," she gravely told Lord Julian after the ordinary greetings had been exchanged.

But Lord Julian answered her as he had answered Major Mallard. "There was no risk, ma'am."

She looked at him in some astonishment. His long, aristocratic face wore a more melancholy, pensive air than usual. He answered the enquiry in her glance:

"So that Blood's ship were allowed to pass the fort, no harm could come to Colonel Bishop. Blood pledged me his word for that."

A faint smile broke the set of her lips, which hitherto had been wistful, and a little colour tinged her cheeks. She would have pursued the subject, but the Deputy-Governor's mood did not permit it. He sneered and snorted at the notion of Blood's word being good for anything, forgetting that he owed to it his own preservation at that moment.

At supper, and for long thereafter he talked of nothing but Blood—of how he would lay him by the heels, and what hideous things he would perform upon his body. And as he drank heavily the while, his speech became increasingly gross and his threats increasingly horrible; until in the end Arabella withdrew, white-faced and almost on the verge of tears. It was not often that Bishop revealed himself to his niece. Oddly enough, this coarse, overbearing planter went in a certain awe of that slim girl. It was as if she had inherited from her father the respect in which he had always been held by his brother.

Lord Julian, who began to find Bishop disgusting beyond endurance, excused himself soon after, and went in quest of the lady. He had yet to deliver the message from Captain Blood, and this, he thought, would be his opportunity. But Miss Bishop had retired for the night, and Lord Julian must curb his impatience—it amounted by now to nothing less—until the morrow.

Very early next morning, before the heat of the day came to render the open intolerable to his lordship, he espied her from his window moving amid the azaleas in the garden. It was a fitting setting for one who was still as much a delightful novelty to him in womanhood as was the azalea among flowers. He hurried forth to join her, and when, aroused from her pensiveness, she had given him a good-morrow, smiling and frank, he explained himself by the announcement that he bore her a message from Captain Blood.

He observed her little start and the slight quiver of her lips, and observed thereafter not only her pallor and the shadowy rings about her eyes, but also that unusually wistful air which last night had escaped his notice.

They moved out of the open to one of the terraces, where a pergola of orange-trees provided a shaded sauntering space that was at once cool and fragrant. As they went, he considered her admiringly, and marvelled at himself that it should have taken him so long fully to realize her slim, unusual grace, and to find her, as he now did, so entirely desirable, a woman whose charm must irradiate all the life of a man, and touch its commonplaces into magic.

He noted the sheen of her red-brown hair, and how gracefully one of its heavy ringlets coiled upon her slender, milk-white neck. She wore a gown of shimmering grey silk, and a scarlet rose, fresh-gathered, was pinned at her breast like a splash of blood. Always thereafter when he thought of her it was as he saw her at that moment, as never, I think, until that moment had he seen her.

In silence they paced on a little way into the green shade. Then she paused and faced him.

"You said something of a message, sir," she reminded him, thus betraying some of her impatience.

He fingered the ringlets of his periwig, a little embarrassed how to deliver himself, considering how he should begin. "He desired me," he said at last, "to give you a message that should prove to you that there is still something left in him of the unfortunate gentleman that... that . ., for which once you knew him."

"That is not now necessary," said she very gravely. He misunderstood her, of course, knowing nothing of the enlightenment that yesterday had come to her.

"I think..., nay, I know that you do him an injustice," said he.

Her hazel eyes continued to regard him.

"If you will deliver the message, it may enable me to judge."

To him, this was confusing. He did not immediately answer. He found that he had not sufficiently considered the terms he should employ, and the matter, after all, was of an exceeding delicacy, demanding delicate handling. It was not so much that he was concerned to deliver a message as to render it a vehicle by which to plead his own cause. Lord Julian, well versed in the lore of womankind and usually at his ease with ladies of the beau-monde, found himself oddly constrained before this frank and unsophisticated niece of a colonial planter.

They moved on in silence and as if by common consent towards the brilliant sunshine where the pergola was intersected by the avenue leading upwards to the house. Across this patch of light fluttered a gorgeous butterfly, that was like black and scarlet velvet and large as a man's hand. His lordship's brooding eyes followed it out of sight before he answered.

"It is not easy. Stab me, it is not. He was a man who deserved well. And amongst us we have marred his chances: your uncle, because he could not forget his rancour; you, because... because having told him that in the King's service he would find his redemption of what was past, you would not afterwards admit to him that he was so redeemed. And this, although concern to rescue you was the chief motive of his embracing that same service."

She had turned her shoulder to him so that he should not see her face.

"I know. I know now," she said softly. Then after a pause she added the question: "And you? What part has your lordship had in this—that you should incriminate yourself with us?"

"My part?" Again he hesitated, then plunged recklessly on, as men do when determined to perform a thing they fear. "If I understood him aright, if he understood aright, himself, my part, though entirely passive, was none the less effective. I implore you to observe that I but report his own words. I say nothing for myself." His lordship's unusual nervousness was steadily increasing. "He thought, then—so he told me—that my presence here had contributed to his inability to redeem himself in your sight; and unless he were so redeemed, then was redemption nothing."

She faced him fully, a frown of perplexity bringing her brows together above her troubled eyes.

"He thought that you had contributed?" she echoed. It was clear she asked for enlightenment. He plunged on to afford it her, his glance a little scared, his cheeks flushing.

"Aye, and he said so in terms which told me something that I hope above all things, and yet dare not believe, for,

God knows, I am no coxcomb, Arabella. He said... but first let me tell you how I was placed. I had gone aboard his ship to demand the instant surrender of your uncle whom he held captive. He laughed at me. Colonel Bishop should be a hostage for his safety. By rashly venturing aboard his ship, I afforded him in my own person yet another hostage as valuable at least as Colonel Bishop. Yet he bade me depart; not from the fear of consequences, for he is above fear, nor from any personal esteem for me whom he confessed that he had come to find detestable; and this for the very reason that made him concerned for my safety."

"I do not understand," she said, as he paused. "Is not that a contradiction in itself?"

"It seems so only. The fact is, Arabella, this unfortunate man has the... the temerity to love you."

She cried out at that, and clutched her breast whose calm was suddenly disturbed. Her eyes dilated as she stared at him.

"I... I've startled you," said he, with concern. "I feared I should. But it was necessary so that you may understand."

"Go on," she bade him.

"Well, then: he saw in me one who made it impossible that he should win you—so he said. Therefore he could with satisfaction have killed me. But because my death might cause you pain, because your happiness was the thing that above all things he desired, he surrendered that part of his guarantee of safety which my person afforded him. If his departure should be hindered, and I should lose my life in what might follow, there was the risk that... that you might mourn me. That risk he would not take. Him you deemed a thief and a pirate, he said, and added that—I am giving you his own words always—if in choosing between us two, your choice, as he believed, would fall on me, then were you in his opinion choosing wisely. Because of that he bade me leave his ship, and had me put ashore."

She looked at him with eyes that were aswim with tears. He took a step towards her, a catch in his breath, his hand held out.

"Was he right, Arabella? My life's happiness hangs upon your answer."

But she continued silently to regard him with those tear-laden eyes, without speaking, and until she spoke he dared not advance farther.

A doubt, a tormenting doubt beset him. When presently she spoke, he saw how true had been the instinct of which that doubt was born, for her words revealed the fact that of all that he had said the only thing that had touched her consciousness and absorbed it from all other considerations was Blood's conduct as it regarded herself.

"He said that!" she cried. "He did that! Oh!" She turned away, and through the slender, clustering trunks of the bordering orange-trees she looked out across the glittering waters of the great harbour to the distant hills. Thus for a little while, my lord standing stiffly, fearfully, waiting for fuller revelation of her mind. At last it came, slowly, deliberately, in a voice that at moments was half suffocated. "Last night when my uncle displayed his rancour and his evil rage, it began to be borne in upon me that such vindictiveness can belong only to those who have wronged. It is the frenzy into which men whip themselves to justify an evil passion. I must have known then, if I had not already learnt it, that I had been too credulous of all the unspeakable things attributed to Peter Blood. Yesterday I had his own explanation of that tale of Levasseur that you heard in St. Nicholas. And now this... this but gives me confirmation of his truth and worth. To a scoundrel such as I was too readily brought to believe him, the act of which you have just told me would have been impossible."

"That is my own opinion," said his lordship gently.

"It must be. But even if it were not, that would now weigh for nothing. What weighs—oh, so heavily and bitterly—is the thought that but for the words in which yesterday I repelled him, he might have been saved. If only I could have spoken to him again before he went! I waited for him; but my uncle was with him, and I had no suspicion that he was going away again. And now he is lost—back at his outlawry and piracy, in which ultimately he will be taken and destroyed. And the fault is mine—mine!"

"What are you saying? The only agents were your uncle's hostility and his own obstinacy which would not study compromise. You must not blame yourself for anything."

She swung to him with some impatience, her eyes aswim in tears. "You can say that, and in spite of his message, which in itself tells how much I was to blame! It was my treatment of him, the epithets I cast at him that drove him. So much he has told you. I know it to be true."

"You have no cause for shame," said he. "As for your sorrow—why, if it will afford you solace—you may still count on me to do what man can to rescue him from this position."

She caught her breath.

"You will do that!" she cried with sudden eager hopefulness. "You promise?" She held out her hand to him impulsively. He took it in both his own.

"I promise," he answered her. And then, retaining still the hand she had surrendered to him—"Arabella," he said very gently, "there is still this other matter upon which you have not answered me."

"This other matter?" Was he mad, she wondered.

Could any other matter signify in such a moment.

"This matter that concerns myself; and all my future, oh, so very closely. This thing that Blood believed, that prompted him..., that... that you are not indifferent to me." He saw the fair face change colour and grow troubled once more.

"Indifferent to you?" said she. "Why, no. We have been good friends; we shall continue so, I hope, my lord."

"Friends! Good friends?" He was between dismay and bitterness. "It is not your friendship only that I ask, Arabella. You heard what I said, what I reported. You will not say that Peter Blood was wrong?"

Gently she sought to disengage her hand, the trouble in her face increasing. A moment he resisted; then, realizing what he did, he set her free.

"Arabella!" he cried on a note of sudden pain.

"I have friendship for you, my lord. But only friendship." His castle of hopes came clattering down about him, leaving him a little stunned. As he had said, he was no coxcomb. Yet there was something that he did not understand. She confessed to friendship, and it was in his power to offer her a great position, one to which she, a colonial planter's niece, however wealthy, could never have aspired even in her dreams. This she rejected, yet spoke of friendship. Peter Blood had been mistaken, then. How far had he been mistaken? Had he been as mistaken in her feelings towards himself as he obviously was in her feelings towards his lordship? In that case... His reflections broke short. To speculate was to wound himself in vain. He must know. Therefore he asked her with grim frankness:

"Is it Peter Blood?"

"Peter Blood?" she echoed. At first she did not understand the purport of his question. When understanding came, a flush suffused her face.

"I do not know," she said, faltering a little.

This was hardly a truthful answer. For, as if an obscuring veil had suddenly been rent that morning, she was permitted at last to see Peter Blood in his true relations to other men, and that sight, vouchsafed her twenty-four hours too late, filled her with pity and regret and yearning.

Lord Julian knew enough of women to be left in no further doubt. He bowed his head so that she might not see the anger in his eyes, for as a man of honour he took shame in that anger which as a human being he could not repress.

And because Nature in him was stronger—as it is in most of us—than training, Lord Julian from that moment began, almost in spite of himself, to practise something that was akin to villainy. I regret to chronicle it of one for whom—if I have done him any sort of justice—you should have been conceiving some esteem. But the truth is that the lingering remains of the regard in which he had held Peter Blood were choked by the desire to supplant and destroy a rival. He had passed his word to Arabella that he would use his powerful influence on Blood's behalf. I deplore to set it down that not only did he forget his pledge, but secretly set himself to aid and abet Arabella's uncle in the plans he laid for the trapping and undoing of the buccaneer. He might reasonably have urged—had he been taxed with it—that he conducted himself precisely as his duty demanded. But to that he might have been answered that duty with him was but the slave of jealousy in this.

When the Jamaica fleet put to sea some few days later, Lord Julian sailed with Colonel Bishop in Vice-Admiral Craufurd's flagship. Not only was there no need for either of them to go, but the Deputy-Governor's duties actually demanded that he should remain ashore, whilst Lord Julian, as we know, was a useless man aboard a ship. Yet both set out to hunt Captain Blood, each making of his duty a pretext for the satisfaction of personal aims; and that common purpose became a link between them, binding them in a sort of friendship that must otherwise have been impossible between men so dissimilar in breeding and in aspirations.

The hunt was up. They cruised awhile off Hispaniola, watching the Windward Passage, and suffering the discomforts of the rainy season which had now set in. But they cruised in vain, and after a month of it, returned empty-handed to Port

Royal, there to find awaiting them the most disquieting news from the Old World.

The megalomania of Louis XIV had set Europe in a blaze of war. The French legionaries were ravaging the Rhine provinces, and Spain had joined the nations leagued to defend themselves from the wild ambitions of the King of France. And there was worse than this: there were rumours of civil war in England, where the people had grown weary of the bigoted tyranny of King James. It was reported that William of Orange had been invited to come over.

Weeks passed, and every ship from home brought additional news. William had crossed to England, and in March of that year 1689 they learnt in Jamaica that he had accepted the crown and that James had thrown himself into the arms of France for rehabilitation.

To a kinsman of Sunderland's this was disquieting news, indeed. It was followed by letters from King William's Secretary of State informing Colonel Bishop that there was war with France, and that in view of its effect upon the Colonies a Governor-General was coming out to the West Indies in the person of Lord Willoughby, and that with him came a squadron under the command of Admiral van der Kuylen to reenforce the Jamaica fleet against eventualities.

Bishop realized that this must mean the end of his supreme authority, even though he should continue in Port Royal as Deputy-Governor. Lord Julian, in the lack of direct news to himself, did not know what it might mean to him. But he had been very close and confidential with Colonel Bishop regarding his hopes of Arabella, and Colonel Bishop more than ever, now that political events put him in danger of being retired, was anxious to enjoy the advantages of having a man of Lord Julian's eminence for his relative.

They came to a complete understanding in the matter, and Lord Julian disclosed all that he knew.

"There is one obstacle in our path," said he. "Captain Blood. The girl is in love with him."

"Ye're surely mad!" cried Bishop, when he had recovered speech.

"You are justified of the assumption," said his lordship dolefully. "But I happen to be sane, and to speak with knowledge."

"With knowledge?"

"Arabella herself has confessed it to me."

"The brazen baggage! By God, I'll bring her to her senses." It was the slave-driver speaking, the man who governed with a whip.

"Don't be a fool, Bishop." His lordship's contempt did more than any argument to calm the Colonel. "That's not the way with a girl of Arabella's spirit. Unless you want to wreck my chances for all time, you'll hold your tongue, and not interfere at all."

"Not interfere? My God, what, then?"

"Listen, man. She has a constant mind. I don't think you know your niece. As long as Blood lives, she will wait for him."

"Then with Blood dead, perhaps she will come to her silly senses."

"Now you begin to show intelligence," Lord Julian commended him. "That is the first essential step."

"And here is our chance to take it." Bishop warmed to a sort of enthusiasm. "This war with France removes all restrictions in the matter of Tortuga. We are free to invest it in the service of the Crown. A victory there and we establish ourselves in the favour of this new government."

"Ah!" said Lord Julian, and he pulled thoughtfully at his lip.

"I see that you understand," Bishop laughed coarsely. "Two birds with one stone, eh? We'll hunt this rascal in his lair, right under the beard of the King of France, and we'll take him this time, if we reduce Tortuga to a heap of ashes."

On that expedition they sailed two days later—which would be some three months after Blood's departure—taking every ship of the fleet, and several lesser vessels as auxiliaries. To Arabella and the world in general it was given out that they were going to raid French Hispaniola, which was really the only expedition that could have afforded Colonel Bishop any sort of justification for leaving Jamaica at all at such a time. His sense of duty, indeed, should have kept him fast in Port Royal; but his sense of duty was smothered in hatred—that most fruitless and corruptive of all the emotions. In the great cabin of Vice-Admiral Craufurd's flagship, the Imperator, the Deputy-Governor got drunk that night to celebrate his conviction that the sands of Captain Blood's career were running out.

XXV

THE SERVICE OF KING LOUIS

Meanwhile, some three months before Colonel Bishop set out to reduce Tortuga, Captain Blood, bearing hell in his soul, had blown into its rockbound harbour ahead of the winter gales, and two days ahead of the frigate in which Wolverstone had sailed from Port Royal a day before him.

In that snug anchorage he found his fleet awaiting him—the four ships which had been separated in that gale off the Lesser Antilles, and some seven hundred men composing their crews. Because they had been beginning to grow anxious on his behalf, they gave him the greater welcome. Guns were fired in his honour and the ships made themselves gay with bunting. The town, aroused by all this noise in the harbour, emptied itself upon the jetty, and a vast crowd of men and women of all creeds and nationalities collected there to be present at the coming ashore of the great buccaneer.

Ashore he went, probably for no other reason than to obey the general expectation. His mood was taciturn; his face grim and sneering. Let Wolverstone arrive, as presently he would, and all this hero-worship would turn to execration.

His captains, Hagthorpe, Christian, and Yberville, were on the jetty to receive him, and with them were some hundreds of his buccaneers. He cut short their greetings, and when they plagued him with questions of where he had tarried, he bade them await the coming of Wolverstone, who would satisfy their curiosity to a surfeit. On that he shook them off, and shouldered his way through that heterogeneous throng that was composed of bustling traders of several nations—English, French, and Dutch—of planters and of seamen of various degrees, of buccaneers who were fruit-selling half-castes, black man slaves, some doll-tearsheets and dunghill-queans from the Old World, and all the other types of the human family that converted the quays of Cayona into a disreputable image of Babel.

Winning clear at last, and after difficulties, Captain Blood took his way alone to the fine house of M. d'Ogeron, there to pay his respects to his friends, the Governor and the Governor's family.

At first the buccaneers jumped to the conclusion that Wolverstone was following with some rare prize of war, but gradually from the reduced crew of the Arabella a very different tale leaked out to stem their satisfaction and convert it into perplexity. Partly out of loyalty to their captain, partly because they perceived that if he was guilty of defection they were guilty with him, and partly because being simple, sturdy men of their hands, they were themselves in the main a little confused as to what really had happened, the crew of the Arabella practised reticence with their brethren in Tortuga during those two days before Wolverstone's arrival. But they were not reticent enough to prevent the circulation of certain uneasy rumours and extravagant stories of discreditable adventures—discreditable, that is, from the buccaneering point of view—of which Captain Blood had been guilty.

But that Wolverstone came when he did, it is possible that there would have been an explosion. When, however, the Old Wolf cast anchor in the bay two days later, it was to him all turned for the explanation they were about to demand of Blood.

Now Wolverstone had only one eye; but he saw a deal more with that one eye than do most men with two; and despite his grizzled head—so picturesquely swathed in a green and scarlet turban—he had the sound heart of a boy, and in that heart much love for Peter Blood.

The sight of the Arabella at anchor in the bay had at first amazed him as he sailed round the rocky headland that bore the fort. He rubbed his single eye clear of any deceiving film and looked again. Still he could not believe what it saw. And then a voice at his elbow—the voice of Dyke, who had elected to sail with him—assured him that he was not singular in his bewilderment.

"In the name of Heaven, is that the Arabella or is it the ghost of her?"

The Old Wolf rolled his single eye over Dyke, and opened his mouth to speak. Then he closed it again without having spoken; closed it tightly. He had a great gift of caution, especially in matters that he did not understand. That this was the Arabella he could no longer doubt. That being so, he must think before he spoke. What the devil should the Arabella be doing here, when he had left her in Jamaica? And was Captain Blood aboard and in command, or had the remainder of her hands made off with her, leaving the Captain in Port Royal?

Dyke repeated his question. This time Wolverstone answered him.

"Ye've two eyes to see with, and ye ask me, who's only got one, what it is ye see!"

"But I see the Arabella."

"Of course, since there she rides. What else was you expecting?"

"Expecting?" Dyke stared at him, open-mouthed. "Was you expecting to find the Arabella here?"

Wolverstone looked him over in contempt, then laughed and spoke loud enough to be heard by all around him. "Of course. What else?" And he laughed again, a laugh that seemed to Dyke to be calling him a fool. On that Wolverstone turned to give his attention to the operation of anchoring.

Anon when ashore he was beset by questioning buccaneers, it was from their very questions that he gathered exactly how matters stood, and perceived that either from lack of courage or other motive Blood, himself, had refused to render any account of his doings since the Arabella had separated from her sister ships. Wolverstone congratulated himself upon the discretion he had used with Dyke.

"The Captain was ever a modest man," he explained to Hagthorpe and those others who came crowding round him. "It's not his way to be sounding his own praises. Why, it was like this. We fell in with old Don Miguel, and when we'd scuttled him we took aboard a London pimp sent out by the Secretary of State to offer the Captain the King's commission if so be him'd quit piracy and be o' good behaviour. The Captain damned his soul to hell for answer. And then we fell in wi' the Jamaica fleet and that grey old devil Bishop in command, and there was a sure end to Captain Blood and to every mother's son of us all. So I goes to him, and 'accept this poxy commission,' says I; 'turn King's man and save your neck and ours.' He took me at my word, and the London pimp gave him the King's commission on the spot, and Bishop all but choked hisself with rage when he was told of it. But happened it had, and he was forced to swallow it. We were King's men all, and so into Port Royal we sailed along o' Bishop. But Bishop didn't trust us. He knew too much. But for his lordship, the fellow from London, he'd ha' hanged the Captain, King's commission and all. Blood would ha' slipped out o' Port Royal again that same night. But that hound Bishop had passed the word, and the fort kept a sharp lookout. In the end, though it took a fortnight, Blood bubbled him. He sent me and most o' the men off in a frigate that I bought for the voyage. His game—as he'd secretly told me—was to follow and give chase. Whether that's the game he played or not I can't tell ye; but here he is afore me as I'd expected he would be."

There was a great historian lost in Wolverstone. He had the right imagination that knows just how far it is safe to stray from the truth and just how far to colour it so as to change its shape for his own purposes.

Having delivered himself of his decoction of fact and falsehood, and thereby added one more to the exploits of Peter Blood, he enquired where the Captain might be found. Being informed that he kept his ship, Wolverstone stepped into a boat and went aboard, to report himself, as he put it.

In the great cabin of the Arabella he found Peter Blood alone and very far gone in drink—a condition in which no man ever before remembered to have seen him. As Wolverstone came in, the Captain raised bloodshot eyes to consider him. A moment they sharpened in their gaze as he brought his visitor into focus. Then he laughed, a loose, idiot laugh, that yet somehow was half a sneer.

"Ah! The Old Wolf!" said he. "Got here at last, eh? And whatcher gonnerdo wi' me, eh?" He hiccoughed resoundingly, and sagged back loosely in his chair.

Old Wolverstone stared at him in sombre silence. He had looked with untroubled eye upon many a hell of devilment in his time, but the sight of Captain Blood in this condition filled him with sudden grief. To express it he loosed an oath. It was his only expression for emotion of all kinds. Then he rolled forward, and dropped into a chair at the table, facing the Captain.

"My God, Peter, what's this?"

"Rum," said Peter. "Rum, from Jamaica." He pushed bottle and glass towards Wolverstone.

Wolverstone disregarded them.

"I'm asking you what ails you?" he bawled.

"Rum," said Captain Blood again, and smiled. "Jus' rum. I answer all your queshons. Why donjerr answer mine? Whatcher gonerdo wi' me?"

"I've done it," said Wolverstone. "Thank God, ye had the sense to hold your tongue till I came. Are ye sober enough to understand me?"

"Drunk or sober, allus 'derstand you."

"Then listen." And out came the tale that Wolverstone had told. The Captain steadied himself to grasp it.

"It'll do as well asertruth," said he when Wolverstone had finished. "And... oh, no marrer! Much obliged to ye, Old Wolf—faithful Old Wolf! But was it worthertrouble? I'm norrer pirate now; never a pirate again. 'S finished'" He banged the table, his eyes suddenly fierce.

"I'll come and talk to you again when there's less rum in your wits," said Wolverstone, rising. "Meanwhile ye'll please to remember the tale I've told, and say nothing that'll make me out a liar. They all believes me, even the men as sailed wi' me from Port Royal. I've made 'em. If they thought as how you'd taken the King's commission in earnest, and for the purpose o' doing as Morgan did, ye guess what would follow."

"Hell would follow," said the Captain. "An' tha's all I'm fit for."

"Ye're maudlin," Wolverstone growled. "We'll talk again tomorrow."

They did; but to little purpose, either that day or on any day thereafter while the rains—which set in that night—endured. Soon the shrewd Wolverstone discovered that rum was not what ailed Blood. Rum was in itself an effect, and not by any means the cause of the Captain's listless apathy. There was a canker eating at his heart, and the Old Wolf knew enough to make a shrewd guess of its nature. He cursed all things that daggled petticoats, and, knowing his world, waited for the sickness to pass.

But it did not pass. When Blood was not dicing or drinking in the taverns of Tortuga, keeping company that in his saner days he had loathed, he was shut up in his cabin aboard the Arabella, alone and uncommunicative. His friends at Government House, bewildered at this change in him, sought to reclaim him. Mademoiselle d'Ogeron, particularly distressed, sent him almost daily invitations, to few of which he responded.

Later, as the rainy season approached its end, he was sought by his captains with proposals of remunerative raids on Spanish settlements. But to all he manifested an indifference which, as the weeks passed and the weather became settled, begot first impatience and then exasperation.

Christian, who commanded the Clotho, came storming to him one day, upbraiding him for his inaction, and demanding that he should take order about what was to do.

"Go to the devil!" Blood said, when he had heard him out. Christian departed fuming, and on the morrow the Clotho weighed anchor and sailed away, setting an example of desertion from which the loyalty of Blood's other captains would soon be unable to restrain their men.

Sometimes Blood asked himself why had he come back to Tortuga at all. Held fast in bondage by the thought of Arabella and her scorn of him for a thief and a pirate, he had sworn that he had done with buccaneering. Why, then, was he here? That question he would answer with another: Where else was he to go? Neither backward nor forward could he move, it seemed.

He was degenerating visibly, under the eyes of all. He had entirely lost the almost foppish concern for his appearance, and was grown careless and slovenly in his dress. He allowed a black beard to grow on cheeks that had ever been so carefully shaven; and the long, thick black hair, once so sedulously curled, hung now in a lank, untidy mane about a face that was changing from its vigorous swarthiness to an unhealthy sallow, whilst the blue eyes, that had been so vivid and compelling, were now dull and lacklustre.

Wolverstone, the only one who held the clue to this degeneration, ventured once—and once only—to beard him frankly about it.

"Lord, Peter! Is there never to be no end to this?" the giant had growled. "Will you spend your days moping and swilling 'cause a white-faced ninny in Port Royal'll have none o' ye? 'Sblood and 'ounds! If ye wants the wench, why the plague doesn't ye go and fetch her?"

The blue eyes glared at him from under the jet-black eyebrows, and something of their old fire began to kindle in them. But Wolverstone went on heedlessly.

"I'll be nice wi' a wench as long as niceness be the key to her favour. But sink me now if I'd rot myself in rum on account of anything that wears a petticoat. That's not the Old Wolf's way. If there's no other expedition'll tempt you, why not Port Royal? What a plague do it matter if it is an English settlement? It's commanded by Colonel Bishop, and there's no lack of rascals in your company'd follow you to hell if it meant getting Colonel Bishop by the throat. It could be done, I tell you. We've but to spy the chance when the Jamaica fleet is away. There's enough plunder in the town to tempt the lads, and there's the wench for you. Shall I sound them on 't?"

Blood was on his feet, his eyes blazing, his livid face distorted. "Ye'll leave my cabin this minute, so ye will, or, by Heaven, it's your corpse'll be carried out of it. Ye mangy hound, d'ye dare come to me with such proposals?"

He fell to cursing his faithful officer with a virulence the like of which he had never yet been known to use. And Wolverstone, in terror before that fury, went out without another word. The subject was not raised again, and Captain Blood was left to his idle abstraction.

But at last, as his buccaneers were growing desperate, something happened, brought about by the Captain's friend

M. d'Ogeron. One sunny morning the Governor of Tortuga came aboard the Arabella, accompanied by a chubby little gentleman, amiable of countenance, amiable and self-sufficient of manner.

"My Captain," M. d'Ogeron delivered himself, "I bring you M. de Cussy, the Governor of French Hispaniola, who desires a word with you."

Out of consideration for his friend, Captain Blood pulled the pipe from his mouth, shook some of the rum out of his wits, and rose and made a leg to M. de Cussy.

"Serviteur!" said he.

M. de Cussy returned the bow and accepted a seat on the locker under the stern windows.

"You have a good force here under your command, my Captain," said he.

"Some eight hundred men."

"And I understand they grow restive in idleness."

"They may go to the devil when they please."

M. de Cussy took snuff delicately. "I have something better than that to propose," said he.

"Propose it, then," said Blood, without interest.

M. de Cussy looked at M. d'Ogeron, and raised his eyebrows a little. He did not find Captain Blood encouraging. But M. d'Ogeron nodded vigorously with pursed lips, and the Governor of Hispaniola propounded his business.

"News has reached us from France that there is war with Spain."

"That is news, is it?" growled Blood.

"I am speaking officially, my Captain. I am not alluding to unofficial skirmishes, and unofficial predatory measures which we have condoned out here. There is war—formally war—between France and Spain in Europe. It is the intention of France that this war shall be carried into the New World. A fleet is coming out from Brest under the command of M.

le Baron de Rivarol for that purpose. I have letters from him desiring me to equip a supplementary squadron and raise a body of not less than a thousand men to reenforce him on his arrival. What I have come to propose to you, my Captain, at the suggestion of our good friend M. d'Ogeron, is, in brief, that you enroll your ships and your force under M. de Rivarol's flag."

Blood looked at him with a faint kindling of interest. "You are offering to take us into the French service?" he asked. "On what terms, monsieur?"

"With the rank of Capitaine de Vaisseau for yourself, and suitable ranks for the officers serving under you. You will enjoy the pay of that rank, and you will be entitled, together with your men, to one-tenth share in all prizes taken."

"My men will hardly account it generous. They will tell you that they can sail out of here tomorrow, disembowel a Spanish settlement, and keep the whole of the plunder."

"Ah, yes, but with the risks attaching to acts of piracy. With us your position will be regular and official, and considering the powerful fleet by which M. de Rivarol is backed, the enterprises to be undertaken will be on a much vaster scale than anything you could attempt on your own account. So that the one tenth in this case may be equal to more than the whole in the other."

Captain Blood considered. This, after all, was not piracy that was being proposed. It was honourable employment in the service of the King of France.

"I will consult my officers," he said; and he sent for them.

They came and the matter was laid before them by M. de Cussy himself. Hagthorpe announced at once that the proposal was opportune. The men were grumbling at their protracted inaction, and would no doubt be ready to accept the service which M. de Cussy offered on behalf of France. Hagthorpe looked at Blood as he spoke. Blood nodded gloomy agreement. Emboldened by this, they went on to discuss the terms.

Yberville, the young French filibuster, had the honour to point out to M. de Cussy that the share offered was too small. For one fifth of the prizes, the officers would answer for their men; not for less.

M. de Cussy was distressed. He had his instructions. It was taking a deal upon himself to exceed them. The buccaneers were firm. Unless M. de Cussy could make it one fifth there was no more to be said. M. de Cussy finally consenting to exceed his instructions, the articles were drawn up and signed that very day. The buccaneers were to be at Petit Goave by the end of January, when M. de Rivarol had announced that he might be expected.

After that followed days of activity in Tortuga, refitting the ships, boucanning meat, laying in stores. In these matters which once would have engaged all Captain Blood's attention, he now took no part. He continued listless and aloof. If he had given his consent to the undertaking, or, rather, allowed himself to be swept into it by the wishes of his officers—it was only because the service offered was of a regular and honourable kind, nowise connected with piracy, with which he swore in his heart that he had done for ever. But his consent remained passive. The service entered awoke no zeal in him. He was perfectly indifferent—as he told Hagthorpe, who ventured once to offer a remonstrance—whether they went to Petit Goave or to Hades, and whether they entered the service of Louis XIV or of Satan.

XXVI

M. DE RIVAROL

Captain Blood was still in that disgruntled mood when he sailed from Tortuga, and still in that mood when he came to his moorings in the bay of Petit Goave. In that same mood he greeted M. le Baron de Rivarol when this nobleman with his fleet of five men-of-war at last dropped anchor alongside the buccaneer ships, in the middle of February. The Frenchman had been six weeks on the voyage, he announced, delayed by unfavourable weather.

Summoned to wait on him, Captain Blood repaired to the Castle of Petit Goave, where the interview was to take place. The Baron, a tall, hawk-faced man of forty, very cold and distant of manner, measured Captain Blood with an eye of obvious disapproval. Of Hagthorpe, Yberville, and Wolverstone who stood ranged behind their captain, he took no heed whatever. M. de Cussy offered Captain Blood a chair.

"A moment, M. de Cussy. I do not think M. le Baron has observed that I am not alone. Let me present to you, sir, my companions: Captain Hagthorpe of the Elizabeth, Captain Wolverstone of the Atropos, and Captain Yberville of the Lachesis."

The Baron stared hard and haughtily at Captain Blood, then very distantly and barely perceptibly inclined his head to each of the other three. His manner implied plainly that he despised them and that he desired them at once to understand it. It had a curious effect upon Captain Blood. It awoke the devil in him, and it awoke at the same time his self-respect which of late had been slumbering. A sudden shame of his disordered, ill-kempt appearance made him perhaps the more defiant. There was almost a significance in the way he hitched his sword-belt round, so that the wrought hilt of his very serviceable rapier was brought into fuller view. He waved his captains to the chairs that stood about.

"Draw up to the table, lads. We are keeping the Baron waiting."

They obeyed him, Wolverstone with a grin that was full of understanding. Haughtier grew the stare of M. de Rivarol. To sit at table with these bandits placed him upon what he accounted a dishonouring equality. It had been his notion that—with the possible exception of Captain Blood—they should take his instructions standing, as became men of their quality in the presence of a man of his. He did the only thing remaining to mark a distinction between himself and them. He put on his hat.

"Ye're very wise now," said Blood amiably. "I feel the draught myself." And he covered himself with his plumed castor.

M. de Rivarol changed colour. He quivered visibly with anger, and was a moment controlling himself before venturing to speak. M. de Cussy was obviously very ill at ease.

"Sir," said the Baron frostily, "you compel me to remind you that the rank you hold is that of Capitaine de Vaisseau, and that you are in the presence of the General of the Armies of France by Sea and Land in America. You compel me to remind you further that there is a deference due from your rank to mine."

"I am happy to assure you," said Captain Blood, "that the reminder is unnecessary. I am by way of accounting myself a gentleman, little though I may look like one at present; and I should not account myself that were I capable of anything but deference to those whom nature or fortune may have placed above me, or to those who being placed beneath me in rank may labour under a disability to resent my lack of it." It was a neatly intangible rebuke. M. de Rivarol bit his lip. Captain Blood swept on without giving him time to reply: "Thus much being clear, shall we come to business?"

M. de Rivarol's hard eyes considered him a moment. "Perhaps it will be best," said he. He took up a paper. "I have here a copy of the articles into which you entered with M. de Cussy. Before going further, I have to observe that M. de Cussy has exceeded his instructions in admitting you to one fifth of the prizes taken. His authority did not warrant his going beyond one tenth."

"That is a matter between yourself and M. de Cussy, my General."

"Oh, no. It is a matter between myself and you."

"Your pardon, my General. The articles are signed. So far as we are concerned, the matter is closed. Also out of regard for M. de Cussy, we should not desire to be witnesses of the rebukes you may consider that he deserves."

"What I may have to say to M. de Cussy is no concern of yours."

"That is what I am telling you, my General."

"But—nom de Dieu!—it is your concern, I suppose, that we cannot award you more than one tenth share." M. de Rivarol smote the table in exasperation. This pirate was too infernally skillful a fencer.

"You are quite certain of that, M. le Baron—that you cannot?"

"I am quite certain that I will not."

Captain Blood shrugged, and looked down his nose. "In that case," said he, "it but remains for me to present my little account for our disbursement, and to fix the sum at which we should be compensated for our loss of time and derangement in coming hither. That settled, we can part friends, M. le Baron. No harm has been done."

"What the devil do you mean?" The Baron was on his feet, leaning forward across the table.

"Is it possible that I am obscure? My French, perhaps, is not of the purest, but..."

"Oh, your French is fluent enough; too fluent at moments, if I may permit myself the observation. Now, look you here, M. le filibustier, I am not a man with whom it is safe to play the fool, as you may very soon discover. You have accepted service of the King of France—you and your men; you hold the rank and draw the pay of a Capitaine de Vaisseau, and these your officers hold the rank of lieutenants. These ranks carry obligations which you would do well to study, and penalties for failing to discharge them which you might study at the same time. They are something severe. The first obligation of an officer is obedience. I commend it to your attention. You are not to conceive yourselves, as you appear to be doing, my allies in the enterprises I have in view, but my subordinates. In me you behold a commander to lead you, not a companion or an equal. You understand me, I hope."

"Oh, be sure that I understand," Captain Blood laughed. He was recovering his normal self amazingly under the inspiring stimulus of conflict. The only thing that marred his enjoyment was the reflection that he had not shaved. "I forget nothing, I assure you, my General. I do not forget, for instance, as you appear to be doing, that the articles we signed are the condition of our service; and the articles provide that we receive one-fifth share. Refuse us that, and you cancel the articles; cancel the articles, and you cancel our services with them. From that moment we cease to have the honour to hold rank in the navies of the King of France."

There was more than a murmur of approval from his three captains.

Rivarol glared at them, checkmated.

"In effect..." M. de Cussy was beginning timidly.

"In effect, monsieur, this is your doing," the Baron flashed on him, glad to have some one upon whom he could fasten the sharp fangs of his irritation. "You should be broke for it. You bring the King's service into disrepute; you force me, His Majesty's representative, into an impossible position."

"Is it impossible to award us the one-fifth share?" quoth Captain Blood silkily. "In that case, there is no need for heat or for injuries to M. de Cussy. M. de Cussy knows that we would not have come for less. We depart again upon your assurance that you cannot award us more. And things are as they would have been if M. de Cussy had adhered rigidly to his instructions. I have proved, I hope, to your satisfaction, M. le Baron, that if you repudiate the articles you can neither claim our services nor hinder our departure—not in honour."

"Not in honour, sir? To the devil with your insolence! Do you imply that any course that were not in honour would be possible to me?"

"I do not imply it, because it would not be possible," said Captain Blood. "We should see to that. It is, my General, for you to say whether the articles are repudiated."

The Baron sat down. "I will consider the matter," he said sullenly. "You shall be advised of my resolve."

Captain Blood rose, his officers rose with him. Captain Blood bowed.

"M. le Baron!" said he.

Then he and his buccaneers removed themselves from the August and irate presence of the General of the King's Armies by Land and Sea in America.

You conceive that there followed for M. de Cussy an extremely bad quarter of an hour. M. de Cussy, in fact, deserves your sympathy. His self-sufficiency was blown from him by the haughty M. de Rivarol, as down from a thistle by the winds of autumn. The General of the King's Armies abused him—this man who was Governor of Hispaniola—as if he were a lackey. M. de Cussy defended himself by urging the thing that Captain Blood had so admirably urged already on his behalf—that if the terms he had made with the buccaneers were not confirmed there was no harm done. M. de Rivarol bullied and browbeat him into silence.

Having exhausted abuse, the Baron proceeded to indignities. Since he accounted that M. de Cussy had proved himself unworthy of the post he held, M. de Rivarol took over the responsibilities of that post for as long as he might remain in Hispaniola, and to give effect to this he began by bringing soldiers from his ships, and setting his own guard in M. de Cussy's castle.

Out of this, trouble followed quickly. Wolverstone coming ashore next morning in the picturesque garb that he affected, his head swathed in a coloured handkerchief, was jeered at by an officer of the newly landed French troops. Not accustomed to derision, Wolverstone replied in kind and with interest. The officer passed to insult, and Wolverstone struck him a blow that felled him, and left him only the half of his poor senses. Within the hour the matter was reported to M. de Rivarol, and before noon, by M. de Rivarol's orders, Wolverstone was under arrest in the castle.

The Baron had just sat down to dinner with M. de Cussy when the black man who waited on them announced Captain Blood. Peevishly M. de Rivarol bade him be admitted, and there entered now into his presence a spruce and modish gentleman, dressed with care and sombre richness in black and silver, his swarthy, clear-cut face scrupulously shaven, his long black hair in ringlets that fell to a collar of fine point. In his right hand the gentleman carried a broad black hat with a scarlet ostrich-plume, in his left hand an ebony cane. His stockings were of silk, a bunch of ribbons masked his garters, and the black rosettes on his shoes were finely edged with gold.

For a moment M. de Rivarol did not recognize him. For Blood looked younger by ten years than yesterday. But the vivid blue eyes under their level black brows were not to be forgotten, and they proclaimed him for the man announced even before he had spoken. His resurrected pride had demanded that he should put himself on an equality with the baron and advertise that equality by his exterior.

"I come inopportunely," he courteously excused himself. "My apologies. My business could not wait. It concerns, M. de Cussy, Captain Wolverstone of the Lachesis, whom you have placed under arrest."

"It was I who placed him under arrest," said M. de Rivarol.

"Indeed! But I thought that M. de Cussy was Governor of Hispaniola."

"Whilst I am here, monsieur, I am the supreme authority. It is as well that you should understand it."

"Perfectly. But it is not possible that you are aware of the mistake that has been made."

"Mistake, do you say?"

"I say mistake. On the whole, it is polite of me to use that word. Also it is expedient. It will save discussions. Your people have arrested the wrong man, M. de Rivarol. Instead of the French officer, who used the grossest provocation, they have arrested Captain Wolverstone. It is a matter which I beg you to reverse without delay."

M. de Rivarol's hawk-face flamed scarlet. His dark eyes bulged.

"Sir, you... you are insolent! But of an insolence that is intolerable!" Normally a man of the utmost self-possession he was so rudely shaken now that he actually stammered.

"M. le Baron, you waste words. This is the New World. It is not merely new; it is novel to one reared amid the superstitions of the Old. That novelty you have not yet had time, perhaps, to realize; therefore I overlook the offensive epithet you have used. But justice is justice in the New World as in the Old, and injustice as intolerable here as there. Now justice demands the enlargement of my officer and the arrest and punishment of yours. That justice I invite you, with submission, to administer."

"With submission?" snorted the Baron in furious scorn.

"With the utmost submission, monsieur. But at the same time I will remind M. le Baron that my buccaneers number eight hundred; your troops five hundred; and M. de Cussy will inform you of the interesting fact that any one buccaneer is equal in action to at least three soldiers of the line. I am perfectly frank with you, monsieur, to save time and hard words. Either Captain Wolverstone is instantly set at liberty, or we must take measures to set him at liberty ourselves. The consequences may be appalling. But it is as you please, M. le Baron. You are the supreme authority. It is for you to say."

M. de Rivarol was white to the lips. In all his life he had never been so bearded and defied. But he controlled himself.

"You will do me the favour to wait in the ante-room, M. le Capitaine. I desire a word with M. de Cussy. You shall presently be informed of my decision."

When the door had closed, the baron loosed his fury upon the head of M. de Cussy.

"So, these are the men you have enlisted in the King's service, the men who are to serve under me—men who do not serve, but dictate, and this before the enterprise that has brought me from France is even under way! What explanations do you offer me, M. de Cussy? I warn you that I am not pleased with you. I am, in fact, as you may perceive, exceedingly angry."

The Governor seemed to shed his chubbiness. He drew himself stiffly erect.

"Your rank, monsieur, does not give you the right to rebuke me; nor do the facts. I have enlisted for you the men that you desired me to enlist. It is not my fault if you do not know how to handle them better. As Captain Blood has told you, this is the New World."

"So, so!" M. de Rivarol smiled malignantly. "Not only do you offer no explanation, but you venture to put me in the wrong. Almost I admire your temerity. But there!" he waved the matter aside. He was supremely sardonic. "It is, you tell me, the New World, and—new worlds, new manners, I suppose. In time I may conform my ideas to this new world, or I may conform this new world to my ideas." He was menacing on that. "For the moment I must accept what I find. It remains for you, monsieur, who have experience of these savage by-ways, to advise me out of that experience how to act."

"M. le Baron, it was a folly to have arrested the buccaneer captain. It would be madness to persist. We have not the forces to meet force."

"In that case, monsieur, perhaps you will tell me what we are to do with regard to the future. Am I to submit at every turn to the dictates of this man Blood? Is the enterprise upon which we are embarked to be conducted as he decrees? Am I, in short, the King's representative in America, to be at the mercy of these rascals?"

"Oh, by no means. I am enrolling volunteers here in Hispaniola, and I am raising a corps of negroes. I compute that when this is done we shall have a force of a thousand men, the buccaneers apart."

"But in that case why not dispense with them?"

"Because they will always remain the sharp edge of any weapon that we forge. In the class of warfare that lies before us they are so skilled that what Captain Blood has just said is not an overstatement. A buccaneer is equal to three soldiers of the line. At the same time we shall have a sufficient force to keep them in control. For the rest, monsieur, they have certain notions of honour. They will stand by their articles, and so that we deal justly with them, they will deal justly with us, and give no trouble. I have experience of them, and I pledge you my word for that."

M. de Rivarol condescended to be mollified. It was necessary that he should save his face, and in a degree the Governor afforded him the means to do so, as well as a certain guarantee for the future in the further force he was raising.

"Very well," he said. "Be so good as to recall this Captain Blood."

The Captain came in, assured and very dignified. M. de Rivarol found him detestable; but dissembled it.

"M. le Capitaine, I have taken counsel with M. le Gouverneur. From what he tells me, it is possible that a mistake has been committed. Justice, you may be sure, shall be done. To ensure it, I shall myself preside over a council to be composed of two of my senior officers, yourself and an officer of yours. This council shall hold at once an impartial investigation into the affair, and the offender, the man guilty of having given provocation, shall be punished."

Captain Blood bowed. It was not his wish to be extreme. "Perfectly, M. le Baron. And now, sir, you have had the night for reflection in this matter of the articles. Am I to understand that you confirm or that you repudiate them?"

M. de Rivarol's eyes narrowed. His mind was full of what M. de Cussy had said—that these buccaneers must prove the sharp edge of any weapon he might forge. He could not dispense with them. He perceived that he had blundered tactically in attempting to reduce the agreed share. Withdrawal from a position of that kind is ever fraught with loss of dignity. But there were those volunteers that M. de Cussy was enrolling to strengthen the hand of the King's General. Their presence might admit anon of the reopening of this question. Meanwhile he must retire in the best order possible.

"I have considered that, too," he announced. "And whilst my opinion remains unaltered, I must confess that since M.

de Cussy has pledged us, it is for us to fulfil the pledges. The articles are confirmed, sir."

Captain Blood bowed again. In vain M. de Rivarol looked searchingly for the least trace of a smile of triumph on those firm lips. The buccaneer's face remained of the utmost gravity.

Wolverstone was set at liberty that afternoon, and his assailant sentenced to two months' detention. Thus harmony was restored. But it had been an unpromising beginning, and there was more to follow shortly of a similar discordant kind.

Blood and his officers were summoned a week later to a council which sat to determine their operations against Spain. M. de Rivarol laid before them a project for a raid upon the wealthy Spanish town of Cartagena. Captain Blood professed astonishment. Sourly invited by M. de Rivarol to state his grounds for it, he did so with the utmost frankness.

"Were I General of the King's Armies in America," said he, "I should have no doubt or hesitation as to the best way in which to serve my Royal master and the French nation. That which I think will be obvious to M. de Cussy, as it is to me, is that we should at once invade Spanish Hispaniola and reduce the whole of this fruitful and splendid island into the possession of the King of France."

"That may follow," said M. de Rivarol. "It is my wish that we begin with Cartagena."

"You mean, sir, that we are to sail across the Caribbean on an adventurous expedition, neglecting that which lies here at our very door. In our absence, a Spanish invasion of French Hispaniola is possible. If we begin by reducing the Spaniards here, that possibility will be removed. We shall have added to the Crown of France the most coveted possession in the West Indies. The enterprise offers no particular difficulty; it may be speedily accomplished, and once accomplished, it would be time to look farther afield. That would seem the logical order in which this campaign should proceed."

He ceased, and there was silence. M. de Rivarol sat back in his chair, the feathered end of a quill between his teeth. Presently he cleared his throat and asked a question.

"Is there anybody else who shares Captain Blood's opinion?"

None answered him. His own officers were overawed by him; Blood's followers naturally preferred Cartagena, because offering the greater chance of loot. Loyalty to their leader kept them silent.

"You seem to be alone in your opinion," said the Baron with his vinegary smile.

Captain Blood laughed outright. He had suddenly read the Baron's mind. His airs and graces and haughtiness had so imposed upon Blood that it was only now that at last he saw through them, into the fellow's peddling spirit. Therefore he laughed; there was really nothing else to do. But his laughter was charged with more anger even than contempt. He had been deluding himself that he had done with piracy. The conviction that this French service was free of any taint of that was the only consideration that had induced him to accept it. Yet here was this haughty, supercilious gentleman, who dubbed himself General of the Armies of France, proposing a plundering, thieving raid which, when stripped of its mean, transparent mask of legitimate warfare, was revealed as piracy of the most flagrant.

M. de Rivarol, intrigued by his mirth, scowled upon him disapprovingly.

"Why do you laugh, monsieur?"

"Because I discover here an irony that is supremely droll. You, M. le Baron, General of the King's Armies by Land and Sea in America, propose an enterprise of a purely buccaneering character; whilst I, the buccaneer, am urging one that is more concerned with upholding the honour of France. You perceive how droll it is."

M. de Rivarol perceived nothing of the kind. M. de Rivarol in fact was extremely angry. He bounded to his feet, and every man in the room rose with him—save only M. de Cussy, who sat on with a grim smile on his lips. He, too, now read the Baron like an open book, and reading him despised him.

"M. le filibustier," cried Rivarol in a thick voice, "it seems that I must again remind you that I am your superior officer."

"My superior officer! You! Lord of the World! Why, you are just a common pirate! But you shall hear the truth for once, and that before all these gentlemen who have the honour to serve the King of France. It is for me, a buccaneer, a sea-robber, to stand here and tell you what is in the interest of French honour and the French Crown. Whilst you, the French King's appointed General, neglecting this, are for spending the King's resources against an outlying settlement of no account, shedding French blood in seizing a place that cannot be held, only because it has been reported to you that there is much gold in Cartagena, and that the plunder of it will enrich you. It is worthy of the huckster who sought to haggle with us about our share, and to beat us down after the articles pledging you were already signed. If I am wrong—let M. de Cussy say so. If I am wrong, let me be proven wrong, and I will beg your pardon. Meanwhile, monsieur, I withdraw from this council. I will have no further part in your deliberations. I accepted the service of the King of France with intent to honour that service. I cannot honour that service by lending countenance to a waste of life and resources in raids upon unimportant settlements, with plunder for their only object. The responsibility for such decisions must rest with you, and with you alone. I desire M. de Cussy to report me to the Ministers of France. For the rest, monsieur, it merely remains for you to give me your orders. I await them aboard my ship—and anything else, of a personal nature, that you may feel I have provoked by the terms I have felt compelled to use in this council. M. le Baron, I have the honour to wish you good-day."

He stalked out, and his three captains—although they thought him mad—rolled after him in loyal silence.

M. de Rivarol was gasping like a landed fish. The stark truth had robbed him of speech. When he recovered, it was to thank Heaven vigorously that the council was relieved by Captain Blood's own act of that gentleman's further participation in its deliberations. Inwardly M. de Rivarol burned with shame and rage. The mask had been plucked from him, and he had been held up to scorn—he, the General of the King's Armies by Sea and Land in America.

Nevertheless, it was to Cartagena that they sailed in the middle of March. Volunteers and black men had brought up the forces directly under M. de Rivarol to twelve hundred men. With these he thought he could keep the buccaneer contingent in order and submissive.

They made up an imposing fleet, led by M. de Rivarol's flagship, the Victorieuse, a mighty vessel of eighty guns. Each of the four other French ships was at least as powerful as Blood's Arabella, which was of forty guns. Followed the lesser buccaneer vessels, the Elizabeth, Lachesis, and Atropos, and a dozen frigates laden with stores, besides canoes and small craft in tow.

Narrowly they missed the Jamaica fleet with Colonel Bishop, which sailed north for Tortuga two days after the Baron de Rivarol's southward passage.

XXVII

CARTAGENA

Having crossed the Caribbean in the teeth of contrary winds, it was not until the early days of April that the French fleet hove in sight of Cartagena, and M. de Rivarol summoned a council aboard his flagship to determine the method of assault.

"It is of importance, messieurs," he told them, "that we take the city by surprise, not only before it can put itself into a state of defence; but before it can remove its treasures inland. I propose to land a force sufficient to achieve this to the north of the city tonight after dark." And he explained in detail the scheme upon which his wits had laboured.

He was heard respectfully and approvingly by his officers, scornfully by Captain Blood, and indifferently by the other buccaneer captains present. For it must be understood that Blood's refusal to attend councils had related only to those concerned with determining the nature of the enterprise to be undertaken.

Captain Blood was the only one amongst them who knew exactly what lay ahead. Two years ago he had himself considered a raid upon the place, and he had actually made a survey of it in circumstances which he was presently to disclose.

The Baron's proposal was one to be expected from a commander whose knowledge of Cartagena was only such as might be derived from maps.

Geographically and strategically considered, it is a curious place. It stands almost four-square, screened east and north by hills, and it may be said to face south upon the inner of two harbours by which it is normally approached. The entrance to the outer harbour, which is in reality a lagoon some three miles across, lies through a neck known as the Boca Chica—or Little Mouth—and defended by a fort. A long strip of densely wooded land to westward acts here as a natural breakwater, and as the inner harbour is approached, another strip of land thrusts across at right angles from the first, towards the mainland on the east. Just short of this it ceases, leaving a deep but very narrow channel, a veritable gateway, into the secure and sheltered inner harbour. Another fort defends this second passage. East and north of Cartagena lies the mainland, which may be left out of account. But to the west and northwest this city, so well guarded on every other side, lies directly open to the sea. It stands back beyond a half-mile of beach, and besides this and the stout Walls which fortify it, would appear to have no other defences. But those appearances are deceptive, and they had utterly deceived M. de Rivarol, when he devised his plan.

It remained for Captain Blood to explain the difficulties when M. de Rivarol informed him that the honour of opening the assault in the manner which he prescribed was to be accorded to the buccaneers.

Captain Blood smiled sardonic appreciation of the honour reserved for his men. It was precisely what he would have expected. For the buccaneers the dangers; for M. de Rivarol the honour, glory and profit of the enterprise.

"It is an honour which I must decline," said he quite coldly.

Wolverstone grunted approval and Hagthorpe nodded. Yberville, who as much as any of them resented the superciliousness of his noble compatriot, never wavered in loyalty to Captain Blood. The French officers—there were six of them present—stared their haughty surprise at the buccaneer leader, whilst the Baron challengingly fired a question at him.

"How? You decline it, 'sir? You decline to obey orders, do you say?"

"I understood, M. le Baron, that you summoned us to deliberate upon the means to be adopted."

"Then you understood amiss, M. le Capitaine. You are here to receive my commands. I have already deliberated, and I have decided. I hope you understand."

"Oh, I understand," laughed Blood. "But, I ask myself, do you?" And without giving the Baron time to set the angry question that was bubbling to his lips, he swept on: "You have deliberated, you say, and you have decided. But unless your decision rests upon a wish to destroy my buccaneers, you will alter it when I tell you something of which I have knowledge. This city of Cartagena looks very vulnerable on the northern side, all open to the sea as it apparently stands. Ask yourself, M. le Baron, how came the Spaniards who built it where it is to have been at such trouble to fortify it to the south, if from the north it is so easily assailable."

That gave M. de Rivarol pause.

"The Spaniards," Blood pursued, "are not quite the fools you are supposing them. Let me tell you, messieurs, that two years ago I made a survey of Cartagena as a preliminary to raiding it. I came hither with some friendly trading Indians, myself disguised as an Indian, and in that guise I spent a week in the city and studied carefully all its approaches. On the side of the sea where it looks so temptingly open to assault, there is shoal water for over half a mile out—far enough out, I assure you, to ensure that no ship shall come within bombarding range of it. It is not safe to venture nearer land than three quarters of a mile."

"But our landing will be effected in canoes and piraguas and open boats," cried an officer impatiently.

"In the calmest season of the year, the surf will hinder any such operation. And you will also bear in mind that if landing were possible as you are suggesting, that landing could not be covered by the ships' guns. In fact, it is the landing parties would be in danger from their own artillery."

"If the attack is made by night, as I propose, covering will be unnecessary. You should be ashore in force before the Spaniards are aware of the intent."

"You are assuming that Cartagena is a city of the blind, that at this very moment they are not conning our sails and asking themselves who we are and what we intend."

"But if they feel themselves secure from the north, as you suggest," cried the Baron impatiently, "that very security will lull them."

"Perhaps. But, then, they are secure. Any attempt to land on this side is doomed to failure at the hands of Nature."

"Nevertheless, we make the attempt," said the obstinate Baron, whose haughtiness would not allow him to yield before his officers.

"If you still choose to do so after what I have said, you are, of course, the person to decide. But I do not lead my men into fruitless danger."

"If I command you..." the Baron was beginning. But Blood unceremoniously interrupted him.

"M. le Baron, when M. de Cussy engaged us on your behalf, it was as much on account of our knowledge and experience of this class of warfare as on account of our strength. I have placed my own knowledge and experience in this particular matter at your disposal. I will add that I abandoned my own project of raiding Cartagena, not being in sufficient strength at the time to force the entrance of the harbour, which is the only way into the city. The strength which you now command is ample for that purpose."

"But whilst we are doing that, the Spaniards will have time to remove great part of the wealth this city holds. We must take them by surprise."

Captain Blood shrugged. "If this is a mere pirating raid, that, of course, is a prime consideration. It was with me. But if you are concerned to abate the pride of Spain and plant the Lilies of France on the forts of this settlement, the loss of some treasure should not really weigh for much."

M. de Rivarol bit his lip in chagrin. His gloomy eye smouldered as it considered the self-contained buccaneer.

"But if I command you to go—to make the attempt?" he asked. "Answer me, monsieur, let us know once for all where we stand, and who commands this expedition."

"Positively, I find you tiresome," said Captain Blood, and he swung to M. de Cussy, who sat there gnawing his lip, intensely uncomfortable. "I appeal to you, monsieur, to justify me to the General."

M. de Cussy started out of his gloomy abstraction. He cleared his throat. He was extremely nervous.

"In view of what Captain Blood has submitted..."

"Oh, to the devil with that!" snapped Rivarol. "It seems that I am followed by poltroons. Look you, M. le Capitaine, since you are afraid to undertake this thing, I will myself undertake it. The weather is calm, and I count upon making good my landing. If I do so, I shall have proved you wrong, and I shall have a word to say to you tomorrow which you may not like. I am being very generous with you, sir." He waved his hand regally. "You have leave to go."

It was sheer obstinacy and empty pride that drove him, and he received the lesson he deserved. The fleet stood in during the afternoon to within a mile of the coast, and under cover of darkness three hundred men, of whom two hundred were negroes—the whole of the black man contingent having been pressed into the undertaking—were pulled away for the shore in the canoes, piraguas, and ships' boats. Rivarol's pride compelled him, however much he may have disliked the venture, to lead them in person.

The first six boats were caught in the surf, and pounded into fragments before their occupants could extricate themselves. The thunder of the breakers and the cries of the shipwrecked warned those who followed, and thereby saved them from sharing the same fate. By the Baron's urgent orders they pulled away again out of danger, and stood about to pick up such survivors as contrived to battle towards them. Close upon fifty lives were lost in the adventure, together with half-a-dozen boats stored with ammunition and light guns.

The Baron went back to his flagship an infuriated, but by no means a wiser man. Wisdom—not even the pungent wisdom experience thrusts upon us—is not for such as M. de Rivarol. His anger embraced all things, but focussed chiefly upon Captain Blood. In some warped process of reasoning he held the buccaneer chiefly responsible for this misadventure. He went to bed considering furiously what he should say to Captain Blood upon the morrow.

He was awakened at dawn by the rolling thunder of guns. Emerging upon the poop in nightcap and slippers, he beheld a sight that increased his unreasonable and unreasoning fury. The four buccaneer ships under canvas were going through extraordinary manoeuvre half a mile off the Boca Chica and little more than half a mile away from the remainder of the fleet, and from their flanks flame and smoke were belching each time they swung broadside to the great round fort that guarded that narrow entrance. The fort was returning the fire vigorously and viciously. But the buccaneers timed their broadsides with extraordinary judgment to catch the defending ordnance reloading; then as they drew the Spaniards' fire, they swung away again not only taking care to be ever moving targets, but, further, to present no more than bow or stern to the fort, their masts in line, when the heaviest cannonades were to be expected.

Gibbering and cursing, M. de Rivarol stood there and watched this action, so presumptuously undertaken by Blood on his own responsibility. The officers of the Victorieuse crowded round him, but it was not until M. de Cussy came to join the group that he opened the sluices of his rage. And M. de Cussy himself invited the deluge that now caught him. He had come up rubbing his hands and taking a proper satisfaction in the energy of the men whom he had enlisted.

"Aha, M. de Rivarol!" he laughed. "He understands his business, eh, this Captain Blood. He'll plant the Lilies of France on that fort before breakfast."

The Baron swung upon him snarling. "He understands his business, eh? His business, let me tell you, M. de Cussy, is to obey my orders, and I have not ordered this. Par la Mordieu! When this is over I'll deal with him for his damned insubordination."

"Surely, M. le Baron, he will have justified it if he succeeds."

"Justified it! Ah, parbleu! Can a soldier ever justify acting without orders?" He raved on furiously, his officers supporting him out of their detestation of Captain Blood.

Meanwhile the fight went merrily on. The fort was suffering badly. Yet for all their manoeuvring the buccaneers were not escaping punishment. The starboard gunwale of the Atropos had been hammered into splinters, and a shot had caught her astern in the coach. The Elizabeth was badly battered about the forecastle, and the Arabella's maintop had been shot away, whilst' towards the end of that engagement the Lachesis came reeling out of the fight with a shattered rudder, steering herself by sweeps.

The absurd Baron's fierce eyes positively gleamed with satisfaction.

"I pray Heaven they may sink all his infernal ships!" he cried in his frenzy.

But Heaven didn't hear him. Scarcely had he spoken than there was a terrific explosion, and half the fort went up in fragments. A lucky shot from the buccaneers had found the powder magazine.

It may have been a couple of hours later, when Captain Blood, as spruce and cool as if he had just come from a levee, stepped upon the quarter-deck of the Victorieuse, to confront M. de Rivarol, still in bedgown and nightcap.

"I have to report, M. le Baron, that we are in possession of the fort on Boca Chica. The standard of France is flying from what remains of its tower, and the way into the outer harbour is open to your fleet."

M. de Rivarol was compelled to swallow his fury, though it choked him. The jubilation among his officers had been such that he could not continue as he had begun. Yet his eyes were malevolent, his face pale with anger.

"You are fortunate, M. Blood, that you succeeded," he said. "It would have gone very ill with you had you failed. Another time be so good as to await my orders, lest you should afterwards lack the justification which your good fortune has procured you this morning."

Blood smiled with a flash of white teeth, and bowed. "I shall be glad of your orders now, General, for pursuing our advantage. You realize that speed in striking is the first essential."

Rivarol was left gaping a moment. Absorbed in his ridiculous anger, he had considered nothing. But he made a quick recovery. "To my cabin, if you please," he commanded peremptorily, and was turning to lead the way, when Blood arrested him.

"With submission, my General, we shall be better here. You behold there the scene of our coming action. It is spread before you like a map." He waved his hand towards the lagoon, the country flanking it and the considerable city standing back from the beach. "If it is not a presumption in me to offer a suggestion..." He paused. M. de Rivarol looked at him sharply, suspecting irony. But the swarthy face was bland, the keen eyes steady.

"Let us hear your suggestion," he consented.

Blood pointed out the fort at the mouth of the inner harbour, which was just barely visible above the waving palms on the intervening tongue of land. He announced that its armament was less formidable than that of the outer fort, which they had reduced; but on the other hand, the passage was very much narrower than the Boca Chica, and before they could attempt to make it in any case, they must dispose of those defences. He proposed that the French ships should enter the outer harbour, and proceed at once to bombardment. Meanwhile, he would land three hundred buccaneers and some artillery on the eastern side of the lagoon, beyond the fragrant garden islands dense with richly bearing fruit-trees, and proceed simultaneously to storm the fort in the rear. Thus beset on both sides at once, and demoralized by the fate of the much stronger outer fort, he did not think the Spaniards would offer a very long resistance. Then it would be for M. de Rivarol to garrison the fort, whilst Captain Blood would sweep on with his men, and seize the Church of Nuestra Senora de la Poupa, plainly visible on its hill immediately eastward of the town. Not only did that eminence afford them a valuable and obvious strategic advantage, but it commanded the only road that led from Cartagena to the interior, and once it were held there would be no further question of the Spaniards attempting to remove the wealth of the city.

That to M. de Rivarol was—as Captain Blood had judged that it would be—the crowning argument. Supercilious until that moment, and disposed for his own pride's sake to treat the buccaneer's suggestions with cavalier criticism, M. de Rivarol's manner suddenly changed. He became alert and brisk, went so far as tolerantly to commend Captain Blood's plan, and issued orders that action might be taken upon it at once.

It is not necessary to follow that action step by step. Blunders on the part of the French marred its smooth execution, and the indifferent handling of their ships led to the sinking of two of them in the course of the afternoon by the fort's gunfire. But by evening, owing largely to the irresistible fury with which the buccaneers stormed the place from the landward side, the fort had surrendered, and before dusk Blood and his men with some ordnance hauled thither by mules dominated the city from the heights of Nuestra Senora de la Poupa.

At noon on the morrow, shorn of defences and threatened with bombardment, Cartagena sent offers of surrender to M. de Rivarol.

Swollen with pride by a victory for which he took the entire credit to himself, the Baron dictated his terms. He demanded that all public effects and office accounts be delivered up; that the merchants surrender all moneys and goods held by them for their correspondents; the inhabitants could choose whether they would remain in the city or depart; but those who went must first deliver up all their property, and those who elected to remain must surrender half, and become the subjects of France; religious houses and churches should be spared, but they must render accounts of all moneys and valuables in their possession.

Cartagena agreed, having no choice in the matter, and on the next day, which was the 5th of April, M. de Rivarol entered the city and proclaimed it now a French colony, appointing M. de Cussy its Governor. Thereafter he proceeded to the Cathedral, where very properly a Te Deum was sung in honour of the conquest. This by way of grace, whereafter M. de Rivarol proceeded to devour the city. The only detail in which the French conquest of Cartagena differed from an ordinary buccaneering raid was that under the severest penalties no soldier was to enter the house of any inhabitant. But this apparent respect for the persons and property of the conquered was based in reality upon M. de Rivarol's anxiety lest a doubloon should be abstracted from all the wealth that was pouring into the treasury opened by the Baron in the name of the King of France. Once the golden stream had ceased, he removed all restrictions and left the city in prey to his men, who proceeded further to pillage it of that part of their property which the inhabitants who became French subjects had been assured should remain inviolate. The plunder was enormous. In the course of four days over a hundred mules laden with gold went out of the city and down to the boats waiting at the beach to convey the treasure aboard the ships.

XXVIII

THE HONOUR OF M. DE RIVAROL

During the capitulation and for some time after, Captain Blood and the greater portion of his buccaneers had been at their post on the heights of Nuestra Senora de la Poupa, utterly in ignorance of what was taking place. Blood, although the man chiefly, if not solely, responsible for the swift reduction of the city, which was proving a veritable treasure-house, was not even shown the consideration of being called to the council of officers which with M. de Rivarol determined the terms of the capitulation.

This was a slight that at another time Captain Blood would not have borne for a moment. But at present, in his odd frame of mind, and its divorcement from piracy, he was content to smile his utter contempt of the French General. Not so, however, his captains, and still less his men. Resentment smouldered amongst them for a while, to flame out violently at the end of that week in Cartagena. It was only by undertaking to voice their grievance to the Baron that their captain was able for the moment to pacify them. That done, he went at once in quest of M. de Rivarol.

He found him in the offices which the Baron had set up in the town, with a staff of clerks to register the treasure brought in and to cast up the surrendered account-books, with a view to ascertaining precisely what were the sums yet to be delivered up. The Baron sat there scrutinizing ledgers, like a city merchant, and checking figures to make sure that all was correct to the last peso. A choice occupation this for the General of the King's Armies by Sea and Land. He looked up irritated by the interruption which Captain Blood's advent occasioned.

"M. le Baron," the latter greeted him. "I must speak frankly; and you must suffer it. My men are on the point of mutiny."

M. de Rivarol considered him with a faint lift of the eyebrows.

"Captain Blood, I, too, will speak frankly; and you, too, must suffer it. If there is a mutiny, you and your captains shall be held personally responsible. The mistake you make is in assuming with me the tone of an ally, whereas I have given you clearly to understand from the first that you are simply in the position of having accepted service under me. Your proper apprehension of that fact will save the waste of a deal of words."

Blood contained himself with difficulty. One of these fine days, he felt, that for the sake of humanity he must slit the comb of this supercilious, arrogant cockerel.

"You may define our positions as you please," said he. "But I'll remind you that the nature of a thing is not changed by the name you give it. I am concerned with facts; chiefly with the fact that we entered into definite articles with you. Those articles provide for a certain distribution of the spoil. My men demand it. They are not satisfied."

"Of what are they not satisfied?" demanded the Baron.

"Of your honesty, M. de Rivarol."

A blow in the face could scarcely have taken the Frenchman more aback. He stiffened, and drew himself up, his eyes blazing, his face of a deathly pallor. The clerks at the tables laid down their pens, and awaited the explosion in a sort of terror.

For a long moment there was silence. Then the great gentleman delivered himself in a voice of concentrated anger.

"Do you really dare so much, you and the dirty thieves that follow you? God's Blood! You shall answer to me for that word, though it entail a yet worse dishonour to meet you. Faugh!"

"I will remind you," said Blood, "that I am speaking not for myself, but for my men. It is they who are not satisfied, they who threaten that unless satisfaction is afforded them, and promptly, they will take it."

"Take it?" said Rivarol, trembling in his rage. "Let them attempt it, and..."

"Now don't be rash. My men are within their rights, as you are aware. They demand to know when this sharing of the spoil is to take place, and when they are to receive the fifth for which their articles provide."

"God give me patience! How can we share the spoil before it has been completely gathered?"

"My men have reason to believe that it is gathered; and, anyway, they view with mistrust that it should all be housed aboard your ships, and remain in your possession. They say that hereafter there will be no ascertaining what the spoil really amounts to."

"But—name of Heaven!—I have kept books. They are there for all to see."

"They do not wish to see account-books. Few of them can read. They want to view the treasure itself. They know—you compel me to be blunt—that the accounts have been falsified. Your books show the spoil of Cartagena to amount to some ten million livres. The men know—and they are very skilled in these computations—that it exceeds the enormous total of forty millions. They insist that the treasure itself be produced and weighed in their presence, as is the custom among the Brethren of the Coast."

"I know nothing of filibuster customs." The gentleman was disdainful.

"But you are learning quickly."

"What do you mean, you rogue? I am a leader of armies, not of plundering thieves."

"Oh, but of course!" Blood's irony laughed in his eyes. "Yet, whatever you may be, I warn you that unless you yield to a demand that I consider just and therefore uphold, you may look for trouble, and it would not surprise me if you never leave Cartagena at all, nor convey a single gold piece home to France."

"Ah, pardieu! Am I to understand that you are threatening me?"

"Come, come, M. le Baron! I warn you of the trouble that a little prudence may avert. You do not know on what a volcano you are sitting. You do not know the ways of buccaneers. If you persist, Cartagena will be drenched in blood, and whatever the outcome the King of France will not have been well served."

That shifted the basis of the argument to less hostile ground. Awhile yet it continued, to be concluded at last by an ungracious undertaking from M. de Rivarol to submit to the demands of the buccaneers. He gave it with an extreme ill-grace, and only because Blood made him realize at last that to withhold it longer would be dangerous. In an engagement, he might conceivably defeat Blood's followers. But conceivably he might not. And even if he succeeded, the effort would be so costly to him in men that he might not thereafter find himself in sufficient strength to maintain his hold of what he had seized.

The end of it all was that he gave a promise at once to make the necessary preparations, and if Captain Blood and his officers would wait upon him on board the Victorieuse tomorrow morning, the treasure should be produced, weighed in their presence, and their fifth share surrendered there and then into their own keeping.

Among the buccaneers that night there was hilarity over the sudden abatement of M. de Rivarol's monstrous pride.

But when the next dawn broke over Cartagena, they had the explanation of it. The only ships to be seen in the harbour were the Arabella and the Elizabeth riding at anchor, and the Atropos and the Lachesis careened on the beach for repair of the damage sustained in the bombardment. The French ships were gone. They had been quietly and secretly warped out of the harbour under cover of night, and three sails, faint and small, on the horizon to westward was all that remained to be seen of them. The absconding M. de Rivarol had gone off with the treasure, taking with him the troops and mariners he had brought from France. He had left behind him at Cartagena not only the empty-handed buccaneers, whom he had swindled, but also M. de Cussy and the volunteers and black men from Hispaniola, whom he had swindled no less.

The two parties were fused into one by their common fury, and before the exhibition of it the inhabitants of that ill-fated town were stricken with deeper terror than they had yet known since the coming of this expedition.

Captain Blood alone kept his head, setting a curb upon his deep chagrin. He had promised himself that before parting from M. de Rivarol he would present a reckoning for all the petty affronts and insults to which that unspeakable fellow—now proved a scoundrel—had subjected him.

"We must follow," he declared. "Follow and punish."

At first that was the general cry. Then came the consideration that only two of the buccaneer ships were seaworthy—and these could not accommodate the whole force, particularly being at the moment indifferently victualled for a long voyage. The crews of the Lachesis and Atropos and with them their captains, Wolverstone and Yberville, renounced the intention. After all, there would be a deal of treasure still hidden in Cartagena. They would remain behind to extort it whilst fitting their ships for sea. Let Blood and Hagthorpe and those who sailed with them do as they pleased.

Then only did Blood realize the rashness of his proposal, and in attempting to draw back he almost precipitated a battle between the two parties into which that same proposal had now divided the buccaneers. And meanwhile those French sails on the horizon were growing less and less. Blood was reduced to despair. If he went off now, Heaven knew what would happen to the town, the temper of those whom he was leaving being what it was. Yet if he remained, it would simply mean that his own and Hagthorpe's crews would join in the saturnalia and increase the hideousness of events now inevitable. Unable to reach a decision, his own men and Hagthorpe's took the matter off his hands, eager to give chase to Rivarol. Not only was a dastardly cheat to be punished but an enormous treasure to be won by treating as an enemy this French commander who, himself, had so villainously broken the alliance.

When Blood, torn as he was between conflicting considerations, still hesitated, they bore him almost by main force aboard the Arabella.

Within an hour, the water-casks at least replenished and stowed aboard, the Arabella and the Elizabeth put to sea upon that angry chase.

"When we were well at sea, and the Arabella's course was laid," writes Pitt, in his log, "I went to seek the Captain, knowing him to be in great trouble of mind over these events. I found him sitting alone in his cabin, his head in his hands, torment in the eyes that stared straight before him, seeing nothing."

"What now, Peter?" cried the young Somerset mariner. "Lord, man, what is there here to fret you? Surely 't isn't the thought of Rivarol!"

"No," said Blood thickly. And for once he was communicative. It may well be that he must vent the thing that oppressed him or be driven mad by it. And Pitt, after all, was his friend and loved him, and, so, a proper man for confidences. "But if she knew! If she knew! O God! I had thought to have done with piracy; thought to have done with it for ever. Yet here have I been committed by this scoundrel to the worst piracy that ever I was guilty of. Think of Cartagena! Think of the hell those devils will be making of it now! And I must have that on my soul!"

"Nay, Peter—'t isn't on your soul; but on Rivarol's. It is that dirty thief who has brought all this about. What could you have done to prevent it?"

"I would have stayed if it could have availed."

"It could not, and you know it. So why repine?"

"There is more than that to it," groaned Blood. "What now? What remains? Loyal service with the English was made impossible for me. Loyal service with France has led to this; and that is equally impossible hereafter. What to live clean, I believe the only thing is to go and offer my sword to the King of Spain."

But something remained—the last thing that he could have expected—something towards which they were rapidly sailing over the tropical, sunlit sea. All this against which he now inveighed so bitterly was but a necessary stage in the shaping of his odd destiny.

Setting a course for Hispaniola, since they judged that thither must Rivarol go to refit before attempting to cross to France, the Arabella and the Elizabeth ploughed briskly northward with a moderately favourable wind for two days and nights without ever catching a glimpse of their quarry. The third dawn brought with it a haze which circumscribed their range of vision to something between two and three miles, and deepened their growing vexation and their apprehension that M. de Rivarol might escape them altogether.

Their position then—according to Pitt's log—was approximately 75 deg. 30' W. Long. by 17 deg. 45' N. Lat., so that they had Jamaica on their larboard beam some thirty miles to westward, and, indeed, away to the northwest, faintly visible as a bank of clouds, appeared the great ridge of the Blue Mountains whose peaks were thrust into the clear upper air above the low-lying haze. The wind, to which they were sailing very close, was westerly, and it bore to their ears a booming sound which in less experienced ears might have passed for the breaking of surf upon a lee shore.

"Guns!" said Pitt, who stood with Blood upon the quarter-deck. Blood nodded, listening.

"Ten miles away, perhaps fifteen—somewhere off Port Royal, I should judge," Pitt added. Then he looked at his captain. "Does it concern us?" he asked.

"Guns off Port Royal... that should argue Colonel Bishop at work. And against whom should he be in action but against friends of ours I think it may concern us. Anyway, we'll stand in to investigate. Bid them put the helm over."

Close-hauled they tacked aweather, guided by the sound of combat, which grew in volume and definition as they approached it. Thus for an hour, perhaps. Then, as, telescope to his eye, Blood raked the haze, expecting at any moment to behold the battling ships, the guns abruptly ceased.

They held to their course, nevertheless, with all hands on deck, eagerly, anxiously scanning the sea ahead. And presently an object loomed into view, which soon defined itself for a great ship on fire. As the Arabella with the Elizabeth following closely raced nearer on their north-westerly tack, the outlines of the blazing vessel grew clearer. Presently her masts stood out sharp and black above the smoke and flames, and through his telescope Blood made out plainly the pennon of St. George fluttering from her maintop.

"An English ship!" he cried.

He scanned the seas for the conqueror in the battle of which this grim evidence was added to that of the sounds they had heard, and when at last, as they drew closer to the doomed vessel, they made out the shadowy outlines of three tall ships, some three or four miles away, standing in toward Port Royal, the first and natural assumption was that these ships must belong to the Jamaica fleet, and that the burning vessel was a defeated buccaneer, and because of this they sped on to pick up the three boats that were standing away from the blazing hulk. But Pitt, who through the telescope was examining the receding squadron, observed things apparent only to the eye of the trained mariner, and made the incredible announcement that the largest of these three vessels was Rivarol's Victorieuse.

They took in sail and hove to as they came up with the drifting boats, laden to capacity with survivors. And there were others adrift on some of the spars and wreckage with which the sea was strewn, who must be rescued.

XXIX

THE SERVICE OF KING WILLIAM

One of the boats bumped alongside the Arabella, and up the entrance ladder came first a slight, spruce little gentleman in a coat of mulberry satin laced with gold, whose wizened, yellow, rather peevish face was framed in a heavy black periwig. His modish and costly apparel had nowise suffered by the adventure through which he had passed, and he carried himself with the easy assurance of a man of rank. Here, quite clearly, was no buccaneer. He was closely followed by one who in every particular, save that of age, was his physical opposite, corpulent in a brawny, vigorous way, with a full, round, weather-beaten face whose mouth was humourous and whose eyes were blue and twinkling. He was well dressed without fripperies, and bore with him an air of vigorous authority.

As the little man stepped from the ladder into the waist, whither Captain Blood had gone to receive him, his sharp, ferrety dark eyes swept the uncouth ranks of the assembled crew of the Arabella.

"And where the devil may I be now?" he demanded irritably. "Are you English, or what the devil are you?"

"Myself, I have the honour to be Irish, sir. My name is Blood—Captain Peter Blood, and this is my ship the Arabella, all very much at your service.

"Blood!" shrilled the little man. "O 'Sblood! A pirate!" He swung to the Colossus who followed him—"A damned pirate, van der Kuylen. Rend my vitals, but we're come from Scylla to Charybdis."

"So?" said the other gutturally, and again, "So?" Then the humour of it took him, and he yielded to it.

"Damme! What's to laugh at, you porpoise?" spluttered mulberry-coat. "A fine tale this'll make at home! Admiral van der Kuylen first loses his fleet in the night, then has his flagship fired under him by a French squadron, and ends all by being captured by a pirate. I'm glad you find it matter for laughter. Since for my sins I happen to be with you, I'm damned if I do."

"There's a misapprehension, if I may make so bold as to point it out," put in Blood quietly. "You are not captured, gentlemen; you are rescued. When you realize it, perhaps it will occur to you to acknowledge the hospitality I am offering you. It may be poor, but it is the best at my disposal."

The fierce little gentleman stared at him. "Damme! Do you permit yourself to be ironical?" he disapproved him, and possibly with a view to correcting any such tendency, proceeded to introduce himself. "I am Lord Willoughby, King William's Governor-General of the West Indies, and this is Admiral van der Kuylen, commander of His Majesty's West Indian fleet, at present mislaid somewhere in this damned Caribbean Sea."

"King William?" quoth Blood, and he was conscious that Pitt and Dyke, who were behind him, now came edging nearer, sharing his own wonder. "And who may be King William, and of what may he be King?"

"What's that?" In a wonder greater than his own, Lord Willoughby stared back at him. At last: "I am alluding to His Majesty King William III—William of Orange—who, with Queen Mary, has been ruling England for two months and more."

There was a moment's silence, until Blood realized what he was being told.

"D'ye mean, sir, that they've roused themselves at home, and kicked out that scoundrel James and his gang of ruffians?"

Admiral van der Kuylen nudged his lordship, a humourous twinkle in his blue eyes.

"His bolitics are fery sound, I dink," he growled.

His lordship's smile brought lines like gashes into his leathery cheeks. "'Slife! hadn't you heard? Where the devil have you been at all?"

"Out of touch with the world for the last three months," said Blood.

"Stab me! You must have been. And in that three months the world has undergone some changes." Briefly he added an account of them. King James was fled to France, and living under the protection of King Louis, wherefore, and for other reasons, England had joined the league against her, and was now at war with France. That was how it happened that the Dutch Admiral's flagship had been attacked by M. de Rivarol's fleet that morning, from which it clearly followed that in his voyage from Cartagena, the Frenchman must have spoken some ship that gave him the news.

After that, with renewed assurances that aboard his ship they should be honourably entreated, Captain Blood led the Governor-General and the Admiral to his cabin, what time the work of rescue went on. The news he had received had set Blood's mind in a turmoil. If King James was dethroned and banished, there was an end to his own outlawry for his alleged share in an earlier attempt to drive out that tyrant. It became possible for him to return home and take up his life again at the point where it was so unfortunately interrupted four years ago. He was dazzled by the prospect so abruptly opened out to him. The thing so filled his mind, moved him so deeply, that he must afford it expression. In doing so, he revealed of himself more than he knew or intended to the astute little gentleman who watched him so keenly the while.

"Go home, if you will," said his lordship, when Blood paused. "You may be sure that none will harass you on the score of your piracy, considering what it was that drove you to it. But why be in haste? We have heard of you, to be sure, and we know of what you are capable upon the seas. Here is a great chance for you, since you declare yourself sick of piracy. Should you choose to serve King William out here during this war, your knowledge of the West Indies should render you a very valuable servant to His Majesty's Government, which you would not find ungrateful. You should consider it. Damme, sir, I repeat: it is a great chance you are given.

"That your lordship gives me," Blood amended, "I am very grateful. But at the moment, I confess, I can consider nothing but this great news. It alters the shape of the world. I must accustom myself to view it as it now is, before I can determine my own place in it."

Pitt came in to report that the work of rescue was at an end, and the men picked up—some forty-five in all—safe aboard the two buccaneer ships. He asked for orders. Blood rose.

"I am negligent of your lordship's concerns in my consideration of my own. You'll be wishing me to land you at Port Royal."

"At Port Royal?" The little man squirmed wrathfully on his seat. Wrathfully and at length he informed Blood that they had put into Port Royal last evening to find its Deputy-Governor absent. "He had gone on some wild-goose chase to Tortuga after buccaneers, taking the whole of the fleet with him."

Blood stared in surprise a moment; then yielded to laughter.

"He went, I suppose, before news reached him of the change of government at home, and the war with France?"

"He did not," snapped Willoughby. "He was informed of both, and also of my coming before he set out."

"Oh, impossible!"

"So I should have thought. But I have the information from a Major Mallard whom I found in Port Royal, apparently governing in this fool's absence."

"But is he mad, to leave his post at such a time?" Blood was amazed.

"Taking the whole fleet with him, pray remember, and leaving the place open to French attack. That is the sort of Deputy-Governor that the late Government thought fit to appoint: an epitome of its misrule, damme! He leaves Port Royal unguarded save by a ramshackle fort that can be reduced to rubble in an hour. Stab me! It's unbelievable!"

The lingering smile faded from Blood's face. "Is Rivarol aware of this?" he cried sharply.

It was the Dutch Admiral who answered him. "Vould he go dere if he were not? M. de Rivarol he take some of our men prisoners. Berhabs dey dell him. Berhabs he make dem tell. Id is a great obbordunidy."

His lordship snarled like a mountain-cat. "That rascal Bishop shall answer for it with his head if there's any mischief done through this desertion of his post. What if it were deliberate, eh? What if he is more knave than fool? What if this is his way of serving King James, from whom he held his office?"

Captain Blood was generous. "Hardly so much. It was just vindictiveness that urged him. It's myself he's hunting at Tortuga, my lord. But, I'm thinking that while he's about it, I'd best be looking after Jamaica for King William." He laughed, with more mirth than he had used in the last two months.

"Set a course for Port Royal, Jeremy, and make all speed. We'll be level yet with M. de Rivarol, and wipe off some other scores at the same time."

Both Lord Willoughby and the Admiral were on their feet.

"But you are not equal to it, damme!" cried his lordship. "Any one of the Frenchman's three ships is a match for both yours, my man."

"In guns—aye," said Blood, and he smiled. "But there's more than guns that matter in these affairs. If your lordship would like to see an action fought at sea as an action should be fought, this is your opportunity."

Both stared at him. "But the odds!" his lordship insisted.

"Id is imbossible," said van der Kuylen, shaking his great head. "Seamanship is imbordand. Bud guns is guns."

"If I can't defeat him, I can sink my own ships in the channel, and block him in until Bishop gets back from his wild-goose chase with his squadron, or until your own fleet turns up."

"And what good will that be, pray?" demanded Willoughby.

"I'll be after telling you. Rivarol is a fool to take this chance, considering what he's got aboard. He carried in his hold the treasure plundered from Cartagena, amounting to forty million livres." They jumped at the mention of that colossal sum. "He has gone into Port Royal with it. Whether he defeats me or not, he doesn't come out of Port Royal with it again, and sooner or later that treasure shall find its way into King William's coffers, after, say, one fifth share shall have been paid to my buccaneers. Is that agreed, Lord Willoughby?"

His lordship stood up, and shaking back the cloud of lace from his wrist, held out a delicate white hand.

"Captain Blood, I discover greatness in you," said he.

"Sure it's your lordship has the fine sight to perceive it," laughed the Captain.

"Yes, yes! Bud how vill you do id?" growled van der Kuylen.

"Come on deck, and it's a demonstration I'll be giving you before the day's much older."

XXX

THE LAST FIGHT OF THE ARABELLA

"VHY do you vait, my friend?" growled van der Kuylen.

"Aye—in God's name!" snapped Willoughby.

It was the afternoon of that same day, and the two buccaneer ships rocked gently with idly flapping sails under the lee of the long spit of land forming the great natural harbour of Port Royal, and less than a mile from the straits leading into it, which the fort commanded. It was two hours and more since they had brought up thereabouts, having crept thither unobserved by the city and by M. de Rivarol's ships, and all the time the air had been aquiver with the roar of guns from sea and land, announcing that battle was joined between the French and the defenders of Port Royal. That long, inactive waiting was straining the nerves of both Lord Willoughby and van der Kuylen.

"You said you vould show us zome vine dings. Vhere are dese vine dings?"

Blood faced them, smiling confidently. He was arrayed for battle, in back-and-breast of black steel. "I'll not be trying your patience much longer. Indeed, I notice already a slackening in the fire. But it's this way, now: there's nothing at all to be gained by precipitancy, and a deal to be gained by delaying, as I shall show you, I hope."

Lord Willoughby eyed him suspiciously. "Ye think that in the meantime Bishop may come back or Admiral van der Kuylen's fleet appear?"

"Sure, now, I'm thinking nothing of the kind. What I'm thinking is that in this engagement with the fort M. de Rivarol, who's a lubberly fellow, as I've reason to know, will be taking some damage that may make the odds a trifle more even. Sure, it'll be time enough to go forward when the fort has shot its bolt."

"Aye, aye!" The sharp approval came like a cough from the little Governor-General. "I perceive your object, and I believe ye're entirely right. Ye have the qualities of a great commander, Captain Blood. I beg your pardon for having misunderstood you."

"And that's very handsome of your lordship. Ye see, I have some experience of this kind of action, and whilst I'll take any risk that I must, I'll take none that I needn't. But..." He broke off to listen. "Aye, I was right. The fire's slackening. It'll mean the end of Mallard's resistance in the fort. Ho there, Jeremy!"

He leaned on the carved rail and issued orders crisply. The bo'sun's pipe shrilled out, and in a moment the ship that had seemed to slumber there, awoke to life. Came the padding of feet along the decks, the creaking of blocks and the hoisting of sail. The helm was put over hard, and in a moment they were moving, the Elizabeth following, ever in obedience to the signals from the Arabella, whilst Ogle the gunner, whom he had summoned, was receiving Blood's final instructions before plunging down to his station on the main deck.

Within a quarter of an hour they had rounded the head, and stood in to the harbour mouth, within saker shot of Rivarol's three ships, to which they now abruptly disclosed themselves.

Where the fort had stood they now beheld a smoking rubbish heap, and the victorious Frenchman with the lily standard trailing from his mastheads was sweeping forward to snatch the rich prize whose defences he had shattered.

Blood scanned the French ships, and chuckled. The Victorieuse and the Medusa appeared to have taken no more than a few scars; but the third ship, the Baleine, listing heavily to larboard so as to keep the great gash in her starboard well above water, was out of account.

"You see!" he cried to van der Kuylen, and without waiting for the Dutchman's approving grunt, he shouted an order: "Helm, hard-a-port!"

The sight of that great red ship with her gilt beak-head and open ports swinging broadside on must have given check to Rivarol's soaring exultation. Yet before he could move to give an order, before he could well resolve what order to give, a volcano of fire and metal burst upon him from the buccaneers, and his decks were swept by the murderous scythe of the broadside. The Arabella held to her course, giving place to the Elizabeth, which, following closely, executed the same manoeuver. And then whilst still the Frenchmen were confused, panic-stricken by an attack that took them so utterly by surprise, the Arabella had gone about, and was returning in her tracks, presenting now her larboard guns, and loosing her second broadside in the wake of the first. Came yet another broadside from the Elizabeth and then the Arabella's trumpeter sent a call across the water, which Hagthorpe perfectly understood.

"On, now, Jeremy!" cried Blood. "Straight into them before they recover their wits. Stand by, there! Prepare to board! Hayton... the grapnels! And pass the word to the gunner in the prow to fire as fast as he can load."

He discarded his feathered hat, and covered himself with a steel head-piece, which a black man lad brought him. He meant to lead this boarding-party in person. Briskly he explained himself to his two guests. "Boarding is our only chance here. We are too heavily outgunned."

Of this the fullest demonstration followed quickly. The Frenchmen having recovered their wits at last, both ships swung broadside on, and concentrating upon the Arabella as the nearer and heavier and therefore more immediately dangerous of their two opponents, volleyed upon her jointly at almost the same moment.

Unlike the buccaneers, who had fired high to cripple their enemies above decks, the French fifed low to smash the hull of their assailant. The Arabella rocked and staggered under that terrific hammering, although Pitt kept her headed towards the French so that she should offer the narrowest target. For a moment she seemed to hesitate, then she plunged forward again, her beak-head in splinters, her forecastle smashed, and a gaping hole forward, that was only just above the water-line. Indeed, to make her safe from bilging, Blood ordered a prompt jettisoning of the forward guns, anchors, and water-casks and whatever else was moveable.

Meanwhile, the Frenchmen going about, gave the like reception to the Elizabeth. The Arabella, indifferently served by the wind, pressed forward to come to grips. But before she could accomplish her object, the Victorieuse had loaded her starboard guns again, and pounded her advancing enemy with a second broadside at close quarters. Amid the thunder of cannon, the rending of timbers, and the screams of maimed men, the half-necked Arabella plunged and reeled into the cloud of smoke that concealed her prey, and then from Hayton went up the cry that she was going down by the head.

Blood's heart stood still. And then in that very moment of his despair, the blue and gold flank of the Victorieuse loomed through the smoke. But even as he caught that enheartening glimpse he perceived, too, how sluggish now was their advance, and how with every second it grew more sluggish. They must sink before they reached her.

Thus, with an oath, opined the Dutch Admiral, and from Lord Willoughby there was a word of blame for Blood's seamanship in having risked all upon this gambler's throw of boarding.

"There was no other chance!" cried Blood, in broken-hearted frenzy. "If ye say it was desperate and foolhardy, why, so it was; but the occasion and the means demanded nothing less. I fail within an ace of victory."

But they had not yet completely failed. Hayton himself, and a score of sturdy rogues whom his whistle had summoned, were crouching for shelter amid the wreckage of the forecastle with grapnels ready. Within seven or eight yards of the Victorieuse, when their way seemed spent, and their forward deck already awash under the eyes of the jeering, cheering Frenchmen, those men leapt up and forward, and hurled their grapnels across the chasm. Of the four they flung, two reached the Frenchman's decks, and fastened there. Swift as thought itself, was then the action of those sturdy, experienced buccaneers. Unhesitatingly all threw themselves upon the chain of one of those grapnels, neglecting the other, and heaved upon it with all their might to warp the ships together. Blood, watching from his own quarter-deck, sent out his voice in a clarion call:

"Musketeers to the prow!"

The musketeers, at their station at the waist, obeyed him with the speed of men who know that in obedience is the only hope of life. Fifty of them dashed forward instantly, and from the ruins of the forecastle they blazed over the heads of Hayton's men, mowing down the French soldiers who, unable to dislodge the irons, firmly held where they had deeply bitten into the timbers of the Victorieuse, were themselves preparing to fire upon the grapnel crew.

Starboard to starboard the two ships swung against each other with a jarring thud. By then Blood was down in the waist, judging and acting with the hurricane speed the occasion demanded. Sail had been lowered by slashing away the ropes that held the yards. The advance guard of boarders, a hundred strong, was ordered to the poop, and his grapnel-men were posted, and prompt to obey his command at the very moment of impact. As a result, the foundering Arabella was literally kept afloat by the half-dozen grapnels that in an instant moored her firmly to the Victorieuse.

Willoughby and van der Kuylen on the poop had watched in breathless amazement the speed and precision with which Blood and his desperate crew had gone to work. And now he came racing up, his bugler sounding the charge, the main host of the buccaneers following him, whilst the vanguard, led by the gunner Ogle, who had been driven from his guns by water in the gun-deck, leapt shouting to the prow of the Victorieuse, to whose level the high poop of the water-logged Arabella had sunk. Led now by Blood himself, they launched themselves upon the French like hounds upon the stag they have brought to bay. After them went others, until all had gone, and none but Willoughby and the Dutchman were left to watch the fight from the quarter-deck of the abandoned Arabella.

For fully half-an-hour that battle raged aboard the Frenchman. Beginning in the prow, it surged through the forecastle to the waist, where it reached a climax of fury. The French resisted stubbornly, and they had the advantage of numbers to encourage them. But for all their stubborn valour, they ended by being pressed back and back across the decks that were dangerously canted to starboard by the pull of the water-logged Arabella. The buccaneers fought with the desperate fury of men who know that retreat is impossible, for there was no ship to which they could retreat, and here they must prevail and make the Victorieuse their own, or perish.

And their own they made her in the end, and at a cost of nearly half their numbers. Driven to the quarter-deck, the surviving defenders, urged on by the infuriated Rivarol, maintained awhile their desperate resistance. But in the end, Rivarol went down with a bullet in his head, and the French remnant, numbering scarcely a score of whole men, called for quarter.

Even then the labours of Blood's men were not at an end. The Elizabeth and the Medusa were tight-locked, and Hagthorpe's followers were being driven back aboard their own ship for the second time. Prompt measures were demanded. Whilst Pitt and his seamen bore their part with the sails, and Ogle went below with a gun-crew, Blood ordered the grapnels to be loosed at once. Lord Willoughby and the Admiral were already aboard the Victorieuse. As they swung off to the rescue of Hagthorpe, Blood, from the quarter-deck of the conquered vessel, looked his last upon the ship that had served him so well, the ship that had become to him almost as a part of himself. A moment she rocked after her release, then slowly and gradually settled down, the water gurgling and eddying about her topmasts, all that remained visible to mark the spot where she had met her death.

As he stood there, above the ghastly shambles in the waist of the Victorieuse, some one spoke behind him. "I think, Captain Blood, that it is necessary I should beg your pardon for the second time. Never before have I seen the impossible made possible by resource and valour, or victory so gallantly snatched from defeat."

He turned, and presented to Lord Willoughby a formidable front. His head-piece was gone, his breastplate dinted, his right sleeve a rag hanging from his shoulder about a naked arm. He was splashed from head to foot with blood, and there was blood from a scalp-wound that he had taken matting his hair and mixing with the grime of powder on his face to render him unrecognizable.

But from that horrible mask two vivid eyes looked out preternaturally bright, and from those eyes two tears had ploughed each a furrow through the filth of his cheeks.

XXXI

HIS EXCELLENCY THE GOVERNOR

When the cost of that victory came to be counted, it was found that of three hundred and twenty buccaneers who had left Cartagena with Captain Blood, a bare hundred remained sound and whole. The Elizabeth had suffered so seriously that it was doubtful if she could ever again be rendered seaworthy, and Hagthorpe, who had so gallantly commanded her in that last action, was dead. Against this, on the other side of the account, stood the facts that, with a far inferior force and by sheer skill and desperate valour, Blood's buccaneers had saved Jamaica from bombardment and pillage, and they had captured the fleet of M. de Rivarol, and seized for the benefit of King William the splendid treasure which she carried.

It was not until the evening of the following day that van der Kuylen's truant fleet of nine ships came to anchor in the harbour of Port Royal, and its officers, Dutch and English, were made acquainted with their Admiral's true opinion of their worth.

Six ships of that fleet were instantly refitted for sea. There were other West Indian settlements demanding the visit of inspection of the new Governor-General, and Lord Willoughby was in haste to sail for the Antilles.

"And meanwhile," he complained to his Admiral, "I am detained here by the absence of this fool of a Deputy-Governor."

"So?" said van der Kuylen. "But vhy should dad dedam you?"

"That I may break the dog as he deserves, and appoint his successor in some man gifted with a sense of where his duty lies, and with the ability to perform it."

"Aha! But id is not necessary you remain for dat. And he vill require no insdrucshons, dis one. He vill know how to make Port Royal safe, bedder nor you or me."

"You mean Blood?"

"Of gourse. Could any man be bedder? You haf seen vhad he can do."

"You think so, too, eh? Egad! I had thought of it; and, rip me, why not? He's a better man than Morgan, and Morgan was made Governor."

Blood was sent for. He came, spruce and debonair once more, having exploited the resources of Port Royal so to render himself. He was a trifle dazzled by the honour proposed to him, when Lord Willoughby made it known. It was so far beyond anything that he had dreamed, and he was assailed by doubts of his capacity to undertake so onerous a charge.

"Damme!" snapped Willoughby, "Should I offer it unless I were satisfied of your capacity? If that's your only objection..."

"It is not, my lord. I had counted upon going home, so I had. I am hungry for the green lanes of England." He sighed. "There will be apple-blossoms in the orchards of Somerset."

"Apple-blossoms!" His lordship's voice shot up like a rocket, and cracked on the word. "What the devil...? Apple-blossoms!" He looked at van der Kuylen.

The Admiral raised his brows and pursed his heavy lips. His eyes twinkled humourously in his great face.

"So!" he said. "Fery boedical!"

My lord wheeled fiercely upon Captain Blood. "You've a past score to wipe out, my man!" he admonished him. "You've done something towards it, I confess; and you've shown your quality in doing it. That's why I offer you the governorship of Jamaica in His Majesty's name—because I account you the fittest man for the office that I have seen."

Blood bowed low. "Your lordship is very good. But..."

"Tchah! There's no 'but' to it. If you want your past forgotten, and your future assured, this is your chance. And you are not to treat it lightly on account of apple-blossoms or any other damned sentimental nonsense. Your duty lies here, at least for as long as the war lasts. When the war's over, you may get back to Somerset and cider or your native Ireland and its potheen; but until then you'll make the best of Jamaica and rum."

Van der Kuylen exploded into laughter. But from Blood the pleasantry elicited no smile. He remained solemn to the point of glumness. His thoughts were on Miss Bishop, who was somewhere here in this very house in which they stood, but whom he had not seen since his arrival. Had she but shown him some compassion...

And then the rasping voice of Willoughby cut in again, upbraiding him for his hesitation, pointing out to him his incredible stupidity in trifling with such a golden opportunity as this. He stiffened and bowed.

"My lord, you are in the right. I am a fool. But don't be accounting me an ingrate as well. If I have hesitated, it is because there are considerations with which I will not trouble your lordship."

"Apple-blossoms, I suppose?" sniffed his lordship.

This time Blood laughed, but there was still a lingering wistfulness in his eyes.

"It shall be as you wish—and very gratefully, let me assure your lordship. I shall know how to earn His Majesty's approbation. You may depend upon my loyal service.

"If I didn't, I shouldn't offer you this governorship."

Thus it was settled. Blood's commission was made out and sealed in the presence of Mallard, the Commandant, and the other officers of the garrison, who looked on in round-eyed astonishment, but kept their thoughts to themselves.

"Now ve can aboud our business go," said van der Kuylen.

"We sail tomorrow morning," his lordship announced.

Blood was startled.

"And Colonel Bishop?" he asked.

"He becomes your affair. You are now the Governor. You will deal with him as you think proper on his return. Hang him from his own yardarm. He deserves it."

"Isn't the task a trifle invidious?" wondered Blood.

"Very well. I'll leave a letter for him. I hope he'll like it."

Captain Blood took up his duties at once. There was much to be done to place Port Royal in a proper state of defence, after what had happened there. He made an inspection of the ruined fort, and issued instructions for the work upon it, which was to be started immediately. Next he ordered the careening of the three French vessels that they might be rendered seaworthy once more. Finally, with the sanction of Lord Willoughby, he marshalled his buccaneers and surrendered to them one fifth of the captured treasure, leaving it to their choice thereafter either to depart or to enrol themselves in the service of King William.

A score of them elected to remain, and amongst these were Jeremy Pitt, Ogle, and Dyke, whose outlawry, like Blood's, had come to an end with the downfall of King James. They were—saving old Wolverstone, who had been left behind at Cartagena—the only survivors of that band of rebels-convict who had left Barbados over three years ago in the Cinco Llagas.

On the following morning, whilst van der Kuylen's fleet was making finally ready for sea, Blood sat in the spacious whitewashed room that was the Governor's office, when Major Mallard brought him word that Bishop's homing squadron was in sight.

"That is very well," said Blood. "I am glad he comes before Lord Willoughby's departure. The orders, Major, are that you place him under arrest the moment he steps ashore. Then bring him here to me. A moment." He wrote a hurried note. "That to Lord Willoughby aboard Admiral van der Kuylen's flagship."

Major Mallard saluted and departed. Peter Blood sat back in his chair and stared at the ceiling, frowning. Time moved on. Came a tap at the door, and an elderly black man slave presented himself. Would his excellency receive Miss Bishop?

His excellency changed colour. He sat quite still, staring at the black man a moment, conscious that his pulses were drumming in a manner wholly unusual to them. Then quietly he assented.

He rose when she entered, and if he was not as pale as she was, it was because his tan dissembled it. For a moment there was silence between them, as they stood looking each at the other. Then she moved forward, and began at last to speak, haltingly, in an unsteady voice, amazing in one usually so calm and deliberate.

"I... I... Major Mallard has just told me..."

"Major Mallard exceeded his duty," said Blood, and because of the effort he made to steady his voice it sounded harsh and unduly loud.

He saw her start, and stop, and instantly made amends. "You alarm yourself without reason, Miss Bishop. Whatever may lie between me and your uncle, you may be sure that I shall not follow the example he has set me. I shall not abuse my position to prosecute a private vengeance. On the contrary, I shall abuse it to protect him. Lord Willoughby's recommendation to me is that I shall treat him without mercy. My own intention is to send him back to his plantation in Barbados."

She came slowly forward now. "I... I am glad that you will do that. Glad, above all, for your own sake." She held out her hand to him.

He considered it critically. Then he bowed over it. "I'll not presume to take it in the hand of a thief and a pirate," said he bitterly.

"You are no longer that," she said, and strove to smile.

"Yet I owe no thanks to you that I am not," he answered. "I think there's no more to be said, unless it be to add the assurance that Lord Julian Wade has also nothing to apprehend from me. That, no doubt, will be the assurance that your peace of mind requires?"

"For your own sake—yes. But for your own sake only. I would not have you do anything mean or dishonouring."

"Thief and pirate though I be?"

She clenched her hand, and made a little gesture of despair and impatience.

"Will you never forgive me those words?"

"I'm finding it a trifle hard, I confess. But what does it matter, when all is said?"

Her clear hazel eyes considered him a moment wistfully. Then she put out her hand again.

"I am going, Captain Blood. Since you are so generous to my uncle, I shall be returning to Barbados with him. We are not like to meet again—ever. Is it impossible that we should part friends? Once I wronged you, I know. And I have said that I am sorry. Won't you... won't you say 'goodbye'?"

He seemed to rouse himself, to shake off a mantle of deliberate harshness. He took the hand she proffered. Retaining it, he spoke, his eyes sombrely, wistfully considering her.

"You are returning to Barbados?" he said slowly. "Will Lord Julian be going with you?"

"Why do you ask me that?" she confronted him quite fearlessly.

"Sure, now, didn't he give you my message, or did he bungle it?"

"No. He didn't bungle it. He gave it me in your own words. It touched me very deeply. It made me see clearly my error and my injustice. I owe it to you that I should say this by way of amend. I judged too harshly where it was a presumption to judge at all."

He was still holding her hand. "And Lord Julian, then?" he asked, his eyes watching her, bright as sapphires in that copper-coloured face.

"Lord Julian will no doubt be going home to England. There is nothing more for him to do out here."

"But didn't he ask you to go with him?"

"He did. I forgive you the impertinence."

A wild hope leapt to life within him.

"And you? Glory be, ye'll not be telling me ye refused to become my lady, when..."

"Oh! You are insufferable!" She tore her hand free and backed away from him. "I should not have come. Goodbye!" She was speeding to the door.

He sprang after her, and caught her. Her face flamed, and her eyes stabbed him like daggers. "These are pirate's ways, I think! Release me!"

"Arabella!" he cried on a note of pleading. "Are ye meaning it? Must I release ye? Must I let ye go and never set eyes on ye again? Or will ye stay and make this exile endurable until we can go home together? Och, ye're crying now! What have I said to make ye cry, my dear?"

"I... I thought you'd never say it," she mocked him through her tears.

"Well, now, ye see there was Lord Julian, a fine figure of a..."

"There was never, never anybody but you, Peter."

They had, of course, a deal to say thereafter, so much, indeed, that they sat down to say it, whilst time sped on, and Governor Blood forgot the duties of his office. He had reached home at last. His odyssey was ended.

And meanwhile Colonel Bishop's fleet had come to anchor, and the Colonel had landed on the mole, a disgruntled man to be disgruntled further yet. He was accompanied ashore by Lord Julian Wade.

A corporal's guard was drawn up to receive him, and in advance of this stood Major Mallard and two others who were unknown to the Deputy-Governor: one slight and elegant, the other big and brawny.

Major Mallard advanced. "Colonel Bishop, I have orders to arrest you. Your sword, sir!"

"By order of the Governor of Jamaica," said the elegant little man behind Major Mallard. Bishop swung to him.

"The Governor? Ye're mad!" He looked from one to the other. "I am the Governor."

"You were," said the little man dryly. "But we've changed that in your absence. You're broke for abandoning your post without due cause, and thereby imperiling the settlement over which you had charge. It's a serious matter, Colonel Bishop, as you may find. Considering that you held your office from the Government of King James, it is even possible that a charge of treason might lie against you. It rests with your successor entirely whether ye're hanged or not."

Bishop rapped out an oath, and then, shaken by a sudden fear: "Who the devil may you be?" he asked.

"I am Lord Willoughby, Governor General of His Majesty's colonies in the West Indies. You were informed, I think, of my coming."

The remains of Bishop's anger fell from him like a cloak. He broke into a sweat of fear. Behind him Lord Julian looked on, his handsome face suddenly white and drawn.

"But, my lord..." began the Colonel.

"Sir, I am not concerned to hear your reasons," his lordship interrupted him harshly. "I am on the point of sailing and I have not the time. The Governor will hear you, and no doubt deal justly by you." He waved to Major Mallard, and Bishop, a crumpled, broken man, allowed himself to be led away.

To Lord Julian, who went with him, since none deterred him, Bishop expressed himself when presently he had sufficiently recovered.

"This is one more item to the account of that scoundrel Blood," he said, through his teeth. "My God, what a reckoning there will be when we meet!"

Major Mallard turned away his face that he might conceal his smile, and without further words led him a prisoner to the Governor's house, the house that so long had been Colonel Bishop's own residence. He was left to wait under guard in the hall, whilst Major Mallard went ahead to announce him.

Miss Bishop was still with Peter Blood when Major Mallard entered. His announcement startled them back to realities.

"You will be merciful with him. You will spare him all you can for my sake, Peter," she pleaded.

"To be sure I will," said Blood. "But I'm afraid the circumstances won't."

She effaced herself, escaping into the garden, and Major Mallard fetched the Colonel.

"His excellency the Governor will see you now," said he, and threw wide the door.

Colonel Bishop staggered in, and stood waiting.

At the table sat a man of whom nothing was visible but the top of a carefully curled black head. Then this head was raised, and a pair of blue eyes solemnly regarded the prisoner. Colonel Bishop made a noise in his throat, and, paralyzed by amazement, stared into the face of his excellency the Deputy-Governor of Jamaica, which was the face of the man he had been hunting in Tortuga to his present undoing.

The situation was best expressed to Lord Willoughby by van der Kuylen as the pair stepped aboard the Admiral's flagship.

"Id is fery boedigal!" he said, his blue eyes twinkling. "Cabdain Blood is fond of boedry—you remember de abble-blossoms. So? Ha, ha!"

THE CHRONICLES OF CAPTAIN BLOOD

CONTENTS

INTRODUCTORY NOTE

The Odyssey of Captain Blood, given to the world some years ago, was derived from various sources, disclosed in the course of its compilation, of which the most important is the log of the Arabella, kept by the young Somersetshire shipmaster Jeremy Pitt. This log amounts to just such a chronicle of Blood's activities upon the Caribbean as that which Esquemeling, in similar case, has left of the exploits of that other great buccaneer, Sir Henry Morgan.

The compilation of the Odyssey, whilst it exhausted all other available collateral sources of information, was very far from exhausting the material left by Pitt. From that log of his were taken only those episodes which bore more or less directly upon the main outline of Blood's story, which it was then proposed to relate and elucidate. The selection presented obvious difficulties; and omissions, reluctantly made, were compelled by the necessity of presenting a straightforward and consecutive narrative.

It has since been felt, however, that some of the episodes then omitted might well be assembled in a supplementary volume which may shed additional light upon the methods and habits of the buccaneering fraternity in general and Captain Blood in particular.

It will be remembered by those who have read the volume entitled Captain Blood: His Odyssey, and it may briefly be repeated here for the information of those who have not, that

Peter Blood was the son of an Irish medicus, who had desired that his son should follow in his own honourable and humane profession. Complying with this parental wish, Peter Blood had received, at the early age of twenty, the degree of baccalaureus medicinae at Trinity College, Dublin. He showed, however, little disposition to practice the peaceful art for which he had brilliantly qualified. Perhaps a roving strain derived from his Somersetshire mother, in whose veins ran the blood of the Frobishers, was responsible for his restiveness. Losing his father some three months after taking his degree, he set out to see the world, preferring to open himself a career with the sword of the adventurer rather than with the scalpel of the surgeon.

After some vague wanderings on the continent of Europe we find him in the service of the Dutch, then at war with France. Again it may have been the Frobisher blood and a consequent predilection for the sea which made him elect to serve upon that element. He enjoyed the advantage of holding a commission under the great De Ruyter, and he fought in the Mediterranean engagement in which that famous Dutch Admiral lost his life. What he learnt under him Pitt's chronicle shows him applying in his later days when he had become the most formidable buccaneer leader on the Caribbean.

After the Peace of Nimeguen and until the beginning of 1685, when he reappears in England, little is known of his fortune, beyond the facts that he spent two years in a Spanish prison—where we must suppose that he acquired the fluent and impeccable Castilian which afterwards served him so often and so well—and that later he was for a while in the service of France, which similarly accounts for his knowledge of the French language.

In January of 1685 we find him at last, at the age of thirty-two, settling down in Bridgewater to practise the profession for which he had been trained. But for the Monmouth Rebellion, in whose vortex he was quite innocently caught up some six months later, this might have been the end of his 'career as an adventurer. And but for the fact that what came to him, utterly uninvited by him, was not in its ultimate manifestation unacceptable, we should have to regard him as one of the victims of the ironical malignity of Fortune aided and abetted, as it ever is, by the stupidity and injustice of man.

In his quality as a surgeon he was summoned on the morning after the battle of Sedgemoor to the bedside of a wounded gentleman who had been out with Monmouth, The dignity of his calling did not permit him to weigh legal quibbles or consider the position in which he might place himself in the eyes of a rigid and relentless law. All that counted with him was that a human being required his medical assistance, and he went to give it.

Surprised in the performance of that humanitarian duty by a party of dragoons who were hunting fugitives from the battle, he was arrested together with his patient. His patient being convicted of high treason for having been in arms against his king, Peter Blood suffered with him the same conviction under the statute which ordains that who succours or comforts a traitor is himself a traitor.

He was tried at Taunton before Judge Jeffreys in the course of the Bloody Assize, and sentenced to death.

Afterwards the sentence was commuted to transportation, not out of any spirit of mercy, but because it was discovered that to put to death the thousands that were implicated in the Monmouth Rebellion was to destroy valuable human merchandise which could be converted into money in the colonies. Slaves were required for work in the plantations, and the wealthy planters overseas who were willing to pay handsomely for the black men rounded up in Africa by slavers would be no less ready to purchase white men. Accordingly, these unfortunate rebels under sentence of death were awarded in batches to this lady or that gentleman of the Court to be turned by them to profitable account.

Peter Blood was in one of these batches, which included also Jeremy Pitt and some others who were later to be associated with him in an even closer bond than that of their present common misfortune.

This batch was shipped to Barbadoes, and sold there. And then, at last, Fate eased by a little her cruel grip of Peter Blood. When it was discovered that he was a man of medicine, and because in Barbadoes a medical man of ability was urgently required, his purchaser perceived how he could turn this slave to better account than by merely sending him to the sugar plantations. He was allowed to practise as a doctor. And since the pursuit of this demanded a certain liberty of action, this liberty, within definite limits, was accorded him. He employed it to plan an escape in association with a number of his fellow slaves.

The attempt was practically frustrated, when the arrival of a Spanish ship of war at Bridgetown and the circumstances attending it suddenly disclosed to the ready wits and resolute will of Peter Blood a better way of putting it into execution.

The Spaniards, having subjected Bridgetown to bombardment, effected a landing there and took possession of the place, holding it to ransom. To accomplish this, and having nothing to fear from a town which had been completely subdued, they left their fine ship, the Cinco Llagas out of Cadiz, at anchor in the bay with not more than a half-score of men aboard to guard her. Nor did these keep careful watch. Persuaded, like their brethren ashore, that there was nothing to be apprehended from the defeated English colonists, they abandoned themselves that night, again like their brethren ashore, to a jovial carousal.

This was Blood's opportunity. With a score of plantation slaves to whom none gave a thought at such a time, he quietly boarded the Cinco Llagas, overpowered the watch and took possession of her.

In the morning, when the glutted Spaniards were returning in boats laden with the plunder of Bridgetown, Peter Blood turned their own guns upon them, smashed their boats with round shot, and sailed away with his crew of rebels-convict to turn their reconquered liberty to such account as Fate might indicate.

I

THE BLANK SHOT

Captain Easterling, whose long duel with Peter Blood finds an important place in the chronicles which Jeremy Pitt has left us, must be regarded as the instrument chosen by Fate to shape the destiny of those rebels-convict who fled from Barbados in the captured Cinco Llagas.

The lives of men are at the mercy of the slenderest chances. A whole destiny may be influenced by no more than the set of the wind at a given moment. And Peter Blood's, at a time when it was still fluid, was certainly fashioned by the October hurricane which blew Captain Easterling's ten-gun sloop into Cayona Bay, where the Cinco Llagas had been riding idly at anchor for close upon a month.

Blood and his associates had run to this buccaneer stronghold of Tortuga, assured of finding shelter there whilst they deliberated upon their future courses. They had chosen it because it was the one haven in the Caribbean where they could count upon being unmolested and where no questions would be asked of them. No English settlement would harbour them because of their antecedents. The hand of Spain would naturally be against them not only because they were English, but, further, because they were in possession of a Spanish ship. They could trust themselves to no ordinary French colony because of the recent agreement between the Governments of France and England for the apprehension and interchange of any persons escaping from penal settlements. There remained the Dutch, who were neutral. But Blood regarded neutrality as the most untrustworthy of all conditions, since it implies liberty of action in any direction. Therefore he steered clear of the Dutch as of the others and made for Tortuga, which, belonging to the French West India Company, was nominally French, but nominally only. Actually it was of no nationality, unless the Brethren of the Coast, as the buccaneering fraternity was called, could be deemed to constitute a nation. At least it can be said that no law ran in Tortuga that was at issue with the laws governing that great brotherhood. It suited the French Government to give the protection of its flag to these lawless men, so that in return they might serve French interests by acting as a curb upon Spanish greed and aggressiveness in the West Indies.

At Tortuga, therefore, the escaped rebels-convict dwelt in peace aboard the Cinco Llagas until Easterling came to disturb that peace and force them into action and into plans for their future, which, without him, they might have continued to postpone.

This Easterling—as nasty a scoundrel as ever sailed the Caribbean—carried under hatches some tons of cacao of which he had lightened a Dutch merchantman homing from the Antilles. The exploit, he realized, had not covered him with glory; for glory in that pirate's eyes was measurable by profit; and the meagre profit in this instance was not likely to increase him in the poor esteem in which he knew himself to be held by the Brethren of the Coast. Had he suspected the Dutchman of being no more richly laden he would have let her pass unchallenged. But having engaged and boarded her, he had thought it incumbent upon him and his duty to his crew of rascals to relieve her of what she carried. That she should have carried nothing of more value than cacao was a contingency for which he blamed the evil fortune which of late had dogged him—an evil fortune which was making it increasingly difficult for him to find men to sail with him.

Considering these things, and dreaming of great enterprises, he brought his sloop Bonaventure into the shelter of the rock-bound harbour of Tortuga, a port designed by very Nature for a stronghold. Walls of rock, rising sheer, and towering like mountains, protect it upon either side and shape it into a miniature gulf. It is only to be approached by two channels demanding skilful pilotage. These were commanded by the Mountain Fort, a massive fortress with which man had supplemented the work of Nature. Within the shelter of this harbour, the French and English buccaneers who made it their lair might deride the might of the King of Spain, whom they regarded as their natural enemy, since it was his persecution of them when they had been peaceful boucan-hunters which had driven them to the grim trade of sea-rovers.

Within that harbour Easterling dismissed his dreams to gaze upon a curious reality. It took the shape of a great red-hulled ship riding proudly at anchor among the lesser craft, like a swan amid a gaggle of geese. When he had come near enough to read the name Cinco Llagas boldly painted in letters of gold above her counter, and under this the port of origin, Cadiz, he rubbed his eyes so that he might read again. Thereafter he sought in conjecture an explanation of the presence of that magnificent ship of Spain in this pirates' nest of Tortuga. A thing of beauty she was, from gilded beak-head above which the brass cannons glinted in the morning sun, to towering sterncastle, and a thing of power as announced by the forty guns which Easterling's practised eye computed her to carry behind her closed ports.

The Bonaventure cast anchor within a cable's length of the great ship, in ten fathoms, close under the shadow of the

Mountain Fort on the harbour's western side, and Easterling went ashore to seek the explanation of this mystery.

In the market-place beyond the mole he mingled with the heterogeneous crowd that converted the quays of Cayona into an image of Babel. There were bustling traders of many nations, chiefly English, French and Dutch; planters and seamen of various degrees; buccaneers who were still genuine boucanhunters and buccaneers who were frankly pirates; lumbermen, beachcombers, Indians, fruit-selling half-castes, black man slaves, and all the other types of the human family that daily loafed or trafficked there. He found presently a couple of well-informed rogues very ready with the singular tale of how that noble vessel out of Cadiz came to ride so peacefully at anchor in Cayona Bay, manned by a parcel of escaped plantation slaves.

To such a man as Easterling, it was an amusing and even an impressive tale. He desired more particular knowledge of the men who had engaged in such an enterprise. He learned that they numbered not above a score and that they were all political offenders—rebels who in England had been out with Monmouth, preserved from the gallows because of the need of slaves in the West Indian plantations. He learned all that was known of their leader, Peter Blood: that he was by trade a man of medicine, and the rest.

It was understood that, because of this, and with a view of resuming his profession, Blood desired to take ship for Europe at the first occasion and that most of his followers would accompany him. But one or two wilder spirits, men who had been trained to the sea, were likely to remain behind and join the Brotherhood of the Coast.

All this Easterling learned in the market-place behind the mole, whence his fine, bold eyes continued to con the great red ship.

With such a vessel as that under his feet there was no limit to the things he might achieve. He began to see visions. The fame of Henry Morgan, with whom once he had sailed and under whom he had served his apprenticeship to piracy, should become a pale thing beside his own. These poor escaped convicts should be ready enough to sell a ship which had served its purpose by them, and they should not be exorbitant in their notions of her value. The cacao aboard the Bonaventure should more than suffice to pay for her.

Captain Easterling smiled as he stroked his crisp black beard. It had required his own keen wits to perceive at once an opportunity to which all others had been blind during that long month in which the vessel had been anchored there. It was for him to profit by his perceptions.

He made his way through the rudely-built little town by the road white with coral dust—so white under the blazing sun that a man's eyes ached to behold it and sought instinctively the dark patches made by the shadows of the limp exiguous palms by which it was bordered.

He went so purposefully that he disregarded the hails greeting him from the doorway of the tavern of The King of France, nor paused to crush a cup with the gaudy buccaneers who filled the place with their noisy mirth. The Captain's business that morning was with Monsieur d'Ogeron, the courtly, middle-aged Governor of Tortuga, who in representing the French West India Company seemed to represent France herself, and who, with the airs of a minister of state, conducted affairs of questionable probity but of unquestionable profit to his company.

In the fair, white, green-shuttered house, pleasantly set amid fragrant pimento trees and other aromatic shrubs, Captain Easterling was received with dignified friendliness by the slight, elegant Frenchman who brought to the wilds of Tortuga a faint perfume of the elegancies of Versailles. Coming from the white glare outside into the cool spacious room, to which was admitted only such light as filtered between the slats of the closed shutters, the Captain found himself almost in darkness until his eyes had adjusted themselves.

The Governor offered him a chair and gave him his attention.

In the matter of the cacao there was no difficulty. Monsieur d'Ogeron cared not whence it came. That he had no illusions on the subject was shown by the price per quintal at which he announced himself prepared to purchase. It was a price representing rather less than half the value of the merchandise. Monsieur d'Ogeron was a diligent servant of the French West India Company.

Easterling haggled vainly, grumbled, accepted, and passed to the major matter. He desired to acquire the Spanish ship in the bay. Would Monsieur d'Ogeron undertake the purchase for him from the fugitive convicts who, he understood, were in possession of her.

Monsieur d'Ogeron took time to reply. "It is possible," he said at last, "that they may not wish to sell."

"Not sell? A God's name what use is the ship to those poor ragamuffins?"

"I mention only a possibility," said Monsieur d'Ogeron. "Come to me again this evening, and you shall have your answer."

When Easterling returned as bidden, Monsieur d'Ogeron was not alone. As the Governor rose to receive his visitor, there rose with him a tall, spare man in the early thirties from whose shaven face, swarthy as a gipsy's, a pair of eyes looked out that were startlingly blue, level, and penetrating. If Monsieur d'Ogeron in dress and air suggested Versailles, his companion as markedly suggested the Alameda. He was very richly dressed in black in the Spanish fashion, with an abundance of silver lace and a foam of fine point at throat and wrists, and he wore a heavy black periwig whose curls descended to his shoulders.

Monsieur d'Ogeron presented him: "Here, Captain, is Mr Peter Blood to answer you in person."

Easterling was almost disconcerted, so different was the man's appearance from anything that he could have imagined. And now this singular escaped convict was bowing with the grace of a courtier, and the buccaneer was reflecting that these fine Spanish clothes would have been filched from the locker of the commander of the Cinco Llagas. He remembered something else.

"Ah yes. To be sure. The physician," he said, and laughed for no apparent reason.

Mr. Blood began to speak. He had a pleasant voice whose metallic quality was softened by a drawling Irish accent. But what he said made Captain Easterling impatient. It was not his intention to sell the Cinco Llagas.

Aggressively before the elegant Mr. Blood stood now the buccaneer, a huge, hairy, dangerous-looking man, in coarse shirt and leather breeches, his cropped head swathed in a red-and-yellow kerchief. Aggressively he demanded Blood's reasons for retaining a ship that could be of no use to him and his fellow convicts.

Blood's voice was softly courteous in reply, which but increased Easterling's contempt of him. Captain Easterling heard himself assured that he was mistaken in his assumptions. It was probable that the fugitives from Barbados would employ the vessel to return to Europe, so as to make their way to France or Holland.

"Maybe we're not quite as ye're supposing us, Captain. One of my companions is a shipmaster, and three others have served, in various ways, in the King's Navy."

"Bah!" Easterling's contempt exploded loudly. "The notion's crazy. What of the perils of the sea, man? Perils of capture? How will ye face those with your paltry crew? Have ye considered that?"

Still Captain Blood preserved his pleasant temper. "What we lack in men we make up in weight of metal. Whilst I may not be able to navigate a ship across the ocean, I certainly know how to fight a ship at need. I learnt it under de Ruyter."

The famous name gave pause to Easterling's scorn. "Under de Ruyter?"

"I held a commission with him some years ago." Easterling was plainly dumbfounded. "I thought it's a doctor ye was."

"I am that, too," said the Irishman simply.

The buccaneer expressed his disgusted amazement in a speech liberally festooned with oaths. And then Monsieur d'Ogeron made an end of the interview. "So that you see, Captain Easterling, there is no more to be said in the matter."

Since, apparently, there was not, Captain Easterling sourly took his leave. But on his disgruntled way back to the mole he thought that although there was no more to be said there was a good deal to be done. Having already looked upon the majestic Cinco Llagas as his own, he was by no means disposed to forgo the prospect of possession.

Monsieur d'Ogeron also appeared to think that there was still at least a word to be added, and he added it after Easterling's departure. "That," he said quietly, "is a nasty and a dangerous man. You will do well to bear it in mind, Monsieur Blood."

Blood treated the matter lightly. "The warning was hardly necessary. The fellow's person would have announced the blackguard to me even if I had not known him for a pirate."

A shadow that was almost suggestive of annoyance flitted across the delicate features of the Governor of Tortuga.

"Oh, but a filibuster is not of necessity a blackguard, nor is the career of a filibuster one for your contempt, Monsieur Blood. There are those among the buccaneers who do good service to your country and to mine by setting a restraint upon the rapacity of Spain, a rapacity which is responsible for their existence. But for the buccaneers, in these waters, where neither France nor England can maintain a fleet, the Spanish dominion would be as absolute as it is inhuman. You will remember that your country honoured Henry Morgan with a knighthood and the deputy-governorship of Jamaica. And he was an even worse pirate, if it is possible, than your Sir Francis Drake, or Hawkins or Frobisher, or several others I could name, whose memory your country also honours."

Followed upon this from Monsieur d'Ogeron, who derived considerable revenues from the percentages he levied by way of harbour dues on all prizes brought into Tortuga, solemn counsels that Mr. Blood should follow in the footsteps of those heroes. Being outlawed as he was, in possession of a fine ship and the nucleus of an able following, and being, as he had proved, a man of unusual resource, Monsieur d'Ogeron did not doubt that he would prosper finely as a filibuster.

Mr. Blood didn't doubt it himself. He never doubted himself. But he did not on that account incline to the notion. Nor, probably, but for that which ensued, would he ever have so inclined, however much the majority of his followers might have sought to persuade him.

Among these, Hagthorpe, Pitt, and the giant Wolverstone, who had lost an eye at Sedgemoor, were perhaps the most persistent. It was all very well for Blood, they told him, to plan a return to Europe. He was master of a peaceful art in the pursuit of which he might earn a livelihood in France or Flanders. But they were men of the sea, and knew no other trade. Dyke, who had been a petty officer in the Navy before he embarked on politics and rebellion, held similar views, and Ogle, the gunner, demanded to know of Heaven and Hell and Mr. Blood what guns they thought the British Admiralty would entrust to a man who had been out with Monmouth.

Things were reaching a stage in which Peter Blood could see no alternative to that of parting from these men whom a common misfortune had endeared to him. It was in this pass that Fate employed the tool she had forged in Captain Easterling.

One morning, three days after his interview with Mr. Blood at the Governor's house, the Captain came alongside the Cinco Llagas in the cockboat from his sloop. As he heaved his massive bulk into the waist of the ship, his bold, dark eyes were everywhere at once. The Cinco Llagas was not only well-found, but irreproachably kept. Her decks were scoured, her cordage stowed, and everything in place. The muskets were ranged in the rack about the mainmast, and the brasswork on the scuttle-butts shone like gold in the bright sunshine. Not such lubberly fellows, after all, these escaped rebels-convict who composed Mr. Blood's crew.

And there was Mr. Blood himself in his black and silver, looking like a Grandee of Spain, doffing a black hat with a sweep of claret ostrich plume about it, and bowing until the wings of his periwig met across his face like the pendulous ears of a spaniel. With him stood Nathaniel Hagthorpe, a pleasant gentleman of Mr. Blood's own age, whose steady eye and clear-cut face announced the man of breeding; Jeremy Pitt, the flaxen-haired young Somerset shipmaster; the short, sturdy Nicholas Dyke, who had been a petty officer and had served under King James when he was Duke of York. There was nothing of the' ragamuffin about these, as Easterling had so readily imagined. Even the burly, rough-voiced Wolverstone had crowded his muscular bulk into Spanish fripperies for the occasion.

Having presented them, Mr. Blood invited the captain of the Bonaventure to the great cabin in the stern, which for spaciousness and richness of furniture surpassed any cabin Captain Easterling had ever entered.

A black man servant in a white jacket—a lad hired here in Tortuga—brought, besides the usual rum and sugar and fresh limes, a bottle of golden Canary which had been in the ship's original equipment and which Mr. Blood recommended with solicitude to his unbidden guest.

Remembering Monsieur d'Ogeron's warning that Captain Easterling was dangerous, Mr. Blood deemed it wise to use him with all civility, if only so that being at his ease he should disclose in what he might be dangerous now.

They occupied the elegantly cushioned seats about the table of black oak, and Captain Easterling praised the Canary liberally to justify the liberality with which he consumed it. Thereafter he came to business by asking if Mr. Blood, upon reflection, had not perhaps changed his mind about selling the ship.

"If so be that you have," he added, with a glance at Blood's four companions, "considering among how many the purchase money will be divided, you'll find me generous."

If by this he had hoped to make an impression upon those four, their stolid countenances disappointed him.

Mr. Blood shook his head. "It's wasting your time, ye are, Captain. Whatever else we decide, we keep the Cinco Llagas."

"Whatever you decide?" The great black brows went up on that shallow brow. "Ye're none so decided than as ye was about this voyage to Europe? Why, then, I'll come at once to the business I'd propose if ye wouldn't sell. It is that with this ship ye join the Bonaventure in a venture—a bonaventure," and he laughed noisily at his own jest with a flash of white teeth behind the great black beard.

"You honour us. But we haven't a mind to piracy."

Easterling gave no sign of offence. He waved a great ham of a hand as if to dismiss the notion. "It ain't piracy I'm proposing."

"What then?"

"I can trust you?"—Easterling asked, and his eyes included the four of them.

"Ye're not obliged to. And it's odds ye'll waste your time in any case."

It was not encouraging. Nevertheless, Easterling proceeded. It might be known to them that he had sailed with Morgan. He had been with Morgan in the great march across the Isthmus of Panama. Now it was notorious that when the spoil came to be divided after the sack of that Spanish city it was found to be far below the reasonable expectations of the buccaneers. There were murmurs that Morgan had not dealt fairly with his men; that he had abstracted before the division a substantial portion of the treasure taken. Those murmurs, Easterling could tell them, were well founded. There were pearls and jewels from San Felipe of fabulous value, which Morgan had secretly appropriated for himself. But as the rumours grew and reached his ears, he became afraid of a search that should convict him. And so, midway on the journey across the Isthmus, he one night buried the treasure he had filched.

"Only one man knew this," said Captain Easterling to his attentive listeners-for the tale was of a quality that at all times commands attention. "The man who helped him in a labour he couldn't ha' done alone. I am that man."

He paused a moment to let the impressive fact sink home, and then resumed.

The business he proposed was that the fugitives on the Cinco Llagas should join him in an expedition to Darien to recover the treasure, sharing equally in it with his own men and on the scale usual among the Brethren of the Coast.

"If I put the value of what Morgan buried at five hundred thousand pieces of eight, I am being modest."

It was a sum to set his audience staring. Even Blood stared, but not quite with the expression of the others.

"Sure, now, it's very odd," said he thoughtfully. "What is odd, Mr. Blood?"

Mr. Blood's answer took the form of another question. "How many do you number aboard the Bonaventure?"

"Something less than two hundred men."

"And the twenty men who are with me make such a difference that you deem it worth while to bring us this proposal?"

Easterling laughed outright, a deep, guttural laugh. "I see that ye don't understand at all." His voice bore a familiar echo of Mr. Blood's Irish intonation. "It's not the men I lack so much as a stout ship in which to guard the treasure when we have it. In a bottom such as this we'd be as snug as in a fort, and I'd snap my fingers at any Spanish galleon that attempted to molest me."

"Faith, now I understand," said Wolverstone, and Pitt and Dyke and Hagthorpe nodded with him. But the glittering blue eye of Peter Blood continued to stare unwinkingly upon the bulky pirate.

"As Wolverstone says, it's understandable. But a tenth of the prize, which, by heads, is all that would come to the Cinco Llagas, is far from adequate in the circumstances."

Easterling blew out his cheeks and waved his great hand in a gesture of bonhomie. "What share would you propose?"

"That's to be considered. But it would not be less than one-fifth."

The buccaneer's face remained impassive. He bowed his gaudily swathed head. "Bring these friends of yours to dine tomorrow aboard the Bonaventure, and we'll draw up the articles."

For a moment Blood seemed to hesitate. Then in courteous terms he accepted the invitation.

But when the buccaneer had departed he checked the satisfaction of his followers.

"I was warned that Captain Easterling is a dangerous man. That's to flatter him. For to be dangerous a man must be clever, and Captain Easterling is not clever."

"What maggot's burrowing under your periwig, Peter?" wondered Wolverstone.

"I'm thinking of the reason he gave for desiring our association. It was the best he could do when bluntly asked the question."

"It could not have been more reasonable," said Hagthorpe, emphatically. He was finding Blood unnecessarily difficult.

"Reasonable!" Blood laughed. "Specious, if you will. Specious until you come to examine it. Faith now, it glitters, to be sure. But it isn't gold. A ship as strong as a fort in which to stow a half-million pieces of eight, and this fortress ship in the hands of ourselves. A trusting fellow this Easterling for a scoundrel!"

They thought it out, and their eyes grew round. Pitt, however, was not yet persuaded. "In his need he'll trust our honour."

Blood looked at him with scorn. "I never knew a man with eyes like Easterling's to trust to anything but possession. If he means to stow that treasure aboard this ship, and I could well believe that part of it, it is because he means to be in possession of this ship by the time he does so. Honour! Bah! Could such a man believe that honour would prevent us from giving him the slip one night once we had the treasure aboard, or even of bringing our weight of metal to bear upon his sloop and sinking her? It's fatuous you are, Jeremy, with your talk of honour."

Still the thing was not quite clear to Hagthorpe. "What, then, do you suppose to be his reason for inviting us to join him?"

"The reason that he gave. He wants our ship, be it for the conveyance of his treasure, if it exists, be it for other reasons. Didn't he first seek to buy the Cinco Llagas? Oh, he wants her, naturally enough; but he wants not us, nor would he keep us long, be sure of that."

And yet, perhaps because the prospect of a share in Morgan's treasure was, as Blood said, a glittering one, his associates were reluctant to abandon it. To gain alluring objects men are always ready to take chances, ready to believe what they hope. So now Hagthorpe, Pitt, and Dyke. They came to the opinion that Blood was leaping to conclusions from a prejudice sown in him by Monsieur d'Ogeron, who may have had reasons of his own to serve. Let them at least dine tomorrow with Easterling, and hear what articles he proposed.

"Can you be sure that we shall not be poisoned?" wondered Blood.

But this was pushing prejudice too far. They mocked him freely. How could they be poisoned by meat and drink that Easterling must share with them? And what end would thus be served? How would that give Easterling possession of the Cinco Llagas?

"By swarming aboard her with a couple of score of his ruffians and taking the men here unawares at a time when there would be none to lead them."

"What?" cried Hagthorpe. "Here in Tortuga? In this haven of the buccaneers? Come, come, Peter! I must suppose there is some honour among thieves."

"You may suppose it. I prefer to suppose nothing of the kind. I hope no man will call me timorous; and yet I'd as soon be called that as rash."

The weight of opinion, however, was against him.

Every man of the rebels-convict crew was as eager for the enterprise when it came to be disclosed as were the three leaders.

And so, despite himself, at eight bells on the morrow, Captain Blood went over with Hagthorpe, Pitt, and Dyke, to dine aboard the Bonaventure. Wolverstone was left behind in charge of the Cinco Llagas.

Easterling welcomed them boisterously, supported by his entire crew of ruffians. Some eight score of them swarmed in the waist, on the forecastle, and even on the poop, and all were armed. It was not necessary that Mr. Blood should point out to his companions how odd it was that all these fellows should have been summoned for the occasion from the taverns ashore which they usually frequented. Their presence and the leering mockery stamped upon their villainous countenances made

Blood's three followers ask themselves at last if Blood had not been justified of his misgivings, and made them suspect with him that they had walked into a trap.

It was too late to retreat. By the break of the poop, at the entrance of the gangway leading to the cabin, stood Captain Easterling waiting to conduct them.

Blood paused there a moment to look up into the pellucid sky above the rigging about which the gulls were circling. He glanced round and up at the grey fort perched on its rocky eminence, all bathed in ardent sunshine. He looked towards the mole, forsaken now in the noontide heat, and then across the crystalline sparkling waters towards the great red Cinco Llagas where she rode in majesty and strength. To his uneasy companions it seemed as if he were wondering from what quarter help might come if it were needed. Then, responding to Easterling's inviting gesture, he passed into the gloom of the gangway, followed by the others.

Like the rest of the ship, which the first glance had revealed for dishevelled and unclean, the cabin was in no way comparable with that of the stately Cinco Llagas. It was so low that there was barely headroom for tall men like Blood and Hagthorpe. It was ill-furnished, containing little more than the cushioned lockers set about a deal table that was stained and hacked. Also, for all that the horn windows astern were open, the atmosphere of the place was heavy with an acrid blend of vile smells in which spunyarn and bilge predominated.

The dinner proved to be much as the surroundings promised. The fresh pork and fresh vegetables had been befouled in cooking, so that, in forcing himself to eat, the fastidious stomach of Mr. Blood was almost turned.

The company provided by Easterling matched the rest. A half-dozen of his fellows served him as a guard of honour. They had been elected, he announced, by the men, so that they might agree the articles on behalf of all. To these had been added a young Frenchman named Joinville, who was secretary to Monsieur d'Ogeron and stood there to represent the Governor and to lend, as it were, a legal sanction to what was to be done. If the presence of this rather vacuous pale-eyed gentleman served to reassure Mr. Blood a little, it served to intrigue him more.

Amongst them they crowded the narrow confines of the cabin, and Easterling's fellows were so placed along the two sides of the table that no two of the men from the Cinco Llagas sat together. Blood and the captain of the Bonaventure immediately faced each other across the board.

Business was left until dinner was over and the black man who waited on them had withdrawn. Until then the men of the Bonaventure kept things gay with the heavily salted talk that passed for wit amongst them. At last, the table cleared of all save bottles, and pens and ink being furnished together with a sheet of paper each to Easterling and Blood, the captain of the Bonaventure opened the matter of the terms, and Peter Blood heard himself for the first time addressed, as Captain. Easterling's first words were to inform him shortly that the one-fifth share he had demanded was by the men of the Bonaventure accounted excessive.

Momentarily Peter Blood's hopes rose.

"Shall we deal in plain terms now, Captain? Do you mean that they'll not be consenting to them?"

"What else should I mean?"

"In that case, Captain, it only remains for us to take our leave, in your debt for this liberal entertainment and the richer for the improvement in our acquaintance."

The elaborate courtesy of those grossly inaccurate terms did not seem to touch the ponderous Easterling. His bold, craftily-set eyes stared blankly from his great red face. He mopped the sweat from his brow before replying.

"You'll take your leave?" There was a sneering undertone to his guttural voice. "I'll trouble you in turn to be plain with me.

I likes plain men and lain words. D'ye mean that yell quit from the business?"

Two or three of his followers made a rumbling challenging echo to his question.

Captain Blood—to give him now the title Easterling had bestowed upon him—had the air of being intimidated. He hesitated, looking as if for guidance to his companions, who returned him only uneasy glances.

"If," he said at length, "you find our terms unreasonable, I must assume ye'll not be wishing to go further, and it only remains for us to withdraw."

He spoke with a diffidence which amazed his own followers, who had never known him other than bold in the face of any odds. It provoked a sneer from Easterling, who found no more than he had been expecting from a leech turned adventurer by circumstances.

"Faith, Doctor," said he, "ye were best to get back to your cupping and bleeding, and leave ships to men as can handle them."

There was a lightning flash from those blue eyes, as vivid as it was transient. The swarthy countenance never lost its faint air of diffidence. Meanwhile Easterling had swung to the Governor's representative, who sat on his immediate right.

"What d'ye think of that, Mossoo Joinville?"

The fair, flabby young Frenchman smiled amiably upon Blood's diffidence. "Would it not be wise and proper, sir, to hear what terms Captain Easterling now proposes?"

"I'll hear them. But—"

"Leave the buts till after, Doctor," Easterling cut in. "The terms we'll grant are the terms I told ye. Your men share equally with mine."

"But that means no more than a tenth for the Cinco Llagas." And Blood, too, now appealed to M. Joinville. "Do you, sir, account that fair? I have explained to Captain Easterling that for what we lack in men we more than make up in weight of metal, and our guns are handled by a gunner such as I dare swear has no compeer in the Caribbean. A fellow named Ogle—Ned Ogle. A remarkable gunner is Ned Ogle. The very devil of a gunner, as you'd believe if you'd seen him pick those Spanish boats off the water in Bridgetown Harbour."

He would have continued upon the subject of Ned Ogle had not Easterling interrupted him. "Hell, man! What's a gunner more or less?"

"Oh, an ordinary gunner, maybe. But this is no ordinary gunner. An eye he has. Gunners like Ogle are like poets: they are born, so they are. He'll put you a shot between wind and water, will Ogle, as neatly as you might pick your teeth."

Easterling banged the table. "What's all this to the point?"

"It may be something. And meanwhile it shows you the valuable ally ye're acquiring." And he was off again on the subject of his gunner. "He was trained in the King's Navy, was Ned Ogle, and a bad day for the King's Navy it was when Ogle took to politics and followed the Protestant champion to Sedgemoor."

"Leave that," growled one of the officers of the Bonaventure, a ruffian who answered to the name of Chard. "Leave it, I say, or we'll waste the day in talk."

Easterling confirmed this with a coarse oath. Captain Blood observed that they did not mean to spare offensiveness, and his speculations on their aims starting from that took a fresh turn.

Joinville intervened. "Could you not compromise with Captain Blood? After all, there is some reason on his side. He might reasonably claim to put a hundred men aboard his ship, and in that case he would naturally take a heavier share."

"In that case he might be worth it," was the truculent answer.

"I am worth it as it is," Blood insisted.

"Ah, bah!" he was answered, with a flick of finger and thumb under his very nose.

He began to suspect that Easterling sought to entice him into an act of rashness, in reply to which he and his followers would probably be butchered where they sat, and M. Joinville would afterwards be constrained to bear witness to the Governor that the provocation had proceeded from the guests. He perceived at last the probable reason for the Frenchman's presence.

But at the moment Joinville was remonstrating. "Come, come, Captain Easterling! Thus you will never reach agreement. Captain Blood's ship is of advantage to you, and we have to pay for what is advantageous. Could you not offer him an eighth or even a seventh share?"

Easterling silenced the growl of disagreement from Chard, and became almost suave. "What would Captain Blood say to that?"

Captain Blood considered for a long moment. Then he shrugged. "I say what you know I must say: that I can say nothing until I have taken the wishes of my followers. We'll resume the discussion when I have done so—another day."

"Oh, s'death!" roared Easterling. "Do you play with us? Haven't you brought your officers with you, and ain't they empowered to speak for your men same as mine? Whatever we settles here, my men abides by. That's the custom of the Brethren of the Coast. And I expect the same from you. And I've the right to expect it, as you can tell him, Mossoo Joinville."

The Frenchman nodded gloomily, and Easterling roared on.

"We are not children, by God! And we're not here to play, but to agree terms. And, by God, we'll agree them before you leave."

"Or not, as the case may be," said Blood quietly. It was to be remarked that he had lost his diffidence by now.

"Or not? What the devil do you mean with your 'or not'?" Easterling came to his feet in a vehemence that Peter Blood believed assumed, as the proper note at this stage of the comedy he was playing.

"I mean or not, quite simply." He accounted that the time had come to compel the buccaneers to show their hand. "If we fail to agree terms, why, that's the end of the matter."

"Oho! The end of the matter, eh? Stab me, but it may prove the beginning of it."

Blood smiled up into his face, and cool as ice he commented: "That's what I was supposing. But the beginning of what, if you please, Captain Easterling?"

"Indeed, indeed, Captain!" cried Joinville. "What can you mean?"

"Mean?" Captain Easterling glared at the Frenchman. He appeared to be extremely angry. "Mean?" he repeated. "Look you, Mossoo, this fellow here, this Blood, this doctor, this escaped convict, made believe that he would enter into articles with us so as to get from me the secret of Morgan's treasure. Now that he's got it, he makes difficulties about the articles. He no longer wants to join us, it seems. He proposes to withdraw. It'll be plain to you why he proposes to withdraw, Mossoo Joinville; just as it'll be plain to you why I can't permit it."

"Why, here's paltry invention!" sneered Blood. "What do I know of his secret beyond his tale of a treasure buried somewhere?"

"Not somewhere. You know where. For I've been fool enough to tell you."

Blood actually laughed, and by his laughter scared his companions, to whom the danger of their situation was now clear enough.

"Somewhere on the Isthmus of Darien! There's precision, on my soul! With that information I can go straight to the spot and set my hand on it! As for the rest, M. Joinville, I invite you to observe it's not myself is making difficulties about the articles. On the one-fifth share which I asked from the outset, I might have been prepared to join Captain Easterling. But now that I'm confirmed in all that I suspected of him and more, why,

I wouldn't join him for a half share in this treasure, supposing it to exist at all, which I do not."

That brought every man of the Bonaventure to his feet as if it had been a signal, and they were clamorous too, until Easterling waved them into silence. Upon that silence cut the tenor voice of M. Joinville.

"You are a singularly rash man, Captain Blood."

"Maybe, maybe," says Blood, light and airily. "Time will show. The last word's not yet been said."

"Then here's to say it," quoth Easterling, quietly sinister on a sudden. "I was about to warn you that ye'll not be allowed to leave this ship with the information ye possess until the articles is signed. But since ye so clearly show your intentions, why, things have gone beyond warnings."

From his seat at the table, which he retained, Captain Blood looked up at the sinister bulk of the captain of the Bonaventure, and the three men from the Cinco Llagas observed with mingled amaze-men and dismay that he was smiling. At first so unusually diffident and timid; now so deliberately and recklessly provoking. He was beyond understanding. It was Hagthorpe who spoke for them.

"What do you mean, Captain? What do you intend by us?"

"Why, to clap you into irons, and stow you under hatches, where you can do no harm."

"My God, sir—" Hagthorpe was beginning, when Captain Blood's crisp pleasant voice cut across his speech.

"And you, M. Joinville, will permit this without protest?"

Joinville spread his hands, thrust out a nether lip, and shrugged. "You have brought it on yourself, Captain Blood."

"So that is what you are here to report to Monsieur d'Ogeron! Well, well!" He laughed with a touch of bitterness.

And then, abruptly, on the noontide stillness outside came the thunder of a gun to shake them all. Followed the screaming of startled gulls, a pause in which men eyed one another, and then, a shade uneasily, came the question from Easterling, addressed to no one in particular:

"What the devil's that?"

It was Blood who answered him pleasantly. "Now don't let it alarm ye, Captain darling. It's just a salute fired in your honour by Ogle, the gunner-the highly skilful gunner—of the Cinco Llagas. Have I told you about him yet?" His eyes embraced the company in the question.

"A salute?" quoth Easterling. "By Hell, what do you mean? A salute?"

"Why, just a courtesy, as a reminder to us and a warning to you. It's reminder to us that we've taken up an hour of your time, and that we must put no further strain upon your hospitality." He got to his feet, and stood, easy and elegant in his Spanish suit of black and silver. "It's a very good day we'll be wishing you, Captain."

Inflamed of countenance, Easterling plucked a pistol from his belt. "You play-acting buffoon! Ye don't leave this ship!"

But Captain Blood continued to smile. "Fith, that will be very bad for the ship, and for all aboard her, including this ingenuous Monsieur Joinville, who really believes you'll pay him the promised share of your phantom treasure for bearing false witness against me, so as to justify you in the eyes of the Governor for seizing the Cinco Llagas. Ye see, I am under no delusions concerning you, my dear Captain. For a rogue ye're a thought too transparent."

Easterling loosed a volley of minatory obscenity, waving his pistol. He was restrained from using it only by an indefinable uneasiness aroused by his guest's bantering manner.

"We are wasting time," Blood interrupted him, "and the moments, believe me, are growing singularly precious. You'd best know where you stand. My orders to Ogle were that if within ten minutes of his firing that salute I and my friends here were not over the side of the Bonaventure, he was to put a round shot into your forecastle along the water-line, and as many more after that as may be necessary to sink you by the head. I do not think that many will be necessary. Ogle is a singularly skilful marksman. He served with distinction as a gunner in the King's Navy. I think I've told you about him."

It was Joinville who broke the moment's silence that followed. "God of my life!" he bleated, bounding to his feet. "Let me out of this!"

"Oh, stow your squealing, you French rat!" snarled the infuriated Easterling. Then he turned his fury upon Blood, balancing the pistol ominously. "You sneaking leech! You college offal! You'd ha' done better to ha' stuck to your cupping and bleedings, as I told you."

His murderous intention was plain. But Blood was too swift for him. Before any could so much as guess his purpose, he had snatched up by its neck the flagon of Canary that stood before him and crashed it across Captain Easterling's left temple.

As the captain of the Bonaventure reeled back against the cabin bulkhead, Peter Blood bowed slightly to him.

"I regret," said he, "that I have no cup; but, as you see, I can practise phlebotomy with a bottle."

Easterling sagged down in a limp unconscious mass at the foot of the bulkhead. The spectacle stirred his officers. There was a movement towards Captain Blood, and a din of raucous voices, and someone laid hands upon him. But above the uproar rang his vibrant voice.

"Be warned! The moments are speeding. The ten minutes have all but fled, and either I and my friends depart, or we all sink together in this bottom."

"In God's name, bethink you of it!" cried Joinville, and started for the door.

A buccaneer who did bethink him of it and who was of a practical turn of mind, seized him about the body and flung him back.

"You there;" he shouted to Captain Blood. "You and your men go first. And bestir yourselves! We've no mind to drown like rats."

They went as they were bidden, curses pursuing them and threats of a reckoning to follow with Captain Easterling.

Either the ruffians aswarm on the deck above were not in the secret of Easterling's intentions, or else a voice of authority forbade them to hinder the departure of Captain Blood and his companions.

In the cock-boat, midway between the two vessels, Hagthorpe found his voice at last.

"On my soul's salvation, Peter, there was a moment when I thought our sands were run."

"Ay, ay," said Pitt with fervour. "And even as it was they might have been." He swung to Peter Blood, where he sat in the sternsheets. "Suppose that for one reason or another we had not got out in those ten minutes, and Ogle had opened fire in earnest? What then?"

"Ah!" said Blood. "Our real danger lay in that he wasn't like to do it."

"But if you so ordered him?"

"Nay, that's just what I forgot to do. All I told him was to loose a blank shot when we had been gone an hour. I thought that however things went it might prove useful. And on my soul, I believe it did. Lord!" He took off his hat, and mopped his brow under the staring eyes of his companions.

"I wonder now if it's the heat that's making me sweat like this."

II

THE TREASURE SHIP

It was a saying of Captain Blood's that the worth of a man manifests itself not so much in the ability to plan great undertakings as in the vision which perceives opportunity and the address which knows how to seize it.

He had certainly displayed these qualities in possessing himself of that fine Spanish ship the Cinco Llagas, and he had displayed them again in foiling the designs of that rascally buccaneer Captain Easterling to rob him of that noble vessel.

Meanwhile his own and his vessel's near escape made it clear to all who followed him that there was little safety for them in Tortuga waters, and little trust to be placed in buccaneers. At a general council held that same afternoon in the ship's waist Blood propounded the simple philosophy that when a man is attacked he must either fight or run.

"And since we are in no case to fight when attacked, as no doubt we shall be, it but remains to play the coward's part if only so that we may survive to prove ourselves brave men some other day."

They agreed with him. But whilst the decision to run was taken, it was left to be determined later whither they should run. At the moment all that mattered was to get away from Tortuga and the further probable attentions of Captain Easterling.

Thus it fell out that in the dead of the following night, which if clear was moonless, the great frigate which lately had been the pride of the Cadiz shipyards weighed anchor as quietly as such an operation might be performed. With canvas spread to the faint favouring breeze from the shore, and with the ebb tide to help the manoeuvre, the Cinco Llagas stood out to sea. If groan of windlass, rattle of chain, and creak of blocks had betrayed the action to Easterling aboard the Bonaventure, a cable's length away, it was not in Easterling's power to thwart Blood's intention.

At least three-quarters of his rascally crew were in the taverns ashore, and Easterling was not disposed to attempt boarding operations with the remnant of his men, even though that remnant outnumbered by two to one the hands of the Cinco Llagas. Moreover, even had his full complement of two hundred been aboard, Easterling would still have offered no opposition to that departure. Whilst in Tortuga waters he might have attempted to get possession of the Cinco Llagas quietly and by strategy, not even his recklessness could consider seizing her violently by force in such a sanctuary, especially as the French Governor, Monsieur d'Ogeron, appeared to be friendly disposed towards Blood and his fellow fugitives.

Out on the open sea it would be another matter; and the tale he would afterwards tell of the manner in which the Cinco Llagas should have come into his possession would be such as no one in Cayona would be in a position to contradict.

So Captain Easterling suffered Peter Blood to depart unhindered, and was well content to let him go. Nor did he display any undue and betraying haste to follow. He made his preparations with leisureliness, and did not weigh anchor until the afternoon of the morrow. He trusted his wits to give him the direction Blood must take and depended upon the greater speed of the Bonaventure to overhaul him before he should have gone far enough for safety. His reasoning was shrewd enough. Since he knew that the Cinco Llagas was not victualled for a long voyage, there could be no question yet of any direct attempt to sail for Europe.

First she must be equipped, and since to equip her Blood dared approach no English or Spanish settlement, it followed that he must steer for one of the neutral Dutch colonies, and there take his only remaining chance. Nor was Blood likely without experienced pilotage to venture among the dangerous reefs of the Bahamas. It was therefore an easy inference that his destination would be the Leeward Islands with intent to put in at San Martin, Saba, or Santa Eustacia. Confident, then, of overtaking him before he could make the nearest of those Dutch settlements, two hundred leagues away, the pursuing Bonaventure steered an easterly course along the northern shores of Hispaniola.

Things, however, were not destined to be so simple as Easterling conjectured. The wind, at first favourable, veered towards evening to the east, and increased throughout the night in vehemence; so that by dawn—an angry dawn with skies ominously flushed—the Bonaventure had not merely made no progress, but had actually drifted some miles out of her course. Then the wind shifted to the south towards noon, and it came on to blow harder than ever. It blew up a storm from the Caribbean, and for twenty-four hours the Bonaventure rode it out with bare yards and hatches battened against the pounding seas that broke athwart her and tossed her like a cork from trough to crest.

It was fortunate that the burly Easterling was not only a stout fighter but also an able seaman. Under his skilled handling the Bonaventure came through the ordeal unscathed, to resume the chase when at last the storm had passed and the wind had settled to a steady breeze from the south-west. With crowded canvas the sloop now went scudding through the heaving seas which the storm had left.

Easterling heartened his followers with the reminder that the hurricane which had delayed them must no less have delayed the Cinco Llagas; that, indeed, considering the lubbers who handled the erstwhile Spanish frigate, it was likely that the storm had made things easier for the Bonaventure.

What exactly the storm had done for them they were to discover on the following morning, when off Cape Engaño they sighted a galleon which at first, in the distance, they supposed to be their quarry, but which very soon they perceived to be some other vessel. That she was Spanish was advertised not only by the towering build, but by the banner of Castile which she flew beneath the Crucifix at the head of her mainmast. On the yards of this mainmast all canvas was close-reefed, and under the spread of only foresail mizzen and spirit she was labouring clumsily towards the Mona Passage with the wind on her larboard quarter.

The sight of her in her partially maimed condition stirred Easterling like a hound at sight of a deer. For the moment the quest of the Cinco Llagas was forgotten. Here was more immediate prey, and of a kind to be easily reduced.

At the poop rail he bawled his orders rapidly. In obedience the decks were cleared with feverish speed and the nettings spread from stem to stern to catch any spars that might be shot down in the approaching action. Chard, Easterling's lieutenant, a short, powerful man, who was a dullard in all things save the handling Of a ship and the wielding of a cutlass, took the helm. The gunners at their stations cleared the leaden aprons from the touchholes and swung their glowing matches, ready for the word of command. For however disorderly and unruly Easterling's crew might be at ordinary times, it knew the need for discipline when battle was to be joined.

Watchful on the poop, the buccaneer captain surveyed the Spaniard upon which he was rapidly bearing down, and observed with scorn the scurry of preparation on her decks. His practised eye read her immediate past history at a glance, and his harsh guttural voice announced what he read to Chard, who stood below him at the whipstaff.

"She would be homing for Spain when the hurricane caught her. She's sprung her mainmast and likely suffered other damage besides, and she's beating back for San Domingo for repairs." Easterling laughed in his throat and stroked his dense black beard. The dark, bold eyes in his great red face glinted wickedly. "Give me a homing Spaniard, Chard. There'll be treasure aboard that hulk. By God, we're in luck at last."

He was indeed. It had long been his grievance, and the true reason of his coveting the Cinco Llagas, that his sloop the Bonaventure was unequal to tackling the real prizes of the Caribbean. And he would never have dared to attack this heavily-armed galleon but that in her crippled condition she was unable to manoeuvre so as to bring her guns to bear upon his flanks.

She, gave him now a broadside from her starboard quarter, and by doing so sealed her own doom. The Bonaventure, coming head on, presented little target, and save for a round shot in her forecastle took no damage. Easterling answered the fire with the chasers on his prow, aiming high, and sweeping the Spaniard's decks. Then, nimbly avoiding her clumsy attempt to go about and change their relative positions, the Bonaventure was alongside on the quarter of her empty guns. There was a rattling, thudding jar, a creak of entangled rigging, a crack and clatter of broken spars and the thud of grapnels rending into the Spaniard's timbers to bind her fast, mid then, tight-locked, the two vessels went drifting down wind, whilst the buccaneers, led by the colossal Easterling, and after discharging a volley of musketry, swarmed like ants over the Spaniard's bulwarks. Two hundred of them there were, fierce fellows in loose leathern breeches, some with shirts as well, but the majority naked to the waist, and by that brown muscular nakedness the more terrific of aspect.

To receive them stood a bare fifty Spaniards in corselet and morion, drawn up in the galleon's waist as if upon parade, with muskets calmly levelled and a hawk-faced officer in a plumed hat commanding them.

The officer spoke an order, and a volley from the muskets momentarily checked the assault. Then, like an engulfing wave, the buccaneer mob went over the Spanish soldiers, and the ship, the Santa Barbara, was taken.

There was not perhaps upon the seas at the time a more cruel, ruthless man than Easterling and those who sailed with him adopted, as men will, their captain's standard of ferocity. Brutally they exterminated the Spanish soldiery, heaving the bodies overboard, and as brutally they dealt with those manning the guns on the main deck below, although these unfortunates readily surrendered in the vain hope of being allowed to keep their lives.

Within ten minutes of the invasion of the Santa Barbara there remained alive upon her of her original crew only the captain, Don Ildefonso de Paiva, whom Easterling had stunned with the butt of a pistol, the navigating officer, and four deck-hands, who had been aloft at the moment of boarding. These six Easterling spared for the present because he accounted that they might prove useful.

Whilst his men were busy in the shrouds about the urgent business of disentangling and where necessary repairing, the buccaneer captain began upon the person of Don Ildefonso the investigation of his capture.

The Spaniard, sickly and pallid and with a lump on his brow where the pistol-butt had smitten him, sat on a locker in the handsome roomy cabin, with pinioned wrists, but striving nevertheless to preserve the haughty demeanour proper to a gentleman of Castile in the presence of an impudent sea-robber. Thus until Easterling, towering over him, savagely threatened to loosen his tongue by the artless persuasions of torture. Then Don Ildefonso, realizing the futility of resistance, curtly answered the pirate's questions. From these answers and his subsequent investigations, Easterling discovered his capture to exceed every hope he could have formed.

There had fallen into his hands—which of late had known so little luck-one of those prizes which had been the dream of every sea-rover since the days of Francis Drake. The Santa Barbara was a treasure-ship from Porto Bello, laden with gold and silver which had been conveyed across the Isthmus from Panama. She had put forth under the escort of three strong ships of war, with intent to call at San Domingo to revictual before crossing to Spain. But in the recent storm which had swept the Caribbean she had been separated from her consorts, and with damaged mainmast had been driven through the Mona Passage by this gale. She had been beating hack for San Domingo in the hope of rejoining there her escort or else awaiting there another fleet for Spain.

The treasure in her hold was computed by Easterling when his gleaming eyes came to consider those ingots at between two and three hundred thousand pieces of eight. It was a prize such as does not come the way of a pirate twice in his career, and it meant fortune for himself and those who sailed with him.

Now the possession of fortune is inevitably attended by anxiety, and Easterling's besetting anxiety at the moment was to convey his prize with all possible speed to the security of Tortuga.

From his own sloop he took two score men to form a prize crew for the Spaniard, and himself remained aboard her because he could not suffer himself to be parted from the treasure. Then, with damage hurriedly repaired, the two ships went about, and started upon their voyage. Progress was slow, the wind being none too favourable and the Santa Barbara none too manageable, and it was past noon before they once more had Cape Raphael abeam. Easterling was uneasy in this near proximity to Hispaniola, and was for taking a wide sweep that would carry them well out to sea, when from the crow's nest of theSanta Barbara came a hail, and a moment later the object first espied by the look-out was visible to them all.

There, rounding Cape Raphael, not two miles away, and steering almost to meet them, came a great red ship under full sail. Easterling's telescope confirmed at once what the naked eye had led him incredulously to suspect. This vessel was the Cinco Llagas, the original object of his pursuit, which in his haste he must have outsailed.

The truth was that, overtaken by the storm as they approached Samana, Jeremy Pitt, who navigated the Cinco Llagas, had run for the shelter of Samana Bay, and under the lee of a headland had remained snug and unperceived, to come forth again when the gale had spent itself.

Easterling, caring little how the thing had happened, perceived in this sudden and unexpected appearance of the Cinco Llagas a sign that Fortune, hitherto so niggardly, was disposed now to overwhelm him with her favours. Let him convey himself and the Santa Barbara's treasure aboard that stout red ship, and in strength he could make good speed home.

Against a vessel so heavily armed and so undermanned as the Cinco Llagas there could be no question of any but boarding tactics, and it did not seem to Captain Easterling that this should offer much difficulty to the swifter and more easily handled Bonaventure, commanded by a man experienced in seamanship and opposed by a lubberly follower who was by trade a surgeon.

So Easterling signalled Chard to be about the easy business, and Chard, eager enough to square accounts with the man who once already had done them the injury of slipping like water through their fingers, put the helm over and ordered his men to their stations.

Captain Blood, summoned from the cabin by Pitt, mounted the poop, and telescope in hand, surveyed the activities aboard his old friend the Bonaventure. He remained in no doubt of their significance. He might be a surgeon, but hardly a lubberly one, as Chard so rashly judged him. His service under de Ruyter in those earlier adventurous days when medicine was neglected by him had taught him more of fighting tactics than Easterling had ever known. He was not perturbed. He would show these pirates how he had profited by the lessons learnt under that great admiral.

Just as for the Bonaventure it was essential to employ boarding tactics, so for the Cinco Llagas it was vital to depend on gunfire. For with no more than twenty men in all, she could not face the odds of almost ten to one, as Blood computed them, of a hand-to-hand engagement. So now he ordered Pitt to put down the helm, and, keeping as close to the wind as possible, to steer a course that would bring them on to the Bonaventure's quarter. To the main deck below he ordered Ogle, that sometime gunner of the King's Navy, taking for his gun crew all but six of the hands who would be required for work above.

Chard perceived at once the aim of the manoeuvre, and swore through his teeth, for Blood had the weather gauge of him. He was further handicapped by the fact that since the Cinco Llagas was to be captured for their own purposes it must be no part of his work to cripple her by gunfire before attempting to board. Moreover, he perceived the risk to himself of the attempt, resulting from the longer range and heavier calibre of the guns of the Cinco Llagas, if she were resolutely handled. And there appeared to be no lack of resolution about her present master.

Meanwhile the distance between the ships was rapidly lessening, and Chard realized that unless he acted quickly he would be within range with his flank exposed. Unable to bring his ship any closer to the wind, he went about on a south-easterly course with intent to circle widely and so get to windward to the Cinco Llagas.

Easterling, watching the manoeuvre from the deck of the Santa Barbara, and not quite understanding its purpose, cursed Chard for a fool. He cursed him the more virulently when he saw the Cinco Llagas veer suddenly to larboard and follow as if giving chase. Chard, however, welcomed this, and taking in sail allowed the other to draw closer. Then with all canvas spread once more, the Bonaventure was off with the wind on her quarter to attempt her circling movement.

Blood understood, and took in sail in his turn, standing so that as the Bonaventure turned north she must offer him her flank within range of his heavy guns. Hence Chard, to avoid this, must put up his helm and run south once more.

Easterling watched the two ships sailing away from him in a succession of such manoeuvres for position, and, purple with rage, demanded of Heaven and Hell whether he could believe his eyes, which told him only Chard was running away from the lubberly leech. Chard, however, was far from any such intention. With masterly patience and self-control he awaited his chance to run in and grapple. And with equal patience and doggedness Blood saw to it that he should be given no such chance.

In the end it became a question of who should commit the first blunder, and it was Chard who committed it. In his almost excessive anxiety to avoid coming broadside on with the Cinco Llagas, he forgot the chasers on her beak-head, and at last in playing for position allowed her to come too near. He realized his blunder when those two guns roared suddenly behind him and the shot went tearing through his shrouds. It angered him, and in his anger he replied with his stern chasers; but their inferior calibre left their fire ineffective. Then, utterly enraged, he swung the Bonaventure about, so as to put a broadside athwart the hawse of the other, and by crippling her sailing powers lay her at the mercy of his boarders.

The heavy ground swell, however, combined with the length of the range utterly to defeat his object, and his broadside thundered forth in impotence to leave a cloud of smoke between himself and the Cinco Llagas. Instantly Blood swung broadside on, and emptied his twenty larboard guns into that smoke-cloud, hoping to attain the Bonaventure's exposed flank beyond. The attempt was equally unsuccessful, but it served to show Chard the mettle of the man he was engaging—a man with whom it was not safe to take such chances. Nevertheless, one more chance he took, and went briskly about, so as to charge through the billowing smoke, and so bear down upon the other ship before she could suspect the design. The manoeuvre, however, was too protracted for success. By the time the Bonaventure was upon her fresh course the smoke had dispersed sufficiently to betray her tactics to Blood, and the Cinco Llagas, lying well over to larboard, was ripping through the water at twice the speed of the Bonaventure, now ill-served by the wind.

Again Chard put the helm over and raced to intercept the other and to get to windward of her. But Blood, now a mile away, and with a safety margin of time, went, about and returned so as to bring his star board guns to bear at the proper moment. To elude this Chard once more headed south and presented no more than his counter as a target.

In this manner the two vessels worked gradually away until the Santa Barbara, with the raging, blaspheming Easterling aboard, was no more than a speck on the northern horizon; and still they were as far as ever from joining battle.

Chard cursed the wind which favoured Captain Blood, and cursed Captain Blood who knew so well how to take and maintain the advantage of his position. The lubberly surgeon appeared possessed of perfect understanding of the situation and uncannily ready to meet each move of his opponent. Occasional shots continued to be exchanged by the chasers of each vessel, each aiming high so as to damage the other's sailing powers, yet, at the long range separating them, without success.

Peter Blood at the poop rail, in a fine back-and-breast and steel cap of black damascened steel, which had been the property of the original Spanish commander of the Cinco Llagas, was growing weary and anxious. To Hagthorpe similarly armed beside him, to Wolverstone whom no armour aboard would fit, and to Pitt at the whipstaff, immediately below, he confessed it in the tone of his question:

"How long can this ducking and dodging continue? And however long it continues what end can it have but one? Sooner or later the wind will drop or veer, or else it's ourselves will drop from sheer weariness. When that happens we'll be at that scoundrel's mercy."

"There's always the unexpected," said young Pitt.

"Why, so there is, and I thank you for reminding me of it, Jerry. Let's put our hopes in it, for all that I can't see whence it's to come."

It was coming at that moment, and coming quickly, although Blood was the only one of them who recognized it when he saw it. They were standing in towards the land at the end of a long westerly run, when round the point of Espada, less than a mile away, a towering heavily-armed ship came sailing as close to the wind as she dared, her ports open and the mouths of a score of guns gaping along her larboard flank, the banner of Castile flapping aloft in the breeze.

At sight of this fresh enemy of another sort Wolverstone loosed an oath that sounded like a groan. "And that's the end of us!" he cried.

"I'm by no means sure, now, that it may not be the beginning," Blood answered him, with something that sounded like laughter in his voice, which when last heard had been jaded and dispirited. And his orders, flowing fast, showed clearly what was in his mind. "Run me the flag of Spain aloft, and bid Ogle empty his chasers at the Bonaventure as we go about."

As Pitt put the helm over, and with straining cordage and creaking blocks the Cinco Llagas swung slowly round, the gold and scarlet banner of Castile broke bravely from her maintruck. An instant later the two guns on her forecastle thundered forth, ineffectually in one way, but very effectually in another. Their fire conveyed very plainly to the Spanish newcomer that here he beheld a compatriot ship in pursuit of an English rover.

Explanations no doubt must follow, especially if upon the discovery of the identity of the Cinco Llagas the Spaniards should happen to be already acquainted with her recent history. But that could not come until they had disposed of the Bonaventure, and Blood was more than content to let the future take care of itself.

Meanwhile the Spanish ship, a guarda-costa from San Domingo, which whilst on patrol had been attracted beyond the Point of Espada by the sound of gunfire out at sea, behaved precisely as was to be expected. Even without the flag now floating at her masthead, the Spanish origin of the Cinco Llagas was plain to read in the lines of her; that she was engaged with this equally obvious English sloop was no less plain. The guarda-costa went into the fight without a moment's hesitation, and loosed a broadside at the Bonaventure as she was in the act of going about to escape this sudden and unforeseen peril.

Chard raged like a madman as the sloop shuddered under blows at stem and stern and her shattered bowsprit hung in a tangle of cordage athwart her bows. In his frenzy he ordered the fire to be returned, and did some damage to the guarda-costa, but not of a kind to impair her mobility. The Spaniard, warming to the battle, went about so as to pound the sloop with her starboard guns, and Chard, having lost his head by now, swung round also so as to return or even anticipate that fire.

Not until he had done so did it occur to him that with empty guns he was helplessly vulnerable to an onslaught from the Cinco Llagas. For Blood, too, espying the opportunity whilst yet it was shaping, had gone about, drawn level, and hurled at him the contents of his heavy artillery. That broadside at comparatively short range swept his deck, shattered the windows of the coach, and one well-placed shot opened a wound in the bows of the Bonaventure almost on the waterline, through which the sea rushed into the hold at every roll of the crippled vessel.

Chard realized that he was doomed, and his bitterness was deepened by perception of the misapprehension at the root of his destruction. He saw the Spanish flag at the masthead of the Cinco Llagas, and grinned in livid malice.

On a last inspiration, he struck his colours in token of surrender. It was his forlorn hope that the guardacosta, accepting this, and ignorant of his strength in men, would rush in to grapple him, in which case he would turn the tables on the Spaniards and, possessing himself of the guarda-costa, might yet come out of the adventure with safety and credit.

But the vigilant Captain Blood guessed, if not the intention, at least the possibility, as well as the alternative possibility of explanations dangerous to himself from the captured Chard to the Spanish commander. To provide against either danger, he sent for Ogle, and under his instructions that skilful gunner crashed a thirty-two-pound shot into the Bonaventure's waterline amidships, so as to supplement the leakage already occurring forward.

The captain of the guarda-costa may have wondered why his compatriot should continue to fire upon a ship that had struck her colours, but the circumstance would hardly seem to him suspicious, although it might be vexatious, for its consequence appeared to be the inevitable destruction of a vessel that might yet have been turned to account.

As for Chard, he had no time for speculations of any kind. The Bonaventure was now making water so fast that his only hope of saving the lives of himself and his men lay in attempting to run her aground before she sank. So he headed her for, the shoals at the foot of the Point of Espada, thanking God that she might now run before the wind, although at an ominously diminishing speed, despite the fact that the buccaneers heaved their cannon overboard to lighten her as they went. She grounded at last in the shallows, with the seas breaking over her stern and forecastles, which alone remained above water. These and the shrouds were now black with the men who had climbed to safety. The guardacosta stood off with idly flapping sails, waiting, her captain wondering to behold the Cinco Llagas half a mile away already heading northwards.

Aboard her presently Captain Blood was inquiring of Pitt if a knowledge of Spanish signals was included in his lore of the sea, and if so would he read the signals that the guarda-costa was flying. The young ship-master confessed that it was not, and expressed the opinion that as a consequence they had but escaped the frying-pan to fall into the fire.

"Now here's a lack of faith in Madame Fortune," said Blood. "We'll just be dipping our flag in salute to them, to imply that we've business elsewhere, and be off to attend to it. We look like honest Spaniards. Even through a telescope, in this Spanish armour, Hagthorpe and I must look like a pair of dons. Let's go and see how it's faring with the ingenious Easterling. I'm thinking the time has come to improve our acquaintance with him."

The guarda-costa, if surprised at the unceremonious departure of the vessel she had assisted in the destruction of that pirate sloop, cannot have suspected her bona-fides. Either taking it for granted that she had business elsewhere, or else because too intent upon making prisoners of the crew of the Bonaventure, she made no attempt to follow.

And so it fell out that some two hours later Captain Easterling, waiting off the coast between Cape Raphael and Cape Engaño, beheld to his stupefaction and horror the swift approach of Peter Blood's red ship. He had listened attentively and in some uneasiness to the distant cannonade, but he had assumed its cessation to that the Cinco Llagas was taken. The sight now of that frigate, sailing briskly, jauntily, and undamaged, defied belief. What had happened to Chard? There was no sign of him upon the sea. Could he have blundered so badly as to have allowed. Captain Blood to sink him?

Speculation on this point was presently quenched by speculation of an infinitely graver character. What might be this damned doctor-convict's present intention? If Easterling had been in case to board him he would have known no apprehension, for even his prize crew on the Santa Barbara outnumbered Blood's men by more than two to one. But the crippled Santa Barbara could never be laid board and board with the Cinco Llagas unless Blood desired it, and if Wood meant mischief as a result of what had happened with the Bonaventure the Santa Barbara must lie at the mercy of his guns.

The reflexion, vexatious enough in itself, was maddening to Easterling when he considered what he carried under hatches. Fortune, it now began to seem, had not favoured him at all. She had merely mocked him by allowing him to grasp something which he could not hold.

But this was by no means the end of his vexation. For now, as if the circumstances in themselves had not been enough to enrage a man, his prize crew turned almost mutinous. Led by a scoundrel named Gunning, a man almost as massive and ruthless as Easterling himself, they furiously blamed their captain and his excessive and improvident greed for the peril in which they found themselves—a peril of death or capture embittered by the thought of the wealth they held. With such a prize in his hands, Easterling should have taken no risks. He should have kept the Bonaventure at hand for protection, and paid no heed to the empty hulk of the Cinco Llagas. This they told him in terms of fiercest vituperation, whose very justice left him without answer other than insults, which he liberally supplied.

Whilst they wrangled, the Cinco Llagas drew nearer, and now Easterling's quartermaster called his attention to the signals she was flying. These demanded the immediate presence aboard her of the commander of the Santa Barbara.

Easterling was taken with panic. The high colour receded from his cheeks, his heavy lips grew purple. He vowed that he would see Doctor Blood in Hell before he went.

His men assured him that they would see him in Hell, and shortly, if he did not go.

Gunning reminded him that Blood could not possibly know what the Santa Barbara carried, and that therefore it should be possible to cozen him into allowing her to go her ways without further molestation.

A gun thundered from the Cinco Llagas, to send a warning shot across the bows of the Santa Barbara. That was enough. Gunning thrust the quartermaster aside, and himself seized the helm and put it over, so that the ship lay hove to, as a first intimation of compliance. After that the buccaneers launched the cock-boat and a half-dozen of them swarmed down to man her, whilst, almost at pistol-point, Gunning compelled Captain Easterling to follow them.

When presently he climbed into the waist of the Cinco Llagas where she lay hove to, a cable's length away across the sunlit waters, there was hell in his eyes and terror in his soul. Straight and tall, in Spanish corselet and headpiece, the despised doctor stood forward to receive him. Behind him stood Hagthorpe and a half-score of his followers. He seemed to smile.

"At last, Captain, ye stand where ye have so long hoped to stand: on the deck of the Cinco Llagas."

Easterling grunted ragefully for only answer to that raillery. His great hands twitched as if he would have them at his Irish mocker's throat. Captain Blood continued to address him.

"It's an ill thing, Captain, to attempt to grasp more than you can comfortably hold. Ye'll not be the first to find himself empty-handed as a consequence. That was a fine fast-sailing sloop of yours, the Bonaventure. Ye should have been content. It's a pity that she'll sail no more; for she's sunk, or will be entirely at high water." Abruptly he asked: '"How many hands are with you?" and he had to repeat the question before he was sullenly answered that forty men remained aboard the Santa Barbara.

"What boats does she carry?"

"Three with the cock-boat."

"That should be enough to accommodate your following. You'll order them into those boats at once if you value their lives, for in fifteen minutes from now I shall open fire on the ship and sink her. This because I can spare no men for a prize crew, nor can I leave her afloat to be repossessed by you and turned to further mischief."

Easterling began a furious protest that was mixed with remonstrances of the peril to him and his of landing on Hispaniola. Blood cropped it short.

"Ye're receiving such mercy as you probably never showed to any whom ye compelled to surrender. Ye'd best profit by my tenderness. If the Spaniards on Hispaniola spare you when you land there, you can get back to your hunting and boucanning, for which ye're better fitted than the sea. Away with you now."

But Easterling did not at once depart. He stood with feet planted wide, swaying on his powerful legs, clenching and unclenching his hands. At last he took his decision.

"Leave me that ship, and in Tortuga, when I get there, I'll pay you fifty thousand pieces of eight. That's better nor the empty satisfaction of turning us adrift."

"Away with you!" was all that Blood answered him, his tone more peremptory.

"A hundred thousand!" cried Easterling.

"Why not a million?" wondered Blood. "It's as easily promised, and the promise as easily broken. Oh, I'm like to take your word, Captain Easterling, as like as I am to believe that ye command such a sum as a hundred thousand pieces of eight."

Easterling's baleful eyes narrowed. Behind his black beard his thick lips tightened. Almost they smiled. Since there was nothing to be done without disclosures, nothing should be done at all. Let Blood sink a treasure which in any case must now be lost to Easterling. There was in the thought a certain bitter negative satisfaction.

"I pray that we may meet again, Captain Blood," he said, falsely, grimly unctuous. "I'll have something to tell you then that'll make you sorry for what you do now."

"If we meet again I've no doubt the occasion will be one for many regrets. Good-day to you, Captain Easterling. Ye've just fifteen minutes, ye'll remember."

Easterling sneered and shrugged, and then abruptly turned and climbed down to the rocking boat that awaited him below.

When he came to announce Blood's message to his buccaneers they stormed and raged so fiercely at the prospect of thus being cheated of everything that they could be heard across the water aboard the Cinco Llagas, to the faintly scornful amusement of Blood, who was far from suspecting the true reason of all this hubbub.

He watched the lowering of the boats, and was thereafter amazed to see the decks of the Santa Barbara empty of that angry vociferous mob. The buccaneers had gone below before leaving each man intent upon taking as much of the treasure as he could carry upon his person. Captain Blood became impatient.

"Pass the word down to Ogle to put a shot into her forecastle. Those rogues need quickening."

The roar of the gun, and the impact of the twenty-four-pound shot as it smashed through the timbers of the high forward structure, brought the buccaneers swarming upon deck again, and thence to the waiting boats with the speed of fear. Yet a certain order they preserved for their safety's sake, for in the sea that was running the capsizing of a boat would have been an easy matter.

They pushed off, their wet oars flashed in the brilliant sunlight, and they began to draw away towards the promontory not more than two miles to windward. Once they were clear, Blood gave the word to open fire, when Hagthorpe clutched his arm.

"Wait, man! Wait! Look! There's someone still aboard her!"

Surprised, Blood looked, first with his naked eye, then through his telescope. He beheld a bareheaded gentleman in corselet and thigh-boots, who clearly was no buccaneer of the kind that sailed with Easterling, and who stood on the poop frantically waving a scarf. Blood with quick to guess his identity.

"It'll be one of the Spaniards who were aboard when Easterling took the ship and whose throat he forgot to cut."

He ordered a boat to be launched, and sent six men with Dyke, who had some knowledge of Spanish, to bring the Spaniard off.

Don Ildefonso, who, callously left to drown in the doomed ship, had worked himself free of the thong that bound his wrists, stood in the forechains to await the coming of that boat. He was quivering with excitement at this deliverance of himself and the vessel in his charge with her precious freight-a deliverance which he regarded as little short of miraculous.

For like the guarda-costa, Don Ildefonso, even if he had not recognized the Spanish lines of this great ship which had come so unexpectedly to the rescue, must have been relieved of all doubt by the flag of Spain which had been allowed to remain floating at the masthead of the Cinco Llagas.

So with speech bubbling eagerly out of him in that joyous excitement of his, the Spanish commander poured into the ears of Dyke, when the boat brought up alongside, the tale of what had happened to them and what they carried. Because of this it was necessary that they should lend him a dozen men so that with the six now under hatches on the Santa Barbara he might bring his precious cargo safely into San Domingo.

To Dyke this was an amazing and exciting narrative. But he did not on that account lose grip of his self-possession. Lest too much Spanish should betray him to Don Ildefonso, he took refuge in curtness.

"Bueno," said he. "I'll inform my captain." Under his breath he ordered his men to push off and head back for the Cinco Llagas.

When Blood heard the tale and had digested his amazement, he laughed.

"So this is what that rogue would have told me if ever we met again. Faith it's a satisfaction to be denied him."

Ten minutes later the Cinco Llagas lay board and board with the Santa Barbara.

In the distance Easterling and his men, observing the operation, rested on their oars to stare and mutter. They saw themselves cheated of even the meagre satisfaction for which they had looked in the sinking of an unsuspected treasure. Easterling burst into fresh profanity.

"It'll be that damned Spaniard I forgot in the cabin who'll ha' blabbed of the gold; Oh, 'sdeath! This is what comes o' being soft-hearted; if only I'd cut his throat now..."

Meanwhile to Don Ildefonso, who had been able to make nothing of this boarding manoeuvre, Captain Blood, save for the light eyes in his bronzed face, looking every inch a Spaniard, and delivering himself in the impeccable Castilian of which he was master, was offering explanations.

He was unable to spare a crew to man the Santa Barbara, for his own following was insufficient. Nor dared he leave her afloat, since in that case she would he repossessed by the abominable pirates whom he had constrained to abandon her. It remained, therefore, before scuttling her only to tranship the treasure with which Don Ildefonso informed him she was laden. At the same time he would be happy to offer Don Ildefonso and his six surviving hands the hospitality of the Cinco Llagas as far as Tortuga, or, if Don Ildefonso preferred it, as seemed probable, Captain Blood would seize a favourable moment for allowing them to take one of his boats and land themselves upon the coast of Hispaniola.

Now this speech was the most amazing thing that had yet happened to Don Ildefonso in that day of amazements.

"Tortuga!" he exclaimed. "Tortuga! You sail to Tortuga, do you say? But what to do there? In God's name who are you, then? What are you?"

"As for who I am, I am called Peter Blood. As for what I am, faith, I scarce know myself."

"You are English!" cried the Spaniard in sudden horror of partial understanding.

"Ah no. That, at least, I am not." Captain Blood drew himself up with great dignity. "I have the honour to be Irish."

"Ah, bah! Irish or English, it is all one."

"Indeed and it is not. There's all the difference in the world between the two."

The Spaniard looked at him with angry eyes. His face was livid, his mouth scornful. "English or Irish, the truth is you are just a cursed pirate."

Blood's eyes looked wistful. He fetched a sigh. "I'm afraid you are right," he admitted. "It's a thing I've sought to avoid. But what am I to do now, when Fate thrusts it upon me in this fashion, and insists that I make so excellent a beginning?"

III

THE KING'S MESSENGER

On a brilliant May morning of the year 1690 a gentleman stepped ashore at Santiago de Porto Rico, followed by a black man servant shouldering a valise. He had been brought to the mole in a cock-boat from the yellow galleon standing in the roadstead, with the flag of Spain floating from her maintruck. Having landed him, the cock-boat went smartly about, and was pulled back to the ship, from which circumstances the gaping idlers on the mole assumed that this gentleman had come to stay.

They stared at him with interest, as they would have stared at any stranger. This, however, was a man whose exterior repaid their attention, a man to take the eye. Even the wretched white slaves toiling half-naked on the fortifications, and the Spanish soldiery guarding them, stood at gaze.

Tall, straight, and vigorously spare, our gentleman was dressed with sombre Spanish elegance in black and silver. The curls of his black periwig fell to his shoulders, and his keen shaven face with its high-bridged nose and disdainful lips was shaded by a broad black hat about the crown of which swept a black ostrich plume. Jewels flashed at his breast, a foam of Mechlin almost concealed his hands, and there were ribbons to the long gold-mounted ebony cane he carried. A fop from the Alameda he must have seemed but for the manifest vigour of him and the air of assurance and consequence with which he bore himself. He carried his dark finery with an indifference to the broiling tropical heat which argued an iron constitution, and his glance was so imperious that the eyes of the inquisitive fell away abashed before it.

He asked the way to the Governor's residence, and the officer commanding the guard over the toiling white prisoners detached a soldier to conduct him.

Beyond the square, which architecturally, and saving for the palm trees throwing patches of black shadow on the dazzling white sun-drenched ground, might have belonged to some little town in Old Spain, past the church with its twin spires and marble steps, they came, by tall, wrought-iron gates, into a garden, and by an avenue of acacias to a big white house with deep external galleries all clad in jessamine. Black man servants in ridiculously rich red-and-yellow liveries admitted our gentleman, and went to announce to the Governor of Porto Rico the arrival of Don Pedro de Queiroz on a mission from King Philip.

Not every day did a messenger from the King of Spain arrive in this almost the least of his Catholic Majesty's overseas dominions. Indeed, the thing had never happened before, and Don Jayme de Villamarga, whilst thrilled to the marrow by the announcement, knew not whether to assign the thrill to pride or to alarm.

A man of middle height, big of head and paunch, and of less than mediocre intelligence, Don Jayme was one of those gentlemen who best served Spain by being absent from her, and this no doubt had been considered in appointing him Governor of Porto Rico. Not even his awe of majesty, represented by Don Pedro, could repress his naturally self-sufficient manner he was pompous in his reception of him, and remained unintimidated by the cold haughty stare of Don

Pedro's eyes—eyes of a singularly deep blue, contrasting oddly with his bronzed face. A Dominican monk, elderly, tall and gaunt, kept his excellency company.

"Sir, I give you welcome." Don Jayme spoke as if his mouth were full. "I trust you will announce to me that I have the honour to meet with his majesty's approbation."

Don Pedro made him a deep obeisance, with a sweep of his plumed hat, which, together with his cane, he thereafter handed to one of the black man lackeys. "It is to signify the royal approbation that I am here, happily, after some adventures. I have just landed from the San Tomas, after a voyage of some vicissitudes. She has gone on to San Domingo, and it may be three or four days before she returns to take me off again. For that brief while I must make free with your excellency's hospitality." He seemed to claim it as a right rather than ask it as a favour.

"Ah!" was all that Don Jayme permitted himself to answer. And with head on one side, a fatuous smile on the thick lips under his grizzled moustache, he waited for the visitor to enter into details of the royal message.

The visitor, however, displayed no haste. He looked about him at the cool spacious room with its handsome furnishings of carved oak and walnut, its tapestries and pictures, all imported from the Old World, and inquired, in that casual manner of the man who is at home in every environment, if he might be seated. His excellency with some loss of dignity made haste to set a chair.

Composedly, with a thin smile which Don Jayme disliked, the messenger sat down and crossed his legs.

"We are," he announced, "in some sort related, Don Jayme."

Don Jayme stared. "I am not aware of the honour."

"That is why I am at the trouble of informing you. Your marriage, sir, established the bond. I am a distant cousin of Doña Hernanda."

"Oh! My wife!" His excellency's tone in some subtle way implied contempt for that same wife and her relations. "I had remarked your name: Queiroz." This also explained to him the rather hard and open accent of Don Pedro's otherwise impeccable Castilian. "You will, then, be Portuguese, like Doña Hernanda?" and again his tone implied contempt of Portuguese, and particularly perhaps of Portuguese who were in the service of the King of Spain, from whom Portugal had re-established her independence a half-century ago.

"Half Portuguese, of course. My family—"

"Yes, yes." Thus the testy Don Jayme interrupted him. "But your message from his majesty?"

"Ah yes. Your impatience, Don Jayme, is natural." Don Pedro was faintly ironical. "You will forgive me that I should have intruded family matters. My message, then. It will be no surprise to you, sir, that eulogistic reports should have reached his majesty, whom God preserve—" he bowed his head in reverence, compelling Don Jayme to do the same—"not only of the good government of this important island of Porto Rico, but also of the diligence employed by you to rid these seas of the pestilent rovers, particularly the English buccaneers who trouble our shipping and the peace of our Spanish settlements."

There was nothing in this to surprise Don Jayme. Not even upon reflection. Being a fool, he did not suspect that Porto Rico was the worst governed of any Spanish settlement in the West Indies. As for the rest, he had certainly encouraged the extirpation of the buccaneers from the Caribbean. Quite recently, and quite fortuitously be it added, he had actually contributed materially to this desirable end, as he was not slow to mention.

With chin high and chest puffed out, he moved, strutting, before Don Pedro as he delivered himself. It was gratifying to be appreciated in the proper quarter. It encouraged endeavour. He desired to be modest. Yet in justice to himself he must assert that under his government the island was tranquil and prosperous. Frey Luis here could bear him out in this. The Faith was firmly planted, and there was no heresy in any form in Porto Rico. And as for the matter of the buccaneers, he had done all that a man in his position could do. Not perhaps as much as he could have desired to do. After all, his office kept him ashore. Had Don Pedro remarked the new fortifications he was building? The work was all but complete, and he did not think that even the infamous Captain Blood would have the hardihood to pay him a visit. He had already shown that redoubtable buccaneer that he was not a man with whom it was prudent to trifle. A party of this Captain Blood's men had dared to land on the southern side of the island a few days ago. But Don Jayme's followers were vigilant. He saw to that. A troop of horse was in the neighbourhood at the time. It had descended upon the pirates and had taught them a sharp lesson. He laughed as he spoke of it; laughed at the thought of it; and Don Pedro politely laughed with him, desiring with courteous and appreciative interest to know more of this.

"You killed them all, of course?" he suggested, his contempt of them implicit in his tone.

"Not yet." His excellency spoke with a relish almost fierce. "But I have them under my hand. Six of them, who were captured. We have not yet decided upon their end. Perhaps the rope. Perhaps an auto-da-fé and the fires of the Faith for them. They are heretics all, of course. It is a matter I am still considering with Frey Luis here."

"Well, well," said Don Pedro, as if the subject began to weary him. "Will your excellency hear the remainder of my message?"

The Governor was annoyed by this suggestion that his lengthy exposition had amounted to an interruption. Stiffly he bowed to the representative of majesty. "My apologies," said he in a voice of ice.

But the lofty Don Pedro paid little heed to his manner. He drew from an inner pocket of his rich coat a folded parchment and a small flat leather case.

"I have to explain, your excellency, the condition in which this comes to you. I have said, although I do not think you heeded it, that I arrive here after a voyage of many vicissitudes. Indeed, it is little short of a miracle that I am here at all, considering what I have undergone. I, too, have been a victim of that infernal dog, Captain Blood. The ship on which I originally sailed from Cadiz was sunk by him a week ago. More fortunate than my cousin Don Rodrigo de Queiroz, who accompanied me and who remains a prisoner in that infamous pirate's hands, I made my escape. It is a long tale with which I will not weary you."

"It would not weary me," exclaimed his excellency, forgetting his dignity in his interest.

But Don Pedro waved aside the implied request for details. "Later! Later, perhaps, if you care to hear of it. It is not important. What is important on your excellency's account is that I escaped. I was picked up by the San Tomas, which has brought me here, and so I am happily able to discharge my mission." He held up the folded parchment. "I but mention it to explain how this has come to suffer by sea-water, though not to the extent of being illegible. It is a letter from his majesty's Secretary of State informing you that our Sovereign, whom God preserve, has been graciously pleased to create you, in recognition of the services I have mentioned, a knight of the most noble order of St. James of Compostella."

Don Jayme went first white, then red, in his incredulous excitement. With trembling fingers he took the letter and unfolded it. It was certainly damaged by sea-water. Some words were scarcely legible. The ink in which his own surname had been written had run into a smear, as had that of his government of Porto Rico, and some other words here and there. But the amazing substance of the letter was indeed as Don Pedro announced, and the royal signature was unimpaired.

As Don Jayme raised his eyes at last from the document, Don Pedro, proffering the leather case, touched a spring in it. It flew open, and the Governor gazed upon rubies that glowed like live coals against their background of black velvet.

"And here," said Don Pedro, "is the insignia; the cross of the most noble order in which you are invested."

Don Jayme took the case gingerly, as if it had been some holy thing, and gazed upon the smouldering cross. The friar came to stand beside him, murmuring congratulatory words. Any knighthood would have been an honourable, an unexpected, reward for Don Jayme's services to the crown of Spain. But that of all orders this most exalted and coveted order of St. James of Compostella should have been conferred upon him was something that almost defied belief. The Governor of Porto Rico was momentarily awed by the greatness of the thing that had befallen him.

And yet when a few minutes later the room was entered by a little lady, young and delicately lovely, Don Jayme had already recovered his habitual poise of self-sufficiency.

The lady, beholding a stranger, an elegant, courtly stranger, who rose instantly upon her advent, paused in the doorway, hesitating, timid. Then she addressed Don Jayme.

"Pardon. I did not know you occupied."

Don Jayme appealed, sneering, to the friar. "She did not know me occupied! I am the King's representative in Porto Rico, his majesty's Governor of this island, and my wife does not know that I am occupied, conceives that I have leisure. It is unbelievable. But come in, Hernanda. Come in." He grew more playful. "Acquaint yourself with the honours the King bestows upon his poor servant. This may help you to realize what his majesty does me the justice to realize, although you may have failed to do so: that my occupations here are onerous."

Timidly she advanced, obedient to his invitation. "What is it, Jayme?"

"What is it?" He seemed to mimic her. "It is merely this." He displayed the order. "His majesty invests me with the cross of Saint James of Compostella, that is all."

She grew conscious that she was mocked. Her pale, delicate face flushed a little. But there was no accompanying sparkle of her great, dark, wistful eyes to proclaim it a flush of pleasure. Rather, thought Don Pedro, she flushed from shame and resentment at being so contemptuously used before a stranger and at the boorishness of a husband who could so use her.

"I am glad, Jayme," she said, in a gentle, weary voice. "I felicitate you. I am glad."

"Ah! You are glad. Frey Alonso, you will observe that Doña Hernanda is glad." Thus he sneered at her without even the poor, grace of being witty. "This gentleman, by whose hand the order came, is a kinsman of yours, Hernanda."

She turned aside, to look again at that elegant stranger. Her gaze was blank. Yet she hesitated to deny him. Kinship when claimed by gentlemen charged by kings with missions of investiture is not lightly to be denied in the presence of such a husband as Don Jayme. And, after all, hers was a considerable family, and must include many with whom she was not personally acquainted.

The stranger bowed until the curls of his periwig met across his face. "You will not remember me, Doña Hernanda. I am, nevertheless, your cousin, and you will have heard of me from our other cousin, Rodrigo. I am Pedro de Queiroz."

"You are Pedro?" She stared the harder. "Why, then..." She laughed a little. "Oh, but I remember Pedro. We played together as children. Pedro and I."

Something in her tone seemed to deny him. But he confronted her unperturbed.

"That would be at Santarem," said he.

"At Santarem it was." His readiness appeared now to bewilder her. "But you were a fat, sturdy boy then, and your hair was golden."

He laughed. "I have become lean in growing, and I favour a black periwig."

"Which makes your eyes a startling blue. I do not remember that you had blue eyes."

"God help us, ninny!" croaked her husband. "You never could remember anything."

She turned to look at him, and for all that her lip quivered, her eyes steadily met his sneering glance. She seemed about to speak, checked herself, and then spoke at last, very quietly. "Oh yes. There are some things a woman never forgets."

"And on the subject of memory," said Don Pedro, addressing the Governor with cold dignity, "I do not remember that there are any ninnies in our family."

"Faith, then, you needed to come to Porto Rico to discover it," his excellency retorted with his loud, coarse laugh.

"Ah!" Don Pedro sighed. "That may not be the end of my discoveries."

There was something in his tone which Don Jayme did not like. He threw back his big 'head and frowned. "You mean?" he demanded.

Don Pedro was conscious of an appeal in the little lady's dark, liquid eyes. He yielded to it, laughed, and answered:

"I have yet to discover where your excellency proposes to lodge me during the days in which I must inflict myself upon you. If I might now withdraw..."

The Governor swung to Doña Hernanda. "You hear? Your kinsman needs to remind us of our duty to a guest. It will not have occurred to you to make provision for him."

"But I did not know... I was not told of his presence until I found him here."

"Well, well. You know now. And we dine in half an hour."

At dinner Don Jayme was in high spirits, which is to say that he was alternately pompous and boisterous, and occasionally filled the room with his loud jarring laugh.

Don Pedro scarcely troubled to dissemble his dislike of him. His manner became more and more frigidly aloof, and he devoted his attention and addressed his conversation more and more exclusively to the despised wife.

"I have news for you," he told her, when they had come to the dessert, "of our Cousin Rodrigo."

"Ah!" sneered her husband. "She'll welcome news of him. She ever had a particular regard for her Cousin Rodrigo, and he for her."

She flushed, keeping her troubled eyes lowered. Don Pedro came to the rescue, swiftly, easily. "Regard for one another is common among the members of our family. Every Queiroz owes a duty to every other, and is at all times ready to perform it." He looked very straightly at Don Jayme as he spoke, as if inviting him to discover more in the words than they might seem to carry. "And that is at the root of what I am to tell you, cousin Hernanda. As I have already informed his excellency, the ship in which Don Rodrigo and I sailed from Spain together was set upon and sunk by that infamous pirate Captain Blood. We were both captured, but I was so fortunate as to make my escape."

"You have not told us how. You must tell us how," the Governor interrupted him.

Don Pedro waved a hand disdainfully. "It is no great matter, and I soon weary of talking of myself. But... if you insist... some other time. At present I am to tell you of Rodrigo. He remains a prisoner in the hands of Captain Blood. But do not be unduly alarmed."

There was need for his reassuring tone. Doña I Hernanda, who had been hanging on his words, had turned deathly white.

"Do not be alarmed. Rodrigo is in good health, and his life is safe. Also, from my own experience, I know that this Blood, infamous pirate though he be, is not without chivalrous ideals, and, piracy apart, he is a man of honour."

"Piracy apart?" Laughter exploded from Don

Jayme. "On my soul, that's humorous! You deal in paradox, Don Pedro. Eh, Frey Alonso?" The lean friar smiled mechanically. Doña Hernanda, pale and piteous, suffered in silence the interruption. Don Pedro frowned.

"The paradox is not in me, but in Captain Blood. An indemoniated robber, yet he practises no wanton cruelty, and he keeps his word. Therefore, I say you need have no apprehension on the score of Don Rodrigo's fate. His ransom has been agreed between himself and Captain Blood, and I have undertaken to procure it. Meanwhile he is well and courteously treated, and, indeed, a sort of friendship has come to exist between himself and his pirate captor."

"Faith, that I can believe!" cried the Governor, Whilst Doña Hernanda sank back in her chair with a sigh of relief. "Rodrigo was ever ready to consort with rogues. Was he not, Hernanda?"

"I..." She bridled indignantly, then curbed herself, "I never observed it."

"You never observed it! I ask myself have you ever observed anything? Well, well, and so Rodrigo's to be ransomed. At what is his ransom fixed?"

"You desire to contribute?" cried Don Pedro with a certain friendly eagerness.

The Governor started as if he had been stung. His countenance became gravely blank. "Not I, by the Virgin! Not I. That is entirely a matter for the family of Queiroz."

Don Pedro's smile perished. He sighed. "True! True! And yet... I've a notion you'll come to contribute something before all is ended."

"Dismiss it," laughed Don Jayme, "for that way lies disappointment."

They rose from table soon thereafter and withdrew to the noontide rest the heat made necessary.

They did not come together again until supper, which was served in that same room, in the comparative cool of eventide and by the light of a score of candles in heavy silver branches brought from Spain.

The Governor's satisfaction at the signal honour of which he was the recipient appeared to have grown with contemplation of it. He was increasingly jovial and facetious, but not on this account did he spare Doña Hernanda his sneers. Rather did he make her the butt of his coarse humours, inviting the two men to laugh with him at the shortcomings he indicated in her. Don Pedro, however, did not laugh. He remained preternaturally grave, indeed almost compassionate, as he observed the tragic patience on that long-suffering wife's sweet face.

She looked so slight and frail in her stiff black satin gown, which rendered more dazzling by contrast the whiteness of her neck and shoulders, even as her lustrous, smoothly-dressed black hair stressed the warm pallor of her gentle countenance. A little statue in ebony and ivory she seemed to Don Pedro's fancy, and almost as lifeless until after supper he found himself alone with her in the deep jessamine-clad galleries that stood open to the cool night breezes blowing from the sea.

His excellency had gone off to indite a letter of grateful acknowledgment to the King, and had taken the friar to assist him. He had commended his guest to the attention of his wife, whilst commiserating with him upon the necessity. She had led Don Pedro out into the scented purple tropic night, and stepping now beside him came at last to life, and addressed him in a breathless anxiety.

"What you told us today of Don Rodrigo de Queiroz, is it true? That he is a prisoner in the hands of Captain Blood, but unhurt and safe, awaiting ransom?"

"Most scrupulously true in all particulars."

"You... you pledge your word for that? Your honour as a gentleman? For I must assume you a gentleman, since you bear commissions from the King."

"And on no other ground?" quoth he, a little taken aback.

"Do you pledge me your word?" she insisted.

"Unhesitatingly. My word of honour. Why should you doubt me?"

"You give me cause. You are not truthful in all things. Why, for instance, do you say you are my cousin?"

"You do not, then, remember me?"

"I remember Pedro de Queiroz. The years might have given you height and slenderness; the sun might have tanned your face, and under your black periwig your hair may still be fair, though I take leave to doubt it. But what, I ask myself, could have changed the colour of your eyes? For your eyes are blue, and Pedro's were dark brown."

He was silent a moment, like a man considering, and she watched his stern, handsome face, made plain by the light beating upon it from the windows of the house. He did not meet her glance. Instead his eyes sought the sea, gleaming under the bright stars and reflecting the twinkling lights of ships in the roadstead, watched the fireflies flitting among the bushes in pursuit of moths, looked anywhere but at the little figure at his side.

At last he spoke, quietly, almost humorously, in admission of the imposture. "We hoped you would have forgotten such a detail."

"We?" she questioned him.

"Rodrigo and I. He is at least my friend. He was hastening to you when this thing befell him. That is how we came to be on the same ship."

"And he desired you to do this?"

"He shall tell you so himself when he arrives. He will be here in a few days, depend on it. As soon as I can ransom him, which will be very soon after my departure. When I was escaping—for, unlike him, I had given no parole—he desired that if I came here I should claim to be your cousin, so as to stand at need in his place until he comes."

She was thoughtful, and her bosom rose and fell in agitation. In silence they moved a little way in step.

"You took a foolish risk," she said, thereby showing her acceptance of his explanation.

"A gentleman," said he sententiously, "will always take a risk to serve a lady."

"Were you serving me?"

"Does it seem to you that I could be serving myself?"

"No. You could not have been doing that."

"Why question further, then? Rodrigo wished it so. He will explain his motives fully when he comes. Meanwhile, as your cousin, I am in his place. If this boorish husband burdens you overmuch..."

"What are you saying?" Her voice rang with alarm.

"That I am Rodrigo's deputy. So that you remember it, that is all I ask."

"I thank you, cousin," she said, and left him.

Three days Don Pedro continued as the guest of the Governor of Porto Rico, and they were much as that first day, saving that daily Don Jayme continued to increase in consciousness of his new dignity as a knight of Saint James of Compostella, and became, consequently, daily more insufferable. Yet Don Pedro suffered him with exemplary fortitude, and at times seemed even disposed to feed the Governor's egregious vanity. Thus, on the third night at supper, Don Pedro cast out the suggestion that his excellency should signalize the honour with which the King had distinguished him by some gesture that should mark the occasion and render it memorable in the annals of the island.

Don Jayme swallowed the suggestion avidly. "Ah yes! That is an admirable thought. What do you counsel that I do?"

Don Pedro smiled with flattering deprecation. "Not for me to counsel Don Jayme de Villamarga. But the gesture should be worthy of the occasion."

"Indeed, yes. That is true." But the dullard's wits are barren of ideas. "The question now is what might be considered worthy?"

Frey' Alonso suggested a ball at Government House, and was applauded in this by Doña Hernanda. Don Pedro, apologetically to the lady, thought a ball would have significance only for those who were bidden to it. Something was required that should impress all social orders in Porto Rico.

"Why not an amnesty?" he inquired at last.

"An amnesty?" The three of them looked at him in questioning wonder.

"Why not? It is a royal gesture, true. But is not a governor in some sort royal, a viceroy, a representative of royalty, the one to whom men look for royal gestures? To mark your accession to this dignity, throw open your gaols, Don Jayme, as do kings upon, their coronation."

Don Jayme conquered his stupefaction at the magnitude of the act suggested, and smote the table with his fist, protesting that here was a notion worth adopting. Tomorrow he would announce it in a proclamation, and set all prisoners free, their sentences remitted.

"That is," he added, "all but six, whose pardon would hardly please the colony."

"I think," said Don Pedro, "that exceptions would stultify the act. There should be no exceptions."

"But these are exceptional prisoners. Can you have forgotten that I told you I had made captive six buccaneers out of a party that had the temerity to land on Porto Rico?"

Don Pedro frowned, reflecting. "Ah, true!" he cried at last. "I remember."

"And did I tell you, sir, that one of these men is that dog Wolverstone?" He pronounced it Volverstohn.

"Wolverstone?" said Don Pedro, who also pronounced it Volverstohn. "You have captured Wolverstone!" It was clear that he was profoundly impressed; as well he might be, for Wolverstone, who was nowadays the foremost of Blood's lieutenants, was almost as well known to Spaniards and as detested by them as Blood himself. "You have captured Wolverstone!" he repeated, and for the first time looked at Don Jayme with eyes of unmistakable respect. "You did not tell me that. Why, in that case, my friend, you have clipped one of Blood's wings. Without Wolverstone he is shorn of half his power. His own destruction may follow now at any moment, and Spain will owe that to you."

Don Jayme spread his hands in an affectation of modesty. "It is something towards deserving the honour his majesty has bestowed upon me."

"Something?" echoed Don Pedro. "If the King had known this, he might have accounted the order of Saint James of Compostella inadequate."

Doña Hernanda looked at him sharply, to see whether he dealt in irony. But he seemed quite sincere, so much so that for once he had shed the hauteur in which he usually arrayed himself. He resumed after a moment's pause.

"Of course, of course, you cannot include these men in the amnesty. They are pot common malefactors. They are enemies of Spain." Abruptly, with a hint of purpose, he asked: "How will you deal with them?"

Don Jayme thrust out a nether lip considering. "I am still undecided whether to hang them out of hand or to let Frey Alonso hold his auto-da-fé upon them and consign them to the fire as heretics. I think I told you so."

"Yes, yes. But I did not then know that Wolverstone is one of them. That makes a difference."

"What difference?"

"Oh, but consider. Give this matter thought. With thought you'll see for yourself what you should do. It's plain enough."

Don Jayme considered awhile as he was bidden. Then shrugged his shoulders.

"Faith, sir, it may be plain enough to you. But I confess that I see no choice beyond that of rope or fire."

"Ultimately, yes. One or the other. But not here in Porto Rico. That is to smother the effulgence of your achievement. Send them to Spain, Don Jayme. Send them to his majesty, as an earnest of the zeal for which he has been pleased to honour you. Show him thus how richly you deserve that honour and even greater honours. Let that be your acknowledgment."

Don Jayme was staring at him with dilating eyes. His face glowed. "I vow to Heaven I should never have thought of it," he said at last.

"Your modesty made you blind to the opportunity."

"It may be that," Don Jayme admitted.

"But you perceive it now that I indicate it?"

"Oh, I perceive it. Yes, the King of Spain shall be impressed."

Frey Alonso seemed downcast. He had been counting upon his auto-da-fé. Doña Hernanda was chiefly intrigued by the sudden geniality of her hitherto haughty and disdainful pretended cousin. Meanwhile Don Pedro piled Pelion upon Ossa.

"It should prove to his majesty that your excellency is wasted in so small a settlement as Porto Rico. I see you as governor of some more important colony. Perhaps as viceroy... Who shall say? You have displayed a zeal such as has rarely been displayed by any Spanish governor overseas."

"But how and when to send them to Spain?" wondered Don Jayme, who no longer questioned the expediency of doing so.

"Why, that is a matter in which I can serve your excellency. I can convey them for you on the San Tomas, which should call for me at any moment now. You will write another letter to his majesty, offering him these evidences of your zeal, and I will bear it together with these captives. Your general amnesty can wait until I've sailed with them. Thus there will be nothing to mar it. It will be complete and properly imposing."

So elated and so grateful to his guest for his suggestion was Don Jayme that he actually went the length of addressing him as cousin in the course of thanking him.

The matter, it seemed, had presented itself for discussion only just in time. For early on the following morning Santiago was startled by the boom of a gun, and turning out to ascertain the reason, beheld again the yellow Spanish ship which had brought Don Pedro coming to anchor in the bay.

Don Pedro himself sought the Governor with the information that this was the signal for his departure, expressing a polite regret that duty did not permit him longer to encroach upon Don Jayme's princely hospitality.

Whilst his black man valet was packing his effects he went to take his leave of Doña Hernanda, and again assured that wistful little lady that she need be under no apprehension on the score of her cousin Rodrigo, who would soon now be with her.

After this Don Jayme, with an officer in attendance, carried Don Pedro off to the town gaol, where the pirates were lodged.

In a dark, unpaved stone chamber, lighted only by a small, heavily-barred, unglazed window set near the ceiling, they were herded with perhaps a score of other malefactors of all kinds and colours. The atmosphere of the place was so indescribably foul and noisome that Don Pedro recoiled as from a blow when it first assailed him. Don Jayme's loud, coarse laugh derided his fastidiousness. Nevertheless, the Governor flicked out a handkerchief that was sprayed with verbena, and thereafter at intervals held it to his nostrils.

Wolverstone and his five associates, heavily loaded with irons, were in a group a little apart from their fellow-prisoners. They squatted against the wall on the foul dank straw that was their bedding. Unshaven, dishevelled and filthy, for no means of grooming themselves had been allowed them, they huddled together there as if seeking strength in union against the common rogues with whom they were confined.

Wolverstone, almost a giant in build, might from his dress have been a merchant. Dyke, that sometime petty officer in the King's Navy, had similarly been arrayed like a citizen of some consequence. The other four wore the cotton shirts and leather breeches which had been the dress of the boucan-hunters before they took to the sea, and their heads were swathed in coloured kerchiefs.

They did not stir when the door creaked on its ponderous hinges and a half-dozen corseletted Spaniards with pikes entered to form a guard of honour as well as a protection for the Governor. When that august personage made his appearance attended by his officer and accompanied by his distinguished-looking guest, the other prisoners sprang up and ranged themselves in awe and reverence. The pirates stolidly sat on. But they were not quite indifferent. As Don Pedro sauntered in, languidly leaning on his beribboned cane, dabbing his lips with a handkerchief, which he, too, had deemed it well to produce, Wolverstone stirred on his foul bed, and his single eye (he had lost the other one at Sedgemoor) rolled with almost portentous ferocity.

Don Jayme indicated the group by a wave of his hand. "There are your cursed pirates, Don Pedro, hanging together like a brood of carrion birds."

"These?" quoth Don Pedro haughtily, and pointed with his cane. "Faith, they look their trade, the villains."

Wolverstone glared more fiercely than ever, but was contemptuously silent. A stubborn rogue, it was plain.

Don Pedro advanced towards them, a superb figure in his black and silver, seeming to symbolise the pride and majesty of Spain. The thick-set Governor, in pale green taffetas, kept pace with him, and presently, when they had come to a halt before the buccaneers, he addressed them.

"You begin to know, you English dogs, what it means to defy the might of Spain. And you'll know it better before all is done.

I deny myself the pleasure of hanging you as I intended, so that you may go to Spain, to feed a bonfire."

Wolverstone leered at him. "You are noble," he said, in execrable, but comprehensible Spanish. "Noble with the nobility of Spain. You insult the helpless."

The Governor raged at him, calling him the unprintably foul names that come so readily to an angry Spaniard's lips. This until Don Pedro checked him with a hand upon his arm.

"Is this waste of breath worth while?" He spoke disdainfully. "It but serves to detain us in this noisome place."

The buccaneers stared at him in a sort of wonder. Abruptly he turned on his heel.

"Come, Don Jayme." His tone was peremptory. "Have them out of this. The San Tomas is waiting, and the tide is on the turn."

The Governor hesitated, flung a last insult at them, then gave an order to the officer, and stalked after his guest, who was already moving away. The officer transferred the order to his men. With the butts of their pikes and many foul words the soldiers stirred the buccaneers. They rose with clank of gyves and manacles, and went stumbling out into the clean air and the sunshine, herded by the pikemen. Hang-dog, foul and weary, they dragged themselves across the square, where the palms waved in the sea breeze, and the islanders stood to watch them pass, and so they came to the mole, where a wherry of eight oars awaited them.

The Governor and his guest stood by whilst they were being packed into the sternsheets, whither the pikemen followed them. Then Don Pedro and Don Jayme took their places in the prow with Don Pedro's black man, who carried his valise. The wherry pushed off and was rowed across the blue water to the stately ship from whose masthead floated the flag of Spain.

They came bumping along her yellow side at the foot of the entrance-ladder, to which a sailor hitched a boathook.

Don Pedro, from the prow of the wherry, called peremptorily for a file of musketeers to stand to order in the waist. A morioned head appeared over the bulwarks to answer him that it was done already. Then, with the pikemen urging them, and moving awkwardly and painfully in their irons, the buccaneer prisoners climbed the ladder and dropped one by one over the ship's side.

Don Pedro waved his black servant after them with the valise, and finally invited Don Jayme to precede him aboard. Himself, Don Pedro followed close, and when at the ladder's head Don Jayme came to a sudden halt, it was Don Pedro's continuing ascent that thrust him forward, and this so sharply that he almost tumbled headlong into the vessel's waist. There were a dozen ready hands to steady him, and a babble of voices to give him laughing welcome. But the voices were English, and the hands belonged to men whose garments and accoutrements proclaimed them buccaneers. They swarmed in the waist, and already some of them were at work to strike the irons from Wolverstone and his mates.

Gasping, livid, bewildered, Don Jayme de Villamarga swung round to Don Pedro who followed. That very Spanish gentleman had paused at the head of the ladder and stood there steadying himself by a ratline, surveying the scene below him. He was calmly smiling.

"You have nothing to apprehend, Don Jayme. I give you my word for that. And my word is good. I am Captain Blood."

He came down to the deck under the stare of the bulging eyes of the Governor, who understood nothing. Before enlightenment finally came his dull, bewildered wits were to understand still less.

A tall, slight gentleman, very elegantly arrayed, stepped forward to meet the Captain. This, to the Governor's increasing amazement, was his wife's cousin, Don Rodrigo. Captain Blood greeted him in a friendly manner.

"I have brought your ransom, as you see, Don Rodrigo," and he waved a hand in the direction of the group of manacled prisoners. "You are free now to depart with Don Jayme. We'll cut short our farewells, for we take up the anchor at once. Hagthorpe, give the order."

Don Jayme thought that he began to understand. Furiously, he turned upon this cousin of his wife's.

"My God, are you in this? Have you plotted with these enemies of Spain to—?"

A hand gripped his shoulder, and a boatswain's whistle piped somewhere forward. "We are weighing the anchor," said Captain Blood. "You were best over the side, believe me. It has been an honour to know you. In future be more respectful to your wife. Go with God, Don Jayme."

The Governor found himself, as in a nightmare, bustled over the side and down the ladder. Don Rodrigo followed him after taking courteous leave of Captain Blood.

Don Jayme collapsed limply in the sternsheets of the wherry as it put off. But soon he roused himself furiously to demand an explanation whilst at the same time overwhelming his companion with threats.

Don Rodrigo strove to preserve his calm. "You had better listen. I was on that ship, the San Tomas, on my way to San Domingo, when Blood captured her. He put the crew ashore on one of the Virgin Islands. But me he retained for ransom because of my rank."

"And to save your skin and your purse you made this infamous bargain with him?"

"I have said that you had better listen. It was not NO at all. He treated me honourably, and we became In some sort friends. He is a man of engaging ways, as you may have discovered. In the course of our talks he gleaned from me a good deal of my private life and yours, which in a way, through my Cousin Hernanda, is linked with it. A week ago, after the capture of the men who had gone ashore with Wolverstone, he decided to use the knowledge he had gained; that and my papers, of which he had, of course, possessed himself. He told me what he intended to do, and promised me that if by the use of my name and the rest he succeeded in delivering those followers of his, he would require no further ransom from me."

"And you? You agreed?"

"Agreed? Sometimes, indeed often, you are fatuous. My agreement was not asked. I was merely informed. Your own foolishness and the order of Saint James of Compostella did the rest. I suppose he conferred it upon you, and so dazzled you with it that you were prepared to believe anything he told you?"

"You were bringing it to me? It was among your papers?" quoth Don Jayme, who thought he began to understand.

There was a grim smile on Don Rodrigo's long, sallow face. "I was taking it to the Governor of Hispaniola Don Jayme de Guzman, to whom the letter was addressed."

Don Jayme's mouth fell open. He turned pale. "Not even that, then? The order was not intended for me? It was part of his infernal comedy?"

"You should have examined the letter more attentively."

"It was damaged by sea-water!" roared the Governor furiously.

"You should have examined your conscience, then. It would have told you that you had done nothing to deserve the cross of Saint James."

Don Jayme was too stunned to resent the gibe. Not until he was home again and in the presence of his wife did he recover himself sufficiently to hector her with the tale of how he had been bubbled. Thus he brought upon himself his worst humiliation.

"How does it come, madam," he demanded, "that you recognized him for your cousin?"

"I did not," she answered him, and dared at last to laugh at him, taking payment in that moment for all the browbeating she had suffered at his hands.

"You did not! You mean that you knew he was not your cousin?"

"That is what I mean."

"And you did not tell me?" The world was rocking about him.

"You would not allow me. When I told him that I did not remember that my Cousin Pedro had blue eyes, you told me that I never remembered anything, and you called me ninny. Because I did not wish to be called ninny again before a stranger I said nothing further."

Don Jayme mopped the sweat from his brow, and appealed in livid fury to her cousin Rodrigo, who stood by. "And what do you say to that?" he demanded.

"For myself, nothing. But I might remind you of Captain Blood's advice to you at parting. I think it was that in future you be more respectful to your wife."

IV

THE WAR INDEMNITY

If it was incredibly gallant, it was no less incredibly foolish of the Atrevida to have meddled with the Arabella, considering the Spaniard's inferior armament and the orders under which she sailed.

The Arabella had once been the Cinco Llagas out of Cadiz, of which Peter Blood had so gallantly possessed himself. He had so re-named her in honour of a lady in Barbados, whose memory was ever to serve him as an inspiration and to set restraint upon his activities as a buccaneer. She was going westward in haste to overtake her consorts, which were a full day ahead, was looking neither to right nor to left, when somewhere about 19° of northern longitude and 66° of western latitude, the Atrevida espied her, turned aside to steer across her course, and opened the attack by a shot athwart her hawse.

The Spaniard's commander, Don Vicente de Casanegra was actuated by a belief in himself that was tempered by no consciousness of his limitations.

The result was precisely what might have been expected. The Arabella went promptly about on a southern tack which presently brought her on to the Atrevida's windward quarter, thus scoring the first tactical advantage. Thence, whilst still out of range of the Spaniard's sakers, the Arabella poured in a crippling fire from her demi-cannons, which went far towards deciding the business. At closer quarters she followed this up with cross-bar and langrel, and so cut and slashed the Atrevida's rigging that she could no longer have fled, even had Don Vicente been prudently disposed to do so. Finally within pistol-range the Arabella hammered her with a broadside that converted the trim Spanish frigate into a staggering impotent hulk. When, after that, they grappled, the Spaniards avoided death by surrender, and it was to Captain Blood himself that the grey-faced, mortified Don Vicente delivered up his sword.

"This will teach you not to bark at me when I am passing peacefully by," said Captain Blood. "I see that you call yourself the Atrevida. But I account you more impudent than daring."

His opinion was even lower when, in the course of investigating his capture, he found among the ship's papers, a letter from the Spanish Admiral, Don Miguel de Espinosa y Valdez, containing Don Vicente's sailing orders. In these he was instructed to join the Admiral's squadron with all speed at Spanish Key off Bieque, for the purpose of a raid upon the English settlement of Antigua. Don Miguel was conveniently expressive in his letter.

Although, he wrote, his Catholic Majesty is at peace with England, yet England makes no endeavour to repress the damnable activities of the pirate Blood in Spanish waters. Therefore it becomes necessary to make reprisals and obtain compensation for all that Spain has suffered at the hands of this indemoniated filibuster.

Having stowed the disarmed Spaniards under hatches—all save the rash Don Vicente, who, under parole, was taken aboard the Arabella—Blood put a prize crew into the Atrevida, patched up her wounds, and set a south-easterly course for the passage between Anegada and the Virgin Islands.

He explained the changed intentions which this implied at a council held that evening in the great cabin and attended by Wolverstone, his lieutenant, Pitt, his shipmaster, Ogle, who commanded on the main-deck, and two representatives of the main body of his followers, one of whom, Albin, was a Frenchman. This because one-third of the buccaneers aboard the Arabella at the time were French.

He met with some opposition when he announced the intention of making for Antigua.

This opposition was epitomized by Wolverstone who banged the table with a fist that was like a ham before delivering himself. "To Hell with King James and all who serve him! It's enough that we never make war upon English ships or English settlements. But I'll be damned if I account it our duty to protect folk whose hands are against us."

Captain Blood explained. "The impending Spanish raid is in the nature of reprisals for damage suffered by Spaniards at our hands. This seems to me to impose a duty upon us. We may not be patriots, as ye say, Wolverstone, and we may not be altruists. If we go to warn and remain to assist, we do so as mercenaries, whose services are to be paid for by a garrison which should be very glad to hire them, thus we reconcile duty with profit."

By these arguments he prevailed.

At dawn, having negotiated the passage, they hove to with the southernmost point of the Virgen Gorda on their starboard quarter, some four miles away. The sea being calm, Captain Blood ordered the boats of the Atrevida to be launched, and her Spanish crew to depart in them, whereafter the two ships proceeded on their way to the Leeward Islands.

Going south of Saba with gentle breezes, they were off the west coast of Antigua on the morning of the next day, and with the Union Jack flying from the maintruck they came to cast anchor in ten fathoms on the north side of the shoal that divides the entrance to Fort Bay.

A few minutes after noon, just as Colonel Courtney, the Captain-General of the Leeward Islands, whose seat of government was in Antigua, was sitting down to dinner with Mrs. Courtney and Captain Macartney, he was astounded by the announcement that Captain Blood had landed at St. John's and desired to wait upon him.

Colonel Courtney, a tall, dried-up man of forty-five, sandy and freckled, stared with pale, red-rimmed eyes at Mr. Ives, his young secretary, who had brought the message. "Captain Blood, did you say? Captain Blood? What Captain Blood? Surely not the damned pirate of that name, the gallows-bird from Barbadoes?"

Mr. Ives permitted himself to smile upon his excellency's excitement. "The same, sir."

Colonel Courtney flung his napkin amid the dishes on the spread table and rose, still incredulous. "And he's here? Here? Is he mad? Has the sun touched him? Stab me, I'll have him in irons for his impudence before I dine, and on his way to England before..." He broke off. "Egad!" he cried, and swung to his second in command. "We'd better have him in, Macartney."

Macartney's round face, as red as his coat, showed an amazement no less than the Governor's. That a rascal with a price on his head should have the impudence to pay a morning call on the governor of an English settlement was something that left Captain Macartney almost speechless and more incapable of thought than usual.

Mr. Ives admitted into the long, cool, sparsely-furnished room a tall, spare gentleman, very elegant in a suit of biscuit-coloured taffetas. A diamond of price gleamed amid the choice lace at his throat, a diamond buckle flashed from the band of the plumed hat he carried, a long pear-shaped pearl hung from his left ear and glowed against the black curls of his periwig. He leaned upon a gold-mounted ebony cane. So unlike a buccaneer was this modish gentleman that they stared in silence into the long, lean, sardonic countenance with its high-bridged nose, and eyes that looked startlingly blue and cold in a face that was burnt to the colour of a Red Indian's. More and more incredulous, the Colonel brought out a question with a jerk.

"You are Captain Blood?"

The gentleman bowed. Captain Macartney gasped and desired his vitals to be stabbed. The Colonel said "Egad!" again, and his pale eyes bulged. He looked at his pallid wife, at Macartney, and then again at Captain Blood. "You're a daring rogue. A daring rogue, egad!"

"I see you've heard of me."

"But not enough to credit this. Ye'll not have come to surrender?"

The buccaneer sauntered forward to the table. Instinctively Macartney rose.

"If you'll be reading this it will save a world of explanations," and he laid before his excellency the letter from the Spanish Admiral. "The fortune of war brought it into my hands together with the gentleman to whom it is addressed."

Colonel Courtney read, changed colour, and handed the sheet to Macartney. Then he stared again at Blood, who spoke as if answering the stare.

"It's here to warn you I am, and at need to serve you."

"To serve me?"

"Ye seem in need of it. Your ridiculous fort will not stand an hour under Spanish gunfire, and after that you'll have these gentlemen of Castile in the town. Maybe you know how they conduct themselves on these occasions. If not, I'll be after telling you."

"But—stab me!" spluttered Macartney; "we're not at war with Spain!"

Colonel Courtney turned in cold fury upon Blood. "It is you who are the author of all our woes. It is your rascalities which bring these reprisals upon us."

"That's why I've come. Although I think I am a pretext rather than a reason." Captain Blood sat down. "You've been finding gold in Antigua, as I've heard. Don Miguel will have heard it too. Your militia garrison is not two hundred strong, and your fort, as I've said, is so much rubbish. I bring you a strong ship very heavily armed, and two hundred of the toughest fighting-men to be found in the Caribbean, or anywhere in the world. Of course I'm a damned pirate, and there's a price on my head, and if ye're fastidiously scrupulous yell have nothing to say to me. But if ye've any sense, as I hope ye have, it's thanking God ye'll be that I've come, and ye'll make terms with me."

"Terms?"

Captain Blood explained himself. His men did not risk their lives for the honour and glory of it, and there were in his following a number who were French, and who therefore lacked all patriotic feeling where a British colony was concerned. They would expect a trifle for the valuable services they were about to render.

"Also, Colonel," Blood concluded, "there's a point of honour for you. Whilst it may be difficult for you to enter into alliance with us, there's no difficulty about hiring us, and you may pursue us again without scruple once this job is done."

The Governor looked at him with gloomy eyes. "If I did my duty I would have you in irons and send you home to England to be hanged."

Captain Blood was unperturbed. "Your immediate duty is to preserve the colony of which ye're governor. Ye'll perceive its danger. And the danger is so imminent that even moments may count. Ye'd do well, faith, not to be wasting them."

The Governor looked at Macartney. Macartney's face was as blank as his mind. Then the lady, who had sat a scared and silent witness, suddenly stood up. Like her husband, she was tall and angular, and a tropical climate had prematurely aged her and consumed her beauty. Apparently, thought Blood, it had not consumed her reason.

"James, how can you hesitate? Think of what will happen to the women-the women and the children—if these Spaniards land. Remember what they did at Bridgetown."

The Governor stood with his chin upon his breast, frowning gloomily. "Yet I cannot enter into alliance with... I cannot make terms with outlaws. My duty here is clear. Quite clear." There was finality in his tone.

"Fiat officium, ruat cœlum," said the classical-minded Blood. He sighed, and rose. "If that's your last word, I'll be wishing you a very good day. I've no mind to be caught unawares by the Caribbean Squadron."

"You don't leave," said the Colonel sharply. "There too my duty is clear. The guard, Macartney."

"Och, don't be a fool now, Colonel." Blood's gesture arrested Macartney.

"I'm not a fool, sir, and I know what becomes me. I must do my duty."

"And is your duty demanding so scurvy a return for the valuable service I've already rendered you by my warning? Give it thought now, Colonel."

Again the Colonel's lady acted as Blood's advocate—and acted passionately in her clear apprehension of the only really material issue.

Exasperated, the Colonel flung himself down into his chair again. "But I cannot. I will not make terms with a rebel, an outlaw, a pirate. The dignity of my office... I... I cannot."

In his heart Captain Blood cursed the stupidity of governments that sent such men as this to represent them overseas.

"Will the dignity of your office restrain the Spanish Admiral, d'ye suppose?"

"And the women, James!" his lady again reminded him. "Surely, James, in this extreme need—a whole squadron coming to attack you—his majesty must approve your enlisting any aid."

Thus she began and thus continued, and now Macartney was moved to alliance with her against his excellency's narrow stubbornness, until in the end the Captain-General was brought to sacrifice dignity to expediency. Still reluctant, he demanded ill-humouredly to know the terms of the buccaneers.

"For myself," said Blood, "I ask nothing. I will organize your defences for the sake of the blood in my veins. But when the Spaniards have been driven off I shall require a hundred pieces of eight for each of my men. I have two hundred of them."

His excellency was scandalized. "Twenty thousand pieces!" He choked, and so far forgot his dignity as to haggle. But Blood was coldly firm, and in the end the price was agreed.

That afternoon he set to work upon the defences of St. John's.

Fort Bay is an inlet some two miles in depth and a mile across its widest part. It narrows a little at the mouth, forming a slight bottle-neck. In the middle of this neck ran a long, narrow spit of sand, partly uncovered at extreme low water, with a channel on either side. The southern channel was safe only for vessels of shallow draught; in the narrow, northern channel, however, at the entrance to which the Arabella now rode at anchor, there was never less than eight fathoms, at times slightly increased by the small tides of this sea, so that this was the only gateway to the bay.

The fort guarded this channel, occupying a shallow eminence on the northern promontory. It was a square, squat, machicolated structure of grey stone, and its armament consisted of a dozen ancient sakers and a half-dozen faucons with an extreme range of two thousand yards—guns these which provoked Captain Blood's contempt. He supplemented them by twelve sakers of more modern fashion, which he brought ashore from the Atrevida.

Twelve more guns he landed from the Spanish ship, including two twelve-pounders. These, however, he reserved for another purpose. Fifty yards west of the fort on the extreme edge of the promontory he set about the construction of earthworks—and set about it at a rate which allowed Colonel Courtney some insight into buccaneer methods and the secret of their success.

He landed a hundred of his men for the purpose and had them toiling almost naked in the broiling sun. To these he added three hundred whites and as many black men from St. John's—practically the whole of its efficient male population—and he had them digging, banking, and filling the wickerwork gabions into the making of which he impressed the women. Others were sent to cut turf and fell trees, and fetch one and the other to the site of these operations. Throughout the afternoon the promontory seethed and crawled like an ant-heap. By sunset all was done. It seemed a miracle to the Captain-General. In six hours, under Blood's direction and the drive of his will, another fort had been constructed which by ordinary methods could not have been built in less than a week.

And it was not only built and armed with the remaining twelve guns brought from the Atrevida and with a half-dozen powerful demi-cannons landed from the Arabella; it was so effectively dissembled that from the sea no suspicion of its existence could be formed. Strips of turf faced it so that it merged into the background of shallow cliff; coconut palm stopped it and rose about it; clumps of white acacia and arnotto trees masked the gun emplacements so effectively as to render them invisible at half a mile.

Colonel Courtney conceived that here was a deal of wasted labour. Why trouble to conceal fortifications whose display should have the effect of deterring an assailant?

Blood explained. "If he's intimidated, he'll merely be postponing attack until some time when I'm not here to defend you. I mean either to destroy him or so to maul him that he'll be glad to leave British settlements alone in future."

That night Blood slept aboard the Arabella at her anchorage under the bluff. In the morning St. John's was awakened and alarmed by the sound of heavy gunfire. The Captain-General ran from his house in a bedgown, conceiving that the Spaniards were already here. The firing, however, proceeded from the new earthworks, and was directed upon the completely dismasted hull of the Atrevida, which had been anchored fore and aft athwart the narrow fairway, right in the middle of the channel.

The Captain-General dressed in haste, took horse, and rode out to the bluff with Macartney. As he reached it the firing ceased. The hulk, riddled with shot, was slowly settling down. She sank with a gurgle, as the now furious Governor flung himself from his horse beside the earthworks. Of Captain Blood, who with a knot of his rude followers was observing the end of the Atrevida, he stormily demanded to know in the name of Heaven and of Hell what folly this might be. Did Captain Blood realize that he had completely blocked the entrance to the harbour for all but vessels of the lightest draught?

"That was the aim," said Blood. "I've been at pains to find the shallowest part of the channel. She lies in six fathoms, reducing the depth to a bare two."

The Captain-General conceived that he was being mocked. Livid, he demanded why so insane a measure should have been taken, and this without consulting him. With a note of weariness in his voice Captain Blood explained what should have been obvious. It gave some pause to the Governor's anger. Yet the suspicions natural to a man of such limited vision were not quieted.

"But if to sink the hulk there was your only object, why in the devil's name did you waste shot and powder on her? Why didn't you scuttle her?"

Blood shrugged. "A little gunnery practice. We accomplished two objects in one."

"Gunnery practice?" His excellency was savage. "At that range? What are you telling me, man?"

"You'll understand better when Don Miguel arrives."

"I'll understand now, if you please. I will so. Stab me! Ye'll observe that I command here in Antigua."

Blood was annoyed. He had never learned to suffer fools gladly. "Faith, then your command outstrips your understanding if my object isn't plain. Meanwhile, there are some other matters yet to be settled, and time may be short." With that he swung on his heel, and left the Captain-General spluttering.

Blood had surveyed the coast and found a snug inlet, known as Willoughby's Cove, not two miles away, where the Arabella could lie concealed and yet so conveniently at hand that he and all his men might remain aboard. This at least was good news to Colonel Courtney, who was in dread of having pirates quartered on the town. Blood demanded that his men should be victualled, and required fifty head of cattle and twenty hogs. The Captain-General would have haggled with him, but was overborne in terms which did not improve their relations. The beasts were duly delivered, and in the days that followed the buccaneers became buccaneers in earnest; the boucan fires were lighted on the shores of Willoughby's Cove, and there the flesh of the slaughtered animals was boucanned, together with a quantity of turtle which the adventurers captured thereabouts.

In these peaceful arts three days were consumed, until the Captain-General began to ask himself if the whole thing were not some evil game to cover nefarious ends of Captain Blood and his pirates. Blood, however, explained the delay. Not until Don Miguel had abandoned hope of being joined by Don Vicente de Casanegra with the Atrevida would he decide to sail without him.

Another four days of inactivity went by, on each of which the Captain-General rode out to Willoughby's Cove to vent his suspicions in searching questions. The interviews increased daily in acrimony. Daily Blood expressed more and more plainly to the Captain-General that he saw little hope for the colonial future of a country which exercised so little discrimination in the election of her overseas governors.

Don Miguel's squadron appeared off Antigua only just in time to avert an open rupture between the Captain-General and his buccaneer ally.

Word being brought of this to Willoughby's Cove, early one Monday morning, by one of the guards left in charge of the earthworks, Captain Blood landed a hundred of his men and marched them across to the bluff. Wolverstone was left in command aboard. Ogle, that formidable gunner, was already quartered at the fort with a gun-crew.

Six miles out at sea, standing directly for the harbour of St. John's, with a freshening breeze from the north-west to temper the increasing heat of the morning sun, came four stately ships under full spread of sail, the banner of Castile afloat from the head of each mainmast.

From the parapet of the old fort Captain Blood surveyed them through his telescope. At his elbow, with Macartney in attendance, stood the Captain-General, persuaded at last that the Spanish menace was a reality.

Don Miguel commanded at the time the Virgen del Pilar, the finest and most powerful vessel in which he had yet sailed since Blood had sunk the Milagrosa some months before. She was a great black-hulled galleon of forty guns, including in her armament several heavy demi-cannon with a range of three thousand yards. Of the other three ships, two, if inferior, were still formidable thirty-gun frigates, whilst the last was really little better than a sloop of ten guns.

Blood closed his telescope and prepared for action in the old fort. The new one was for the moment left inactive.

Within a half-hour battle was joined. Don Miguel's advance had all the rashness which Blood knew of old. He made no attempt to shorten sail until within two thousand yards. He conceived, no doubt, that he was taking the place entirely unawares, and that the antiquated guns of the fort would probably be inadequate. Nevertheless, he must dispose of them before attempting to enter the harbour. To be sure of making short work of it, he continued to advance until Blood computed him within a thousand yards.

"On my soul," said Blood, "he'll be meaning to get within pistol-range, or else he thinks the fort of no account at all. Wake him up, Ogle. Let him have a salute."

Ogle's crew had been carefully laying their guns, and they had followed the advance with the twelve sakers from the Atrevida. Others stood at hand with linstocks, rammers and water-tubs, to serve the gunners.

Ogle gave the word, and the twelve guns were touched off as one, with a deafening roar. Within that easy range even the five-pound shot of these comparatively small cannon did some little damage to two of the Spanish ships. The moral effect of thus surprising those who came to surprise was even greater. The Admiral instantly signalled them to go about. In doing so they poured broadside after broadside into the fort, and for some minutes the place was a volcano, smoke and dust rising in a dense column above the flying stones and crumbling masonry. Blinded by it, the buccaneers had no vision of what the Spaniards might be doing. But Blood guessed it, and cleared every man from the fort into shelter behind it during the brief respite before the second broadsides came.

When that was over he drove them back again into the battered fortress, which for awhile now had nothing more to fear, and the original antiquated guns of St. John's were brought into action. The faucons were fired at random through the cloud of dust that hid them merely as a display and to let the

Spaniards know that the fort was still alive. Then, as the cloud lifted, the five-pounders spoke, in twos and threes, carefully aimed at the ships which were now beating to windward. They did little damage; but this was less important than to keep the Spaniards in play.

Meanwhile the gun-crews were busy with the sakers from the Atrevida. Water-tubs had been emptied over them, and now with swabs and wads and rammers at work the reloading was proceeding.

The Captain-General, idle amid this terrific activity, required presently to know why powder was so ineffectively being wasted by these pop-guns, when in the earthworks there were cannon of long range which might be hammering the Spaniards with twenty-four and thirty-pound shot. When he was answered evasively, he passed from suggestion to command, whereupon he was invited not to interfere with carefully laid plans.

An altercation was saved by the return of the Spaniards to the attack and a repetition of all that had gone before. Again the fort was smashed and pounded, and this time two black men were killed and a half-dozen buccaneers were injured by flying masonry, despite Blood's precaution to get them out of the place before the broadsides came.

When the second attack had been beaten off and the Spaniards were again retiring to reload, Blood resolved to withdraw the guns from the fort in which another half-dozen broadsides might completely bury them. Black men and buccaneers and men of the Antiguan militia were indiscriminately employed on the business and harnessed to the guns. Even so it took an hour to get them all dear of the rubble and emplaced anew on the landward side of the fort, where Ogle and his men proceeded once more to load and carefully to lay them. The body of the fort meanwhile served to screen the operation from the Spaniards as they sailed in for the third time. Now the English held their fire whilst another storm of metal crashed upon those battered but now empty ramparts. When it was over, the fort was a shapeless heap of rubble, and the little army lying concealed behind the ruins heard the Spanish cheer that announced their conviction that all was done, since no single shot had been fired to answer their bombardment.

Proudly, confidently, Don Miguel came on. No need now to stand off to reload. Already the afternoon was well advanced and he would house his men in St. John's before nightfall. The haze of dust and smoke, whilst serving to screen the defenders and their new emplacements from the sight of the enemy, could yet be penetrated at close quarters by the watchful eyes of the buccaneers. The Virgen del Pilar was within five hundred yards of the harbour's mouth, when six sakers, charged now with langrel, chain and cross-bar, swept her decks with murderous effect and some damage to her shrouds. Six faucons, similarly charged, followed after a moment's pause, and if their fire was less effective yet it served to increase the confusion and the alarm of so unexpected an attack.

In the pause they could hear the blare of a trumpet aboard the Virgen, screeching the Admiral's orders to the other ships of his squadron. Then, as in the haste of their manoeuvre to go about the Spaniards yawed a moment, broadside on, Blood gave the signal, and two by two the remaining sakers sent their five-pound round shot in search of Spanish timbers. Odd ones took effect, and one very fortunate cannon-ball smashed the mainmast of one of the frigates. In her rippled state and the desperate haste resulting from it, she fouled the sloop, and before the two vessels could disentangle themselves and follow the retreat of the others, their decks had been raked again and again by langrel and cross-bar from water-cooled and hurriedly reloaded guns.

Blood, who had been crouching with the rest, stood up at last as the firing ceased, its work temporarily accomplished. He looked into the long, solemn face of Colonel Courtney and laughed.

"Faith! It's another slaughter of the innocents, so it is!"

The Captain-General smiled sourly back at him. "If you had done as I desired you—"

Blood interrupted without ceremony. "On my soul, now! Are ye not content? If I'd done as you desired me, I'd have put all my cards on the table by now. It's saving my trumps I am until the Admiral plays as I want him to."

"And if the Admiral doesn't, Captain Blood?"

"He will, for one thing because it's in the nature of him; for another because there's no other way to play at all. And so ye may go home and sleep in peace, placing your trust in Providence and me."

"I do not care for the association, sir," said the Governor frostily.

"But you will. On my soul, you will. For we do fine things when we work together, Providence and I."

An hour before sunset the Spaniards were hove to a couple of miles out at sea, and becalmed. The Antiguans, white and black, dismissed by Blood, went home to sup—all but some two score whom he retained for emergencies. Then his buccaneers sat down under the sky to a generous supply of meat and a limited amount of rum.

The sun went down into the jade waters of the Caribbean, and darkness followed almost as upon the extinction of a lamp—the soft, purple darkness of a moonless night irradiated by a myriad stars.

Captain Blood stood up and nosed the air. The north-westerly breeze, which had died down towards evening, was springing up again. He ordered all res and lights to be extinguished, so as to encourage that for which he hoped.

Out at sea in the fine cabin of the Virgen del Pilar, the proud, noble, brave, incompetent admiral of the Caribbean held a council of war which was no council, for he had summoned his captains merely so that he might impose his will upon them. At dead midnight, by when all in St. John's should be asleep, in the conviction that no further attack would come until morning, they would creep past the fort under cover of darkness and with all lights extinguished. Daylight should find them at anchor a mile or more beyond it, in the bay, with their guns trained upon the town. That must be checkmate to the Antiguans.

Upon this they acted, and with sails trimmed to the favouring breeze, and shortened so as to lessen the gurgle of water at their prows, they nosed gently forward through the velvety gloom. With the Virgen leading they reached the entrance of the harbour and the darker waters between the shadowy bluffs on either side. Here all was deathly still. Not a light showed save the distant phosphorescent line where the waters met the shore; not a sound disturbed the stillness save the silken rustle of the sea against their sides.

Already within two hundred yards of the fort, and of the spot where the Atrevida had been sunk to block the channel, the Virgen crept on, her bulwarks lined with silent, watchful men, Don Miguel, leaning immovable as a statue upon the poop-rail. He was abreast of the fort and counting the victory already won, when suddenly his keel grated, and, grating ever harder, drove shuddering onwards for some yards, to be finally gripped and held as if by some monstrous hand in the depths below, whilst overhead under pressure of a wind to which the vessel no longer yielded, the sails drummed loudly to an accompaniment of groaning cordage and clattering blocks.

And then, before the Admiral could even conjecture what had happened to him, the gloom to larboard was split by flame, the silence smashed by a roar of guns, the rending of timbers, and the crashing of spars, as the demi-cannons landed from the Arabella, and held in reserve until now in the dissembled earthworks, hurled their thirty-two-pound shot into the Spanish flagship at merciless short range. The deadly accuracy of these guns might have revealed to Colonel Courtney precisely why Captain Blood had elected to sink the Atrevida by gunfire instead of scuttling her. Thus he had obtained the exact range which enabled him to fire so accurately through the darkness.

One frantic, wildly-aimed broadside the Virgen discharged in answer before, smashed and riddled and held above water only by the hulk on which she had stuck fast, the Admiral abandoned her. With his survivors he clambered aboard one of the frigates, the Indiana, which, unable to check her way in time, had crashed into him astern. Moving very slowly, the Indiana had suffered little damage beyond a smashed bowsprit, and her captain, acting promptly, had taken in what little sail he carried.

Mercifully at that moment the guns ashore were reloading. In that brief respite the Indiana received the fugitives from the flagship, whilst the sloop which had been next in line, perceiving the situation, took in all sail at once, and getting out her sweeps, warped the Indiana astern from her entanglement, and out into the open, where the other frigate lay hove to firing desultorily in the direction of the now silent earthworks on the bluff. The only effect of this was to betray her whereabouts to the buccaneers, and presently the demi-cannons were roaring again, though no longer collectively. A shot from one of them completed the crippling of the Indiana by smashing her rudder; so that having been warped out of the harbour she had to be taken in tow by her sister ship.

The firing ceased on both sides, and the peace and silence of the tropical night would again have descended on St. John's but that all in the town were now afoot and hastening out to the bluff for information.

When daylight broke the only ship on the blue expanse of the Caribbean within the vision of Antigua was the red-hulled Arabella at anchor in the shadow of the bluff to receive the demi-cannons she had lent the enterprise, and the battered

Virgen del Pilar listing heavily to starboard where she had stuck on the submerged hull of the Atrevida. About the wrecked flagship swarmed a fleet of small boats and canoes in which the buccaneers were salving every object of value to be found aboard her. They brought all ashore: arms and armour, some of great price, a service of gold plate, vessels of gold and silver, two steel-bound coffers being, presumably, the treasury of the squadron and containing some six thousand pieces of eight, besides jewels, clothes, oriental carpets and rich brocades from the great cabin. All were piled up beside the fort for subsequent division as provided by the articles under which the buccaneers sailed.

A string of four pack-mules came along the shallow cliff as the salving was concluded and drew up beside the precious heap.

"What's this?" quoth Blood, who was present at the spot.

"From his excellency the Captain-General," replied the black man muleteer, "fo' dah conveying ob dah treasure."

Blood was taken aback. When he recovered: "Much obliged," said he, and ordered the mules to be laden and conducted to the end of the bluff, to the boats which were to carry the spoils aboard the Arabella.

After that he went to wait upon the Captain-General.

He was shown into a long narrow room from one end of which a portrait of his late sardonic majesty King Charles II looked into a mirror on the other. There was a long, narrow table on which stood some books, a guitar, a bowl of heavily-scented white acacia, and there were some tall-backed chairs of black oak without upholstery.

The Captain-General came in followed by Macartney. His face looked longer and narrower than ever.

Captain Blood, telescope under his arm and plumed hat in his hand, bowed low.

"I come to take my leave, your excellency."

"I was about to send for you." The Colonel's pale eyes sought to meet the Captain's steady gaze, but failed. "I hear of considerable treasure taken from the Spanish wreck. I am told your men have carried this aboard your ship. You are aware, sir—or are you not?—that these spoils are the property of the King?"

"I am not aware of it," said Captain Blood. "You are not? Then I inform you of it now." Captain Blood shook his head, smiling tolerantly.

"It is a prize of war."

"Exactly. And the war was being waged on behalf of his majesty and in defence of this his majesty's colony."

"Save that I did not hold the King's commission."

"Tacitly, and temporarily, I granted it you when I consented to enlist you and your men in the defence of the island."

Blood stared at him in amused astonishment.

"What were you, sir, before they made you Captain-General of the Leeward Islands? A lawyer?"

"Captain Blood, I think you mean to be insolent."

"You may be sure I do, and more. You consented to enlist me, did you? Here's condescension! Where should you be now if I hadn't brought you the assistance you consented to receive?"

"We will take one thing at a time, if you please." The Colonel was coldly prim. "When you entered the service of King James, you became subject to the laws that govern his forces. Your appropriation of treasure from the Spanish flagship is an act of brigandage contrary to all those laws and severely punishable under them."

Captain Blood found the situation increasingly humorous. He laughed.

"My clear duty," added Colonel Courtney, "is to place you under arrest."

"But I hope you're not thinking of performing it?"

"Not if you choose to take advantage of my leniency, and depart at once."

"I'll depart as soon as I receive the twenty thousand pieces of eight for which I hired you my services."

"You have chosen, sir, to take payment in another fashion. You have committed a breach of the law. I have nothing more to say to you, Captain Blood."

Blood considered him with narrowing eyes. Was the man so utterly a fool, or was he merely dishonest?

"Oh, sharper than the serpent's tooth!" he laughed. "Sure now I must spend the remainder of my days in succouring British colonies in distress. Meanwhile, here I am and here I stay until I have my twenty thousand pieces." He flung his hat on the table, drew up a chair, sat down, and crossed his legs. "It's a warm day, Colonel, so it is."

The Colonel's eyes flashed. "Captain Macartney, the guard is waiting in the gallery. Be good enough to call it."

"Will ye be intending to arrest me?"

The Colonel's eyes gloomed at him. "Naturally, sir. It is my clear duty. It has been my duty from the moment that you landed here. You show me that I should have considered nothing else whatever my own needs." He waved a hand to the soldier who had paused by the door. "If you please, Captain Macartney."

"Oh, a moment yet, Captain Macartney. A moment yet, Colonel." Blood raised his hand. "This amounts to a declaration of war."

The Colonel shrugged contemptuously. "You may so regard it if you choose. It is not material."

Captain Blood's doubts about the man's honesty were completely dissipated. He was just a fool with a mental vision that could perceive one object only at a time.

"Indeed, and it's most material. Since you declare war on me, war you shall have; and I warn you that you'll find me as ruthless an opponent as the Spaniards found me yesterday when I was your ally."

"By God!" swore Macartney. "Here's fine talk from a man whose person we hold!"

"Others have held me before, Captain Macartney. Don't be attaching too much importance to that." He paused to smile, and then resumed. "It's fortunate now for Antigua that the war you have declared on me may be fought without bloodshed. Indeed, you may perceive at a glance that it has been fought already, that the strategic advantages lie with me, and, therefore, that nothing remains for you but capitulation."

"I perceive nothing of the kind, sir."

"That is because you are slow to perceive the obvious. I am coming to think that at home they regard this as a necessary qualification in a Colonial Governor. A moment's patience, Colonel, while I point out to you that my ship is off the harbour. She carries two hundred of the toughest fighting-men, who would devour your spineless militia at a gulp. She carries forty guns, the half of which could be landed on the bluff within an hour, and within another hour St. John's would be a dust-heap. If you think they would hesitate because this colony is English, I'll remind you that a third of my following is French and the other two-thirds are outlaws like myself. They would sack this town with pleasure, firstly because it is held in the name of King James, a name detestable to all of them, and secondly because the gold you have been finding in Antigua should make it well worth the sacking."

Macartney, purple in the face, was fingering his sword-hilt. But it was the Colonel, livid with passion, who answered, waving one of his bony freckled hands.

"You infamous pirate scoundrel! You damned escaped convict! You've forgot one thing: that until you can get back to your pestilential buccaneers none of this can happen."

"We have to thank him for the warning, sir," Captain Macartney jeered.

"Ah, bah! Ye've no imagination, as I suspected yesterday. Your muleteer gave me a glimpse of what to expect from you. I took my measures accordingly, so I did. I left orders with my lieutenant to assume at twelve o'clock that war had been declared, and to land the guns and haul them to the fort, whence they command the town. I left your mules with him for the purpose." He glanced at the timepiece on the overmantel. "It's nearly half-past twelve already. From your windows here you can see the fort." He stood up and proffered his telescope. "Assure yourself that what I have said is happening."

There was a pause in which the Captain-General considered him with eyes of hate. Then in silence he took the telescope and went to the window. When he turned from it again he was fierce as a rattlesnake. "But you forget one thing still. That we hold you. I'll send word to your pirate scum that at the first shot from them I'll hang you. The guard, Macartney. There's been talk enough."

"Oh, a moment yet," Blood begged. "Ye're so plaguily hasty in your conclusions. Wolverstone has my orders, and no threat to my life will swerve him from them by a hair's breadth. Hang me if you will." He shrugged. "If I set great store by life I should hardly follow the trade of a buccaneer. But when you've hanged me be sure that not one stone of St. John's will be left upon another, not man, woman or child will my buccaneers spare in avenging me. Consider that, and consider at the same time your duty to this colony and to your King—this duty by which you rightly set such store."

The Governor's pale eyes stabbed him as if they would reach his soul. Calm and intrepid he stood before them, so calm in all the circumstances as almost to intimidate.

The Colonel looked at Macartney, as if for help. He found none there. Irritably he broke out at last: "Oh, stab me! I am well served for dealing with a pirate. To be rid of you, I'll pay you your twenty thousand pieces, and so farewell and be damned to you."

"Twenty thousand pieces!" Blood raised his eyebrows in surprise. "But that was whilst I was your ally; that was before ye declared war upon me."

"What the devil do you mean now?"

"That since ye admit defeat, we will pass to the discussion of terms."

"Terms! What terms?" The Captain-General's exasperation was swiftly mounting.

"You shall hear them. First, the twenty thousand pieces of eight that you owe my men for services rendered. Next, thirty thousand for the redemption of the town from the bombardment that is preparing."

"What? By God, sir!..."

"Next," Captain Blood pursued relentlessly, "ten thousand pieces for your own ransom, ten thousand for the ransom of your own family, and five thousand for that of other persons of consequence in St. John's, including Captain Macartney here. That makes seventy-five thousand pieces of eight, and they must be paid within the next hour, since later will be too late."

The Captain-General looked unutterable things. He tried to speak. But speech failed him. He sat down heavily. At last he found his voice. It came thick and quavering.

"You... you abuse my patience. You surely... You think me mad?"

"Best hang him, Colonel, and have done," Macartney exploded.

"And thereby destroy the colony it is your duty at all costs—at all costs, mark you—to preserve."

The Captain-General passed a hand across his wet, pallid brow, and groaned.

They talked, of course, for some time yet; but ever within the circle of what had been said already, until in the end Colonel Courtney broke into a laugh that was almost hysterical.

"Stab me, sir! It only remains to marvel at your moderation. You might have asked seven hundred thousand pieces, or seven millions—"

"True," Blood interrupted him. "But then I am by nature moderate, and also I have a notion of the resources of your treasury."

"But the time!" cried the Governor desperately, to show that he had yielded. "How can I collect the sum within an hour?"

"I'll be reasonable. Send me the money to the bluff by sunset, and I'll withdraw. And now I'll take my leave at once, so as to suspend the operations. It's a very good day I'll be wishing you."

They let him go, perforce. And at sunset Captain Macartney rode out to the gun emplacements of the buccaneers followed by a black man leading a mule on which the gold was laden.

Captain Blood came forward alone to receive him. "It isn't what you'd have got from me," said the choleric captain through his teeth.

"I'll remember that in case you should ever command a settlement. And now, sir, to business. What do these sacks hold?"

"You'll find five thousand pieces in each."

"Then set me down four of them: the twenty thousand pieces for which I agreed to serve Antigua. The rest you can take back to the Captain-General with my compliments. Let the experience teach him, and you too, Captain darling, that a man's first duty is less to his office than to his own honour, and that he cannot perform it unless he fulfils the engagements of his word."

Captain Macartney sucked in his breath. "Gads-life!" he exclaimed huskily. "And you're a pirate!"

Sternly came the vibrant metallic voice of the buccaneer. "I am Captain Blood."

V

BLOOD MONEY

Captain Blood was pleased with the world—which is but another way of saying that he was pleased with himself.

He stood on the mole at Cayona and surveyed the shipping in the rockbound harbour. With pride he considered the five great ships that now made up his fleet, every spar and timber of which had once been the property of Spain. There was his own flagship, the Arabella, of forty guns, that once had been the Cinco Llagas out of Cadiz, with her red bulwarks and gilded ports aflame in the evening sunlight, with the scarcely less powerful blue and white Elizabeth beside her. Beyond them rode the three smaller twenty-gun vessels captured in the great affair at Maracaybo from which Blood was lately returned. These ships, originally named the Infanta, the San Felipe, and the Santo Niño, Blood had renamed after the three Parcae, the Clotho, the Lachesis, and the Atropos, by which it was his intention playfully to convey that they were the arbiters of the fate of any Spaniard henceforth encountered by them upon the seas.

Captain Blood took satisfaction in his own delicate, scholarly humour. He was, as I have said, well pleased with himself. His following numbered close upon a thousand men, and he could double this number whenever he pleased. For his luck was passing into a proverb, and luck is the highest quality that can be sought in a leader of hazardous enterprises. Not the great Henry Morgan himself in his best days had wielded such authority and power. Not even Montbar—surnamed by Spain the Exterminator—had been more dreaded by Spaniards in his day that was Don Pedro Sangre, as they translated Peter Blood's name, accounting it most apt.

Order, he knew, was being taken against him. Not only the King of Spain, of whose power he had made a mock, but also the King of England, whom he accounted, and with some reason, a contemptible fellow, were concerting measures for his destruction; and news had lately come to Tortuga that, nearer at hand, the Spanish Admiral, Don Miguel de Espinosa, who had been the latest and most terrible sufferer at his hands, had proclaimed that he would pay ten thousand pieces of eight to any man who should deliver up to him the person of Captain Blood alive. Don Miguel's was a vindictiveness that was not to be satisfied by mere death.

Peter Blood was not intimidated, nor on that account was he likely to mistrust his luck so much as to let himself run to rust in the security of Tortuga. For that which he had suffered—and he had suffered much—at the hands of man, he had chosen to make Spain the scapegoat. Thus he accounted that he served a twofold purpose. He took compensation, and at the same time served, not indeed the Stuart King, whom he despised—although himself born an Irishman and bred a Papist—but England, and, for that matter, all the rest of civilized mankind, which cruel, treacherous, greedy, bigoted Castile sought to debar from intercourse with the New World.

He was turning from the mole, almost deserted by now of its usual bustling heterogeneous crowd, when the voice of Hayton, the boatswain of the Arabella, called after him from the boat that had brought him ashore.

"Back at eight bells, Captain?"

"At eight bells," said Blood over his shoulder, and sauntered on, swinging his long ebony cane, elegant and courtly in a suit of grey and silver.

He took his way up towards the town, saluted as he went by most of those whom he met, and stared at by the rest. He chose to go by way of the wide, unpaved Rue du Roi de France, which the townsfolk had sought to embellish by flanking it with rows of palm-trees. As he approached the tavern of The King of France the little crowd about its portals drew to attention. From within came a steady drone of voices as a muffled accompaniment to foul exclamations, snatches of coarse songs, and the shrill, foolish laughter of women. Through all ran the rattle of dice and the clinking of drinking-cans.

Blood realized that his buccaneers were making merry with the gold they had brought back from Maracaybo. The ruffians overflowing from that house of infamy hailed him with a ringing cheer. Was he not the king of all the ruffians that made up the great Brotherhood of the Coast?

He acknowledged their greeting by a lift of the hand that held the cane, and passed on. He had business with M. d'Ogeron, the Governor, and this business took him now to the handsome white house crowning the eminence to the east of the town.

The Captain was an orderly, provident man, and he was busily providing against the day when the death or downfall of King James II might make it possible for him to return home. For some time now it had been his practice to make over the bulk of his share of prizes to the Governor against bills of exchange on France, which he forwarded to Paris for collection and deposit. Peter Blood was ever a welcome visitor at the Governor's house, not only because these transactions were profitable to M. d'Ogeron, but in a still deeper measure because of a signal service that the Captain had once done him and his in rescuing his daughter Madeleine from the hands of a ruffianly pirate who had attempted to carry her off. By M.

d'Ogeron, his son and his two daughters, Captain Blood had ever since been regarded as something more than an ordinary friend.

It was therefore nowise extraordinary that when, his business being transacted, he was departing on this particular evening, Mademoiselle d'Ogeron should choose to escort Captain Blood down the short avenue of her father's fragrant garden.

A pale-faced, black-haired beauty, tall and statuesque of figure, and richly gowned in the latest mode of France, Mademoiselle d'Ogeron was as romantic of appearance as of temperament. And as she stepped gracefully beside the Captain in the gathering dusk she showed her purpose to be not without a certain romantic quality also.

"Monsieur," she said in French, hesitating a little, "I have come to implore you to be ever on your guard. You have too many enemies."

He halted and, half-turning, hat in hand, he bowed until his long black ringlets almost met across his clear-cut, gipsy-tinted face.

"Mademoiselle, your concern is flattering; but so flattering." Erect again, his bold eyes, so startlingly light under their black brows and in a face so burnt and swarthy, laughed into her own. "I do not want for enemies, true. It is the penalty of greatness. Only he who is without anything is without enemies. But at least they are not in Tortuga."

"Are you so very sure of that?"

Her tone gave him pause. He frowned, and considered her solemnly for an instant before replying.

"Mademoiselle, you speak as if from some knowledge."

"Hardly so much. My knowledge is but the knowledge of what a slave told me today. He says that the Spanish Admiral has placed a price upon your head."

"That is just the Spanish Admiral's notion of flattery, mademoiselle."

"And that Cahusac has been heard to say he will make you rue the wrong you did him at Maracaybo."

"Cahusac?"

The name revealed to him the rashness of his assertion that he had no enemy in Tortuga. He had forgotten Cahusac; but he realized that Cahusac would not be likely to have forgotten him. Cahusac had been with him at Maracaybo, and had been trapped with him there by the arrival of Don Miguel de Espinosa's fleet. The French rover had taken fright, had charged Blood with rashness in his conduct of the enterprise, had quarrelled with him and had made terms with the Spanish Admiral for himself and his own French contingent. Granted a safe-conduct by Don Miguel, he had departed empty-handed, leaving Captain Blood to his fate. But it proved not at all as the timorous Cahusac conceived it. Captain Blood had not only broken out of the Spanish trap, but he had sorely mauled the Admiral, captured three of his ships, and returned to Tortuga laden with rich spoils of victory.

To Cahusac this was gall and wormwood. With the faculty for confusing cause and effect which is the chief disability of stupid egoists, he came to account himself cheated by Captain Blood. And he was making no secret of his unfounded resentment.

"He is saying that, is he?" said Captain Blood. "Now, that is indiscreet of him. Besides, all the world knows he was not wronged. He was allowed to depart in safety as he wished when he thought the situation grew too dangerous."

"But by doing so he sacrificed his share of the prizes, and for that he and his companions have since been the mock of Tortuga. Can you not conceive what must be that ruffian's feelings?"

They had reached the gate.

"You will take precautions? You will guard yourself?" she begged him.

He smiled upon her friendly anxiety.

"If only so that I may live on to serve you." With formal courtesy he bowed low over her hand and kissed it.

Seriously concerned, however, by her warning he was not. That Cahusac should be vindictive he could well believe. But that Cahusac should utter threats here in Tortuga was an indiscretion too dangerous to be credible in the case of a cur who took no risks.

He stepped out briskly through the night that was closing down, soft and warm, and came soon within sight of the lights of the Rue du Roi de France. As he reached the head of that now deserted thoroughfare a shadow detached itself from the mouth of a lane on his right to intercept him.

Even as he checked: prepared to fall on guard, he made out the figure to be a woman's, and heard his name called softly in a woman's voice.

"Captain Blood!"

As he halted she came closer, and addressed him quickly, breathlessly. "I saw you pass two hours since. But I dursn't be seen speaking to you in daylight here in the street. So I have been on the watch for your return. Don't go on, Captain. You are walking into danger; walking to your death."

At last his puzzled mind recognized her: and before the eyes of his memory flashed a scene enacted a week ago at The King of France. Two drunken ruffians had quarrelled over a woman—a fragment of the human wreckage of Europe washed up on the shores of the New World—an unfortunate creature of a certain comeliness, which, however, like the castoff finery she wore, was tarnished, soiled, and crumpled. The woman, arrogating a voice in a dispute of which she was the object, was brutally struck by one of her companions, and Blood, upon an impulse of chivalrous anger, had felled her assailant and escorted her from the place.

"They're lying in wait for you down yonder," she was saying, "and they mean to kill you."

"Who does?" he asked her, Mademoiselle d'Ogeron's words of warning sharply recalled.

"There's a score of them. And if they was to know—if they was to see me here a-warning you—my own throat would be cut before morning."

She peered fearfully about her through the gloom as she spoke, and fear quivered in her voice. Then she cried out huskily, as if with mounting terror.

"Oh, don't let us stand here! Come with me; I'll make you safe until daylight. Then you can go back to your ship, and if you're wise you'll stay on board after this, or else come ashore in company. Come!" she ended, and caught him by the sleeve.

"Whisht now! Whisht!" said he, resisting the pressure on his arm. "Whither will you be taking me!"

"Oh, what odds, so long as I make you safe?" She was dragging on him with all her weight. "You was kind to me, and I can't leave you to be killed. And we'll both be murdered unless you come."

Yielding at last, as much for her sake as his own, he allowed her to lead him from the wide street into the byway from which she had issued to intercept him. It was a narrow lane with little one-storied houses that were mostly timber standing at wide intervals along one side of it. Along the other ran a palisade enclosing a plantation.

At the second house she stopped. The little door stood open, and the interior was dimly lighted by the naked flame of a brass oil lamp set upon a table.

"Go in," she bade him in a shuddering whisper.

Two steps led down to the floor of the house, which was below the level of the street. Down these went Captain Blood, and on into the room, whose air was rank with the reek of stale tobacco and the sickly odour of the little oil lamp. The woman followed, and closed the door. And then, before Captain Blood could turn to inspect his surroundings in that dim light, he was struck over the head from behind with something heavy and hard-driven, which, if it did not stun him outright, at least stretched him sick and faint upon the grimy naked earth of the unpaved floor.

At the same moment a woman's scream, that ended abruptly in a stifled gurgle, cut sharply upon the silence.

In an instant, before Captain Blood could move to help himself, before he could even recover from his bewildered surprise, swift, sinewy, skilful hands had done their work upon him. Thongs of hide lashed his ankles and his wrists, which' had been dragged behind him. Then he was rolled over on to his back, lifted, forced into a chair, and lashed by the waist to that.

A man of low stature and powerful, apelike build, long in the body and short in the legs, was leaning over him. The sleeves of his blue shirt were rolled to the elbows of his prodigious, long, muscular and hairy arms. Little black eyes twinkled wickedly in a broad face that was almost as flat and sallow as a mulatto's. A red and blue scarf swathed his head, completely concealing his hair; heavy gold rings hung in the lobes of the great ears.

Captain Blood considered him for a long moment, setting a curb upon the violent rage that rose in him in a measure as his senses cleared. Instinctively he realized that violence and passion would help him not at all, and that at all costs they must be suppressed. And he suppressed them.

"Cahusac!" he said slowly. And then added: "This is an unexpected pleasure entirely!"

"Ye've dropped anchor at last, Captain," said Cahusac, and he laughed softly with infinite malice.

Blood looked beyond him towards the door, where the woman was writhing in the grasp of Cahusac's companion.

"Will you be quiet, you slut, or must I quiet you?" the ruffian was threatening.

"What are you going to do with him, Sam?" she whimpered.

"No business of yours, my girl."

"Oh yes, it is! You told me he was in danger, and I believed you, you lying tyke!"

"Well, so he was. But he's safe and snug now. You go in there, Molly." He pointed across the room to the black entrance of an alcove.

"I'll not—" she was beginning angrily.

"Go on," he snarled, "or it'll be the worse for you!"

He seized her roughly again at neck and waist and thrust her, still resisting, across the room and into the alcove. He closed the door and bolted it.

"Stay you there, you slut, and keep quiet, or I'll quiet you once for all."

From behind the door he was answered by a moan. Then there was the creak of a bed as the woman flung herself violently upon it, and thereafter silence.

Captain Blood accounted her part in this business explained, and more or less ended. He looked up into the face of his sometime associate, and his lips smiled to simulate a calm he was far from feeling.

"Would it be an impertinence to inquire what ye're intending, Cahusac?" said he.

Cahusac's companion laughed, and lounged across the table, a tall, loose-limbed fellow, with a long face of an almost Indian cast of features. His dress implied the hunter. He answered for Cahusac, who glowered, morosely silent.

"We intend to hand you over to Don Miguel de Espinosa."

He stooped to give his attention to the lamp, pulling up the wick and trimming it, so that the light in the shabby little room was suddenly increased.

"C'est ça!" said Cahusac. "And Don Miguel, no doubt, he'll intend to hang you from the yardarm."

"So Don Miguel's in this, is he? Glory be! I suppose it's the blood-money that's tempted ye. Sure now, it's the very work that ye're fitted for, devil a doubt. But have ye considered all? There are reefs ahead, my lad. Hayton was to have met me with a boat at the mole at eight bells. I'm late as it is. Eight bells was made an hour ago and more. Presently they'll take alarm. They knew where I was going. They'll follow and track me. To find me, the boys will be turning Tortuga inside out like a sack. And what'll happen to ye then, Cahusac? Have you thought of that? The pity of it is that ye're entirely without foresight. It was lack of foresight that sent ye away empty-handed from Maracaybo. And even then, but for me, ye'd be hauling at the oar of a Spanish galley this very minute. Yet ye're aggrieved, being a poor-spirited, cross-grained cur, and to vent your spite you're running straight upon destruction. If ye've a spark of sense you'll haul in sail, my lad, and heave-to before it's too late."

Cahusac leered at him for only answer, and then in silence went through the Captain's pockets. The other, meanwhile, sat down on a three-legged stool of pine.

"What's o'clock, Cahusac?" he asked.

Cahusac consulted the Captain's watch.

"Near half-past nine, Sam."

"Plague on it!" grumbled Sam. "Three hours to wait!"

"There's dice in the cupboard," said Cahusac, "and here's something to be played for."

He jerked his thumb towards the yield of Captain Blood's pockets, which made a little pile upon the table. There were some twenty gold pieces, a little silver, an onion-shaped gold watch, a gold tobacco-box, a pistol, and, lastly, a jewel which Cahusac had detached from the lace at the Captain's throat, besides a sword and rich balrick of grey leather heavily wrought in gold.

Sam rose, went to a cupboard, and fetched thence the dice. He set them on the table, and drawing up his stool, again resumed his seat. The money he divided into two equal halves. Then he added the sword and the watch to one pile, and the jewel, the pistol, and the tobacco-box to the other.

Blood, very alert and watchful—so concentrated, indeed, upon the problem of winning free from this trap that he was hardly conscious of the pain in' his head from the blow that had felled him—began to speak again. Resolutely he refused to admit the fear and hopelessness that were knocking at his heart.

"There's another thing ye've not considered," said he slowly, almost drawlingly, "and that is that I might be willing to ransom myself at a far more handsome price than the Spanish Admiral has offered for me."

But they weren't impressed. Cahusac merely mocked him.

"Tiens! And your certainty that Hayton will come to your rescue then? What of that?"

He laughed, and Sam laughed with him.

"It's probable," said Blood, "most probable. But not certain; nothing is, in this uncertain world. Not even that the Spaniard will pay you the ten thousand pieces of eight they tell me he has been after offering for me. You could make a better bargain with me, Cahusac."

He paused, and his keen, watchful glance observed the sudden gleam of covetousness in the Frenchman's eye, as well as the frown contracting the brow of the other ruffian. Therefore he continued.

"You might make such a bargain as would compensate you for what you missed at Maracaybo. For every thousand pieces that the Spaniard offers, sure now I'll offer two."

Cahusac's jaw fell, his eyes widened.

"Twenty thousand pieces!" he gasped in blank amazement.

And then Sam's great fist crashed down upon the rickety table, and he swore foully and fiercely.

"None of that!" he roared. "I've made my bargain, and I abides by it. It'll be the worse for me if I doesn't—ay, and for you, Cahusac. Besides, are you such a gull that you think this pretty hawk'll keep faith with you?"

"He knows that I would," said Blood, "he's sailed with me. He knows that my word is accounted good even by Spaniards."

"Maybe. But it's not accounted good by me." Sam stood over him, the long, evil face, with its sloping brows and heavy eyelids, grown dark and menacing. "I'm pledged to deliver you safely at midnight, and when I pledges myself to a job I does it. Understand?"

Captain Blood looked up at him, and actually smiled.

"Faith," said he. "You don't leave much to a man's imagination."

And he meant it literally; for what he had clearly gathered was that it was Sam who had entered into league with the Spanish agents, and dared not for his life's sake break with them.

"Then that's as well," Sam assured him. "If you want to be spared the discomfort of a gag for the next three hours, you'll just hold your plaguey tongue. Understand that?"

He thrust his long face forward into his captive's, sneering and menacing.

Understanding, Captain Blood abandoned his desperate clutch of the only slender straw of hope that he had discovered in the situation. He realized that he was to wait here, helpless in his bonds, until the time appointed for his delivery to someone who should carry him off to Don Miguel de Espinosa. Upon what would happen to him then he scarcely dared to dwell. He knew the revolting cruelties of which a Spaniard was capable, and he could guess what a spur of rage would be the Spanish admiral's. A sweat of horror broke upon his skin. Was he indeed to end his gloriously hazardous career in this mean way? Was he, who had so proudly sailed the seas of the Main as a conqueror, to founder thus in a dirty backwater? He could found no hope upon the search that. Hayton and the others would presently be making. That, as he had said, they would turn the place inside out, he never doubted. But he never doubted, either, that they would come too late. They might hunt down his betrayers, and wreak a terrible vengeance upon them. But how should that avail him?

The fogs of passion thickened in his mind; despair smothered the power of thought. He had close upon a thousand devoted men here in Tortuga, almost within hail, and he bound and helpless, and so to be delivered to the vindictive justice of Castile! That insistent, ever-recurring thought beat backwards and forwards like a pendulum in his brain, distracting it.

And then, in a sense, he came to himself again. His mind grew clear once more, preternaturally clear and active. Cahusac he knew for a venal scoundrel, who would keep faith with none if he saw profit in treachery. And the other was probably no better; indeed, probably worse, since interest alone—that Spanish blood-money—had lured him to his present task. He concluded that he had too soon abandoned the attempt to outbid the Spanish admiral. That way he might yet throw a bone of contention to these mangy curs, over which they would perhaps end by tearing at each other's throats.

A moment he surveyed them now, observing the evil greed in the eyes of each as they watched the fall of the dice over their trifling stakes from the gold and trinkets of which they had rifled him, and over which they were gaming to beguile the time of waiting.

And then he heard his own crisp voice breaking the silence.

"You gamble there for halfpence with a fortune within your reach."

"Are you beginning again?" growled Sam. But the Captain went on undaunted.

"I'll outbid the Spanish admiral's blood-money by forty thousand pieces. I offer you fifty thousand pieces of eight for my life."

Sam, who had risen in anger, stood suddenly arrested by the mention of so vast a sum.

Cahusac had risen too, and now both men stood, one on each side of the table, tense with excitement, which, if unexpressed as yet, was none the less to be read in the sudden pallor of their faces and dilation of their eyes. At last the Frenchman broke the silence.

"God of God! Fifty thousand pieces of eight!" He uttered the words slowly, as if to impress the figure upon his own and his companion's mind. And he repeated. "Fifty thousand pieces of eight! Twenty-five thousand for each! Pardi! but that is worth some risk! Eh, Sam?"

"A mort of money, true," said Sam, thoughtfully. And then he recovered. "Bah! What's a promise, anyhow? Who's to trust him? Once he's free, who's to make him pay, and he's—"

"Oh, I pay," said Blood. "Cahusac will tell you that I always pay." And he continued. "Consider that such a sum, even when divided, will make each of you wealthy, to lead a life of ease and plenty. Muchoviño, muchas mugeres!" he laughed in Spanish. "To be sure now, you'll be wise."

Cahusac licked his lips and looked at his companion. "It could be done," he muttered persuasively. "It's not yet ten, and between this and midnight we could put ourselves beyond the reach of your Spanish friends."

But Sam was not to be persuaded. He had been thinking; yet, tempting as he must find the lure, he dared not yield, discerning a double peril within it. Committed now by Spain to this venture, he dared neither draw back nor shift his course. Between the certain rage of the Spaniards should he play them false, and the probable resentment of Blood once he was restored to liberty, Sam saw himself inevitably crushed. Better an assured five thousand pieces to be enjoyed in comparative safety than a possible twenty-five thousand accompanied by such intolerable risks.

"It could not be done at all!" he cried angrily. "So let us hear no more about it. I've warned you once already."

"Mordieu!" cried Cahusac thickly. "But I say it could! And I say it's worth the risk."

"You say so, do you? And where's the risk for you? The Spaniards do not even know that you're in the business. It's easy for you, my lad, to talk about risks that you won't be called upon to run. But it's not quite the same for me. If I fails the Don, he'll want to know the reason. And, anyhow, I've pledged myself, and I'm a man of my word. So let's hear no more about it."

He towered there, fierce and determined, and Cahusac, after a scowling stare into that long, resolute face, uttered a sigh of exasperation, and sat down again.

Blood perceived quite clearly the inward rage that consumed the Frenchman. Vindictive though he might be towards the Captain, the venal scoundrel preferred his enemy's gold to his blood, and it was easy to guess the bitterness in which he saw himself compelled to forgo the more tangible satisfaction, simply because of the risks with which acceptance would be fraught for his associate.

For a while there was no word spoken between the twain, nor did Blood judge that he could further serve his ends by adding anything to what he had already said. He took heart, meanwhile, from the clear perception of the mischief he had already made.

When at last he broke the brooding silence, his words seemed to have no bearing whatever upon the situation.

"Though you may mean to sell me to Spain, sure there's no reason why ye should let me die of thirst in the meantime. I've a throat that's like the salt ponds on Saltatudos, so I have."

Although he had a definite purpose to serve, to which he made his thirst a pretext, yet that thirst itself was real, and it was suffered by his captors in common with himself. The air of the room, whose door and window were tight-barred, was stifling. Sam passed a hand across his dank brow and swept away the moisture.

"Hell! The heat!" he muttered. "And now I thirst myself."

Cahusac licked his dry lips.

"Is there nothing in the house?" he asked.

"No. But it's only a step to The King of France."

He rose. "I'll go fetch a jack of wine."

Hope soared wildly in the breast of Captain Blood.

It was precisely for this that he had played. Knowing their drinking habit, and how easily suggestion must arouse their desire to indulge it, he had hoped to send one of them upon that errand, and that the one to go would be Sam. With Cahusac he was sure he could make a deal at once.

And then Cahusac, the fool, ruined all by his excessive eagerness. He, too, was on his feet.

"A jack of wine! Yes, yes!" he cried. "Make haste. I, too, am thirsty."

Almost was there a quiver in his voice. Sam's ears detected it. He stood arrested, pondering his associate, and reading in his face the little rascal's treacherous intent.

He smiled a little.

"On second thoughts," said he, slowly, "it will be best if you goes and I stays on guard."

Cahusac's mouth fell open; almost he turned pale. Inwardly Captain Blood cursed him for a triple fool. "D'ye mean that ye don't trust me?" he demanded. "It ain't that—not exactly," he was answered.

"But it's me that stays."

Cahusac became really and vehemently angry. "Ah, ca! Name of God! If you don't trust me with him, I don't trust you neither."

"You don't need to. You know that I dursn't be tempted by his promises. That's why I'm the one to stay."

For a long moment the two ruffianly associates glowered at each other in angry silence. Then Cahusac's glance became sullen. He shrugged and turned aside, as if grudgingly admittingly that Sam's reasoning was unanswerable. He stood pondering with narrowed eyes. Finally he bestirred himself as if with sudden resolve.

"Ah, bah, I go!" he declared, and abruptly went.

As the door closed on the departing Frenchman, Sam resumed his seat at the table. Blood listened to the quickly receding footsteps until they had faded in the distance; then he broke the silence with a laugh that startled his companion.

Sam looked up sharply.

"What's amusing you now, Captain?"

Blood would have preferred, as we know, to deal with Cahusac. Cahusac was a certainty. Sam was hardly a possibility, obsessed as he obviously was by the fear of Spain. Still, that possibility must be exploited, however slender it might appear.

"Your rashness, bedad!" answered Captain Blood. "Yell not trust him to remain on guard, yet ye trust him out of your sight."

"And what harm can he do?"

"He might not return alone," said the Captain darkly.

"Blister me!" cried Sam. "If he tries any such tricks, I'll pistol him at sight. That's how I serves them that gets tricky with me."

"Ye'd be wise to serve him so in any case. He's a treacherous tyke, Sam, as I should know. Ye've baffled him tonight, and he's not the man to forgive. Ye should know that from his betrayal of me. But ye don't know. Ye've eyes, Sam, but no more sight than a blind puppy. And a head, Sam, but no more brains than are contained in a melon, or you'd never hesitate between Spain and me."

"Oh, that's it, is it?"

"Just that. Just fifty thousand pieces of eight that I offer, and that I pledge my honour to pay you, as well as pledging my honour to bear no malice and seek no vengeance. Even Cahusac assures you that my word is good, and was ready enough to accept it."

He paused. The rascally hunter was considering him silently, his face clay-coloured and the perspiration standing in beads upon his brow.

Presently he spoke hoarsely.

"Fifty thousand pieces, you said?" quoth he softly.

"To be sure. For where's the need to share with the French cur? D'ye dream he'd share with you if he could make it all his own by slipping a knife into your back? Come, Sam, make a bold bid for fortune. Damn your fears of Spain! Spain's a phantom! I'll protect you from Spain. You can lie safe aboard my flagship."

Sam's eyes flashed momentarily, then grew troubled again by thought.

"Fifty thousand. Ah, but the risk!"

"Sure, there's no risk at all," said Blood. "Not half the risk you run when it comes out that you sold me to Spain, as come out it will. Man, ye'll never leave Tortuga alive. And if ye did, my buccaneers would hunt ye to the end of the earth."

"But who's to tell?"

"There's always someone. Ye were a fool to undertake this job, a bigger fool to have taken Cahusac for partner. Hasn't he talked openly of vengeance? And won't he, therefore, be the first man suspected? And when they get him, as get him they will, isn't it as sure as judgment that he'll tell on you?"

"By Heaven, I believe you in that!" cried the man, presented with facts which he had never paused to consider.

"Faith, you may believe me in the rest as readily, Sam."

"Wait! Let me think!"

As once before, Captain Blood judged wisely that he had said enough for the moment. So far his success with Sam had been greater than he had dared to hope. The seed he had sown might now be left awhile to germinate.

The minutes sped, and Sam, elbows on the table and head in his hand, sat still and thoughtful. When at last he looked up, and the yellow light beat once more upon his face, Blood saw that it was pallid and gleaming. He tried to conjecture how far the poison he had dropped into Sam's mind might have done its work. Presently Sam plucked a pistol from his belt and examined the priming. This seemed to Blood significant. But it was more significant still that he did not replace the pistol in his belt. He sat nursing it, his yellowish face grimly set, his coarse lips tight with purpose.

"Sam," said Captain Blood softly, "what have you decided?"

"I'll put it out of the power of that French mongrel to bubble me," said the ruffian.

"And nothing else?"

"The rest can wait."

With difficulty Captain Blood bridled his eagerness to force the pace.

Followed an apparently interminable time of waiting, in a silence broken only by the ticking of the Captain's watch where it lay upon the table. Then, faintly at first, but swiftly growing louder as it drew nearer, came a patter of steps in the lane outside. The door was pushed open, and Cahusac appeared carrying a great black jack.

Sam was already on his feet beyond the table, his right hand behind him.

"You've been a long time gone!" he grumbled. "What kept you?"

Cahusac was pale, and breathing rather hard, as if he had been running. Blood, whose mind was preternaturally alert, knowing that he had not run, looked elsewhere for a reason, and guessed it to lie in either fear or excitement.

"I made all haste," was the Frenchman's answer. "But I was athirst myself, and I stayed to quench it. Here's your wine."

He set the leathern jack upon the table.

And on the instant, almost at point-blank range, Sam shot him through the heart.

Through the rising cloud of smoke, whose acrid smell took him sharply in the throat and set him coughing, Blood saw a picture that he was to retain in his mind to the end of his days. Face downwards on the floor lay Cahusac with twitching limbs, whilst Sam leaned forward, across the table to watch him, a grin on his long, animal face.

"I take no risk with French swines like you," he explained himself, as if his victim could still hear him. Then he put down the pistol and reached for the jack. He raised it to his mouth, and poured a full draught down his parched throat. Noisily he smacked his lips as he set down the vessel. Then as a bitter after-taste caught him in the throat he made a grimace, and apprehension charged suddenly through his mind and spread upon his countenance. He snatched up the jack again and thrust his nose into it, sniffing audibly like a questing dog. Then, with eyes dilating in horror, he stared at Blood out of a countenance that was leather-hued, and in an awful voice screamed a single word:

"Manzanilla!"

Then he swung round, and, uttering horrible, blood-curdling blasphemies, he hurled the jack and the remainder of its contents at the dead man on the floor.

A moment later he was doubled up by pain, and his hands were clawing and clutching at his stomach. Then he mastered himself, and without any thought now for Blood, or anything but the torment at work upon his vitals, he reeled across the room and pulled the door wide. The effort seemed to increase his agony. Again he was taken by a cramp that doubled him until his chest was upon his knees, and he howled the while, blaspheming at first, but presently uttering mere inarticulate, animal noises. He collapsed at last upon the floor, a raving, writhing lunatic.

Captain Blood considered him grimly, amazed but no whit intrigued. The riddle did not even require the key supplied by the single word that Sam had ejaculated. It was very plain to read.

Never had poetic retribution more fitly and promptly overtaken a pair of villains. Cahusac had loaded the wine with the poison of the manchineel apple, so readily procurable in Tortuga. With this, and so that he might be free to make a bargain with Captain Blood, and secure to himself the whole of the ransom the Captain offered, he had murdered his associate in the very moment in which, with the same intent, his associate had murdered him.

If Captain Blood had his own wits to thank for much, he had his luck to thank for more.

Gradually and slowly, as it seemed to the captive spectator, though in reality very quickly, the poisoned man's struggles grew fainter. Presently they were merely, and ever decreasingly, sporadic, and finally they ceased altogether, as did his breathing, which at the last had grown stertorous. He lay quite still in a cramped huddle against the open door.

By then Captain Blood was giving his attention to himself, and he had already wasted some moments and some strength in ineffectual straining at his bonds. A drumming on the door of the alcove reminded him of the presence of the woman who had been used unconsciously to decoy him. The shot and Sam's utterances had aroused her into activity. Captain Blood called to her.

"Break down the door! There's no one left here but myself."

Fortunately, that door was but a feeble screen of slender planks, and it yielded quickly to the shoulder that she set against it. Wild-eyed and dishevelled, she broke at 'last into the room, then checked and screamed at what she beheld there.

Captain Blood spoke sharply, to steady her.

"Now, don't be screeching for nothing, my dear. They're both as dead as the planks of the table, and dead men never harmed anyone. There's a knife yonder. Just be slipping it through these plaguey thongs."

In an instant he was free and on his feet, shaking out his ruffled plumage. Then he recovered his sword, his pistol, his watch, and his tobacco-box. The gold and the jewels he pushed together in a little heap upon the table.

"Ye'll have a home somewhere in the world, no doubt. This will help you back to it, my girl."

She began to weep. He took up his hat, picked up his ebony cane from the floor, bade her goodnight, and stepped out into the lane.

Ten minutes later he walked into an excited, torch-lit mob of buccaneers upon the mole, whom Hagthorpe and Wolverstone were organizing into search-parties to scour the town. Wolverstone's single eye fiercely conned the Captain.

"Where the devil have you been?" he asked. "Observing the luck that goes with blood-money," said Captain Blood.

VI

THE GOLD AT SANTA MARIA

The buccaneer fleet of five tall ships rode snugly at anchor in a sequestered creek on the western coast of the Gulf of Darien. A cable's length away, across gently heaving, pellucid waters, shot with opalescence by the morning sun, stretched a broad crescent of silver-grey sand; behind this rose the forest, vividly green from the rains now overpast, abrupt and massive as a cliff. At its foot, among the flaming rhododendrons thrusting forward like outposts of the jungle, stood the tents and rude log huts, palmetto thatched—the buccaneer encampment during that season of careening, of refitting, and of victualling with the fat turtles abounding thereabouts. The buccaneer host, some eight hundred strong, surged there like a swarming hive, a motley mob, English and French in the main, but including odd Dutchmen, and even a few West Indian half-castes. There were boucan-hunters from Hispaniola, lumbermen from Campeachy, vagrant seamen, runagate convicts from the plantations, and proscribed outlaws from the Old World and the New.

Out of the jungle into their midst stepped, on that glowing April morning, three Darien Indians, the foremost of whom was of a tall, commanding presence, broad in the shoulder and long in the arm. He was clad in drawers of hairy, untanned hide, and a red blanket served him for a cloak. His naked breast was streaked in black and reds in his nose he wore a crescent-shaped plate of beaten gold that hung down to his lip, and there were massive gold rings in his ears. A tuft of eagle's feathers sprouted from his sleek black hair, and he was armed with a javelin which he used as a stag.

He advanced calmly and without diffidence into their staring midst, and in primitive Spanish announced himself as the cacique Guanahani, called by the Spaniards Brazo Largo. He begged to be taken before their captain, to whom he referred also by his Hispanicised name of Don Pedro Sangre.

They conducted him aboard the flagship, the Arabella, and there, in the captain's cabin, the Indian cacique was courteously made welcome by a spare gentleman of a good height, very elegant in the Spanish fashion, whose resolute face, in cast of features and deep coppery tan, might, but for the eyes of a vivid blue, have been that of a Darien Indian.

Brazo Largo came to the point with a directness and economy of words to which his limited knowledge of Spanish constrained him.

"Usted venir conmigo. Yo llevar usted mucho oro Espanol. Caramba!" said he, in deep, guttural tones. Literally this may be rendered: "You to come with me. I take you much Spanish gold," with the added vague expletive "Caramba!"

The blue eyes flashed with interest. And, in the fluent Spanish acquired in less unregenerate days, Captain Blood answered him with a laugh:

"You are very opportune. Caramba! Where is this Spanish gold?"

"Yonder." The cacique pointed vaguely westward. "March ten days."

Blood's face grew overcast. Remembering Morgan's exploit across the isthmus, he leapt at a conclusion.

"Panama?" quoth he.

But the Indian shook his head, a certain impatience in his sternly wistful features.

"No. Santa Maria."

And he proceeded clumsily to explain that there, on the river of that name, was collected all the gold mined in the mountains of the district for ultimate transmission to Panama. Now was the time when the accumulations were heaviest. Soon the gold would be removed. If Captain Blood desired it—and Brazo Largo knew that there was a prodigious store—he must come at once.

Of the Indian's sincerity and goodwill towards himself Captain Blood entertained no single doubt. The bitter hatred of Spain smouldering in the breast of all Indians under Spanish rule made them the instinctive allies of any enemy of Spain.

Captain Blood sat on the locker under the stern windows and looked out over the sun-kissed waters of the lagoon.

"How many men would be required?" he asked at last.

"Forty ten, fifty ten, perhaps," said Brazo Largo, from which the Captain adduced that he meant four or five hundred.

He questioned him closely as to the nature of the country they would have to cross and the fortifications defending Santa Maria. Brazo Largo put everything in the most favourable light, smoothed away all difficulties, and promised not only himself to guide them, but to provide bearers to convey their gear. And all the time, with gleaming, anxious eyes, he kept repeating to Captain Blood:

"Much gold. Much Spanish gold. Caramba!"

So often did he repeat this parrot-cry, and with such obvious intent to allure, that Blood began to ask himself did not this Indian protest too vehemently for utter honesty.

Pondering him, the Captain voiced his suspicion in a question.

"You are very eager that we should go, my friend?"

"Go. Yes. Go you," the Indian answered. "Spaniards love gold. Guanahani no love Spaniards."

"So that you want to spite them? Indeed, you seem to hate them very bitterly."

"Hate!" said Brazo Largo. His lips writhed, and he made guttural noises of emphatic affirmation. "Huh! Huh!"

"Well, well, I must consider."

He called the boatswain and delivered the cacique into his care for entertainment.

A council, summoned by bugle-call from the quarter-deck of the Arabella, was held as soon there after as those concerned were come aboard.

Assembled about the oak table in the admiral's cabin, they formed a motley group, truly representative of the motley host encamped ashore. Blood, at the table's head, looking like a grande of Spain in the sombre richness of his black and silver, the long ringlets of his sable hair reaching to his collar of fine point; young Jerry Pitt, ingenuous of face, and in plain grey homespun, like the West of England Puritan that he had been; Hagthorpe, stiffly built, stern-faced, wearing showy clothes without grace, looked the simple, downright captain of fortune he was become; Wolverstone, herculean of build, bronzed of skin, and picturesquely untidy of person, with a single eye of a fierceness far beyond his nature, was perhaps the only one whose appearance really sorted with his trade; Mackett and James had the general appearance of mariners; lastly, Yberville, who commanded a French contingent, vying in elegance with Blood, had more the air and manner of a Versailles exquisite than of a leader of desperate and bloody pirates.

The admiral—for such was the title by now bestowed by his following upon Captain Blood—laid before them the proposal brought by Brazo Largo. He merely added that it came opportunely, inasmuch as they were without immediate plans.

Opposition sprang naturally enough from those who were, first and foremost, seamen—from Pitt, Mackett, and James. Each in turn dwelt upon the hardships and the dangers attending long overland expeditions. Hagthorpe and Wolverstone, intent upon striking the Spaniard where he most would feel it, favoured the proposal, and reminded the council of Morgan's successful raid upon Panama. Yberville, a French Huguenot proscribed and banished for his faith, and chiefly intent upon slitting the throats of Spanish bigots, wherever and whenever it might be done, proclaimed himself also for the venture in accents as mild and gentle as his words were hot and bloodthirsty.

Thus stood the council equally divided, and it remained for Blood to cast the vote that should determine the matter. But the admiral hesitated, and in the end resolved to leave the decision to the men themselves. He would call for volunteers, and if their numbers reached the necessary, he would lead them across the isthmus, leaving the others with the ships.

The captains approving this, they went ashore at once, taking the Indians with them. There Blood harangued the buccaneers, fairly expounding what was to be said for and what against the venture.

"I myself," he announced, "have resolved to go if so be that I am sufficiently supported." And then, after the manner of Pizarro on a similar occasion, he whipped out his rapier, and with the point of it drew a line in the sand. "Let those who choose to follow me across the isthmus, step now to windward of this line."

A full half of them responded noisily to his invitation. They included to a man the boucan-hunters from Hispaniola—who were by now amphibious fighters, and the hardiest of all that hardy host—and most of the lumbermen from Campeachy, for whom swamp and jungle had no terrors.

Brazo Largo, his coppery face aglow with satisfaction, departed to collect his bearers; and he marched them, fifty stalwart savages, into the camp next morning. The adventurers were ready. They were divided into three companies, each commanded respectively by Wolverstone, Yberville—who had shred his fripperies and dressed himself in the leather garb of the hunter—and Hagthorpe.

In this order they set out, preceded by the Indian bearers, who carried their heavier gear—their tents, six small brass cannons of the kind known as sakers, cans for fireballs, good store of victuals—doughboys and strips of dried turtle-and the medicine-chest. From the decks of the fleet bugles called farewell, and, in pure ostentation, Pitt, who was left in charge, fired a salute from his guns as the jungle swallowed the adventurers.

Ten days later, having covered a distance of some 160 miles, they encamped within striking distance of their destination.

The first part of the journey had been the worst, when their way lay over precipitous mountains, laboriously scaled on the one side and almost as laboriously descended on the other. On the seventh they rested in a great Indian village, where dwelt the king or chief cacique of the Indians of Darien, who, informed by Brazo Largo of their object, received and treated them with all honour and consideration. Gifts were exchanged, knives, scissors, and beads on the one side, against plantains and sugarcane on the other; and, reinforced here by scores of Indians, the buccaneers pushed on.

They came on the morrow to the river of Santa Maria, on which they embarked in a fleet of some seventy canoes of Indian providing. But it was a method of travelling that afforded at first little of the ease it had seemed to promise. All that day and the next they were constrained, at the distance of every stone's cast, to turn out, to haul the boats over shallows or rocks or over trees that had fallen across the channel. At last the navigation grew clearer, and presently, the river becoming broad and deep, the Indians discarded the poles, with which hitherto they had guided the canoes, and took to paddles and oars.

And so they came at length by night within sakershot of Santa Maria. The town stood on the riverbank a half-mile beyond the next bend.

The buccaneers proceeded to unload their arms, which were fast lashed to the insides of the canoes, the locks, as well as their cartridge-boxes and powder-horns, well cased and waxed down. Then, not daring to make a fire lest they should betray their presence, they posted sentries, and lay down to rest until daybreak.

It was Blood's hope to take the Spaniards so completely by surprise as to seize their town before they could put themselves in posture of defence, and so snatch a bloodless victory. This hope, however, was dispelled at dawn, when a distant discharge of musketry, followed by a drum beating frenziedly a travailler within the town, warned the buccaneers that they had not stolen upon the Spaniards as unobserved as they imagined.

To Wolverstone fell the honour of leading the vanguard, and two score of his men were equipped with firepots—shallow cylindrical cans filled with resin and gunpowder—whilst others bore forward the sakers, which were under the special command of Ogle, the gunner from the Arabella. Next came Hagthorpe's company, whilst Yberville's brought up the rear.

They marched briskly through the woods to the very edge of the savannah, where, at a distance of perhaps two furlongs, they beheld their Eldorado.

Its appearance was disappointing. Here was no handsome city of New Spain, such as they had been expecting, but a mere huddle of one-storeyed wooden buildings, thatched with wild cane and palmetto royal, clustering about a church, and defended by a fort. The place existed solely as a receiving station for the gold produced by the neighbouring mountains, and it numbered few inhabitants apart from the garrison and the slaves who worked in the goldfields. Fully half the area occupied by the town was taken up by the mud fort, which, whilst built to front the river, presented its flank to the savannah. For further defence against the very hostile Indians of Darien, Santa Maria was encircled by a stout palisade, some twelve feet high, pierced by loopholes for musketry at frequent intervals.

Within the town drums had ceased, but a hum of human movement reached the buccaneers as they reconnoitred from the wood's edge before adventuring upon the open ground. On the parapet of the fort stood a little knot of men in morion and corselet. Above the palisade quivered a thin line of smoke, to announce that Spanish musketeers were at their posts with matches ready lighted.

Blood ordered the sakers forward, having decided to breach the palisade towards the north-east angle, where a storming party would be least attainable by the gunners of the fort. Accordingly, Ogle mounted his battery at a point where a projecting spur of the forest on his left gave him cover. But now a faint easterly breeze beginning to stir carried forward the smoke of their fuses, to betray their whereabouts and invite the speculative fire of the Spanish musketeers. Bullets were already flicking and spattering through the branches about them when Ogle opened with his guns. At that short range it was an easy matter to smash a breach through wooden pales that had never been constructed to resist such weapons. Into that breach, to hold it, rushed the badly-captained Spanish troops. A withering volley from the buccaneers scattered them, whereupon Blood ordered Wolverstone to charge.

"Fireballs to the van! Scatter as you advance, and keep low. God speed you, Ned! Forward!"

Forth they leapt at the double, and they were halfway across the open before the Spaniards brought any considerable body of fire to bear upon them. Then they dropped, and lay supine in the short gamma grass until that frenzied musketry had slackened, when they leapt up again, and on at speed before the Spaniards could reload. And meanwhile Ogle had swung his sakers round to the right, and he was freely hurling his five-pound shot into the town on the flank of the advancing buccaneers.

Seven of Wolverstone's men lay on the ground where they had paused, ten more were picked off, during that second forward rush, and now Wolverstone was at the breach. Over went a score of fireballs to scatter death and terror, and before the Spaniards could recover from the confusion caused by these, the dread enemy was upon them, yelling as they burst through the cloud of smoke and dust.

Nevertheless, the Spanish commander, a courageous if unimaginative officer named Don Domingo Fuentes, rallied his men so effectively that for a quarter of an hour the battle swayed furiously backwards and forwards in the breach.

But in a battle of cold steel there were no troops in the world that, in anything approaching equality of numbers, could have stood long against these hardy, powerful, utterly reckless fellows. Gradually, but relentlessly and inevitably, the cursing, screaming Spaniards were borne back by Wolverstone, supported now by the main host, with Blood himself in command.

Back and back they were thrust, fighting with a wild fury of despair, until the beaten-out line of their resistance suddenly snapped. They broke and scattered, to re-form again, and by a rearguard action gain the shelter of the fort, leaving the buccaneers in possession of the town.

Within the fort, with the two hundred demoralized survivors of his garrison of three hundred men, Don Domingo Fuentes took counsel, and presently sent a flag of truce to Captain Blood, offering to surrender with the honours of war.

But this was more than Blood could prudently concede. He knew that his men would probably be drunk before night, and he could not take the risk of having two hundred armed Spaniards in the neighbourhood at such a time. Being, however, averse to unnecessary bloodshed, and eager to make an end without further fighting, he returned a message to Don Domingo, pledging his word that if he would surrender at discretion, no violence should be done to the life or ultimate liberty of the garrison or the inhabitants of Santa Maria.

The Spaniards piled arms in the great square within the fort, and the buccaneers marched in with banners flying and trumpets blaring. The commander stood forward to make formal surrender of his sword. Behind him were ranged his two hundred disarmed men, and behind these again the scanty inhabitants of the town, who had sought refuge with them. They numbered not more than sixty, amongst whom were perhaps a dozen women, a few black men, and three friars in the black-and-white habit of Saint Dominic. The black slave population, it was presently ascertained, were at the mines in the mountains, whither they had just returned.

Don Domingo, a tall, personable man of thirty, in corselet and headpiece of black steel, with a little peaked beard that added length to his long, narrow face, addressed Captain Blood almost contemptuously.

"I have accepted your word," he said, "because, although you are a pirate scoundrel and a heretic in every other way dishonourable, you have at least the reputation of observing your pledges."

Captain Blood bowed. He was not looking his best. Half the coat had been torn from his back, and he had taken a scalp wound in the battle. But, however begrimed with blood and sweat, dust and gunpowder, his grace of deportment remained unimpaired.

"You disarm me by your courtesy," said he.

"I have no courtesies for pirate rogues," answered the uncompromising Castilian. Whereupon Yberville, that fierce hater of all Spaniards, thrust himself forward, breathing hard, but was restrained by Captain Blood.

"I am waiting," Don Domingo intrepidly continued, "to learn your detestable purpose here; to learn why you, the subject of a nation at peace with Spain, dare to levy war upon Spaniards."

Blood laughed.

"Faith, now, it's just the lure of gold, which is as potent with pirates as with more respectable scoundrels all the world over—the very lure that has brought you Spaniards to plant this town conveniently near the goldfields. To be plain, Captain, we've come to relieve you of the season's yield, and as soon as ye've handed it over we'll relieve you also of our detestable presence."

The Spaniard laughed, and looked round at his men as if inviting them to laugh with him. "To be sure, you conceive me a fool!" he said.

"Far from it. I'm hoping, for your own sake, that ye're not."

"Do you think that, forewarned as I was of your coming, I kept the gold at Santa Maria?" He was derisive. "You are too late, Captain Blood. It is already on its way to Panama. We embarked it in canoes during the night, and sent a hundred men to guard it. That is how my garrison comes to be depleted, and that is why I have not hesitated to surrender."

He laughed again, observing Blood's rueful countenance.

A gust of rage swept through the ranks of the buccaneers pressing behind their leader. The news had run as swiftly as flame over gunpowder, and with similar effect in the explosion it produced. With yells of execration and sinister baring of weapons, they would have flung themselves upon the Spanish commander, who—in their view—had cheated them, and they would have torn him there and then to pieces, had not

Blood swung round and made of his own body a shield for Don Domingo.

"Hold!" he commanded, in a voice that blared like a trumpet. "Don Domingo is my prisoner, and I have pledged my word that he shall suffer no violence!"

Yberville it was who fiercely voiced the common thought.

"Will you keep faith with a Spanish dog who has cheated us? Let him be hanged!"

"It was his duty, and I'll have no man hanged for doing no more than that!"

For a moment Blood's voice was drowned in uproar. But he stood his ground impassively, his light eyes stern, his hand upheld, imposing some measure of restraint upon them.

"Silence, there, and listen! You are wasting time. The harm is far from being beyond repair. The gold has but a few hours' start. You, Yberville, and you, Hagthorpe, re-embark your companies at once, and follow. You should come up with them before they reach the Gulf, but even if you don't, it is still a far cry to Panama, and you'll overtake them long before they're in sight of it. Away with you! Wolverstone's company will await your return here with me."

It was the only thing that could have stayed their fury and prevented a massacre of the unarmed Spaniards. They did not wait to be told a second time, but poured out of the fort and out of the town faster than they had poured into it. The only grumblers were the six score men of Wolverstone's company who were bidden to remain behind. They locked up the Spaniards, all together, in one of the long pent-houses that made up the interior of the fort. Then they scattered about the little town in quest of victuals and such loot as there might be.

Blood turned his attention to the wounded. These, both his own men and the Spaniards, had been carried into another of the pent-houses, where beds of hay and dried leaves had been improvised for them. There were between forty and fifty of them in all, of which number one quarter were buccaneers. In killed and wounded the Spanish loss had been upwards of a hundred men; that of the buccaneers between thirty and forty.

With a half dozen assistants, of whom one was a Spaniard who had some knowledge of medicine, Blood went briskly to work to set limbs and patch up wounds. Absorbed in his task, he paid no heed to the sounds outside, where the Indians, who had gone to earth during the fighting, were now encamped, until suddenly a piercing scream disturbed him.

Before he could move or speak, the door of the hut was wrenched open, and a woman, hugging an infant to her breast, reeled in, calling him wildly by his Hispanicised name.

"Don Pedro! Don Pedro Sangre!" Then, as he stepped forward, frowning, she gasped for breath, clutched her throat, and fell on her knees before him, crying agonizedly in Spanish: "Save him! They are murdering him—murdering him!"

She was a lithe young thing that had scarcely yet crossed the threshold of womanhood, whom at a casual glance you might, from her apparel and general appearance, have supposed a Spaniard of the peasant class. Her blue-black hair and liquid black eyes were such as you might see in many an Andalusian, nor was her skin much swarthier. Only the high cheekbones and peculiar, dusky lips proclaimed, upon a closer inspection, her real race.

"What is it?" said Blood. "Whom are they murdering?"

A shadow darkened the sunlit doorway and Brazo Largo entered, dignified and grimly purposeful.

Overmastering terror of the advancing Indian froze the crouching woman's tongue.

Now he was standing over her. He stooped and set his hand upon her shrinking shoulder. He spoke to her swiftly in the guttural tongue of Darien, and though Blood understood no word of it, yet he could not mistake the note of stern command.

Wildly, a mad thing, she looked up at Captain Blood.

"He bids me go to see them roasting him alive! Mercy, Don Pedro! Save him!"

"Save whom?" barked the Captain, almost in exasperation.

Brazo Largo answered him, explaining:

"She to be my daughter—this. Captain Domingo, he come village, one year now, and carry her away with him. Caramba! Now I roast him, and take her home." He turned to the girl. "Vamos," he commanded, continuing to use his primitive Spanish, "you to come with me. You see him roast, then you come back village."

Captain Blood found the explanation ample. In a flash he recalled Guanahani's excessive eagerness to conduct him to the Spanish gold at Santa Maria, and how that eagerness had momentarily awakened suspicion in him. Now he understood. In urging this raid on Santa Maria, Brazo Largo had used him and his buccaneers to exploit a private vengeance and to recover an abducted daughter from Domingo Fuentes. But however deserving of punishment that abduction might appear, it was also revealed that, whether the girl had gone off willingly or not with the Spanish captain, his subsequent treatment of her had been such that she now desired to stay with him, and was concerned to the point of madness for his life and safety.

"Is it true what he says—that Don Domingo is your lover?" the Captain asked her.

"He is my husband, my married husband, and my love," she answered, a passion of entreaty in her liquid eyes. "This is our little baby. Do not let them kill him, Don Pedro! Oh, if they do," she moaned, "I shall kill myself!"

Captain Blood looked across at the grim-faced Indian.

"You hear? The Spaniard has been good to her. She desires his life. And his offence being as you say, it is her will that decked his fate. What have you done with him?"

Both clamoured at once, the father in angry, almost incoherent, remonstrance, the girl in passionate gratitude. She sprang up and caught Blood's arm to drag him thence.

But Brazo Largo, still protesting, barred the way. He conveyed that in his view Captain Blood was violating the alliance between them.

"Alliance!" snorted Blood. "You have been using me for purposes of your own. You should have been frank with me and told me of your quarrel with Don Domingo before I pledged myself that he should suffer no violence. As it is..."

He shrugged, and went out quickly with the young mother. Brazo Largo stalked after them, glowering and thoughtful.

Outside, Blood ran into Wolverstone and a score of men who were returning from the town. He ordered them to follow him, telling them that the Indians were murdering the Spanish captain.

"Good luck to them!" quoth Wolverstone, who had been drinking.

Nevertheless, he followed, and his men with him, being in reality less bloody in deed than in speech.

Beyond the breach in the palisade they came upon the Indians—some forty of them—kindling a fire. Near at hand lay the helpless Don Domingo, bound with leather thongs. The girl sped to him, crooning soft Spanish endearments. He smiled in answer out of a white face that yet retained something of scornful calm. Captain Blood, more practical, followed with a knife and slashed away the prisoner's bonds.

There was a movement of anger among the Indians, instantly quelled by Brazo Largo. He spoke to them rapidly, and they stood disappointed but impassive. Wolverstone's men were there, musket in hand, blowing on their fuses.

They escorted Don Domingo back to the fort, his little wife tripping between him an the buccaneer captain, whom she enlightened on the score of the Indians' ready obedience to her father.

"He told them that you must have your way since you had pledged your word that Domingo's life should be safe. But that presently you would depart. Then they would return and deal with him and the other few Spaniards left here."

"We must provide against it," said Captain Blood, to reassure her.

When they got back to the fort they found that, in their absence, the remainder of the Indians, numbering rather more than a score, had broken into the shed where the Spaniards were confined. Fortunately the business had only just begun, and the Spaniards, although unarmed, were sufficiently numerous to offer a resistance, which, so far, had been effective. Nevertheless, Captain Blood came no more than in time to prevent a general massacre.

When he had driven off his savage allies, the Spanish commander desired a word with him.

"Don Pedro," he said, "I owe you my life. It is difficult to thank you."

"Pray don't give yourself the trouble," said Captain Blood. "I did what I did, not for your sake, but for the sake of my pledged word, though concern for your little Indian wife may have had some part in it."

The Spaniard smiled almost wistfully as his glance rested on her standing near him, her fond eyes devouring him.

"I was discourteous to you this morning. I beg your pardon."

"That is an ample amend."

The Captain was very dignified.

"You are generous. May I ask, sir, what is your intention regarding us—myself and the others?"

"Nothing against your liberty, as I promised. So soon as my men return, we shall march away and leave you."

The Spaniard sighed.

"It is what I feared. You will leave us, weakened in strength, our defences wrecked, at the mercy of Brazo Largo and his Indians, who will butcher us the moment your backs are turned. For don't imagine that they will leave Santa Maria until that is done."

Captain Blood considered, frowning.

"You have certainly stirred up a personal vengeance, which Brazo Largo will prosecute without pity. But what can I do?"

"You could suffer us to depart for Panama at once, whilst you are here to cover our retreat from your Indian allies."

Captain Blood made a gesture of impatience.

"Ah, wait, Don Pedro! I would not propose it did I not deem you, from what I have seen, to be a man of heart, a gallant gentleman, pirate though you may be. Also you will observe that, since you have disavowed any intention of retaining us as prisoners, I am really not asking for anything at all."

It was quite true, and, upon turning it over in his mind, Captain Blood came to the conclusion that they would be much better off at Santa Maria without these Spaniards, who had to be guarded on the one hand and protected on the other. Therefore he consented. Wolverstone demurred. But when Blood asked him what possible purpose could be served by keeping the Spaniards at Santa Maria, Wolverstone confessed that he did not know. All that he could say was that he trusted no living Spaniard, which did not seem to have any bearing on the question.

So Captain Blood went off to find Brazo Largo, who was sulking on the wooden jetty below the fort.

The Indian rose at his approach, an exaggerated impassivity on his countenance.

"Brazo Largo," said the Captain, "your men have set my word at naught and put my honour in danger."

"I not understand," the Indian answered him. "You make friends with Spanish thieves?"

"Make friends! No. But when they surrendered to me I promised, as the condition of their surrender, that no harm should come to them. Your men would have murdered them in violation of that promise had I not prevented it."

The Indian was contemptuous.

"Huh! Huh! You not my friend. I bring you to Spanish gold, and you turn against me."

"There is no gold," said Blood. "But I am not quarrelling on that. You should have told me, my friend, before we came this journey, that you were using me so that we might deliver up to you your Spanish enemy and your daughter. Then I should not have passed my word to Don Domingo that he would be safe, and you could have drunk the blood of every Spaniard in the place. But you deceived me, Brazo Largo."

"Huh! Huh!" said Brazo Largo. "I not say anything more."

"But I do. There are your men. After what has happened, I cannot trust them. And my pledged word compels me to defend the Spaniards so long as I am here."

The Indian bowed.

"Perfectamente! So long as you here. What then?"

"If there is trouble again, there may be shooting, and some of your braves may be hurt. I should regret that more than the loss of the Spanish gold. It must not happen, Brazo Largo. You must summon your men, and let me consign them to one of the huts in the fort for the present—for their own sakes."

Brazo Largo considered. Then he nodded. He was a very reasonable savage. And so the Indians were assembled, and Brazo Largo, smiling the smile of a man who knew how to wait, submitted to confinement with them in one of the pent-houses.

The assembled buccaneers murmured a little among themselves, and Wolverstone ventured to express the general disapproval.

"Ye're pushing matters rather far, Captain, to risk trouble with the Indians for the sake of those Spanish dogs!"

"Oh, not for their sake. For the sake of my pledged word, and that bit of an Indian girl with her baby. The Spanish commander has been good to her, and he's a gallant fellow."

"God help us!" said Wolverstone, and swung away in disgust.

An hour later the Spaniards were embarking from the jetty, under the eyes of the buccaneers, who, from the mud wall of the fort, watched their departure with some misgivings. The only weapons Blood allowed the voyagers were half a dozen fowling-pieces. They took with them, however, a plentiful supply of victuals, and Don Domingo, like a prudent captain, was very particular in the matter of water. Himself he saw the casks stowed aboard the canoes. Then he took his leave of Captain Blood.

"Don Pedro," he said, "I have no words in which to praise your generosity. I am proud to have had you for my enemy."

"Let us say that you are fortunate."

"Fortunate, too. I shall tell it wherever there are Spaniards to hear me that Don Pedro Sangre is a very gallant gentleman."

"I shouldn't," said Captain Blood. "For no one will believe you."

Protesting still, Don Domingo stepped aboard the piragua that carried his Indian wife and their half-caste baby. His men pushed the vessel off into the current, and he started on his journey to Panama, armed with a note in Captain Blood's hand, ordering Yberville and Hagthorpe to pass him unscathed in the event of his coming up with them.

In the cool of the evening the buccaneers sat down to a feast in the open square of the fort. They had found great stores of fowls in the town, and some goats, besides several hogsheads of excellent wine in the house of the Dominican fathers. Blood, with Wolverstone and Ogle, supped in the departed commander's well-equipped quarters, and through the open windows watched with satisfaction the gaiety of his feasting followers. But his satisfaction was not shared by Wolverstone, whose humour was pessimistic.

"Stick to the sea in future, Captain, says I," he grumbled between mouthfuls. "There's no packing off a treasure there when we come within saker-shot. Here we are, after ten days' marching, with another ten days' marching in front of us! And I'll thank God if we get back as light as we came, for as likely as not we shall have differences to settl with old Brazo Largo, and we'll be lucky if we get back at all, ever. Ye've bungled it this time, Captain."

"Ye're just a foolish heap of brawn, Ned," said the Captain. "I've bungled nothing at all. And as for Brazo Largo, he's an understanding savage, so he is, who'll keep friends with us if only because he hates the Spaniards."

"And ye behave as if ye loved 'em," said Wolverstone. "Ye're all smirks and bows for this plaguey commander who cheated us out of the gold, and ye—"

"Sure now, he was a gallant fellow, Spaniard or no Spaniard," said Blood. "In packing off the gold when he heard of our approach he did his duty. Had he been less gallant, he would have gone off with it himself, instead of remaining here at his post. Gallantry calls to gallantry; and that's all I have to say about it."

And then, before Wolverstone could make answer, sharp and clear above the noise the buccaneers were making rang the note of a bugle from the side of the river. Blood leapt to his feet.

"It will be Hagthorpe and Yberville returning!" he cried.

"Pray God they've got the gold at last!" said Wolverstone.

They dashed out into the open and made for the parapet, to which the men were already swarming. As Blood reached it, the first of the returning canoes swung alongside of the jetty, and Hagthorpe sprang out of it.

"Ye're soon returned," cried Blood, leaping down to meet him. "What luck?"

Hagthorpe, tall and square, his head swathed in a yellow kerchief, faced him in the dusk.

"Certainly not the luck that you deserve, Captain." His tone was curious.

"Do you mean that you didn't overtake them?" Yberville, stepping ashore at that moment, answered for his fellow-leader.

"There was nobody to overtake, Captain. He fooled you, that treacherous Spaniard; he lied when he told you that he had sent off the gold; and you—you believed him—you believed a Spaniard!"

"If ye'd come to the point now!" said Captain Blood. "Did I hear ye say he had not sent off the gold? D'ye mean that it is still here?"

"No," said Hagthorpe. "What we mean is that, after he had so fooled you with his lies that ye didn't even trouble to make search, you allowed them to go off scot-free, taking the gold with them."

"What?" the Captain barked at him. "How do you know this?"

"A dozen miles or so from here we came upon an Indian village; and we had the wit to stop and inquire how long it might be since a Spanish fleet of canoes had gone that way. They answered that no such fleet had passed today, or yesterday, or any day since the last rains. That's how we knew that your gallant Spaniard had lied. We put about at once to return, and midway back we ran into Don Domingo's party. The meeting took him by surprise. He had not reckoned that we'd seek information so soon. But he was as smooth and specious as ever, and a deal more courteous. He confessed quite frankly that he had lied to you, adding that subsequently, after our departure, he had purchased his liberty, and that of all who accompanied him, by surrendering the gold to you. He was instructed by you, he said, to order us to return at once; and he showed us your note of hand, which made him safe."

And then Yberville took up the tale.

"But we being not quite so trustful of Spaniards, and arguing that he who lies once will lie again, took them ashore and subjected them to a search."

"And d'ye tell me that you found the gold?" cried Blood, aghast.

Yberville paused a moment and smiled.

"You had permitted them to victual themselves generously against that journey. Did you observe at what spring Don Domingo filled his water-casks?"

"His water-casks?" quoth Blood.

"Were casks of gold—there's six or seven hundred-weight of it at the least. We've brought it with us."

By the time the joyous uproar excited by that announcement had settled down, Captain Blood had recovered from his chagrin. He laughed.

"I give you best," he said to Hagthorpe and Yberville. "And the least I can do, by way of amends for having suffered myself to be so utterly fooled, is to forgo my share of the booty." And then, on a graver note: "What did you do with Don Domingo?"

"I would have shot him for his perfidy!" said Hagthorpe fiercely. "But Yberville here—Yberville, of all men—turned mawkish, and besought me to let him go."

Shamefacedly the young Frenchman hung his head, avoiding the Captain's glance of questioning surprise.

"Oh, but after all," he flung out, defiant almost in self-defence, "what would you? There was a lady in the case—his little Indian wife."

"Faith, now, it was of her that I was thinking," said Blood. "And for her sake and his—oh, and also for our own—it will be best to tell Brazo Largo that Don Domingo and his wife were slain in the fight for the gold. The sight of the recovered water-casks will amply confirm the story. Thus there should be peace for all concerned, himself included."

And so, although they brought back that rich booty from Santa Maria, Blood's part in that transaction was rated as one of his few failures. Not so, however, did he himself account it.

VII

THE LOVE STORY OF JEREMY PITT

The love-story of Jeremy Pitt, the young Somerset shire shipmaster, whose fate had been linked with Peter Blood's since the disastrous night of Sedgemoor, belongs to the later days of Blood's career as a buccaneer, to the great days when he commanded a fleet of five ships and over a thousand men of mixed nationality, held in a discipline to which his skill and good fortune made them willing to submit.

He had lately returned from a very successful raid upon the Spanish pearling fleet in the Rio de la Hache. He had come back to Tortuga to refit, and this not before it was necessary. There were several other buccaneer vessels in the harbour of Cayona at the time, and the little town was boisterous with their revelry. Its taverns and rum-shops throve, whilst the taverners and the women, white and half-castes, as mixed in origin and nationality as the buccaneers themselves, eased the rovers of a good deal of the plunder of which they had eased the Spaniards, who, again, were seldom better than robbers.

Usually these were unquiet times for Monsieur d'Ogeron, the agent of the French West India Company and Governor of Tortuga.

Ogeron himself, as we know, did very well out of the buccaneers in the percentages on their prizes which they very readily paid as harbour dues, and in other ways. But M. d'Ogeron had two daughters, the dark and stately Madeleine and the slight and joyous brunette Lucienne. Now Madeleine, for all her stateliness, had once succumbed to the wooing of a ruffianly buccaneer named Levasseur. To abstract her from this danger her father had shipped her off to France. But Levasseur, getting wind of it in time, had followed, seized the ship that carried her, and the worst might have befallen her but for the timely intervention of Captain Blood, who delivered her, unscathed, from his clutches and restored her, sobered by the experience, to her father.

Since then M. d'Ogeron had sought to practise discretion in the guests he received in the big white house set in its fragrant garden just above the town.

Captain Blood, by the service he had rendered the family on that occasion, had come to be regarded almost as a member of it. And since his officers, all of them driven to their trade as a consequence of transportation suffered for a political offence, were men of a different stamp from the ordinary buccaneer, they, too, were well received.

Now this in itself created a difficulty. If Monsieur d'Ogeron's house was open to the captains who followed Blood, he could not without offence close it to other buccaneer commanders. Therefore he was constrained to tolerate the visits of some whom he neither liked nor trusted, and this despite the protests of a guest from France, the fastidious and delicate Monsieur de Mercceur, who cared little for the company of any of them.

Monsieur de Mercoeur was the son of one of the governors of the French West India Company, sent by his father on a voyage of instruction to the settlements in which the company was interested. The frigateCygne, which had brought him a week ago, had been at anchor since in Cayona Bay, and would continue there until the young gentleman should see fit to depart again. From this his social consequence may be inferred. Obviously he was a person whose wishes a colonial governor would do his utmost to respect. But how was he to respect them, for instance, where such a truculent, swaggering fellow as Captain Tondeur of the Reine Margot was concerned? Monsieur d'Ogeron did not quite see how he could forbid him the house, as Monsieur de Mercceur would have desired, not even when it became apparent that the rascal was attracted thither by Mademoiselle Lucienne.

Another who was yielding to the same attraction was young Jeremy Pitt. But Pitt was a fellow of a very different stamp, and if his courtship of Lucienne occasioned Monsieur d'Ogeron some distress, at least it caused him no such uneasiness as that begotten by Tondeur.

If ever there was a man designed by nature for a lover, that man was Jeremy Pitt, with his frank, smooth, comely face, his ingenuous blue eyes, his golden locks and his neatly-apparelled, graceful figure. With the vigour of a man he combined the gentleness of a woman. Anything less like a conspirator, which he had been, and a buccaneer, which he was, it would be impossible to conceive. He had, too, ingratiating ways and a gift of almost poetical expression to complete his equipment as the ideal lover.

His instincts—or it may have been his hopes—and perhaps something in the lady's kindly manner, led him to believe that Lucienne was not indifferent to him; and so one evening, under the fragrant pimento trees in her father's garden, he told her that he loved her, and whilst she was still breathless from the effects of that avowal he kissed her lips.

Quivering and troubled she stood before him after that operation. "Monsieur Jeremy... you... you should not... you should not have done that." In the fading light Mr. Pitt saw that there were tears in her eyes. "If my father knew..."

Jeremy interrupted her with emphasis.

"He shall. I mean him to know. He shall know now." And as Monsieur de Mercoeur and Madeleine were at that moment approaching, Jeremy departed at once in quest of the Governor of Tortuga.

Monsieur d'Ogeron, that slight, elegant gentleman who had brought with him to the New World the courtliness of the old, could scarcely dissemble his distress. Monsieur d'Ogeron had grown wealthy in his governorship and he had ambitions for his motherless daughters, whom he contemplated removing before, very long to France.

He said so, not crudely or bluntly, but with an infinite delicacy calculated to spare Mr. Pitt's feelings, and he added that she was already promised in marriage.

Jeremy's face was overspread by blank astonishment.

"Promised! But she told me nothing of this!" He forgot that he had never really given her such opportunity.

"It may be that she does not realize. You know how these things are contrived in France."

Mr. Pitt began an argument upon the advantages of natural selection, nipped by Monsieur d'Ogeron before he had properly developed it.

"My dear Mr. Pitt, my friend, consider, I beg, your position in the world. You are a filibuster in—short, an adventurer. I do not use the term offensively. I merely mean that you are a man who lives by adventure. What prospect of security, of domesticity, could you offer a delicately-nurtured girl? If you, yourself, had a daughter, should you gladly give her to such a man?"

"If she loved him," said Mr. Pitt.

"Ah! But what is love, my friend?"

Although perfectly aware of what it was from his late rapture and present misery, Jeremy found a difficulty in giving expression to his knowledge. Monsieur d'Ogeron smiled benignly upon his hesitation.

"To a lover, love is sufficient, I know. To a parent, more is necessary so as to quiet his sense of responsibility. You have done me an honour, Monsieur Pitt. I am desolated that I must decline it. It will be better that we do not trouble our mutual esteem by speaking of this again."

Now when a young man discovers that a certain woman is necessary to his existence, and when he believes with pardonable egotism that he is equally necessary to hers, he does not abandon the quest at the first obstacle.

At the moment, however, the matter could be pursued no further because of the interruption afforded by the entrance of the stately Madeleine accompanied by Monsieur de Meroceur. The young Frenchman's eyes and voice sought Lucienne. He had charming eyes and a charming voice, and was altogether a charming person, impeccable as to dress and manners. In build he was almost tall, but so slight and frail that he looked as if a strong wind might blow him over; yet he possessed an assurance of address oddly at variance with his almost valetudinarian air.

He seemed surprised not to find Lucienne with her father. He desired, he announced, to persuade her to sing again some of those Provençal songs with which last night she had delighted them. His gesture took in the harpsichord standing in a corner of the well-appointed room. Madeleine departed to seek her sister. Mr. Pitt rose to take his leave. In his present mood he did not think he could bear to sit and hear Lucienne singing Provençal songs for the delight of Monsieur de Mercoeur.

He went off with his woes to Captain Blood, whom he found in the great cabin of the Arabella, that splendid red-hulled ship which once had been the Cinco Llagas, but since re-named by Blood after the little lady to whom all his life he remained faithful, as has been elsewhere related.

The Captain laid down his well-thumbed copy of Horace to lend an ear to the plaint of his young friend and shipmaster. Lounging on the cushioned locker under the sternports,

Captain Blood thereafter delivered himself, as sympathetic in manner as he was uncompromising in matter. Monsieur d'Ogeron was entirely right, the Captain opined, when he said that Jeremy's occupation in life did not justify him in taking a wife.

"And that's only half the reason for abandoning this notion. The other is that Lucienne charming and seductive child though she may be, is a thought too light to promise any peace and security to a husband not always at hand to guard and check her. That fellow Tondeur goes daily to the Governor's house. It hasn't occurred to you, now, to ask yourself what is attracting him? And why does this frail French dandy, Monsieur de Mercoeur, linger in Tortuga? Oh, and there are others I could name who have had, no doubt, your own delectable experience with a lady who's never reluctant to listen to a tale of love."

"Now devil take your lewdness!" roared out Pitt, with all a lover's unbounded indignation. "By what right do you say such a thing as that?"

"By the right of sanity and an unclouded vision. Ye'll not be the first to have kissed Mademoiselle Lucienne's lips; and ye'll not be the last neither, not even if ye marry her. She has a beckoning eye, so she has, and it's the uneasy husband I should be at sea if she were my wife. Be thankful ye're not the husband of her father's choice. Lovely things like Lucienne d'Ogeron were created just to trouble the world."

Jeremy would listen to no more of this blasphemy. It was like Blood, whom he bitterly denounced as without faith and without ideals, to think so vilely of the sweetest, purest saint in all the world. On that he flung out of the cabin, and left the Captain free to return to his Horace.

Blood, however, had planted a rankling seed in our young lover's heart. The clear perception of grounds for jealousy is a sword that can slay love at a stroke; but the mere suspicion of their existence is a goad to drive a lover on. Feverishly, then, on the morrow, and utterly oblivious of Monsieur d'Ogeron's rejection of his suit, Mr. Pitt made his way betimes to the white house above the town. It was earlier than his wont, and he came upon the lady of his dreams walking in the garden. With her walked Captain Tondeur, that man of sinister reputation. It was said of him that once he had been a fencing-master in Paris, and that he had taken to the sea so as to escape the justice it was desired to mete out to him by the family of a gentleman he had killed in a duel. He was a man of middle height and deceptive slimness, for he was as tough as whipcord. He dressed with a certain raffish elegance and moved with agile grace. His countenance was undistinguished save for the eyes, which, if small and round and black ere singularly penetrating. They were penetrating Mr. Pitt now with an arrogant stare that seemed to invite him to depart again. The Captain's right arm was about the waist of Mademoiselle Lucienne. It remained there notwithstanding Mr. Pitt's appearance, until presently, after a moments surprised pause, the lady disengaged herself in some embarrassment.

"It is Monsieur Jeremy!" she cried, and added, quite needlessly, thought Mr. Pitt: "I was not expecting you."

Jeremy took the hand she proffered and bore it to his lips, more or less mechanically, whilst mumbling a greeting in his indifferent French. Followed an exchange of commonplaces, and then an awkward pause, at the end of which said Tondeur with a scowl:

"When a lady tells me that I am unexpected, I understand her to mean that I am inopportune."

"No doubt a common experience in your life." Captain Tondeur smiled. Your practised, duellist is always self-possessed.

"At least not a subject for pertness. It is not always wise to be pert. The moment's glitter may lead to painful instruction."

Lucienne intervened. She was a little breathless. Her eyes were scared.

"But what is this? What are you saying? You are wrong, Monsieur le Capitaine, to assume Monsieur Jeremy inopportune. Monsieur Jeremy is my friend, and my friends are never inopportune."

"Not perhaps to you, Mademoiselle. But to other friends of yours they can be monstrously so."

"Again you are mistaken." Her manner was frigid. "He is no friend of mine to whom other friends of mine are unwelcome in my presence."

The Captain bit his lip, and Jeremy took a fragment of comfort, for all that he still hotly remembered that arm about the waist of the woman whose lips he had kissed last night and also Captain Blood's condemnation of her.

The elements of a very pretty quarrel were shattered by the sudden appearance of Monsieur d'Ogeron and Monsieur de Meroceur. Both were out of breath as if they had been hurrying. They checked, however, and seemed relieved when they saw who was present. It was as if Monsieur d'Ogeron found not quite what he had expected, and relief upon the safety for Lucienne which is believed to reside in numbers. Their advent put an end to acrimony, and perhaps because he was in the humour for little else, Captain Tondeur presently took his leave. A smile of disquieting significance accompanied his parting words to Jeremy.

"I shall look forward, monsieur, to an early opportunity of continuing our interesting discussion." Anon, when Jeremy, too, would have departed, Monsieur d'Ogeron detained him. "Remain yet a moment, Monsieur Pitt."

He took the young man by the arm in a friendly manner and drew him away from Monsieur de Meroceur and Lucienne. They moved up the avenue and entered a tunnel fashioned of over-arching orange trees imported from Europe; a cool place this where the ripe fruit glowed like lamps against the dusky green.

"I did not like the parting words of Captain Tondeur, nor yet his smile. That is a very dangerous man. You would be wise to beware of him."

Jeremy bridled a little. "Do you suppose I fear him?"

"I suppose you would be prudent to do so. A very dangerous man. A canaille. He comes here too much."

"Regarding him as you do, why do you permit it?"

Monsieur d'Ogeron made a grimace. "Regarding him as I do, I cannot do otherwise."

"You are afraid of him?"

"I confess it. Oh, not for myself, Monsieur Pitt. But there is Lucienne. He pays his court to her."

Jeremy quivered with fury. "Could you not forbid him your house?"

"Of course." Monsieur d'Ogeron smiled crookedly. "I did something of the kind once before, in the case of Levasseur. You know the story."

"Oh, but... Oh, but..." Jeremy encountered a difficulty, but finally surmounted it. "Mademoiselle Madeleine was so misguided as to lend herself to the scheme of Levasseur. You do not dream that Mademoiselle Lucienne—"

"Why should I not dream it? This Tondeur canaille though he be, is not without attraction, and he has over Levasseur the advantage that he was once a gentleman and can still display the manners of one when it suits him. An inexperienced child like Lucienne is easily allured by your bold, enterprising wooer."

Mr. Pitt was a little sick at heart and bewildered. "Yet what good can temporising do? Sooner or later you will have to reject him. And then... What then?"

"It is what I ask myself," said Monsieur d'Ogeron almost lugubriously. "Yet an evil that is postponed may ultimately be removed by chance." And then, suddenly, his manner changed. "Oh, but your pardon, my dear Mr. Pitt. Our talk is taking a turn very far from what I intended. A father's anxiety! I meant to do no more than utter a warning, and I beg that you will heed it."

Mr. Pitt thought he understood. What was in Monsieur d'Ogeron's mind was that Tondeur scented a rival in Jeremy and that such a man would take prompt means to eliminate a rival.

"I am obliged to you, Monsieur d'Ogeron. I can take care of myself."

"I trust so. Sincerely I trust so." And on that they parted.

Jeremy went back to dine on board the Arabella, and after dinner, pacing the poop with Blood, he told him what had passed.

Captain Blood was thoughtful. "There is cause enough to warn you. Though why the Governor should be troubling to do so is just a trifle odd. I'll pay him a visit, so I will. I may be able to help him, though I don't yet see how. Meanwhile, Jerry, if ye're prudent, ye'll be keeping the ship. Devil a doubt but Tondeur will be looking for you."

"And I am to avoid him, am I?" snorted Jeremy.

"If ye're wise."

"If I'm a coward."

"Now isn't a live coward better than a dead fool, which is what ye'll be if ye come to grips with Master Tondeur? Ye'll not be forgetting the man's a fencing-master; whilst you... Pshaw! It would be just murder, so it would. And where's the glory of suffering that?"

Pitt knew it in his heart and yet would not admit the humiliating knowledge. Therefore, neglecting Blood's advice, he went ashore on the morrow, and was sitting with Hagthorpe and Wolverstone in the tavern of the King of France when Tondeur found him.

It was in the neighbourhood of noon, and the common-room was thronged with buccaneers, a few ordinary seamen from the Cygne, beachcombers and the land-sharks of both sexes who prey upon seafaring men, and particularly upon buccaneers, who are ever prodigal of their broad pieces of eight. The air of the ill-lighted place was heavy with the reek of rum, tobacco, spun-yarn and humanity.

Tondeur came forward leisurely, his left hand resting on his hilt, exchanging nods and bringing up at last before Jeremy's table.

"You permit?" quoth he, and without waiting for an answer, he drew up a stool and sat down. "I am fortunate so soon to be able to resume the little discussion that yesterday was interrupted."

Jeremy, understanding perfectly what was coming, stared at him uneasily. His two companions, understanding nothing, stared with him.

"We discussed inopportuneness, I think, and your sluggishness in perceiving that your presence was not required."

Jeremy leaned forward. "What we discussed is no matter. You are here, I think, to pick a quarrel with me."

"I?" Captain Tondeur stared and frowned. "Why should you suppose that? You do me no harm. It is not in your power to do me harm. Yo are not even in my way. If you were, I should crack you like a flea." He laughed contemptuously, offensively, and by that laugh flung Jeremy, as he intended, into a passion.

"I am no flea for your cracking."

"Are you not?" Tondeur got up. "Then be careful not to pester me again, or you may find yourself under my thumbnail. You have your warning." He spoke loudly, so that all might hear him, and his tone brought a hush upon the crowded room.

He was turning away contemptuously when Jeremy's answer arrested him.

"You insolent dog!"

Captain Tondeur checked. He raised his brows. A snarling smile lifted an end of his little moustache. And meanwhile the burly Wolverstone, still understanding nothing, sought instinctively to restrain Jeremy, who had also risen.

"Dog?" said the Captain slowly. "Dog, eh? It is apt enough. The dog and the flea. All the same, I do not like dog. You will be so good as to retract' dog. You will retract it at once. I am not a patient man, Monsieur Pitt."

"Certainly I will retract it," said Jeremy. "I'll not insult an animal."

"Meaning me?"

"Meaning the dog. I'll substitute instead—"

"Substitute rat," said a sharp voice from the background, which made Tondeur spin round where he stood.

Just within the doorway lounged Captain Blood, tall and elegant in his black and silver, leaning upon his ebony cane. The intensely blue eyes in his clear-cut, sun-tanned face met and held the stare of Captain Tondeur. He sauntered forward, speaking easily and without stress as he came.

"Rat, I think, describes you better, Captain Tondeur." And he stood waiting for the Frenchman's answer.

It came presently in the wake of a sneering laugh. "I see. I see. The little shipmaster here is to be protected. Papa Blood intervenes to save the little coward."

"Certainly he is to be protected. I will not have my shipmaster murdered by a bully-swordsman. That is why I intervene. You might have foreseen it, Captain Tondeur. As for cowardice, you paltry rascal, that is the attribute of the rat to which I liken you. You trade upon a certain skill with the sword; but you are careful to employ it only against those you have reason to believe unskilled. That is the coward's way. Oh, and the murderer's, which is, I believe, what they call you in France."

"That's a lie, anyway," said Tondeur, livid.

Captain Blood was unperturbed. He was deliberately playing Tondeur's own game of baiting an opponent into fury. "You may proceed to prove it upon me, in which case I shall retract, either before or after killing you. Thus you will die in honour, having lived in dishonour. The inner room there is spacious and empty. We can—"

But Tondeur interrupted him, sneering. "I am not so easily distracted. My affair is with Mr. Pitt."

"Let it wait until you have settled mine."

Tondeur contained himself. He was white with passion and breathing hard.

"Look you, Captain Blood: I have been insulted by this shipmaster of yours, who called me dog in the presence here of these. You deliberately seek to thrust yourself into a quarrel that does not concern you. It is not to be tolerated. I appeal me to the company."

It was a shrewd move and the result justified it. The company was on his side. Such of Captain Blood's own men who were present kept silent, whilst the remainder loudly gave the Frenchman reason. Not even Hagthorpe and Wolverstone could do more than shrug, and Jeremy made matters utterly hopeless by declaring himself on the side of the enemy.

"Captain Tondeur is in the right, Peter. You are not concerned in this affair."

"You hear?" cried Tondeur.

"I am concerned, whatever may be said. You mean murder, you scum, and I mean to prevent it." Captain Blood abandoned his cane, and carried his hand to his sword.

But dozens sprang to restrain him, protesting so forcibly and angrily that, finding himself without even the support of his own followers, Captain Blood was forced to give way.

Even the staunch and loyal Wolverstone was muttering in his ear: "Nay, Peter! A God's name! Ye'll provoke a riot for naught. Ye were just too late. The lad had committed himself."

"And what were you doing to let him? Well, well! There he goes, the rash fool."

Pitt was already leading the way to the inner room: a lamb not merely going to the slaughter, but actually conducting the butcher. Hagthorpe was with him. Tondeur followed closely, and others brought up the rear.

Captain Blood, with Wolverstone at his side, went with the crowd, controlling himself now with difficulty.

The inner room was spacious and almost bare. What few chairs and tables it contained were swiftly thrust aside. The place was little more than a shed or pent-house built of wood, and open from the height of some three feet along the whole of one side. Through this opening the afternoon sun was flooding the place with light and heat.

Sword in hand, stripped to the waist, the two men faced each other on the bare earthen floor, Jeremy, the taller of the two, sturdy and vigorous; the other, light, sinewy and agile as a cat. The taverner and the drawers were among the press of onlookers ranged against the inner wall; two or three young viragos were in the crowd, but most of the women had remained in the common-room.

Captain Blood and Wolverstone had come to stand towards the upper end of the room at a table on which there were various objects cleared from the others: some drinking-cans, a couple of flagons, a jack and a pair of brass candlesticks with wide saucer-like stands. In the moments of waiting, whilst preliminaries were being settled, Blood, pale under his tan and with a wicked look in his blue eyes, had glanced at these objects, idly fingering one or two of them as if he would have employed them as missiles.

Hagthorpe was seconding Jeremy. Ventadour, the lieutenant of the Reine Margot, stood by Tondeur. The antagonists faced each other along the length of the room, with the sunlight on their flank. As they took up their positions, Jeremy's eyes sought

Blood's. The lad smiled to him. Blood, unsmiling, answered by a sign. For a moment there was inquiry in Jeremy's glance, then understanding followed.

Ventadour gave the word: "Allez, messieurs!" and the blades rang together.

Instantly, obeying that signal which he had received from his captain, Jeremy broke ground, and attacked Tondeur on his left. This had the effect of causing Tondeur to veer to that side, with the result that he had the sun in his eyes. Now was Jeremy's chance if he could take it, as Blood had foreseen when he had signalled the manoeuvre. Jeremy did his best, and by the assiduity of his endeavours kept his opponent pinned in that position of disadvantage. But Tondeur was too strong for him. The practised swordsman never lost touch of the opposing blade, and presently, venturing a riposte, availed himself of the ensuing disengage to break ground in his turn, and thus level the position, the antagonists having now completely changed places.

Blood ground his teeth to see Jeremy lose the only advantage he possessed over the sometime fencing-master who was bent on murdering him. Yet the end did not come as swiftly as he expected. Jeremy had certain advantages of reach and vigour. But these did not account for the delay, nor yet did the fact that the fencing-master may have been a little rusty from lack of recent practice. Tondeur played a closely circling blade which found openings everywhere in the other's wide and clumsy guard. Yet he did not go in to finish. Was he deliberately playing with his victim as cat with mouse, or was it perhaps that, standing a little in awe of Blood and of possible consequences should he kill Pitt outright, he aimed merely at disabling him?

The spectators, beholding what they beheld, were puzzled by the delay. They were puzzled still more when Tondeur again broke ground, so as to place his back to the sun and turn his helpless opponent into the position of disadvantage in which Tondeur had erstwhile found himself. To the onlookers this seemed a refinement of cruelty.

Blood, who now directly faced Tondeur, picked up in that moment one of the brass candlesticks from the table beside him. None observed him, every eye being upon the combatants. Blood alone appeared entirely to have lost interest in them. His attention was bestowed entirely upon the candlestick. So as to examine the socket intended for the candle, he raised the object until its broad saucer-like base was vertical. At that moment, for no apparent reason, Tondeur's blade faltered in its guard, and failed to deflect a clumsy thrust with which Jeremy was mechanically in the act of countering. Meeting no opposition, Jeremy's blade drove on until some inches of it came out through Tondeur's back.

Almost before the amazed company had realized this sudden and unexpected conclusion, Captain Blood was on his knees beside the prostrate man. He called for water and clean linen, the surgeon in him now paramount whilst Jeremy—the most amazed in that amazed crowd—stood foolishly looking on beside him.

Whilst Blood was dressing the wound, Tondeur recovered from his momentary swoon he stared with eyes that slowly focussed the man who was bending over him.

"Assassin!" he said through his teeth, and then his head lolled limply on his shoulder once more.

"On the contrary," said Blood, his finger deftly swathing the body which Ventadour was supporting, "I'm your preserver." And to the company he announced: "He will not die of this, for all that it went through him.. With luck he'll be ruffling it again within the month. But he'd best not be moved from here for some days, and he'll need care."

Jeremy never knew how he found himself once more aboard the Arabella. The events of the afternoon were dim to him as the transactions of a dream. He had looked, as he conceived, into the grim face of death, and yet he had survived. That evening at supper in the great cabin he made philosophy upon it.

"It serves," he said, "to show the advantages of never losing heart or admitting defeat in an encounter. I might so easily have been slain today; and it would have been simply and solely by a preconception: the preconception that Tondeur was the better swordsman."

"It is still possible that he was," said Blood.

"Then how came I to run him through so easily?"

"How indeed, Peter?" demanded Wolverstone, and the other half-dozen present echoed the question, whilst Hagthorpe enlarged upon the theme.

"The fact is the rascal's reputation for swordsmanship rested solely upon his own boasting. It's the source of many a reputation." And there the discussion was allowed to drop.

In the morning Captain Blood suggested that they should pay a visit to Monsieur d'Ogeron, and render their account to him of what had taken place. As Governor of Tortuga, some formal explanation was due to him, even though his acquaintance with the combatants should render it almost unnecessary. Jeremy, at all times ready to visit the Governor's house on any pretext, was this morning more than willing, the events having set about him a heroic halo.

As they were being rowed ashore Captain Blood observed that the Cygne was gone from her moorings in the bay, which would mean, Jeremy opined with faint interest, that Monsieur de Meroceur had at last departed from Tortuga.

The little Governor gave them a very friendly welcome. He had heard of the affair at The King of France. They need not trouble themselves with any explanations. No official cognizance would be taken of the matter. He knew but too well the causes which had led to it.

"Had things gone otherwise," he said quite frankly, "it would have been different. Knowing who would be the aggressor—as I warned you, Monsieur Pitt—I must have taken some action against Tondeur, and I might have had to call upon you, Captain Blood, to assist me. Order must be preserved even in such a colony as this. But as it is, why, the affair could not have had a more fortunate conclusion. You have made me very happy, Monsieur Pitt."

This augured so well that Mr. Pitt presently asked leave to pay his homage to Mademoiselle Lucienne.

Monsieur d'Ogeron looked at him as if surprised by the request.

"Lucienne? But Lucienne has gone. She sailed for France this morning on the Cygne with her husband."

"Her... her husband?" echoed Jeremy, with a sudden feeling of nausea.

"Monsieur de Mercoeur. Did I not tell you she was promised? They were married at cock-crow by Father Benoit. That is why I say you have made me very happy, Monsieur Pitt. Until Captain Tondeur was laid by the heels I dared not permit this thing to take place. Remembering Levasseur, I could not allow Lucienne to depart before. Like Levasseur, it is certain that Tondeur would have followed, and on the high seas would have dared that which he dared not here in Tortuga."

"Therefore," said Captain Blood, in his driest tone, "you set the other two by the ears, so that whilst they were quarrelling over the bone, the third dog might make off with it. That, Monsieur d'Ogeron, was more shrewd than friendly."

"You are angry with me, Captain!" Monsieur d'Ogeron appeared genuinely distressed. "But I had to think of my child, and besides, I had no doubt of the issue. This dear Monsieur Pitt could not fail to prevail against a man like Tondeur."

"This dear Monsieur Pitt," said Captain Blood, "might very easily have lost his life for love of your daughter so as to forward your marriage schemes for her. There's a pretty irony in the thought." He linked his arm through that of his young shipmaster, who stood there white and hang-dog. "You see, Jerry, the pitfalls injudicious loving can dig for a man. Let's be going, my lad. Good day to you, Monsieur d'Ogeron."

He almost dragged the boy away. Then, because he was very angry, he paused when they had reached the door, and there was an unpleasant smile on the face he turned to the Governor.

"Why do you suppose that I should not do on Mr. Pitt's behalf what you feared Tondeur might do? Why shouldn't I go after the Cygne and capture your daughter for my shipmaster?"

"My God!" ejaculated Monsieur d'Ogeron, suddenly appalled by the prospect of so merited a vengeance. "You would never do that!"

"No, I would not. But do you know why?"

"Because I've trusted you. Because you are a man of honour."

"Honour! Bah! I'm just a pirate. It's because I don't think she is good enough for Mr. Pitt, as I told him from the outset, and as I hope he now believes."

That was all the revenge he took of Monsieur d'Ogeron for his foxy part in the affair. Having taken it, he departed, and the stricken Jeremy suffered himself to be led away.

But by the time they had reached the mole the lads numbness had given place to rage. He had been duped and tricked, his very life had been put in pawn to serve the schemes of those others, and somebody must pay.

"If ever I meet Monsieur de Meroceur..." he was raging.

"You'll do fine things," the Captain mocked him. "I'll serve him as I served that dog Tondeur." And now Captain Blood stood still that he might laugh.

"Oh! It's the fine swordsman ye've become all at once, Jerry. The very butcher of a silk button. I'd best be disillusioning you, my young Tybalt, before ye swagger into mischief."

"Disillusioning me?" Jeremy stared at him, a frown darkening that fair, honest face. "Did I, or did I not, lay low that French duellist yesterday?"

And Blood, still laughing, answered him: "You did not!"

"I did not? I did not?" Jeremy set his arms akimbo. "Well ye tell me, then, who did?"

"I did," said the Captain, and on that grew serious. "I did it with the bright bottom of a brass candlestick. I flashed enough reflected sunlight into his eyes to blind him whilst you were doing the business."

He saw Jeremy turn pale, and added the reminder: "He would have murdered you else." Then there was a whimsical twist of his firm lips, a queer flash from his vivid eyes, and he added on a note of conscious pride: "I am Captain Blood."

VIII

THE EXPIATION OF MADAME DE-COULEVAIN

On a day-bed under the wide square sternposts of the luxurious cabin of the Estremadura lounged Don Juan de la Fuente, Count of Medians, twanging a beribboned guitar and singing an indelicate song, well known in Malaga at the time, in a languorous baritone voice.

He was a young man of thirty, graceful and elegant, with soft dark eyes and full red lips that were half veiled by small moustaches and a little peaked black beard. Face, figure, dress and posture advertised the voluptuary, and the setting afforded him by the cabin of the great forty-gun galleon he commanded was proper to its tenant. From bulkheads painted an olive green detached gilded carvings of cupids and dolphins, fruit and flowers, whilst each stanchion was in the shape of a fish-tailed caryatid. Against the forward bulkhead a handsome buffet was laden with gold and silver plate; between the doors of two cabins on the larboard side hung a painting of Aphrodite; the floor was spread with a rich Eastern carpet; a finer one covered the quadrangular table, above which was suspended a ponderous lamp of chiselled silver. There were books in a rack: the *Ars Amatoria* of Ovid, the *Satiricon*, a Boccaccio and a Poggio, to bear witness to the classico-licentious character of this student. The chairs, like the daybed on which Don Juan was sprawling, were of Cordovan leather, painted and gilded, and although the sternports stood open to the mild airs that barely moved the galleon, the place was heavy with ambergris and other perfumes.

Don Juan's song extolled life's carnal joys and, in particular, bewailed the Pope's celibacy amid opulence:

"Vida sin niña no es vida, es muerte,
Y del Padre Santo muy triste es la suerte."

That was its envoy and at the same time its mildest ribaldry. You conceive the rest.

Don Juan was singing this song of his to Captain Blood, who sat with an elbow leaning on the table and a leg thrown across a second chair. On his dark aquiline face there was a set mechanical smile, put on like a mask, to dissemble his weariness and disgust. He wore a suit of grey camlet with silver lace, which had come from Don Juan's wardrobe, for they were much of the same height and shape as they were akin in age, and a black periwig, that was likewise of Don Juan's providing, framed his countenance.

A succession of odd chances had brought about this incredible situation, in which that detested enemy of Spain came to find himself an honoured guest aboard a Spanish galleon, crawling north across the Caribbean, with the Windward Islands some twenty miles abeam. Let it be explained at once that the langourous Don who entertained him was very far from suspecting whom he entertained.

The tale of how he came there, set forth at great and almost tedious length by Pitt in his chronicle, must here be briefly summarized.

A week ago, on Margarita, in a secluded cove of which his own great ship the Arabella was careened to clear her keel of accumulated foulness, word had been brought him by some friendly Carib Indians of a Spanish pearling fleet at work in the Gulf of Cariaco, which had already collected a rich harvest.

The temptation to raid it proved irresistible to Captain Blood. In his left ear he wore a great pear-shaped pearl of enormous price that was part of the magnificent haul they had once made from a similar fleet in the Rio de la Hacha. So with three piraguas and forty men carefully picked from his crew of close upon two hundred, Blood slipped one night across the narrow sea between Margarita and the Main, and lay most of the following day under the coast, to creep towards evening into the Gulf of Cariaco. There, however they were surprised by a Spanish guarda-costa whose presence they had been far from suspecting.

They put about in haste, and ran for the open. But the guardship gave chase in the brief dusk, opened fire, and shattered the frail boats that bore the raiders. Of the forty buccaneers, some must have been shot, some drowned, and others picked up to be made prisoners. Blood himself had spent the night clinging to a stout piece of wreckage. A stiffish southerly breeze had sprung up at sunset, and driven by this and borne by the currents, he had miraculously been washed ashore at dawn, exhausted, benumbed, and almost pickled by the long briny immersion, on one of the diminutive islands of the Hermanos group.

It was an island not more than a mile and a half in length and less than a mile across, sparsely grown with coconut palms and aloes, and normally uninhabited save by sea-birds and turtles. But at the time of Blood's arrival there, it happened to be tenanted in addition by a couple of castaway Spaniards. These unfortunates had escaped in a sailing pinnace from the English settlement of Saint Vincent, where they had been imprisoned. Ignorant of navigation, they had entrusted themselves to the sea, and with water and provisions exhausted, and at the point of death from thirst and hunger, they had fortuitously made their landfall a month ago. Not daring after that experience to venture forth again, they had subsisted there on shell-fish taken from the rocks and on coconuts, yams, and berries.

Since Captain Blood could not be sure that Spaniards, even when in these desperate straits, would not slit his throat if they guessed his real identity, he announced himself as shipwrecked from a Dutch brig which had been on its way to Curaco, gave himself the name of Peter Vandermeer, and attributed to himself a mixed parentage of Dutch father and Spanish mother, thus accounting for the fluent Castilian which he spoke.

Finding the pinnace in good order, he provisioned her with a store of yams and of turtle, which he himself boucanned, filled her water-casks, and put to sea with the two castaways. By sun and stars he trusted to steer a course due east for Tobago, whose Dutch settlers were sufficiently neutral to, give them shelter. He deemed it prudent, however to inform his trusting companions that he was making for Trinidad.

But neither Trinidad nor Tobago was to prove their destination. On the third day out they were picked up by the Spanish galleon Estremadura, to the jubilation of the two Spaniards and the dismay at first of Captain Blood. However he put a bold face on the matter and trusted to fortune and to the ragged condition in which he went aboard the galleon to escape recognition. When questioned he maintained the fictions of his shipwreck, his Dutch nationality and his mixed parentage, and conceiving that since he was plunging he might as well plunge deeply, and that since he claimed a Spanish mother, he might as well choose one amongst the noblest Spain could afford, he announced her a Trasmiera of the family of the Duke of Arcos, who, therefore, was his kinsman.

The authoritative bearing, which not even his ragged condition could diminish, his intrepid aquiline countenance, dark skin and black hair, and, above all, his fluent, cultured Castilian, made credible the imposture. And, anyway, since he desired no more than to be set ashore on some Dutch or French settlement, whence he could resume his voyage to Curacao, there seemed no reason why he should magnify his identity.

The sybaritic Don Juan de la Fuente who commanded the Estremadura, impressed by this shipwrecked gentleman's tale of high connections, treated him generously, placed a choice and extensive wardrobe at his disposal, gave him a stateroom off the main cabin, and used him in every way as one person of distinction should use another. It contributed to this that Don Juan found in Peter Vandermeer a man after his own heart. He insisted upon calling him Don Pedro, as if to stress the Spanish part in him, swearing that his Vandermeer blood had been entirely beneaped by that of the Trasmieras. It was a subject on which the Spanish gentleman made some ribaldries. Indeed, ribaldry flowed from him naturally and copiously on all occasions, and infected his officers, four of whom, young gentlemen of lineage, dined and supped with him daily in the great cabin.

Proclivities which in a raw lad of eighteen Blood might have condoned, trusting to time to correct them, he found frankly disgusting in this man of thirty. Under the courtly elegant exterior he perceived the unclean spirit of the rakehell. But he was far indeed from betraying his contempt. His own safety, resting precariously as it did upon maintaining the good impression he had made at the outset, compelled him to adapt himself to the company, to represent himself as a man of their own licentious kidney.

Thus it came about that during those days when, almost becalmed on the tropical sea, they crawled slowly north under a mountain of canvas that was often limp, something akin to a friendship sprang up between Don Juan and this Don Pedro. Don Juan found much to admire in him: his obvious vigour of body and of spirit, the deep knowledge of men and of the world which he displayed, his ready wit and the faintly cynical philosophy which his talk revealed. Spending long hours together daily, their intimacy grew at the rate peculiar to growths in that tropical region.

And that, briefly, is how you come to find these two closeted together on this the sixth day of Blood's voyage as a guest of honour in a ship in which he would have been travelling in irons had his identity been so much as suspected. Meanwhile her commander wearied him with lascivious songs, whilst Blood pondered the amusing side of the situation, which, nevertheless, it would be well to end at the earliest opportunity.

So presently, when the song had ceased and the Spaniard was munching Peruvian sweetmeats from a silver box beside him, Captain Blood approached the question. The pinnace in which he had travelled with the castaway Spaniards had been taken in tow by the Estremadura, and the time, he thought, had come to use it.

"We should now be abeam of Martinique," he said. "It cannot be more than six or seven leagues to land."

"Very true, thanks to this cursed lack of wind. I could blow harder from my own lungs."

"You cannot, of course, put in for me," said Blood. There was war at the time between France and Spain, which Blood understood to be one of the reasons of Don Juan's presence in these waters. "But in this calm sea I could easily pull myself ashore in the boat that brought me. Suppose, Don Juan, I take my leave of you this evening."

Don Juan looked aggrieved. "Here's a sudden haste to leave us! Was it not agreed that I carry you to Saint Martin?"

"True. But, thinking of it, I remember that ships are rare there, and I may be delayed some time in finding a vessel for Curacao; whereas from Martinique..."

"Ah, no," he was peevishly interrupted. "You shall land, if you please, at Mariegalante, where I myself have business, or at Guadeloupe if you prefer it, as I think you may. But I vow I do not let you go just yet."

Captain Blood had checked in the act of filling himself a pipe of finest Sacerdotes tobacco from a jar of broken leaf upon the table. "You have business at Mariegalante?" So surprised was he that he abandoned for that question the matter more personal to himself. "What business is possible at present between you and the French?"

Don Juan smiled darkly. "The business of war, my friend. Am I not a man of war?"

"You are going to raid Mariegalante?"

The Spaniard was some time in answering. Softly he stirred the chords of his guitar into sound. The smile still hovered about his full red lips, but it had assumed a faintly cruel character and his dark eyes glowed.

"The garrison at Basseterre is commanded by a dog named Coulevain with whom I have an account to settle. It is over a year old, but at last we are approaching pay-day. The war gives me my opportunity. I serve Spain and myself at a single stroke."

Blood kindled a light, applied it to his pipe, and fell to smoking. It did not seem to him to be a very commendable service to Spain to risk one of her ships in an attack upon so negligible a settlement as Mariegalante. When presently he spoke, however, it was to utter the half of his thought upon another subject, and he said nothing more of landing on Martinique.

"It will be something to add to my experience, to have been aboard a ship in action. It will be something not easily forgotten—unless we are sunk by the guns of Basseterre."

Don Juan laughed. For all his profligacy, the fellow seemed of a high stomach, not easily disturbed at the imminence of a fight. Rather did the prospect fill him now with glee. This increased when that evening, at last, the breeze freshened and they began to make better speed, and that night in the cabin of the Estremadura spirits ran high, boisterously led by Don Juan himself. There was deep drinking of heady Spanish wines and a deal of easily excited laughter.

Captain Blood conjectured that heavy indeed must be the account of the French commander of Mariegalante with Don Juan if the prospect of a settlement could so exalt the Spaniard. His own sympathies went out freely to the French settlers who were about to suffer one of those revolting raids by which the Spaniards had rendered themselves so deservedly detested in the New World. But he was powerless to raise a finger or utter a word in their defence, compelled to join in this brutal mirth at the prospect of French slaughter, and to drink damnation to the French in general and to Colonel de Coulevain in particular.

In the morning, when he went on deck, Captain Blood beheld the long coastline of Dominica, ten or twelve miles away on the larboard quarter, and in the distance ahead a vague grey mass which he knew to be the mountain that rises in the middle of the round Island of Mariegalante. They had come south of Dominica in the night, and so had passed out of the Caribbean Sea into the open Atlantic.

Don Juan, in high spirits and apparently none the worse for last night's carouse, came to join him on the poop and to inform him of that which he already knew, but of which he was careful to betray no knowledge.

For a couple of hours they held to their course, driving straight before the wind with shortened sail. When within ten miles of the island, which now seemed to rise from the turquoise sea like a wall of green, the crew became active under sharp words of command and shrill notes from the boatswain's pipe. Nettings were spread above the Estremadura's decks to catch any spars that might be brought down in action; the shot-racks were filled; the leaden aprons were cleared from the guns, and buckets for seawater were distributed beside them.

From the carved poop-rail, at Don Juan's side, Captain Blood looked on with interest and approval as the musketeers in corselet and peaked headpiece were marshalled in the waist. And all the while Don Juan was explaining to him the significance of things with which no man afloat was better acquainted than Captain Blood.

At eight bells they went below to dine, Don Juan less boisterous now that action was imminent. His face had lost some of its colour, and there was a restlessness about his long slender hands, a feverish glitter in his velvet eyes. He ate little, and this little quickly; but he drank copiously; and he was still at table when one of his officers, a squat youngster named Veraguas, who had remained on duty, came to announce that it was time for him to take command.

He rose, and, with the aid of his black man steward Absolom, armed himself quickly in back and breast and steel cap; then went on deck. Captain Blood accompanied him, despite the Spaniard's warning that he should not expose himself without body-armour.

The Estremadura had come within three miles of the port of Basseterre. She flew no flag, from a natural reluctance to advertise her nationality more than it was advertised already by her lines and rig. Within a mile Don Juan could, through his telescope, survey the whole of the wide-mouthed harbour, and he announced that at least no ships of war were present. The fort would be the only antagonist in the preliminary duel.

A shot just then across the Estremadura's bows proclaimed that at least the commandant of the fort was a man who understood his business. Despite that definite signal to heave to, the Estremadura raced on and met the roar of a dozen guns. Unscathed by the volley, she held to her course, reserving her fire. Thus Don Juan earned the unspoken approval of Captain Blood. He ran the gauntlet of a second volley, and still held his fire until almost at point-blank range. Then he loosed a broadside, went smartly about, loosed another, and then ran off, close-hauled, to reload, offering only the narrow target of his stern to the French gunners.

When he returned to the attack he trailed astern the three boats that hitherto had been on the booms amidship, in addition to the useful pinnace in which Captain Blood had travelled.

He suffered now some damage to the mizzen yards, and the tall deck structures of his ornate forecastle were heavily battered. But there was nothing in this to distress him, and, handling his ship with great judgment, he smashed at the fort with two more heavy broadsides of twenty guns each, so well-delivered that he effectively silenced it for the moment.

He was off again, and when next he returned the boats in tow were filled with his musketeers. He brought them to within a hundred yards of the cliff, to seaward of the fort and at an angle at which the guns could hardly reach him, and sending the boats ashore, he stood there to cover their landing. A party of French that issued from the half-ruined fortress to oppose them were mown down by a discharge of gangrel and case-shot. Then the Spaniards were ashore and swarming up the gentle slope to the attack whilst the empty boats were being rowed back for reinforcements.

Whilst this was happening, Don Juan moved forward again and crashed yet another broadside at the fort to create a diversion and further to increase the distress and confusion there. Four or five guns answered him, and a twelve-pound shot came to splinter his bulwarks amidships; but he was away again without further harm, and going about to meet his boats. He was, still loading them with a further contingent when the musketry ashore fell silent. Then a lusty Spanish cheer came over the water, and soon thereafter the ring of hammers upon metal to announce the spiking of the fort's now undefended guns...

Hitherto Captain Blood's attitude had been one of dispassionate criticism of proceedings in which he was something of an authority. Now, however, his mind turned to what must follow, and from his knowledge of the ways of Spanish soldiery on a raid, and his acquaintance with the rakehell who was to lead them, he shuddered, hardened buccaneer though he might be, at the prospective sequel. To him war was war, and he could engage in it ruthlessly against men as ruthless. But the sacking of towns with the remorselessness of a brutal inflamed soldiery towards peaceful colonists and their women was something he had never tolerated.

That Don Juan de la Fuente, delicately bred gentleman of Spain though he might be, shared no particle of Blood's scruples was evident. For Don Juan, his dark eyes aglow with expectancy, went ashore with his reinforcements, personally to lead that raid. At the last, with a laugh, he invited his guest to accompany him, promising him rare sport and a highly diverting addition to his experiences of life. Blood commanded himself and remained outwardly cold.

"My nationality forbids it, Don Juan. The Dutch are not at war with France."

"Why, who's to know you're Dutch? Be entirely a Spaniard for once, Don Pedro, and enjoy yourself. Who is to know?"

"I am," said Blood. "It is a question of honour." Don Juan stared at him as if he were ludicrous. "You must be the victim of your scruples, then;" and still laughing he went down the accommodation ladder to the waiting boat.

Captain Blood remained upon the poop, whence he could watch the town above the shore, less than a mile away; for the Estremadura now rode at anchor in the roadstead. Of the officers, only Veraguas remained aboard, and of the men not more than fourteen or fifteen. But they kept a sharp watch, and there was a master gunner amongst them for emergencies.

Don Sebastian Veraguas bewailed his fate that he should have been left out of the landing party, and spoke wistfully of the foul joys that might have been his ashore. He was a sturdy, bovine fellow of five and-twenty, prominent of nose and chin, and he chattered self-sufficiently whilst Blood kept his glance upon the little town. Even at that distance they could hear the sounds of the horrid Spanish handiwork, and already more than one house was in flames. Too well Blood knew what was taking place at the instigation of a gentleman of Spain, and as grim-faced he watched, he would have given much to have had a hundred of his buccaneers at hand with whom to sweep this Spanish rubbish from the earth. Once before he had witnessed at close quarters such a raid, and he had sworn then that never thereafter would he show mercy to a Spaniard. To that oath he had been false in the past; but he vowed now that he would not fail to keep it in future.

And meanwhile the young man at his elbow, whom he could gladly have strangled with his hands, was calling down the whole heavenly hierarchy to witness his disappointment at being absent from that Hell.

It was evening when the raiders returned, coming, as they had gone, by the road which led to the now silent fort, and there taking boat to cross a hundred yards of jade-green water to the anchored ship. They sang as they came, boisterous and hilarious, a few of them with bandaged wounds, many of them flushed with wine and rum, and all of them laden with spoils. They made vile jests of the desolation they had left behind and viler boasts of the abominations they had practised. No buccaneers in the world, thought Blood, could ever have excelled them in brutality. The raid had been entirely successful and they had lost not more than a half-dozen men whose deaths had been terribly avenged.

And then in the last boat came Don Juan. Ahead of him up the accommodation ladder went two of his men bearing a heaving bundle, which Blood presently made out to be a woman whose head and shoulders were muffled in a cloak. Below the black folds of this he beheld a petticoat of flowered silk and caught a glimpse of agitated legs in silken hose and dainty high-heeled shoes. In mounting horror he judged from this that the woman was a person of quality.

Don Juan, with face and hands begrimed with sweat and powder, followed closely. From the head of the ladder he uttered a command: "To my cabin."

Blood saw her borne across the deck, through the ranks of men who jeered their ribaldries, and then she vanished in the arms of her captors down the gangway.

Now whatever he may have been towards men, towards women Blood had never been other than chivalrous. This, perhaps, for the sake of that sweet lady in Barbadoes to whom he accounted himself nothing, but who was to him an inspiration to more honour than would be thought possible in a buccaneer. That chivalry arose in him now full-armed. Had he yielded to it completely and blindly he would there and then have fallen upon Don Juan, and thus wrecked at once all possibility of being of service to his unfortunate captive. Her presence here could be no mystery to any. She was the particular prize that the profligate Spanish commander reserved to himself, and Blood felt his flesh go crisp and cold at the thought.

Yet when presently he came down the companion and crossed the deck to the gangway he was calm and smiling. In that narrow passage he joined Don Juan's officers, the three who had been ashore with him as well as Veraguas. They were all talking at once and laughing boisterously, and the subject of their approving mirth was their captain's vileness.

Together they burst into the cabin, Blood coming last. The black man servant had laid the table for supper with the usual six places, and had just lighted the great silver lamp, for with sunset the daylight faded almost instantly.

Don Juan was emerging at that moment from one of the larboard cabins. He closed the door, and stood for a dozen heart-beats with his back to it, surveying that invasion almost mistrustfully. It determined him to turn the key in the lock, draw it out and put it in his pocket. From that lesser cabin, in which clearly the lady had been bestowed, there came no sound.

"She's quiet at last, God be praised," laughed one of the officers.

"Worn out with screeching," explained another. "Lord! Was there ever such a wild-cat? A woman of spirit that, from the way she fought; a little devil worth the taming. It's a task I envy you, Juan."

Veraguas hailed the prize as well-deserved by such brilliant leadership, and then whilst questionable quips and jests were still being bandied, Don Juan, smiling grimly, introspectively, ordered them to table.

"We'll sup briefly, if you please," he announced, as he unbuckled his harness, and by the remark produced a fresh storm of hilarity on the subject of his haste and at the expense of the poor victim beyond that door.

When at last they sat down Captain Blood thrust himself upon Don Juan's notice with a question: "And Colonel de Coulevain?"

The handsome face darkened. "A malediction on him! He was away from Basseterre, organizing defences at Les Carmes."

Blood raised his brows, adopted a tone of faint concern. "Then the account remains unsettled in spite of all your brave efforts."

"Not quite. Not quite."

"By Heaven, no!" said another with a laugh. "Madame de Coulevain should give an ample quittance."

"Madame de Coulevain?" said Blood, although the question was unnecessary as were the glances that travelled towards the locked cabin door to answer him. He laughed. "Now that..." He paused. "That is an artistic vengeance, Don Juan, whatever the offence." And, with Hell in his soul, he laughed again, softly, in admiring approval.

Don Juan shrugged and sighed. "Yet I would I had found him and made him pay in full."

But Captain Blood would not leave it there. "If you really hate the man, think of the torment to which you have doomed him, always assuming that he loves his wife. Surely by comparison with that the peace of death would be no punishment at all."

"Maybe, maybe." Don Juan was short. Disappointment seemed to have spoiled his temper, or perhaps impatience fretted him. "Give me wine, Absolom. God of my life! How I thirst!"

The black man poured for them. Don Juan drained his bumper at a draught. Blood did the same, and the goblets were replenished.

Blood toasted the Spanish commander in voluble terms. He was no great judge, he declared, of an action afloat; but he could not conceive that the one he had witnessed that day could have been better fought by any commander living.

Don Juan smiled his gratification; the toast was drunk with relish, and the cups were filled again. Then others talked, and Blood lapsed into thought.

He reflected that soon now, supper being done, Don Juan would drive them all to their quarters. Captain Blood's own were on the starboard side of the great cabin. But would he be suffered to remain there now, so near at hand? If so, he might yet avail that unhappy lady, and already he knew precisely how. The danger lay in that he might be sent elsewhere tonight.

He roused himself and broke in upon the talk, called noisily for more wine, and after that for yet more, in which the others who had sweated profusely in that day's action kept him company gladly enough. He broke into renewed eulogies of Don Juan's skill and valour, and it was presently observed that his speech was slurred and indistinct, and that he hiccoughed and repeated himself foolishly.

Thus he provoked ridicule, and when it was forthcoming he displayed annoyance, and appealed to Don Juan to inform these merry and befuddled gentlemen that he at least was sober; but his speech grew thicker even whilst he was protesting.

When Veraguas taxed him with being drunk he grew almost violent, spoke of his Dutch origin to remind them that he came of a nation of great drinkers, and offered to drink any man in the Caribbean under the table. Boastfully, to prove his words, he called for more wine, and having drunk it lapsed gradually into silence. His eyelids dropped heavily, his body sagged, and presently, to the hilarity of all who beheld here a boaster confounded, he slid from his chair and came to rest upon the cabin floor, nor attempted to rise again.

Veraguas stirred him contemptuously and ungently with his foot. He gave no sign of life. He lay inert as a log, breathing stertorously.

Don Juan got up abruptly. "Put the fool to bed. And get you gone too; all of you."

Don Pedro was borne, insensible, amid laughter and some rude handling, to his cabin. His neckcloth was loosed, and so they left him, closing the door upon him.

Then, in compliance with Don Juan's renewed command, they all departed noisily, and the commander locked the door of the now empty great cabin.

Alone, he came slowly back to the table, and stood a moment listening to the uncertain steps and the merry voices retreating down the gangway. His goblet stood half-full. He picked it up and drank. Then, setting it down, and proceeding without haste, he drew from his pocket the key of the cabin in which Madame de Coulevain had been bestowed. He crossed the floor, thrust the key into the lock and turned it. But before he could throw open the door a sound behind him made him turn again.

His drunken guest was leaning against the bulkhead beside the open door of his stateroom. His clothes were in disorder, his face vacuous, and he stood so precariously that it was a wonder the gentle heave of the ship did not pitch him off his balance. He moved his lips like a man nauseated, and parted them with a dry click.

"Wha's o'clock?" was his foolish question.

Don Juan relaxed his stare to smile, although a thought impatiently.

The drunkard babbled on: "I... I don't... remember..." He broke off. He lurched forward. "Thousand devils! I... I thirst!"

"To bed with you! To bed!" cried Don Juan. "To bed? Of... of course to bed. Whither... else? Eh? But first... a cup."

He reached the table. He lurched round it, a man carried forward by his own impetus, and came to rest opposite the Spaniard, whose velvet eyes watched him with angry contempt. He found a goblet and a jug, a heavy, encrusted silver jug, shaped like an amphora with a handle on either side of its long neck. He poured himself wine, drank, and set down the cup; then he stood swaying slightly, and put forth his right hand as if to steady himself. It came to rest on the neck of the silver jug.

Don Juan, watching him ever with impatient scorn, may have seen for the fraction of a second the vacuity leave that countenance, and the vivid blue eyes under their black brows grow cold and hard as sapphires. But before the second was spent, before the brain could register what the eyes beheld, the body of that silver jug had crashed into his brow, and the commander of the Estremadura knew nothing more.

Captain Blood, without a trace now of drunkenness in face or gait, stepped quickly round the table, and went down on one knee beside the man he had felled. Don Juan lay quite still on the gay Eastern carpet, his handsome face clay-coloured with a trickle of blood across it from the wound between the half-closed eyes. Captain Blood contemplated his work without pity or compunction. If there was cowardice in the blow which had taken the Spaniard unawares from a hand which he supposed friendly, that cowardice was born of no fear for himself, but for the helpless lady in that larboard cabin. On her account he could take no risk of Don Juan's being able to give the alarm; and, anyway, this cruel, soulless profligate deserved no honourable consideration.

He stood up briskly, then stooped and placed his hand under the inert Spaniard's armpits. Raising the limp body, he dragged it with trailing heels to the stern window, which stood open to the soft, purple, tropical night. He took Don Juan in his arms, and, laden with him, mounted the day-bed. A moment he steadied his heavy burden upon the sill; then he thrust it forth, and, supporting himself by his grip of a stanchion, leaned far out to observe the Spaniard's fall.

The splash he made in the phosphorescent wake of the gently moving ship was merged into the gurgle of water about the vessel. For an instant as it took the sea the body glowed, sharply defined in an incandescence that was as suddenly extinguished. Phosphorescent bubbles arose and broke in the luminous line astern; then all was as it had been.

Captain Blood was still leaning far out, still peering down, when a voice in the cabin behind him came to startle him. It brought him instantly erect, alert; but he did not yet turn round. Indeed, he checked himself in the very act, and remained stiffly poised, his left hand supporting him still upon the stanchion, his back turned squarely upon the speaker.

For the voice was the voice of a woman. Its tone was tender, gentle, inviting. The words it had uttered in French were:

"Juan! Juan! Why do you stay? What do you there? I have been waiting. Juan!"

Speculation treading close upon amazement, he continued to stand there, waiting for more that should help him to understand. The voice came again, more insistently now.

"Juan! Don't you hear me? Juan!"

He swung round at last, and beheld her near the open door of her cabin, from which she had emerged: a tall, handsome woman, in the middle twenties, partly dressed, with a mantle of unbound golden tresses about her white shoulders. He had imagined this lady cowering, terror-stricken, helpless, probably pinioned, in the cabin to which the Spanish ravisher had consigned her. Because of that mental picture, intolerable to his chivalrous nature, he had done what he had done. Yet there she stood, not merely free, nor merely having come forth of her own free will, but summoning Don Juan in accents that are used to a lover.

Horror stunned him: horror of himself and of the dreadful murderous blunder he had committed in his haste to play at knight-errantry: to usurp the place of Providence.

And then another deeper horror welled up to submerge the first: horror of this woman as she stood suddenly revealed to him. That dreadful raid on Basseterre had been no more than a pretext to cloak her elopement, and must have been undertaken at her invitation. The rest, her forcible conveyance aboard, her bestowal in the cabin, had all been part of a loathly comedy she had played—a comedy set against a background of fire and rape and murder, by all of which she remained so soullessly unperturbed that she could come forth to coo her lover's name on that seductive note.

It was for this harpy, who waded complacently through blood and the wreckage of a hundred lives to the fulfilment of her desires, that he had soiled his hands. The situation seemed to transmute his chivalrously-inspired deed into a foulness.

He shivered as he regarded her, and she, confronted by that stern aquiline face and those ice-cold blue eyes, that were certainly not Don Juan's, gasped, recoiled, and clutched her flimsy silken body-garment chosen to her generous breast.

"Who are you?" she demanded. "Where is Don Juan de la Fuente?"

He stepped down from the day-bed, and something bodeful in his countenance changed her surprise to incipient alarm.

"You are Madame de Coulevain?" he asked, using her own language. He must make no mistake.

She nodded. "Yes, yes." Her tone was impatient, but the fear abode in her eyes. "Who are you? Why do you question me?" She stamped her foot. "Where is Don Juan?"

He knew that truth is commonly the shortest road, and he took it. He jerked a thumb backwards over his shoulder. "I've just thrown him through the window."

She stared and stared at this cold, calm man about whom she perceived something so remorseless and terrifying that she could not doubt his incredible words.

Suddenly she loosed a scream. It did not disconcert or even move him. He began to speak again, and, dominated by those brilliant intolerable eyes which were like points of steel, she controlled herself to listen.

"You are supposing me one of Don Juan's companions; perhaps even that, covetous of the noble prize he took today at Basseterre I have murdered him to possess it. That far indeed from the truth. Deceived like the rest by the comedy of your being brought forcibly aboard, imagining you the unhappy victim of a man I knew for a profligate voluptuary, I was moved to unutterable compassion on your behalf, and to save you from the horror I foresaw for you I killed him. And now," he added with a bitter smile, "it seems that you were in no need of saving, that I have thwarted you no less than I have thwarted him. This comes of playing Providence."

"You killed him!" she said. She staggered where she stood, and, ashen-faced, looked as if she would swoon. "You killed him! Killed him! Oh, my God! My God! You've killed my Juan." Thus far she had spoken dully, as if she were repeating something so that she might force it upon her own understanding. But now she wrought herself to frenzy. "You beast! You assassin!" she screamed. "You shall pay! I'll rouse the ship! You shall answer, as God's in Heaven!"

She was already across the cabin hammering on the door; already her hand was upon the key when he came up with her.

She struggled like a wild-cat in his grip, screaming the while for help. At last he wrenched her away, swung her round and hurled her from him. Then he withdrew, and pocketed the key.

She lay on the floor, by the table, where he had flung her, and sent scream after scream to alarm the ship.

Captain Blood surveyed her coldly. "Aye, aye, breathe your lungs, my child," he bade her. "It will do you good and me no harm."

He sat down to await the exhaustion of her paroxysm. But his words had already quieted her. Her round eyes asked a question. He smiled sourly as he answered it.

"No man aboard this ship will stir a foot for all your cries, or even heed them, unless it be as a matter for amusement. That is the kind of men they are who follow Don Juan de la Fuente."

He saw by her stricken expression how well she understood. He nodded with that faint sardonic smile which she found hateful. "Aye, madame. That's the situation. You were best bring yourself to a calm contemplation of it."

She got to her feet, and stood leaning heavily against the table, surveying him with rage and loathing. "If they do not come tonight, they will come tomorrow. Some time they must come. And when they come it will be very ill for you, whoever you may be."

"Will it not also be very ill for you?" quoth Blood.

"For me? I did not murder him."

"You'll not be accused of it. But in him you've lost your only protector aboard this ship. What will betide you, do you suppose, when you are alone and helpless in their power, a prisoner of war, the captive of a raid, in the hands of these merry gentlemen of Spain?"

"God of Heaven!" She clutched her breast in terror.

"Quiet you," he bade her, almost contemptuously. "I did not rescue you, as I supposed, from one wolf, merely to fling you to the pack. That will not happen—unless you yourself prefer it to returning to your husband."

She grew hysterical.

"To my husband? Ah, that, no! Never that! Never that!"

"It is that or..."—he pointed to the door—"... The pack. I perceive no choice for you save between those alternatives."

"Who are you?" she asked abruptly. "What are you, you devil, who have destroyed me and yet torment me?"

"I am your saviour, not your destroyer. Your husband, for his own sake, shall be left to suppose, as all have been led to suppose, that you were violently carried off. He will receive you back with relief of his own anguish and with tenderness, and make amends to you for all that the poor fool will fancy you have suffered."

She laughed on a note of hysteria.

"Tenderness! Tenderness in my husband! If he had ever been tender I should not be where I now am." And suddenly, to his surprise, she was moved to explain, to exculpate herself. "I was married to a cold, gross, stupid, cruel animal. That is Monsieur de Coulevain, a fool who has squandered his possessions and is forced to accept a command in these raw barbarous colonies to which he has dragged me.

"Oh, you think the worst of me, of course. You account me just a light woman. But you shall know the truth.

"At the height of my disillusion some few months after my marriage, Don Juan de la Fuente came to us at Pau, where we lived, for my husband is a Gascon. My Don Juan was travelling in France. We loved each other from our first meeting. He saw my unhappiness, which was plain to all. He urged me to fly to Spain with him, and I would to Heaven I had yielded then, and so put an end to misery. Foolishly I resisted. A sense of duty kept me faithful to my vows. I dismissed him. Since then my cup of misery and shame has overflowed, and when a letter from him was brought to me here at Basseterre on the outbreak of war with Spain, to show me that his fond, loyal, noble heart had not forgotten, I answered him, and in my despair I bade him come for me whenever he would."

She paused a moment, looking at Captain Blood with tragic eyes from which the tears were flowing.

"Now, sir, you know precisely what you have done, what havoc you have made."

Blood's expression had lost some of its sternness. His voice, as he answered her, assumed a gentler note.

"The havoc exists only in your mind, madame. The change which you conceived to be from hell to heaven would have been from hell to deeper hell. You did not know this man, this loyal, noble heart, this Don Juan de la Fuente. You were taken by the external glitter of him. But it was the glitter, I tell you of decay, for at the core the man was rotten, and in his hands your fate would have been infamy."

"Do you mend your case or mine by maligning the man you've murdered?"

"Malign him? Nay, madame. Proof of what I say is under my hand. You were in Basseterre today. You know something of the bloodshed, the slaughter of almost defenceless men, the dreadful violence to women..."

Faintly she interrupted him. "These things... in the way of war..."

"The way of war?" he roared. "Madame, undeceive yourself. Look truth boldly in the face though it condemn you both. Of what consequence Mariegalante to Spain? And, having been taken, is it held? War served your lover as a pretext. He let loose his dreadful soldiery upon the ill-defended place, solely so that he might answer your invitation. Men who today have been wantonly butchered, and unfortunate women who have suffered brutal violence, would now be sleeping tranquilly in their beds but for you and your evil lover. But for you—"

She interrupted him. She had covered her face with her hands while he was speaking, and sat rocking herself and moaning feebly. Now suddenly she uncovered her face again, and he saw that her eyes were fierce.

"No more!" she commanded, and stood up. "I'll hear no more. It's false! False what you say! You distort things to justify your own wicked deed."

He considered her grimly with those cold, penetrating eyes of his.

"Your kind," he said slowly, "will always believe what it chooses to believe. I do not think that I need pity you too much. But since I know that I have distorted nothing, I am content that expiation now awaits you. You shall choose the form of it, madame. Shall I leave you to these Spanish gentlemen, or will you come with me to your husband?"

She looked at him, her eyes distraught, her bosom in tumult. She began to plead with him. Awhile he listened; then he cut her short.

"Madame, I am not the arbiter of your fate. You have shaped it for yourself. I but point out the only two roads it leaves you free to tread."

"How... how can you take me back to Basseterre?" she asked him presently.

He told her, and without waiting for her consent, which he knew could not be withheld, he made swift preparation. He flung some provisions into a napkin, took a skin of wine, and a little cask of water, and by a rope which he fetched from his state-room lowered these things to the pinnace, which was again in tow, and which he drew under the counter of the galleon.

Next he lashed the shortened tow-rope to a cleat on one of the stanchions, then summoned her to make with him the airy passage down that rope.

It appalled her. But he conquered her fears, and when she had come to stand beside him, he seized the rope and swung out on it and slid down a little way to make room for her above him. At his command, although almost sick with terror, she grasped the rope and placed her feet on his shoulders. Then she slid down between the rope and him, until his hold embraced her knees and held her firmly.

Gently now, foot by foot, they began to descend. From the decks above came the sound of voices raised in song. The men were singing some Spanish scrannel in chorus.

At last his toe was on the gunwale of the pinnace. He worked her nose forward with that foot, sufficiently to enable him to plant the other firmly in the foresheets. After that it was an easy matter to step backwards, drawing her after him whilst still she clung to the rope. Thus he hauled the boat a little farther under the counter until he could take his companion about the waist and gently lower her.

After that he attacked the tow-rope with a knife and sawed it swiftly through. The galleon with its glowing sternport and the three great golden poop lamps sped serenely on close-hauled to the breeze, leaving them gently oscillating in her wake.

When he had recovered breath he bestowed Madame de Coulevain in the sternsheets, then hoisting the sail and trimming it, he broached to, and with his eyes on the brilliant stars in the tropical sky he steered a course which, with the wind astern, should bring them to Basseterre before sunrise.

In the sternsheets the woman was now gently weeping. With her, expiation had begun, as it does when it is possible to sin no more.

IX

THE GRATITUDE OF MONSIEUR DE COULEVAIN

All through the tepid night the pinnace, gently driven by the southerly breeze, ploughed steadily through a calm sea, which after moonrise became of liquid silver.

At the tiller sat Captain Blood. Beside him in the stern-sheets crouched the woman, who between silences was now whimpering, now vituperative, now apologetic. Of the gratitude which he accounted due to him he perceived no sign. But he was a tolerant, understanding man, and he did not, therefore, account himself aggrieved. Madame de Coulevain's case, however regarded, was a hard one; and she had little, after all, for which to be thankful to Fate or to Man.

Her mixed and alternating emotions did not surprise him.

He perceived quite clearly the sources of the hatred that rang in her voice whenever in the darkness she upbraided him and that glared in her pallid face when the dawn at last began to render it visible.

They were then within a couple of miles of land: a green flat coast with a single great mountain towering in the background. To larboard a tall ship was sweeping past them, steering for the bay ahead, and in her lines and rig Captain Blood read her English nationality. From her furled topsails he assumed that her master, evidently strange to these waters, was cautiously groping his way in. And this was confirmed by the seaman visible on the starboard forechains, leaning far out to take soundings. His chanting voice reached them across the sunlit waters as he told the fathoms.

Madame de Coulevain, who latterly had fallen into a drowsy stupor, roused herself to stare across at the frigate, aglow in the golden glory of the risen sun.

"No need for fear, madame. She is not Spanish."

"Fear?" She glared at him, blear-eyed from sleeplessness and weeping. She was a handsome woman, golden-headed and built on the generous lines of Hebe. Her full lips writhed into bitterness. "What have I to fear more than the fate you thrust upon me?"

"I, madame? I thrust no fate upon you. You are overtaken by the fate your own actions have invited."

Fiercely she interrupted him. "Have I invited this? That I should return to my husband?"

Captain Blood sighed in weariness. "Are we to have the argument all over again? Must I remind you that yourself you refused the only alternative, which was to remain at the mercy of those Spanish gallants on that Spanish ship? For the rest, your husband shall be left to suppose that you were carried off against your will."

"It if had not been for you, you assassin..."

"If it had not been for me, madame, your fate would have been even worse than you tell me that it is going to be."

"Nothing could be worse! Nothing! This man who has brought me out to these savage lands because, discredited and debt-ridden as he is, there was no longer a place for him at home, is... Oh, but why do I talk to you? Why do I try to explain to one who obstinately refuses to understand, to one who desires only to blame?"

"Madame, I do not desire to blame. I desire that you should blame yourself, for the horror you brought upon Basseterre. If you will accept whatever comes as an expiation, you may find some peace of mind."

"Peace of mind! Peace of mind!" Her scorn was fulminating.

He became sententious. "Expiation cleanses conscience. And when that has happened calm will return to your spirit."

"You preach to me! You! A filibuster, a sea-robber! And you preach of things you do not understand. I owe no expiation. I have done no wrong. I was a desperate woman, hard-driven by a man who is a beast, a cruel drunken beast, a broken gamester without honour; not even honest. I took my only chance to save my soul. Was I to know that Don Juan was what you say he is? Do I know it even now?"

"Do you not?" he asked her. "Did you see the ruin and desolation wantonly wrought in Basseterre, the horrors that he loosed his men to perpetrate, and do you still doubt his nature? And can you contemplate that havoc wrought so as to give you to your lover's arms, and still protest that you did no wrong? That, madame, is the offence that calls for expiation; not anything that may lie between yourself and your husband, or yourself and Don Juan."

Her mind refused admission to a conviction which it dared not harbour. Therefore she ranted on. Blood ceased to listen. He gave his attention to the sail; hauled it a little closer, so that the craft heeled over and headed straight for the bay.

It was an hour later when they brought up at the mole. A longboat was alongside, manned by English sailors from the frigate which in the meantime had come to anchor in the roadstead.

Odd groups of men and women, white and black, idling, cowed, at the waterside, with the horror of yesterday's events still heavy upon them, stared round-eyed at Madame de Coulevain as she was handed from the boat by her stalwart, grim-faced escort, in his crumpled coat of silver-laced grey camlett and black periwig that was rather out of curl.

The little mob moved forward in wonder, slowly at first, then with quickening steps, to crowd about the unsuspected author of their woes with questions of welcome and thanksgiving for this miracle of her return, of her deliverance, as they accounted it.

Blood waited, grim and silent, his eyes upon the sparse town which showed yesterday's ugly wounds as yet unscarred. Houses displayed shattered doors and broken windows, whilst here and there a heap of ashes smouldered where a house had stood. Pieces of broken furniture lay about in the open. From the belfry of the little church standing amid the acacias in the open square came the mournful note of a passing-bell. Within the walled enclosure about it there was an ominous activity, and black men could be seen at work there with pick and shovel.

Captain Blood's cold blue eyes played swiftly over all this and more. Then, almost roughly, he extricated the lady from that little mob of stricken questioning sympathisers who little guessed to what extent she was the author of their woes. At once conducted and conducting, he made his way up the gently rising ground. They passed a party of British sailors filling water-casks at a fountain which had been contrived by the damming of a brook. They passed the church with its busy graveyard. They passed a company of militia at drill; men in blue coats with red facings who had been hurriedly brought over by Colonel de Coulevain from Les Carmes after the harm was done.

Delayed on the way by others whom they met and who must stop to cry out in wonder at sight of Madame de Coulevain, accompanied by this tall, stern stranger, they came at last by a wide gateway into a luxuriant garden, and by an avenue of palms to a long, low house of stone and timber.

There were no signs of damage here. The Spaniards who had yesterday invaded the place, if, indeed, they had invaded it, had wrought no other mischief than to carry off the Governor's lady. The elderly black man who admitted them broke into shrill cries upon beholding his dishevelled mistress in her crumpled gown of flowered silk. He laughed and wept at once. He uttered scraps of prayer. He capered like a dog. He caught her hand and slobbered kisses on it.

"You appear to be loved, madame," said Captain Blood when at last they stood alone in the long dining-room.

"Of course that must surprise you," she sneered, with that twist of her full lips which he had come to know.

The door of a connecting-room was abruptly flung open, and a tall, heavily-built man with prominent features and sallow, deeply-lined cheeks stood at gaze. His militia coat, of blue with red facings, was stiff with tarnished gold lace. His dark bloodshot eyes opened wide at sight of her. He turned pale under his tan.

"Antoinette!" he ejaculated. He came forward unsteadily and took her by the shoulders. "Is it really you? They told me... But where have you been since yesterday?"

"Where they told you I was, no doubt." There was little in her tone besides weariness. "Fortunately, or unfortunately, this gentleman delivered me, and he has brought me safely back."

"Fortunately or unfortunately?" he echoed, and scowled. His lip curled. The dislike of her in his eyes was not to be mistaken. He took his hands from her shoulders, and half turned to consider her companion. "This gentleman?" Then his glance darkened further. "A Spaniard?"

Captain Blood met the frown with a smile. "A Dutchman, sir," he lied. But the rest of his tale was true. "By great good fortune I was aboard that Spanish ship, the Estremadura. I had been picked up by her at sea a few days before. I had access to the great cabin in which the Spanish commander had locked himself with Madame your wife. I interrupted his amorous intentions. In fact, I killed him with my hands." And he added a brief account of how, thereafter, he had conveyed her from the galleon.

Monsieur de Coulevain swore profoundly to express his wonder; stood silently pondering the thing he had been told; then swore again. Blood accounted him a dull, brutish fellow whom any woman would be justified in leaving. If the Colonel felt any tenderness towards his wife, or thankfulness for her delivery from the dreadful fate to which he must suppose her to have been exposed, he kept the emotions to himself. He showed presently, however, that he could be emotional enough over the memory of yesterday's catastrophe. This Blood accounted reasonable until he came to perceive that the man's real concern was less with the sufferings of the people of Basseterre than with the possible consequences to himself when an account of his stewardship should come to be asked of him by the French Government.

Madame, her beauty sadly impaired by her pallor, her weariness and dishevelled condition, interrupted his lament, to recall him to the demands of common courtesy.

"You have not yet thanked this gentleman for the heroic service he has rendered us."

Blood caught the sneer and perceived its double edge. At last he found it in his heart to pity her a little, to understand the despair which had driven her, reckless of what might betide others, so that she should escape from this boorish egotist.

Belatedly and clumsily M. de Coulevain expressed his thanks. When that was done, Madame took her leave of them. She confessed herself exhausted, and it was the old black man, who had remained in attendance in the background, who came forward to proffer his arm and to assist her. On the threshold a black woman waited, all tenderness and solicitude, to put her weary mistress to bed.

Coulevain, heavy-eyed, watched her depart, and remained staring until Captain Blood's brisk voice aroused him.

"If you were to offer me some breakfast, sir, that would be a practical measure of repayment."

Coulevain swore. "Death of my life! How negligent I am! These troubles, sir... the ruin of the town... the abduction of my wife... It is too much, sir. You'll understand. It discomposes a man. You forgive me, Monsieur... I have not the honour to know your name."

"Vandermeer. Peter Vandermeer, at your service."

And then another voice cut in, a voice that spoke French with a rasping English accent. "Are you quite sure that that is your name?"

Blood span round. On the threshold of the adjacent room from which Colonel de Coulevain had earlier issued stood now the stocky figure of a youngish man in a red coat that was laced with silver. In the plump, florid countenance Captain Blood recognized at a glance his old acquaintance Captain Macartney, who had been second in command at Antigua when some months before Captain Blood had slipped through the fingers of the British there. His momentary surprise at finding Macartney here was dispelled by remembrance of the English frigate which had passed him as they were approaching Basseterre.

The officer was smiling hatefully. "Good morning, Captain Blood. This time you have no buccaneers at your heels, no ships, no demi-cannons with which to intimidate us."

So ominous was the tone, so clear its hint of the speaker's intention, that Blood's hand flew instinctively to his left side. The Englishman's smile became a laugh.

"Not even a sword, Captain Blood."

"Its absence will no doubt encourage your impertinences."

But now the Colonel was intervening. "Captain Blood, did you say? Captain Blood? Not the filibuster? Not...?"

"The filibuster indeed; the buccaneer, the transported rebel, the escaped convict on whose head the British Government has placed the price of a thousand pounds."

"A thousand pounds!" Coulevain sucked his breath. His dark, blood-injected eyes returned to the contemplation of his wife's preserver. "Sir, sir! Is this true, sir?"

Blood shrugged. "Of course it's true. Who else do you suppose could have done what I have told you that I did last night?"

Coulevain continued to stare at him with increasing wonder. "And you contrived to pass yourself off as a Dutchman on a Spanish ship?"

"Who else but Captain Blood could have done that?"

"My God!" said Coulevain.

"I hope, none the less, you'll give me some breakfast, my Colonel?"

"Aboard the Royal Duchess," said Macartney, evilly facetious, "you shall have all the breakfast you require."

"Much obliged. But I have a prior claim on the hospitality of Colonel de Coulevain, for services rendered to his wife."

Major Macartney—he had been promoted since Blood's last meeting with him—smiled. "My claim can wait, then, until your fast is broken."

"What claim is that?" quoth Coulevain.

"To do my duty by arresting this damned pirate, and delivering him to the hangman."

M. de Coulevain seemed shocked. "Arrest him? You want to laugh, I think. This, sir, is France. Your warrant does not run on French soil."

"Perhaps not. But there is an agreement between France and England for the prompt exchange of any prisoners who may have escaped from a penal settlement. Under that agreement, sir, you dare not refuse to surrender Captain Blood to me."

"Surrender him to you? My guest? The man who has served me so nobly? Who is here as a direct consequence of that service? Sir, it... it is unthinkable." Thus he displayed to Captain Blood certain remains of decent feeling.

Macartney was gravely calm. "I perceive your scruples. I respect them. But duty is duty."

"I care nothing for your duty, sir."

The Major's manner became more stern. "Colonel de Coulevain, you will forgive me for pointing out to you that I have the means at hand to enforce my demand, and my duty will compel me to employ it."

"What?" Colonel de Coulevain was aghast. "You would land your men under arms on French soil?"

"If you are obstinate in your misplaced chivalry you will leave me no choice."

"But... God of my life! That would be an act of war. War between the nations would be the probable result."

Macartney shook his round head. "The certain result would be the cashiering of Colonel de Coulevain for having made the act necessary in defiance of the existing agreement." He smiled maliciously. "I think you will be sufficiently under a cloud already, my Colonel, for yesterday's events here."

Coulevain sat down heavily, dragged forth a handkerchief and mopped his brow. He was perspiring freely. He appealed in his distress to Captain Blood. "Death of my life! What am I to do?"

"I am afraid," said Captain Blood, "that his reasoning is faultless." He stifled a yawn. "You'll forgive me. I was out in the open all night." And he, too, sat down. "Do not permit yourself to be distressed, my Colonel. This business of playing Providence is seldom properly requited by Fortune."

"But what am I to do, sir? What am I to do?"

Under his sleepy exterior, Captain Blood's wits were wide-awake and busy. It was within his experience of these officers sent overseas that they belonged almost without exception to one of two classes: they were either men who, like Coulevain, had dissipated their fortunes, or else younger sons with no fortunes to dissipate. Now, as he afterwards expressed it, he heaved the lead so as to sound the depth of Macartney's disinterestedness and honesty of purpose.

"You will give me up, of course, my Colonel. And the British Government will pay you the reward of a thousand pounds—five thousands pieces of eight."

Each officer made a sharp movement at that, and from each came an almost inarticulate ejaculation of inquiry.

Captain Blood explained himself. "It is so provided by the agreement under which Major Macartney claims my surrender. Any reward for the apprehension of an escaped prisoner is payable to the person surrendering him to the authorities. Here, on French soil, it will be you, my Colonel, who will surrender me. Major Macartney is merely the representative of the authorities—the British Government—to whom I am surrendered."

The Englishman's face lost some of its high colour; it lengthened; his mouth drooped; his very breathing quickened. Blood had heaved the lead to some purpose. It had given him the exact depth of Macartney, who stood now tongue-tied and crestfallen, forbidden by decency from making the least protest against the suddenly vanished prospect of a thousand pounds which he had been reckoning as good as in his pocket.

But this was not the only phenomenon produced by Blood's disclosure of the exact situation. Colonel de Coulevain, too, was oddly stricken. The sudden prospect of so easily acquiring this magnificent sum seemed to have affected him as oddly as the contrary had affected Macartney. This was an unexpected complication to the observant Captain Blood. But it led him at once to remember that Madame de Coulevain had described her husband as a broken gamester harassed by creditors. He wondered what would be the ultimate clash of the evil forces he was releasing, and almost ventured to hope that in that, when it came, as once before in a similar situation, would lie his opportunity.

"There is no more to be said, my Colonel," he drawled. "Circumstances have been too much for me. I know when I've lost, and I must pay." He yawned again. "Meanwhile, if I might have a little food and rest, I should be grateful. Perhaps Major Macartney will give me leave until this evening, when he can come to fetch me with an escort."

Macartney swung aside, and paced towards the open windows. The elation, the masterfulness, had completely left him. He dragged his feet. His shoulders drooped. "Very well," he said sourly, and checked his aimless wandering to turn towards the door. "I'll return for you at six o'clock."

But on the threshold he paused..."You'll play me no tricks, Captain Blood?"

"Tricks? What tricks can I play?" The Captain smiled wistfully. "I have no buccaneers, no ship, no demi-cannon. Not even a sword, as you remarked, Major. For the only trick I might yet play you..." He broke off, and changed his tone to add more briskly: "Major Macartney, since there's no thousand pounds to be earned by you for taking me, should you not be a fool to refuse a thousand pounds for leaving me? For forgetting that you have seen me?"

Macartney flushed. "What the devil do you mean?"

"Now don't be getting hot, Major. Think it over until this evening. A thousand pounds is a deal of money. You don't earn it every day, or every year, in the service of King James; and you perceive quite clearly by now that you won't earn it by arresting me."

Macartney bit his lip, looking searchingly meanwhile at the Colonel. "It... it's unthinkable!" he exploded. "I am not to be bribed. Unthinkable! If it were known..."

Captain Blood chuckled. "Is that what's troubling you? But who's to tell? Colonel de Coulevain owes me silence at least."

The brooding Colonel roused himself. "Oh, at least, at least. Have no doubt of that, sir."

Macartney looked from one to the other of them, a man plainly in the grip of temptation. He swore in his throat. "I'll return at six," he announced shortly.

"With an escort, Major, or alone?" was Blood's sly question.

"That's... that's as may be."

He strode out, and they heard his angrily-planted feet go clattering across the hall. Captain Blood winked at the Colonel, and rose. "I'll wager you a thousand pounds that there will be no escort."

"I cannot take the wager since I am of the same opinion."

"Now that's a pity, for I shall require the money, and I don't know how else to obtain it. It is possible he may consent to accept my note of hand."

"No need to distress yourself on that score."

Captain Blood searched the Colonel's heavy, blood-hound countenance. It wore a smile, a smile intended to be friendly. But somehow Captain Blood did not like the face any better on that account.

The smile broadened to an increasing friendliness. "You may break your fast and take your rest with an easy mind, sir. I will deal with Major Macartney when he returns."

"You will deal with him? Do you mean that you will advance the money?"

"I owe you no less, my dear Captain."

Again Captain Blood gave him a long searching stare before he bowed and spoke his eloquent thanks. The proposal was amazing. So amazing coming from a broken gamester harassed by creditors, that it was not to be believed-at least not by a man of Captain Blood's experience.

When, having broken his fast, he repaired to the curtained bed which Abraham had prepared for him in a fair room above stairs, he lay despite his weariness for some time considering it all. He recalled the subtle sudden betraying change in Coulevain's manner when it was disclosed that the reward would go to him; he saw again the oily smile on the Colonel's face when he had announced that he would deal with Major Macartney. If he knew men at all, Coulevain was the last whom he would trust. Of himself he was aware that he was an extremely negotiable security. The British Government had set a definite price upon his head. But it was widely known that the Spaniards whom he had harassed and pillaged without mercy would pay three or four times that price for him alive, so that they might have the pleasure of roasting him in the fires of the Faith. Had this scoundrel Coulevain suddenly perceived that the advent in Mariegalante of this saviour of his wife's honour was something in the nature of a windfall with which to repair his battered fortunes? If the half of what Madame de Coulevain had said of her husband in the course of that night's sailing was true there was no reason to suppose that any nice scruples would restrain him.

The more he considered, the more the Captain's uneasiness increased. He began to perceive that he was in an extremely tight corner. He even' went so far as to ask himself if the most prudent course might not be to rise, weary as he was, slip down to the mole, get aboard the pinnace which already had served him so well, and trust himself in her to the mercies of the ocean. But whither steer a course in that frail cockleshell? Only the neighbouring islands were possible, and they were all either French or British. On British soil he was certain of arrest with the gallows to follow, whilst on French soil he could hardly expect to fare better, considering his experience here where the commander was so deeply in his debt. If only he had money with which to purchase a passage on some ship that might pick him up at sea, money enough to induce a shipmaster to ask no questions whilst landing him off Tortuga. But he had none. The only thing of value in his possession was the great pearl in his left ear, worth perhaps five hundred pieces.

He was disposed to curse that raid in canoes upon the pearl fisheries of Cariaco which had resulted in disaster, had separated him from his ship, and had left him since adrift. But since cursing past events was the least profitable method of averting future ones, he decided to take the sleep of which he stood in need, hoping for the counsel which sleep is said to bring.

He timed himself to awaken at six o'clock, the hour at which Major Macartney was to return, and, his well-trained senses responding to that command, he awakened punctually. The angle of the sun was his sufficient dock. He slipped from the bed, found his shoes, which Abraham had cleaned, his coat, which had been brushed, and his periwig, which had been combed by the good black man. He had scarcely donned them when through the open window floated up to him the sound of a voice. It was the voice of Macartney, and it was answered instantly by the Colonel's with a hearty: "Come you in, sir. Come in."

In the nick of time, thought Blood; and he accepted the circumstances as a good omen. Cautiously he made his way below, meeting no one on the stairs or in the hall. Outside the door of the dining-room he stood listening. A hum of voices reached him. But they were distant. They came from the room beyond. Noiselessly he opened the door and slid across the threshold. The place was empty, as he had expected. The door of the adjacent room stood ajar. Through this came now the Major's laugh, and upon the heels of it the Colonel's voice.

"Depend upon it. He is under my hand. Spain, as you've said, will pay three times this sum, or even more, for him. Therefore he should be glad to ransom himself for, say, five times the amount of this advance." He chuckled, adding: "I have the advantage of you, Major, in that I can hold him to ransom, which your position as a British officer makes impossible to you. All things considered, you are fortunate, yes, and wise, to earn a thousand pounds for yourself."

"My God!" said Macartney, rendered suddenly virtuous by envy. "And that's how you pay your debts and reward the man for preserving your wife's life and honour! Faith, I'm glad I'm not your creditor."

"Shall we abstain from comments?" the Colonel suggested sourly.

"Oh, by all means. Give me the money, and I'll go my ways."

There was a chinking squelch twice repeated, as of moneybags that are raised and set down again. "It is in rolls of twenty double moidores. Will you count them?"

There followed a mumbling pause, and at the end of it came the Colonel's voice again. "If you will sign this quittance, the matter is at an end."

"Quittance?"

"I'll read it to you." And the Colonel read: "I acknowledge, and give Colonel Jerome de Coulevain this quittance for the sum of five thousand pieces of eight, received from him in consideration of my forbearing from any action against Captain Blood, and of my undertaking no action whatever hereafter for as long as he may remain the guest of Colonel de Coulevain on the Island of Mariegalante or elsewhere. Given under my hand and seal this tenth day of July of 1688."

As the Colonel's voice trailed off there came an explosion from Macartney.

"God's death, Colonel! Are you mad, or do you think that I am?"

"What do you find amiss? Is it not a correct statement?"

Macartney banged the table in his vehemence. "It puts a rope round my neck."

"Only if you play me false. What other guarantee have I that when you've taken these five thousand pieces you will keep faith with me?"

"You have my word," said Macartney in a passion. "And my word must content you."

"Your word! Your word!" The Frenchman's sneer was unmistakable. "Ah, that, no. Your word is not enough."

"You want to insult me!"

"Pish! Let us be practical, Major. Ask yourself: Would you accept the word of a man in a transaction in which his own part is dishonest?"

"Dishonest, sir? What the devil do you mean?"

"Are you not accepting a bribe to be false to your duty? Is not that dishonesty?"

"By god! This comes well from you, considering your intentions."

"You make it necessary. Besides, have I played the hypocrite as to my part? I have been unnecessarily frank, even to appearing a rogue. But, as in your own case, Major, necessity knows no law with me."

A pause followed upon those conciliatory words. Then: "Nevertheless," said Macartney, "I do not sign that paper."

"You'll sign and seal it, or I do not pay the money. What do you fear, Major? I give you my word—"

"Your word! Hell and the devil! In what is your word better than mine?"

"The circumstances make it better. On my side there can be no temptation to break faith, as on yours. It cannot profit me."

It was clear by now to Blood that since Macartney had not struck the Frenchman for his insults, he would end by signing. Only a desperate need of money could so have curbed the Englishman. He therefore heard with surprise Macartney's angry outburst.

"Give me the pen. Let us have done."

Another pause followed, then the Colonel's voice: "And now seal it here, where I have set the wax. The signet on your finger will serve."

Captain Blood waited for no more. The long windows stood open to the garden over which the dusk was rapidly descending. He stepped noiselessly out and vanished amid the shrubs. About the stem of a tall silk-cotton tree he found a tough slender liana swarming like a snake. He brought out his knife, slashed it near the root, and drew it down.

As Captain Macartney, softly humming to himself, a heavy leathern bag in the crook of each arm, came presently down the avenue between the palms where the evening shadows were deepest, he tripped over what he conceived to be a rope stretched taut across the path, and spread-eagled forward with a crash.

Lying momentarily half-stunned by the heavy fall, a weight descended on his back, and in his ear a pleasant voice was murmuring in English, with a strong Irish accent: "I have no buccaneers, Major, no ship, no demi-cannon, and, as you remarked, not even a sword. But I still have my hands and my wits, and they should more than suffice to deal with a paltry rogue like you."

"By God!" swore Macartney, though half-choked. "You shall hang for this, Captain Blood! By God, you shall!" Frenziedly he struggled to elude the grip of his assailant. His sword being useless in his present position, he sought to reach the pocket in which he carried a pistol, but, by the movement, merely betrayed its presence. Captain Blood possessed himself of it.

"Will you be quiet now?" he asked. "Or must I be blowing out your brains?"

"You dirty Judas! You thieving pirate! Is this how you keep faith?"

"I pledged you no faith, you nasty rogue. Your bargain was with the French colonel, not with me. It was he who bribed you to be false to your duty. I had no part in it."

"Had you not? You lying dog! You're a pretty pair of scoundrels, on my soul! Working in con-conjunction."

"Now that," said Blood, "is needlessly and foolishly offensive."

Macartney broke into fresh expletives.

"You talk too much," said Captain Blood, and tapped him twice over the head with the butt of the pistol, using great science. The Major sank forward gently, like a man asleep.

Captain Blood rose, and peered about him through the dusk. All was still. He went to pick up the leather bags which Macartney had dropped as he fell. He made a sling for them with his scarf, and so hung them from his neck. Then he raised the unconscious Major, swung him skilfully to his shoulder, and, thus burdened, went staggering down the avenue and out into the open.

The night was hot and Macartney was heavy. The sweat ran from Blood's pores. But he went steadily ahead until he reached the low wall of the churchyard, just as the moon was beginning to rise. On to the summit of this wall he eased himself of his burden, toppled it over into the churchyard, and then climbed after it. What he had to do there was quickly done by the light of the moon under the shelter of that wall. With the man's own sash he trussed him up at wrists and ankles. Then he stuffed some of the Major's periwig into his mouth, using the fellow's neckcloth to hold this unpleasant gag in position and taking care to leave his nostrils free.

As he was concluding the operation, Macartney opened his eyes and glared at him.

"Sure now it's only me: your old friend, Captain Blood. I'm just after making you comfortable for the night. When they find you in the morning, ye can tell them any convenient lie that will save you the trouble of explaining what can't be explained at all. It's a very good night I'll be wishing you, Major darling."

He went over the wall and briskly down the road that led to the sea.

On the mole lounged the British sailors who manned the longboat from the Royal Duchess, awaiting the Major's return. Further on, some men of Mariegalante were landing their haul from a fishing-boat that had just come in. None gave heed to Blood as he stepped along to the mole's end where that morning he had moored the pinnace. In the locker, where he stowed the heavy bags of gold, there was still some of the food that he had brought away last night from the Estremadura. He could not take the risk of adding to it. But he filled the two small water-casks at the fountain.

Then he stepped aboard, cast off and got out the sweeps. Another night on the open sea lay ahead of him. The wind, however, was still in the same quarter as last night and would favour the run to Guadeloupe upon which he had determined.

Once out of the bay he hoisted sail, and ran northward along the coast and the shallow cliffs which cast an inky shadow against the moon's white radiance. On he crawled through a sea of rippling quicksilver until he reached the island's end; then he headed straight across the ten miles of intervening water.

Off Grand Terre, the eastern of the two main islands of Guadeloupe, he lay awaiting sunrise. When it came, bringing a freshening of the wind, he ran close past Saint Anne, which was empty of shipping, and, hugging the coast, sailed on in a north-easterly direction until he came, some two hours later, to Port du Moule.

There were half a dozen ships in the harbour, and Blood scanned them with anxiety until his glance alighted on a black brigantine that was bellied like a Flemish alderman. Those lines were a sufficient advertisement of her Dutch origin, and Captain Blood, sweeping alongside, hailed her with confidence and climbed to her deck.

"I am in haste," he informed her sturdy captain, "to reach the northern coast of French Hispaniola, and I will pay you well for a passage thither."

The Dutchman eyed him without favour. "If you're in haste you had better seek what you need elsewhere. I am for Curacao."

"I've said I'll pay you well. Five thousand pieces of eight should compensate you for delays."

"Five thousand pieces!" The Dutchman stared. The sum was as much as he could hope to earn by his present voyage. "Who are you, sir?"

"What's that to the matter? I am one who will pay five thousand pieces."

The skipper of the brigantine screwed up his little blue eyes. "Will you pay in advance?"

"The half of it. The other half I shall obtain when my destination is reached. But you may hold me aboard until you have the money." Thus he ensured that the Dutchman, ignorant of the fact that the entire sum was already under his hand, should keep faith.

"I could sail tonight," said the other slowly.

Blood at once produced one of the two bags. The other he had stowed in one of the water-casks in the locker of the pinnace, and there it remained unsuspected until four days later, when they were in the narrow seas between Hispaniola and Tortuga.

Then Captain Blood, announcing that he would put himself ashore, paid over the balance of the money, and climbed down the side of the brig to re-enter the pinnace. When, presently, the Dutchman observed him to be steering not, indeed, towards Hispaniola, but a northerly course in the direction of Tortuga, that stronghold of the buccaneers, his growing suspicions may have been fully confirmed. He remained, however, untroubled, the only man who, in addition to Blood himself, had really profited by that transaction on the Island of Mariegalante.

Thus Captain Blood came back at last to Tortuga and to the fleet that was by now mourning him as dead. With that fleet of five tall ships he sailed into the harbour of Basseterre a month later with intent to settle a debt which he conceived to lie between Colonel de Coulevain and himself.

His appearance there in such force fluttered both the garrison and the inhabitants. But he came too late for his purposes. Colonel de Coulevain was no longer there to be fluttered. He had been sent back to France under arrest.

Captain Blood was informed of this by Colonel Sancerre, who had succeeded to the military command of Mariegalante, and who received him with the courtesy due to a filibuster who comes backed by the powerful fleet that Blood had anchored in the roadstead.

Captain Blood fetched a sigh when he heard the news. "A pity! I had a little word to say to him; a little debt to settle."

"A little debt of five thousand pieces of eight, I think," said the Frenchman.

"On my faith, you are well informed."

The Colonel explained. "When the General of the Armies of France in America came here to inquire into the matter of the Spanish raid on Mariegalante, he discovered that Colonel de Coulevain had robbed the French Colonial Treasury of that sum. There was proof of it in a quittance that was found among M. de Coulevain's papers."

"So that's where he got the money!"

"I see that you understand." The Commandant looked grave. "Robbery is a serious, shameful matter, Captain Blood."

"I know it is. I've practised a good deal of it myself."

"And I've little doubt that they will hang M. de Coulevain, poor devil."

Captain Blood nodded. "No doubt of that. But we'll save our tears to water some nobler grave, my Colonel."

Colonel Sancerre eyed him with cold disapproval. "This hardly comes well from you, Captain Blood. It was to save you from the English that Colonel de Coulevain paid over the money, was it not?"

"Hardly to save me from them. To buy me from them so that he might sell me again to Spain at a handsome profit. He had an eye to a profit, your Colonel de Coulevain."

"But what do you tell me?" cried Sancerre.

"That it's entirely a poetic thing that the quittance he took on my behalf should be the means of hanging him."

X

GALLOWS KEY

It is impossible now to determine whether Gallows Key took its name from the events I am about to relate or bore it already previously among seafaring men. Jeremy Pitt in his log gives no hint, and the miniature island is not now to be identified with precision. All that we know positively, and this from Pitt's log of the Arabella, is that it forms part of the group known as the Albuquerque Keys, lying in 12° northern latitude and 85° western longitude, some sixty miles north-west of Porto Bello.

It is little more than a barren rock, frequented only by sea-birds and the turtles that come to deposit their eggs in the golden sand of the reef-enclosed lagoon on its eastern side. This strip of beach shelves rapidly to a depth of some sixty fathoms, and the entrance to the lagoon is by a gap of not more than twenty yards in the rocky amphitheatre which goes to form it.

Into this secure if desolate haven sailed Captain Easterling one April day of the year 1688 in his thirty-gun frigate the Avenger, followed by the two ships that made up his fleet: the Hermes, a frigate of twenty-six guns, commanded by Roger Galloway, and the Valiant, a brigantine carrying twenty, in charge of Crosby Pike, who once had sailed with Captain Blood and was realizing his mistake in making a change of admiral.

You will remember this scoundrel Easterling, how once he had tried a fall with Peter Blood, when Blood was on the very threshold of his career as a buccaneer, and how, as a consequence, Easterling's ship had been blown from under him and himself swept from the seas.

But laboriously, with the patience and tenacity found in bad men as in good, Easterling had won back to his old position, and was afloat once more and in greater strength than ever before upon the Caribbean.

He was, in Peter Blood's own words, just a filthy pirate, a ruthless, bloodthirsty robber, without a spark even of that honour which is said to prevail among thieves. His followers made up a lawless mob, of mixed nationalities, subject to no discipline and obeying no rules save those which concerned the division of their spoils. They practised no discrimination in their piracy. They would attack an English or Dutch merchantman as readily as a Spanish galleon, and deal out the same ruthless brutality to the one as to the other.

Now, despite his ill-repute even among buccaneers, he had succeeded in luring away from Blood's following the resolute Crosby Pike, with his twenty-gun ship and well-disciplined crew of a hundred and thirty men. The lure had been that old story of Morgan's treasure with which Easterling once had unsuccessfully attempted to beguile Blood.

Again he told that hoary tale of how he had sailed with Henry Morgan and had been with him at the sack of Panama; how—as was well known—on the return march across the isthmus there had been all but mutiny among Morgan's followers on a suspicion that the booty divided among them was very far from being all the booty taken; how it was murmured that Morgan had secretly abstracted a great portion for himself; how Morgan, becoming alarmed lest a mutinous search of his personal baggage should reveal the truth of the rumour, had taken Easterling into his confidence and sought his aid in what he was to do. Between them they had buried that treasure—a treasure of pearls and precious stones of the fabulous value of at least half a million pieces of eight—at a spot on the banks of the Chagres River. They were to return to unearth it later when opportunity should serve. Morgan, however, swept by destiny along other profitable pursuits, was still postponing his return when death overtook him. Easterling had never returned because never before had he commanded the necessary force for the penetration of Spanish territory, or the necessary strength of ships for the safe conveyance of the treasure once it was reclaimed.

Such had been the tale to which Blood had scorned to lend an ear but to which Pike succumbed, in spite of Blood's warning against joining forces with so unscrupulous a rogue and his freely expressed conviction that no such treasure existed.

Pitying Pike for his credulity, Blood bore him no resentment for his defection, and feared rather than hoped that the sequel would punish him sufficiently.

Blood himself at this time had been planning an expedition to Darien. But since Easterling's activities on the isthmus might put the Spaniards on the alert, he found it prudent to postpone the business. His fleet, consisting in those days of five stout ships, scattered and went a-roving without definite objective. This was at the beginning of April, and it was concerted that they should reassemble at Mosquito Keys, at the end of May, when the expedition to Darien could be considered anew.

The Arabella, going south by the Windward Passage, and then east along the southern coast of Hispaniola, came, some twenty miles beyond Cape Tiburon, upon an English merchantman in a foundering condition. She was kept precariously afloat so long as the sea was calm by the shifting of her guns and all other heavy gear to larboard, so as to keep above water the gaping wounds in her starboard quarter. Her broken spars and fractured mainmast told an eloquent tale, and Blood imagined that Spaniards had been at work. He discovered instead, when he went to her assistance, that she had yesterday been attacked and plundered by Easterling, who had put half her crew to the sword and brutally killed her captain for not having struck his colours when summoned to do so.

The Arabella towed her within ten miles of Port Royal, and daring to go no nearer, lest she should draw down upon herself the Jamaica Squadron, left her there to complete alone what little remained of the voyage to safety.

That done, however, the Arabella did not sail east again, but headed south for the Main. To Pitt, his shipmaster, Blood explained his motives.

"We'll be keeping an eye on this blackguard Easterling, so we will, Jerry, and maybe more than an eye."

And south they sailed, since that was the way Easterling had gone. To the tale of his treasure, Blood, as we know, attached no faith. He regarded it as an invention to gull such credulous fellows as Pike into association. In this, however, he was presently to be proven wrong.

Creeping down the Mosquito Coast, he found a snug anchorage in a cove of one of the numerous islands in the Lagoon of Chiriqui. There for the moment he elected to lie concealed, and thence he watched the operations of Easterling, twenty miles away, through the eyes of friendly Mosquito Indians whom he employed as scouts. From these he learned that Easterling had cast anchor a little to westward of the mouth of the Chagres, that he had landed a force of three hundred and fifty men, and that he was penetrating with them into the isthmus. From his knowledge of Easterling's total strength, Blood computed that hardly more than a hundred men had been left behind to guard the waiting ships.

Whilst waiting in his turn, Blood took his ease. On a cane day-bed set under an improvised awning on the poop (for the weather was growing hot) the buccaneer found sufficient adventure for his spirit in the verse of Horace and the prose of Suetonius. When physical activity was desired, he would swim in the clear, jade-green waters of the lagoon, or, landing on the palm-fringed shore of that uninhabited island, he would take a hand with his men in the capture of turtle, or in the hewing of wood to provide the fuel for the boucan fires in which their succulent flesh was being cured.

Meanwhile his Indians brought him news, first of a skirmish between Easterling's men and a party of Spaniards who evidently had got wind of the presence on Darien of the buccaneers. Then came word that Easterling was marching back to the coast; a couple of days later he was informed of another encounter between Easterling and a Spanish force, in which the buccaneers had suffered severely, although in the end they had beaten off the attack. Lastly came news of yet a third engagement, and this was brought, together with other precious details, by one who had taken part in it.

He was one of Pike's men, a hard-bitten old adventurer, who had given up logwood-cutting to take to the sea. His name was Cunley, and he had been rendered helpless by a gunshot wound in the thigh and left by Easterling's retreating force to die where he had fallen. Overlooked by the Spaniards, he had dragged himself into the scrub for shelter and thus into the hands of the watchful Indians. They had handled him tenderly, so that he should survive to tell his tale to Captain Blood, and they had quieted his alarms with assertions in their broken Spanish that it was to Don Pedro Sangre that he was being conveyed.

Tenderly they hoisted the crippled fellow aboard the Arabella, where Blood's first care was to employ his surgeon's skill to dress the hideous festering wound. Thereafter, in the ward-room, converted for the moment into a sick bay, Cunley told in bitterness the tale of the adventure.

Morgan's treasure was real enough. The buccaneers were bearing it back to the waiting ships, and in value it exceeded all that Easterling had represented. But it was being dearly bought—most dearly by Pike's contingent, whence the bitterness investing Cunley's tale. Going and coming they had been harassed by Spaniards and once by a party of hostile Indians. Further, they had been reduced by fever and sickness on that difficult march through a miasmic country where mosquitoes had almost eaten them alive. Of the three hundred and fifty men who had left the ships, Cunley computed that after the last engagement, in which he had been wounded, not more than two hundred remained alive. But the ugly fact was that not more than twenty of these men were Pike's. Yet Pike had brought ashore by Easterling's orders the heaviest of the three contingents, landing a hundred and thirty men, and leaving a bare score to guard the Valiant, whilst fifty men at least had been left on each of the other ships.

Easterling had so contrived that Pike's contingent was ever in the van, so that it had borne the brunt of every attack the buccaneers had suffered. It was not to be supposed that Pike had submitted to this without remonstrances. Protests had grown increasingly bitter as the ill continued. But Easterling, backed by his earlier associate, Roger Galloway, who commanded the Hermes, had browbeaten Pike into submission, whilst the ruffianly followers of those two captains, by preponderance of numbers remaining at comparatively full strength, had easily imposed their will upon the dwindling force of the Valiant. If all her present survivors got back to the ship, the Valiant could now muster a crew of barely forty hands, whilst the other two combined a strength of nearly three hundred men.

"Ye see, Captain," Cunley concluded grimly, "how this Easterling has used us. As the monkey used the cat. And now him and Galloway—them two black-hearted bastards—is in such strength that Crosby Pike dursn't say a word o' protest.

It was a black day for all of us, Captain, when the Valiant left your fleet to join that blackguard Easterling's, treasure or no treasure."

"Treasure or no treasure," Captain Blood repeated. "And I'm thinking that for Captain Pike no treasure it will prove."

He rose from his chair by the sick man's bed, tall, graceful and vigorous in his black small clothes, silver-broidered waistcoat and full white cambric sleeves. His coat of black and silver he had discarded before commencing his surgical ministrations. He waved away the white-clad black man who attended with bowl and lint and forceps, and, alone with Cunley, he paced to the wardroom ports and back. His long supple fingers toyed thoughtfully with the curls of his black periwig; his eyes, blue as sapphires, were now as hard.

"I thought that Pike would prove a minnow in the jaws of Easterling. It but remains for Easterling to swallow him, and faith, it's what he'll be doing."

"Ye've said it, Captain. It's plaguey little o' that treasure me and my mates o' the Valiant or Captain Pike himself 'll ever see. The thirty that's left of us 'll be lucky if they gets away alive. That's my faith, Captain."

"And mine, bedad," said Captain Blood. But his mouth was grim.

"Can ye do nothing for the honour of the Brethren of the Coast and for the sake o' justice, Captain?"

"It's thinking of it, I am. If the fleet were with me I'd sail in this minute and take a hand. But with just this one ship..." He broke off and shrugged. "The odds are a trifle heavy. But I'll watch, and I'll consider."

Cunley's opinion that it was a black day for the Valiant when she joined Easterling's fleet was now being shared by every survivor of her crew, and by none more fully than by Captain Pike himself. He had become. apprehensive of the final issue of the adventure, and his apprehensions received the fullest confirmation on the morrow of their sailing from the Chagres, when they came to anchorage in that lagoon of Gallows Key to which I have alluded.

Easterling's Avenger led the way into that diminutive circular harbour, and anchored nearest to the shore. Next came the Hermes. The Valiant, now bringing up the rear, was compelled, for lack of room within, to anchor in the narrow roadstead. Thus again Pike was given the most vulnerable station in the event of attack—a station in which his ship must act as a shield for the others.

Trenam, Pike's sturdy young Cornish lieutenant, who from the outset had been against association with Easterling, perceiving the object of this disposition, was not ashamed to urge Pike to take up anchor and be off in the night, abandoning Easterling and the treasure before worse befell them. But Pike, as obstinate as he was courageous, repudiated this for a coward counsel.

"By God!" he swore. "It's what Easterling desires! We've earned our share of that treasure, and we're not sailing without it."

But the practical Trenam, shook his fair head. "That will be as Easterling chooses. He's got the strength to enforce his will, and the will to play the rogue, or I'm a fool else."

Pike silenced him by making oath that he was not afraid of twenty Easterlings.

And his air was as truculent when next morning, in response to a signal from the flagship, he went aboard the Avenger.

He was awaited in the cabin not only by Easterling, arrayed in tawdry splendour, but by Galloway, who favoured the loose leather breeches and cotton shirt that made up the habitual garb of a boucan-hunter. Easterling was massively built and swarthy—a man still young, with fine eyes and a full black beard, behind which, when he laughed, there was a flash of strong white teeth. Galloway, squat and broad, was not apelike in build, with his long arms and short powerful legs, but oddly apelike in countenance, out of which two bright little wicked eyes sparkled under a shallow wrinkled brow.

They received Captain Pike with every show of friendliness, sat him down at the greasy table, poured rum for him and pledged him, whereafter Easterling came promptly to business.

"We've sent for ye, Captain Pike, because at present we're carrying, as it were, all our eggs in one basket. This treasure," and he waved a hand in the direction of the chests containing it, "is best divided without more ado, so that each of us can go about his business."

Pike took heart at this promising beginning. "Ye mean to break up the fleet, then?" said he indifferently.

"Why not, since the job's done? Roger here and me has decided to quit piracy. We're for home with the fortune we've made. I'll belike turn farmer somewhere in Devon." He laughed.

Pike smiled, but offered no comment. He was not at any time a man of many words, as his long, dour, weatherbeaten face announced.

Easterling cleared his throat and resumed. "Me and Roger's been considering that some change in the provisions o' the articles would be only fair. They do run that one-third of what's left over after I've taken my fifth goes to each of the three ships."

"Ay, that's how they run, and that's fair enough for me," said Pike.

"That's not our opinion, Roger's and mine, now that we comes to think it over."

Pike opened his mouth to answer, but Easterling, giving him no time, ran on:

"Roger and me don't see as you should take a third to share among thirty men, while we share each of us the same among a hundred and fifty."

Captain Pike was swept by sudden passion. "Was, that why ye saw to it that my men were always put where the Spaniards could kill them until we're reduced to less than a quarter of our strength at the outset?"

Easterling's black brows met above eyes that were suddenly malevolent.

"Now what the devil do you mean by that, Captain Pike, if you please?"

"It's an imputation," said Galloway dryly. "A nasty imputation."

"No imputation at all," said Pike. "It's a fact."

"A fact, eh?" Easterling was smiling, and the lean, tough, resolute Pike grew uneasy under that smile. Galloway's bright little ape's eyes were considering him oddly. The very air of that untidy, evil-smelling cabin became charged with menace. Pike had a vision of brutalities witnessed in the course of his association with Easterling, wanton, unnecessary brutalities springing from the sheer lust of cruelty. He recalled words in which Captain Blood had warned him against association with a man whom he described as treacherous and foul by nature. If he had hugged a doubt of the deliberate calculation by which is own men had been sacrificed on Darien, that doubt was now dispelled.

He was as a sleepwalker who awakens suddenly to find himself on the edge of a precipice into which another step must have projected him. The instinct of self-preservation made him recoil from an attitude of truculence which might lead to his being pistolled on the spot. He pushed back the hair from his moist brow and commanded himself to answer in level tones.

"What I mean is that if my men have been reduced, they've suffered this in the common cause. They will consider it unfair to break the articles on any such grounds."

He argued on. He reminded Easterling of the practice of matelotage among buccaneers, whereby every man enters into a partnership with another in which the two make common cause and under which each is the other's heir. In this alone lay reason why many of his men who were to inherit should feel defrauded by any change in the articles.

Easterling's evil grin gave way again to a scowl. "What's it to me what any of your mangy followers may feel? I'm admiral of this fleet, and my word is law."

"So it is," said Pike. "And your word is in the articles under which we sailed with you."

"To hell with the articles!" roared Captain Easterling.

He rose and stood over Pike, towering and menacing, his head almost touching the ceiling of the cabin. He spoke deliberately. "I'm telling you things is changed since we signed them articles. What I says is more nor any articles, and what I says is that the Valiant can have a tenth share of the plunder. Ye'd be wise to take it, remembering the saying that who tries to grasp too much ends by holding nothing."

Pike stared up at him with fallen jaw. He had turned pale from the stress of the conflict within him between rage and prudence.

"By God, Easterling..." He broke off abruptly.

Easterling scowled down upon him. "Continue," he commanded. "Finish what ye has to say."

Pike shrugged despondently. "Ye know I dursn't accept your offer. Ye know my men would tear me in pieces if I did so without consulting them."

"Then away with you to consult them. I've a mind to slit your pimpish ears so that they may see what happens to them as gets pert with Captain Easterling. You may tell your scum that if they has the impudence to refuse my offer they needn't trouble to send you here again. They can up anchor and be off to Hell. Remind 'em of what I says: that who tries to grasp too much ends by holding nothing. Away with you, Captain Pike, with that message."

Not until he was back aboard his own ship did Captain Pike release the rage from which he all but bursted. And the sound of it, the tale he told in the ship's waist with the survivors of his crew about him, aroused in his violent followers a rage to match his own. Trenam added fuel to the flames by the views he expressed.

"If the swine means to break faith is it likely he'll stop half-way? Depend on it, if we accept this tenth, he'll find a pretext to cheat us of all. Captain Blood was in the right. We should never ha' put our trust in that son of a dog."

One of the hands spoke up, voicing the feelings of all. "But since we've put it, we've got to see he keeps it."

Pike, who was leaning by now to Trenam's despondent view of their case, waited for the chorus of angry approval to subside.

"Will you tell me how we are to do it? We are some forty men against three hundred. A twenty-gun brig against two frigates with fifty guns of heavier weight between them."

This gave them pause until another bold one spoke. "He says a tenth or naught. Our answer is a third or naught. There's honour among buccaneers, and we hold him to his pledge, to the articles upon which the dirty thief enlisted us."

As one man the crew supported him. "Go you back with that answer, Captain."

"And if he refuses?"

It was Trenam who now thought he held the answer.

"There's ways of compelling him. Tell him we'll raise the whole Brotherhood of the Coast against him. Captain Blood will see that we have justice. Captain Blood's none so fond of him, as he well knows. Remind him of that, Captain. Go you back and tell him."

It was a powerful card to play. Pike realized this: yet he confessed that he did not relish the task of playing it. But his men turned upon him with up-braidings. It was he who had persuaded them to follow Easterling. It was he who had not known how to make a stand against Easterling's encroachments from the outset. They had done their part. It was for him to see to it that they were not cheated of their pay.

So back from the Valiant at her anchorage in the very neck of the harbour went Captain Pike in the cockboat to convey his men's answer to Captain Easterling, and to hoist the bogey of Captain Blood and the Brethren of the Coast, upon which he depended now for his own safety.

The interview took place in the waist of the Avenger before an audience of her crew and in the presence of Captain Galloway, who was still aboard her. It was short and violent.

When Captain Pike had stated that his men insisted upon the fulfilment of the terms of the articles, Easterling laughed. His crew laughed with him; some there were who cheered Pike ironically.

"If that's their last word, my man," said Easterling, "they can up anchor and away to the devil. I've no more to say to them."

"It'll be the worse for you, Captain, if they go," said Pike steadily.

"D'ye threaten, by God!" The man's great bulk seemed to swell with rage.

"I warn you, Captain."

"You warn me? Warn me of what?"

"That the Brethren of the Coast, the whole buccaneering fraternity, will be raised against you for this breach of faith."

"Breach of faith!" Easterling's voice soared in pitch. "Breach of faith, ye bastard scum! D'ye dare stand before my face and say that to me?" He plucked a pistol from his belt. "Be off this ship at once, and tell your blackguards that if the Valiant is still there by noon I'll blow her out of the water. Away with you."

Pike, choking with indignation, and made bold by it, played his master card.

"Very well," said he. "You'll have Captain Blood to deal with for this."

Pike had reckoned upon intimidating, but neither upon the extent to which his words would achieve it, nor the blind fury that follows panic in such natures as that of the man with whom he dealt.

"Captain Blood?" Easterling spoke through his teeth, his great face purple. "You'll go whining to Captain Blood, will you? Go whine in Hell, then."

And on the word, at point-blank range, he shot Pike through the head.

The buccaneers standing about them recoiled in momentary horror as the man's body went backwards across the hatch coaming. Easterling jeered coarsely at their squeamishness. Galloway looked on, his little eyes glittering, his face inscrutable.

"Take up that carrion." Easterling pointed with his still smoking pistol. "Hang it from the yard-arm. Let it serve as a warning to those swine on the Valiant of what happens to them as gets pert with Captain Easterling."

A long-drawn cry, in which anger, fear and pity were all blended, went up from the deck of Pike's ship when her crew, crowding the larboard bulwarks, perceived through the rigging of the Hermes, the limp body of their captain swinging from the yardarm of the Avenger. So intent were these men that they paid no heed to the two long Indian canoes that came alongside to starboard, or even to the tall gentleman in black and silver who stepped from the accommodation ladder to the deck behind them. Not until his crisp dry voice rang out were they aware of him.

"I arrive a trifle late, it seems."

They turned and beheld him on the hatch-coaming, his left hand on the pummel of his rapier, his face in the shadow of his broad plumed hat, his eyes hard and cold with anger. Asking themselves how he came there, they stared at him as if he were an apparition, mystified, incredulous, doubting their vision.

At last young Trenam sprang towards him, his eyes blazing with excitement in his grey face. "Captain Blood! Is it indeed you? But how—?"

Captain Blood quieted him by a wave of the long supple hand emerging from the foam of lace at his wrist. "I've never been far from you ever since you landed on Darien. I know your case, and this is no more than I foresaw. But I had hoped to avert it."

"You'll call a reckoning from that treacherous dog?"

"To be sure I will, and at once. That hideous gesture demands an instant answer." His voice was as grim as his countenance. "You have men here to lay the guns. Get them below at once."

The Valiant had been swinging with the first of the gentle ebb when Blood stepped aboard; she stood now. In the line of the channel, so that the operation of opening the gun-ports could not be discerned from the other ships.

"The guns?" gasped Trenam. "But, Captain, we're in no case to fight. We've neither the men nor the metal."

"Enough for what's to do. Men and guns are not all that count in these affairs. Easterling gave you this station so that you should cover the other ships." Blood uttered a short stern laugh. "He shall learn the strategic disadvantages of it, so he shall. Get your gun crew below." Then he gave other orders briskly. "Eight of you to man the longboat. There are two canoes astern well-manned to assist you warp your ship broadside when the time comes. The ebbing tide will help you. Send aloft every man you can spare, to loose sail once we're out of the channel. Bestir, Trenam! Bestir!"

He dived below to the main deck, where the gun crew was already at work clearing the guns for action. He stimulated the men by his words and manner, and received unquestioning obedience from them; for, without understanding what might be afoot, they were stirred almost to enthusiasm by their confidence in him and their assurance that he would avenge upon Easterling their captain's murder and their own wrongs.

When all was ready and the matches glowing he went on deck again.

The two canoes manned by Mosquito Indians and the Valiant's longboat were astern under her counter and invisible to those aboard the other two ships. Towing-ropes had been attached, and the men waited for the word of command.

At Blood's suggestion Trenam, did not wait to take up anchor, but slipped his cable, and the oarsmen bent to their task of warping the ship round. Labours which would not in themselves have sufficed were made easy by the ebb, and slowly the brigantine began to swing broadside across the channel. Already Blood was below again, directing the hands that manned the starboard guns. Five of these were to be concentrated on the rudder of the Hermes, the other five were to sweep her shrouds.

As the Valiant swung about and the warping operations became apparent to the men on the other ships it was assumed by them that, panic-stricken by the fate of their captain, the crew of the brigantine had resolved on flight. From the decks of the Hermes a derisive valedictory cheer rang out. But scarcely had it died away, and just as it was being taken up by the Avenger, it was answered by the roar of ten guns at point-blank range.

The Hermes rocked and shuddered under the impact of that unexpected broadside, and the fierce outcries of her men were mingled with the hoarse voices of the startled sea-birds that rose to circle in alarm.

Blood was on deck again almost before the reverberations had rolled away. He peered through the rising cloud of smoke and smiled. The rudder of the Hermes had been shattered, her mainmast was broken and hung precariously suspended in her shrouds, whilst a rent showed in the bulwarks of her forecastle.

"And now?" quoth Trenam in uneasy excitement.

Blood looked round. They were moving steadily if slowly down the short channel, and were already almost in the open sea. A steady breeze was blowing from the north. "Crowd on sail, and let her run before the wind."

"They'll follow," said the young mariner. "Why, so I trust. But not yet awhile. Take a look at their plight."

It was only the that Trenam understood precisely what Blood had done. With her broken rudder and shattered mainmast, the Hermes, whilst being herself unmanageable, was blocking the way and making it impossible for the raging Easterling to get past her and attack the Valiant.

Trenam perceived and admired, but was still far from easy. "If you've invited pursuit, it's true that you've certainly delayed it. But it will surely come, and we shall be as surely sunk when it does. It's just what that devil Easterling desires."

"Indeed, and I hope so; and, anyway, I've quickened those same desires of his."

They had picked up the crew of the longboat, whilst the Indian canoes could be seen making off to the north along the reef. The Valiant was now running before the wind and Gallows Key was dropping swiftly astern. All hands were on deck. From the pooprail, where he leaned beside Trenam, Blood spoke to the man at the whipstaff below.

"Put up the helm. We go about." Perceiving Trenam's alarm, he smiled. "Quiet you. Have faith in me, and man the larboard guns. They'll not yet have disentagled themselves, and we'll give them a salute in passing. Faith now, ye may trust me. It's by no means the first action I've fought, and I know the fool I'm engaging. It won't have occurred to him that we might have the impudence to return, and I'll wager your share of Morgan's treasure that he won't have so much as opened his ports as yet."

It fell out as he foretold. When they ran in, close-hauled, they saw that the Hermes had only just been warped aside to give passage to the Avenger, which with sprit-sail, sweeps, and the ebb to assist her, was crawling towards the channel.

Easterling must have rubbed his eyes at this reappearance of the Valiant, which he was imagining in full flight; he must have ground his strong white teeth when she hung there an instant with slatting sails and poured a broadside athwart his decks before going off again on a north-easterly tack. He replied in haste and ineffectively with his chasers, and whilst the mess made by the Valiant's guns was being cleared up, he settled down vindictively to a pursuit which must end in the sinking of the audacious brigantine with every hand aboard.

The Valiant was perhaps a mile away to the northeast when Trenam beheld the Avenger emerge from the narrow roadstead and take the open sea to come ploughing after them with crowded yards. It was a dismaying vision. He turned to Captain Blood.

"And now, Captain? What remains?"

"To go about again," was the surprising answer. "Bid the helmsman steer for the northernmost point of the Key yonder."

"That will bring us within range."

"No matter. We'll run the gauntlet of his fire. At need we can round the point. But I've a notion the need will not present itself."

They went about, and ran in once more, Blood scanning the rocky coast of the island the while through the telescope. Trenam stood fretful at his elbow.

"What do you look for, Captain?" he wondered with faint hope.

"My Indian friends. They've made good speed. They've gone. All should be well."

To Trenam it seemed that things would be anything but well. The Avenger had veered a point nearer to the wind, so as to shorten the work of intercepting them. From her forward ports a gun boomed, and a round shot flung up the spray half a cable's length astern of the Valiant.

"He's getting the range," said Blood indifferently.

"Aye," agreed Trenam with bitter dryness. "We've let you have your way unquestioned, Captain. But what's to be the end?"

"I fancy it's coming yonder under full sail," said Captain Blood, and he pointed with the telescope.

Round the northern point of Gallows Key came a great red-hulled ship under a mountain of canvas that gleamed like snow in the noontide sunshine. Veering south as she appeared, she swept majestically on before the wind, a thing of beauty and of power, from gilded beak-head to lofty poop-lantern. She was abeam of the Valiant between the brigantine and island, before the dumbfounded Trenam found his voice, and before the voices of the crew were raised to cheer and cheer again.

Pale with excitement, his eyes sparkling, Trenam swung to Captain Blood. "The Arabella!"

Blood smiled upon him quizzically. "To be sure ye supposed I swam here, or crossed the ocean in a canoe; or may be ye thought I wanted to be chased by Easterling just for the fun of running away and the joy of being drowned at the end of it. Ye hadn't thought about these things maybe. Neither, had Easterling. But he's thinking about them now, so he is. Thinking hard, I dare swear."

But Easterling was doing nothing of the kind. His wits were paralysed. In the madness of despair, seeing himself beset by that formidable ship, which, moreover, had the weather gauge of him, he attempted to run for shelter back to the harbour from which he had been lured. Once there, with the guns of the Hermes to support his own, he might have held the narrow roadstead against all comers. But he should have known that he would never be allowed to reach it. When he ignored the shot athwart his bows, summoning him to strike his colours, a broadside of twenty heavy guns crashed into his exposed flank, and wrought such damage in it that he was bereft of even the satisfaction of replying. The Arabella, well handled by old Wolverstone, who was in command of her, went promptly about, and at still closer range poured in a second broadside to complete the business. Hard hit between wind and water, the Avenger was seen to be settling down by the head.

A sound like a wail arose from the deck of the Valiant. It startled Blood.

"What is it? What do they cry?"

"The treasure!" Trenam answered him. "Morgan's treasure!"

Blood frowned. "Faith, Wolverstone must ha' forgotten it in his fury." Then the frown cleared. He sighed and shrugged. "Ah well! It's gone now, so it has. Bad cess to it."

The Arabella hove to and lowered her boats to pick up the survivors struggling in the water. Easterling, lacking the courage to drown, was amongst them, and by Blood's direction he was brought aboard theValiant. Thus was the iron driven deep into his soul. But deeper still was it to be driven when he stepped on to the deck of Pike's ship to find himself confronting Captain Blood. It had been no bogey, then, with which Pike's last words had threatened him. He recoiled as if at last, and for once in his life, afraid. The dark eyes smouldered in his grey face with the mingled fury and terror to be seen in those of a trapped animal.

"So it was you!" he ejaculated.

"If ye mean it was I who took Pike's place when ye murdered him, ye're right. Ye'd had done better to have been honest with him. There's a maxim ye should have learnt at school, that honesty is the best policy. Though perhaps ye never were at school. But there's another maxim of which I made you a present years ago and which they tell me that ye're fond of quoting: Who seeks to grasp too much ends by holding nothing."

He waited for a reply, but none came. Easterling, his great bulk sagging, glowered at him silently with those dark feral eyes.

Blood sighed, and moved towards the head of the accommodation ladder.

"Ye're no affair of mine. I leave ye to these men you have wronged, and whose leader you have murdered. It is for them to judge you."

He went down to the boat that had brought Easterling aboard, and so back to the Arabella, his task accomplished, and his long duel with Easterling at last concluded.

An hour later the Arabella and the Valiant were running south together. Gallows Key was falling rapidly astern, and Galloway and his crew aboard the crippled Hermes imprisoned in the lagoon were left to conjecture what had happened outside and to extricate themselves as best they could from their own difficulties.

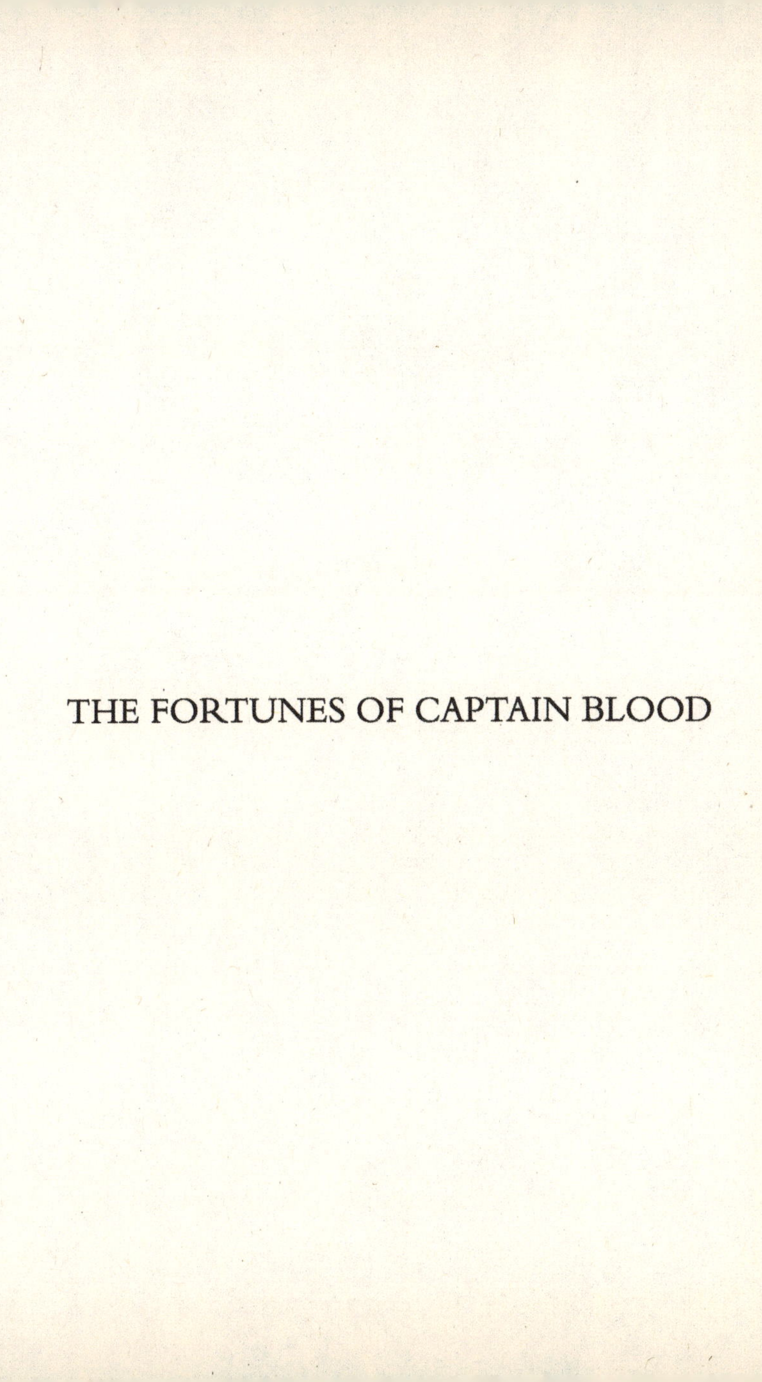

THE FORTUNES OF CAPTAIN BLOOD

CONTENTS

Episode 1

THE DRAGON'S JAW

I

She was a beautiful ship, in the frigate class, fashioned, not merely in her lines, but in her details, with an extreme of that loving care that Spanish builders not infrequently bestowed. She had been named, as if to blend piety with loyalty, the San Felipe, and she had been equipped with a fastidiousness to match the beauty of her lines.

The great cabin, flooded with sunlight from the tall stern windows of horn, which now stood open above the creaming wake, had been made luxurious by richly carved furnishings, by hangings of green damask and by the gilded scrollwork of the bulkheads. Here Peter Blood, her present owner, bending over the Spaniard who reclined on a day bed by the stern locker, was reverting for the moment to his original trade of surgery. His hands, as strong as they were shapely, and by deftness rendered as delicate of touch as a woman's, had renewed the dressing of the Spaniard's thigh, where the fractured bone had pierced the flesh. He made now a final adjustment of the strappings that held the splint in place, stood up, and by a nod dismissed the black man steward who had been his acolyte.

'It is very well, Don Ilario.' He spoke quietly in a Spanish that was fluent and even graceful. 'I can now give you my word that you will walk on your two legs again.'

A wan smile dispelled some of the shadows from the hollows which suffering had dug in the patient's patrician countenance. 'For that,' he said, 'the thanks to God and you. A miracle.'

'No miracle at all. Just surgery.'

'Ah! But the surgeon, then? That is the miracle. Will men believe me when I say I was made whole again by Captain Blood?'

The Captain, tall and lithe, was in the act of rolling down the sleeves of his fine cambric shirt. Eyes startlingly blue under black eyebrows, in a hawk-face tanned to the colour of mahogany, gravely considered the Spaniard.

'Once a surgeon, always a surgeon,' he said, as if by way of explanation. 'And I was a surgeon once, as you may have heard.'

'As I have discovered for myself, to my profit. But by what queer alchemy of Fate does a surgeon become a buccaneer?'

Captain Blood smiled reflectively. 'My troubles came upon me from considering only—as in your case—a surgeon's duty; from beholding in a wounded man a patient, without concern for how he came by his wounds. He was a poor rebel who had been out with the Duke of Monmouth. Who comforts a rebel is himself a rebel. So runs the law among Christian men. I was taken red-handed in the abominable act of dressing his wounds, and for that I was sentenced to death. The penalty was commuted, not from mercy. Slaves were needed in the plantations. With a shipload of other wretches, I was carried overseas to be sold in Barbados. I escaped, and I think I must have died at somewhere about the time that Captain Blood came to life. But the ghost of the surgeon still walks in the body of the buccaneer, as you have found, Don Ilario.'

'To my great profit and deep gratitude. And the ghost still practises the dangerous charity that slew the surgeon?'

'Ah!' The vivid eyes flashed him a searching look, observed the flush on the Spaniard's pallid cheekbones, the queer expression of his glance.

'You are not afraid that history may repeat itself?'

'I do not care to be afraid of anything,' said Captain Blood, and he reached for his coat. He settled to his shoulders the black satin garment rich with silver lace, adjusted before a mirror the costly Mechlin at his throat, shook out the curls of his black periwig, and stood forth, an elegant incarnation of virility, more proper to the ante-chambers of the Escurial than to the quarter-deck of a buccaneer ship.

'You must rest now and endeavour to sleep until eight bells is made. You show no sign of fever. But tranquillity is still my prescription for you. At eight bells I will return.'

The patient, however, showed no disposition to be tranquil.

'Don Pedro... Before you go... Wait. This situation puts me to shame. I cannot lie so under this great obligation to you. I sail under false colours.'

Blood's shaven lips had an ironic twist. 'I have, myself, found it convenient at times.'

'Ah, but how different! My honour revolts.' Abruptly, his dark eyes steadily meeting the Captain's, he continued: 'You know me only as one of four shipwrecked Spaniards you rescued from that rock of the St Vincent Keys and have generously undertaken to land at San Domingo. Honour insists that you should know more.'

Blood seemed mildly amused. 'I doubt if you could add much to my knowledge. You are Don Ilario de Saavedra, the King of Spain's new Governor of Hispaniola. Before the gale that wrecked you, your ship formed part of the squadron of the Marquis of Riconete, who is to co-operate with you in the Caribbean in the extermination of that endemonized pirate and buccaneer, that enemy of God and Spain, whose name is Peter Blood.'

Don Ilario's blank face betrayed the depth of his astonishment. 'Virgen Santissima—Virgin Most Holy! You know that?'

'With commendable prudence you put your commission in your pocket when your ship was about to founder. With a prudence no less commendable, I took a look at it soon after you came aboard. We are not fastidious in my trade.'

If the simple explanation removed one astonishment, it replaced it by another. 'And in spite of that, you not only use me tenderly, you actually convey me to San Domingo!' Then his expression changed. 'Ah, I see. You trust my gratitude, and...'

But there Captain Blood interrupted him. 'Gratitude?' He laughed. 'It is the last emotion in which I should put my trust. I trust to nothing but myself, sir. I have told you that I do not care to be afraid of anything. Your obligation is not to the buccaneer, it is to the surgeon; and that is an obligation to a ghost. So dismiss it. Do not trouble your mind with problems of where your duty lies: whether to me or to your king. I am forewarned. That is enough for me. Give yourself peace, Don Ilario.'

He departed, leaving the Spaniard bewildered and bemused.

Coming out into the waist, where some two score of his buccaneers, the half of the ship's full company, were idling, he detected a sullenness in the air, which earlier had been fresh and clear. There had, however, been no steadiness in the weather since the hurricane some ten days ago, on the morrow of which he had rescued the injured Don Ilario and his three companions from the rocky islet on which the storm had cast them up. It was due to these country winds of some violence, with intermittent breathless calms, that the San Felipe was still no nearer to her destination than a point some twenty miles south of Saona. She was barely crawling over a gently heaving oily sea of deepest violet, her sails alternately swelling and sagging. The distant highlands of Hispaniola on the starboard quarter, which earlier had been clearly visible, had vanished now behind an ashen haze.

Chaffinch, the sailing master, standing by the whip staff at the break of the poop, spoke to him as he passed. 'There's more mischief coming, Captain. I begin to doubt if we'll ever make San Domingo. We've a Jonah aboard.'

So far as the mischief went, Chaffinch was not mistaken. It came on to blow from the west at noon, and brought up such a storm that his lightly expressed doubt of ever making San Domingo came before midnight to be seriously entertained by every man aboard. Under a deluge of rain, to the crash of thunder, and with great seas pounding over her, the San Felipe rode out a gale that bore her steadily northwestwards. Not until daybreak did the last of the hurricane sweep past her, leaving her, dipping and heaving on a black sea of long smooth rollers, to cast up her damage and lick her wounds. Her poop-rail had been shorn away, and her swivel-guns had gone with it overboard. From the boom amidships one of her boats had been carried off, and some parts of the wreckage of another lay tangled in the forechains.

But of all that she had suffered above deck the most serious damage was to her mainmast. It had been sprung, and was not merely useless but a source of danger. Against all this, however, they could set it that the storm had all but swept them to their destination. Less than five miles ahead, to the north, stood El Rosarto, beyond which lay San Domingo. Into the Spanish waters of that harbour and under the guns of King Philip's fortresses, Don Ilario, for his own sake, must supply them with safe conduct.

It was still early morning, brilliant now and sparkling after the tempest, when the battered ship, with mizzen and foresails ballooning to the light airs, but not a rag on her mainmast save the banner of Castile at its summit, staggered past the natural breakwater, which the floods of the Ozama have long since eroded, and came by the narrow eastern passage that was known as the Dragon's Jaw into the harbour of San Domingo.

She found eight fathoms close alongside of a shore that was reared like a mole on a foundation of coral, forming an island less than a quarter of a mile in width by nearly a mile in length, with a shallow ridge along the middle of it crowned by some clusters of cabbage-palms. Here the San Felipe dropped anchor and fired a gun to salute the noblest city of New Spain across the spacious harbour.

White and fair that city stood in its emerald setting of wide savannahs, a place of squares and palaces and churches that might have been transported from Castile, dominated by the spire of the cathedral that held the ashes of Columbus.

There was a stir along the white mole, and soon a string of boats came speeding towards the San Felipe, led by a gilded barge of twenty oars, trailing the red-and-yellow flag of Spain. Under a red awning fringed with gold sat a portly, swarthy, blue-jowled gentleman in pale-brown taffetas and a broad plumed hat, who wheezed and sweated when presently he climbed the accommodation-ladder to the waist of the San Felipe.

There Captain Blood, in black-and-silver splendour, stood to receive him beside the day-bed on which the helpless Don Ilario had been carried from the cabin. In attendance upon him stood his three shipwrecked companions, and for background there was a file of buccaneers, tricked out in headpieces and corselets to look like Spanish infantry, standing with ordered muskets.

But Don Clemente Pedroso, the retiring Governor, whom Don Ilario came to replace, was not deceived. A year ago, off Puerto Rico, on the deck of a galleon that Captain Blood had boarded and sacked, Pedroso had stood face to face with the buccaneer, and Blood's was not a countenance that was easily forgotten. Don Clemente checked abruptly in his advance.

Into his swarthy, pear-shaped face came a blend of fear and fury.

Urbanely, plumed hat in hand, the Captain bowed to him.

'Your Excellency's memory honours me, I think. But do not suppose that I fly false colours.' He pointed aloft to the flag which had earned the San Felipe the civility of this visit. 'That is due to the presence aboard of Don Ilario de Saavedra, King Philip's new Governor of Hispaniola.'

Don Clemente lowered his eyes to the pallid, proud face of the man on the day-bed, and stood speechless, breathing noisily, whilst Don Ilario in a few words explained the situation and proffered a commission still legible if sadly blurred by seawater. The three Spaniards who had been rescued with him were also presented, and there was assurance that all further confirmation would be supplied by the Marquis of Riconete, the Admiral of the Ocean-Sea, whose squadron should very soon be at San Domingo.

In a scowling silence Don Clemente listened; in scowling silence he scanned the new Governor's commission. Thereafter he strove, from prudence, to wrap in a cold dignity the rage which the situation and the sight of Captain Blood aroused in him.

But he was in obvious haste to depart. 'My barge, Don Ilario, is at your Excellency's orders. There is, I think, nothing to detain us.'

And he half turned away scorning in his tremendous dignity further to notice Captain Blood.

'Nothing,' said Don Ilario, 'beyond expressions of gratitude to my preserver and provision for his requital.'

Don Clemente, without turning, answered sourly. 'Naturally, I suppose, it becomes necessary to permit him a free withdrawal.'

'I should be shamed by so poor and stingy an acknowledgment,' said Don Ilario, 'especially in the present condition of his ship.

It is a poor enough return for the great service he has rendered me to permit him to supply himself here with wood and water and fresh victuals and with boats to replace those which he has lost. He must also be accorded sanctuary at San Domingo to carry out repairs.'

Captain Blood interposed. 'For those repairs I need not be troubling San Domingo. The island here will excellently serve, and, by your leave, Don Clemente, I shall temporarily take possession of it.'

Don Clemente, who had stood fuming during Don Ilario's announcement, swung about now and exploded. 'By my leave?' His face was yellow. 'I render thanks to God and His Saints that I am relieved of that shame since Don Ilario is now the Governor.'

Saavedra frowned. He spoke with languid sternness.

'You will bear that in your memory, if you please, Don Clemente, and trim your tone to it.'

'Oh, your Excellency's servant.' The deposed Governor bowed in raging irony. 'It is, of course, yours to command how long this enemy of God and of Spain shall enjoy the hospitality and protection of His Catholic Majesty.'

'For as long as he may need so as to carry out his repairs.'

'I see. And once these are effected, he is, of course, to be free to depart, so that he may continue to harass and plunder the ships of Spain?'

Frostily Saavedra answered: 'He has my word that he shall be free to go, and that for forty-eight hours thereafter there shall be no pursuit or other measure against him.'

'And he has your word for that? By all the Hells! He has your word...'

Blandly Captain Blood cut in. 'And it occurs to me that it would be prudent to have your word as well, my friend.'

He was moved by no fear for himself, but only by generosity to Don Ilario: to link the old Governor and the new in responsibility, so that Don Clemente might not hereafter make for his successor the mischief of which Blood perceived him capable.

Don Clemente was aghast. Furiously he waved his fat hands. 'My word? My word!' He choked with rage. His countenance swelled as if it would burst. 'You think I'll pass my word to a pirate rogue? You think...'

'Oh, as you please. If you prefer it I can put you under hatches and in irons, and keep both you and Don Ilario aboard until I am ready to sail again.'

'It's an outrage.'

Captain Blood shrugged. 'You may call it that. I call it holding hostages.'

Don Clemente glared at him with increasing malice. 'I must protest. Under constraint...'

'There's no constraint at all. You'll give me your word, or I'll put you in irons. Ye've a free choice. Where's the constraint?'

Then Don Ilario cut in. 'Come, sir, come! This wrangling is monstrously ungracious. You'll pledge your word, sir, or take the consequences.'

And so, for all his bitterness, Don Clemente suffered the reluctant pledge to be wrung from him.

After that, in contrast with his furious departure was Don Ilario's gracious leave-taking when they were about to lower his day-bed in slings to the waiting barge. He and Captain Blood parted with mutual compliments and expressions of goodwill, which it was perfectly understood should nowise hinder the active hostility imposed by duty upon Don Ilario once the armistice were at an end.

Blood smiled as he watched the red barge with its trailing flag ploughing with flash of oars across the harbour towards the mole. Some of the lesser boats went with it. Others, laden with fruit and vegetables, fresh meat and fish, remained on the flank of the San Felipe, little caring, in their anxiety to trade their wares, that she might be a pirate.

Wolverstone, the one-eyed giant who had shared Blood's escape from Barbados and had since been one of his closest associates, leaned beside him on the bulwarks. 'Ye'll not be trusting overmuch, I hope, to the word of that flabby, blue-faced Governor?'

'It's hateful, so it is, to be by nature suspicious, Ned. Hasn't he pledged himself, and would ye do him the wrong to suspect his bona fides? I cry shame on you, Ned; but all the same we'll be removing temptation from him, so we will, by fortifying ourselves on the island here.'

II

They set about it at once, with the swift, expert activity of their kind. Gangways were constructed, connecting the ship with the island, and on that strip of sand and coral they landed the twenty-four guns of the San Felipe, and so emplaced them that they commanded the harbour. They erected a tent of sail-cloth, felling palms to supply the poles, set up a forge, and, having unstepped the damaged mast, hauled it ashore so that they might repair it there. Meanwhile the carpenters aboard went about making good the damage to the upper works, whilst parties of buccaneers in the three boats supplied to them by the orders of Don Ilario went to procure wood and water and the necessary stores, for all of which Captain Blood scrupulously paid.

For two days they laboured without disturbance or distraction. When on the morning of the third day the alarm came, it was not from the harbour or the town before them, but from the open sea at their backs.

Captain Blood was fetched ashore at sunrise, so that from the summit of the ridge he might survey the approaching peril. With him went Wolverstone and Chaffinch, Hagthorpe, the West Country gentleman who shared their fortunes, and Ogle, who once had been a gunner in the King's Navy.

Less than a mile away they beheld a squadron of five tall ships approaching in a bravery of ensigns and pennants, all canvas spread to the light but quickening morning airs. Even as they gazed, a white cloud of smoke blossomed like a cauliflower on the flank of the leading galleon, and the boom of a saluting gun came to arouse a city that as yet was barely stirring.

'A lovely sight,' said Chaffinch.

'For a poet or a shipmaster,' said Blood. 'But I'm neither of those this morning. I'm thinking this will be King Philip's Admiral of the Ocean-Sea, the Marquis of Riconete.'

'And he's pledged no word not to molest us,' was Wolverstone's grim and unnecessary reminder.

'But I'll see to it that he does before ever we let him through the Dragon's Jaw.' Blood turned on his heel, and, making a trumpet of his hands, sounded his orders sharp and clearly to some two or three score buccaneers who stood also at gaze, some way behind them, by the guns.

Instantly those hands were seething to obey, and for the next five minutes all was a bustle of heaving and hauling to drag the San Felipe's two stern chasers to the summit of the ridge. They were demi-cannon, with a range of fully a mile and a half, and they were no sooner in position than Ogle was laying one of them. At a word from Blood he touched off the gun, and sent a thirty-pound shot athwart the bows of the advancing Admiral, three-quarters of a mile away.

There is no signal to lie hove to that will command a more prompt compliance. Whatever the Marquis of Riconete's astonishment at this thunderbolt from a clear sky, it brought him up with a round turn. The helm was put over hard, and the Admiral swung to larboard with idly flapping sails. Faintly over the sunlit waters came the sound of a trumpet, and the four ships that followed executed the same manoeuvre. Then from the Admiral a boat was lowered, and came speeding towards the reef to investigate this portent.

Peter Blood, with Chaffinch and a half-score men, was at the water's edge when the boat grounded. Wolverstone and Hagthorpe had taken station on the other side of the island, so as to watch the harbour and the mole, which was now all agog.

An elegant young officer stepped ashore to request on the Admiral's behalf an explanation of the sinister greeting he had received. It was supplied.

'I am here refitting my ship by permission of Don Ilario de Saavedra, in return for some small service I had the honour to do him when he was lately shipwrecked. Before I can suffer the Admiral of the Ocean-Sea to enter this harbour I must possess his confirmation of Don Ilario's sanction and his pledge that he will leave me in peace to complete my repairs.'

The young officer stiffened with indignation. 'These are extraordinary words, sir. Who are you?'

'My name is Blood. Captain Blood, at your service.'

'Captain... Captain Blood!' The young man's eyes were round. 'You are Captain Blood?' Suddenly he laughed. 'You have the effrontery to suppose...'

He was interrupted. 'I do not like "effrontery". And as for what I suppose, be good enough to come with me. It will save argument.' He led the way to the summit of the ridge, the Spaniard sullenly following. There he paused. 'You were about to tell me, of course, that I had better be making my soul, because the guns of your squadron will blow me off this island. Be pleased to observe.'

He pointed with his long ebony cane to the activity below, where a motley buccaneer host was swarming about the landed cannon. Six of the guns were being hauled into a new position so as completely to command at point-blank range the narrow channel of the Dragon's Jaw. On the seaward side, whence it might be assailed, this battery was fully protected by the ridge.

'You will understand the purpose of these measures,' said Captain Blood. 'And you may have heard that my gunnery is of exceptional excellence. Even if it were not, I might without boasting assert—and you, I am sure, are of intelligence to perceive—that the first ship to thrust her bowsprit across that line will be sunk before she can bring a gun to bear.' He leaned upon his tall cane, the embodiment of suavity. 'Inform your Admiral, with my service, of what you have seen, and assure him from me that he may enter the harbour of San Domingo the moment he has given me the pledge I ask; but not a moment sooner.' He waved a hand in dismissal. 'God be with you, sir. Chaffinch, escort the gentleman to his boat.'

In his anger the Spaniard failed to do justice to so courteous an occasion. He muttered some Spanish mixture of theology and bawdiness, and flung away in a pet, without farewells. Back to the Admiral he was rowed. But either he did not report accurately or else the Admiral was of those who will not be convinced. For an hour later the ridge was being ploughed by round-shot, and the morning air shaken by the thunder of the squadron's guns. It distressed the gulls and set them circling and screaming overhead. But it distressed the buccaneers not at all, sheltered behind the natural bastion of the ridge from that storm of iron.

During a slackening of the fire, Ogle wriggled snakewise up to the demi-cannons which had been so emplaced that they thrust their muzzles and no more above the ridge. He laid one of them with slow care. The Spaniards, formed in line ahead for the purposes of their bombardment, three-quarters of a mile away, offered a target that could hardly be missed. Ogle touched off the unsuspected gun, and a thirty-pound shot crashed amidships into the bulwarks of the middle galleon. It went to warn the Marquis that he was not to be allowed to practise his gunnery with impunity.

There was a blare of trumpets and a hasty going about of the entire squadron to beat up against the freshening wind. To speed them, Ogle fired the second gun, and although lethally the shot was harmless, morally it could scarcely fail of its alarming purpose. Then he whistled up his gun-crew to re-load at leisure in that moment of the enemy's fleeing panic.

All day the Spaniards remained hove to a mile and a half away, where they accounted themselves out of range. Blood took advantage of this to order six more guns to be hauled to the ridge, and so as to form a breastwork half the palms on the island were felled. Whilst the main body of the buccaneers, clothed only in loose leather breeches, made short work of this, the remainder under the orders of the carpenter calmly pursued the labours of refitting. The fire glowed in the forge, and the anvils pealed bell-like under the hammers.

Across the harbour and into this scene of heroic activity came towards evening Don Clemente Pedroso, greatly daring and more yellow-faced than ever. Conducted to the ridge, where Captain Blood with the help of Ogle was still directing the construction of the breastwork, his Excellency demanded furiously to know what the buccaneers supposed must be the end of this farce.

'If you think you're propounding a problem,' said Captain Blood, 'ye're mistook. It'll end when the Admiral gives me the pledge I've asked that he'll not molest me.'

Don Clemente's black eyes were malevolent, and malevolent was the crease at the base of his beaky nose. 'You do not know the Marquis of Riconete.'

'What's more to the matter is that the Marquis does not know me. But I think we shall soon be better acquainted.'

'You deceive yourself. The Admiral is bound by no promise made you by Don Ilario. He will never make terms with you.'

Captain Blood laughed in his face. 'In that case, faith, he can stay where he is until he reaches the bottom of his water-casks. Then he can either die of thirst or sail away to find water. Indeed, we may not have to wait so long. You've not observed perhaps that the wind is freshening from the south.

If it should come to blow in earnest, your Marquis may be in some discomfort off this coast.'

Don Clemente wasted some energy in vague blasphemies. Captain Blood was amused. 'I know how you suffer. You were already counting upon seeing me hanged.'

'Few things in this life would bring me greater satisfaction.'

'Alas! I must hope to disappoint your Excellency. You'll stay to sup aboard with me?'

'Sir, I do not sup with pirates.'

'Then you may go sup with the devil,' said Captain Blood. And on his short fat legs Don Clemente stalked in dudgeon back to his barge.

Wolverstone watched his departure with a brooding eye.

'Odslife, Peter, you'ld be wise to hold that Spanish gentleman. His pledge binds him no more than would a cobweb. The treacherous dog will spare nothing to do us a mischief, pledge or no pledge.'

'You're forgetting Don Ilario.'

'I'm thinking Don Clemente may forget him, too.'

'We'll be vigilant,' Blood promised confidently

That night the buccaneers slept as usual in their quarters aboard, but they left a gun-crew ashore and set a watch in a boat anchored in the Dragon's Jaw, lest the Admiral of Ocean-Sea should attempt to creep in. But although the night was clear, other risks apart, the Spaniards would not attempt the hazardous channel in the dark.

Throughout the next day, which was Sunday, the condition of stalemate continued. But on Monday morning the exasperated Admiral once more plastered the island with shot, and then stood boldly in to force a passage.

Ogle's battery had suffered no damage because the Admiral knew neither its position nor extent. Nor did Ogle now disclose it until the enemy was within a half-mile. Then four of his guns blazed at the leading ship. Two shots went wide, a third smashed into her tall forecastle, and the fourth caught her between wind and water and opened a breach through which the sea poured into her. The other three Spaniards veered in haste to starboard, and went off on an easterly tack. The crippled listed galleon went staggering after them, jettisoning in desperate haste her guns, and what other heavy gear she could spare, so as to bring the wound in her flank above the water-level.

Thus ended that attempt to force a way in, and by noon the Spaniards had gone about again and were back in their old position a mile and a half away. They were still there twenty-four hours later when a boat went out from San Domingo with a letter from Don Ilario in which the new Governor required the Marquis of Riconete to accord Captain Blood the terms he demanded. The boat had to struggle against a rising sea, for it was coming on to blow again, and from the south dark, ominous banks of cloud were rolling up. Apprehensions on the score of the weather may well have combined with Don Ilario's letter in persuading the Marquis to yield where obstinacy seemed to promise only humiliation.

So the officer by whom Captain Blood had already been visited came again to the island at the harbour's mouth, bringing him the required letter of undertaking from the Admiral, as a result of which the Spanish ships were that evening allowed to come into shelter from the rising storm. Unmolested they sailed through the Dragon's Jaw, and went to drop anchor across the harbour, by the town.

III

The wounds in the pride of the Marquis of Riconete were raw, and at the Governor's Palace that night there was a discussion of some heat. It beat to and fro between the dangerous doctrine expounded by the Admiral and supported by Don Clemente that an undertaking obtained by threats was not in honour binding, and the firm insistence of the chivalrous Don Ilario that the terms must be kept.

Wolverstone's mistrust of the operation of the Spanish conscience continued unabated, and nourished his contempt of Blood's faith in the word that had been pledged. Nor would he account sufficient the measures taken in emplacing the guns anew, so that all but six still left to command the Dragon's Jaw were now trained upon the harbour. His single eye remained apprehensively watchful in the three or four peaceful days that followed, but it was not until the morning of Friday, by when, the mast repaired, they were almost ready to put to sea, that he observed anything that he could account significant. What he observed then led him to call Captain Blood to the poop of the San Felipe.

'There's a queer coming and going of boats over yonder, between the Spanish squadron and the mole. Ye can see it for yourself. And it's been going on this half-hour and more. The boats go fully laden to the mole, and come back empty to the ships. Maybe ye'll guess the meaning of it.'

'The meaning's plain enough,' said Blood. 'The crews are being put ashore.'

'It's what I was supposing,' said Wolverstone. 'But will you tell me what sense or purpose there can be in that? Where there's no sense there's usually mischief. There'ld be no harm in having the men stand to their arms on the island tonight.'

The cloud on Blood's brow showed that his lieutenant had succeeded in stirring his suspicions. 'It's plaguily odd, so it is. And yet... Faith, I'll not believe Don Ilario would play me false.'

'I'm not thinking of Don Ilario, but of that bile-laden curmudgeon Don Clemente. That's not the man to let a pledged word thwart his spite. And if this Riconete is such another, as well he may be...'

'Don Ilario is the man in authority now.'

'Maybe. But he's crippled by a broken leg, and those other two might easily overbear him, knowing that King Philip himself would condone it.'

'But if they mean mischief, why should they be putting the crews ashore?'

'That's what I hoped you might guess, Peter.'

'Since I can't, I'd better go and find out.' A fruit-barge had just come alongside. Captain Blood leaned over the rail. 'Hey, you!' he hailed the owner. 'Bring me your yams aboard.'

He turned to beckon some of the hands in the waist and issued orders briefly whilst the fruit-seller was climbing the accommodation-ladder with a basket of yams balanced on his head. He was invited aft to the Captain's cabin, and, unsuspecting, went, after which he was seen no more that day. His half-caste mate, who had remained in the barge, was similarly lured aboard, and went to join his master under hatches. Then an unclean, bare-legged, sunburned fellow in the greasy shirt, loose calico breeches and swathed head of a waterside hawker went over the side of the San Felipe, climbed down into the barge, and pulled away across the harbour towards the Spanish ships, followed by anxious eyes from the bulwarks of the buccaneer vessel.

Bumping alongside of the Admiral, the hawker bawled his wares for some time in vain. The utter silence within those wooden walls was significant. After a while steps rang out on the deck. A sentry in a headpiece looked over the rail to bid him take his fruit to the devil, adding the indiscreet but already superfluous information that if he were not a fool he would know that there was no one aboard.

Bawling ribaldries in return, the hawker pulled away for the mole, climbed out of the barge, and went to refresh himself at a wayside tavern that was thronged with Spaniards from the ships. Over a pot of wine he insinuated himself into a group of these seamen, with an odd tale of wrongs suffered at the hands of pirates and a fiercely rancorous criticism of the Admiral for suffering the buccaneers to remain on the island at the harbour's mouth instead of blowing them to perdition.

His fluent Spanish admitted of no suspicion. His truculence and obvious hatred of pirates won him sympathy.

'It's not the Admiral,' a petty officer assured him. 'He'ld never have parleyed with these dogs. It's this weak-kneed new Governor of Hispaniola who's to blame. It's he who has given them leave to repair their ship.'

'If I were an Admiral of Castile,' said the hawker, 'I vow to the Virgin I'd take matters into my own hands.'

There was a general laugh, and a corpulent Spaniard clapped him on the back. 'The Admiral's of the same mind, my lad.'

'In spite of his flabbiness the Governor,' said a second.

'That's why we're all ashore,' nodded a third.

And now in scraps which the hawker was left to piece together forth came the tale of mischief that was preparing for the buccaneers.

So much to his liking did the hawker find the Spaniards, and so much to their liking did they find him, that the afternoon was well advanced before he rolled out of the tavern to find his barge and resume his trade. The pursuit of it took him back across the harbour, and when at last he came alongside the San Felipe he was seen to have a second and very roomy barge in tow. Making fast at the foot of the accommodation-ladder, he climbed to the ship's waist, where Wolverstone received him with relief and not without wrath.

'Ye said naught of going ashore, Peter. Where the plague was the need o' that? You'll be thrusting your head into a noose once too often.'

Captain Blood laughed. 'I've thrust my head into no noose at all. And if I had the result would have been worth the risk. I'm justified of my faith in Don Ilario. It's only because he's a man of his word that we may all avoid having our throats cut this night. For if he had given his consent to employ the men of the garrison, as Don Clemente wished, we should never have known anything about it until too late. Because he refused, Don Clemente has made alliance with that other forswarn scoundrel, the Admiral. Between them they've concocted a sweet plan behind Don Ilario's back. And that's why the Marquis has taken his crews ashore, so as to hold them in readiness for the job.

'They're to slip out to sea in boatloads at midnight by the shallow western passage, land on the unguarded southwest side of the island, and then, having entered by the back door as it were, creep across to surprise us on board the San Felipe and cut our throats whilst we sleep. There'll be some four hundred of them at the least. Practically every mother's son from the squadron. The Marquis of Riconete means to make sure that the odds are in his favour.'

'And we with eighty men in all!' Wolverstone rolled his single eye. 'But we're forewarned. We can shift the guns so as to smash them as they land.'

Blood shook his head. 'It can't be done without being noticed. If they saw us move the guns they must suppose we've got wind of what's coming. They'd change their plans, and that wouldn't suit me at all.'

'Wouldn't suit you! Does this camisado suit you?'

'Let me see the trap that's set for me, and it's odd if I can't turn it against the trapper. Did ye notice that I brought a second barge back with me? Forty men can pack into those two bottoms, the remainder can go in the four boats we have.'

'Go? Go where? D'ye mean to run, Peter?'

'To be sure I do. But no farther than will suit my purpose.'

He cut things fine. It wanted only an hour to midnight when he embarked his men. And even then he was in no haste to set out. He waited until the silence of the night was disturbed by a distant creak of rowlocks, which warned him that the Spaniards were well upon their way to the shallow passage on the western side of the island. Then, at last, he gave the word to push off, and the San Felipe was abandoned to the enemy stealing upon her through the night.

It would be fully an hour later, when the Spaniards, having landed, came like shadows over the ridge, some to take possession of the guns, others to charge across the gangways. They preserved a ghostly silence until they were aboard the San Felipe. Then they gave tongue loudly as stormers will, to encourage themselves. To their surprise, however, not all the din they made sufficed to arouse these pirate dogs, who, apparently, were all asleep so trustfully that they had set no watch.

A sense of something outside their calculations began to pervade them as they stood at fault, unable to understand this lack of life aboard the ship they had invaded. Then, suddenly, the darkness of the night was split by tongues of flame from across the harbour, and with a roar as of thunder a broadside of twenty guns crashed its metal into the flank of the San Felipe.

The surprise-party thus, itself, surprised, filled the night with a screaming babel of imprecations, and turned in frenzy to escape from a vessel that was beginning to founder. In the mad panic of men assailed by forces of destruction which they cannot understand, the Spaniards fought one another to reach the gangways and regain the comparative safety of the shore without thought or care for those who had been wounded by that murderous volley.

The Marquis of Riconete, a tall, gaunt man, strove furiously to rally them.

'Stand firm! In the name of God, stand firm, you dogs!'

His officers plunged this way and that into the fleeing mob, and with blows and oaths succeeded in restoring some measure of order. Whilst the San Felipe was settling down in eight fathoms, the men, ashore and re-formed at last, stood to their arms, waiting. But they no more knew for what they waited than did the Marquis, who was furiously demanding of Heaven and Hell the explanation of happenings so unaccountable.

It was soon afforded. Against the blackness of the night loomed ahead, in deeper blackness, the shape of a great ship that was slowly advancing towards the Dragon's Jaw. The splash of oars and the grating of rowlocks told that she was being warped out of the harbour, and to the straining ears of the Spaniards the creak of blocks and the rattle of spars presently bore the message that she was hoisting sail.

To the Marquis, peering with Don Clemente through the gloom, the riddle was solved. Whilst he had been leading the men of his squadron to seize a ship that he supposed to be full of buccaneers, the buccaneers had stolen across the harbour to take possession of a ship that they knew to be untenanted, and to turn her guns upon the Spaniards in the San Felipe. It was in that same vessel, the Admiral's flagship, the magnificent Maria Gloriosa of forty guns, with a fortune in her hold, that those accursed pirates were now putting to sea under the Admiral's impotent nose.

He said so in bitterness, and in bitterness raged awhile with Don Clemente, until the latter suddenly remembered the guns that Blood had trained upon the passage, guns that would still be emplaced and of a certainty loaded, since they had not been used. Frantically he informed the Admiral of how he might yet turn the tables on the buccaneers, and at the information the Admiral instantly took fire.

'I vow to Heaven,' he cried, 'that those dogs shall not leave San Domingo, though I have to sink my own ship. Ho there! The guns! To the guns!'

He led the way at a run, half a hundred men stumbling after him in the dark towards the channel battery. They reached it just as the Maria Gloriosa was entering the Dragon's Jaw. In less than five minutes she would be within point-blank range.

A miss would be impossible at such close quarters, and six guns stood ready trained.

'A gunner!' bawled the Marquis. 'At once a gunner, to sink me that infernal pirate into Hell.'

A man stood briskly forward. From the rear came a gleam of light, and a lantern was passed forward from hand to hand until it reached the gunner. He snatched it, ignited from its flames a length of fuse, then stepped to the nearest gun.

'Wait,' the Marquis ordered. 'Wait until she is abreast.'

But by the light of the lantern the gunner perceived at once that waiting could avail them nothing. With an imprecation he sprang to the nearest gun, shed light upon the touch-hole, and again passed on. Thus from gun to gun he sped until he had reached the last. Then he came back, swinging the lantern in one hand and the spluttering fuse in the other, so slowly that the Marquis was moved to frenzy.

Not a hundred yards away the Maria Gloriosa was slowly passing, her hull a dark shadow, her sails faintly grey above.

'Make haste, fool! Make haste! Touch them off!' roared the Admiral of the Ocean-Sea.

'Look for yourself, Excellency.' The gunner set down the lantern on the gun so that its light fell directly upon the touch-hole. 'Spiked. A soft nail has been rammed home. It is the same with all of them.'

The Admiral of the Ocean-Sea swore with the picturesque and horrible fervour that only a Spaniard can achieve. 'He forgets nothing, that endemonized pirate dog.'

A musket-shot, carefully aimed by a buccaneer from the bulwarks of the passing ship, came to shatter the lantern. It was followed by an ironic cheer and a burst of still more ironic laughter from the deck of the Maria Gloriosa as she passed on her stately way through the Dragon's Jaw to the open sea.

Episode 2

THE PRETENDER

I

Mobility, as everyone knows, is a quality that has been in all times a conspicuous factor of success with most great commanders by land and sea. So, too, with Captain Blood. There were occasions when his onslaught was sudden as the stoop of a hawk. And there was a time, coinciding with his attainment of the summit of his fame, when this mobility assumed proportions conveying such an impression of ubiquity that it led the Spaniards to believe and assert that only a compact with Satan could enable a man so miraculously to annihilate space.

Not content to be mildly amused by the echoes that reached him from time to time of the supernatural powers with which Spanish superstition endowed him, Captain Blood was diligent to profit where possible by the additional terror in which his name came thus to be held. But when shortly after his capture at San Domingo of the Maria Gloriosa, the powerful, richly laden flagship of the Spanish Admiral of the Ocean-Sea, the Marquis of Riconete, he heard it positively and circumstantially reported that on the very morrow of his sailing from San Domingo he had been raiding Cartagena, two hundred miles away, it occurred to him that one or two other fantastic tales of his doings that had lately reached his ears might possess a foundation less vague than was supplied by mere superstitious imaginings.

It was in a water-side tavern at Christianstadt on the island of Sainte Croix, where the Maria Gloriosa (impudently re-named the Andalusian Lass, and as impudently flying the flag of the Union) had put in for wood and water, that he overheard an account of horrors practised by himself and his buccaneers at Cartagena in the course of that same raid.

He had sought the tavern in accordance with his usual custom when roving at a venture, without definite object. These resorts of seafaring men were of all places the likeliest in which to pick up scraps of information that might be turned to account. Nor was this the first time that the information he picked up concerned himself, though never yet had it been of quite so surprising a nature.

The narrator was a big Dutchman, red of hair and face, named Claus, master of a merchant ship from the Scheldt, and he was entertaining with his lurid tale of pillage, rape and murder two traders of the town, members of the French West India Company.

Uninvited, Blood thrust himself into this group with the object of learning more, and the intrusion was not merely accepted with the tolerance that prevailed in such resorts, but welcomed by virtue of the elegance of this stranger's appointments and the quiet authority of his manner.

'My greetings, messieurs.' If his French had not the native fluency of his Spanish, acquired during two years at Seville in a prison of the Holy Office, yet it was serviceably smooth. He drew up a stool, sat down without ceremony, and rapped with his knuckles on the stained deal table to summon the taverner. 'When do you say that this occurred?'

'Ten days ago it was,' the Dutchman answered him.

'Impossible.' Blood shook his periwigged head. 'To my certain knowledge, Captain Blood ten days ago was at San Domingo. Besides, his ways are hardly as villainous as those you describe.'

Claus, that rough man, of a temper to match his fiery complexion, displayed impatience of the contradiction. 'Pirates are pirates, and all are foul.' He spat ostentatiously upon the sanded floor, as if to mark his nausea.

'Faith, I'll not argue with you on that. But since I know that ten days ago Captain Blood was at San Domingo, it follows that he could not at the same time have been at Cartagena.'

'Cock-sure, are you not?' the Dutchman sneered. 'Then let me tell you, sir, that I had the tale two days since at San Juan de Puerto Rico from the captain of one of two battered Spanish plate-ships that had been beset in Cartagena by the raiders. You'll not pretend to know better than he. Those two galleons ran into San Juan for shelter. They had been hunted across the Caribbean by that damned buccaneer, and they would never have escaped him but that a lucky shot of theirs damaged his foremast and compelled him to shorten sail.'

But Blood was not impressed by this citation of an eyewitness. 'Bah!' said he. 'The Spaniards were in a mistake. That's all.'

The traders looked uneasily at the dark face of this newcomer, whose eyes, so vividly blue under their black eyebrows, were coldly contemptuous. The timely arrival of the taverner brought a pause to the discussion, and Blood softened the mounting irritation of the Dutchman by inviting these habitual rum-drinkers to share with him a bottle of more elegant Canary Sack.

'My good sir,' Claus insisted, 'there could be no mistake. Blood's big red ship, the Arabella, is not to be mistaken.'

'If they say that the Arabella chased them, they make it the more certain that they lied. For, again to my certain knowledge, the Arabella is at Tortuga, careened for graving and refitting.'

'You know a deal,' said the Dutchman, with his heavy sarcasm.

'I keep myself informed,' was the plausible answer, civilly delivered. 'It's prudent.'

'Ay, provided that you inform yourself correctly. This time you're sorely at fault. Believe me, sir, at present Captain Blood is somewhere hereabouts.'

Captain Blood smiled. 'That I can well believe. What I don't perceive is why you should suppose it.'

The Dutchman thumped the table with his great fist. 'Didn't I tell you that somewhere off Puerto Rico his foremast was strained, in action with these Spaniards? What better reason than that? He'll have run to one of these islands for repairs. That's certain.'

'What's much more certain is that your Spaniards, in panic of Captain Blood, see an Arabella in every ship they sight.'

Only the coming of the Sack made the Dutchman tolerant of such obstinacy in error. When they had drunk, he confined his talk to the plate-ships. Not only were they at Puerto Rico for repairs, but after their late experience, and because they were very richly laden, they would not again put to sea until they could be convoyed.

Now here, at last, was matter of such interest to Captain Blood that he was not concerned to dispute further about the horrors imputed to him at Cartagena and the other falsehood of his engagement with those same plate-ships.

That evening in the cabin of the Andalusian Lass, in whose splendid equipment of damasks and velvets, of carved and gilded bulkheads, of crystal and silver, was reflected the opulence of the Spanish Admiral to whom she had so lately belonged, Captain Blood summoned a council of war. It was composed of the one-eyed giant Wolverstone, of Nathaniel Hagthorpe, that pleasant mannered West Country gentleman, and of Chaffinch, the little sailing master, all of them men who had been transported with Blood for their share in the Monmouth rising. As a result of their deliberations, the Andalusian Lass weighed anchor that same night, and slipped away from Sainte Croix, to appear two days later off San Juan de Puerto Rico.

Flying now the red and gold of Spain at her maintruck, she hove to in the roads, fired a gun in salute, and lowered a boat.

Through his telescope, Blood scanned the harbour for confirmation of the Dutchman's tale. There he made out quite clearly among the lesser shipping two tall yellow galleons, vessels of thirty guns, whose upper works bore signs of extensive damage, now in course of repair. So far, then, it seemed, Mynheer Claus had told the truth. And this was all that mattered.

It was necessary to proceed with caution. Not only was the harbour protected by a considerable fort, with a garrison which no doubt would be kept more than usually alert in view of the presence of the treasure-ships, but Blood disposed of no more than eighty hands aboard the Andalusian Lass, so that he was not in sufficient strength to effect a landing, even if his gunnery should have the good fortune to subdue the fortress. He must trust to guile rather than to strength, and in the lowered cock-boat Captain Blood went audaciously ashore upon a reconnaissance.

II

It was so improbable as to be accounted impossible that news of Captain Blood's capture of the Spanish flagship at San Domingo could already have reached Puerto Rico; therefore the white-and-gold splendours, and the pronouncedly Spanish lines, of the Maria Gloriosa should be his sufficient credentials at the outset. He had made free with the Marquis of Riconete's extensive wardrobe, and he came arrayed in a suit of violet taffetas, with stockings of lilac silk and a baldrick of finest

Cordovan of the same colour that was stiff with silver bullion. A broad black hat with a trailing claret feather covered his black periwig and shaded his weathered, high-bred face.

Tall, straight, and vigorously spare, his head high, and authority in every line of him, he came to stand, leaning upon his tall gold-headed cane, before the Captain-General of Puerto Rico, Don Sebastian Mendes, and to explain himself in that fluent Castilian so painfully acquired.

Some Spaniards, making a literal translation of his name, spoke of him as Don Pedro Sangre, others alluded to him as El Diablo Encarnado. Humorously blending now the two, he impudently announced himself as Don Pedro Encarnado, deputy of the Admiral of the Ocean-Sea, the Marquis of Riconete, who could not come ashore in person because chained to his bed aboard by an attack of gout. From a Dutch vessel, spoken off Sainte Croix, his Excellency the Admiral had heard of an attack by scoundrelly buccaneers upon two ships of Spain from Cartagena, which had sought shelter here at San Juan. These ships he had seen in the harbour, but the Marquis desired more precise information in the matter.

Don Sebastian supplied it tempestuously. He was a big, choleric man, flabby and sallow, with little black moustachios surmounting lips as thick almost as an African's, and he possessed a number of chins, all of them blue from the razor.

His reception of the false Don Pedro had been marked, first by all the ceremony due to the deputy of a representative of the Catholic King, and then by the cordiality proper from one Castilian gentleman to another; he presented him to his dainty, timid, still youthful little wife, and kept him to dinner, which was spread in a cool white patio under the green shade of a trellis of vines, and served by liveried black man slaves at the orders of a severely formal Spanish majordomo.

At table the tempestuousness aroused in Don Sebastian by his visitor's questions was maintained. It was true enough—por

Dios!—that the plate-ships had been set upon by buccaneers, the same vile hijos de puta who had lately transformed Cartagena into the likeness of Hell. There were nauseating details, which the Captain-General supplied without regard for the feelings of Doña Leocadia, who shuddered and crossed herself more than once while his horrible tale was telling.

If it shocked Captain Blood to learn that such things were being imputed to him and his followers, he forgot this in the interest aroused in him by the information that there was bullion aboard those plate-ships to the value of two hundred thousand pieces of eight, to say nothing of pepper and spices worth almost the like amount.

'What a prize would not that have been for that incarnate devil Blood, and what a mercy of the Lord it was that the ships were able not only to get away from Cartagena, but to escape his subsequent pursuit of them!'

'Captain Blood?' said the visitor. 'Is it certain, then, that this was his work?'

'Not a doubt of it. Who else is afloat today who would dare so much? Let me lay hands on him, and as Heaven hears me I'll have the skin off his bones to make myself a pair of breeches.'

'Sebastian, my love!' Doña Leocadia shudderingly remonstrated. 'What horror!'

'Let me lay hands on him,' Don Sebastian fiercely repeated.

Captain Blood smiled amiably. 'It may come to pass. He may be nearer to you than you suppose.'

'I pray God he may be.' And the Captain-General twirled his absurd moustache.

After dinner the visitor took a ceremonious leave, regretfully, but of necessity since he must report to his Admiral. But on the morrow he was back again, and when the boat that brought him ashore had returned to the white-and-gold flagship, the great galleon was observed by the idlers on the mole to take up her anchor and to be hoisting sail. Before the freshening breeze that set a sparkling ruffle on the sunlit violet waters, she moved majestically eastwards along the peninsula on which San Juan is built.

Penmanship had occupied some of Captain Blood's time aboard since yesterday, and the Admiral's writing-coffer had supplied his needs: the Admiral's seal and a sheet of parchment surmounted by the arms of Spain. Hence an imposing document, which he now placed before Don Sebastian. Explanations plausibly accompanied it.

'Your assurance that Captain Blood is in these waters has persuaded the Admiral to hunt him out. In his Excellency's absence, he commands me, as you observe, to remain here.'

The Captain-General was poring over the parchment with its great slab of red wax bearing the arms of the Marquis of Riconete. It ordered Don Sebastian to make over to Don Pedro Encarnado the command of the military establishment of San Juan de Puerto Rico, the Fort of Santo Antonio, and its garrison.

It was not an order that Don Sebastian could be expected to receive with equanimity. He frowned and blew out his fat lips. 'I do not understand this at all. Colonel Vargas who commands the fort under my orders is a competent, experienced officer. Besides,' he bristled, 'I have been under the impression that it is I who am Captain-General of Puerto Rico, and that it is for me to appoint my officers.'

No speech or manner could have been more conciliatory than Captain Blood's. 'In your place, Don Sebastian, I must confess—oh, but entirely between ourselves—that I should feel precisely as you do. But... What would you? It is necessary to have patience. The Admiral is moved to excessive anxiety for the safety of the plate-ships.'

'Is not their safety in San Juan my affair? Am I not the King's representative in Puerto Rico? Let the Admiral command as he pleases on the ocean; but here on land...'

Suavely Captain Blood interrupted him, a hand familiarly upon his shoulder. 'My dear Don Sebastian!' He lowered his voice to a confidential tone. 'You know how it is with these royal favourites.'

'Royal...' Don Sebastian choked down his annoyance in sudden apprehension. 'I never heard that the Marquis of Riconete is a royal favourite.'

'A lap-dog to his Majesty. That, of course, between ourselves. Hence his audacity. I should not blame you for holding the opinion that he abuses the King's affection for him. You know how the royal favour goes to a man's head.' He paused and sighed. 'It distresses me to be the instrument of this encroachment upon your province but I am as helpless as yourself, my friend.'

Thus brought to imagine that he trod dangerous ground, Don Sebastian suppressed the heat begotten of this indignity to his office, and philosophically consented, as Captain Blood urged him, to take comfort in the thought that the Admiral's interference possessed at least the advantage for him of relieving him of all responsibility for what might follow.

After this, and in the two succeeding days, Peter Blood displayed a tact that made things easy, not only for the Captain-General, but also for Colonel Vargas, who at first had been disposed to verbal violence on the subject of his supersession. It reconciled the Colonel, at least in part, to discover that the new commandant showed no inclination to interfere with any of his military measures. Far from it, having made a close inspection of the fort, its armament, garrison, and munitions, he warmly commended all that he beheld, and generously confessed that he should not know how to improve upon the Colonel's dispositions.

It was on the first Friday in June that the false Don Pedro had come ashore to take command. On the following Sunday morning in the courtyard of the Captain-General's quarters, a breathless young officer reeled from the saddle of a lathered, spent, and quivering horse. To Don Sebastian, who was at breakfast with his lady and his temporary Commandant, this messenger brought the alarming news that a powerfully armed ship that flew no flag and was manifestly a pirate was threatening San Patrico, fifty miles away. It had opened a bombardment of the settlement, so far without damage because it dared not come within range of the fire maintained by the guns of the harbour fort. Lamentably, however, the fort was very short of ammunition, and once this were exhausted there was no adequate force in men to resist a landing.

Such was Don Sebastian's amazement that it transcended his alarm. 'In the devil's name, what should pirates seek at San Patrico? There's nothing there but sugarcane and maize.'

'I think I understand,' said Captain Blood. 'San Patrico is the back door to San Juan and the plate-ships.'

'The back door?'

'Don't you see? Because these pirates dare not venture a frontal attack against your heavily armed fort of Santo Antonio here, they hoped to march overland from San Patrico and take you in the rear.'

The Captain-General was profoundly impressed by this prompt display of military acumen.

'By all the Saints, I believe you explain it.' He heaved himself up, announcing that he would take order at once, dismissed the officer to rest and refreshment, and despatched a messenger to fetch Colonel Vargas from the fort.

Stamping up and down the long room, which was kept in cool shadow by the slatted blinds, he gave thanks to his patron saint, the martyred centurion, that Santo Antonio was abundantly munitioned, thanks to his foresight, and could spare all the powder and shot that San Patrico might require so as to hold these infernal pirates at bay.

The timid glance of Doña Leocadia followed him about the room, then was turned upon the new commandant when his voice, cool and calm, invaded the Captain-General's pause for breath.

'With submission, sir, it would be an error to take munitions from Santo Antonio. We may require all that we have. Several things are possible. These buccaneers may change their plans, when they find the landing at San Patrico less easy than they suppose. Or'—and now he stated what he knew to be the case, since it was precisely what he had commanded—'the attack on San Patrico may be no more than a feint, to draw thither your strength.'

Don Sebastian stared blankly, passing a jewelled hand over his ponderous blue jowl. 'That is possible. Yes, God help me!' And thankful now for the presence of this calm, discerning commandant, whose coming at first had so offended him, he cast himself entirely upon the man's resourcefulness.

Don Pedro was prompt to take command. 'I have a note of the munitions aboard the plate-ships. They are considerable. Abundant for the needs of San Patrico, and useless at present to the vessels. We will take not only their powder and shot, but their guns as well, and haul them at once to San Patrico.'

'You'll disarm the plate-ships?' Don Sebastian stared alarm.

'What need to keep them armed whilst in harbour here? It is the fort that will defend the entrance if it should come to need defending. The emergency is at San Patrico.' He became more definite. 'You will be good enough to order the necessary mules and oxen for the transport. As for men, there are two hundred and thirty at Santo Antonio and a hundred and twenty aboard the plate-ships. What is the force at San Patrico?'

'Between forty and fifty.'

'God help us! If these buccaneers intend a landing, it follows that they must be four or five hundred strong. To oppose them San Patrico will need every man we can spare. I shall have to send Colonel Vargas thither with a hundred and fifty men from Santo Antonio and a hundred men from the ships.'

'And leave San Juan defenceless?' In his horror Don Sebastian could not help adding: 'Are you mad?'

Captain Blood's air was that of a man whose knowledge of his business places him beyond all wavering. 'I think not. We have the fort with a hundred guns, half of them of powerful calibre. A hundred men should abundantly suffice to serve them. And lest you suppose that I subject you to risks I am not prepared to share, I shall, myself, remain here to command them.'

When Vargas came, he was as horrified as Don Sebastian at this depletion of the defence of San Juan. In the heat of his arguments against it he became almost discourteous. He looked down his nose at the Admiral's deputy, and spoke of the Art of War as if from an eminence where it had no secrets. From that eminence, the new commandant coolly dislodged him. 'If you tell me that we can attempt to resist a landing at San Patrico with fewer than three hundred men, I shall understand that you have still to learn the elements of your profession. And, anyway,' he added, rising, so as to mark the end of the discussion, 'I have the honour to command here, and the responsibility is mine. I shall be glad if you will give my orders your promptest obedience.'

Colonel Vargas bowed stiffly, biting his lip, and the Captain-General returned explosive thanks to Heaven that he held a parchment from the Admiral of the Ocean-Sea which must relieve him of all blame for whatever consequences might attend this rashness.

As the Cathedral bells were summoning the faithful to High Mass, and notwithstanding the approaching sweltering heat of noontide, the matter admitting of no delay, Colonel Vargas marched his men out of San Juan. At the head of the column, and followed by a long train of mules, laden with ammunition, and of oxen-teams hauling the guns, the Colonel took the road across the gently undulating plains to San Patrico, fifty miles away.

III

You will have conceived that the pirate threatening San Patrico was the erstwhile flagship of the Spanish Admiral of the Ocean-Sea, now the Andalusian Lass, despatched thither on that business by Captain Blood. Wolverstone had been placed in command of her, and his orders were to maintain his demonstration and keep the miserable little fort of San Patrico in play for forty-eight hours. At the end of that time, and under cover of night, he was to slip quietly away before the arrival of the reinforcements from San Juan, which by then would be well upon their way, and, abandoning the feint, come round at speed to deliver the real blow at the now comparatively defenceless San Juan.

Messengers from San Patrico arriving at regular intervals throughout Monday brought reports that showed how faithfully Wolverstone was fulfilling his instructions. The messages gave assurance that the constant fire of the fort was compelling the pirates to keep their distance.

It was heartening news to the Captain-General, persuaded that every hour that passed increased the chances that the raiders would be caught red-handed by the Admiral of the Ocean-Sea, who must be somewhere in the neighbourhood, and incontinently destroyed. 'By tomorrow,' he said, 'Vargas will be at San Patrico with the reinforcements and the pirates' chance of landing will be at an end.'

But what the morrow brought was something very different from the expectations of all concerned. Soon after daybreak, San Juan was awakened by the roar of guns. Don Sebastian's first uplifting thought, as he thrust a leg out of bed, was that here was the Marquis of Riconete announcing his return by a fully royal salute. The continuous bombardment, however, stirred his misgivings even before he reached the terrace of his fine house. Once there, and having seen what his telescope could show him in detail, his misgivings were changed to stark consternation.

Captain Blood's first awakening emotions had been the very opposite to Don Sebastian's. But his annoyed assumptions were at once dismissed. Even if Wolverstone should have left San Patrico before midnight, which was unlikely, it was impossible, in the teeth of the keen westerly wind now blowing, that he could reach San Juan for another twelve hours. Moreover, Wolverstone was not the man to act in such careless disregard of his instructions.

Half dressed, Captain Blood made haste to seek at Don Sebastian's side the explanation of this artillery, and there experienced a consternation no whit inferior to the Captain-General's, though vastly different of source. For the great red ship whose guns were pounding the fort from the roads, a half-mile away, had all the appearance of his own Arabella, which he had left careened in Tortuga less than a month ago.

He remembered the false current tale of a raid by Captain Blood on Cartagena, and he asked himself was it possible that Pitt and Dyke and other associates whom he had left behind had gone roving in his absence, conducting their raids with inhuman cruelties such as those which had disgraced Morgan and Montbars. He could not believe it of them; and yet here stood his ship under a billowing cloud of smoke from her own gunfire, delivering broadsides that were bringing down the walls of a fort that had the appearance of being massive and substantial, but the mortar of which, as he had been glad to ascertain when inspecting it, was mere adobe.

At his side the Captain-General of Puerto Rico was invoking alternately all the saints in the calendar and all the fiends in Hell to bear witness that here was that incarnate devil Captain Blood.

Tight-lipped, that incarnate devil at his very elbow gave no heed to his imprecations. With a hand to his brow, so as to shade his eyes from the morning sun, he scanned the lines of that red ship from gilded beak-head to towering poop. It was the Arabella, and yet it was not the Arabella. The difference eluded him, yet a difference he perceived.

As he looked, the great vessel came broadside on in the act of going about. Then, even without counting her gunports, he obtained a clear assurance. She carried four guns less than his own flagship.

'That is not Captain Blood,' he said.

'Not Captain Blood? You'll tell me that I am not Sebastian Mendes. Is not his ship named the Arabella?'

'That is not the Arabella.'

Don Sebastian looked him over with a contemptuous, blood-injected eye. Then he proffered his telescope.

'Read the name on the counter for yourself.'

Captain Blood took the glass. The ship was swinging, so as to bring her starboard guns to bear, and her counter came fully into view. In letters of gold, he read there the name Arabella, and his bewilderment was renewed.

'I do not understand,' he said. But the roar of her broadside drowned his words and loosened some further tons of the fort's masonry. And then, at last, the guns of the fort thundered in their turn for the first time. The fire was wild and wide of the mark, but at least it had the effect of compelling the attacking ship to stand off, so as to get out of range.

'By God, they're awake at last!' cried Don Sebastian, with bitter irony.

Blood departed in search of his boots, ordering the scared servants who stood about to find and saddle him a horse.

When, five minutes later, booted, but still not more than half dressed, he was setting his foot to the stirrup, the Captain-General surged beside him. 'It's your responsibility,' he raged.

'Yours and your precious Admiral's. Your fatuous measures have left us defenceless. I hope you'll be able to answer for it. I hope so.'

'I hope so too; and to that brigand, whoever he may be.' Captain Blood spoke through his teeth in an anger more bitter if less boisterous than the Captain-General's. For he was experiencing the condition of being hoist with his own petard and all the emotions that accompany it. He had been at such elaborate and crafty pains to disarm San Juan, merely, it seemed, so as to make it easy for a pestilential interloper to come and snatch from under his very nose the prize for which he played. He could not conjecture the identity of the interloper, but he had more than a suspicion that it was not by mere coincidence that this red ship was named the Arabella, and not a doubt but that her master was the author of those horrors in Cartagena which were being assigned to Captain Blood.

However that might be, what mattered now was to do what might be done so as to frustrate this most inopportune of interlopers. And so, by a singular irony, Captain Blood rode forth upon the hope, rendered forlorn by his own contriving, of organizing the defences of a Spanish place against an attack by buccaneers.

He found the fortress in a state of desolation and confusion. Half the guns were already out of action under the heaped rubble. Of the hundred men that had been left to garrison it, ten had been killed and thirty disabled. The sixty that remained whole were resolute and steady men—there were no better troops in the world than those of the Spanish infantry—but reduced to helplessness by the bewildered incompetence of the young officer in command.

Captain Blood came amongst them just as another broadside shore away twenty yards of ramparts. In the well-like courtyard, half choked with the dust of crumbling masonry and the acrid fumes of gunpowder, he stormed at the officer who ran to meet him.

'Will you keep your company cowering here until men and guns are all buried together in these ruins?'

Captain Araña bridled. He threw a chest. 'We can die at our posts, sir, to pay for your errors.'

'So can any fool. But if you had as much intelligence as impertinence you would be saving some of the guns. They'll be needed presently. Haul a score of them out of this, and have them posted in that cover.' He pointed to a pimento grove less than a half-mile away in the direction of the city. 'Leave me a dozen hands to serve the guns that remain, and take every other man with you. And get your wounded out of this death-trap. When you're in the grove send out for teams of mules, horses, oxen, what you will, against the need for further haulage. Load with canister. Use your wits, man, and waste no time. About it!'

If Captain Araña lacked imagination to conceive, at least he possessed energy to execute the conceptions of another. Dominated by the commandant's brisk authority fired by admiration for measures whose simple soundness he at once perceived, he went diligently to work, whilst Blood took charge of a battery of ten guns emplaced on the southern rampart which best commanded the bay. A dozen men, aroused from their inertia by his vigour, and stimulated by his own indifference to danger, carried out his orders calmly and swiftly.

The buccaneer, having emptied her starboard guns, was going about so as to bring her larboard broadside to bear. Taking advantage of the manoeuvre, and gauging as best he could the station from which her next fire would be delivered, Blood passed from gun to gun, laying each with his own hands, deliberately and carefully. He had just laid the last of them when the red ship, having put the helm over, presented her larboard flank. He snatched the spluttering match from the hand of a musketeer, and instantly touched off the gun at that broad target. If the shot was not as lucky as he hoped, yet it was lucky enough. It shore away the pirate's bowsprit. She yawed under the shock and listed slightly, and this at the very moment that her broadside was delivered. As a consequence of that fortuitously altered elevation, the discharge soared harmlessly over the fort and went to plough the ground away in its rear. At once she swung downwind so as to run out of range.

'Fire!' roared Blood, and the other nine guns blazed as one.

The buccaneer's stern presenting but a narrow mark, Blood could hope for little more than a moral effect. But again luck favoured him, and if eight of the twenty-four-pound missiles merely flung up the spray about the ship, the ninth crashed into her stern-coach, to speed her on her way.

The Spaniards sent up a cheer. 'Viva Don Pedro!' And it was actually with laughter that they set about reloading, their courage resurrected by that first if slight success.

There was no need now for haste. It took the buccaneer some time to clear the wreckage of her bowsprit, and it was quite an hour before she was beating back, close-hauled against the breeze, to take her revenge.

In that most valuable respite, Araña had got the guns into the cover of the grove a quarter of a mile away. Thither Blood might have retreated to join him. But, greatly daring, he stayed, first to repeat his earlier tactics. This time, however, his fire went wide, and the full force of the red ship's broadside came smashing into the fort to open another wound in its crumbling flank. Then, infuriated perhaps by the mishap suffered, and judging, no doubt, from the fort's previous volley that only a few of its guns remained effective and that these would now be empty the buccaneer ran in close, and, going about, delivered her second broadside at point-blank range.

The result was an explosion that shook the buildings in San Juan, a mile away.

Blood felt as if giant hands had seized him, lifted him and cast him violently from them upon the subsiding ground. He lay winded and half stunned, while rubble came spattering down in a titanic hailstorm; and to the roar as of a continuous cataract, the walls of the fort slid down as if suddenly turned liquid, and came to rest in a shapeless heap of ruin.

An unlucky shot had found the powder-magazine. It was the end of the fort.

The cheer that came over the water from the buccaneer ship was like an echo of the explosion.

Blood roused himself, shook himself free of the mortar and rubble in which he was half buried, coughed the dust from his throat, and made a mental examination of his condition. His hip was hurt, but the gradually subsiding pain assured him that there was no permanent damage. He got slowly to his knees, still half dazed, then, at last, to his feet. Badly shaken, his hands cut and bleeding, smothered in dust and grime, he was, at least, whole. He had broken nothing. But of the twelve who had been with him he found only five as sound as they had been before the explosion; a sixth lay groaning with a broken thigh, a seventh sat nursing a dislocated shoulder. The other five were gone, buried in that heaped-up mound.

He collected wits that had been badly scattered, straightened his dusty periwig, and decided that there could be no purpose in lingering on this rubbish-heap that lately had been a fort. To the five survivors he ordered the care of their two crippled fellows, saw these borne away towards the pimento grove, and went staggering after them.

By the time he reached the shelter of that belt of perfumed trees, the buccaneers were disposing for the tactics that logically followed upon the destruction of the fort. Their preparations for landing were clearly discernible to Blood as he paused on the edge of the grove to observe them, shading his eyes from the glare of the sun. He saw that five boats had been lowered, and that, manned to over-crowding, these were pulling away for the beach, whilst the red ship rode now at anchor to cover the landing.

There was no time to lose. Blood entered the cool green shade of the plantation, where Araña and his men awaited him. He approved the emplacement there of the guns unsuspected by the buccaneers, and charged with canister as he had directed. Carefully judging the spot, less than a mile away, where the enemy should come ashore, he ordered and himself supervised the training of the guns upon it. He took for mark a fishing-boat that stood upside down upon the beach, half a cable's length from the water's creamy edge.

'We'll wait,' he explained to Araña, 'until those sons of dogs are in line with it, and then we'll give them a passport into Hell.' From that, so as to beguile the waiting moments, he went on to lecture the Spanish captain upon the finer details of the art of war.

'You begin to perceive the advantages that may lie in departing from school-room rules and preconceptions, and in abandoning a fort that can't be held, so as to improvise another one that can be. By these tactics we hold those ruffians at our mercy. In a moment you'll see them swept to perdition, and victory plucked from the appearance of defeat.'

No doubt it is what would have happened but for the supervention of the unexpected. As a matter of fact, Captain Araña was having an even more instructive morning than Captain Blood intended. He was now to receive a demonstration of the futility of divided command.

IV

The trouble came from Don Sebastian, who, meanwhile, had unfortunately not been idle. As Captain-General of Puerto Rico he conceived it to be his duty to arm every man of the town who was able to lift a weapon. Without taking the precaution of consulting Don Pedro, or even of informing him of what he proposed, he had brought the improvised army, some five or six score strong, under cover of the white buildings, to within a hundred yards of the water. There he held them in ambush, to launch them in a charge against the landing buccaneers at the very last moment. In this way he calculated to make it impossible for the ship's artillery to play upon his force, and he was exultantly proud of his tactical conception.

In themselves these tactics were as sound as they were obvious; but they suffered from the unsuspected disadvantage that in serving to baulk the buccaneer gunners on the ship, they no less baulked the Spanish battery in the grove. Before Blood could deliver the fire he was holding, he beheld to his dismay the yelling improvised army of Puerto Rican townsfolk go charging down the beach upon the invader, so that in a moment all was a heaving, writhing, battling, screaming press, in which friend and foe were inextricably mixed.

In this confusion that fighting mob surged up the beach slowly at first, but steadily gathering impetus in a measure as Don Sebastian's forces gave way before the fury of little more than half their number of buccaneers. Firing, and shouting, they all vanished together into the town, leaving some bodies behind them on the sands.

Whilst Captain Blood was cursing Don Sebastian's untimely interference, Captain Araña was urging a rescue. He received yet another lesson.

'Battles are not won by heroics, my friend, but by calculation. The ruffians aboard will number at least twice those that have been landed; and these are by now masters of the situation, thanks to the heroics of Don Sebastian. If we march in now, we shall be taken in the rear by the next landing-party and thus find ourselves caught between two fires. So we'll wait, if you please, for the second landing-party, and when we've destroyed that, we'll deal with the blackguards who are by now in possession of the town. Thus we make sure.'

The time of waiting, however, was considerable. In each of the boats only two men had been left to pull back to the ship, and their progress was slow. Slow, too, was the second loading and return. So that close upon two hours had passed since the first landing before the second party leapt ashore.

It may have appeared to this second party that there was no need for haste, since all the signs went clearly to show that the feeble opposition offered by San Juan had already been fully overcome.

Therefore no haste they made even when their keels grated on the beach. In leisurely fashion they climbed out of the boats, a motley crowd, like that which had composed the first landing-party: some in hats, some few in morions, others with heads swathed in dirty, gaudy scarves, and offering the same variety in the remainder of their dress. It was representative of every class, from the frank buccaneer in cotton shirt and raw-hide breeches to the hidalgo in a laced coat, whilst here and there a back-and-breast supplied a more military equipment. They were uniform at least in that everybody was scarved by a bandoleer, every shoulder bore a musket, and from every belt hung a sword of some description.

They numbered perhaps fifty, and one who seemed set in authority, and wore a gaudy scarlet coat with tarnished lace, marshalled them at the water's edge into a parody of military formation, then, placing himself at their head, waved his sword and gave the word to march.

They marched, breaking into song, so as to supply a rhythm. Raucously bawling their lewd ditty, they advanced in close order, whilst in the pimento grove the gunners blew on their matches, their eyes on Captain Blood, who watched and waited, his right arm raised. At last the raiders were in line with the boat which had served the Spaniards for a mark. Blood's arm fell, and five guns were touched off as one.

That hail of canister swept away the head of the column together with the sword-waving leader in his fine red coat. The unexpectedness of the blow struck the remainder with a sudden palsy, from which few recovered in time. For twice more did Blood's arm rise and fall, and twice more did the charge of five guns mow through those too serried ranks, until almost all that remained of them were heaped about the beach below, some writhing and some still. A few, a half-dozen perhaps, escaped miraculously whole and unscathed, and these, not daring to return to the boats which stood unmanned and empty where they had been drawn up, were making for the shelter of the town, and wriggling on their stomachs lest yet another murderous blast should sweep death across that beach. Captain Blood smiled terribly into the startled eyes of Captain Araña. He resumed the military education of that worthy Spanish officer.

'We may advance now with confidence, Captain, since we have made our rear secure from attack. You may have observed that with deplorable rashness the pirates have employed all their boats in their landings. What men remain aboard that ship are safely marooned in her.'

'But they have guns,' objected Araña. 'What if in vindictiveness they open fire upon the town?'

'Whilst their captain and his first landing-party are in it? Not likely. Still, so as to make sure, we'll leave a dozen men here to serve these guns. If those on board should turn desperate and lose their heads, a volley or two will drive them out of range.'

Dispositions made, an orderly company of fifty Spanish musketeers, unsuspected by the buccaneers to have survived the demolition of the fort, were advancing from the pimento grove at the double upon the town.

V

The pirate captain—whose name has not survived—was set down by Blood as a lubberly idiot, who, like all idiots, took too much for granted, otherwise he would have been at pains to make sure that the force which had opposed his landing comprised the full strength of San Juan.

Ludicrous, too, was the grasping covetousness which had inspired that landing. In this Captain Blood accounted him just a cheap thief, who stayed to rake up crumbs where a feast was spread. With the great prize for which the scoundrel played, the two treasure-ships which he had chased across the Caribbean from Cartagena now lying all but at his mercy, it was a stupid rashness not to have devoted all his energy to making himself master of them at once. From the circumstance that those ships had never fired a gun, he must have inferred—if he was capable of inferences—that the crews were ashore; and if he was not capable of inferences, his telescope—and Captain Blood supposed that the fellow would at least possess a telescope—should have enabled him to ascertain the fact by observation.

But here Blood's reasoning is possibly at fault. For it may well have been the actual perception that the ships were unmanned, and easily to be reduced into possession, which induced the captain to let them wait until his excessive greed should have been satisfied by the plunder of the town. After all, he will have remembered, there was often great store of wealth in these cities of New Spain, and there would be a royal treasury in the keeping of the governor. It would be just such a temptation as this which had led him to plunder the city of Cartagena whilst those treasure-ships were putting to sea. Evidently not even this had sufficed to teach him that who seeks to grasp too much ends by holding nothing; and here he was in San Juan pursuing the same inexpert methods, and pursuing them in the same disgusting manner as that in which at Cartagena he had dishonoured—as Captain Blood was now fully persuaded—the name of the great buccaneer leader which he had assumed.

I will not say that in what he had done Captain Blood was not actuated by the determination that no interloper should come and snatch from him the prize for which he had laboured and the capture of which his dispositions had rendered easy, but I account it beyond doubt that his manner of doing it gathered an unusual ferocity because of his deep resentment of that foul impersonation at Cartagena and the horrors perpetrated there in his name. The sins of a career which harsh fortune had imposed upon him were heavy enough already. He could not patiently suffer that still worse offences should be attributed to him as a result of the unrestrained methods of this low pretender and his crew of ruthless blackguards.

So it was a grimly resolute, not to say a vindictive, Captain Blood who marched that little column of Spanish musketeers to clean up a place which his impersonator would now be defiling. As they approached the town gate the sounds that met them abundantly justified his assumptions of the nature of the raider's activities.

The buccaneer captain had swept invincibly through a place whose resistance had been crushed at the outset. Finding it at his mercy, he had delivered it to his men for pillage. Let them make holiday here awhile in their brutal fashion before settling down to the main business of the raid and possessing themselves of the plate-ships in the harbour. And so that evil crew, composed of the scourings of the gaols of every land, had broken up into groups which had scattered through the town on a voluptuous course of outrage, smashing, burning, pillaging and murdering in sheer lust of destruction.

For himself the leader marked down what should prove the richest prize in San Juan. With a half-dozen followers he broke into the house of the Captain-General, where Don Sebastian had shut himself up after the rout of his inopportunely improvised force.

Having laid violent hands upon Don Sebastian and his comely, panic-stricken little lady, the captain delivered over the main plunder of the house to the men who were with him. Two of these, however, he retained, to assist him in the particular kind of robbery upon which he was intent, whilst the other four were left remorselessly to pillage the Spaniard's property and guzzle the fine wines that he had brought from Spain.

A tall, swarthy raffish fellow of not more than thirty, who had announced himself as Captain Blood, and who flaunted the black and silver that was notoriously Blood's common wear, the pirate sprawled at his ease in Don Sebastian's dining-room. He sat at the head of the long table of dark oak, one leg hooked over the arm of his chair, his plumed hat cocked over one eye, and a leer on his thick, shaven lips.

Opposite to him, at the table's foot, between two of the captain's ruffians, stood Don Sebastian in shirt and breeches, without his wig, his hands pinioned behind him, his face the colour of lead, yet with defiance in his dark eyes.

Midway between them, but away from the table, in a tall chair, with her back to one of the open windows, sat Doña Leocadia in a state of terror that brought her to the verge of physical sickness but otherwise robbed her of movement.

The captain's fingers were busy with a length of whipcord, making knots in it. In slow, mocking tones and in clumsy, scarcely intelligible Spanish, he addressed his victim.

'So you won't talk, eh? You'ld put me to the trouble of pulling down this damned hovel of yours stone by stone so as to find what I want. Your error, my hidalgo. You'll not only talk, you'll be singing presently. Here's to provide the music.'

He flung the knotted whipcord up the table, signing to one of his men to take and use it. In a moment it was tightly encircling the Captain-General's brow, and the grinning ape whose dirty fingers had bound it there took up a silver spoon from the Spaniard's sideboard, and passed the handle of it between the cord and the flesh.

'Hold there,' his captain bade him. 'Now Don Gubernador, you know what's coming if you don't loose your obstinate tongue and tell me where you hide your pieces of eight.' He paused, watching the Spaniard from under lowered eyelids, a curl of contemptuous amusement on his lip. 'If you prefer it, we can give you a lighted match between the fingers, or a hot iron to the soles of your feet. We've all manner of ingenious miracles for restoring speech to the dumb. It's as you please, my friend. But you'll gain nothing by being mute. Come now. These doubloons. Where do you hide them?'

But the Spaniard, his head high, his lips tight, glared at him in silent detestation.

The pirate's smile broadened in deepening, contemptuous menace. He sighed. 'Well, well! I'm a patient man. You shall have a minute to think it over. One minute.' He held up a dirty forefinger. 'Time for me to drink this.' He poured himself a bumper of dark, syrupy Malaga from a silver jug, and quaffed it at a draught. He set down the lovely glass so violently that the stem snapped. He used it as an illustration. 'And that's how I'll serve your ugly neck in the end, you Spanish pimp, if you play the mule with me. Now then: these doubloons. Vamos, maldito! Soy Don Pedro Sangre, yo! Haven't you heard that you can't trifle with Captain Blood.'

Hate continued to glare at him from Don Sebastian's eyes. 'I've heard nothing of you that's as obscene as the reality, you foul pirate dog. I tell you nothing.'

The lady stirred, and made a whimpering, incoherent sound, that presently resolved itself into speech. 'For pity's sake, Sebastian! In God's name, tell him. Tell him. Let him take all we have. What does it matter?'

'What, indeed, if ye've no life with which to enjoy it?' the captain mocked him. 'Give heed to your pullet's better sense. No?' He banged the table in anger. 'So be it! Squeeze it out of his cuckoldy head, my lads.' And he settled himself more comfortably in his chair, in expectation of entertainment.

One of the brigands laid hands upon the spoon he had thrust between cord and brow. But before he had begun to twist it the captain checked him again.

'Wait. There's perhaps a surer way.' The cruel coarse mouth broadened in a smile. He unhooked his leg from the chair-arm, and sat up. 'These dons be mighty proud o' their women.' He turned, and beckoned Doña Leocadia. 'Aqui, muger! Aqui!' he commanded.

'Don't heed him, Leocadia,' cried her husband. 'Don't move.'

'He... he can always fetch me,' she answered, pathetically practical in her disobedience.

'You hear, fool? It's a pity you've none of her good sense. Come along, madam.'

The frail, pallid little woman, quaking with fear, dragged herself to the side of his chair. He looked up at her with his odious smile, and in his close-set eyes there was insulting appraisal of this dainty, timid wisp of womanhood. He flung an arm about her waist and pulled her to him.

'Come closer, woman. What the devil!'

Don Sebastian closed his eyes, and groaned between pain and fury. For a moment he strove desperately in the powerful hands that held him.

The captain, handling the little lady as if she were invertebrate, as indeed horror had all but rendered her, hauled her to sit upon his knee.

'Never heed his jealous bellowing, little one. He shan't harm you, on the word of Captain Blood.' He tilted up her chin, and smiled into dark eyes that panic was dilating. This and his lingering kiss she bore as a corpse might have borne them. 'There'll be more o' that to follow, my pullet, unless your loutish husband comes to his senses. I've got her, you see, Don Gubernador, and I dare swear she'd enjoy a voyage with me. But you can ransom her with the doubloons you hide. You'll allow that's generous, now. For I can help myself to both if I've a mind to it.'

The threatened woolding could not have put Don Sebastian in a greater anguish.

'You dog! Even if I yield, what assurance have I that you will keep faith?'

'The word of Captain Blood.'

A sudden burst of gunfire shook the house. It was closely followed by a second and yet a third.

Momentarily it startled them.

'What the devil...' the captain was beginning, when he checked, prompt to find the explanation. 'Bah! My children amuse themselves. That's all.'

But he would hardly have laughed as heartily as he did could he have guessed that those bursts of gunfire had mown down some fifty of those children of his, in the very act of landing to reinforce him, or that some fifty Spanish musketeers were advancing at the double from the pimento grove, led by the authentic Captain Blood, who came to deal with the pirates scattered through the town. And deal with them he did with sharp efficiency as fast as he came upon them, in groups of four, or six, or ten at most. Some were shot at sight, and the remainder rounded up and taken prisoners, so that no chance was ever theirs to assemble and offer an organized resistance.

In the Captain-General's dining-room, the buccaneer captain, unhurried because deriving more and more evil relish from the situation in a measure as he grew more fuddled by the heady Malaga wine, gave little heed to the increasing sounds outside, the shots, the screams and the bursts of musketry. In his complete persuasion that all power of resistance had been crushed, he supposed these to be the ordinary indications that his children continued to amuse themselves. Idle gunfire was a common practice among jubilant filibusters, and who but his own men should now have muskets to fire in San Juan?

So he continued at his leisure to savour the voluptuous humour of tormenting the Captain-General with a choice between losing his wife or his doubloons until at last Don Sebastian's spirit broke, and he told them where the King's treasure-chest was stored.

But the evil in the buccaneer was not allayed. 'Too late,' he declared. 'You've been trifling with me overlong. And in the meantime I've grown fond of this dainty piece of yours. So fond that I couldn't bear now to be parted from her. Your life you may have, you Spanish dog. And after your cursed obstinacy that's more than you deserve. But your money and your women go with me, like the plate-ships of the King of Spain.'

'You pledged me your word!' cried the demented Spaniard.

'Ay ay! But that was long since. You didn't accept when the chance was yours. You chose to trifle with me.' Thus the filibuster mocked him, and in the room none heeded the quick approach of steps. 'And I warned you that it is not safe to trifle with Captain Blood.'

The last word was not out of him when the door was flung open, and a crisp, metallic voice was answering him on a grimly humorous note.

'Faith, I'm glad to hear you say it, whoever you may be.' A tall man in a dishevelled black periwig without a hat, his violet coat in rags, his lean face smeared with sweat and grime, came in, sword in hand. At his heels followed three musketeers in Spanish corselets and steel caps. The sweep of his glance took in the situation.

'So. So. No more than in time, I think.'

Startled, the ruffian flung Doña Leocadia from him and bounded to his feet, a hand on one of the pistols he carried slung before him at the ends of an embroidered stole.

'What's this? In Hell's name, who are you?'

The newcomer stepped close to him, and out of that begrimed countenance eyes blue as sapphires and as hard sent a chill through him. 'You poor pretender! You dung-souled impostor!'

Whatever the ruffian may or may not have understood, he was in no doubt that here was need for instant action. He plucked forth the pistol on which his hand was resting. But before he could level it, Captain Blood had stepped back. His rapier licked forth, sudden as a viper's tongue, to transfix the pirate's arm, and the pistol clattered from a nerveless hand.

'You should have had it in the heart, you dog, but for a vow I've made that, God helping me, Captain Blood shall never be hanged by any hand but mine.'

One of the musketeers closed with the disabled man, and bore him down, snarling and cursing, whilst Blood and the others dealt swiftly and efficiently with his men.

Above the din of that brutal struggle rang the scream of Doña Leocadia, who reeled to a chair, fell into it, and fainted.

Don Sebastian, scarcely in better case when his bonds were cut, babbled weakly an incoherent mixture of thanksgivings for this timely miracle and questions upon how it had been wrought.

'Look to your lady,' Blood advised him, 'and give yourself no other thought. San Juan is cleared of this blight. Some thirty of these scoundrels are safe in the town gaol, the others, safer still, in Hell. If any have got away at all, they'll find a party waiting for them at the boats. We've the dead to bury, the wounded to attend, the fugitives from the town to recall. Look to your lady and your household, and leave the rest to me.'

He was away again, as abruptly as he had come, and gone too were his musketeers, bearing the raging captive with them.

VI

He came back at suppertime to find order restored to the Captain-General's house, the servants at their posts once more, and the table spread. Doña Leocadia burst into tears at sight of him, still all begrimed from battle. Don Sebastian hugged him to his ample bosom, the grime notwithstanding, proclaiming him the saviour of San Juan, a hero of the true Castilian pattern, a worthy representative of the great Admiral of the Ocean-Sea. And this, too, was the opinion of the town, which resounded that night with cries of 'Viva Don Pedro! Long live the hero of San Juan de Puerto Rico!'

It was all very pleasant and touching, and induced in Captain Blood, as he afterwards confessed to Jeremy Pitt, a mood of reflection upon the virtue of service to the cause of law and order. Cleansed and re-clothed, in garments at once too loose and too short, borrowed from Don Sebastian's wardrobe, he sat down to supper at the Captain-General's table, ate heartily and did justice to some excellent Spanish wine that had survived the raid upon the Captain-General's cellar.

He slept peacefully, in the consciousness of a good action performed and the assurance that, being without boats and very short of men, the pretended Arabella was powerless to accomplish upon the treasure-ships the real object of her descent upon San Juan. So as to make doubly sure, however, a Spanish company kept watch at the guns in the pimento grove. But there was no alarm, and when day broke it showed them the pirate ship hull down on the horizon, and, in a majesty of full sail, the sometime Maria Gloriosa entering the roads.

At breakfast, when he came to it, Don Pedro Encarnado was greeted by Don Sebastian with news that his Admiral's ship had just dropped anchor in the bay.

'He is very punctual,' said Don Pedro, thinking of Wolverstone.

'Punctual? He's behind the fair. He arrives just too late to complete your glorious work by sinking that pirate craft. I shall hope to tell him so.'

Don Pedro frowned. 'That would be imprudent, considering his favour with the King. It is not well to ruffle the Marquis. Fortunately he is not likely to come ashore. The gout, you see.'

'But I shall pay him a visit aboard his ship.'

There was no make-believe in Captain Blood's frown. Unless he could turn Don Sebastian from that reasonable intention the smooth plan he had evolved would be disastrously wrecked.

'No, no. I shouldn't do that,' he said.

'Not do it? Of course I shall. It is my duty.'

'Oh no, no. You would derogate. Think of the great position you occupy Captain-General of Puerto Rico; which is to say, Governor, Viceroy almost. It is not for you to wait upon admirals, but for admirals to wait upon you. And the Marquis of Riconete is well aware of it. That is why, being unable, from his plaguey gout, to come in person, he sent me to be his deputy. What you have to say to the Marquis, you can say here, at your ease, to me.'

Impressed, Don Sebastian passed a reflective hand over his several chins. 'There is, of course, a certain truth in what you say. Yes, yes. Nevertheless, in this case I have a special duty to perform, which must be performed in person. I must acquaint the Admiral very fully with the heroic part you have played in saving Puerto Rico and the King's treasury here, not to mention the plate-ships. Honour where honour is due. I must see, Don Pedro, that you have your deserts.'

And Doña Leocadia, remembering with a shudder the horrors of yesterday which the gallantry of Don Pedro had cut short, and further possible horrors which his timely coming had averted, was warm and eager in reinforcement of her husband's generous intentions.

But before that display of so much goodwill Don Pedro's face grew more and more forbidding. Sternly he shook his head.

'It is as I feared,' he said—'something which I cannot permit. If you insist, Don Sebastian, you will affront me. What I did yesterday was no more than was imposed upon me by my office. Neither thanks nor praise are due for a performance of bare duty. They are heroes only who without thought of risk to themselves or concern for their own interests, perform deeds which are not within their duties. That, at least, is my conception. And, as I have said, to insist upon making a ballad of my conduct yesterday would be to affront me. You would not, I am sure, wish to do that, Don Sebastian.'

'Oh, but what modesty!' exclaimed the lady, joining her hands and casting up her eyes. 'How true it is that the great are always humble.'

Don Sebastian looked crestfallen. He sighed. 'It is an attitude worthy of a hero. True. But it disappoints me, my friend. It is a little return that I could make...'

'No return is due, Don Sebastian.' Don Pedro was forbiddingly peremptory. 'Let us speak of it no more, I beg of you.' He rose. 'I had better go aboard at once, to receive the Admiral's orders. I will inform him, in my own terms, of what has taken place here. And I can point to the gallows you are erecting on the beach for this pestilent Captain Blood. That will be most reassuring to his Excellency.'

Of how reassuring it was Don Pedro brought news when towards noon he came ashore again, no longer in the borrowed ill-fitting clothes, but arrayed once more in all the glories of a grandee of Spain.

'The Marquis of Riconete asks me to inform you that since the Caribbean is happily delivered of the infamous Captain Blood, his Excellency's mission in these waters is at an end, and nothing now prevents him from yielding to the urgency of returning to Spain at once. He has decided to convoy the plate-ships across the ocean, and he begs you to instruct their captains to be ready to weigh anchor on the first of the ebb: this afternoon at three.'

Don Sebastian was aghast. 'But did you not tell him, sir, that it is impossible?'

Don Pedro shrugged. 'One does not argue with the Admiral of the Ocean-Sea.'

'But, my dear Don Pedro, more than half the crews are absent and the ships are without guns.'

'Be sure that I did not fail to inform his Excellency of that. It merely annoyed him. He takes the view that since each ship carries hands enough to sail her, no more is necessary. The Maria Gloriosa is sufficiently armed to protect them.'

'He does not pause, then, to reflect what may happen should they become separated?'

'That also I pointed out. It made no impression. His Excellency is of a high confidence.'

Don Sebastian blew out his cheeks. 'So! So! To be sure, it is his affair. And I thank God for it. The plate-ships have brought trouble enough upon San Juan de Puerto Rico, and I'll be glad to see the last of them. But permit me to observe that your Admiral of the Ocean-Sea is a singularly rash man. It comes, I suppose, of being a royal favourite.'

Don Pedro's sly little smile suggested subtly complete agreement. 'It is understood, then, that you will give orders for the promptest victualling of the ships. His Excellency must not be kept waiting, and, anyway, the ebb will not wait even for him.'

'Oh, perfectly,' said Don Sebastian. Irony exaggerated his submission. 'I will give the orders at once.'

'I will inform his Excellency. He will be gratified. I take my leave, then, Don Sebastian.' They embraced. 'Believe me,

I shall long treasure the memory of our happy and profitable association. My homage to Doña Leocadia.'

'But will you not stay to see the hanging of Captain Blood? It is to take place at noon.'

'The Admiral expects me aboard at eight bells. I dare not keep him waiting.'

But on his way to the harbour, Captain Blood paused at the town gaol. By the officer in charge he was received with the honour due to the saviour of San Juan, and doors were unlocked at his bidding.

Beyond a yard in which the heavily ironed, dejected prisoners of yesterday's affray were herded, he came to a stone chamber lighted by a small window set high and heavily barred. In this dark, noisome hole sat the great buccaneer, hunched on a stool, his head in his manacled hands. He looked up as the door groaned on its hinges, and out of a livid face he glared at his visitor. He did not recognize his grimy opponent of yesterday in this elegant gentleman in black and silver, whose sedulously curled black periwig fell to his shoulders and who swung a gold-headed ebony cane as he advanced.

'Is it time?' he growled in his bad Spanish.

The apparent Castilian nobleman answered him in the English that is spoken in Ireland. 'Och now, don't be impatient. Ye've still time to be making your soul; that is, if ye've a soul to make at all; still time to repent the nasty notion that led you into this imposture. I could forgive you the pretence that you are Captain Blood. There's a sort of compliment in that. But I can't be forgiving you the things you did in Cartagena: the wantonly murdered men, the violated women, the loathsome cruelties for cruelty's sake by which you slaked your evil lusts and dishonoured the name you assumed.'

The ruffian sneered. 'You talk like a canting parson sent to shrive me.'

'I talk like the man I am, the man whose name ye've befouled with the filth of your nature. I'll be leaving you to ponder, in the little time that's left you, the poetic justice by which mine is the hand that hangs you. For I am Captain Blood.'

A moment still he remained inscrutably surveying the doomed impostor whom amazement had rendered speechless; then, turning on his heel, he went to rejoin the waiting Spanish officer.

Thence, past the gallows erected on the beach, he repaired to the waiting boat, and was pulled back to the white-and-gold flagship in the roads.

And so it befell that on that same day the false Captain Blood was hanged on the beach of San Juan de Puerto Rico, and the real Captain Blood sailed away for Tortuga in the Maria Gloriosa, or Andalusian Lass, convoying the richly laden plate-ships, which had neither guns nor crews with which to offer resistance when the truth of their situation was later discovered to their captains.

Episode 3

THE DEMONSTRATION

I

'Fortune,' Captain Blood was wont to say, 'detests a niggard. Her favours are reserved for the man who knows how to spend nobly and to stake boldly.'

Whether you hold him right or wrong in this opinion, it is at least beyond question that he never shrank from acting upon it. Instances of his prodigality are abundant in that record of his fortunes and hazards which Jeremy Pitt has left us, but none is more recklessly splendid than that supplied by his measures to defeat the West Indian policy of Monsieur de Louvois when it was threatening the great buccaneering brotherhood with extinction.

The Marquis de Louvois, who succeeded the great Colbert in the service of Louis XIV, was universally hated whilst he lived, and as universally lamented when he died. Than this conjunction of estimates there can be, I take it, no higher testimonial to the worth of a minister of State. Nothing was either too great or too small for Monsieur de Louvois' attention. Once he had set the machinery of State moving smoothly at home, he turned in his reorganizing lust to survey the French possessions in the Caribbean, where the activities of the buccaneers distressed his sense of orderliness.

Thither, in the King's twenty-four-gun ship the Béarnais, he dispatched the Chevalier de Saintonges, an able, personable gentleman in the early thirties, who had earned a confidence which Monsieur de Louvois did not lightly bestow, and who bore now clear instructions upon how to proceed so as to put an end to the evil, as Monsieur de Louvois accounted it.

To Monsieur de Saintonges, whose circumstances in life were by no means opulent, this was to prove an unsuspected and Heaven-sent chance of fortune; for in the course of serving his King to the best of his ability he found occasion, with an ability even greater, very abundantly to serve himself. During his sojourn in Martinique, which the events induced him to protract far beyond what was strictly necessary, he met, wooed at tropical speed, and married, Madame de Veynac. This young and magnificently handsome widow of Hommaire de Veynac had inherited from her late husband those vast West Indian possessions which comprised nearly a third of the island of Martinique, with plantations of sugar, spices, and tobacco producing annual revenues that were nothing short of royal. Thus richly endowed, she came to the arms of the stately but rather impecunious Chevalier de Saintonges.

The Chevalier was too conscientious a man and too profoundly imbued with the sense of the importance of his mission to permit this marriage to be more than a splendid interlude in the diligent performance of the duties which had brought him to the New World. The nuptials having been celebrated in Saint Pierre with all the pomp and luxury proper to the lady's importance, Monsieur de Saintonges resumed his task with the increased consequence which he derived from the happy change in his circumstances. He took his bride aboard the Béarnais, and sailed away from Saint Pierre to complete his tour of inspection before setting a course for France and the full enjoyment of the fabulous wealth that was now his.

Dominica, Guadeloupe, and the Grenadines he had already visited, as well as Sainte Croix, which properly speaking was the property not of the French Crown but of the French West India Company. The most important part of his mission, however, remained yet to be accomplished at Tortuga, that other property of the French West India Company, which had become the stronghold of those buccaneers, English, French and Dutch, for whose extermination it was the Chevalier's duty to take order.

His confidence in his ability to succeed in this difficult matter had been materially augmented by the report that Peter Blood, the most dangerous and enterprising of all these filibusters, had lately been caught by the Spaniards and hanged at San Juan de Puerto Rico.

In calm but torrid August weather the Béarnais made a good passage and came to drop anchor in the Bay of Cayona, that rockbound harbour which Nature might have designed expressly to be a pirates' lair.

The Chevalier took his bride ashore with him, bestowing her in a chair expressly procured, for which his seamen opened a way through the heterogeneous crowd of Europeans, Black men, Maroons, and Mulattos of both sexes who swarmed to view this great lady from the French ship. Two half-caste porters, all but naked, bore the chair with its precious cargo, whilst the rather pompous Monsieur de Saintonges, clad in the lightest of blue taffetas, cane in one hand and the hat with which he fanned himself in the other, stalked beside it, damning the heat, the flies, and the smells. A tall, florid man, already inclining slightly at this early age to embonpoint, he perspired profusely, and his head ran wet under his elaborate golden periwig.

Up the gentle acclivity of the main unpaved street of Cayona with its fierce white glare of coral dust and its fringe of languid palms, he toiled to the blessed fragrant shade of the Governor's garden and eventually to the cool twilight of chambers from which the sun's ardour was excluded by green, slatted blinds. Here cool drinks, in which rum and limes and sugar-cane were skilfully compounded, accompanied the cordial welcome extended by the Governor and his two handsome daughters to these distinguished visitors.

But the heat in which Monsieur de Saintonges arrived was destined to be only temporarily allayed. Soon after Madame de Saintonges had been carried off by the Governor's daughters, a discussion ensued which reopened all the Chevalier's pores.

Monsieur d'Ogeron, who governed Tortuga on behalf of the French West India Company, had listened with a gravity increasing to gloom to the forcible expositions made by his visitor in the name of Monsieur de Louvois.

A slight, short, elegant man was this Monsieur d'Ogeron, who retained in this outlandish island of his rule something of the courtly airs of the great world from which he came, just as he surrounded himself in his house and its equipment with the elegancies proper to a French gentleman of birth. Only breeding and good manners enabled him now to dissemble his impatience. At the end of the Chevalier's blunt and pompous peroration, he fetched a sigh in which there was some weariness.

'I suspect,' he ventured, 'that Monsieur de Louvois is indifferently informed upon West Indian conditions.'

Monsieur de Saintonges was aghast at this hint of opposition. His sense of the importance and omniscience of Monsieur de Louvois was almost as high as his sense of his own possession of these qualities.

'I doubt, sir, if there are any conditions in the world upon which Monsieur le Marquis is not fully informed.'

Monsieur d'Ogeron's smile was gentle and courteous. 'All the world is of course aware of Monsieur de Louvois' high worth. But his Excellency does not possess my own experience of these remotenesses, and this, I venture to think, lends some value to my opinion.'

By an impatient gesture the Chevalier waved aside the matter of Monsieur d'Ogeron's opinions. 'We lose sight of the point, I think. Suffer me to be quite blunt, sir. Tortuga is under the flag of France. Monsieur de Louvois takes the view, in which I venture to concur, that it is in the last degree improper... In short, that it is not to the honour of the flag of France that it should protect a horde of brigands.'

Monsieur d'Ogeron's gentle smile was still all deprecation. 'Sir, sir, it is not the flag of France that protects the filibusters, but the filibusters that protect the flag of France.'

The tall, blond, rather imposing representative of the Crown came to his feet, as if to mark his indignation. 'Monsieur, that is an outrageous statement.'

The Governor's urbanity remained unimpaired. 'It is the fact that is outrageous, not the statement. Permit me to observe to you, monsieur, that a hundred and fifty years ago, His Holiness the Pope bestowed upon Spain the New World of Columbus' discovery. Since then other nations, the French, the English, the Dutch, have paid less heed to that papal bull than Spain considers proper. They have attempted, themselves, to settle some of these lands—lands of which the Spaniards have never taken actual possession. Because Spain insists upon regarding this as a violation of her rights, the Caribbean for years has been a cockpit.

'These buccaneers themselves, whom you regard with such contempt, were originally peaceful hunters, cultivators, and traders. The Spaniards chased them out of Hispaniola, drove them, English and French, from St Christopher and the Dutch from Sainte Croix, by ruthless massacres which did not spare even their women and children. In self-defence these men forsook their peaceful boucans, took arms, banded themselves together into a brotherhood, and hunted the Spaniard in their turn. That the Virgin Islands today belong to the English Crown is due to these Brethren of the Coast, as they call themselves, these buccaneers who took possession of those lands in the name of England. This very island of Tortuga, like the island of Sainte Croix, came to belong to the French West India Company, and so to France, in the same way.

'You spoke, sir, of the protection of the French flag enjoyed by these buccaneers. There is here a confusion of ideas. If there were no buccaneers to hold the rapacity of Spain in check, I ask myself, Monsieur de Saintonges, if this voyage of yours would ever have been undertaken, for I doubt if there would have been any French possessions in the Caribbean to be visited.' He paused to smile upon the blank amazement of his guest. 'I hope, monsieur, that I have said enough to justify the opinion, which I take the liberty of holding in opposition to that of Monsieur de Louvois, that the suppression of the buccaneers might easily result in disaster to the French West Indian colonies.'

At this point Monsieur de Saintonges exploded. As so commonly happens, it was actually a sense of the truth underlying the Governor's argument that produced his exasperation. The reckless terms of his rejoinder lead us to doubt the wisdom of Monsieur de Louvois in choosing him for an ambassador.

'You have said enough, monsieur... more than enough to persuade me that a reluctance to forgo the profits accruing to your Company and to yourself personally from the plunder marketed in Tortuga, is rendering you negligent of the honour of France, upon which this traffic is a stain.'

Monsieur d'Ogeron smiled no longer. Stricken in his turn by the amount of truth in the Chevalier's accusation; he came to his feet suddenly, white with anger. But, a masterful, self-contained little man, he was without any of the bluster of his tall visitor. His voice was as cold as ice and very level.

'Such an assertion, monsieur, can be made to me only sword in hand.'

Saintonges strode about the long room, and waved his arms.

'That is of a piece with the rest! Preposterous! If that's your humour, you had better send your cartel to Monsieur de Louvois. I am but his mouthpiece. I have said what I was charged to say, and what I would not have said if I had found you reasonable. You are to understand, monsieur, that I have not come all the way from France to fight duels on behalf of the Crown, but to explain the Crown's views and issue the Crown's orders. If they appear distasteful to you, that is not my affair. The orders I have for you are that Tortuga must cease to be a haven for buccaneers. And that is all that needs to be said.'

'God give me patience, sir,' cried Monsieur d'Ogeron in his distress. 'Will you be good enough to tell me at the same time how I am to enforce these orders?'

'Where is the difficulty? Close the market in which you receive the plunder. If you make an end of the traffic, the buccaneers will make an end of themselves.'

'How simple! But how very simple! And what if the buccaneers make an end of me and of this possession of the West India Company? What if they seize the island of Tortuga for themselves, which is no doubt what would happen? What then, if you please, Monsieur de Saintonges?'

'The might of France will know how to enforce her rights.'

'Much obliged. Does the might of France realize how mighty it will have to be? Has Monsieur de Louvois any conception of the strength and organization of these buccaneers? Have you never, for instance, heard in France of Morgan's march on Panama? Is it realized that there are in all some five or six thousand of these men afloat, the most formidable sea-fighters the world has ever seen? If they were banded together by such a menace of extinction, they could assemble a navy of forty or fifty ships that would sweep the Caribbean from end to end.'

At last the Governor had succeeded in putting Monsieur de Saintonges out of countenance by these realities. For a moment the Chevalier stared chapfallen at his host. Then he rallied obstinately. 'Surely, sir, surely you exaggerate.'

'I exaggerate nothing. I desire you to understand that I am actuated by something more than the self-interest you so offensively attribute to me.'

'Monsieur de Louvois will regret, I am sure, the injustice of that assumption when I report to him fully, making clear what you have told me. For the rest, sir, however, you have your orders.'

'But surely, sir, you have been granted some discretion in the fulfilment of your mission. Finding things as you do, as I have explained them, it seems to me that you would do no disservice to the Crown in recommending to Monsieur de Louvois that until France is in a position to place a navy in the Caribbean so as to protect her possessions, she would be well-advised not to disturb the existing state of things.'

The Chevalier merely stiffened further. 'That, monsieur, is not a recommendation that would become me. You have the orders of Monsieur de Louvois, which are that this mart for the plunder of the seas must at once be closed. I trust that you will enable me to assure Monsieur de Louvois of your immediate compliance.'

Monsieur d'Ogeron was in despair before the stupidity of this official intransigence. 'I must still protest, monsieur, that your description is not a just one. No plunder comes here but the plunder of Spain to compensate us for all the plunder we have suffered and shall continue to suffer at the hands of the gentlemen of Castile.'

'That, sir, is fantastic. There is peace between Spain and France.'

'In the Caribbean, Monsieur de Saintonges, there is never peace. If we abolish the buccaneers, we lay down our arms and offer our throats to the knife. That is all.'

There were, however, no arguments that could move Monsieur de Saintonges from the position he had taken up. 'I must regard that as a personal opinion, more or less coloured—suffer me to say it without offence—by the interests of your Company and yourself. Anyway, the orders are clear. You realize that you will neglect them at your peril.'

'And also that I shall fulfil them at my peril,' said the Governor, with a twist of the lips. He shrugged and sighed. 'You place me, sir, between the sword and the wall.'

'Do me the justice to understand that I discharge my duty,' said the lofty Chevalier de Saintonges, and the concession of those words was the only concession Monsieur d'Ogeron could wring from his obstinate self-sufficiency.

II

Monsieur de Saintonges sailed away with his wife that same evening from Tortuga, setting a course for Port au Prince, where he desired to pay a call before finally steering for France and the opulent ease which he could now command there. Admiring himself for the firmness with which he had resisted all the Governor of Tortuga's special pleading, he took Madame de Saintonges into his confidence in the matter, so that she too might admire him.

'That little trafficker in brigandage might have persuaded me from my duty if I had been less alert,' he laughed. 'But I am not easily deceived. That is why Monsieur de Louvois chose me for a mission of this importance. He knew the difficulties I should meet, and knew that I should not be duped by misrepresentations however specious.'

She was a tall, handsome, languorous lady, sloe-eyed, black-haired, with a skin like ivory and a bosom of Hebe. Her languishing eyes considered in awe and reverence this husband from the great world, who was to open for her social gates in France that would have been closed against the wife of a mere planter, however rich. Yet for all her admiring confidence in his acumen, she ventured to wonder was he correct in regarding as purely self-interested the arguments which Monsieur d'Ogeron had presented. She had not spent her life in the West Indies without learning something of the predatoriness of Spain, although perhaps she had never until now suspected the extent to which the activities of the buccaneers might be keeping that predatoriness in check. Spain maintained a considerable fleet in the Caribbean, mainly for the purpose of guarding her settlements from filibustering raids. The suppression of the filibusters would render that fleet comparatively idle, and in idleness there is no knowing to what devilry men may turn, especially if they be Spaniards.

Thus, meekly, Madame de Saintonges to her adored husband. But the adored husband, with the high spirit that rendered him so adorable, refused to be shaken.

'In such an event, be sure that the King of France, my master, will take order.'

Nevertheless, his mind was no longer quite at rest. His wife's very submissive and tentative support of Monsieur d'Ogeron's argument had unsettled him. It was easy to gird at the self-interest of the Governor of Tortuga, and to assign to it his dread of Spain. Monsieur de Saintonges, because, himself, he had acquired a sudden and enormous interest in French West Indian possessions, began to ask himself whether, after all, he might not have been too ready to believe that Monsieur d'Ogeron had exaggerated.

And the Governor of Tortuga had not exaggerated. However much his interests may have jumped with his arguments, there can be no doubt whatever that these were well founded. Because of this he could perceive ahead of him no other course but to resign his office and return at once to France, leaving Monsieur de Louvois to work out the destinies of the French West Indies and of Tortuga in his own fashion. It would be a desertion of the interests of the West India Company. But if the new minister's will prevailed, very soon the West India Company would have no interests to protect.

The little Governor spent a disturbed night, and slept late on the following morning, to be eventually aroused by gunfire.

The boom of cannon and the rattle of musketry were so continuous that it took him some time to realize that the din did not betoken an attack upon the harbour, but a feu-de-joie such as the rocks of Cayona had never yet echoed. The reason for it, when he discovered it, served to dispel some part of his dejection. The report that Peter Blood had been taken and hanged at San Juan de Puerto Rico was being proven false by the arrival in Cayona of Peter Blood himself. He had sailed into the harbour aboard a captured Spanish vessel, the sometime Maria Gloriosa, lately the flagship of the Marquis of Riconete, the Admiral of the Ocean-Sea, trailing in her wake the two richly laden Spanish galleons, the plate-ships taken at Puerto Rico.

The guns that thundered their salutes were the guns of Blood's own fleet of three ships, which had been refitting at Tortuga in his absence and aboard which during the past week all had been mourning and disorientation.

Rejoicing as fully as any of those jubilant buccaneers in this return from the dead of a man whom he too had mourned—for a real friendship existed between the Governor of Tortuga and the great Captain—Monsieur d'Ogeron and his daughters prepared for Peter Blood a feast of welcome, to which the Governor brought some of those bottles 'from behind the faggots', as he described the choice wines that he received from France.

The Captain came in great good humour to the feast, and entertained them at table with an account of the queer adventure in Puerto Rico, which had ended in the hanging of a poor scoundrelly pretender to the name and fame of Captain Blood, and had enabled him to sail away unchallenged with the two plate-ships that were now anchored in the harbour of Tortuga.

'I never made a richer haul, and I doubt if many richer have ever been made. Of the gold alone my own share must be a matter of twenty-five thousand pieces of eight, which I'll be depositing with you against bills of exchange on France. Then the peppers and spices in one of the galleons should be worth over a hundred thousand pieces to the West India Company. It awaits your valuation, my friend.'

But an announcement which should have increased the Governor's good humour merely served to precipitate him visibly into the depths of gloom by reminding him of how the circumstances had altered. Sorrowfully he looked across the table at his guest, and sorrowfully he shook his head.

'All that is finished, my friend. I am under a cursed interdict.' And forth in fullest detail came the tale of the visit of the Chevalier de Saintonges with its curtailment of Monsieur d'Ogeron's activities. 'So you see, my dear Captain, the markets of the West India Company are now closed to you.'

The keen, shaven, suntanned face in its frame of black curls showed an angry consternation.

'Name of God! But didn't you tell this lackey from Court that—'

'There was nothing I did not tell him to which a man of sense should have listened, no argument that I did not present. To all that I had to say he wearied me with insistence that he doubted if there were any conditions in the world upon which

Monsieur de Louvois is not informed. To the Chevalier de Saintonges there is no god but Louvois, and Saintonges is his prophet. So much was plain. A consequential gentleman this Monsieur de Saintonge, like all these Court minions. Lately in Martinique he married the widow of Hommaire de Veynac. That will make him one of the richest men in France. You know the effect of great possessions on a self-sufficient man.' Monsieur d'Ogeron spread his hands. 'It is finished, my friend.'

But with this Captain Blood could not agree. 'That is to bend your head to the axe. Oh no, no. Defeat is not to be accepted so easily by men of our strength.'

'For you, who dwell outside the law, all things are possible. But for me... Here in Tortuga I represent the law of France. I must serve and uphold it. And the law has pronounced.'

'Had I arrived a day sooner the law might have been made to pronounce differently.'

D'Ogeron was wistfully sardonic. 'You imagine, in spite of all that I have said, that you could have persuaded this coxcomb of his folly?'

'There is nothing of which a man cannot be persuaded if the proper arguments are put before him in the proper manner.'

'I tell you that I put before him all the arguments that exist.'

'No, no. You presented only those that occurred to you.'

'If you mean that I should have put a pistol to the head of this insufferable puppy...'

'Oh, my friend! That is not an argument. It is a constraint. We are all of us self-interested, and none are more so than those who, like this Chevalier de Saintonges, are ready to accuse others of that fault. An appeal to his interests might have been persuasive.'

'Perhaps. But what do I know of his interests?'

'What do you know of them? Oh, but think. Have you not, yourself, just told me that he lately married the widow of Hommaire de Veynac? That gives him great West Indian interests. You spoke vaguely and generally of Spanish raids upon the settlements of other nations. You should have been more particular. You should have dwelt upon the possibility of a raid upon wealthy Martinique. That would have given him to think. And now he's gone, and the chance is lost.'

But d'Ogeron would see no reason for sharing any regrets of that lost opportunity.

'His obstinacy would have prevented him from taking fright. He would not have listened. The last thing he said to me before he sailed for Port au Prince...'

'For Port au Prince!' ejaculated Captain Blood, to interrupt him, 'He's gone to Port au Prince?'

'That was his destination when he departed yesterday. It's his last port of call before he sails for France.'

'So, so!' The Captain was thoughtful. 'That means, then, that he will be returning by way of the Tortuga Channel?'

'Of course, since in the alternative he would have to sail round Hispaniola.'

'Now, glory be, I may not be too late, after all. Couldn't I intercept him as he returns, and try my persuasive arts on him?'

'You'd waste your time, Captain.'

'You make too sure. It's the great gift of persuasion I have. Sustain your hopes awhile, my friend, until I put Monsieur de Saintonges to the test.'

But to raise from their nadir the hopes of Monsieur d'Ogeron something more was necessary than mere light-hearted assurances. It was with the sigh of an abiding despondency that he bade farewell that day to Captain Blood, and without confidence that he wished him luck in whatever he might adventure.

What form the adventure might take, Captain Blood, himself, did not yet know when he quitted the Governor's house and went aboard his own splendid forty-gun ship the Arabella, which, ready for sea, fitted, armed and victualled, had been standing idle during his late absence. But the thought he gave the matter was to such good purpose that late that same afternoon, with a definite plan conceived, he held a council of war in the great cabin, and assigned particular duties to his leading associates.

Hagthorpe and Dyke were to remain in Tortuga in charge of the treasure-ships. Wolverstone was given command of the Spanish Admiral's captured flagship, the Maria Gloriosa, and was required to sail at once, with very special and detailed instructions. To Yberville, the French buccaneer who was associated with him, Blood entrusted the Elizabeth, with orders to make ready to put to sea.

That same evening, at sunset, the Arabella was warped out of the swarm of lesser shipping that had collected about her anchorage. With Blood, himself, in command, with Pitt for sailing master and Ogle for master gunner, she set sail from Cayona, followed closely by the Elizabeth. The Maria Gloriosa was already hull down on the horizon.

Beating up against gentle easterly breezes, the two buccaneer ships, the Arabella and her consort, were off Point Palmish on the northern coast of Hispaniola by the following evening. Hereabouts, where the Tortuga Channel narrows to a mere five miles between Palmish and Portugal Point, Captain Blood decided to take up his station for what was to be done.

III

At about the time that the Arabella and the Elizabeth were casting anchor in that lonely cove on the northern coast of Hispaniola, the Béarnais was weighing at Port au Prince. The smells of the place offended the delicate nostrils of Madame de Saintonges, and on this account—since wives so well endowed are to be pampered—the Chevalier cut short his visit even at the cost of scamping the King's business. Glad to have set a term to this at last, with the serene conviction of having discharged his mission in a manner that must deserve the praise of Monsieur de Louvois, the Chevalier now turned his face towards France and his thoughts to lighter and more personal matters.

With a light wind abeam, the progress of the Béarnais was so slow that it took her twenty-four hours to round Cape St Nicholas at the Western end of the Tortuga Channel; so that it was somewhere about sunset on the day following that of her departure from Port au Prince when she entered that narrow passage.

Monsieur de Saintonges at the time was lounging elegantly on the poop, beside a day-bed set under an awning of brown sailcloth. On this day-bed reclined his handsome Creole wife. There was about this superbly proportioned lady, from the deep mellowness of her voice to the great pearls entwined in her glossy black hair, nothing that did not announce her opulence. It was enhanced at present by profound contentment in this marriage in which each party so perfectly complemented the other. She seemed to glow and swell with it as she lay there luxuriously, faintly waving her jewelled fan, her rich laugh so ready to pay homage to the wit with which her bridegroom sought to dazzle her.

Into this idyll stepped, more or less abruptly, and certainly intrusively, Monsieur Luzan, the Captain of the Béarnais, a lean, brown, hook-nosed man something above the middle height, whose air and carriage were those of a soldier rather than a seaman. As he approached, he took the telescope from under his arm and pointed aft with it.

'Yonder is something that is odd,' he said. And he held out the glass. 'Take a look, Chevalier.'

Monsieur de Saintonges rose slowly, and his eyes followed the indication. Some three miles to westward a sail was visible.

'A ship,' he said, and languidly accepted the proffered telescope. He stepped aside, to the rail, whence the view was clearer and where he could find a support on which to steady his elbow.

Through the glass he beheld a big white vessel very high in the poop. She was veering northward, on a starboard tack against the easterly breeze, and so displayed a noble flank pierced for twenty-four guns, the ports gleaming gold against the white. From her maintopmast, above a mountain of snowy canvas, floated the red-and-gold banner of Castile, and above this a crucifix was mounted.

The Chevalier lowered the glass. 'A Spaniard,' was his casual comment. 'What oddness do you discover in her, Captain?'

'Oh, a Spaniard manifestly. But she was steering south when first we sighted her. A little later she veered into our wake and crowded sail. That is what is odd. For the inference is that she decided to follow us.'

'What then?'

'Just so. What then?' He paused as if for a reply, then resumed. 'From the position of her flag she is an admiral's ship. You will have observed that she is of a heavy armament. She carries forty-eight guns besides stern and forechasers.' Again he paused, finally to add with some force: 'When I am followed by a ship like that I like to know the reason.'

Madame stirred languidly on her day-bed to an accompaniment of deep, rich laughter. 'Are you a man to start at shadows, Captain?'

'Invariably, when cast by a Spaniard, Madame.' Luzan's tone was sharp. He was of a peppery temper, and this was stirred by the reflection upon his courage which he found implied in Madame's question.

The Chevalier, disliking the tone, permitted himself some sarcasms where he would have been better employed in inquiring into the reasons for the Captain's misgivings. Luzan departed in annoyance.

That night the wind dropped to the merest breath, and so slow was their progress that by the following dawn they were still some five or six miles to the west of Portugal Point and the exit of the straits. And daylight showed them the big Spanish ship ever at about the same distance astern. Uneasily and at length Captain Luzan scanned her once more, then passed his glass to his lieutenant.

'See what she can tell you.'

The lieutenant looked long, and whilst he looked he saw her making the addition of stunsails to the mountain of canvas that she already carried. This he announced to the Captain at his elbow, and then, having scanned the pennant on her foretopmast, he was able to add the information that she was the flagship of the Spanish Admiral of the Ocean-Sea, the Marquis of Riconete.

That she should put out stunsails so as to catch the last possible ounce of the light airs increased the Captain's suspicion that her aim was to overhaul him, and being imbued, as became an experienced seaman, whilst in these waters with a healthy mistrust of the intentions of all Spaniards, he took his decision. Crowding all possible sail, and as close-hauled as he dared run, he headed south for the shelter of one of the harbours of the northern coast of French Hispaniola. Thither this Spaniard, if she was indeed in pursuit, would hardly dare to follow him. If she did, she would scarcely venture to display hostility. The manoeuvre would also serve to apply a final test to her intentions.

The result supplied Luzan with almost immediate certainty. At once the great galleon was seen to veer in the same direction, actually thrusting her nose yet a point nearer to such wind as there was. It became as clear that she was in pursuit of the Béarnais as that the Béarnais would be cut off before ever she could reach the green coast that was now almost ahead of her, but still some four miles distant.

Madame de Saintonges, greatly incommoded in her cabin by the apparently quite unnecessary list to starboard, demanded impatiently to be informed by Heaven or Hell what might be amiss that morning with the fool who commanded the Béarnais. The uxorious Chevalier, in bed-gown and slippers, and with a hurriedly donned periwig, the curls of which hung like a row of tallow candles about his flushed countenance, made haste to go and ascertain.

He reeled along the almost perpendicular deck of the gangway to the ship's waist, and stood there bawling angrily for Luzan.

The Captain appeared at the poop-rail to answer him with a curt account of his apprehensions.

'Are you still under that absurd persuasion?' quoth Monsieur de Saintonges. 'Absurd! Why should a Spaniard be in pursuit of us?'

'It will be better to continue to ask ourselves that question than to wait to discover the answer,' snapped Luzan, thus, by his lack of deference, increasing the Chevalier's annoyance.

'But it is imbecile, this!' raved Saintonges. 'To run away from nothing. And it is infamous to discompose Madame de Saintonges by fears so infantile.'

Luzan's patience completely left him. 'She'll be infinitely more discomposed,' he sneered, 'if these infantile fears are realized.' And he added bluntly: 'Madame de Saintonges is a handsome woman, and Spaniards are Spaniards.'

A shrill exclamation was his answer, to announce that Madame herself had now emerged from the companionway. She was in a state of undress that barely preserved the decencies; for without waiting to cast more than a wrap over her night-rail, and with a mane of lustrous black hair like a cloak about her splendid shoulders, she had come to ascertain for herself what might be happening.

Luzan's remark, overheard as she was stepping into the ship's waist, brought upon him now a torrent of shrill abuse, in the course of which he heard himself described as a paltry coward and a low, coarse wretch. And before she had done, the Chevalier was adding his voice to hers.

'You are mad, sir. Mad! What can we possibly have to fear from a Spanish ship, a King's ship, you tell me, an Admiral? We fly the flag of France, and Spain is not at war with France.'

Luzan controlled himself to answer as quietly as he might. 'In these waters, sir, it is impossible to say with whom Spain may be at war. Spain is persuaded that God created the Americas especially for her delight. I have been telling you this ever since we entered the Caribbean.'

The Chevalier remembered not only this, but also that from someone else he had lately heard expressions very similar. Madame, however, was distracting his attention. 'The fellow's wits are turned by panic,' she railed in furious contempt. 'It is terrible that such a man should be entrusted with a ship. He would be better fitted to command a kitchen battery.'

Heaven alone knows what might have been the answer to that insult and what the consequences of it if at that very moment the boom of a gun had not come to save Luzan the trouble of a reply, and abruptly to change the scene and the tempers of the actors.

'Righteous Heaven!' screamed Madame, and 'Ventredieu!' swore her husband.

The lady clutched her bosom. The Chevalier, with a face of chalk, put an arm protectingly about her. From the poop the Captain whom they had so freely accused of cowardice laughed outright with a well-savoured malice.

'You are answered, Madame. And you, sir. Another time perhaps you will reflect before you call my fears infantile and my conduct imbecile.'

With that he turned his back upon them, so that he might speak to the lieutenant who had hastened to his elbow. He bawled an order. It was instantly followed by the whistle of the boatswain's pipe, and in the waist about Saintonges and his bride there was a sudden jostling stir as the hands came pouring from their quarters to be marshalled for whatever the Captain might require of them. Aloft there was another kind of activity. Men were swarming the ratlines and spreading nets whose purpose was to catch any spars that might be brought down in the course of action.

A second gun boomed from the Spaniard and then a third; after that there was a pause, and then they were saluted by what sounded like the thunder of a whole broadside.

The Chevalier lowered his white and shaking wife, whose knees had suddenly turned to water, to a seat on the hatch-coaming. He was futilely profane in his distress.

From the rail Luzan, taking pity on them, and entirely unruffled, uttered what he believed to be reassurance.

'At present she is burning powder to no purpose. Mere Spanish bombast. She'll come within range before I fire a shot. My gunners have their orders.'

But, far from reassuring them, this was merely to increase the Chevalier's fury and distress.

'God of my life! Return her fire? You mustn't think of it. You can't deliver battle.'

'Can't I? You shall see.'

'But you cannot go into action with Madame de Saintonges on board.'

'You want to laugh,' said Luzan. 'If I had the Queen of France on board I must still fight my ship. And I have no choice, pray observe. We are being overhauled too fast to make harbour in time. And how do I know that we should be safe even then?'

The Chevalier stamped in rage.

'But they are brigands, then, these Spaniards?'

There was another roar of artillery at closer quarters now which if still not close enough for damage was close enough to increase the panic of Monsieur and Madame de Saintonges.

The Captain was no longer heeding them. His lieutenant had clutched his arm, and was pointing westward. Luzan with the telescope to his eye was following that indication.

A mile or so off on their starboard beam, midway between the Béarnais and the Spanish Admiral, a big red forty-gun ship under full sail was creeping into view round a headland of the Hispaniola coast. Close in her wake came a second ship of an armament only a little less powerful. They flew no flag, and it was in increasing apprehension that Luzan watched their movements, wondering were they fresh assailants. To his almost incredulous relief, he saw them veer to larboard, heading in the direction of the Spaniard half hidden still in the smoke of her last cannonade, which that morning's gentle airs were slow to disperse.

Light though the wind might be, the newcomers had the advantage of it, and with the weather-gauge of the Spaniard they advanced upon him, like hawks stooping to a heron, opening fire with their forechasers as they went.

Through a veil of rising smoke the Spaniard could be discerned easing up to receive them; then a half-dozen guns volleyed from her flank, and she was again lost to view in the billowing white clouds they had belched. But she seemed to have fired wildly in her excessive haste, for the red ship and her consort held steadily for some moments on their course, evidently unimpaired, then swung to starboard, and delivered each an answering broadside at the Spaniard.

By now, under Luzan's directions, and despite the protests of Monsieur de Saintonges, the Béarnais too had eased up, until she stood with idly flapping sails, suddenly changed from actor to spectator in this drama of the seas.

'Why do you pause, sir?' cried Saintonges. 'Keep to your course. Take advantage of this check to make that harbour.'

'Whilst others fight my battles for me?'

'You have a lady on board,' Saintonges raged at him. 'Madame de Saintonges must be placed in safety.'

'She is in no danger at present. And we may be needed. A while ago you accused me of cowardice. Now you would persuade me to become a coward. For the sake of Madame de Saintonges I will not go into battle save in the last extremity. But for that last extremity I must stand prepared.'

He was so grimly firm that Saintonges dared insist no further. Instead, setting his hopes upon those Heaven-sent rescuers, he stood on the hatch-coaming, and from that elevation sought to follow the fortunes of the battle which was roaring away to westward. But there was nothing to be seen now save a great curtain of smoke, like a vast spreading, deepening cloud that hung low over the sea and extended for perhaps two miles in the sluggish air. From somewhere within the heart of it they continued for awhile to hear the thunder of the guns. Then came a spell of silence, and after a while on the southern edge of the cloud two ships appeared that were at first as the wraiths of ships. Gradually rigging and hulls assumed definition as the smoke rolled away from them, and at about the same time the heart of the cloud began to assume a rosy tint, deepening swiftly to orange, until through the thinning smoke it was seen to proceed from the flames of a ship on fire.

From the poop-rail, Luzan's announcement brought relief at last to the Chevalier. 'The Spanish Admiral is burning. It is the end of her.'

IV

One of the two ships responsible for the destruction of the Spanish galleon remained hove to on the scene of action, her boats lowered and ranging the waters in her neighbourhood. This Luzan made out through his telescope. The other and larger vessel, emerging from that brief decisive engagement without visible scars, headed eastward, and came beating up against the wind towards the Béarnais,her red hull and gilded beakhead aglow in the morning sunshine. Still she displayed no flag, and this circumstance renewed in Monsieur de Saintonges the apprehensions which the issue of the battle had allayed.

With his lady still in half-clad condition, he was now on the poop at Luzan's side, and to the Captain he put the question was it prudent to remain hove to whilst this ship of undeclared nationality advanced upon them.

'But hasn't she proved a friend? A friend in need?' said the Captain.

Madame de Saintonges had not yet forgiven Luzan his plain speaking. Out of her hostility she answered him. 'You assume too much. All that we really know is that she proved an enemy to that Spanish ship. How do you know that these are not pirates to whom every ship is a prey? How do we know that since fire has robbed them of their Spanish prize they may not be intent now upon compensating themselves at our expense?'

Luzan looked at her without affection. 'There is one thing I know,' said he tartly. 'Her sailing powers are as much in excess of our own as her armament. It would avail us little to turn a craven tail if she means to overtake us. And there is another thing. If they meant us mischief one of those ships would not have remained behind. The two of them would be heading for us. So we need not fear to do what courtesy dictates.'

This argument was reassuring, and so the Béarnais waited whilst in the breeze that was freshening now the stranger came rippling forward over the sunlit water. At a distance of less than a quarter of a mile she hove to. A boat was lowered to the calm sea and came speeding with flash of yellow oars towards the Béarnais. Out of her a tall man climbed the Jacob's ladder of the French vessel, and stood at last upon the poop in an elegance of black and silver, from which you might suppose him to come straight from Versailles or the Alameda rather than from the deck of a ship in action.

To the group that received him there—Monsieur de Saintonges and his wife in their disarray, with Luzan and his lieutenant—this stately gentleman bowed until the curls of his periwig met across his square chin, whilst the claret feather in his doffed hat swept the deck.

'I come,' he announced in fairly fluent French, 'to bear and receive felicitations, and to assure myself before sailing away that you are in no need of further assistance and that you suffered no damage before we had the honour to intervene and dispose of that Spanish brigand who was troubling you.'

Such gallant courtesy completely won them, especially the lady. They reassured him on their own score and were solicitous as to what hurts he might have taken in the fight, for all that none were manifest.

Of these he made light. He had suffered some damage on the larboard quarter, which they could not see, but so slight as not to be worth remarking, whilst his men had taken scarcely a scratch. The fight, he explained, had been as brief as, in one sense, it was regrettable. He had hoped to make a prize of that fine galleon. But before he could close with her, a shot had found and fired her powder-magazine, and so the little affair ended almost before it was well begun. He had picked up most of her crew, and his consort was still at that work of rescue.

'As for the flagship of the Admiral of the Ocean-Sea, you see what's left of her, and very soon you will not see even that.'

They carried off this airy, elegant preserver to the great cabin, and in the wine of France they pledged his opportuneness and the victory which had rescued them from ills unnamable. Yet throughout there was from black-and-silver no hint of his identity or nationality, although this they guessed from his accent to be English. Saintonges, at last, approached the matter obliquely.

'You fly no flag, sir,' he said, when they had drunk.

The swarthy gentleman laughed. He conveyed the impression that laughter came to him readily. 'Sir, to be frank with you, I am of those who fly any flag that the occasion may demand. It might have been reassuring if I had approached you under French colours. But in the stress of the hour I gave no thought to it. You could hardly mistake me for a foe.'

'Of those that fly no flag?' the Chevalier echoed, staring bewilderment.

'Just so.' And airily he continued: 'At present I am on my way to Tortuga, and in haste. I am to assemble men and ships for an expedition to Martinique.'

It was the lady's turn to grow round-eyed. 'To Martinique?' She seemed suddenly a little out of breath. 'An expedition to Martinique? An expedition? But to what end?'

Her intervention had the apparent effect of taking him by surprise. He looked up, raising his brows. He smiled a little, and his answer had the tone of humouring her.

'There is a possibility—I will put it no higher—that Spain may be fitting out a squadron for a raid upon Saint Pierre. The loss of the Admiral which I have left in flames out yonder may delay their preparations, and so give us more time. It is what I hope.'

Rounder still grew her dark eyes, paler her cheeks. Her deep bosom was heaving now in tumult.

'Do you say that Spaniards propose a raid upon Martinique? Upon Martinique?'

And the Chevalier in an excitement scarcely less marked than his wife's added at once: 'Impossible, sir. Your information must be at fault. God of my life! That would be an act of war. And France and Spain are at peace.'

The dark brows of their preserver were raised again as if in amusement at their simplicity. 'An act of war. Perhaps. But was it not an act of war for that Spanish ship to fire upon the French flag this morning? Would the peace that prevails in Europe have availed you in the West Indies if you had been sunk?'

'An account—a strict account—would have been asked of Spain.'

'And it would have been rendered, not a doubt. With apologies of the fullest and some lying tales of a misunderstanding. But would that have set your ship afloat again if she had been sunk this morning, or restored you to life so that you might expose the lies by which Spanish men of State would cover the misdeed? Has this not happened, too, and often, when Spain has raided the settlements of other nations?'

'But not of late, sir,' Saintonges retorted.

Black-and-silver shrugged. 'Perhaps that is just the reason why the Spaniards in the Caribbean grow restive.'

And by that answer Monsieur de Saintonges was silenced, bewildered.

'But Martinique!' wailed the lady.

Black-and-silver shrugged expressively. 'The Spaniards call it Martinico, Madame. You are to remember that Spain believes that God created the New World especially for her profit, and that the Divine Will approves her resentment of all interlopers.'

'Isn't that just what I told you, Chevalier?' said Luzan. 'Almost my own words to you this morning when you would not believe there could be danger from a Spanish ship.'

There was an approving gleam from the bright blue eyes of the swarthy stranger as they rested on the French captain.

'So, so. Yes. It is hard to believe. But you have now the proof of it, I think, that in these waters, as in the islands of the Caribbean Sea, Spain respects no flag but her own unless force is present to compel respect. The settlers of every other nation have experienced in turn the Spaniards' resentment of their presence here. It expresses itself in devastating raids, in rapine, and in massacre. I need not enumerate instances. They will be present in your mind. If today it should happen, indeed, to be the turn of Martinico, we can but wonder that it should not have come before. For that is an island worth plundering and possessing, and France maintains no force in the West Indies that is adequate to restrain these conquistadores. Fortunately we still exist. If it were not for us...'

'For you?' Saintonges interrupted him, his voice suddenly sharp. 'You exist, you say. Of whom do you speak, sir? Who are you?'

The question seemed to take the stranger by surprise.

He stared, expressionless, for a moment; then his answer, for all that it confirmed the suspicions of the Chevalier and the convictions of Luzan, was nevertheless as a thunderbolt to Saintonges.

'I speak of the Brethren of the Coast, of course. The buccaneers, sir.' And he added, almost it seemed with a sort of pride: 'I am Captain Blood.'

Blankly, his jaw fallen, Saintonges looked across the table into that dark, smiling face of the redoubtable filibuster who had been reported dead.

To be faithful to his mission he should place this man in irons and carry him a prisoner to France. But not only would that in the circumstances of the moment be an act of blackest ingratitude, it would be rendered impossible by the presence at hand of two heavily armed buccaneer ships. Moreover, in the light so suddenly vouchsafed to him, Monsieur de Saintonges perceived that it would be an act of grossest folly. He considered what had happened that morning: the direct and very disturbing evidence of Spain's indiscriminate predatoriness; the evidence of a buccaneer activity which he could not now regard as other than salutary, supplied by that burning ship a couple of miles away; the further evidence of one and the other contained in this news of an impending Spanish raid on Martinique and the intended buccaneer intervention to save it where France had not the means at hand.

Considering all this—and the Martinique business touched him so closely and personally that from being perhaps the richest man in France he might find himself as a result of it no better than he had been before this voyage—it leapt to the eye that for once, at least, the omniscient Monsieur de Louvois had been at fault. So clear was it, and so demonstrable, that Saintonges began to conceive it his duty to shoulder the burden of that demonstration.

Something of all these considerations and emotions quivered in the hoarse voice in which, still staring blankly at Captain Blood, he ejaculated: 'You are that brigand of the sea!'

Blood displayed no resentment. He smiled. 'Oh, but a benevolent brigand, as you perceive. Benevolent, that is, to all but Spain.'

Madame de Saintonges swung in a breathless excitement to her husband, clutching his arm. In the movement the wrap slipped from her shoulders, so that still more of her opulent charms became revealed. But this went unheeded by her. In such an hour of crisis modesty became a negligible matter.

'Charles, what will you do?'

'Do?' said he dully.

'The orders you left in Tortuga may mean ruin to me, and...'

He raised a hand to stem this betrayal of self-interest. In whatever might have to be done, of course, no interest but the interest of his master the King of France must be permitted to sway him.

'I see, my dear. I see. Duty becomes plain. We have received a valuable lesson this morning. Fortunately before it is too late.'

She drew a deep breath of relief, and swung excitedly, anxiously to Captain Blood, 'You have no doubt in your mind, sir, that your buccaneers can ensure the safety of Martinique?'

'None, Madame.' His voice was of a hard confidence. 'The Bay of Saint Pierre will prove a mousetrap for the Spaniards if they are so rash as to sail into it. I shall know what is to do. And the plunder of their ships alone will richly defray the costs of the expedition.'

And then Saintonges laughed.

'Ah, yes,' said he. 'The plunder, to be sure. I understand. The ships of Spain are a rich prey, when all is said. Oh, I do not sneer, sir. I hope I am not so ungenerous.'

'I could not suppose it, sir,' said Captain Blood. He pushed back his chair, and rose. 'I will be taking my leave. The breeze is freshening and I should seize the advantage. If it holds I shall be in Tortuga this evening.'

He stood, inclined a little, before Madame de Saintonges, awaiting the proffer of her hand, when the Chevalier took him by the shoulder.

'A moment yet, sir. Keep Madame company whilst I write a letter which you shall carry for me to the Governor of Tortuga.'

'A letter!' Captain Blood assumed astonishment. 'To commend this poor exploit of ours? Sir, sir, never be at so much trouble.'

Monsieur de Saintonges was for a moment ill at ease. 'It... it has a further purpose,' he said at last.

'Ah! If it is to serve some purpose of your own, that is another matter. Pray command me.'

V

In the faithful discharge of that courier's office Captain Blood laid the letter from the Chevalier de Saintonges on the evening of that same day before the Governor of Tortuga, without any word of explanation.

'From the Chevalier de Saintonges, you say?' Monsieur d'Ogeron was frowning thoughtfully. 'To what purpose?'

'I could guess,' said Captain Blood. 'But why should I, when the letter is in your hands? Read it, and we shall know.'

'In what circumstances did you obtain this letter?'

'Read it. It may tell you, and so save my breath.'

D'Ogeron broke the seal and spread the sheet. With knitted brows he read the formal retraction by the representative of the Crown of France of the orders left with the Governor of Tortuga for the cessation of all traffic with the buccaneers. Monsieur d'Ogeron was required to continue relations with them as heretofore pending fresh instructions from France. And the Chevalier added the conviction that these instructions when and if they came would nowise change the existing order of things. He was confident that when he had fully laid before the Marquis de Louvois the demonstration he had received of the conditions prevailing in the West Indies, his Excellency would be persuaded of the inexpediency at present of enforcing his decrees against the buccaneers.

Monsieur d'Ogeron blew out his cheeks. 'But will you tell me, then, how you worked this miracle with that obstinate numskull?'

'Every argument depends, as I said to you, upon the manner of its presentation. You and I both said the same thing to the Chevalier de Saintonges. But you said it in words. I said it chiefly in action. Knowing that fools learn only by experience, I supplied experience for him. It was thus.' And he rendered a full account of that early morning sea-fight off the northern coast of Hispaniola.

The Governor listened, stroking his chin. 'Yes,' he said slowly, when the tale was done. 'Yes. That would be persuasive. And to scare him with this bogey of a raid on Martinque and the probable loss of his new-found wealth was well conceived. But don't you flatter yourself a little, my friend, on the score of your shrewdness? Are you not forgetting how amazingly fortunate it was for you that in such a place and at such a time a Spanish galleon should have had the temerity to attack the Béarnais? Amazingly fortunate! It fits your astounding luck most oddly!'

'Most oddly, as you say,' Blood solemnly agreed.

'What ship was this you burnt and sank? And what fool commanded her? Do you know?'

'Oh yes. The Maria Gloriosa, the flagship of the Marquis of Riconete, the Spanish Admiral of the Ocean-Sea.'

D'Ogeron looked up sharply. 'The Maria Gloriosa? What are you telling me? Why, you captured her yourself at San Domingo, and came back here in her when you brought the treasure-ships.'

'Just so. And therefore I had her in hand for this little demonstration of Spanish turpitude and buccaneer prowess. She sailed with Wolverstone in command and just enough hands to work her and to man the half-dozen guns I spared her for the sacrifice.'

'God save us! Do you tell me, then, that it was all a comedy?'

'Mostly played behind a curtain of the smoke of battle. It was a very dense curtain. We supplied an abundance of smoke from guns loaded with powder only, and the light airs assisted us. Wolverstone set fire to the ship at the height of the supposed battle, and under cover of that friendly smoke came aboard the Arabella with his crew.'

The Governor continued to glare amazement. 'And you tell me that this was convincing?'

'That it was convincing, no. That it convinced.'

'And you deliberately—deliberately burnt that splendid Spanish ship.'

'That is what convinced. Merely to have driven her off might not have done it.'

'But the waste! Oh my heavens, the waste!'

'Do you complain? Will you be cheese-paring? Do you think that it is by economies that great enterprises are carried through? Look at the letter in your hand again. It amounts to a Government charter for a traffic against which there was a Government decree. Do you think such things can be obtained by fine phrases? You tried them, and you know what came of it.' He slapped the little Governor on the shoulder. 'Let's come to business. For now I shall be able to sell you my spices, and I warn you that I shall expect a good price for them: the price of three Spanish ships at least.'

Episode 4

THE DELIVERANCE

I

For a year and more after his escape from Barbados with Peter Blood, it was the abiding sorrow of Nathaniel Hagthorpe, that West Country gentleman whom the force of adversity had made a buccaneer, that his younger brother Tom should still continue in the enslaved captivity from which, himself, he had won free.

Both these brothers had been out with Monmouth, and being taken after Sedgemoor, both had been sentenced to be hanged for their share in that rebellion. Then came the harsh commutation of the sentence which doomed them to slavery in the plantations, and with a shipload of other rebels-convict they had been sent out to Barbados, and there had passed into the possession of the brutal Colonel Bishop. But by the time that Blood had come to organize the escape of himself and his fellows from that island, Tom Hagthorpe was no longer there.

Colonel Sir James Court, who was deputy in Nevis for the Governor of the Leeward Islands, had come on a visit to Bishop in Barbados and had brought with him his young wife. She was a dainty, wilful piece of mischief, too young by far to have mated with so elderly a man, and having been raised by her marriage to a station above that into which she had been born, she was the more insistent upon her ladyhood and of exactions and pretensions at which a duchess might have paused.

Newly arrived in the West Indies, she was resentfully slow to adapt herself to some of the necessities of her environment, and among her pretensions arising out of this was the lack of a white groom to attend her when she rode abroad. It did not seem fitting to her that a person of her rank should be accompanied on those occasions by what she contemptuously termed a greasy blackamoor.

Nevis, however, could offer her no other, fume as she might. Although by far the most important slave-mart in the West Indies, it imported this human merchandise only from Africa. Because of this it had been omitted by the Secretary of State at home from the list of islands to which contingents of the West Country rebels had been shipped. Lady Court had a notion that this might be repaired in the course of that visit to Barbados, and it was Tom Hagthorpe's misfortune that her questing eyes should have alighted admiringly upon his clean-limbed almost stripling grace when she beheld him at work, half naked, among Colonel Bishop's golden sugar-cane. She marked him for her own, and thereafter gave Sir James no peace until he had bought the slave from the planter who owned him. Bishop made no difficulty about the sale. To him one slave was much as another, and there was a delicacy about this particular lad which made him of indifferent value in a plantation and easily replaced.

Whilst the separation from his brother was a grief to Tom, yet at first the brothers were so little conscious of his misfortune that they welcomed this deliverance from the lash of the overseer; and although a gentleman born, yet so abjectly was he fallen that they regarded it as a sort of promotion that he should go to Nevis to be a groom to the Colonel's lady. Therefore

Nat Hagthorpe, taking comfort in the assurance of the lad's improved condition, did not grievously bewail his departure from Barbados until after his own escape, when the thought of his brother's continuing slavery was an abiding source of bitterness.

Tom Hagthorpe's confidence that at least he would gain by the change of owners and find himself in less uneasy circumstances seems soon to have proved an illusion. We are without absolute knowledge of how this came about. But what we know of the lady, as will presently be disclosed, justifies a suspicion that she may have exercised in vain the witchery of her long narrow eyes on that comely lad; in short that he played Joseph to her Madam Potiphar, and thereby so enraged her that she refused to have him continue in attendance. He was clumsy she complained, ill-mannered and disposed to insolence.

'I warned you,' said Sir James a little wearily, for her exactions constantly multiplying were growing burdensome, 'that he was born a gentleman, and must naturally resent his degradation. Better to have left him in the plantations.'

'You can send him back to them,' she answered. 'For I've done with the rascal.'

And so, deposed from the office for which he had been acquired, he went to toil again at sugar-cane under overseers no whit less brutal than Bishop's, and was given for associates a gang of gaolbirds, thieves, and sharpers lately shipped from England.

Of this, of course, his brother had no knowledge, or he must have been visited by a deeper dejection on Tom's behalf and a fiercer impatience to see him delivered from captivity. For that was an object constantly before Nat Hagthorpe, and one that he constantly urged upon Peter Blood.

'Will you be patient now?' the Captain would answer him, himself driven to the verge of impatience by this reiteration of an almost impossible demand. 'If Nevis were a Spanish settlement, we could set about it without ceremony. But we haven't come yet to the point of making war on English ships and English lands. That would entirely ruin our prospects.'

'Prospects? What prospects have we?' growled Hagthorpe. 'We're outlawed, or aren't we?'

'Maybe, maybe. But we discriminate by being the enemy of Spain alone. We're not hostis humani generis yet, and until we become that, we need not abandon hope, like others of our kind, that one day this outlawry will be lifted. I'll not be putting that in jeopardy by a landing in force on Nevis, not even to save your brother Nat.'

'Is he to languish there until he dies, then?'

'No, no. I'll find the way. Be sure I'll find it. But we'd be wise to wait awhile.'

'For what?'

'For Chance. It's a great faith I have in the lady. She's obliged me more than once, so she has; and she'll maybe oblige me again. But she's not a lady you can drive. Just put your faith in her, Nat, as I do.'

And in the end he was shown to be justified of that faith. The Chance upon which he depended came with unexpected suddenness to his assistance, soon after the affair of San Juan de Puerto Rico. The news that Captain Blood had been caught by the Spaniards and had expiated his misdeeds on a gallows on the beach of San Juan had swept like a hurricane across the Caribbean, from Hispaniola to the Main. In every Spanish settlement there was exultation over the hanging of the most formidable agent of restraint upon Spain's fierce predatoriness that had ever sailed the seas. For the same reason there was much secret unavowed regret among the English and French colonists, by whom the buccaneers were, at least tacitly, encouraged.

Before very long it must come to be discovered that the treasure-ships which had sailed from San Juan under the convoy of the flagship of the Admiral of the Ocean-Sea had cast anchor not in Cadiz Bay, but in the harbour of Tortuga, and that it was not the Admiral of the Ocean-Sea, but Captain Blood, himself, who had commanded the flagship at the very time when his body could be seen dangling from that gallows on the beach. But until the discovery came, Captain Blood was concerned, like a wise opportunist, to profit by the authoritative report of his demise. He realized that there was no time to be lost if he would take full advantage of the present relaxation of vigilance throughout New Spain, and so he set out from the buccaneer stronghold of Tortuga on a projected descent upon the Main.

He took the seas in the Arabella, but she bore a broad white stripe painted along her water-line so as to dissemble her red hull, and on her counter the name displayed was now Mary of Modena, so as to supply an ultra-Stuart English antidote to her powerful, shapely Spanish lines. With the white, blue, and red of the Union flag at her maintruck, she put in at St Thomas, ostensibly for wood and water, actually to see what might be picked up. What she picked up was Mr Geoffrey Court, who came to supply the chance for which Nathaniel Hagthorpe had prayed and Captain Blood had confidently waited.

II

Over the emerald water that sparkled in the morning sunlight, in a boat rowed by four moistly gleaming black men, came Mr Geoffrey Court, a consequential gentleman in a golden periwig and a brave suit of mauve taffetas with silver buttonholes.

Whilst the black men steadied the boat against the great hull, he climbed the accommodation ladder in the prow, and stepped aboard, fanning himself with his plumed hat, inviting Heaven to rot him if he could support this abominable heat, and peremptorily demanding the master of this pestilential vessel.

The adjective was merely a part of his habitual and limited rhetoric. For the deck on which he stood was scrubbed clean as a trencher; the brass of the scuttle-butts and the swivel-guns on the poop-tail gleamed like polished gold; the muskets in the rack about the mainmast could not have been more orderly or better furbished had this been a King's ship; and all the gear was stowed as daintily as in a lady's chamber.

The men lounging on the forecastle and in the waist, few of them wearing more than a cotton shirt and pair of loose calico drawers, observed the gentleman's arrogance with a mild but undisguised amusement to which he was happily blind.

A black man steward led him by a dark gangway to the main cabin astern, which surprised him by its space and the luxury of its appointments. Here, at a table spread with snowy napery on which crystal and silver sparkled, sat three men, and one of these, spare and commanding of height, very elegant in black and silver, his sunburned hawk face framed in the flowing curls of a black periwig, rose to receive the visitor. The other two, who remained seated, if less imposing were yet of engaging aspect. They were Jeremy Pitt, the ship-master, young and fair and slight of build, and Nathaniel Hagthorpe, older and broader and of a graver countenance.

Our gentleman in mauve lost none of his assurance under the calm survey to which those three pairs of eyes subjected him. His self-sufficiency proclaimed itself in the tone in which he desired to be informed whither the Mary of Modena might be bound. That he supplied a reason for the question seemed on his part a mere condescension.

'My name is Court. Geoffrey Court, to serve you, sir. I am in haste to reach Nevis, where my cousin commands.'

The announcement made something of a sensation upon his audience. It took the breaths of the three men before him, and from Hagthorpe came a gasping 'God save us!' whilst his sudden pallor must have been apparent even with his face in shadow, for he sat with the tall stern windows at his back. Mr Court, however, was too much engrossed in himself to pay heed to changes in the aspect of another. He desired to impress them with his consequence.

'I am cousin to Sir James Court, who is Deputy in Nevis for the Governor of the Leeward Islands. You will have heard of him, of course.'

'Of course,' said Blood.

Hagthorpe's impatience was not content to wait. 'And you want us to carry you to Nevis?' he cried, out of breath, in an eagerness that would have been noticed by any man less obtuse.

'If your course lies anywhere in that direction. It's this way with me: I came out from home, may I perish, on a plaguey half-rotten ship that met foul weather and all but went to pieces under it. Her seams opened under the strain, and she was leaking like a colander when we ran in here for safety. You can see her at anchor yonder. May I rot if she'll ever be fit to take the seas again. The most cursed luck it was to have sailed in such a worm-eaten wash-tub.'

'And you're in haste to get to Nevis?' quoth Blood.

'In desperate haste, may I burn. I've been expected there this month past.'

It was Hagthorpe who answered him in a voice hoarse with emotion. 'Odslife, but you're singularly in luck, sir. For Nevis is our next port of call.'

'Stab me! And is that so?'

There was a grim smile on Blood's dark face. 'It's a strange chance, so it is,' he said. 'We weigh at eight bells, and if this wind holds it's tomorrow morning we'll be dropping anchor at Charlestown.'

'Nothing, then, could be more fortunate. Nothing, may I perish.' The florid countenance was all delight. 'Fate owes me something for the discomforts I have borne. By your leave, I'll fetch my portmantles at once.' Magnificently he added: 'The price of the passage shall be what you will.'

As magnificently Blood waved a graceful hand that was half smothered in a foam of lace. 'That's a matter of no moment at all. Ye'll take a morning whet with us?'

'With all my heart, Captain...'

He paused there, waiting for the name to be supplied to him; but Captain Blood did not appear to heed. He was giving orders to the steward.

Rum and limes and sugar were brought, and over their punch they were reasonably merry, saving Hagthorpe, who was fathoms deep in preoccupation. But no sooner had Mr Court departed than he roused himself to thank Blood for what he supposed had been in his mind when he so readily consented to carry this passenger.

'Didn't I say, now, that if you'ld put your faith in Chance, she'ld be serving us sooner or later? It's not myself ye should be thanking, Nat. It's Fortune. She's just tumbled Mr Court out of her cornucopia into your lap.' He laughed as he mimicked Mr Court: "The price of the passage shall be what you will." What you will, Nat; and I'm thinking it's Sir James Court we'll be asking to pay it.'

III

At the very moment that Mr Geoffrey Court was drinking that morning whet in the cabin of the Arabella, his cousin Sir James, a tall, spare man of fifty, as vigorous still of body as he was irresolute of mind, sat at his breakfast-table with a satchel of letters that had just arrived from England. They were letters long overdue, for the ship that had brought them, delayed and driven out of her course by gales, had exceeded by fully two months the normal time of the voyage.

Sir James had emptied the satchel on to the table, and had spread the contents for a general preliminary glance. A package bulkier than the rest drew his attention, and he took it up. He scanned the superscription with a frown that gradually drew together his heavy, grizzled brows. He hesitated, passing a brown, bony hand along his chin; then, as if abruptly taking a decision, he broke the seals and tore away the wrapper. From this husk he extracted a dainty volume bound in vellum, with some gold tooling on the spine and the legend, also in gold, The Poems of Sir John Suckling.

He sniffed contemptuously, and contemptuously tossed the thing aside. But as it fell, the volume partly opened, and at what he saw his narrow face grew attentive. He took it up again. The fold of vellum on the inner side of the cover had become detached and had slightly curled away from the board. The paste securing that fold had perished, and as he fingered the curled edge the entire flap forming the side of the cover came loose. Between this and the board a folded sheet was now disclosed.

That sheet was still in James' hand ten minutes later, when the room was abruptly invaded by the dainty lady who might have been, in years, his daughter, but was, in fact, his wife. She was scarcely of the middle height and virginally slight of figure, clear-eyed and of a delicate tint unblemished by the climate of the tropics. She was dressed for riding, her face in the shadow of a wide hat, a whip in her hand.

'I have to speak to you,' she announced, her voice musical, but its tone shrewish.

Sir James, sitting with his back to the door, had not turned to see who entered. At the sound of her voice he dropped a napkin over the volume of poems. Then, still without turning, he spoke. 'In that case the King's business may go to the devil.'

'Must you always sneer, sir?' The shrewish note grew sharper. 'Do you transact the King's business at the breakfast-table?'

Always calm, even lethargic, of spirit, Sir James replied: 'Not always. No. But just as often as you must be peremptory.'

'I don't want for cause.' She swept forward and round the table so that she might directly face him. She stood there, very straight, her riding-whip in her gloved hands, held across her slim, vigorous young body. There was a petulance on the sensual lips, an aggressive forward thrust of the little pointed chin.

'I have been insulted,' she announced.

Grey-faced, Sir James considered her. 'To be sure,' he said at last.

'What do you mean—"To be sure"?'

'Doesn't it happen every time that you ride out?'

'And if it does, who shall wonder when yourself you set the example?'

He avoided the offered argument. Argument, at least, was something that he had learnt to refuse this winsome termagant of half his age whom he had married five years ago and who had since poisoned his life with the bad manners and ill-temper brought from her tradesman-father's home.

'Who was it today?' asked his weary voice.

'That dog Hagthorpe. I would to God I had left him rotting in Barbados.'

'Instead of bringing him to rot here. Yes? What did he say to you?'

'Say? You don't conceive he had the effrontery to speak to me?'

He smiled a little sourly. In these days of disillusion he was able to perceive that most of the trouble came from her being too consciously a lady without proper preparation for the role.

'But if he insulted you?'

'It was in the cursed impudent way he looked at me, with a half-smile on his insolent face.'

'A half-smile?' The bushy brows went up. 'It may have been no more than a greeting.'

'You would say that. You would take sides even with your slaves against your wife. Happen what may, I am never in the right. Oh no. Never. A greeting?' she sniffed. 'This was no greeting. And if it was, is a low slave to greet me with smiles?'

'A half-smile, I think you said. And as for low, he may be a slave—poor devil!—but he was born a gentleman.'

'Fine gentleman to be sure! A damned rebel who should have been hanged.'

His deep-set eyes gravely considered her daintiness. 'Are you quite without pity?' he asked her. 'I wonder sometimes. And is there no constancy in you either? You were so taken with the lad when first we saw him in Barbados that nothing would content you until I had bought him so that you might make of him your groom and lavish favours on him only to—'

Her whip crashed down on the table to interrupt him. 'I'll listen to no more of this. It's cowardly always to browbeat and bully me, and put me in the wrong. But I shall know what to do another time. I'll lay my whip across that rogue's smug face. That will teach him to leer at me.'

'It will be worthy,' was the bitter comment. 'It will be brave, towards an unfortunate who must bear whatever comes lest worse should follow.'

But she was no longer listening. The stroke of her whip had scattered some of the letters heaped upon the table. Her attention was sharply diverted.

'Has a packet come from England?' Her breathing seemed to quicken as he watched her.

'I spoke, I think, of the King's business. Here you see it. At the breakfast-table.'

She was already rummaging through the heap, scanning each package in turn. 'Are there letters for me?'

It was a second or two before his suddenly compressed lips parted again to reply evasively: 'I haven't seen all of them yet.'

She continued her search, whilst he watched her from under his brows. At the end she looked at him again.

'Nothing?' she asked, on a note of surprised, aggrieved inquiry. Her brows were knit, her delicate chin seemed to grow more pointed. 'Nothing?'

'You have looked for yourself,' he said.

She turned slowly away, her lip between finger and thumb. He was grimly amused to observe that the furious grievance with which she had sought him was forgotten; that her wrath on the matter of the slave had been quenched in another preoccupation. Slowly she moved to the door, passing out of his range of sight. Her hand upon the knob, she paused. She spoke in a voice that was soft and amiable. 'You have no word from Geoffrey?' He answered without turning. 'I have told you that I have not yet looked through all the letters.'

Still she lingered. 'I did not see his hand on any of them.'

'In that case he has not written to me.'

'Odd!' she said slowly, 'It is very odd. We should have had word by now of when to expect him.'

'I'll not pretend to anxiety for that news.'

'You'll not?' A flush slowly inflamed her face in the pause she made. Then her anger lashed him again. 'And I? You've no thought, of course, for me, chained in this hateful island, with no society but the parson and the commandant and their silly wives. Haven't I sacrificed enough for you that you should grudge me even the rare company of someone from the world, who can give me news of something besides sugar and pepper and the price of blackamoors?' She waited through a silent moment. 'Why don't you answer me?' she shrilled.

He had turned pale under his tan. He swung slowly round in his chair.

'You want an answer, do you?' There was an undertone of thunder in his voice.

Evidently she didn't. For at the mere threat of it she went abruptly out, and slammed the door. He half rose, and she little knew in what peril she stood at that moment from the anger that flamed up in him. Emotion of any kind, however, was short-lived in this lethargic-minded man. An imprecation fluttered from him on a sigh as he sagged back again into his chair. Again unfolding the sheet which his hand had retained during her presence in the room, he resumed his scowling study of it. Then, having sat gloomily in thought for a long while, he rose and went to lock both the letter and the vellum-bound volume in a secretaire that stood between the open windows. After that, at last, he gave his attention to the other packages that awaited him.

IV

Lady Court's yearnings for society from the great world, which were at the root of a good deal of the wretchedness of that household, received some satisfaction on the morrow, when the Mary of Modena reached the island of Nevis—that vast green mountain rising from the sea—and came to cast anchor in Charlestown Bay.

Mr Court, all a quivering eagerness to go ashore, was in the very act of ordering Jacob, the steward, to take up his portmantles, when Captain Blood sauntered into the cabin.

'That will be for tomorrow perhaps,' said he.

'Tomorrow?' Mr Court stared at him. 'But this is Nevis, isn't it?'

'To be sure. This is Nevis. But before we set you ashore there's the trifling matter of the price of your passage.'

'Oh! That!' Mr Court was contemptuous. 'Didn't I say you might make it what you please?'

'You did. And, faith, I may be taking you at your word.'

Mr Court did not like the Captain's smile. He interpreted it in his own fashion.

'If you mean to be—ah—extortionate...'

'Och, not extortionate at all. Most reasonable, to be sure. Sit down, sir, whilst I explain.'

'Explain? Explain what?'

'Sit down, sir.' Blood's tone and manner were compelling. Bewildered, Mr Court sat down.

'It's this way,' said Captain Blood, and sat down also, on the stern locker, with his back to the open window, the sunshine, the glittering sea and the hawkers' boats that with fruit and vegetables and fowls came crowding about the ship. 'It's this way: For the moment I'll trouble you to be considering yourself, in a manner of speaking, a hostage, Mr Court. A hostage for a very good friend of mine, who at this moment is a slave in the hands of your cousin, Sir James. You've told us how highly Sir James esteems and loves you; so there's no cause for uneasiness at all. In short, sir: my friend's freedom is the price I'll be asking Sir James for your passage. That's all.'

'All?' There was fury in Mr Court's tone, in his prominent eyes. 'This is an outrage!'

'I'll not be depriving you of the comfort of calling it that.'

Mr Court set an obvious restraint upon his feelings. 'And supposing that Sir James should refuse?'

'Och, why will you be vexing your soul by supposing anything so unpleasant? The one certain thing at present is that if Sir James consents you'll be landed at once on Nevis.'

'I am asking you, sir, what will happen if he doesn't.'

Captain Blood smiled amiably. 'I'm an orderly man, and so I like to take one thing at a time. Speculation's mostly a waste of thought. We'll leave that until it happens, for the excellent reason that it may never happen at all.'

Mr Court came to his feet in exasperation.

'But this... this is monstrous. Od rot me, sir, you'll do me this violence at your peril.'

'I am Captain Blood,' he was answered, 'so you'll not be supposing that a little peril more or less will daunt me.'

The announcement released some fresh emotions in Mr Court. His eyes threatened to drop from his flushed, angry face.

'You are Captain Blood! Captain Blood! That damned pirate! You may be but, may I perish, I care nothing who you are...'

'Why should you now? All I'm asking of you is that you'll step into your cabin. Of course I shall have to place a guard at the door, but there'll be no other restraints, and your comforts shall not suffer.'

'Do you suppose I'll submit to this?'

'I can put you in irons if you prefer it,' said Captain Blood suavely.

Mr Court, having furiously considered him, decided that he would not prefer it.

Captain Blood was rowed ashore, and took his way to the Deputy-Governor's house on the water-front: a fine white house with green slatted sun-blinds set back in a fair garden where azaleas flamed and all was fragrance of orange and pimento.

He found access to Sir James an easy matter. To a person of his obvious distinction, in his becoming coat of dark-blue camlett, his plumed hat and his long sword slung from a gold-embroidered baldrick, colonial doors were readily opened. He announced himself as Captain Peter, which was scarcely false, and he left it to be supposed that his rank was naval and to be understood that the ship in which he now sailed was his own property. His business in Nevis, the most important slave-market of the West Indies, he declared to be the acquisition of a lad of whom he might make a cabin boy. He had been informed that Sir James, himself, did a little slave-dealing, but even if this information were not correct, he had the presumption to hope that he might deserve Sir James' assistance in his quest.

His person was so elegantly engaging, his manner, perfectly blending deference with dignity, so winning, that Sir James professed himself entirely at Captain Peter's service. Just now there were no slaves available, but at any moment a cargo of blacks from the Coast of Guinea should be arriving, and if Captain Peter were not pressed for a day or two there was no doubt that his need would be supplied. Meanwhile, of course, Captain Peter would stay to dine.

And to dine Captain Peter stayed, meeting Lady Court, whom he impressed so favourably that before dinner was over the invitation extended by her husband had been materially enlarged by her.

Meanwhile, considering the ostensible object of Captain Peter's visit to Nevis, it was natural that the conversation should turn to slaves, and to a comparison of the service to be obtained from them with that afforded by European servants. Sir James, by opining that the white man was so superior as to render any comparison ridiculous, opened the way for the Captain's searching probe.

'And yet all the white men out here as a result of the Monmouth rebellion are being wasted in the plantations. It is odd that no one should ever have thought of employing any of them in some other capacity.'

'They are fit for nothing else,' said her ladyship. 'You can't make ordinary servants of such mutinous material. I know because I tried.'

'Ah! Your ladyship tried. Now that is interesting. But you'll not be telling me that the wretches you so rescued from the plantations were so indifferent to this good fortune as not to give good service?'

Sir James interposed. 'My wife's experience is more limited than her assertion might lead you to suppose. She judges from a single trial.'

She acknowledged the hostile criticism by a disdainful glance, and the Captain came gallantly to her support.

'Ab uno omnes, you know, Sir James. That is often true.' He turned to the lady, who met him smiling. 'What was this single trial? What manner of man was it who proved so lacking in grace?'

'One of those rebels-convict shipped to the plantations. We found him in Barbados, and I bought him to make a groom of him. But he was so little grateful, so little sensible of that betterment of his fortunes that in the end I sent him back to work at sugar-cane.'

The Captain's grave nod approved her. 'Faith, he was rightly served. And what became of him?'

'Just that. He's repenting his bad manners on Sir James' plantation here. A surly, mutinous dog.'

Again Sir James spoke, sadly: 'The poor wretch was a gentleman once, like so many of his misguided fellow-rebels. It was a poor mercy not to have hanged them.'

On that he changed the subject, and Captain Blood having obtained the information that he sought was content to allow him to do so.

But whatever the matter of which they talked, the lady's rare young beauty, combined with a sweet, ingenuous charm of manner, which seemed to bring a twist to the lip of Sir James as he watched her, commanded from their visitor the attentive regard which no man of any gallantry could have withheld. She rewarded him by insisting that whilst he waited in Charlestown he should take up his quarters in their house. She would admit of no refusal. She vowed that all the favour would be of the Captain's bestowing. Too rarely did a distinguished visitor from across the ocean come to relieve the monotony of their life on Nevis.

As a further inducement, she enlarged upon the beauties of this island. She must be the Captain's guide to its scented groves, its luxuriant plantations, its crystal streams, so that he should realize what an earthly Paradise was this which her husband had so often heard her denounce a desolate Hell.

Sir James, without illusions, covering his contempt of her light arts with a mask of grave urbanity, confirmed her invitation, whereupon she announced that she would give orders at once to have a room prepared and the Captain must send aboard for what he needed.

Captain Blood accepted this hospitality in graceful terms and without reluctance. Whilst so much may not have been absolutely necessary for the accomplishment of his purpose in Nevis, yet there could be no doubt that residence in the household of Sir James Court might very materially assist him.

V

We have heard Captain Blood expressing his faith in Fortune, or Chance, as he named it to Hagthorpe. Nevertheless, he did not carry his faith to the lengths of sitting still for Fortune to come seeking him. Chances, he knew, were to be created, or at least attracted, by intelligence and diligence, and betimes on the following morning he was afoot and booted, so as to lose no time in his quest. He knew, from the information gathered yesterday, in what direction it should be pursued, and soon after sunrise he was making his way to Sir James' stables to procure the necessary means.

There could be nothing odd in that a guest of early-rising habits should choose to go for a gallop before breakfast, or that for the purpose he should borrow a mount from his host. The fact that he should elect in his ride to go by way of Sir James' plantation could hardly suggest an interest in one of the slaves at work in it.

So far, then, he could depend upon himself. Beyond that—for sight and perhaps speech of the slave he sought—he put his faith again in Fortune.

At the outset it looked as if Fortune that morning were in no kindly mood. For early though the hour, Lady Court, be it because of matutinal habits, because meticulous in her duty as a hostess, or because of an unconquerable and troublesome susceptibility to such attractiveness in the male as her guest displayed, came fresh and sprightly to take him by surprise in the stables, and to call for a horse so that she might ride with him. It was vexatious, but it did not put him out of countenance. When she joyously announced that she would show him the cascades, he secretly cursed her sprightliness. Very politely he demurred on the ground that his first interest was in the plantations.

She puckered her perfect nose in mock disdain of him. 'I vow, sir, you disappoint me. I conceived you more poetical, more romantical, a man to take joy in beauty, in the wild glories of nature.'

'Why, so I am, I hope. But I'm practical as well; and also something of a student. I can admire the orderliness of man's contriving, and inform myself upon it.'

This led to argument; a very pretty and equally silly battle of words, which Captain Blood, with a definite purpose in view, found monstrous tedious. It ended in a compromise. They rode out first to the cascades, in which she could not spur the Captain into more than languid interest, and then home to breakfast by way of the sugar-plantations, in which no interest could have been more disappointingly keen to her than his. For he wasted time there, and her ladyship was growing sharp-set.

So that he might view at leisure every detail, he proceeded at no more than a walking pace through the broad lanes between the walls of cane that were turning golden, past gangs of slaves, of whom a few were white, who were toiling at the irrigation trenches. From time to time the Captain would try the lady's patience by drawing rein, so that he might look about him more searchingly, and once he paused by an overseer, to question him, first on the subject of the cultivation itself, then on that of the slaves employed, their numbers and quality. He was informed that the white ones were transported convicts.

'Rebel knaves, I suppose,' said the Captain. 'Some of those psalm-singers who were out with the Duke of Monmouth.'

'Nay, sir. We've only one o' they; one as came from Barbados wi' a parcel o' thieves and cozeners. That gang's down yonder, at the end of this brake.'

They rode on and came to the group, a dozen or so half-naked unkempt men, some of them burnt so black by the sun that they looked like pale-coloured black men, and more than one back a criss-cross of scars from the overseer's lash. It was amongst these that Captain Blood's questing eyes alighted on the man he sought in Nevis.

My lady, who could never long sustain a role of amiable docility, was beginning to manifest her loss of patience at these futilities. That loss was complete when her companion now drew rein yet again, and gave a courteous good morning to the burly overseer of these wretched toilers. Almost at once her annoyance found an outlet. A young man, conspicuous for his athletic frame and sun-bleached golden hair, stood leaning upon his hoe, staring up wide-eyed and open-mouthed at the Captain.

She urged her mare forward.

'Why do you stand idle, oaf? Will you never learn not to stare at your betters? Then here's to improve your manners.'

Viciously her riding-switch cut across his naked shoulders. It was raised again, to repeat the stroke; but the slave, who had half swung round so as fully to face her, parried the blow on his left forearm as it descended, whilst his hand, simultaneously closing upon the switch, wrenched it from her with a jerk that almost pulled her from the saddle.

If the other toilers fell idle, to stare in awe, there was instant action from the watchful overseer. With an oath he sprang for the young slave, uncoiling the thong of his whip.

'Cut the flesh from his bones, Walter!' shrilled the lady.

Before this menace the goaded youth flung away the silver-mounted switch and swung his hoe aloft. His light eyes were blazing. 'Touch me with that whip and I'll beat your brains out.'

The big overseer checked. He knew reckless resolve when he saw it, and here it glared at him plainly. The slave, maddened by pain and injustice, was no more in case to count the cost of doing as he threatened than of having dared to employ the threat. The overseer attempted to dominate him by words and tone, so as to gain time until the frenzy should have passed.

'Put down that hoe, Hagthorpe. Put it down at once.'

But Hagthorpe laughed at him; and then my lady laughed too, on a note that was horrible in its evil, spiteful glee.

'Don't argue with the dog. Pistol him. You've my warrant for it, Walter. I'm witness to his mutiny. Pistol him, man.'

Thus insistently and imperatively ordered, the man carried a hand to the holster of his belt. But even as he drew the weapon, the Captain leaned over from the saddle, and the butt of his heavy riding-crop crashed upon the overseer's hand, sending the pistol flying. The fellow cried out in pain and amazement.

'Be easy now,' said Blood. 'I've saved your life, so I have. For it would have cost you no less if you had fired that pistol.'

'Captain Peter!' It was a cry of indignant, incredulous protest from Lady Court.

He turned to her, and the scorn in his eyes, so vividly blue under their black brows, struck her like a blow.

'What are you? A woman? Od's blood, ma'am, in London Town I've seen poor street-walkers carted that were more womanly.'

She gasped. Then fury rallied her courage to answer him. 'I have a husband, sir, I thank God. You shall answer to him for that.' She drove a vicious spur into her horse, and departed at the gallop, leaving him to follow as he listed.

'Sure and I'll answer to all the husbands in the world,' he called after her, and laughed.

Then he beckoned Hagthorpe forward. 'Here, my lad. You'll come and answer with me. I am going to see justice done, and I know better than to leave you at the mercy of an overseer while I'm about it. Take hold of my stirrup-leather. You're coming with me to Sir James. Stand back there, my man, or I'll ride you down. It's to your master I'll be accounting for my actions, not to you.'

Still nursing his hand, the overseer, his face sullen, fell aside before that threat, and Captain Blood moved on at an easy pace down the golden lane with Tom Hagthorpe striding beside him clinging to his stirrup-leather. Out of earshot the young man hoarsely asked a question.

'Peter, by what miracle do you happen here?'

'Miracle, is it? Now didn't ye suppose that sooner or later one or another of us would be coming to look for you?' He laughed. 'I've not only had the luck to find you. That sweet, womanly creature has supplied a pretext for my interest in you. It makes things easy. And, anyway, easy or difficult, by my soul, I'm not leaving Nevis without you.'

VI

In the hall of the Deputy-Governor's house, when they came to it, Captain Blood left the lad to wait for him, whilst, guided by my lady's strident scolding voice, he strode to the dining-room. There he found Sir James seated, cold and sneering, before a neglected breakfast and her ladyship pacing the room as she railed. The opening of the door momentarily checked her. Then with heaving breast and eyes that flamed in a white face she exploded at the intruder.

'You have the effrontery to present yourself?'

'I thought that I might be expected.'

'Expected? Ha!'

He bowed a little. 'I'm far from wishing to intrude. But I supposed that some explanation might be desired of me.'

'Some explanation indeed!'

'And it's not in my sensitive heart to disappoint a lady.'

'A while ago you had another name for me.'

'A while ago you deserved another.'

Sir James rapped the table. His dignity both as Deputy-Governor and as husband demanded, he conceived, this intervention. 'Sir!' His tone was a reproof. Peremptorily he added: 'A plain tale, if you please.'

'Faith, I'll make it plainer than may please you, Sir James. I'll not be mincing words at all.' And forth came a scrupulous account of the events, in the course of rendering which he was more than once compelled to overbear her ladyship's interruptions.

At the end her husband looked at her where she stood fuming, and there was no sympathy in his glance. It was cold and hard and laden with dislike. 'Captain Peter supplies what the tale lacked to make it hang together.'

'It should suffice at least to show you that satisfaction is required, unless you're a poltroon.'

Whilst the Deputy-Governor was wincing at the insult, Captain Blood was making haste to interpose.

'Sir James, I am at your service for satisfaction of whatever sort you choose. But first, for my own satisfaction, let me say that if under the spur of emotions which I trust you will account humane, I have done aught that is offensive, my apologies are freely offered.'

Sir James remained singularly cold and stern. 'You have done little good, and perhaps a deal of harm, by your intervention. This wretched slave, encouraged to mutiny by your action, cannot be suffered to escape the consequences. There would be an end to order and discipline in the plantation if his conduct were overlooked. You perceive that?'

'Does it matter what he perceives?' railed the lady

'What I perceive is that if I had not intervened this man would have been shot on the spot by her ladyship's orders, and this because innocent of all offence he resisted the threat—again by her ladyship's orders—of having the flesh cut from his bones. Those were her gentle words.'

'It is certainly what will happen to him now,' she spitefully announced. 'That is, unless Sir James prefers to hang him.'

'As a scapegoat for me, because I intervened?' demanded the Captain of Sir James, and Sir James, stung by the sneer, made haste to answer: 'No, no. For threatening the overseer.'

This brought down upon him a fresh attack from her ladyship.

'His insolence to me, of course, is of no account. Nor, it seems, is this gentleman's.'

Between the two of them, Sir James was in danger of losing his stern habitual calm. He slapped the table so that the dishes rattled.

'One thing at a time, madam, if you please. The situation is nasty enough, God knows. I've warned you more than once against venting your spleen upon this fellow Hagthorpe. Now you force me to choose between flogging him for an insubordination that I cannot regard as other than fully provoked, and imperilling all discipline among the slaves. Since I cannot afford that, I have to thank your tantrums, madam, for compelling me to be inhuman.'

'Whilst I have none but myself to thank for having mated with a fool.'

'That, madam, is a matter we may presently have occasion to argue,' said he, and there was something so mysteriously minatory in his tone that her astonishment deprived her pertness of an answer.

Softly Blood's voice cut into the pause. 'I might be able, Sir James, to lift you from the horns of this dilemma.' And he went on to explain himself. 'You'll remember that it was to buy a cabin-boy I landed here. I had thought of a black man; but this Hagthorpe seems a likely lad. Sell him to me, and I'll take him off your hands.'

The elderly man considered a moment, and his gloom was seen to lighten a little. 'Egad! It's a solution.'

'You have but to name your price, then, Sir James.'

But her ladyship was there with her spite to close that easy exit.

'What next? The man's a rebel-convict, doomed for life to service in the plantations. You have a clear duty. You dare not be a party to his leaving the West Indies.'

In the troubled hesitation of that irresolute man, Blood saw that all was not yet done, as he had hoped. Cursing the spite of the lovely termagant, he advanced to the foot of the table, and, folding his arms on the tall back of the chair that stood there, he looked grimly from one to other of them.

'Well, well!' said he. 'And so this unfortunate lad is to be flogged.'

'He's to be hanged,' her ladyship corrected.

'No, no,' Sir James protested. 'A flogging will suffice.'

'I see that I can do no more,' said Blood, and his manner became ironically smooth. 'So I'll take my leave. But before I go, Sir James, there's something I'd almost forgot. I found a cousin of yours at St Thomas who was in haste to get to Nevis.'

He intended to surprise them; and he succeeded; but their surprise was no greater than his own at the abrupt and utter change of manner his announcement produced in her ladyship.

'Geoffrey!' she cried, a catch in her voice. 'Do you mean Geoffrey Court?'

'That is his name. Geoffrey Court.'

'And he's at St Thomas, you say?' Again it was her ladyship who questioned him, the change in her manner growing more ludicrously marked. There was a change too in the aspect of Sir James. He was observing his wife from under his bushy eyebrows, the ghost of a sneer on his thin lips.

'No, no,' Blood corrected. 'Mr Court is here. Aboard my ship. I gave him passage from St Thomas.'

'Then...' She paused. She was out of breath, and her brows were knit in a puzzled frown. 'Then why has he not landed?'

'I'm disposed to think it's by a dispensation of Providence. Just as it was by a dispensation of Providence that he requested a passage of me. All that need matter to you, Sir James, is that he's still aboard.'

'But is he ill, then?' cried my lady

'As healthy as a fish, ma'am. But he may not so continue. Aboard that ship, Sir James, I am as absolute as you are here ashore.'

It was impossible to misunderstand him. Taken aback, they stared at him a moment, then her ladyship, panting and quavering, exploded.

'There are laws to restrain you, I suppose.'

'No laws at all, ma'am. You have only half my name. I am Captain Peter, yes. Captain Peter Blood.' It had become necessary to disclose himself if his threat was to carry weight. He smiled upon their silent stupefaction. 'Perhaps you'll be seeing the need, for the sake of Cousin Geoffrey, of being more humane in the matter of this unfortunate slave. For I give you my word that whatever you do to young Hagthorpe that same will I do to Mr Geoffrey Court.'

Sir James actually and incomprehensibly laughed, whilst her ladyship gaped in terror for a moment before bracing herself to deal practically with the situation.

'Before you can do anything you'll have to reach your ship again, and you'll never leave Charlestown until Mr Court is safely ashore. You'd forgot to...'

'Och, I've forgotten nothing,' he interrupted, with a wave of the hand. 'You're not to suppose that I'm the man to walk into a gin without taking precautions to see that it can't be sprung on me. The Mary of Modena carries forty guns in her flanks, all of them demi-cannons. Two of her broadsides will make of Charlestown just a heap of rubble. And it's what'll happen if they have no word of me aboard before eight bells is made. You'll come away from that bell-pull, my lady, if you're prudent.'

She came away white and trembling, whilst Sir James, grey-faced, but still with that suggestion of a sneering smile about his lips, looked up at Captain Blood.

'You play the highwayman, sir. You put a pistol to our heads.'

'No pistol at all. Just forty demi-cannons, and every one of them loaded.'

But for all his bravado Captain Blood fully realized that in the pass to which things were come he might yet have to pistol Sir James so as to win free. He would deplore the necessity; but he was prepared for it. What he was not prepared for was the Deputy-Governor's abrupt and easy acquiescence.

'That simplifies the issue, which is, I think, that whatever I do to Hagthorpe you will do to my cousin.'

'That is the issue exactly.'

'Then if I were to hang Hagthorpe...'

'There would be a yard-arm for your cousin.'

'Only one decision, of course, is possible.'

Her ladyship's gasp of relief from her mounting fears was clearly audible. 'You prevail, sir,' she cried. 'We must let Hagthorpe go.'

'On the contrary,' said Sir James. 'I must hang him.'

'You must...' She choked as she stared at him, open-mouthed, the horror back again in her wide blue eyes.

'I have a clear duty, madam, as you reminded me. As you said, I dare not be a party to Hagthorpe's leaving the plantations. He must hang. Fiat justitia, ruat coelum. I think that's how it runs. What happens afterwards will not be on my conscience.'

'Not on your conscience!' She was distraught. 'But Geoffrey!' She wrung her hands. 'Geoffrey!' Her tone had become a wail. Then, rallying, she turned in fury on her husband. 'You're mad. Mad! You can't do this. You can't. Hagthorpe must go. What does he matter, after all? What's a slave more or less? In God's name, let him go.'

'And my duty, then? My clear duty?'

His sternness broke her spirit. 'Oh God!' She flung herself on her knees beside his chair, clawing his arm in her anguish.

He cast her off and answered her with a laugh that in its contemptuous mockery was horrible to hear.

Afterwards Captain Blood boasted, perhaps unduly that it was this cruel amusement at the woman's panic that brought light to a situation full of mystery, explained the ready acceptance of it by Sir James, and made plain much else that had been puzzling.

Having laughed his wicked fill, the Deputy-Governor rose, and waved a hand in dismissal of the Captain. 'The matter's settled, then. You'll desire to return to your ship, and I'll not detain you. Yet, stay. You might take a message to my cousin.' He went to unlock the secretaire that stood between the windows. Thence he took a copy of The Poems of Sir John Suckling on one of the sides of which the vellum curled away from the board. 'Condole with him on my behalf, and restore him this. I was waiting for him, to hand it to him myself. But it will be much better this way. Assure him from me that the letter it contained, almost as poetical as the volume itself, has now been faithfully delivered.' And to her ladyship he held out a folded sheet. 'It is for you, ma'am. Take it.' She shrank in fear. 'Take it,' he insisted, and flung it at her. 'We will discuss its contents presently. Meanwhile, it will help you to understand my strict regard for that clear duty of which you reminded me.'

Crouching where he had left her beside his empty chair, her shaking fingers unfolded the sheet. She lowered her eyes to the writing; then, after a moment, with a whimpering sound, let the sheet fall.

Captain Blood was taking in his hands the volume that Sir James had proffered. It was now, I think, that full understanding came to him, and for a moment he was in a dilemma. If the unexpected had helped him at the commencement, the unexpected had certainly come to thwart him now, when in sight of the end.

'I'll wish you a very good day, sir,' said Sir James. 'There is nothing to detain you longer.'

'You're in a mistake, Sir James. There's just one thing. I've changed my mind. I may have done many things in my time for which I should take shame. But I've never yet been anyone's hangman, and I'll be damned if I fill that office in your service. I was quite ready to hang this cousin of yours as an act of reprisal. But I'm damned if I'll hang him to oblige you. I'll send him ashore, Sir James, so that you may hang him yourself.'

The sudden dismay in Sir James' face was no more than Captain Blood expected. Having thus wrecked that sweet plan of vengeance, the Captain went on to show where consolation lay.

'If now that I've changed my mind you were to change yours, and sell me this lad to be my cabin-boy, I'ld not only carry your cousin away with me, but I think I could induce him not to trouble you again.'

Sir James' deep-set eyes questioningly searched the face of the buccaneer.

Captain Blood smiled. 'It's entirely a friendly proposal, Sir James,' he said, and the assurance bore conviction to the troubled mind of the Deputy-Governor.

'Very well,' he said at last. 'You may take the lad. On those terms I make you a gift of him.'

VII

Realizing that husband and wife would be having a good deal to say to each other, and that to linger at such a time would be intrusive, Captain Blood took an immediate tactful leave, and departed.

In the hall he summoned the waiting Tom Hagthorpe to accompany him, and the lad, understanding nothing of this amazing deliverance, went with him.

None hindering them, they hired a boat at the mole, and so came to the Mary of Modena, in the waist of which the two brothers, reunited, fell into each other's arms, whilst Captain Blood looked on with all the sense of being a beneficent deity.

On the verge of tears, Nat demanded to know by what arts Peter Blood had accomplished this deliverance so speedily and without violence.

'I'll not be saying there was no violence,' said Blood. 'There was, in fact, a deal of it. But it was violence of the emotions. And there's some more of the same kind to be borne yet. But that's for Mr Court.' He turned to the bo'sun who was standing by. 'Pipe the hands to quarters, Jake. We weigh at once.'

He went off to the cabin to which Mr Court was confined. He dismissed the guard posted at the door, and unlocked it. A very furious gentleman greeted him.

'How much longer do you keep me here, you damned scoundrel?'

'And where would you be going now?' wondered Captain Blood.

'Where would I be going? D'ye mock me, you cursed pirate? I'm going ashore, as you well know.'

'Do I, now? I wonder.'

'D'ye mean still to prevent me?'

'Faith, there may not be the need. I have a message for you from Sir James: a message and a book of poetry.'

Faithfully he delivered both. Mr Court changed colour, went limp, and sat down suddenly on a locker.

'Perhaps you'll be less eager now to land on Nevis. It may begin to occur to you that the West Indies are not the healthiest region for dalliance. Jealousy in the tropics can be like the climate—mighty hot and fierce. You'll wisely prefer, I should think, to find a ship somewhere that will carry you safely home to England.'

Mr Court wiped the perspiration from his brow

'Then you're not putting me ashore?'

The thudding of the capstan and the rattle of the anchor chain reached them through the open port of the cabin. Captain Blood's gesture drew attention to the sound.

'We are weighing now. We shall be at sea in half-an-hour.'

'Perhaps it's as well,' Mr Court resignedly admitted.

Episode 5

SACRILEGE

I

Never in the whole course of his outlawry did Captain Blood cease to regard it as distressingly ironical that he who was born and bred in the Romish Faith should owe his exile from England to a charge of having supported the Protestant Champion and should be regarded by Spain as a heretic who would be the better for a burning.

He expatiated at length and aggrievedly upon this to Yberville, his French associate, on a day when he was constrained by inherent scruples to turn his back upon a prospect of great and easy plunder to be made at the cost of a little sacrilege.

Yet Yberville, whose parents had hoped to make a churchman of him, and who had actually been in minor orders before circumstances sent him overseas and turned him into a filibuster instead, was left between indignation and amusement at scruples which he accounted vain. Amusement, however, won the day with him; for this tall and vigorous fellow, already inclining a little to portliness, was of as jovial and easy-going a nature as his humorous mouth and merry brown eye announced. Undoubtedly—although in the end he was to provoke derision by protesting it—a great churchman had been lost in him.

They had put into Bieque, and, ostensibly for the purpose of buying stores, Yberville had gone ashore to see what news might be gleaned that could be turned to account. For this was at a time when the Arabella was sailing at a venture, without definite object. A Basque who had spent some years across the border in Spain, Yberville spoke a fluent Castilian which enabled him to pass for a Spaniard when he chose, and so equipped him perfectly for this scouting task in a Spanish settlement.

He had come back to the big red-hulled ship at anchor in the roadstead, with the flag of Spain impudently flaunted from her maintruck, with news that seemed to him to indicate a likely enterprise. He had learnt that Don Ignacio de la Fuente, sometime Grand Inquisitor of Castile, and now appointed Cardinal-Archbishop of New Spain, was on his way to Mexico on the eighty-gun galleon the Santa Veronica, and in passing was visiting the bishoprics of his province. His Eminence had been at San Salvador, and he was now reported on his way to San Juan de Puerto Rico, after which he was expected at San Domingo, perhaps at Santiago de Cuba, and certainly at Havana, before finally crossing to the Main.

Unblushingly Yberville disclosed the profit which his rascally mind conceived might be extracted from these circumstances.

'Next to King Philip himself,' he opined, 'or, at least, next to the Grand inquisitor, the Cardinal-Archbishop of Seville, there is no Spaniard living who would command a higher ransom than this Primate of New Spain.'

Blood checked in his stride. The two were pacing the high poop of the Arabella in the bright November sunshine of that region of perpetual summer. Yberville's tall vigour was still set off by the finery of lilac satin in which he had gone ashore, a purple love-knot in his long brown curls. Forward at the capstan and at the braces was the bustle of preparation to get the great ship under way; and in the forechains, Snell, the bo'sun, his bald pate gleaming in a circlet of untidy grey curls, was ordering in obscene and fragmentary Castilian some bumboats to stand off.

Blood's vivid eyes flashed disapproval upon the jovial countenance of his companion. 'What then?' he asked.

'Why, just that. The Santa Veronica carries a sacerdotal cargo as rich as the plate in any ship that ever came out of Mexico.' And he laughed.

But Blood did not laugh with him. 'I see. And it's your blackguardly notion that we should lay her board and board, and seize the Archbishop?'

'Just that, my faith! The place to lie in wait for the Santa Veronica would be the straits north of Saona. There we should catch his Eminence on his way to San Domingo. It should offer little difficulty.'

Under the shade of his broad hat Blood's countenance had become forbidding. He shook his head. 'That is not for us.'

'Not for us? Why not? Are you deterred by her eighty guns?'

'I am deterred by nothing but the trifle of sacrilege concerned. To lay violent hands on an archbishop, and hold him to ransom! I may be a sinner, God knows; but underneath it all I hope I'm a true son of the Church.'

'You mean a son of the true Church,' Yberville amended. 'I hope I'm no less myself, but not on that account would I make a scruple of holding a Grand Inquisitor to ransom.'

'Maybe not. But then you had the advantage of being bred in a seminary. That makes you free, I suppose, with holy things.'

Yberville laughed at the sarcasm. 'It makes me discriminate between the Faith of Rome and the Faith of Spain. Your Spaniard with his Holy House, his autos de fé and his faggots is very nearly a heretic in my eyes.'

'A sophistry, to justify the abduction of a Cardinal. But I'm not a sophist, Ybervïlle, whatever else I may be. We'll keep out of sacrilege, so we will.'

Before the determination in his tone and face, Yberville fetched a sigh of resignation. 'Well, well! If that's your feeling... But it's a great chance neglected.'

And it was now that Captain Blood dilated upon the irony of his fate, until from the capstan to interrupt him came the bo'sun's cry: 'Belay there!' Then his whistle shrilled, and men swarmed aloft to let go the clewlines. The Arabella shook out her sails as a bird spreads its wings, and stood out for the open sea, to continue at a venture, without definite aim.

In leisurely fashion, with the light airs prevailing, they skimmed about the Virgin Islands, keeping a sharp look-out for what might blow into their range; but not until some three or four days later, when perhaps a score of miles to the south of Puerto Rico, did they sight a likely quarry. This was a small two-masted carack, very high in the poop, carrying not more than a dozen guns, and obviously a Spaniard, from the picture of Our Lady of Sorrows on the ballooning mainsail.

The Arabella shifted a point or two nearer to the wind, hoisted the Union Flag, and coming within range put a shot across the Spaniard's bows, as a signal to heave to.

Considering the presumed Englishman's heavy armament and superior sailing power, it is not surprising that the carack should have been prompt to obey that summons. But it was certainly a surprising contradiction to the decoration of her mainsail that simultaneously with her coming up into the wind the Cross of St George should break from her maintruck. After that she lowered a boat, and sent it speeding across the quarter-mile of gently ruffled sapphire water to the Arabella.

Out of his boat, a short, stockily built man, red of hair and of face, decently dressed in bottle green, climbed the Jacob's ladder of Blood's ship. With purposefulness in every line of him, he rolled forward on short, powerful legs towards Captain Blood, who, in a stateliness of black and silver, waited to receive him in the ship's waist. Blood was supported there by the scarcely less splendid Yberville, the giant Wolverstone, who had left an eye at Sedgemoor and boasted that with the one remaining he could see twice as much as any ordinary man, and Jeremy Pitt, the sailing-master of theArabella, from whose entertaining chronicles we derive this account of the affair.

Pitt sums up this newcomer in a sentence. 'Not in all my life did I ever see a hotter man.' There was a scorching penetration in the glance of his small eyes under their beetling sandy brows as they raked his surroundings: the deck that was clean-scoured as a trencher, the gleaming brass of the scuttle butts and of the swivel-gun on the poop-rail, the orderly array of muskets in the rack about the mainmast. All may well have led him to suppose that he was aboard a King's ship.

Finally his questing hazel eyes returned to a second and closer inspection of the waiting group.

'My name is Walker,' he announced with a truculent air and in an accent that proclaimed a northern origin. 'Captain Walker. And I'll be glad to know who the devil you may be that ye're so poxy ready with your gunfire. If ye've put a shot athwart my bows 'cause o' they emblems o' Popery on my mains'l, supposing me a Spaniard, faith, then ye're just the men I be looking for.'

Blood was austere. 'If you are the captain of that ship, it's glad I'd be to learn how that comes to be the case.'

'Ay, ay. So ye may, ecod! It's a long tale, Cap'n, and an ugly.'

Blood took the hint. 'Come below,' he said, 'and let us have it.'

It was in the great cabin of the Arabella with its carved and gilded bulkheads, its hangings of green damask, its costly plate and books and pictures and other sybaritic equipment such as the rough little North Country seaman had never dreamed could be found under a ship's deck, that the tale was told. It was told to the four who had received this odd visitor, and after Blood had presented himself and his associates, thereby momentarily abating some of the little shipmaster's truculence. But he recovered all his heat and fury when they came to sit about the table, on which the black man steward had set Canary Sack and Nantes brandy and a jug of meg, and it roared in him as he related what he had endured.

He had sailed, he told them, from Plymouth, six months earlier, bound in the first instance for the Coast of Guinea, where he had taken aboard three hundred able-bodied young black men, bought with beads and knives and axes from an African chieftain with whom he had already previously done several similar tradings. With this valuable cargo under hatches he was making his way to Jamaica, where a ready market awaited him, when, at the end of September, somewhere off the Bahamas, he was caught by an early storm, forerunner of the approaching hurricane season.

'By the mercy o' God we came through it afloat. But we was so battered and feckless that I had to jettison all my guns. Under the strain we had sprung a leak that kept us pumping for our lives; most o' my upper works was gone, and my mizzen was in such a state that I couldna' wi' safety ha' spread a night-shift on it. I must run to the nearest port for graving, and the nearest port happened to be Havana.

'When the port Alcalde had come aboard, seen for hisself my draggle-tailed condition, and that, anyway, wi'out guns I were toothless, as ye might say, he let me come into the shelter o' the lagoon, and there, without careening, we set about repairs.

'To pay for what we lacked I offered to trade the Alcalde some o' they blacks I carried. Now happen, as I was to learn, that the mines had been swept by a plague o' some kind—smallpox or yellow fever or summut—and they was mighty short o' slaves to work them. The Alcalde would buy the lot, he says, if I would sell. Seeing how it was with me, I were glad enough to lighten the ship by being rid o' the whole cargo, and I looked on the Alcalde's need as a crowning mercy to get me out of all my difficulties. But that weren't the end o' the windfall, as I supposed it. Instead o' gold, the Alcalde proposed to me that I takes payment in green hides, which, as ye may know, is the chief product of the island of Cuba. Naught could ha' suited me better, for I knew as I could sell the hides in England for three times the purchase price, and maybe a trifle over. So he gives me a bill o' lading for the hides, which it were agreed we should take aboard so soon as we was fit to sail.

'I pushed on wi' repairs, counting my fortune made, and looking on a voyage that at one time had seemed as if it must end in shipwreck, like to prove the most profitable as I had ever made.

'But I were reckoning without Spanish villainy. For when we was at last in case to put to sea again, and I sends word to the Alcalde that we was ready to load the hides of his bill of lading, the mate, which I had sent ashore, comes me back wi' a poxy message that the Captain-General—as they call the Governor in Cuba—would not allow the shipment, seeing as how it was against the law for any foreigner to trade in a Spanish settlement, and the Alcalde advised us to put to sea at once, whilst the Captain-General was in a mind to permit it.

'Ye'll maybe guess my feelings. Tom Walker, I may tell ye, bain't the man to let hisself be impudently robbed by anyone, whether pick-pocket or Captain-General. So I goes ashore myself. Not to the Alcalde. Oh no. I goes straight to the Captain-General hisself, a high-and-mighty Castilian grande, wi' a name as long as my arm. For short, they calls him Don Ruiz Perera de Valdoro y Peñascon, no less, and he's Count of Marcos too. A grande of the grandest.

'I slaps down my bill o' lading afore him, and tells him straightly how the thieving Alcalde had dealt by me, certain sure in my fecklessness that justice would be done at once.

'But from the way he shrugged and smiled I knew him for a villain afore ever he spoke. "Ye've been told the law, I believe," says he, wi' a leering curl to his mangy lip. "And ye've been rightly told. It is forbidden us by decree of His Catholic Majesty to buy from or sell to any foreign trader. The hides may not be shipped."

'It were a sour disappointment to me, seeing the profit on which I'd reckoned. But I keeps my temper to myself. "So be it," says I, "although it comes mighty hard on me and the law might ha' been thought of afore I were given this poxy bill o' lading. Howsomever, here it be; and ye can have it back in return for my three hundred black man's."

'At that he scowls and tries to stare me down, twirling his moustachios the while. "God gi' me patience wi' you!" says he. "That transaction too were illegal. Ye had no right to trade your slaves here."

'"I traded them at the Alcalde's request, Excellency," I reminds him.

'"My friend," says he, "if you was to commit murder at someone else's request, would that excuse the crime?"

'"It's not me what's broke the law," says I, "but him which bought the slaves from me."

'"Ye're both guilty. Therefore, neither must profit. The slaves is confiscate to the State."

'Now, I've told ye, sirs, as how I was making no ado about suffering the loss of my lawful profit on the hides. But to be stripped naked, as it were, by that heuck-fingered Spanish gentleman, robbed o' a cargo o' blacks, the worth o' which I had agreed at ten thousand pieces of eight—Od rot my soul!—that was more nor I could stomach. My temper got the better o' me, and I ups and storms in a mighty rage at that fine Castilian nobleman—Don Ruiz Perera de Valdoro y Peñascon—crying shame on him for such iniquity, and demanding that at least he pay me in gold the price o' my slaves.

'The cool villain lets me rant myself out, then shows me his teeth again in another o' his wicked, fleering smiles.

'"My friend," says he, "ye've no cause to make this pother, no cause to complain at all. Why, you heretic fool, let me tell you as I am doing far less than my strict duty, which would be to seize your ship, your crew and your person, and send you to Cadiz or Seville there to purge the heresies wi' which your kind be troubling the world."'

Captain Walker paused there, to compose himself a little from the passion into which his memories had whipped him. He mopped his brow, and took a pull at the bumbo before resuming.

'Od rot me for a coward, but my courage went out o' me like sweat at they words. "Better be robbed," says I to myself, "than be cast into the Fires o' the Faith in a fool's coat." So I takes my leave of his Excellency afore his sense o' duty might get the better o' what he calls his compassion—damn his dirty soul!'

Again he paused, and then went on. 'Ye may be supposing that the end o' my trouble. But bide a while; for it weren't, nor yet the worst.

'I gets back aboard in haste, as ye'll understand. We weighs at once, and slips out to sea without no interference from the forts. But we've not gone above four or five miles, when on our heels comes a carack of a guarda-costa and opens fire on us as soon as ever she's within range. It's my belief she had orders from the muckety Captain-General to sink us. And for why? Because the talk of the Holy Office and the Fires of the Faith was so much bluster. The last thing as that thief would wish would be as they should find out in Spain the ways by which he is becoming rich in the New World.

'Howsomever, there was the guarda-costa, pumping round-shot into us as fast and hard as bad Spanish gunnery could contrive it. Without guns as we was it were easy as shooting woodcock. Or so they thought. But, having the weather-gauge o' them, I took the only chance left us. I put the helm hard over, and ran straight for her. Not a doubt but those muck-scutcheons counted on shooting us to pieces afore ever we could reach her, and, on my soul, they all but did. We was sinking fast, leaking like a colander, wi' our decks awash when at last we bumps alongside o' her. But by the mercy o' God to heretics, what were left o', my poor ship got a hold on that guarda-costa's timbers wi' her grapnels, what time we climbs aboard her. After that it were red hell on them decks, for we was all mad wi' rage at those cold-blooded murderers. From stem to stern we swept her wi' cold steel. I had five men killed and a half-score wounded; but the only Spaniards left alive was them as went overboard to drown.'

The slaver paused again, and his fiery eye flung a glance of challenge at his audience. 'That's about all, I think. We kept the carack, of course, my own ship being sunk, and that'll explain they emblems o' Popery on our mainsail. I knew as they'ld bring us trouble afore long. And yet, when, as I supposed, it was on account o' they that ye put a shot athwart my hawse, it came to me that maybe I had found a friend.'

II

The tale was told, and the audience, thrilled and moved by it, sat in silence a while, still under the spell of it after Walker had ceased to speak.

It was Wolverstone, at last, who stirred and growled. 'As ugly a story as I've heard of Castilian subtlety. That Captain-General would be the better for a keel-hauling.'

'Better still for a roasting over a slow fire,' said Yberville. 'It's the only way to give savour to this New Christian pig.'

Blood looked at him across the table. 'New Christian?' he echoed. 'You know him, then?'

'No more than you.' And the sometime seminarist explained. 'In Spain when a Jew is received into the Church he must take a new name. But his choice is not entirely free. The name he takes must be the name of a tree or plant, or the like, so that the source of his house may still be known. This Captain-General bears the name of Perera: Pear tree. The Valdaro and Peñascon have been subsequently added. They are always the readiest, these renegadoes, with threats of the Fires of the Faith.'

Blood gave his attention once more to Captain Walker.

'You'll have a purpose, sir, in giving yourself the trouble of telling us this nasty tale. What service do you seek of us?'

'Why, just a spare set o' sails, if so be ye have them, as I'm supposing ye will. I'll pay you what they're worth; for, burn me, it's inviting trouble to try to cross the ocean with those I carry.'

'And is that all, now! Faith, it was in my mind ye might be asking us to recover the value of your slaves from this Captain-General of Havana, with perhaps just a trifle over for our trouble in the interests of poetic justice. Havana is a wealthy city.'

Walker stared at him. 'Ye're laughing at me, Captain. I know better than to ask the impossible.'

'The impossible!' said Blood, with a lift of his black brows. Then he laughed. 'On my soul, it's almost like a challenge.'

'No challenge at all. Ye'll be bonny fighters, like enough; but the devil himself wouldn't venture to sail a buccaneer ship into Havana.'

'Ah!' Blood rubbed his chin. 'Yet this fellow needs a lesson, bad cess to him. And to rob a thief is a beckoning adventure.' He looked at his associates. 'Will we be paying him a visit, now?'

Pitt's opposition was immediate. 'Not unless we've taken leave of our senses. You don't know Havana, Peter. If there's a Spanish harbour in the New World that may be called impregnable, that harbour is Havana. In all the Caribbean there are no defences more formidable, as Drake discovered already in his day.'

'And that's the fact,' said Walker, whose red eye had momentarily gleamed at Blood's words. 'The place is an arsenal. The entrance is by a channel not more than half a mile across, with three forts, no less, to defend it: the Moro, the Puntal, and El Fuerte. Ye wouldn't stay afloat an hour there.'

Blood's eyes were dreamy. 'Yet you stayed afloat some days.'

'Ay, man. But the circumstances.'

'Glory be, now. Couldn't we be contriving circumstances? It wouldn't be the first time. The thing needs thought, and it's worth thinking about with no other enterprise to engage us.'

'That,' said Yberville, who had never been able to reconcile himself to the neglect of the opportunity presented by the voyage of the Archbishop, 'is only because you're mawkish. The Primate of the New World is still at sea. Let him pay for the sins of his countrymen. His ransom need be no less than the plunder of Havana would yield us, and we could include in it compensation for Captain Walker for the slaves of which they've robbed him.'

'Faith, ye have it,' said Wolverstone, who, being a heretic, was undaunted by any thought of sacrilege. 'It's like burning candles to Satan to be delicate with a Spaniard just because he's an archbishop.'

'And it need not end there,' said Pitt, that other heretic, in a glow of sudden inspiration. 'If we had the Archbishop in the hold, we could sail into Havana without fear of their forts. They'ld never dare to fire on a ship that housed his holiness.'

Blood was pensively toying with a curl of his black periwig. He smiled introspectively. 'I was thinking that same.'

'So!' crowed Yberville. 'Religious scruples begin to yield to reason. Heaven be praised.'

'Faith, now, I'll not say that it might not be worth a trifle of sacrilege—just a trifle, mark you—to squeeze his plunder out of this rogue of a Captain-General. Yes, I think it might be done.' He got up suddenly. 'Captain Walker, if ye've a mind to come with us on this venture and seek to recover what ye've lost, ye'd best be scuttling that guarda-costa and fetching your hands aboard the Arabella. Ye can trust us to provide you with a ship to take you home when this is over.'

'Man!' cried the tough little slaver, all the natural fierceness of him sunk fathoms deep in his amazement. 'Ye're not serious?'

'Not very,' said Captain Blood. 'It's just a whim of mine. But a whim that is like to cost this Don What's-his-name Perera dear. So you can come with us to Havana, and take your chance of sailing home again in a tall ship with a full cargo of hides, your fortunes restored, or you can have the set of sails ye're asking for, and go home empty-handed. The choice is yours.'

Looking up at him almost in awe, Captain Walker yielded at once to the vigorous vitality and full-blooded confidence of the buccaneer. The adventurous spirit in him answered to the call. No risk, he swore, was too great that offered a chance to wipe off the score against that forsworn Captain-General.

Yberville, however, was frowning. 'But the Archbishop, then?'

Blood smiled with tight lips. 'The Archbishop certainly. We can do nothing without the Archbishop.' He turned to Pitt with an order that showed how fully he had already resolved not only upon what was to do, but upon how it should be done. 'Jerry you'll lay me a course for Sainte Croix.'

'Why that?' quoth Yberville. 'It's much farther east than we need to go for his Eminence.'

'To be sure it is. But one thing at a time. There's some gear we'll be needing, and Sainte Croix is the place to provide it.'

III

They did not, after all, scuttle the Spanish carack, as Captain Blood proposed. The thrifty nature of the little North Country seaman revolted at the thought of such waste, whilst his caution desired to know how he and his hands were ever to get back to England if Blood's scheme should, after all, miscarry even in part and no such tall ship as he promised should be forthcoming.

For the rest, however, the events followed the course that Captain Blood laid down. Steering in a north-easterly direction, the Arabella, with the guarda-costa following, came a couple of days later to the French settlement of Sainte Croix, of which the buccaneers were free. Forty-eight hours they remained there, and Captain Blood, with Yberville and the bald-headed little bo'sun, Snell, who knew his way about every port of the Caribbean, spent most of the time ashore.

Then, leaving the carack to await their return, Walker and his hands transferred themselves to the Arabella. She set sail, and laid a westward course once more, in the direction of Puerto Rico. After that she was seen no more until a fortnight later, when her great red hull was sighted off the undulating green hills of the northern coast of Cuba.

In the genial, comparatively temperate airs of that region she sailed along those fertile shores, and so came at last to the entrance of the lagoon on which Havana stood in a majesty of limestone palaces, of churches, monasteries, squares, and market-places that might have been transported bodily from Old Castile to the New World.

Scanning the defences as they approached, Blood realized for himself how little either Walker or Jeremy Pitt had exaggerated their massive strength. The mighty Moro Fort, with its sullen bastions and massive towers, occupied a rocky eminence at the very mouth of the channel; opposite to it stood the Puntal, with its demi-lunar batteries; and facing the entrance loomed El Fuerte, no less menacing. Whatever might have been the strength of the place in the time of Drake, he would be rash, indeed, who would run the gauntlet of those three formidable guardians now.

The Arabella hove to in the roadstead, announced herself by firing a gun as a salute, hoisted the Union flag, and awaited events.

They followed soon in the shape of a ten-oared barge, from under the awning of which stepped the Alcalde of the port, Walker's old friend, Don Hieronimo. He puffed his way up the Jacob's ladder, and came aboard to inquire into the purpose of this ship in these waters.

Captain Blood, in a splendour of purple and silver, received him in the waist, attended by Pitt and Wolverstone. A dozen half-naked seamen hovered above the trim decks, and a half-dozen more were aloft dewing up the royals.

Nothing could have exceeded the courtliness with which the Alcalde was made welcome. Blood, who announced himself casually as on his way to Jamaica with a valuable cargo of slaves, had been, he said, constrained by lack of wood and water to put in at Havana. He would depend upon the kindliness and courtesy of the Alcalde for these and also for some fresh victuals for which they would be the better, and he would gladly pay in gold for what they took.

The black-coated Don Hieronimo, pasty-faced and flabby, some five and a half feet high and scarcely less round the belly, with the dewlap of an ox, was not to be seduced by the elegant exterior or courteous phrases of any damned heretical foreigner. He responded coldly, his expression one of consequential malevolence, whilst his shrewd black eyes scoured every corner of those decks suspiciously. Thus until the slaves were mentioned. Then a curious change took place; a measure of affability overspread his forbidding surliness. He went so far as to display his yellow teeth in a smile.

To be sure the Señor Captain could purchase whatever he required in Havana. To be sure he was at liberty to enter the port when he pleased, and then not a doubt but that the bumboats would be alongside and able to supply all that he lacked. If not, the Alcalde would be happy to afford him every facility ashore.

Upon these assurances the seaman at the whipstaff was ordered to put down the helm, and Pitt's clear voice rang out in command to the men at the braces to let go and haul. Catching the breeze again, the Arabella crept forward past those formidable forts, with the Alcalde's barge in tow, what time the Alcalde with ever-increasing affability was slyly seeking to draw from Captain Blood some information touching this cargo of slaves in his hold. But so vague and lethargic was Captain Blood upon the subject, that in the end, Don Hieronimo was forced to come out into the open and deal frankly.

'I may seem persistent in questioning you about these slaves,' he said. 'But that is because it occurs to me that if you choose, you need not be at the cost of carrying them to Jamaica. You would find a ready market for them here in Havana.'

'In Havana?' Blood raised his eyebrows. 'But is it not against the laws of His Catholic Majesty?'

The Alcalde pursed his thick, dusky lips. 'The law was made when there was no thought for our present difficulties. There has been a scourge of smallpox in the mines, and we are short of hands. Of necessity we must waive the law. If, then, you would care to trade, sir captain, there is no obstacle.'

'I see,' said Blood, without enthusiasm.

'And the prices will be good,' added Don Hieronimo, so as to stir him from his lethargy. 'In fact, they will be unusual.'

'So are my slaves. Very unusual.'

'And that's the fact,' Wolverstone confirmed him in his halting Spanish. 'They'll cost you dear, Señor Alcalde. Though I don't suppose ye'll grudge the price when you've had a look at them.'

'If I might see them,' begged the Spaniard.

'Oh, but why not?' was Blood's ready agreement.

The Arabella had come by now through the bottle-neck into the great blue lagoon that is the Bay of Havana, a full three miles across. The leadsman in the forechains was calling the fathoms, and it occurred to Blood that it might be prudent to go no farther. He turned aside for a moment, to order Pitt to anchor where they stood, well away from the forest of masts and spars reared by the shipping over against the town. Then he came back to the Alcalde.

'If you will follow me, Don Hieronimo,' said he, and led the way to a scuttle.

By a short narrow ladder they dropped to the main-deck below, where the gloom was shot by shafts of sunlight from the open gunports, crossed by others from the gratings overhead. The Alcalde looked along that formidable array of cannon, and at the lines of hammocks slung behind them on either side, in some of which men were even now reposing.

Stooping to avoid the stanchions in that shallow place, he followed his tall leader aft, and was followed in turn by the massive Wolverstone. Presently Blood paused, and turned, to ask a curious question.

'Does it happen, sir, that you are acquainted with the Cardinal-Archbishop Don Ignacio de la Fuente, the new Primate of New Spain?'

'Not yet, sir. He has not yet reached Havana. But we look daily now for the honour of receiving him.'

'It may be yours even sooner than you think.'

'But not sooner than we hope. What, sir, do you know of the Cardinal-Archbishop's voyage?'

Blood, however, had already resumed his progress aft, and did not answer him.

They came at last to the door of the wardroom, which was guarded by two musketeers. A muffled sound of chanting, Gregorian of character, which had mystified the Alcalde as they approached, was now so distinct that as they halted he could even distinguish the words of that droned supplication:

'Hostem repellas longius
Pacemque dones protinus;
Ductore sic te praevio
Vitemus omne noxium.'

He frowned, and stared up at Blood. 'Por Dios! Are they your slaves who sing?'

'They appear to find consolation in it.'

Don Hieronimo was suspicious without knowing what to suspect. Something here was not as it should be. 'Oddly devout, are they not?' said he.

'Certainly devout. Not oddly.'

At a sign from him, one of the musketeers had unbarred the door, and as he now flung it wide, the chanting abruptly broke off on the word 'Saeculorum'. The Amen to that hymn was never uttered.

Ceremoniously Blood waved the Alcalde forward. In haste to resolve this riddle, Don Hieronimo stepped boldly and quickly across the threshold, and there abruptly checked, at gaze with horror-stricken, bulging eyes.

In the spacious but sparsely furnished ward-room, invaded by the smell of bilge-water and spunyarn, and lighted by a window astern, he beheld a dozen men in the white woollen habit and black cloak of the order of St Dominic. In two rows they sat, silent and immovable as lay-figures, their hands folded within their wide sleeves, their heads bowed and cowled, all save one who stood uncovered and as if in immediate attendance upon a stately figure that sat apart, enthroned on a tall chair. A tall, handsome man of perhaps forty, he was from head to foot a flame of scarlet. A scarlet skullcap covered the tonsure to be presumed in his flowing locks of a rich brown that was almost auburn; a collar of finest point adorned the neck of his silken cassock; a gold cross gleamed on his scarlet breast. His very hands were gloved in red, and on the annular finger of his right flashed the episcopal sapphire, worn over his glove. His calm and the austerity in which he was enveloped lent him a dignity of aspect almost superhuman.

His handsome eyes surveyed the gross fellow who had so abruptly and unceremoniously stumbled into that place. But their lofty calm remained unperturbed. It was as if he left human passions to lesser mortals, such as a bare-headed, red-faced, rather bibulous-looking friar behind him, a man, relieved by nature from recourse to the tonsuring razor, whose hairless pate rose brown and gleaming from a crown of grey, greasy curls. A very human brother, this, to judge by the fierce scowl with which he surveyed the intruder.

Forcibly Captain Blood thrust forward the palsied Alcalde, so as to gain room to enter. Hat in hand, he stepped past him some little way, then turned to beckon him forward.

But before he could speak, the Alcalde, apoplectic and out of breath, was demanding to know what this might mean.

Blood was smilingly bland before that indignation. 'Is it not plain? I understand your surprise. But you'll remember that I warned you that my slaves are unusual.'

'Slaves? These?' The Alcalde seemed to choke. 'For sale? In God's name, who are you that you dare so impious, so infernal a jest?'

'I am called Blood, sir. Captain Blood.' And he added, with a bow, 'To serve you.'

'Blood!' The black eyes grew almost invisible in that congested countenance. 'You are Captain Blood? You are that endemonized pirate out of hell?'

'That is how Spain describes me. But Spain is prejudiced. Leave that, sir, and come.' Again he beckoned him, and what he said confirmed the Alcalde's worst fearful suspicions. 'Let me have the honour of presenting you to His Eminence the Cardinal-Archbishop Don Ignacio de la Fuente, the Primate of New Spain. I told you that it might be yours to welcome him sooner than you thought.'

'God of mercy!' gurgled the Alcalde.

Stately as a Court usher, Blood advanced a pace, and bowed low to the Cardinal. 'Eminence, condescend to receive a poor sinner who is, nevertheless, a person of some consequence in these parts: the Alcalde of the port of Havana.'

At the same moment Don Hieronimo was thrust violently forward by the herculean arm of Wolverstone, who bawled after him: 'On your knees, sir, to ask a blessing of his Eminence.'

The prelate's calm, inscrutable, deep-set eyes were considering the horrified officer who was now on his knees before him.

'Eminence!' gasped Don Hieronimo, almost in tears. 'Eminence!'

As steady as the glance was the deep, rich voice that murmured: 'Pax tibi, filius meus,' whilst in slow majesty the hand that bore the cardinalitial ring was extended to be kissed.

Faltering 'Eminence!' yet again, the Alcalde fell upon it and bore it to his mouth as if he would eat it. 'What horror!' he wailed. 'My God, what horror! What sacrilege!'

A smile infinitely wistful, infinitely compassionate and saintly broke upon the prelate's handsome face. 'We offer up these ills for our sins, my son, thankful, since that is so, that they are given us to endure. We are for sale, it seems, I and these poor brethren of St Dominic who accompany me and share my duress at the hands of our heretical captors. We must pray for grace to bear it with becoming fortitude, remembering that those great Apostles St Peter and St Paul also suffered incarceration in the fulfilment of their sacred missions.'

Don Hieronimo was scrambling to his feet, moving sluggishly not only from his obesity but also from overpowering emotion. 'But how could such a horror come to pass?' he groaned.

'Let it not distress you, my son, that I should be a prisoner in the hands of this poor, blind heretic.'

'Three errors in three words, Eminence,' was Blood's comment. 'Behold how easy is error, and let it serve as a warning against hasty judgements when you are called upon to judge, as presently you shall be. I am not poor. I am not blind. I am not a heretic. I am a true son of Mother Church. And if I have reluctantly laid violent hands upon your Eminence, it was not only so that you might be a hostage for the righting of a monstrous wrong that has been done in the name of the Catholic King and the Holy Faith, but so that in your wisdom and piety you might, yourself, deliver judgement upon the deed and the doer.'

Through his teeth the bareheaded, red-faced little friar, leaning forward and snarling like a terrier, uttered three words of condemnation. 'Perro hereje maldito!'

Instantly the Cardinal's gloved hand was raised imperiously to rebuke and restrain him. 'Peace, Frey Domingo!

'I spoke, sir, of poverty and blindness of the spirit, not of the flesh,' he quietly answered Blood, and continued, addressing him in the second person singular, as if more signally to mark the gulf between them: 'For in that sense poor and blind thou art.' He sighed. More sternly still he added: 'That thou shouldst confess thyself a son of the True Church is but to confess this outrage more scandalous than I had supposed it.'

'Suspend your judgement, Eminence, until all my motive is disclosed,' said Blood, and taking a step or two in the direction of the open door he raised his voice to call. 'Captain Walker!'

In answer, a bow-legged, red-haired little man, all fire and truculence, advanced with a rolling gait to nod curtly to the scarlet presence, and then, arms akimbo, to confront the Alcalde.

'Good day to you, Don Ladrin, which is what I calls you. You'ld not be expecting to see me again so soon, ye murdering villain. Ye didna know maybe that an English sailor has as many lives as a cat. I've come back for my hides, ye thief. My hides, and my tall ship as your rascals sank under me.'

If anything at that moment could have added to the Alcalde's distress and rage and to the confusion of his wits this reappearance of Captain Walker certainly supplied it. Yellow-faced and shaking from head to foot, he stood gasping and mouthing, desperately seeking words in which to answer. But Captain Blood gave him little time to strain his wits.

'So now, Don Hieronimo, perhaps you begin to understand,' he said. 'We are here in quest of restitution of what was stolen, of reparation for a crime. And for this his Eminence there is no more than a hostage in our hands.

'I will not trouble you to restore the hides out of which you and your Captain-General between you swindled this poor seaman. But you'll pay in gold the price they would have fetched in England; that is twenty thousand pieces of eight. And you'll provide a ship of a burthen at least equal to that which your guarda-costa sank by orders of your Captain-General, this ship to be of not less than twenty guns, all found, armed and victualled for a voyage. Time enough, when that is done, to discuss putting his Eminence ashore.'

There was a streak of blood on the Alcalde's chin, from the wound his teeth had made in his lip. Yet frenzied though he might be by impotent rage, yet he was not so blinded but that he perceived that the guns of the mighty forts of Havana, and of the Admiral's squadron within range of which this pirate vessel impudently rode at anchor, were powerless against her whilst the sacred person of the Primate of New Spain was in her hold. Similarly to attempt to take her by assault must be fraught by a like deadly peril for the Cardinal at the hands of men so desperate and bloody as these. At whatever cost, his Eminence must be delivered, and this with the least delay. In all the circumstances it was perhaps a matter for thankfulness that the pirate's demands should be as modest as they were.

He strove for dignity, drew himself up and thrust out his paunch, and spoke to Blood in the tone of a man addressing his lackey. 'I do not parley with you. I will inform his Excellency the Captain-General.' He turned to the Cardinal, with a change to utmost humility. 'Give me leave, Eminence, accepting my assurance that you will not be allowed to remain in this scandalous duress one moment longer than may be avoidable. Give me leave.' He bowed very low, and would have withdrawn. But the Cardinal gave him no such leave just yet. He had been listening with obvious attention to what passed.

'Wait, sir. Wait. There is something here that I do not understand.' A puzzled frown stood between his brows. 'This man speaks of restitution, of reparation. Has he the right to use such words?'

It was Blood who answered him. 'I desire your Eminence to be the judge of that. That is the judgement to which I alluded. It is so that you may deliver it that I have ventured to lay hands upon your sacred person, for which I shall hope for your absolution in the end.' Thereupon, in a dozen crisp, incisive sentences, he sketched the tale of the robbery of Captain Walker under the cloak of legal justification.

When he had done the Cardinal looked at him with scorn, and from him turned to the fuming Alcalde. His gentle voice was warm with indignation.

'That tale of course is false. Impossible. It does not deceive me. No Castilian man of honour placed by His Catholic Majesty in authority could be guilty of such turpitude. You hear, sir Alcalde, how this misguided pirate imperils his immortal soul by bearing false witness.'

The perspiring Alcalde's answer did not come as promptly as his Eminence expected it. 'But is it possible that you hesitate?' he asked, as if startled, leaning forward.

Desperately Don Hieronimo broke into stumbling speech. 'It is that... Dios mio! The tale is grossly exaggerated. It—'

'Exaggerated!' The gentle voice was suddenly and sharply raised. 'Exaggerated? Not wholly false, then?'

The only answer he received was a cringing hunch of the Alcalde's shoulders and a glance that fell in fear under the prelate's stern eyes.

The Cardinal-Archbishop sank back into his chair, his face inscrutable, his voice of an ominous quiet.

'You have leave to go. You will request the Captain-General of Havana to wait upon me here in person. I require to know more of this.'

'He... he may require safe-conduct,' stuttered the unfortunate Alcalde.

'It is granted him,' said Captain Blood.

'You hear? I shall expect him at the earliest.' And the scarlet hand with its sapphire ring majestically waved Don Hieronimo away.

Daring no more, the Alcalde bowed himself double and went out backwards as if from a royal presence.

IV

If the tale borne by Don Hieronimo to the Captain-General, of Captain Blood's outrageous and sacrilegious violence to the Cardinal-Archbishop of New Spain filled Don Ruiz with amazement, dismay, and horrified indignation, the summons on which it concluded, and the reasons for it, supplied a stimulus that presently moved his Excellency to almost superhuman activity. If he delayed four hours in answering in person that summons, at least the answer that he then delivered was of such a fullness that it would have taken an ordinary Spaniard in ordinary circumstances as many days to have prepared it.

His conscience shaken into uneasiness by what his subordinate told him, Don Ruiz Perera de Valdoro y Peñascon, who was also Count of Marcos, deemed it well to omit in the Cardinal-Archbishop's service no effort that might be calculated to conciliate his Eminence. It occurred to him, naturally enough, that nothing could be more conciliatory, nothing would be more likely to put the Cardinal in a good humour with him, than if he were to present himself in the role of his Eminence's immediate deliverer from the hands of that abominable pirate who held him captive.

Therefore by exertions unprecedented in all his experience Don Ruiz so contrived that in seeking the Cardinal-Archbishop aboard the Arabella he was actually able to fulfil all the conditions upon which he understood that Captain Blood had consented to restore his prisoner to liberty. So great an achievement must fill the Primate with a wonder and gratitude that would leave no room for petty matters.

Thus, then, it fell out almost incredibly that when some four hours after the Alcalde's departure from the Arabella the Captain-General came alongside in his barge, a broad-beamed, two-masted, square-rigged brigantine was warped to a station a cable's length from the buccaneer's larboard quarter. In addition to this, Don Ruiz, who climbed the ladder with the Alcalde in close attendance, was followed by two alguaziles, each of whom shouldered a wooden coffer of some weight.

Captain Blood had taken his precautions against treachery. His gun-ports had been opened on the larboard side, and twenty threatening muzzles had been run out. As his Excellency stepped down into the waist, his contemptuous eyes saw the bulwarks lined by men, some half naked, some fully clothed, and some actually in armour, but all with muskets poised and matches glowing.

A tall, narrow-faced gentleman with a bold nose, Don Ruiz came dressed as was demanded by an occasion of such ceremony. He was magnificent in gold-laced black. He wore the cross of St James on his breast, and a gold-hilted sword swung at his side. He carried a long cane in one hand and a gold-edged handkerchief in the other.

Under his little black moustachios his thin lips curled in disdain as he acknowledged the bow with which Captain Blood received him. The deepening sallowness of his face bore witness to the wicked humour upon which he strove to set that mask of lofty contempt.

He delivered himself without preamble. 'Your impudent conditions are fulfilled, Sir Pirate. There is the ship you have demanded, and here in these coffers is the gold—the twenty thousand pieces. It is now for you to keep your part of the bargain struck, and so make an end of the sacrilegious infamy of which you have been guilty.'

Without answering him, Captain Blood turned and beckoned forward the little North-Country shipmaster from the background, where he stood glowering at Don Ruiz.

'You hear, Captain Walker.' He pointed to the coffers, which the alguaziles had set down upon the hatch-coaming. 'There, says his Excellency, is your gold. Verify it, then take it, put your men aboard that brigantine, spread your sails, and be off whilst I am still here to make your departure safe.'

For a moment amazement and emotion before such munificence rendered the little slaver dumb. Then speech bubbled out of him in a maudlin gush of wonder and gratitude which Blood made haste to stem.

'It's wasting good time ye are, my friend. Sure, don't I know all that: that I'm great and noble and that it was the lucky day for you when I put a shot athwart your hawse? Away with you now, and say a good word for Peter Blood in England when ye get there.'

'But this gold,' Walker still protested. 'Ye'll take the half of it at least?'

'Och, now! What's a trifle of gold? I'll know how to repay myself for my trouble, ye may be sure. Gather your hands and be off, and God be with you, my friend.'

When at last he had wrenched his fingers from the crushing grip into which the slaver packed all the emotion that he could not properly utter, Blood gave his attention to Don Ruiz, who had stood aloof with the Alcalde, disdainful of eye and lip.

'If you will follow me, I will conduct you to his Eminence.'

He led the way below, and Pitt and Wolverstone went with them.

In the ward-room, at sight of that majestic figure, glittering in scarlet splendour against the humble monkish background, Don Ruiz, with an inarticulate cry, ran forward to cast himself upon his knees.

'Benedictus sis,' murmured the Primate, and gave him his ring to kiss.

'My lord! Eminence! That these incarnate devils should have subjected your saintliness to such indignity!'

'That is not important, my son,' said the gentle, musical voice. 'By me and these my brethren in Christ suffering is accepted thankfully, as something of which to make an offering to the Throne of Grace. What is important, what gives me deep concern, is the reason pretexted for it, which I learned only this morning here. I have been told, Lord Count, that in the King's name delivery was refused of merchandise that had been sold to an English seaman, that the moneys he had already paid, as the price of that merchandise, were confiscated, that he was driven empty away with threats of prosecution by the Holy Office, and that even when, thus robbed, he had departed, his ship was pursued and sunk by one of your guarda-costas.

'These things I have heard, my son; but although your Alcalde did not contradict them, I must refuse to believe that a gentleman of Spain and a representative of His Catholic Majesty in these parts could be guilty of such conduct.'

Don Ruiz got to his feet. Sallower than ever was his narrow face. But he contrived that his tone should be easy and his manner imposing. By a certain loftiness he hoped to wave the matter away.

'That is all overpast, Eminence. If error there was, it has now been corrected, and with generous interest, as this buccaneer captain will bear me witness. I am here to give myself the honour of escorting your Eminence ashore to the joyous welcome that awaits you and the great reception which expectant Havana has been preparing for some weeks.'

But his ingratiatory smile found no reflection in the Primate's lofty countenance. It remained overcast, sadly grave. 'Ah! You admit the error, then. But you do not explain it.'

Choleric by nature and imperious from long habit of command, the Captain-General was momentarily in danger of forgetting that he stood in the presence of one who was virtually the Pope of the New World, a man whose powers there were inferior only to the King's, and before whom in certain matters even the King, himself, must bow. Although he remembered it in time, a hint of tartness still invested his reply.

'Explanation must prove tedious to your Lordship, and perhaps obscure, since these are matters concerned with my legal office. Your Eminence's great and renowned enlightenment will scarcely cover what is a matter of jurisprudence.'

The most wistful of smiles broke upon that handsome face. 'You are indifferently informed, I fear, Don Ruiz. You can never have heard that I have held the exalted office of Grand Inquisitor of Castile, or you would know—since it must follow—that I am a doctor not only of canon, but also of civil law. Be under no apprehension, then, that I shall fail to follow your legal exposition of the event, and even less on the score of tedium. Many of my duties are tedious, my son; but they are not on that account avoided.'

To that cold, relentless insistence the Captain-General saw himself under the necessity of submitting. He swallowed his annoyance, steadied himself, and provided himself with a scapegoat who would not dare, on his life, to deny him.

'In brief, Eminence, these transactions were permitted without my knowledge by my Alcalde.' The audible gasp from Don Hieronimo, who stood behind him, did not deter his Excellency. He went steadily on. 'When I learned of them, I had no choice but to cancel them, since it is my duty to insist upon the law which forbids all foreigners to trade in His Catholic Majesty's dominions.'

'With that there could be no quarrel. But I understand that this English seaman had already paid for the merchandise.'

'He had traded slaves for them, Eminence.'

'No matter what he had traded. Were his slaves restored to him when the transaction was cancelled by you?'

'The laws which he defied when he traded them decreed their confiscation likewise.'

'Ordinarily that might be so. But this, if I am rightly informed, is no ordinary case. I am told that he was urged to trade his slaves by your Alcalde.'

'Just as I,' Blood interposed, 'was urged by him this morning to trade mine.' And the sweep of his hand indicated the Cardinal-Archbishop and his attendant monks.

'He does not learn by his errors, then, this Alcalde of yours. Perhaps you do not desire that he shall.'

Ostentatiously Don Ruiz turned his shoulder upon Blood, ignoring him. 'Your Eminence cannot account me bound by the illegality of a subordinate.' Then permitting himself a little smile, he added the sophism which he had already used with Captain Walker. 'If a man commit murder it cannot exculpate him to say that he had the sanction of another.'

'That is to be subtle, is it not? I must take thought upon this, Don Ruiz. We will talk of it again.'

Don Ruiz bowed low, his lip in his teeth. 'At your Eminence's disposal,' he said. 'Meanwhile, my barge is waiting to carry your Eminence ashore.'

The Cardinal rose, imposingly tall in his robes, and drew his scarlet cloak about him. The cowled Dominicans, who had stood like statues, stirred responsively into life. His Eminence turned to them.

'Be mindful, my children, to return thanks for this safe deliverance. Let us go.'

And he stepped forward, to be checked at once by Captain Blood. 'Patience yet awhile, Eminence. All is not done.'

The Cardinal threw up his head, a frown darkening his brow. 'How? What, then, remains?'

Blood's answer was delivered rather to the scowling Captain-General than to the prelate. 'So far we have had no more than restitution. Come we now to the question of compensations.'

'Compensations!' cried the Primate, and for once the splendid calm of him was ruffled. Sternly he added the questions:

'What is this? Do you break faith sir?'

'That, at least, has never yet been said of me. I break no faith. On the contrary, I am punctilious. What I told the Alcalde was that when restitution was made we would discuss the matter of your Eminence's landing. That we would discuss it. No more than that.'

Don Ruiz smiled in rage and malice, a smile that displayed his white teeth. 'Ingenious. Yes. And then, you brigand?'

'I could not without disrespect to his Eminence, the Primate of New Spain, set his ransom at less than a hundred thousand ducats.'

Don Ruiz sucked in his breath. He went livid. His jaw fell loose. 'A hundred thousand ducats!'

'That is today. Tomorrow I may not be so modest.'

The Captain-General in his fury swung to the Cardinal, his gestures wild. 'Your Eminence hears what this thief now demands?'

But the Cardinal, having now resumed his unworldly calm, was not again to be shaken from it. 'Patience, my son. Patience! Let us beware the mortal sin of anger, which will scarcely hasten my release for the apostolic labours that await me in Havana.'

It would have needed a great deal more than this to bring Don Ruiz to yield had not the very fury that now possessed him, craving an orgy of vengeance, shown him the way. Trembling a little in his suppressed wrath, yet he was sufficiently master of himself to bow as if to an order, and to promise in comparatively civil terms that the money should at once be forthcoming, in order that his Eminence's deliverance should be procured at the earliest moment.

V

But in his barge as he was returning to shore with the Alcalde, the Captain-General betrayed the fact that it was not the deliverance of the Cardinal-Archbishop that spurred him so much as his eagerness to crush this impudent pirate who defeated him at his own game.

'The fool shall have the gold, so that destruction may overtake him.'

Gloomily the Alcalde shook his head. 'It's a terrible price to pay God of my life! A hundred thousand pieces!'

'There's no help for that.' Almost Don Ruiz implied by his manner that he accounted cheap at the price the destruction of a man who had brought him to such humiliation that he, the Captain-General of Havana, lord of life and death in those parts, had been made to look no better than a schoolboy standing to be birched. 'Nor is it so exorbitant. The Admiral of the Ocean-Sea is willing to pay fifty thousand pieces for the head of Captain Blood. I but double it—out of the royal Treasury.'

'But what the Marquis of Riconete pays would not be lost. Whilst this will be sunk with that scoundrel.'

'But perhaps not beyond recovery. It depends upon where we sink him. Where he's anchored now there's not above four fathoms, and it's all shallow on that side as far as the bar. But that's no matter. What matters is to get the Cardinal-Archbishop out of that ship, so as to put an end to this cursed dog's immunity.'

'Are you so sure that it will end then? That sly devil will demand pledges, oaths.'

Don Ruiz laughed savagely from livid lips. 'He shall have them. All the pledges, all the oaths that he requires. An oath sworn under constraint has never been accounted binding on any man.'

But the Alcalde's gloom was not relieved. 'That will not be his Eminence's view.'

'His Eminence?'

'Can you doubt that this damned pirate will ask a pledge from him—a pledge of safe-conduct for himself? You've seen the man this Cardinal is: a narrow, bigoted zealot, a slave to the letter of a contract. It's an ill thing to set up priests as judges. They're so unfitted for the office. There's no humanity in them, no breadth of understanding. What this prelate swears, that he will do; no matter where or how the oath may have been exacted.'

For a moment dismay darkened still further the Captain-General's soul. A little thought, however, and his tortuous mind had found a way. He laughed again.

'I thank you, Don Hieronimo, for that forewarning. I am not pledged yet, nor will those be upon whom I shall depend, and who shall have my instant orders.'

Back in his palace before coming to the matter of the Cardinal's ransom, he summoned one of his officers.

'The Cardinal-Archbishop of New Spain will land this evening at Havana,' he announced. 'To do him honour, and so that the city may be apprised of this happy event, I shall require a salute to be fired from the gun on the mole. You will take a gunner, and station yourself there. The moment his Eminence sets foot on land you will order the gun to be touched off.'

On that he dismissed the officer, and summoned another one.

'You will take horse at once, and ride to El Fuerte, to the Moro, and the Puntal. In my name you will order the commandant of each of those forts to train his guns on that red ship at anchor yonder, flying the English flag. After that they are to wait for the signal, which will be the firing of the gun on the mole, when the Cardinal-Archbishop of New Spain comes ashore. As soon as they hear it, but not before, they are to open fire upon that pirate ship and sink her. Let there be no mistake.'

Upon the officer's assurance that all was perfectly clear, Don Ruiz dismissed him to carry those orders, and then turned his attention to raiding the royal treasury for the gold which was to deliver the Cardinal from his duress.

So expeditiously did he go about this matter that he was alongside the Arabella again by the first dog-watch, and out of his barge four massive chests were hoisted to the deck of the buccaneer.

It had enheartened both him and the Alcalde, who again faithfully accompanied him, to behold, as they approached, the Cardinal-Archbishop on the poop-deck. Mantled and red-hatted, his crozier borne before him by the bareheaded Frey Domingo, and the other Dominicans modestly cowled and ranged behind him, it was clear that already his Eminence was ready and waiting to go ashore. This, and the measure of liberty which his presence on deck announced had already been accorded to him, finally assured Don Ruiz that once the ransom were paid there would be an end of the sacrilege of His Eminence's detention and no further obstacle would delay his departure from that accursed ship. With the removal of that protecting consecrated presence the immunity of the Arabella would be at an end and the guns of the Havana forts would make short work of her timbers.

Exulting in this thought, Don Ruiz could not refrain from taking with Blood, who received him at the head of the entrance ladder, the tone proper from a royal representative to a pirate.

'Maldito ladron—accursed thief—there is your gold, the price of a sacrilege for which you'll burn in Hell through all eternity. Verify it, and let us begone.'

Captain Blood gave no hint that he was so much as touched by that insulting speech. He stooped to the massive chests, unlocked each in turn, and cast a casual yet appraising glance over the gleaming contents. Then he beckoned his shipmaster forward. 'Jerry, here is the gold. See it stowed.' Almost disdainfully he added: 'We assume the count to be correct.'

Thereupon he turned to the poop and to the scarlet figure at the rail, and raised his voice. 'My Lord Cardinal, the ransom has been received and the Captain-General's barge waits to take you ashore. You have but to pledge me your word that I shall be allowed to depart without let, hindrance, or pursuit.'

Under his little black moustachios the Captain-General's lip curled in a little smile. The slyness of the man displayed itself in the terms, so calculated to avert suspicion, in which he chose to give expression to his venom.

'You may now depart without let or hindrance, you rogue. But if ever we meet again upon the seas, as meet we shall...'

He left his sentence there. But Captain Blood completed it for him. 'It is probable that I shall have the satisfaction of hanging you from that yard-arm, like the forsworn, dishonoured thief that you are, you gentleman of Spain.'

At the head of the companion the advancing Cardinal paused to reprove him for those words.

'Captain Blood, that threat is as ungenerous as I hope the terms of it are untrue.'

Don Ruiz caught his breath, aghast, more enraged even by the reproof than by the offensive terms of the threat that had provoked it.

'You hope!' he cried. 'Your Eminence hopes!'

'Wait!' Slowly the Cardinal descended the steps of the companion, his monks, following him, and came to stand in the waist, a very incarnation of the illimitable power and majesty of the Church.

'I said I hoped that the accusation is untrue, and that implies a doubt, which has offended you. For that doubt, Don Ruiz, I shall hope presently to seek your pardon. But first, since last you were here something has been troubling me which I must ask you to resolve.'

'Ashore, your Eminence will find me ready fully to answer your every question.' And Don Ruiz strode away to place himself at the head of the ladder by which the Cardinal was to descend. Captain Blood at the same moment, hat in hand, passed to its other side and took up his station there, as the courteous speeding of a departing guest demanded.

But the Primate did not move from where he stood. 'Don Ruiz, there is one question that must be answered before I consent to land in a province that you govern.' And so stern and commanding was his mien that Don Ruiz, at whose nod a population trembled, stood in dismay before him, waiting.

The Cardinal's glance passed from him to the attendant Don Hieronimo, and it was to him that the crucial question was set.

'Señor Alcalde, weigh well your answer to me, for your office and perhaps even more will depend upon your accuracy. What was done with the merchandise—the property of that

English seaman—which the Captain-General ordered you to confiscate?'

Don Hieronimo's uneasy eyes looked anywhere but at his questioner. Intimidated, he dared not be other than prompt and truthful in his reply. 'It was sold again, Eminence.'

'And the gold it fetched? What became of that?'

'I delivered it to his Excellency, the Captain-General. Some twelve thousand ducats.'

In the hushed pause that followed, Don Ruiz bore the searching scrutiny of those stern, sad eyes, with his head high and a scornful, defiant curl to his lip. But the Primate's next question wiped the last vestige of that arrogance from his countenance.

'And is, then, the Captain-General of Havana also the King's Treasurer?'

'Not so, of course, Eminence,' said Don Ruiz, perforce.

'Then, sir, did you in your turn surrender to the Treasury this gold received for goods you confiscated in the name of the King, your master?'

He dared not prevaricate where verification of his word must so shortly follow. His tone, nevertheless, was surly with resentment of such a question.

'Not yet, Eminence. But...'

'Not yet!' The Cardinal allowed him to go no further, and there was an undertone of thunder in that gentle, interrupting voice. 'Not yet? And it is a full month since those events. I am answered, sir. Unhappily I did you no wrong by my doubt, which was that an officer of the Crown who interprets the laws with such sophistries as that which you uttered to me this morning cannot possibly be honest.'

'Eminence!' It was a roar of anger. In his excitement, his face livid, he advanced a step. Such words wherever uttered to him must have moved his wrath. But to be admonished and insulted by this priest in public, to be held up to the scorn and derision of these ruffianly buccaneers, was something beyond the endurance of any Castilian gentleman. In his fury he was seeking words in which to answer the indignity as it deserved, when, as if divining his mind, the Primate launched a scornful fulmination that withered his anger and turned it into fear.

'Silence, man! Will you raise your voice to us? By such means as these you no doubt grow rich in gold, but still richer in dishonour. And there is more. So that this unfortunate English seaman should quietly suffer himself to be robbed, you threatened him with prosecution by the Holy Office and the Fires of the Faith. Even a New Christian, and a New Christian more than any other, should know that to invoke the Holy Office for such base ends is to bring himself within the scope of its just resentment.'

That terrible threat on the lips of a sometime Grand Inquisitor, and the terms in which it was delivered, with its hint of old Christian scorn of New Christian blood, was the lightning-stroke that reduced the Captain-General's heart to ashes. He stood appalled, in fancy already seeing himself dishonoured, ruined, sent home to be arraigned in an auto de fé, stripped of every dignity before being flung to the secular arm for execution. 'My lord!' It was the piteous wail of a broken man. He held out hands in supplication. 'I did not see...'

'That I can well believe. Oculos habent et non videbunt. No man who saw would incur that peril.' Then his normal calm descended upon him again. Awhile he stood thoughtful, and about him all was respectful silence. Then he sighed, and advanced to take the stricken Count of Marcos by the arm. He led him away towards the forecastle, out of earshot of the others. He spoke very gently. 'Believe me, my heart bleeds for you, my son. Humanum est errare. Sinners are we all. I practise mercy where I can, against my own need of mercy. Therefore, the little that I can do to help you, I will do. Once I am ashore in Cuba, whilst you are its Captain-General, I must discover it to be my clear duty as Inquisitor of the Faith to take action in this matter. And that action of necessity must break you. To avoid this, my son, I will not land whilst you hold office here. But this is the utmost that I can do. Perhaps even in doing so much I am guilty of a sophistry myself. But I have to think not only of you, but also of the proud Castilian name and the honour of Spain herself, which must suffer in the dishonour of one of her administrators. At the same time, you will see that I cannot suffer that one who has so grossly abused the King's trust should continue in authority, or that his offence should go entirely unpunished.'

He paused a moment, whilst Don Ruiz stood in abjection with lowered head to bear the sentence that he knew must follow.

'You will resign your governorship this very day, on any pretext that you choose, and you will take the first ship to Spain. Then, so long as you do not return to the New World or assume any public office at home, so long shall I avoid official knowledge of your offence. More I cannot do. And may God forgive me if already I do too much.'

If the sentence was harsh, yet the broken man who listened heard it almost in relief, for he had not dared to expect to be so lightly quit. 'So be it, Eminence,' he faltered, his head still bowed. Then he raised eyes of despair and bewilderment to meet the Cardinal's compassionate eyes. 'But if your Eminence does not land... ?'

'Do not be concerned for me. I have already sounded this Captain Blood against my possible need. Now that I have taken my resolve, he shall carry me to San Domingo. When my work there is done I can take ship to return here to Havana and by that time you will have departed.'

Thus Don Ruiz saw himself cheated even of his vengeance upon that accursed sea-robber who had brought this ruin upon him. He began a last, weak, despairing attempt to avert at least that.

'But will you trust these pirates, who already have... ?'

He was interrupted. 'In this world, my son, I have learnt to place my trust in Heaven rather than in man. And this buccaneer, for all the evil in him, is a son of the true Church, and he has shown me that he is a scrupulous observer of his word. If there are risks I must accept them. See to it by your future conduct that I accept them in a good cause. Now go with God, Don Ruiz. There is no reason why I should detain you longer.'

The Captain-General went down on his knees to kiss the Cardinal's ring and ask a blessing. Over his bowed head the Primate of New Spain extended his right hand, two fingers and the thumb extended, and made the Sign of the Cross.

'Benedictus sis. Pax Domini sit sempre tecum. May the light of grace show you better ways in future. Depart with God.'

But for all the penitence displayed in his attitude at the Cardinal's feet, it is to be doubted if he departed as admonished. Stumbling like a blind man to the entrance-ladder, with a curt summons to the Alcalde to attend him and not so much as a glance or word to anybody else, he went over the side and down to his waiting barge.

And whilst he and the Alcalde raged in mutual sympathy, and damned the Cardinal-Archbishop for a vain, muddling priest, the Arabella was weighing anchor. Under full sail she swaggered past the massive forts and out of the bay of Havana, safe from molestation since, because of the imposing scarlet figure that paced the poop, the signal gun could not be fired.

And that is how it came to pass that when a fortnight later that great galleon the Santa Veronica, in a bravery of flags and pennants and with guns thundering in salute, sailed into the bay of Havana there was no Captain-General to welcome the arriving Primate of New Spain. To deepen the annoyance of that short, corpulent, choleric little prelate, not only was there no proper preparation for his welcome, but the Alcalde who came aboard in an anguish of bewilderment was within an ace of treating his Eminence as an impostor.

Aboard the Arabella in those days, Yberville, divested of his scarlet splendours, which, like the monkish gowns, had been hurriedly procured in Sainte Croix, was giving himself airs and vowing that a great churchman had been lost to the world when he became a buccaneer. Captain Blood, however, would concede no more than that the kiss was that of a great comedian. And in this the bo'sun Snell, whom Nature had so suitably tonsured for the part of Frey Domingo, being a heretic, entirely concurred with Captain Blood.

Episode 6

THE ELOPING HIDALGA

I

Word was brought to Tortuga by a half-caste Indian, who had shipped as one of the hands on a French brig, of the affair in which the unfortunate James Sherarton lost his life. It was a nasty story with which we are only indirectly concerned here, so that it need be no more than briefly stated. Sherarton and the party of English pearl-fishers he directed were at work off one of the Espada Keys near the Gulf of Maracaybo. They had already garnered a considerable harvest, when a Spanish frigate came upon them, and, not content with seizing their sloop and their pearls, ruthlessly put them to the sword. And there were twelve of them, honest, decent men who were breaking no laws from any but the Spanish point of view, which would admit no right of any other nation in the waters of the New World.

Captain Blood was present in the Tavern of the King of France at Cayona when the half-caste told in nauseous detail the story of that massacre.

'Spain shall pay,' he said. And his sense of justice being poetic, he added: 'And she shall pay in pearls.'

Beyond that he gave no hint of the intention which had leapt instantly to his mind. The inspiration was as natural as it was sudden. The very mention of pearl-fisheries had been enough to call to his mind the Rio de la Hacha, that most productive of all the pearl-fisheries in the Caribbean from which such treasures were brought to the surface, to the profit of King Philip.

It was not the first time that the notion of raiding that source of Spanish wealth had occurred to him; but the difficulties and dangers with which the enterprise was fraught had led him hitherto to postpone it in favour of some easier immediate task. Never, however, had those difficulties and dangers been heavier than at this moment, when it almost seemed that the task was imposed upon him by a righteously indignant Nemesis. He was not blind to this. He knew how fiercely vigilant was the Spanish Admiral of the Ocean-Sea, the Marquis of Riconete, who was cruising with a powerful squadron off the Main. So rudely had Captain Blood handled him in that affair at San Domingo that the Admiral dared not show himself again in Spain until he had wiped out the disgrace of it. The depths of his vindictiveness might be gauged from the announcement, which he had published far and wide, that he would pay the enormous sum of fifty thousand pieces of eight for the person of Captain Blood, dead or alive, or for information that should result in his capture.

If, then, a raid on Rio de la Hacha were to succeed, it was of the first importance that it should be carried out smoothly and swiftly. The buccaneers must be away with their plunder before the Admiral could even suspect their presence off the coast. With a view to making sure of this, Captain Blood took the resolve of first reconnoitring the ground in person, and rendering himself familiar with its every detail, so that there should be no fumbling when the raid took place.

Moulting his normal courtly plumage, discarding gold lace and Mechlin, he dissembled his long person in brown homespun, woollen stockings, plain linen bands, and a hat without adornment. He discarded his periwig, and replaced it by a kerchief of black silk that swathed his cropped head like a skullcap.

In this guise, leaving at Tortuga his fleet, which consisted in those days of four ships manned by close upon a thousand buccaneers, he sailed alone for Curaçao in a trading-vessel and there transferred himself to a broad-beamed Dutchman, the Loewen, that made regular voyages to and fro between that island and Carthagena. He represented himself as a trader in hides and the like, and assumed the name of Tormillo and a mixed Dutch and Spanish origin.

It was on a Monday that he landed from the Dutchman at Rio de la Hacha. The Loewen would be back from Carthagena on the following Friday, and even if no other business should bring her to Rio de la Hacha, she would call there again so as to pick up Señor Tormillo, who would be returning in her to Curaçao. He had contrived, largely at the cost of drinking too much bumbo, to establish the friendliest relations with the Dutch skipper, so as to ensure the faithful observance of this arrangement.

Having been put ashore by the Dutchman's cockboat, he took lodgings at the Escudo de Leon, a decent inn in the upper part of the town, and gave out that he was in Rio de la Hacha to purchase hides. Soon the traders flocked to him, and he won their esteem by the quantity of hides he agreed to purchase, and their amused contempt by the liberal prices he agreed to pay. In the pursuit of his business he went freely and widely about the place, and in the intervals between purchases he contrived to observe what was to be observed and to collect the information that he required.

So well did he employ his time that by the evening of Thursday he had fully accomplished all that he came to do. He was acquainted with the exact armament and condition of the fort that guarded the harbour, with the extent and quality of the military establishment, with the situation and defences of the royal treasury, where the harvest of pearls was stored; he had even contrived to inspect the fishery where the pearling-boats were at work under the protection of a ten-gun guarda-costa; and he had ascertained that the Marquis of Riconete, having flung out swift scouting-vessels, had taken up his headquarters at Carthagena, a hundred and fifty miles away to the south-west. Not only this, but he had fully evolved in his mind the plan by which the Spanish scouts were to be eluded and the place surprised, so that it might quickly be cleaned up before the Admiral's squadron could supervene to hinder.

Content, he came back to the Escudo de Leon on that Thursday evening for his last night in his lodgings there. In the morning the Dutchman should be back to take him off again, his mission smoothly accomplished. And then that happened which altered everything and was destined to change the lives and fortunes of persons of whose existence at that hour he was not even aware.

The landlord met him with the news that a Spanish gentleman, Don Francisco de Villamarga, had just been seeking him at the inn, and would return again in an hour's time. The mention of that name seemed suddenly to diminish the stifling heat of the evening for him. But, at least, he kept his breath and his countenance.

'Don Francisco de Villamarga?' he slowly repeated, giving himself time to think. Was it possible that there were in the New World two Spaniards of that same distinguished name? 'I seem to remember that a Don Francisco de Villamarga was deputy-governor of Maracaybo.'

'It is the same, sir,' the landlord answered him. 'Don Francisco was governor there, or, at least Alcalde, until about a year ago.'

'And he asked for me?'

'For you, Señor Tormillo. He came back from the interior today, he says, with a parcel of green hides which he desires to offer you.'

'Oh!' It was almost a gasp of relief. The Captain breathed more freely, but not yet freely enough. 'Don Francisco with hides to sell? Don Francisco de Villamarga a trader?'

The fat little vintner spread his hands. 'What would you, sir? This is the New World. Here such things can happen to a hidalgo when he is not fortunate. And Don Francisco, poor gentleman, has had sad misfortune, through no fault of his own. The province of his governorship was raided by Captain Blood, that accursed pirate, and Don Francisco fell into disgrace. What would you? It is the way of these things. There is no mercy for a governor who cannot protect a place entrusted to him.'

'I see.' Captain Blood took off his broad hat, and mopped his brow that was beaded with sweat below the line of the black scarf.

So far all was well, thanks to the fortunate chance of his absence when Don Francisco had called. But the danger of recognition which so far had been safely run was now only just round the corner. And there were few men in New Spain by whom Captain Blood would be more reluctant to be recognized than by this sometime deputy-governor of Maracaybo, this proud Spanish gentleman who had been constrained, for the reasons given by the inn-keeper, to soil his hands in trade. The impending encounter was likely to be as sweet for Don Francisco as it would certainly be bitter for Captain Blood. Even in prosperity Don Francisco would not have been likely to spare him. In adversity the prospect of earning fifty thousand pieces of eight would serve to sharpen the vindictiveness of this official who had fallen upon evil days.

Shuddering at the narrowness of the escape, thankful for that timeliest of warnings, Captain Blood perceived that there was only one thing to be done. Impossible now to await the coming of the Dutchman in the morning. In some sort of vessel, alone if need be in an open boat, he must get out of Rio de la Hacha at once. But he must not appear either startled or in flight.

He frowned annoyance. 'What misfortune that I should have been absent when Don Francisco called! It is intolerable to put a gentleman born to the trouble of seeking me again. I will wait upon him at once, if you will tell me where he is lodged.'

'Oh, certainly. You will find his house in the Calle San Bias; that is the first turning on your right; anyone there will show you where Don Francisco lives.'

The Captain waited for no more. 'I go at once,' he said, and stepped out.

But either he forgot or he mistook the landlord's directions, for instead of turning to his right, he turned to his left and took his way briskly down a street, at this hour of supper almost deserted, that led towards the harbour.

He was passing an alley, within fifty yards of the mole, when from the depths of it came ominous sounds of strife; the clash of steel on steel, a woman's cry, a man's harsh, vituperative interjections.

The concern supplied him by his own situation might well have reminded him that these murderous sounds were no affair of his, and that he had enough already on his hands to get out of Rio de la Hacha with his life. But the actual message of the vituperative exclamation overheard arrested his flight.

'Perro inglés! Dog of an Englishman!'

Thus Blood learnt that in that dark alley it was a compatriot who was being murdered. It was enough. In foreign lands, to any man who is not dead to feeling, a compatriot is a brother. He plunged at once into the gloom of that narrow way, his hand groping for the pistol inside the breast of his coat.

As he ran, however, it occurred to him that here was noise enough already. The last thing he desired was to attract spectators by increasing it. So he left the pistol in his pocket and whipped out his rapier instead.

By the little light that lingered, he could make out the group as he advanced upon it. Three men were assailing a fourth, who, with his back to a closed door, and his left arm swathed in his coat so as to make a buckler, offered a defence that was as desperate as it must ultimately prove futile. That he could have stood so long even against such odds was evidence of an unusual toughness.

At a little distance beyond that brawling quartet, the slight figure of a woman, cloaked and hooded by a light mantle of black silk, leaned in helplessness against the wall.

Blood's intervention was stealthy, swift, and practical. He announced his arrival by sending his sword through the back of the nearest of the three assailants.

'That will adjust the odds,' he explained, and cleared his blade just in time to engage a gentleman who whirled to face him, spitting blasphemies with that fluency in which the Castilian's only rival is the Catalan.

Blood broke ground nimbly, enveloped the vicious thrust in a counter-parry, and, in the movement, drove his steel through the blasphemer's sword-arm.

Out of action, the man reeled back, gripping the arm from which the blood was spurting, and cursing more fluently than ever, whilst the only remaining Spaniard, perceiving the sudden change in the odds, from three to one on his side to two to one against it, and not relishing this at all, gave way before Blood's charge. In the next moment he and his wounded comrade were in flight, leaving their friend to lie where he had fallen.

At Blood's side the man he had rescued, breathing in gasps, almost collapsed against him.

'Damned assassins!' he panted. 'Another minute would ha' seen the end of me.'

Then the woman who had darted forward surged at his other side.

'Vamos, Jorgito! Vamos!' she cried in fearful urgency. Then shifted from Spanish to fairly fluent English. 'Quick, my love! Let us get to the boat. We are almost there. Oh, come!'

This mention of a boat was an intimation to Blood that his good action was not likely to go unrewarded. It gave him every ground for hoping that in helping a stranger he had helped himself; for a boat was, of all things, what he most needed at the moment.

His hands played briskly over the man he was supporting, and came away wet from his left shoulder. He made no more ado. He hitched the fellow's right arm round his neck, gripped him about the waist to support him, and bade the girl lead on.

Whatever her panic on the score of her man's hurt, the promptitude of her obedience to the immediate need of getting him away was in itself an evidence of her courage and practical wit. One or two windows in the alley had been thrust open, and from odd doorways white faces dimly seen in the gloom were peering out to discover the cause of the hubbub. These witnesses, though silent, and perhaps timid, stressed the need for haste.

'Come,' she said. 'This way. Follow me.'

Half supporting, half carrying the wounded man, Blood kept pace with her speed, and so came out of the alley and gained the mole. Across this, disregarding the stare of odd wayfarers who paused and turned as they went by, she led him to a spot where a long-boat waited.

Two men rose out of it: Indians, or half-castes, their bodies naked from shoulder to waist. One of them sprang instantly ashore, then checked, peering in the dusk at the man Captain Blood was supporting.

'Que tal el patron?' he asked gruffly

'He has been hurt. Help him down carefully. Oh, make haste! Make haste!'

She remained on the quay, casting fearful glances over her shoulder whilst Blood and the Indians were bestowing the wounded man in the sternsheets. Then Blood, standing in the boat, proffered her his hand.

'Aboard, ma'am.' He was peremptory, and so as to save time and argument he added: 'I am coming with you.'

'But you can't. We sail at once. The boat will not return. We dare not linger, sir.'

'Faith, no more dare I. It is very well. I've said I am coming with you. Aboard, ma'am!' and without more ado, he almost pulled her into the boat, ordering the men to give way.

II

If she found the matter bewildering, she did not pursue it. Concern enough for her at the moment lay in the condition of her Englishman and the evidently urgent need of getting him away before his assailants returned, reinforced, to finish him. She could not waste moments so precious in arguing with an eccentric: possibly she had not even any thoughts to spare him.

As the boat shot away from the mole, she sank down in the sternsheets at the side of her companion, who had swooned. On his other side, Blood was kneeling, and the deft fingers of the buccaneer, who once had been a surgeon, located and gropingly examined that wound, high in the shoulder.

'Give yourself peace,' he comforted the girl. 'This is no great matter. A little bloodletting has made him faint. That is all. You'll soon have him well again.'

She breathed a little prayer of thanks, 'Gracias a Dios,' then, with a backward glance in the direction of the mole, urged the men to greater effort.

As the boat sped over the dark water towards a ship's lantern a half-mile away, the Englishman stirred and looked about him.

'What the plague...' he began, and struggled to rise.

Blood's hand restrained him. 'Quiet,' he said. 'There's no need for alarm. We're taking you aboard.'

'Taking me aboard? Who the devil are you?'

'Jorgito,' the girl cried, 'it is the gentleman who saved your life.'

'Odso! You're there, Isabelita?' His next question showed that he took in the situation. 'Are they following?'

When she had reassured him and pointed ahead to the ship's lantern towards which they were heading, he laughed softly, then cursed the Indians.

'Faster, Bend your backs to it, you louts.'

The rowers increased their effort, breathing stertorously. The man laughed again, softly, as before, a fleering, mocking sound.

'So, so. We've had the luck to win clear of that gin with no more than a scratch. Yet, God's my life, it's more than a scratch. I'm bleeding like a Christian martyr.'

'It's nothing,' Blood reassured him. 'You've lost some blood. But once aboard we'll staunch the wound and make you comfortable.'

'Faith, you talk like a sawbones.'

'It's what I am.'

'Gadso! Was there ever greater luck. Eh, Isabelita? A swordsman to rescue me and a doctor to heal me, all in one. There's a providence watching over me this night. An omen, sweetheart.'

'A mercy,' she corrected on a crooning note, and drew closer to him.

And now from their scraps of talk, Blood pieced together the tale of their exact relationship. They were an eloping pair, these two—this Englishman, whose name was George Fairfax, and this little hidalga of the great family of Sotomayor. His late assailants were her brother and two friends, bent upon frustrating the elopement. Her brother was the Spaniard who had escaped uninjured from the encounter, and it was his pursuit in force which she dreaded and for which she continually looked back towards the receding mole. By the time, however, that agitated lights came dancing at last along the water's edge, the long-boat was in the black shadow of a two-masted brig, bumping against her side, whilst from her deck a gruff English voice was hailing them.

The lady was the first to swarm the accommodation ladder. Then followed Fairfax, with Blood immediately and so closely behind as to support him and, indeed, partly carry him aboard.

At the head of the ladder they were received by a large man with a face that showed hot in the light of a lantern slung from the mainmast, who overwhelmed them with alarmed questions.

Fairfax, steadying himself against the bulkhead, gasped for breath, and broke into that interrogatory flow sharply to rap out his orders.

'Get under way at once, Tim. No time to get the boat aboard. Take her in tow. And don't stay to take up anchor. Cut the cable. Hoist sail and let's away. Thank God the wind serves. We shall have the Alcalde and all the alguaziles of la Hacha aboard if we delay. So stir your damned bones.'

Tim's roaring voice was passing on the orders and men were leaping to obey, when the lady set a hand on her lover's arm.

'But this gentleman, George. You forget him. He does not know where we go.'

Fairfax supported himself with a hand on Blood's shoulder. He turned his head to peer into the countenance of his preserver, and there was a scowl on the lean, dark face.

'Ye'll have gathered I can't be delayed,' he said.

'Faith, it's very glad to gather it I've been,' was the easy answer. 'And it's little I'm caring where you go, so long as it's away from Rio de la Hacha.'

The dark face lightened. The man laughed softly. 'Running away too, are you? Damn my blood! You're most accommodating. It seems all of a piece. Look alive, Tim. Can't these lubbers of yours move no faster?'

There was a blast from the master's whistle, and naked feet pattered at speed across the deck. Tim spoke briskly and savagely, to stimulate their efforts, then sprang to the side to shout his orders to the Indians still in the boat alongside.

'Get you below, sir,' he begged his employer. 'I'll come to you as soon as we are under way and the course is set.'

It was Blood who assisted Fairfax to the cabin—a place of fair proportions if rudely equipped, lighted by a slush-lamp that swung above the bare table. The lady, breathing tenderest solicitude, followed closely.

To receive them a black man lad emerged from a stateroom on the larboard side. He cried out at sight of the blood with which his master's shirt was drenched, and stood arrested, teeth and eyeballs flashing in that startled dusky face.

Assuming authority, Blood ordered him to lend a hand, and between them they carried Fairfax, whose senses were beginning to swim again, through the doorway which the steward had left open, and there removed his shoes and got him to bed.

Then Blood despatched the boy, who answered to the name of Alcatrace, to the galley for hot water and to the Captain of the ship's medicine-chest.

On the narrow bed, Fairfax, a man as tall and well-knit as Blood himself, reclined in a sitting posture, propped by all the pillows available. He wore his own hair, and the reddish-brown cloud of it half veiled his pallid, bony countenance as with eyes half closed his head lolled weakly forward.

Having disposed of him comfortably, Blood cut away his sodden shirt and laid bare his vigorous torso.

When the steward returned with a can of water, some linen and a cedar box containing the ship's poor store of medicines, the lady followed him into the stateroom, begging to be allowed to help. Through the ports that stood open to the purple tropical night, she heard the creak of blocks and the thud of the sails as they took the wind, and it was with immense relief that she felt at last under her feet the forward heave of the unleashed brig. One anxiety at least was now allayed, and the danger of recapture overpast.

Courteously Blood welcomed her assistance. Observing her now in the light, he found her to agree with the impressions he had already formed. A slight wisp of womanhood, little more than a child, and probably not long out of the hands of the nuns, she showed him a winsome, eager face, and two shining eyes intensely black against the waxen pallor in which they were set. Her gold-laced gown of black, with beautiful point of Spain at throat and wrists, and, some pearls of obvious price entwined in her glossy tresses, were, like the proud air investing her, those of a person of rank.

She proved quick to understand Blood's requirements and deft to execute them, and thus, with her assistance, he worked upon the man for love of whom this little hidalga of the great house of Sotomayor was apparently burning her boats. Carefully, tenderly, he washed the purple lips of the wound in the shoulder, which was still oozing. In the medicine-chest held for him by Alcatrace he discovered at least some arnica, and of this he made a liberal application. It produced a fiercely reviving effect. Fairfax threw up his head.

'Hell-fire!' he cried. 'Do you burn me, damn you?'

'Patience, sir. Patience. It's a healing cautery.'

The lady's arm encircled the patient's head, supporting and soothing him. Her lips lightly touched his dank brow. 'My poor Jorgito,' she murmured.

He grunted for answer, and closed his eyes.

Blood was tearing linen into strips. Out of these, he made a pad for the wound, applied a bandage to hold it in position, and then a second bandage, like a sling, to keep the left arm immovable against the patient's breast. Then Alcatrace found him a fresh shirt, and they passed it over the Englishman's head, leaving the left sleeve empty. The surgical task was finished.

Blood made a readjustment of the pillows. 'Ye'll sleep in that position if you please. And you'll avoid movement as much as possible. If we can keep you quiet, you should be whole again in a week or so. Ye've had a near escape. Had the blade taken you two inches lower, it's another kind of bed we'ld be making for you this minute. Ye've been lucky, so you have.'

'Lucky? May I burn!'

'There's even, perhaps, something for which to render thanks.'

If the quiet reminder brought from Fairfax no more than a grumbled oath, it stirred the lady to a sort of violence. She leaned across the narrow bed to seize both of Blood's hands. Her pale, dark face was solemnly intense. Her lips trembled, as did her voice.

'You have been so good, so brave, so noble.'

Before he could guess her intent, she had carried his hands to her lips and kissed them. Protesting, he wrenched them away. She smiled up at him wistfully.

'But shall I not kiss them, then, those hands? Have they not save' my Jorgito's life? Have they not heal' his wounds? All my life I shall love those hands. All my life I shall be grateful to them.'

Captain Blood had his doubts about this. He was not finding Jorgito prepossessing. The fellow's shallow, sloping animal brow and wide, loose-lipped mouth inspired no confidence, for all that in its total sum, and in a coarse raffish way, the face might be described as handsome. It was a face of strongly marked bone structures, the nose boldly carved, the cheekbones prominent, the jaw long and powerful. In age, he could not have passed the middle thirties.

His eyes, rather close-set and pale, shifted under Blood's scrutiny, and he began to mutter belated acknowledgments, reminded by the lady's outburst of what was due from him.

'I vow, sir, I am deeply in your debt. Damn my blood! That's nothing new for me, God knows. I've been in somebody's debt ever since I can remember. But this—may I perish—is a debt of another kind. If only you had skewered for me the guts of that pimp who got away, I'ld be still more grateful to you. The world could very well do without Don Serafino de Sotomayor. Damn his blood!'

'Señor Jesus! No digas eso, querido!' Quick and shrill came the remonstrance from the little hidalga. 'Don't say such things, my love.' To soften her protest, she stroked his cheek as she ran on, 'No, no, Jorgito. If that have happen never more will my conscience be quiet. If my brother's blood have been shed, it will kill me.'

'And what of my blood, then? Hasn't there been enough of that shed by him and his plaguey bullies. And didn't he hope to shed it all, the damned cut-throat?'

'Querido,' she soothed him. 'That was for protect me. He think it his duty. I could not have forgive him ever if he kill you. It would have broke my heart, Jorgito, you know. Yet I can understand Serafino. Oh, let us thank God—God and this so brave gentleman—that no worse have happen.'

And then Tim, the big red ship-master, rolled in to inquire how Mr Fairfax fared, and to report that the course was set, that the Heron was moving briskly before a steady southerly breeze, and that already La Hacha was half a dozen miles astern. 'So all's well that ends well, sir. And we've to find quarters for this gentleman who came aboard with you. I'll have a hammock slung for him in the cuddy. See to it, Alcatrace.' He drove the black man out upon that task. 'Pronto Vamos!'

Fairfax reclined with half-closed eyes. 'All's well that ends well,' he echoed. He laughed softly, and Blood observed that always when he laughed his loose mouth seemed to writhe in a sneer. He was recovering vigour of body and of mind with every moment now, since he had been made comfortable and the bleeding had been checked. His hand closed over the lady's where it lay upon the counterpane. 'Ay. All's well that ends well,' he repeated. 'Ye'll have the jewels safe, sweetheart?'

'The jewels?' She started, caught her breath, and for a moment her brows were knit in thought. Then, with consternation overspreading her countenance and a hand on her heart, she came to her feet. 'The jewels!'

Fairfax slewed his head round to look at her fully, his pale eyes suddenly wide, the brows raised. 'What now?' His voice was a croak. 'Ye have them safe?'

Her lip quivered. 'Valga me Dios! I must have drop' the casket when Serafino overtake us.'

There was a long hushed pause, which Blood felt to be of the kind that is the prelude of a storm. 'Ye dropped the casket!' said Fairfax. His tone was ominously quiet. He was staring at her in stupefaction, his jaw loose. 'Ye dropped the casket?' Gradually a blaze kindled in his light eyes. 'D'ye say ye dropped the casket?' This time his voice rose and cracked. 'Damn my blood! It passes belief. Hell! Ye can't have dropped it.'

The sudden fury of him shocked her. She looked at him with frightened eyes. 'You are angry, Jorgito,' she faltered. 'But you must not be angry. That is not right. Think of what happen'. I was distracted. Your life was in danger. What were the jewels then? How can I think of jewels? I let the casket fall. I did not notice. Then when you are wounded, and I think perhaps you will die, can I think of jewels then? You see, Jorgito? It is lastima, yes. But they do not matter. We have each other. They do not matter. Let them go.'

Her fond hand was stealing about his neck again. But in a rage he flung it off.

'Don't matter!' he roared, his loose mouth working. 'Rot my bones! You lose a fortune; you spill thirty thousand ducats in the kennel, and you say it don't matter! Hell and the devil, girl! If that don't matter, tell me what does.'

Blood thought it time to intervene. Gently, but very firmly, he pressed the wounded man back upon his pillows. 'Will you be quiet now, ye bellowing calf? Haven't you spilt enough of your blood this night?'

But Fairfax raged and struggled. 'Quiet? Damn my soul! You don't understand. How can I be quiet? Quiet, when this little fool has...'

She interrupted him there. She had drawn herself stiffly erect. Her lips were steady now her eyes more intensely black than ever.

'Is it so much to you that I lose my jewels, George? They were my jewels. You'll please to remember that. If I lose them, I lose them, and it is my affair, my loss. And I should not count it loss in a night when I have gain' so much. Or have I not, George? Were the jewels such great matter to you? More than I, perhaps?'

That challenge brought him to his senses. He beat a retreat before it, in the best order he could contrive, paused, and then broke into a laugh that to Blood was pure play-acting. 'What the devil! Are you angry with me, Isabelita? Plague on it! I am like that. Hot and quick. That's my nature. And thirty thousand ducats is a loss to make a man forget his manners for the moment. But the jewels? Bah! Rot the jewels. If they've gone, they've gone.' He held out a coaxing hand. 'Come, Isabelita. Kiss and forgive, sweetheart. I'll soon be buying you all the jewels you could want.'

'I want no jewels, George.' She was not more than half-mollified. Something of the ugly suspicion he had aroused in her still lingered. But she went to him, and suffered him to put an arm about her. 'You must not be angry with me again, ever, Jorgito. If I had love' you less, I would have think more of the casket.'

'To be sure you would, chick. To be sure.'

Tim shuffled uncomfortably. 'I'd best get back on deck, sir.' He made shift to go, but in the doorway paused to turn to Captain Blood. 'That blackamoor will ha' slung your hammock for you.'

'You may be showing me the way, then. There's no more I can do here for tonight.'

Whilst the ship-master waited, holding the door, he spoke again. 'If this wind holds, we should make Port Royal by Sunday night or Monday morning.'

Blood was brought to a standstill. 'Port Royal?' said he slowly. 'I'ld not care to land there.'

Fairfax looked at him. 'Why not? It's an English settlement. You should have nothing to fear in Jamaica.'

'Still I'ld not care to land there. What port will you be making after that?'

The question seemed to amuse Fairfax. Again he uttered his unpleasant, fleering laugh. 'Faith, that'll depend upon a mort o things.'

Blood's steadily rising dislike of the man sharpened his rejoinder.

'I'ld thank you to make it depend a little upon my convenience, seeing that I'm here for yours.'

'For mine?' Fairfax raised his light brows. 'Od rot me, now! Didn't I understand you was running away too? But we'll see what we can do. Where was you wishing to be put ashore?'

By an effort Blood stifled his indignation and kept to the point. 'From Port Royal, it would be no great matter for you to carry me through the Windward Passage, and land me either on the northwest coast of Hispaniola or even on Tortuga.'

'Tortuga!' There was such a quickening of the light, shifty eyes, that Blood instantly regretted that he should have mentioned the place. Fairfax was pondering him intently, and behind that searching glance it was obvious that his mind was busy. 'Tortuga, eh? So ye've friends among the buccaneers?' He laughed. 'Well, well! That's your affair, to be sure. Let the Heron make Port Royal first, and then we'll be obliging you.'

'I'll be in your debt,' said Blood, with more than a hint of sarcasm. 'Give you good night, sir. And you, ma'am.'

III

For a considerable time after the door had closed upon the departing men, Fairfax lay very still and very thoughtful, his eyes narrowed, a mysterious smile on his lips.

At long last Doña Isabela spoke softly. 'You should sleep, Jorgito. Of what do you think?'

He made her an answer that seemed to hold no sense.

'Of the difference the lack of a periwig makes to a man who's an Irishman and a surgeon and wants to be landed on Tortuga.'

For a moment she wondered whether he had a touch of fever, and it increased her concern that he should sleep. She proposed to leave him. But he would not hear of it. He cursed the burning thirst he discovered in himself, and begged her to give him to drink. That same thirst continued thereafter to torment him and to keep him wakeful, so that she stayed at his side and gave him frequent draughts of water, mixed with the juice of limes, and once, on his insistent demand, with brandy.

The night wore on, with little said between them, and after some three hours of it he turned so quiet that she thought he slept at last and was preparing to creep away, when suddenly he announced his complete wakefulness by an oath and a laugh and ordered her to summon Tim. She obeyed only because to demur would be to excite him.

When Tim returned with her, Fairfax required to know what o'clock it might be and how far the master reckoned they had travelled. Eight bells, said Tim, had just been made, and they had put already a good forty miles between the Heron and La Hacha.

Then came a question that was entirely odd: 'How far to Carthagena?'

'A hundred miles maybe. Maybe a trifle more.'

'How long to make it?'

The ship-master's eyes became round with surprise. 'With the wind as it blows, maybe twenty-four hours.'

'Make it, then,' was the astounding order. 'Go about at once.'

The surprise in Tim's hot face was changed to concern.

'Ye've the fever, Captain, surely. What should we be doing back on the Main?'

'I've no fever, man. Ye've heard my order. Go about and lay a course for Carthagena.'

'But Carthagena...' The mate and Doña Isabel exchanged glances.

Surprising this, and perceiving what was in their minds, Fairfax's mouth twisted ill-humouredly. 'Od rot you! Wait!' he growled, and fell to thinking.

Had he been in full possession of his vigour he would have admitted no partner to the evil enterprise he had in mind. He would have carried it through single-handed, keeping his own counsel. But his condition making him dependent upon the ship-master left him no choice, as he saw it, but to lay his cards upon the table.

'Riconete is at Carthagena, and Riconete will pay fifty thousand pieces of eight for Captain Blood, dead or alive. Fifty thousand pieces of eight.' He paused a moment, and then added: 'That's a mort o' money, and there'll be five thousand pieces for you, Tim, when it's paid.'

Tim's suspicions were now a certainty. 'To be sure. To be sure.'

Exasperated, Fairfax snarled at him. 'God rot your bones, Tim! Are you humouring me! Ye think I have the fever. Ye'ld be the better yourself for a touch of the fever that's burning me. It might sharpen your paltry wits and quicken your sight.'

'Ay ay,' said Tim. 'But where do we find Captain Blood?'

'In the cuddy where you've bestowed him.'

'Ye're light-headed, sir.'

'Will you harp on that? Damn you for a fool. That is Captain Blood, I tell you. I recognized him the moment he asked to be landed at Tortuga. I'ld ha' known him sooner if I'ld ha' been more than half awake. He wouldn't care to land at Port Royal, he said. Of course he wouldn't. Not while Colonel Bishop is Governor of Jamaica. That'll maybe help you to understand.'

Tim was foolishly blinking his amazement and loosed an oath or two of surprised conviction. 'Ye recognize him, d'ye say?'

'That's what I say, and ye may believe I'm not mistook. Be off now, and put about. That first. Then you'd better see to making this fellow fast. If you take him in his sleep, it'll save trouble. Away with you.'

'Ay, ay,' said Tim, and bustled off in a state of excitement that was tempered by no scruples.

Doña Isabela, in a horror that had been growing steadily with understanding of what she heard, came suddenly to her feet.

'Wait, wait! What is it you will do?'

'No matter for you, sweetheart,' said Fairfax, and a peremptory wave of his sound hand dismissed Tim from the doorway where her voice had arrested him.

'But it is matter for me. I understand. You cannot do this, George.'

'Can't I? Why, the rogue'll be asleep by now. It should be easy. There'll be a surprised awakening for him; there will so.' And his fleering laugh went to increase her horror.

'But—Dios mio!—you cannot, you cannot. You cannot sell the man who save' your life.'

He turned his head to consider her with sneering amusement. Too much of a scoundrel to know how much of a scoundrel he was, he imagined himself opposed by a foolish, sentimental qualm that would be easily allayed. He was confident, too, of his complete ascendancy over a mind whose innocence he mistook for simplicity.

'Rot me, child, it's a duty, no less. You don't understand. This Blood is a pirate rogue, buccaneer, thief, and assassin. The sea'll be cleaner without him.'

She became only more vehement. 'He may be what you say—pirate, buccaneer, and the rest. Of that I know nothing. I care nothing. But I know he save' your life, and I care for that. He is here in your ship because he save' your life.'

'That's a lie, anyway,' growled Fairfax. 'He's here because he's took advantage of my condition. He's come aboard the Heron so as to escape from the Main and the justice that is after him. Well, well. He'll find out his mistake tomorrow.'

She wrung her hands, a fierce distress in her white face. Then, growing steadier, she pondered him very solemnly with an expression he had never yet seen on that eager face, an expression that annoyed him.

The faith in this man, of whom, after all, she knew but little, the illusions formed about him in the course of being swept off her maiden feet by a whirlwind wooing, which had made her cast everything away so that at his bidding she might link her fortunes with his own, had been sorely disturbed by the spectacle of his coarse anger at the loss of the jewels. That faith was now in danger of being finally and tragically shattered by this revelation of a nature which must fill her with dread and loathing once she admitted to herself the truth of what she beheld. Against this admission she was still piteously struggling. For if George Fairfax should prove, indeed, the thing she was being compelled to suspect, what could there be for her who was now so completely and irrevocably in his power?

'George,' she said quietly, in a forced calm to which the tumult of her bosom gave the lie, 'it matters not what this man is. You owe him your life. Without him you would lie dead now in that alley in La Hacha. You cannot do what you say. It would be infamy.'

'Infamy? Infamy be damned!' He laughed his ugly, contemptuous laugh. 'Ye just don't understand. It's a duty, I tell you—the duty of every honest gentleman to lay this pirate rogue by the heels.'

Scorn deepened in the dark eyes that continued so disconcertingly to regard him. 'Honest? You say that! Honest to sell the man who save' your life? For fifty thousand pieces of eight, was it not? That is honest? Honest as Judas, who sell the Saviour for thirty pieces.'

He glowered at her in resentment. Then found, as rogues will, an argument to justify himself. 'If you don't like it, you may blame yourself. If in your stupidity you hadn't lost the jewels I shouldn't need to do this. As it is, it's just a providence. For how else am I to find money for Tim and the hands, buy stores at Jamaica, and pay for the graving of the Heron against the ocean voyage? How else?'

'How else!' There was a bitter edge to her voice now 'How else since I lost my jewels, eh? It is so. It was for that? My jewels were for that? Que verguenza?' A sob shook her. 'Dios mio, que viltad! Ay de mi! Ay de mi!'

Then, hoping against hope in her despair, she caught his arm in her two hands and changed her tone to one of pleading.

'Jorgito...'

But Mr Fairfax, you'll have gathered, was not a patient man. He would be plagued no further. He flung her off with a violence that sent her hurtling against the bulkhead at her back. His evil temper was now thoroughly aroused, and it may have been rendered the more savage because his impetuous movement brought a twinge of pain to his wounded shoulder.

'Enough of that whining, my girl. Devil take you if you haven't set me bleeding again. Ye'll meddle in things you understand and not in my affairs. D'ye think a man's to be pestered so? Ye'll have to learn different afore we're acquainted much longer. Ye will so, by God?' Peremptorily he ended: 'Get you to bed.'

As she still lingered, winded where he had flung her, white-faced, aghast, incredulous, annoying him by the reproach of her stare, he raised his voice in fury. 'D'ye hear me? Get you to bed, rot you! Go!'

She went without another word, so swiftly and quietly that she left him with a sense of something ominous. Uneasy, a sudden suspicion of treachery crossing his mind, he got gingerly down from his bed, despite his condition, and staggered to the door, to spy upon her thence. He was just in time to see her vanish through the doorway of the stateroom opposite, and a moment later, from beyond her closed door, a sound of desolate sobbing reached him across the cabin.

His upper lip curled as he listened. At least, it had not occurred to her to betray his intentions to Captain Blood. Not that it would matter much if she did. Tim and the six hands aboard would easily account for the buccaneer if he should make trouble. Still, the notion might come to her, and it would be safer to provide.

He bawled the name of Alcatrace, who lay stretched, asleep, on the stern locker. The steward, awakened by the call, leapt up to answer it, and received from Fairfax stern, clear orders to remain awake and on guard so as to see that Doña Isabela did not leave the couch. At need, he was to employ violence to prevent it.

Then, with the help of Alcatrace, Fairfax crawled back to his bed, re-settled himself, and soon a heavy list to starboard informing him that they had gone about, this man who accounted his fortune made allowed himself to sink at last into an exhausted sleep.

IV

It should have occurred to them that the list to starboard so reassuring to Mr George Fairfax must present a riddle to Captain Blood if he should happen still to be awake. And awake it happened that he was.

He had doffed no more than his coat and his shoes, and he lay in shirt and breeches in the hammock they had slung for him in the stuffy narrow spaces of the cuddy, vainly wooing a slumber that held aloof. He was preoccupied, and not at all on his own behalf. Not all the rude ways that he had followed and the disillusions that he had suffered had yet sufficed to extinguish the man's sentimental nature. In the case of the little lady of the house of Sotomayor, he found abundant if disturbing entertainment for it this night. He was perplexed and perturbed by the situation in which he discovered her, so utterly in the power of a man who was not merely and unmistakably a scoundrel, but a crude egotist of little mind and less heart. Captain Blood reflected upon the misery and heart-break that so often will follow upon an innocent girl's infatuation for just such a man, who has obtained empire over her by his obvious but flashy vigour and the deceptive ardour of his wooing. In the buccaneer's sentimental eyes she was as a dove in the talons of a hawk, and he would give a deal to deliver her from them before she was torn to pieces. But it was odds that in her infatuation she would not welcome that deliverance, and even if, proving an exception to the rule, she should lend an ear to the sense that Blood could talk to her, he realized that he was in no case to offer her assistance, however ardently he might desire to do so.

With a sigh, he sought to dismiss a problem to which he could supply no happy solution; but it persisted until that list to starboard of a ship that hitherto had ridden on an even keel came to divert his attention into other channels. Was it possible, he wondered, that the wind could have veered with such suddenness? It must be so, because nothing else would explain the fact observed; at least, nothing else that seemed reasonable.

Nevertheless, he was moved to ascertain. He eased himself out of the hammock, groped for his coat and his shoes, put them on, and made his way by the gangway to the ship's waist.

Here one of the hands squatted on the hatch-coaming, softly singing, and at the break of the low poop the helmsman stood at the whipstaff. But Blood asked no questions of either of them. He preferred instead to obtain from the heavens the information that he sought, and the clear, starry sky told him all that he required to know. The North Star was abeam on the starboard quarter. Thus he obtained the surprising knowledge that they had gone about.

Always prudently mistrustful of anything that appeared to be against reason, he climbed the poop in quest of Tim. He beheld him pacing there, a burly silhouette against the light from the two tall stern lanterns, and he stepped briskly towards him.

To the ship-master, Captain Blood's advent was momentarily disconcerting. At that very instant he had been asking himself whether sufficient time had been given their passenger to be fast asleep, so that they might tie him up in his hammock without unnecessary ado. Recovering from his surprise, Tim jovially hailed the Captain as he advanced across the canting deck.

'A fine night, sir.'

Blood took a devious way to his ends, by an answer that applied a test. 'I see the wind has changed.'

'Ay,' the ship-master answered with alacrity. 'It was uncommon sudden. It's come to blow hard from the south.'

'That'll be delaying us in making Port Royal.'

'If it holds. But maybe it'll change again.'

'Maybe it will,' said Blood. 'We'll pray for it.'

Pacing together; they had come to the rail. They leaned upon it, and looked down at the dark water and the white, luminous edge of the wave that curled away from the ship's flank.

Blood made philosophy. 'A queer, uncertain life, this seafaring life, Tim, at the mercy of every wind that blows, driving us now in one direction, now in another, sometimes helping, sometimes hindering, and sometimes defeating and destroying us. I suppose you love your life, Tim?'

'What a question! To be sure I love my life.'

'And ye'll have the fear of death that's common to us all?'

'Od rot me! Ye're talking like a parson.'

'Maybe. Ye see it's opportune to remind you that ye're mortal, Tim. We're all apt to forget it at times and place our self in dangers that are entirely unnecessary. Mortal dangers. Just such a danger as you stand in this very minute, Tim.'

'What's that?' Tim took his elbows from the rail.

'Now don't be moving,' said Blood gently. His hand was inside the breast of his coat, and from the region of it, under cover of the cloth, something hard and tubular was pressed closely into the mate's side just below the ribs. 'My finger's on the trigger, Tim, and if ye were to move suddenly ye might startle me into pulling it. Put your elbows back on the rail, Tim darling while we talk. Ye've nothing to fear. I've no notion of hurting you; that is, provided ye're reasonable, as I think ye will be. Tell me now: Why are we going back to the Main?'

Tim was gasping in mingled surprise and fear, and his fear was greater perhaps than it need have been because he knew now beyond doubt with whom he had to deal. The sweat stood in cold beads on his brow.

'Going back to the Main?' he faltered stupidly

'Just so. Why have ye gone about? And why did ye lie to me about a south wind? D'ye think I'm such a lubber that I can't tell north from south on a clear night like this? Ye're no better than a fool, it seems. But unless ye get sense enough not to lie to me again, ye'll never tell another lie to anyone after this night. Now I'll be asking you again: Why are we going back to the Main? And don't tell me it's Fairfax you're selling.'

There was on Tim's part a thoughtful, hard-breathing pause. Blood might have made him afraid to lie, but he was still more afraid to speak the truth since it was what it was. 'Who else should it be?' he growled.

'Tim, Tim! Ye're lying to me again despite my warning. And your lies have the queer quality of telling me the truth. For if ye were meaning to sell Fairfax, it's La Hacha ye'ld be making for; and if ye were making for La Hacha ye'ld never be reaching so far on this westerly tack unless ye're a lubberly idiot, which I perceive ye're not. I'm saving you the trouble of lying again, Tim, for that—I vow to God—would certainly be the death of you. D'ye know who I am? Let me have the truth of that too. Do you?'

It was just because he did know who his questioner was that, having twice been so easily caught out in falsehood by this man's acuteness, the master stood chilled and palsied, never doubting that if he moved his inside would be blown out by that pistol in his flank. Fear at last tore the truth from him.

'I do, Captain. But...'

'Whisht now! Don't be committing suicide by telling me another falsehood; and there's no need. There's no need to tell me more. I know the rest. Ye're heading for Carthagena, of course. That's the market for the goods you carry, and the Marquis of Riconete is your buyer. If the notion is yours, Tim, I can forgive it. For you owe me nothing, and there's no reason in the world why ye shouldn't be earning fifty thousand pieces of eight by sellin' me to Spain. Is the notion yours, now?'

Vehemently Tim invoked the heavenly hierarchy to bear witness that he had done no more than obey the orders of Fairfax, who alone had conceived this infamous notion of making for Carthagena. He was still protesting when Blood cut into that flow of blasphemy-reinforced assertion.

'Yes, yes. I believe you. I had a notion that he recognized me when I spoke of landing on Tortuga. It was incautious of me. But, bad cess to him!—I'd saved his mangy life, and I thought that even the worst blackguard in the Caribbean would hesitate before... No matter. Tell me this: What share were you to have of the blood money, Tim?'

'Five thousand pieces, he promised,' said Tim, hang-dog.

'Glory be! Is that all! Ye can't be much of a hand at a bargain; and that's not the only kind of fool you are. How long did you think you'ld live to enjoy the money? Or perhaps you didn't think. Well, think now, Tim, and maybe it'll occur to you that when it was known, as known it would be, how he'd earned it, my buccaneers would hunt you to the ends of the seas. Ye should reflect on these things, Tim, when ye go partners with a scoundrel. Ye'll be wiser to throw in your lot with me, my lad. And if it's five thousand pieces you want, faith, you may still earn them by taking my orders whilst I'm aboard this brig. Do that, and you may call for the money at Tortuga when you please, and be sure of safe-conduct. You have my word for that. And I am Captain Blood.'

Tim required no time for reflection. From the black shadow of imminent death that had been upon him, he saw himself suddenly not only offered safety but a reward as great as that which villainy would have brought him, and free from those overlooked risks to which Blood had just drawn his attention.

'I take the Almighty to be my witness...' he was beginning with fervour, when again Blood cut him short.

'Now don't be wasting breath on oaths, for I put no trust in them. My trust is in the gold I offer on the one hand and the lead on the other. I'm not leaving your side from this moment, Tim. I've conceived a kindness for you, my lad. And if I take my pistol from your ribs, don't be presuming upon that. It stays primed and cocked. Ye've no pistols of your own about you, I hope.' He ran his left hand over the master's body, as he spoke, so as to assure himself. 'Very well. We'll not go about again as you might be supposing, because we are still going back to the Main. But not to Carthagena. It's for La Hacha that we'll be steering a course. So you'll just be stepping to the poop-rail with me, and bidding them put the helm over. Ye've run far enough westward. It's more than time we were on the other tack if we are to make La Hacha by morning. Come along now.'

Obediently the master went with him, and from the rail, piped the hands to quarters. When all was ready, his deep voice rang out.

'Let go, and haul!' and a moment later, in response, the foreyards ran round noisily, the deck came level and then canted to larboard, and the brig was heading southwest.

V

All through that clear June night Captain Blood and the master of the Heron remained side by side on the poop of the brig, whether sitting or standing or going ever and anon to the rail to issue orders to the crew. And though the voice was always Tim's the orders were always Captain Blood's.

Tim gave him no trouble, it never being in his mind to change a state of things which suited his rascality so well. The reckoning there might have to be with Fairfax gave him no concern. In the main there was silence between them. But when the first grey light of dawn was creeping over the sea, Tim ventured a question that had been perplexing him.

'Sink me if I understand why ye should be wanting to go back to La Hacha. I thought as you was running away from it. Why else did ye ever consent to stop aboard when we weighed anchor?'

Blood laughed softly. 'Maybe it's as well ye should know. Ye'll be the better able to explain things to Mr Fairfax in case they should not be altogether clear to him.

'Ye may find it hard to believe from what you know of me, but there's a streak of chivalry in my nature, a remnant from better days; for indeed, it was that same chivalry that made me what I am. And ye're not to suppose that it's Fairfax I'm taking back to La Hacha and the vengeance of the house of Sotomayor. For I don't care a louse what may happen to the blackguard, and I'm not by nature a vindictive man.

'It's the little hidalga I'm concerned for. It's entirely on her account that we're going back, now that I've sounded the nasty depths of this fellow to whom in a blind evil hour she entrusted herself. We're going to restore her to her family, Tim, safe and undamaged, God be praised. It's little thanks I'm likely to get for it from her. But that may come later, when with a riper knowledge of the world she may have some glimpse of the hell from which I am delivering her.'

Here was something beyond Tim's understanding. He swore in his amazement. Also it placed in jeopardy, it seemed to him, the five thousand pieces he was promised.

'But if ye was running away from La Hacha, there must be danger for ye there. Are ye forgetting that?'

'Faith, I never yet knew a danger that could prevent me from doing what I'm set on. And I'm set on this.'

It persuaded Tim of that streak of chivalry of which Blood had boasted, a quality which the burly master of the Heron could not help regarding as a deplorable flaw in a character of so much rascally perfection.

Ahead the growing daylight showed the loom of the coastline. But seven bells had been made before they were rippling through the greenish water at the mouth of the harbour of Rio de la Hacha, with the sun already high abeam on the larboard side.

They ran in to find an anchorage, and from the pooprail the now weary and blear-eyed Tim continued to be the mouthpiece of the tall man who clung to him like his shadow.

'Bid them let go.'

The order was issued, a rattle followed from the capstan, and the Heron came to anchor within a quarter of a mile of the mole.

'Summon all hands to the waist.'

When the six men who composed the crew of the brig stood assembled there, Blood's next instructions followed. 'Bid them take the cover from the main hatch.'

It was done at once.

'Now order them all down into the hold. Tell them they are to stow it for cargo to be taken aboard.'

It may have puzzled them, but there was no hesitation to obey, and as the last man disappeared into the darkness, Blood drew the master to the companion. 'You'll go and join them, Tim, if you please.'

There was a momentary rebellion. 'Sink me, Captain, can't you—'

'You'll go and join them,' Blood insisted. 'At once.'

Under the compulsion of that tone and of the eyes so blue and cold that looked with deadly menace into his own, Tim's resistance crumbled, and obediently he climbed down into the hold.

Captain Blood, following close upon his heels, dragged the heavy wooden cover over the hatchway again, and dumped it down, insensible to the storm of howling from those he thus imprisoned in the bowels of the brig.

The noise they made aroused Mr Fairfax from an exhausted slumber, on one side of the cabin, and Doña Isabela from a despondent listlessness on the other.

Mr Fairfax, realizing at once that they were at anchor, and puzzled to the point of uneasiness by the fact, wondering, indeed, whether he could have slept the round of the clock, got stiffly from his couch and staggered to the port. It happened to look out towards the open sea, so that all that he beheld was the green, ruffled water, and some boats at a little distance. Clearly, then, they were in harbour. But in what harbour? It was impossible that they could be in Carthagena. But if in Carthagena, where the devil were they?

He was still asking himself this question when his attention was caught by sounds in the main cabin. He could hear the liquid voice of Alcatrace raised in alarmed, insistent protest.

'De orders, ma'am, are dat you not leabe de cabin. Cap'n's orders, ma'am.'

Doña Isabela, who from her port on the brig's other side had seen and recognized the mole of Rio de la Hacha, without understanding how they came there and without thought even to inquire, had flung in breathless excitement from her stateroom. The resolute black man confronting her and arresting her intended flight almost turned her limp with the sickness of frustration.

'Please, Alcatrace. Please!' On an inspiration she snatched at the pearls in her hair and tore them free. She held them out to him.

'I give you these, Alcatrace. Let me pass.'

What she would do when she had passed and even if she gained the deck she did not stay to think. She was offering all that remained her to bribe a passage of the first obstacle.

The black man's eyes gleamed covetously. But the fear of Fairfax, who might be awake and overhearing, was stronger than his greed. He closed his eyes and shook his head.

'Cap'n's orders, ma'am,' he repeated.

She looked to right and left as a hunted thing will, seeking a way of escape, and her desperate eyes alighted on a brace of pistols on the buffet against the forward bulkhead of the cabin. It was enough. Moving so suddenly as to take him by surprise, she sprang for them, caught them up, and wheeled again to face him with one in each hand, whilst the pearls that had failed her rolled neglected across the cabin floor.

'Out of my way, Alcatrace!'

Before that formidable menace the black man fell back in squealing alarm, and the lady swept out unhindered and made for the deck.

Out there Blood was concluding his preparations for what was yet to do. Most of his anxiety about the immediate future was allayed by the sight of the broad-beamed Dutch ship that was to carry him back to Curaçao beating up into the roads, faithful to the engagement made with him.

But before he could think of boarding the Dutchman, he would take the eloping hidalga ashore, whether she liked it or not, and even if he had to employ force with her. So he went about his preparations. He disengaged the tow-rope of the long-boat from its bollard, and warped the boat forward to the foot of the Jacob's ladder. This done, he made for the gangway leading aft in quest of the lady in whose service the boat was to be employed. He was within a yard of the door when it was suddenly and violently flung open, and he found himself to his amazement confronted by Doña Isabela and her two pistols.

Waving these weapons at him, her voice strident, she addressed him much as she had addressed Alcatrace.

'Out of my way! Out of my way!'

Captain Blood in his time had faced weapons of every kind with imperturbable intrepidity. But he was to confess afterwards that a panic seized him before the threat of those pistols brandished by a woman's trembling hands. Spurred by it to nimbleness, he leapt aside, and flattened himself against a bulkhead in promptest obedience.

He had been prepared for the utmost resistance to his kindly intentions for her, but not for a resistance expressed in so uncompromising and lethal a manner. It was the surprise of it that for a moment put him so utterly out of countenance. When he had recovered from it, he contrived to stand grimly calm before the quivering panic he now perceived in the lady with the pistols.

'Where is Tim?' she demanded. 'I want him. I must be taken ashore at once. At once!'

Blood loosed a breath of relief. 'Glory be! Have ye come to your senses, then, of your own accord? But maybe ye don't know where we are.'

'Oh, I know where I am. I know—' And there, abruptly, she broke off, staring round-eyed at this man whose place and part aboard this ship were suddenly borne in upon her excited senses. His presence, confronting her now, served only to bewilder her. 'But you... You...' she faltered, breathless, 'You don't know. You are in great danger, sir.'

'I am that, ma'am, for ye will be wagging those pistols at me. Put them down. Put them down, ma'am, a God's name, before we have an accident.' As she obeyed him and lowered her hands, he caught her by the arm. 'Come on ashore with you, then, since that's where ye want to be going. Glory be! Ye're saving me a deal of trouble, for it was ashore I meant to take you whether ye wanted to go or not. Come on.'

But in her amazement she resisted, turning heavy to the suasion of his hand, demanding explanation. 'You meant to take me ashore, you say?'

'Why else do you suppose I brought you back to La Hacha? For it's by my contriving, that we're back here this morning. They say the night brings counsel, but I hardly hoped that a night aboard the brig would bring you such excellent counsel as ye seem to have had.' And again impatiently he sought to hustle her forward.

'You brought me back? You? Captain Blood!'

That gave him pause. His grip of her arm relaxed. His eyes narrowed. 'Ye know that, do you? To be sure he would tell you. Did the blackguard tell you at the same time that he meant to sell me?'

'That,' she said, 'is why I want to go ashore. That is why I thank God to be back in La Hacha.'

'I see. I see.' But his eyes were still grave. 'And when I've put you ashore, can I trust you to hold your tongue until I'm away again?'

There was angry reproach in her glance. She thrust forward her little pointed chin. 'You insult me, sir. Should I betray you? Can you think that?'

'I can't. But I'd like to be sure.'

'I told you last night what I thought of you.'

'So ye did. And heaven knows ye've cause to think better of me still this morning. Come away, then.'

He swept her across the deck, past the hatchway from which the angry sounds of the imprisoned men were still arising, to the Jacob's ladder, and so down into the waiting long-boat.

It was as well they had delayed no longer, for he had no sooner cast off than two faces looked down at them from the head of the ladder in the waist, one black, the other ghastly white in its pallor and terrible in the fury that convulsed it. Mr Fairfax with the help of Alcatrace had staggered to the deck just as Blood and the lady reached the boat.

'Good morning to you, Jorgito!' Blood hailed him. 'Doña Isabela is going ashore with me. But her brother and all the Sotomayors will be alongside presently and devil a doubt but they'll bring the Alcalde with them. They'll be correcting the mistake I made last night when I saved your nasty life.'

'Oh, not that! I do not want that,' Dona Isabela appealed to him.

Blood laughed as he bent his oars. 'D'ye suppose he'll wait? It'll quicken him in getting the cover off the hatch, so as to get under way again. Though the devil knows where he'll go now. Certainly not to Carthagena. It was the notion he took to go there persuaded me he was not the right kind of husband for your ladyship, and decided me to bring you back to your family.'

'That is what made me wish to return,' she said, her dark eyes very wistful. 'All night I prayed for a miracle, and behold my prayer is answered. By you.' She looked at him, a growing wonder in her vivid little face. 'I do not yet know how you did it.'

'Ah!' he said, and rested for a moment on his oars. He drew himself up and sat very erect in the thwart, his lean, intrepid face lighted by a smile half humorous, half complacent. 'I am Captain Blood.'

But before they reached the mole her persistency had drawn a fuller explanation from him, and it brought a great tenderness to eyes that were aswim in tears.

He brought his boat through the swarm of craft with their noisy tenants to the sea-washed steps of the mole, and sprang out under the stare of curious questioning eyes, to hand her from the sternsheets.

Still holding her hand, he said: 'Ye'll forgive me if I don't tarry.'

'Yes, yes. Go. And God go with you.' But she did not yet release her clasp. She leaned nearer. 'Last night I thought you were sent by Heaven to save... that man. Today I know that you were sent to save me. Always I shall remember.'

The phrase must have lingered pleasantly in his memory, as we judge from the answer he presently returned to the greeting of the master of the Dutch brig. For with commendable prudence, remembering that Don Francisco de Villamarga was in La Hacha, he denied himself the satisfaction of such thanks as the family of Sotomayor might have been disposed to shower upon him, and pulled steadily away until he brought up against the bulging hull of that most opportunely punctual Dutchman.

Classens, the master, was in the waist to greet him when he climbed aboard.

'Ye're early astir, sir,' the smiling, rubicund Dutchman commended him.

'As becomes a messenger of Heaven,' was the cryptic answer, in which for long thereafter Mynheer Classens vainly sought the jest he supposed to be wrapped in it.

They were in the act of weighing anchor when the Heron, crowding canvas, went rippling past them out to sea, a disgruntled, raging, fearful Heron in full flight from the neighbourhood of the hawks. And in all this adventure that was Captain Blood's only regret.